P9-DMF-392

ALSO BY MICHAEL CHABON

MICHAEL CHABON

PICADOR

NEW YORK

Praise for *The Amazing Adventures of Kavalier & Clay*

"Starts out as one of the most pleasurable novels of the past few years. It ends as one of the most moving."
—*Atlanta Journal-Constitution*

"A lyrical [novel] that's exquisitely patterned . . . composed with detailed scenes, and spotted with some rapturous passages."
—*Entertainment Weekly*

"The kind of prose that leaps 600 pages of fantasy and social history in a single bound . . . never before told with as much imagination, verve, and affection."
—*Time* Magazine

"[A] seamless performance, richly imagined and unexpectedly moving, *Kavalier & Clay* shows a thoroughbred author writing at the peak of his talents."
—*San Francisco Chronicle*

"Michael Chabon's new novel is the product of sparkling intelligence, undeniable talent, and consummate skill . . . a triumph both of style and storytelling."
—*Sun-Sentinel* (Ft. Lauderdale, Florida)

"Mr. Chabon has fashioned a big, ripe, excitingly imaginative novel."
—*The New York Times*

"[Chabon's] biggest and most ambitious work so far. High-spirited, fantastic yet historically grounded, written in a charming, fluent, witty prose, it is a highly engaging and entertaining book.
—*Newsday*

"Chabon's highly propelled, magnificently furnished, linguistically unbuttoned, and joyfully melancholy tale . . . is not merely hypnotically compelling but, even better, fall-on-the-floor-funny-but-with-a-lump-in-your-throat."
—*The Commercial Appeal* (Memphis)

"Chabon takes center stage as a literary Houdini. It's a crowd-wowing performance, one that pushes the author toward the top ranks of his generation of American writers."

—Denver Post

"Well researched and deeply felt, this rich, expansive, and hugely satisfying novel will delight a wide range of readers."

—Publishers Weekly (starred review)

"A superb new novel."

—Star-Ledger (Newark)

"*Kavalier & Clay* is full of the kind of exquisitely figurative language and gorgeous sentences for which Chabon is deservedly celebrated."

—Philadelphia Inquirer

"*Kavalier & Clay* is more than a novel about the American Dream. . . . It's a grand novel about dreamers selling dreams, reminding us that part of the thrill of dreaming is not the dream itself, but the realization that we *can* dream."

—CNN.com

"This is a glad-hearted novel, rich in story and character and invention, and a great escape."

—Pittsburgh Tribune

"A stroke of sheer conceptual genius . . . a huge enthralling third novel."

—Kirkus Reviews (starred review)

THE AMAZING ADVENTURES OF KAVALIER & CLAY

The AMAZING ADVENTURES of KAVALIER & CLAY

A NOVEL

This is a work of fiction. Names, characters, places, and incidents
are the products of the author's imagination or are used fictitiously.
Any resemblance to actual events, locales, or persons, living
or dead, is entirely coincidental.

THE AMAZING ADVENTURES OF KAVALIER & CLAY. Copyright © 2000 by Michael
Chabon. All rights reserved. Printed in the United States of America. For
information, address Picador, 175 Fifth Avenue, New York, N.Y. 10010.

www.picadorusa.com

Picador® is a U.S. registered trademark and is used by St. Martin's Press
under license from Pan Books Limited.

For information on Picador Reading Group Guides, as well as ordering,
please contact the Trade Marketing department at St. Martin's Press.
Phone: 1-800-221-7945 extension 763
Fax: 212-677-7456
E-mail: trademarketing@stmartins.com

Library of Congress Cataloging-in-Publication Data

Chabon, Michael.
    The amazing adventures of Kavalier & Clay: a novel / Michael Chabon.
        p. cm.
    ISBN 0-312-28299-0
    1. Comic books, strips, etc.–Authorship–Fiction. 2. Heroes in mass media–
Fiction. 3. Czech Americans–Fiction. 4. New York (N.Y.)–Fiction. 5. Young
men–Fiction. 6. Artists–Fiction. I. Title.

PS3553.H15 A82 2000
813'.54–dc21   00-029063
CIP

First published in the United States by Random House, Inc., New York, and
simultaneously in Canada by Random House of Canada Limited, Toronto.

28 27 26 25 24 23 22 21

To my father

*We have this history of impossible solutions
for insoluble problems.*
—WILL EISNER, in conversation

Wonderful escape!
—NATHANIEL HAWTHORNE, "Wakefield"

CONTENTS

PART I

The

ESCAPE
ARTIST

I N LATER YEARS, holding forth to an interviewer or to an audience of aging fans at a comic book convention, Sam Clay liked to declare, apropos of his and Joe Kavalier's greatest creation, that back when he was a boy, sealed and hog-tied inside the airtight vessel known as Brooklyn, New York, he had been haunted by dreams of Harry Houdini. "To me, Clark Kent in a phone booth and Houdini in a packing crate, they were one and the same thing," he would learnedly expound at WonderCon or Angoulême or to the editor of *The Comics Journal.* "You weren't the same person when you came out as when you went in. Houdini's first magic act, you know, back when he was just getting started. It was called 'Metamorphosis.' It was never just a question of escape. It was also a question of *transformation.*" The truth was that, as a kid, Sammy had only a casual interest, at best, in Harry Houdini and his legendary feats; his great heroes were Nikola Tesla, Louis Pasteur, and Jack London. Yet his account of his role—of the role of his own imagination—in the Escapist's birth, like all of his best fabulations, rang true. His dreams *had* always been Houdiniesque: they were the dreams of a pupa struggling in its blind cocoon, mad for a taste of light and air.

Houdini was a hero to little men, city boys, and Jews; Samuel Louis Klayman was all three. He was seventeen when the adventures began: bigmouthed, perhaps not quite as quick on his feet as he liked to imagine, and tending to be, like many optimists, a little excitable. He was not, in any conventional way, handsome. His face was an inverted triangle, brow large, chin pointed, with pouting lips and a blunt, quarrelsome nose. He slouched, and wore clothes badly: he always looked as though he had just been jumped for his lunch money. He went forward each morning with the hairless cheek of innocence itself, but by noon a clean shave was no more than a memory, a hoboish penumbra on the jaw not quite sufficient to make him look tough. He thought of himself as ugly, but this was because he had never seen his face in repose. He had delivered the *Eagle* for most of 1931 in order to afford a set of dumbbells, which he had hefted every morning for the next eight years until his arms, chest, and shoulders were ropy and strong; polio had left him with the legs of a delicate boy. He stood, in his socks, five feet five inches tall. Like all of his friends, he considered it a compliment when somebody called him a wiseass. He possessed an incorrect but fervent understanding of the workings of television, atom power, and antigravity, and harbored the ambition—one of a thousand—of ending his days on the warm sunny beaches of the Great Polar Ocean of Venus. An omnivorous reader with a self-improving streak, cozy with Stevenson, London, and Wells, dutiful about Wolfe, Dreiser, and Dos Passos, idolatrous of S. J. Perelman, his self-improvement regime masked the usual guilty appetite. In his case the covert passion—one of them, at any rate—was for those two-bit argosies of blood and wonder, the pulps. He had tracked down and read every biweekly issue of *The Shadow* going back to 1933, and he was well on his way to amassing complete runs of *The Avenger* and *Doc Savage*.

The long run of Kavalier & Clay—and the true history of the Escapist's birth—began in 1939, toward the end of October, on the night that Sammy's mother burst into his bedroom, applied the ring and iron knuckles of her left hand to the side of his cranium, and told him to move over and make room in the bed for his cousin from Prague. Sammy sat up, heart pounding in the hinges of his jaw. In the livid light of the fluorescent tube over the kitchen sink, he made out a slender young man of about his own age, slumped like a question mark against the door frame, a disheveled pile of newspapers pinned under one arm, the other thrown as if in shame across his face. This, Mrs. Klayman said, giving Sammy a helpful shove toward the wall, was Josef Kavalier, her brother Emil's son, who had arrived in New York tonight on a Greyhound bus, all the way from San Francisco.

"What's the matter with him?" Sammy said. He slid over until his shoulders touched cold plaster. He was careful to take both of the pillows with him. "Is he sick?"

"What do you think?" said his mother, slapping now at the vacated expanse of bedsheet, as if to scatter any offending particles of himself that Sammy might have left behind. She had just come home from her last night on a two-week graveyard rotation at Bellevue, where she worked as a psychiatric nurse. The stale breath of the hospital was on her, but the open throat of her uniform gave off a faint whiff of the lavender water in which she bathed her tiny frame. The natural fragrance of her body was a spicy, angry smell like that of fresh pencil shavings. "He can barely stand on his own two feet."

Sammy peered over his mother, trying to get a better look at poor Josef Kavalier in his baggy tweed suit. He had known, dimly, that he had Czech cousins. But his mother had not said a word about any of them coming to visit, let alone to share Sammy's bed. He wasn't sure just how San Francisco fitted into the story.

"There you are," his mother said, standing up straight again, apparently satisfied at having driven Sammy onto the easternmost five inches of the mattress. She turned to Josef Kavalier. "Come here. I want to tell you something." She grabbed hold of his ears as if taking a jug by the handles, and crushed each of his cheeks in turn with her lips. "You made it. All right? You're here."

"All right," said her nephew. He did not sound convinced.

She handed him a washcloth and went out. As soon as she left, Sammy reclaimed a few precious inches of mattress while his cousin stood there, rubbing at his mauled cheeks. After a moment, Mrs. Klayman switched off the light in the kitchen, and they were left in darkness. Sammy heard his cousin take a deep breath and slowly let it out. The stack of newsprint rattled and then hit the floor with a heavy thud of defeat. His jacket buttons clicked against the back of a chair; his trousers rustled as he stepped out of them; he let fall one shoe, then the other. His wristwatch chimed against the water glass on the nightstand. Then he and a gust of chilly air got in under the covers, bearing with them an odor of cigarette, armpit, damp wool, and something sweet and somehow nostalgic that Sammy presently identified as the smell, on his cousin's breath, of prunes from the leftover ingot of his mother's "special" meatloaf—prunes were only a small part of what made it so very special—which he had seen her wrap like a parcel in a sheet of wax paper and set on a plate in the Frigidaire. So she had known that her nephew would be arriving tonight, had even been expecting him for supper, and had said nothing about it to Sammy.

Josef Kavalier settled back against the mattress, cleared his throat once, tucked his arms under his head, and then, as if he had been unplugged, stopped moving. He neither tossed nor fidgeted nor even so much as flexed a toe. The Big Ben on the nightstand ticked loudly. Josef's breathing thickened and slowed. Sammy was just wondering if anyone could possibly fall asleep with such abandon when his cousin spoke.

"As soon as I can fetch some money, I will find a lodging, and leave the bed," he said. His accent was vaguely German, furrowed with an odd Scots pleat.

"That would be nice," Sammy said. "You speak good English."

"Thank you."

"Where'd you learn it?"

"I prefer not to say."

"It's a secret?"

"It is a personal matter."

"Can you tell me what you were doing in California?" said Sammy. "Or is that confidential information too?"

"I was crossing over from Japan."

"Japan!" Sammy was sick with envy. He had never gone farther on his soda-straw legs than Buffalo, never undertaken any crossing more treacherous than that of the flatulent poison-green ribbon that separated Brooklyn from Manhattan Island. In that narrow bed, in that bedroom hardly wider than the bed itself, at the back of an apartment in a solidly lower-middle-class building on Ocean Avenue, with his grandmother's snoring shaking the walls like a passing trolley, Sammy dreamed the usual Brooklyn dreams of flight and transformation and escape. He dreamed with fierce contrivance, transmuting himself into a major American novelist, or a famous smart person, like Clifton Fadiman, or perhaps into a heroic doctor; or developing, through practice

and sheer force of will, the mental powers that would give him a preter-
natural control over the hearts and minds of men. In his desk drawer
lay—and had lain for some time—the first eleven pages of a massive autobiographical novel to be entitled either (in the Perelmanian mode)
Through Abe Glass, Darkly or (in the Dreiserian) *American Disillusionment* (a subject of which he was still by and large ignorant). He had devoted an embarrassing number of hours of mute concentration—brow
furrowed, breath held—to the development of his brain's latent powers
of telepathy and mind control. And he had thrilled to that *Iliad* of medical heroics, *The Microbe Hunters*, ten times at least. But like most na-
tives of Brooklyn, Sammy considered himself a realist, and in general
his escape plans centered around the attainment of fabulous sums of
money.

From the age of six, he had sold seeds, candy bars, houseplants,
cleaning fluids, metal polish, magazine subscriptions, unbreakable
combs, and shoelaces door-to-door. In a Zharkov's laboratory on the
kitchen table, he had invented almost functional button-reattachers,
tandem bottle openers, and heatless clothes irons. In more recent years,
Sammy's commercial attention had been arrested by the field of professional illustration. The great commercial illustrators and cartoonists—
Rockwell, Leyendecker, Raymond, Caniff—were at their zenith, and
there was a general impression abroad that, at the drawing board, a
man could not only make a good living but alter the very texture and
tone of the national mood. In Sammy's closet were stacked dozens of
pads of coarse newsprint, filled with horses, Indians, football heroes,
sentient apes, Fokkers, nymphs, moon rockets, buckaroos, Saracens,
tropic jungles, grizzlies, studies of the folds in women's clothing, the
dents in men's hats, the lights in human irises, clouds in the western
sky. His grasp of perspective was tenuous, his knowledge of human
anatomy dubious, his line often sketchy—but he was an enterprising
thief. He clipped favorite pages and panels out of newspapers and comic
books and pasted them into a fat notebook: a thousand different exem-
plary poses and styles. He had made extensive use of his bible of clippings in concocting a counterfeit *Terry and the Pirates* strip called *South
China Sea*, drawn in faithful imitation of the great Caniff. He had
knocked off Raymond in something he called *Pimpernel of the Planets*

and Chester Gould in a lockjawed G-man strip called *Knuckle Duster Doyle*. He had tried swiping from Hogarth and Lee Falk, from George Herriman, Harold Gray, and Elzie Segar. He kept his sample strips in a fat cardboard portfolio under his bed, waiting for an opportunity, for his main chance, to present itself.

"Japan!" he said again, reeling at the exotic Caniffian perfume that hung over the name. "What were you doing *there?*"

"Mostly I was suffering from the intestinal complaint," Josef Kavalier said. "And I suffer still. Particular in the night."

Sammy pondered this information for a moment, then moved a little nearer to the wall.

"Tell me, Samuel," Josef Kavalier said. "How many examples must I have in my portfolio?"

"Not Samuel. Sammy. No, call me Sam."

"Sam."

"What portfolio is that?"

"My portfolio of drawings. To show your employer. Sadly, I am obligated to leave behind all of my work in Prague, but I can very quickly do much more that will be frightfully good."

"To show my boss?" Sammy said, sensing in his own confusion the persistent trace of his mother's handiwork. "What are you talking about?"

"Your mother suggested that you might to help me get a job in the company where you work. I am an artist, like you."

"An artist." Again Sammy envied his cousin. This was a statement he himself would never have been able to utter without lowering his fraudulent gaze to his shoe tops. "My mother told you I was an artist?"

"A commercial artist, yes. For the Empire Novelties Incorporated Company."

For an instant Sammy cupped the tiny flame this secondhand compliment lit within him. Then he blew it out.

"She was talking through her hat," he said.

"Sorry?"

"She was full of it."

"Full of . . . ?"

"I'm an inventory clerk. Sometimes they let me do pasteup for an ad. Or when they add a new item to the line, I get to do the illustration. For that, they pay me two dollars per."

"Ah." Josef Kavalier let out another long breath. He still had not moved a muscle. Sammy couldn't decide if this apparent utter motionlessness was the product of unbearable tension or a marvelous calm. "She wrote a letter to my father," Josef tried. "I remember she said you create designs of superb new inventions and devices."

"Guess what?"

"She talked into her hat."

Sammy sighed, as if to suggest that this was unfortunately the case; a regretful sigh, long-suffering—and false. No doubt his mother, writing to her brother in Prague, had believed that she was making an accurate report; it was Sammy who had been talking through his hat for the last year, embroidering, not only for her benefit but to anyone who would listen, the menial nature of his position at Empire Novelties. Sammy was briefly embarrassed, not so much at being caught out and having to confess his lowly status to his cousin, as at this evidence of a flaw in the omniveillant maternal loupe. Then he wondered if his mother, far from being hoodwinked by his boasting, had not in fact been *counting* on his having grossly exaggerated the degree of his influence over Sheldon Anapol, the owner of Empire Novelties. If he were to keep up the pretense to which he had devoted so much wind and invention, then he was all but obliged to come home from work tomorrow night clutching a job for Josef Kavalier in his grubby little stock clerk's fingers.

"I'll try," he said, and it was then that he felt the first spark, the tickling finger of possibility along his spine. For another long while, neither of them spoke. This time, Sammy could feel that Josef was still awake, could almost hear the capillary trickle of doubt seeping in, weighing the kid down. Sammy felt sorry for him. "Can I ask you a question?" he said.

"Ask me what?"

"What was with all the newspapers?"

"They are your New York newspapers. I bought them at the Capitol Greyhound Terminal."

"How many?"

For the first time, he noticed, Josef Kavalier twitched. "Eleven."

Sammy quickly calculated on his fingers: there were eight metropolitan dailies. Ten if you counted the *Eagle* and the *Home News*. "I'm missing one."

"Missing . . . ?"

"*Times, Herald-Tribune*"—he touched two fingertips—"*World-Telegram, Journal-American, Sun.*" He switched hands. "*News, Post.* Uh, *Wall Street Journal.* And the Brooklyn *Eagle.* And the *Home News* in the Bronx." He dropped his hands to the mattress. "What's eleven?"

"The Woman's Daily Wearing."

"*Women's Wear Daily?*"

"I didn't know it was like that. For the garments." He laughed at himself, a series of brief, throat-clearing rasps. "I was looking for something about Prague."

"Did you find anything? They must have had something in the *Times.*"

"Something. A little. Nothing about the Jews."

"The Jews," said Sammy, beginning to understand. It wasn't the latest diplomatic maneuverings in London and Berlin, or the most recent bit of brutal posturing by Adolf Hitler, that Josef was hoping to get news of. He was looking for an item detailing the condition of the Kavalier family. "You know Jewish? Yiddish. You know it?"

"No."

"That's too bad. We got four Jewish newspapers in New York. They'd probably have something."

"What about German newspapers?"

"I don't know, but I'd imagine so. We certainly have a lot of Germans. They've been marching and having rallies all over town."

"I see."

"You're worried about your family?"

There was no reply.

"They couldn't get out?"

"No. Not yet." Sammy felt Josef give his head a sharp shake, as if to end the discussion. "I find I have smoked all my cigarettes," he went on, in a neutral, phrase-book tone. "Perhaps you could—"

"You know, I smoked my last one before bed," said Sammy. "Hey, how'd you know I smoke? Do I smell?"

"Sammy," his mother called, "sleep."

Sammy sniffed himself. "Huh. I wonder if Ethel can smell it. She doesn't like it. I want to smoke, I've got to go out the window, there, onto the fire escape."

"No smoking in bed," Josef said. "The more reason then for me to leave it."

"You don't have to tell me," Sammy said. "I'm dying to have a place of my own."

They lay there for a few minutes, longing for cigarettes and for all the things that this longing, in its perfect frustration, seemed to condense and embody.

"Your ash holder," Josef said finally. "Ashtray."

"On the fire escape. It's a plant."

"It might be filled with the . . . *spacek*? . . . *kippe*? . . . the stubbles?"

"The butts, you mean?"

"The butts."

"Yeah, I guess. Don't tell me you'd smoke—"

Without warning, in a kind of kinetic discharge of activity that seemed to be both the counterpart and the product of the state of perfect indolence that had immediately preceded it, Josef rolled over and out of the bed. Sammy's eyes had by now adjusted to the darkness of his room, which was always, at any rate, incomplete. A selvage of gray-blue radiation from the kitchen tube fringed the bedroom door and mingled with a pale shaft of nocturnal Brooklyn, a compound derived from the halos of streetlights, the headlamps of trolleys and cars, the fires of the borough's three active steel mills, and the shed luster of the island kingdom across the river, which came slanting in through a parting in the curtains. In this faint glow that was, to Sammy, the sickly steady light of insomnia itself, he could see his cousin going methodically through the pockets of the clothes he had earlier hung so carefully from the back of the chair.

"The lamp?" Josef whispered.

Sammy shook his head. "The mother," he said.

Josef came back to the bed and sat down. "Then we must to work in the darkness."

He held between the first fingers of his left hand a pleated leaf of cigarette paper. Sammy understood. He sat up on one arm, and with the other tugged the curtains apart, slowly so as not to produce the telltale creak. Then, gritting his teeth, he raised the sash of the window beside his bed, letting in a chilly hum of traffic and a murmuring blast of cold October midnight. Sammy's "ashtray" was an oblong terra-cotta pot, vaguely Mexican, filled with a sterile compound of potting soil and soot and the semipetrified skeleton, appropriately enough, of a cineraria that had gone unsold during Sammy's houseplant days and thus predated his smoking habit, still a fairly recent acquisition, by about three years. A dozen stubbed-out ends of Old Golds squirmed around the base of the withered plant, and Sammy distastefully plucked a handful of them—they were slightly damp—as if gathering night crawlers, then handed them in to his cousin, who traded him for a box of matches that evocatively encouraged him to EAT AT JOE'S CRAB ON FISHERMAN'S WHARF, in which only one match remained.

Quickly, but not without a certain showiness, Josef split open seven butts, one-handed, and tipped the resultant mass of pulpy threads into the wrinkled scrap of Zig Zag. After half a minute's work, he had manufactured them a smoke.

"Come," he said. He walked on his knees across the bed to the window, where Sammy joined him, and they wriggled through the sash and thrust their heads and upper bodies out of the building. He handed the cigarette to Sammy and, in the precious flare of the match, as Sammy nervously sheltered it from the wind, he saw that Josef had prestidigitated a perfect cylinder, as thick and straight and nearly as smooth as if rolled by machine. Sammy took a long drag of True Virginia Flavor and then passed the magic cigarette back to its crafter, and they smoked it in silence, until only a hot quarter inch remained. Then they climbed back inside, lowered the sash and the blinds, and lay back, bedmates, reeking of smoke.

"You know," Sammy said, "we're, uh, we've all been really worried . . . about Hitler . . . and the way he's treating the Jews and . . . and all that. When they, when you were . . . invaded. . . . My mom was . . . we all . . ." He shook his own head, not sure what he was trying to say. "Here." He sat up a little, and tugged one of the pillows out from under the back of his head.

Josef Kavalier lifted his own head from the mattress and stuffed the pillow beneath it. "Thank you," he said, then lay still once more.

Presently, his breathing grew steady and slowed to a congested rattle, leaving Sammy to ponder alone, as he did every night, the usual caterpillar schemes. But in his imaginings, Sammy found that, for the first time in years, he was able to avail himself of the help of a confederate.

I T WAS A CATERPILLAR SCHEME—a dream of fabulous escape—
that had ultimately carried Josef Kavalier across Asia and the Pacific
to his cousin's narrow bed on Ocean Avenue.

As soon as the German army occupied Prague, talk began, in certain
quarters, of sending the city's famous Golem, Rabbi Loew's miraculous
automaton, into the safety of exile. The coming of the Nazis was attended by rumors of confiscation, expropriation, and plunder, in particular of Jewish artifacts and sacred objects. The great fear of its secret
keepers was that the Golem would be packed up and shipped off to or-
nament some *institut* or private collection in Berlin or Munich. Already
a pair of soft-spoken, keen-eyed young Germans carrying notebooks
had spent the better part of two days nosing around the Old-New Synagogue, in whose eaves legend had secreted the long-slumbering champion of the ghetto. The two young Germans had claimed to be merely
interested scholars without official ties to the Reichsprotektorat, but
this was disbelieved. Rumor had it that certain high-ranking party
members in Berlin were avid students of theosophy and the so-called
occult. It seemed only a matter of time before the Golem was discovered, in its giant pine casket, in its dreamless sleep, and seized.

There was, in the circle of its keepers, a certain amount of resistance to the idea of sending the Golem abroad, even for its own pro-
tection. Some argued that since it had originally been formed of the
mud of the River Moldau, it might suffer physical degradation if removed from its native climate. Those of a historical bent—who, like
historians everywhere, prided themselves on a levelheaded sense of
perspective—reasoned that the Golem had already survived many
centuries of invasion, calamity, war, and pogrom without being ex-

posed or dislodged, and they counseled against rash reaction to another momentary downturn in the fortunes of Bohemia's Jews. There
were even a few in the circle who, when pressed, admitted that they
did not want to send the Golem away because in their hearts they had
not surrendered the childish hope that the great enemy of Jew-haters
and blood libelers might one day, in a moment of dire need, be revived
to fight again. In the end, however, the vote went in favor of removing
the Golem to a safe place, preferably in a neutral nation that was out
of the way and not entirely devoid of Jews.

It was at this point that a member of the secret circle who had ties to
Prague's stage-magic milieu put forward the name of Bernard Kornblum as a man who might be relied upon to effect the Golem's escape.

Bernard Kornblum was an *Ausbrecher*, a performing illusionist who
specialized in tricks with straitjackets and handcuffs—the sort of act
made famous by Harry Houdini. He had recently retired from the stage
(he was seventy, at least) to settle in Prague, his adopted home, and
await the inescapable. But he came originally, his proponent said, from
Vilna, the holy city of Jewish Europe, a place known, in spite of its reputation for hardheadedness, to harbor men who took a cordial and
sympathetic view of golems. Also, Lithuania was officially neutral, and
any ambitions Hitler might have had in its direction had reportedly
been forsworn by Germany, in a secret protocol to the Molotov-
Ribbentrop pact. Thus Kornblum was duly summoned, fetched from
his inveterate seat at a poker table in the card room of the Hofzinser
Club to the secret location where the circle met—at Faleder Monuments, in a shed behind the headstone showroom. The nature of the job
was explained to Kornblum: the Golem must be spirited from its hiding
place, suitably prepared for transit, and then conveyed out of the country, without attracting notice, to sympathetic contacts in Vilna. Necessary official documents—bills of lading, customs certificates—would be
provided by influential members of the circle, or by their highly placed
friends.

Bernard Kornblum agreed at once to take on the circle's commis-
sion. Although like many magicians a professional unbeliever who rev-
erenced only Nature, the Great Illusionist, Kornblum was at the same
time a dutiful Jew. More important, he was bored and unhappy in re-

tirement and had in fact been considering a perhaps ill-advised return to the stage when the summons had come. Though he lived in relative penury, he refused the generous fee the circle offered him, setting only two conditions: that he would divulge nothing of his plans to anyone, and accept no unsolicited help or advice. Across the entire trick he would draw a curtain, as it were, lifting the veil only when the feat had been pulled off.

This proviso struck the circle as not only charming, in a certain way, but sensible as well. The less any of them knew about the particulars, the more easily they would be able, in the event of exposure, to disavow knowledge of the Golem's escape.

Kornblum left Faleder Monuments, which was not far from his own lodgings on Maisel Street, and started home, his mind already beginning to bend and crimp the armature of a sturdy and elegant plan. For a brief period in Warsaw in the 1890s, Kornblum had been forced into a life of crime, as a second-story man, and the prospect of prizing the Golem out of its current home, unsuspected, awoke wicked old memories of gaslight and stolen gems. But when he stepped into the vestibule of his building, all of his plans changed. The *gardienne* poked her head out and told him that a young man was waiting to see him in his room. A good-looking boy, she said, well spoken and nicely dressed. Ordinarily, of course, she would have made the visitor wait on the stair, but she thought she had recognized him as a former student of Herr Professor.

Those who make their living flirting with catastrophe develop a faculty of pessimistic imagination, of anticipating the worst, that is often all but indistinguishable from clairvoyance. Kornblum knew at once that his unexpected visitor must be Josef Kavalier, and his heart sank. He had heard months ago that the boy was withdrawing from art school and emigrating to America; something must have gone wrong.

Josef stood when his old teacher came in, clutching his hat to his chest. He was wearing a new-looking suit of fragrant Scottish tweed. Kornblum could see from the flush in his cheeks and the excess of care he took to avoid knocking his head against the low sloping ceiling that the boy was quite drunk. And he was hardly a boy anymore; he must be nearly nineteen.

"What is it, son?" said Kornblum. "Why are you here?"

"I'm not here," Josef replied. He was a pale, freckled boy, black-haired, with a nose at once large and squashed-looking, and wide-set blue eyes half a candle too animated by sarcasm to pass for dreamy. "I'm on a train for Ostend." With an outsize gesture, Josef pretended to consult his watch. Kornblum decided that he was not pretending at all. "I'm passing Frankfurt right about now, you see."

"I see."

"Yes. My family's entire fortune has been spent. Everyone who must be bribed has been bribed. Our bank accounts have been emptied. My father's insurance policy has been sold. My mother's jewelry, her silver. The pictures. Most of the good furniture. Medical equipment. Stocks. Bonds. All to ensure that I, the lucky one, can be sitting on this train, you see? In the smoking car." He blew a puff of imaginary smoke. "Hurtling through Germany on my way to *the good old U.S.A.*" He finished in twanging American. To Kornblum's ear, his accent sounded quite good.

"My boy—"

"With all of my papers in order, *you betcha.*"

Kornblum sighed. "Your exit visa?" he guessed. He had heard stories of many such last-minute denials in recent weeks.

"They said I was missing a stamp. One stamp. I told them this couldn't be possible. Everything was in order. I had a checklist, prepared for me by the Underassistant Secretary for Exit Visas himself. I showed this checklist to them."

"But?"

"They said the requirements were changed *this morning.* They had a directive, a telegram from Eichmann himself. I was put off the train at Eger. Ten kilometers from the border."

"Ah." Kornblum eased himself down onto the bed—he suffered from hemorrhoids—and patted the coverlet beside him. Josef sat down. He buried his face in his hands. He let out a shuddering breath, his shoulders grew taut, cords stood out on the back of his neck. He was struggling with the desire to cry.

"Look," the old magician said, hoping to forestall tears, "look now. I am quite certain you will be able to correct the predicament." The words of consolation came out more stiffly than Kornblum would have liked, but he was starting to feel a little apprehensive. It was well past midnight, and the boy had an air of desperation, of impending explosion, that could not fail to move Kornblum, but also made him nervous. Five years earlier, he had been involved in a misadventure with this reckless and unlucky boy, to his undiminished regret.

"Come," Kornblum said. He gave the boy a clumsy little pat on the shoulder. "Your parents are sure to be worrying. I'll walk you home."

This did it; with a sharp intake of breath, like a man leaping in terror from a burning deck into a frozen sea, Josef began to cry.

"I already left them once," he said, shaking his head. "I just can't do it to them again."

All morning, in the train carrying him west toward Ostend and America, Josef had been tormented by the bitter memory of his farewell. He had neither wept, nor tolerated especially well, the weeping of his mother and grandfather, who had sung the role of Vitek in the 1926 premiere of Janáček's *Věc Makropulos* at Brno and tended, as is not uncommon among tenors, to wear his heart on his sleeve. But Josef, like many boys of nineteen, was under the misapprehension that his heart had been broken a number of times, and he prided himself on the imagined toughness of that organ. His habit of youthful stoicism kept him cool in the lachrymose embrace of his grandfather that morning at the Bahnhof. He had also felt disgracefully glad to be going. He was not happy to be leaving Prague so much as he was thrilled to be headed for America, for the home of his father's sister and an American cousin named Sam, in unimaginable Brooklyn, with its nightspots and tough guys and Warner Bros. verve. The same buoyant Cagneyesque callousness that kept him from marking the pain of leaving his entire family, and the only home he knew, also allowed him to tell himself that it would be only a matter of time before they all joined him in New York. Besides, the situation in Prague was undoubtedly as bad now as it was ever going to get. And so, at the station, Josef had kept his head erect and his cheeks dry and puffed on a cigarette, resolutely affecting greater notice of the other travelers on the train platform, the steam-shrouded locomotives, the German soldiers in their elegant coats, than of the members of his own family. He kissed his grandfather's scratchy cheek, withstood his mother's long embrace, shook hands with his father and with his younger brother, Thomas, who handed Josef an envelope. Josef stuck it in a coat pocket with a studied absentmindedness, ignoring the trembling of Thomas's lower lip as the envelope vanished. Then, as Josef was climbing into the train, his father had taken hold of his son's coattails and pulled him back down to the platform. He reached around from behind Josef to accost him with a sloppy hug. The shock of his father's tear-damp mustache against Josef's cheek was mortifying. Josef had pulled away.

"See you in the funny papers," he said. Jaunty, he reminded himself; always jaunty. In my panache is their hope of salvation.

As soon as the train pulled away from the platform, however, and Josef had settled back in the second-class compartment seat, he felt, like a blow to the stomach, how beastly his conduct had been. He seemed at once to swell, to pulse and burn with shame, as if his entire body were in rebellion against his behavior, as if shame could induce the same catastrophic reaction in him as a bee's sting. This very seat had cost, with the addition of departure imposts and the recent "transfer excise," precisely what Josef's mother had been able to raise from the pawning of an emerald brooch, her husband's gift to her on their tenth anniversary. Shortly before that triste anniversary, Frau Dr. Kavalier had miscarried in her fourth month of pregnancy, and abruptly the image of this unborn sibling—it would have been a sister—arose in Josef's mind, a curl of glinting vapor, and fixed him with a reproachful emerald gaze. When the emigration officers came on at Eger to take him off the train—his name was one of several on their list—they found him between two cars, snot-nosed, bawling into the crook of his elbow.

The shame of Josef's departure, however, was nothing compared to the unbearable ignominy of his return. On the journey back to Prague, crowded now into a third-class car of an airless local, with a group of strapping, loud Sudeten farm families headed to the capital for some kind of religious rally, he spent the first hour relishing a sense of just punishment for his hard-heartedness, his ingratitude, for having abandoned his family at all. But as the train passed through Kladno, the inevitable homecoming began to loom. Far from offering him the opportunity to make up for his unpardonable behavior, it seemed to him, his surprise return would be an occasion only to bring his family further sorrow. For the six months since the start of occupation, the focus of the Kavaliers' efforts, of their collective existence, had been the work of sending Josef to America. This effort had, in fact, come to represent a necessary counterbalance to the daily trial of mere coping, a hopeful inoculation against its wasting effects. Once the Kavaliers had determined that Josef, having been born during a brief family sojourn in the Ukraine in 1920, was, by a quirk of politics, eligible to emigrate to the United States, the elaborate and costly process of getting him there had restored a measure of order and meaning to their lives. How it would crush them to see him turn up on their doorstep not eleven hours after he had left! No, he thought, he could not possibly disappoint them by coming home. When the train at last crawled back into the Prague station early that evening, Josef remained in his seat, unable to move, until a passing conductor suggested, not unkindly, that the young gentleman had better get off.

Josef wandered into the station bar, swallowed a liter and a half of beer, and promptly fell asleep in a booth at the back. After an indefinite period, a waiter came over to shake him, and Josef woke up, drunk. He wrestled his valise out into the streets of the city that he had, only that morning, seriously imagined he might never see again. He drifted along Jerusalem Street, into the Josefov, and somehow, almost inevitably, his steps led him to Maisel Street, to the flat of his old teacher. He could not dash the hopes of his family by letting them see his face again; not, at any rate, on this side of the Atlantic Ocean. If Bernard Kornblum could not assist him in escaping, at least he would be able to help him to hide.

Kornblum handed Josef a cigarette and lit it for him. Then he went over to his armchair, settled carefully into it, and lit another for himself. Neither Josef Kavalier nor the Golem's keepers were the first to have approached Kornblum in the desperate expectation that his expertise with jail cells, straitjackets, and iron chests might somehow be extended to unlocking the borders of sovereign nations. Until this night, he had turned all such inquiries aside as not merely impractical, or beyond his expertise, but extreme and premature. Now, however, sitting in his chair, watching his former student shuffle helplessly through the flimsy scraps of triplicate paper, train tickets, and stamped immigration cards in his travel wallet, Kornblum's keen ears detected the sound, unmistakable to him, of the tumblers of a great iron lock clicking into place. The Emigration Office, under the directorship of Adolf Eichmann, had passed from mere cynical extortion to outright theft, taking applicants for everything they had in return for nothing at all. Britain and America had all but closed their doors—it was only through the persistence of an American aunt and the geographic fluke of his birth in the Soviet Union that Josef had been able to obtain a U.S. entry visa. Meanwhile, here in Prague, not even a useless old lump of river mud was safe from the predatory snout of the invader.

"I can get you to Vilna, in Lithuania," Kornblum said at last. "From there you will have to find your own way. Memel is in German hands now, but perhaps you can find passage from Priekule."

"Lithuania?"

"I am afraid so."

After a moment the boy nodded, and shrugged, and stubbed out the cigarette in an ashtray marked with the kreuzer-and-spade symbol of the Hofzinser Club.

" 'Forget about what you are escaping *from*,' " he said, quoting an old maxim of Kornblum's. " 'Reserve your anxiety for what you are escaping *to*.' "

3

JOSEF KAVALIER'S determination to storm the exclusive Hofzinser Club had reached its height one day back in 1935, over breakfast, when he choked on a mouthful of omelette with apricot preserves. It was one of those rare mornings at the sprawling Kavalier flat, in a lacy secession-style building off the Graben, when everyone sat down to eat breakfast together. The Doctors Kavalier maintained exacting professional schedules and, like many busy parents, were inclined at once to neglect and indulge their children. Herr Dr. Emil Kavalier was the author of *Grundsätzen der Endikronologie,* a standard text, and the identifier of Kavalier's acromegaly. Frau Dr. Anna Kavalier was a neurologist by training who had been analyzed by Alfred Adler and had since gone on to treat, on her paisley divan, the cream of cathected young Prague. That morning, when Josef suddenly hunched forward, gagging, eyes watering, scrabbling for his napkin, the father reached out from behind his *Tageblatt* and idly pounded Josef on the back. His mother, without looking up from the latest number of *Monatsschrift für Neurologie und Psychiatrie,* reminded Josef, for the ten thousandth time, not to bolt his food. Only little Thomas noticed, in the instant before Josef brought the napkin to his lips, the glint of something foreign in his brother's mouth. He got up from the table and went around to Josef's chair. He stared at his brother's jaws as they slowly worked over the offending bit of omelette. Josef ignored him and tipped another forkful into his mouth.

"What is it?" Thomas said.

"What is what?" said Josef. He chewed with care, as if bothered by a sore tooth. "Go away."

Presently Miss Horne, Thomas's governess, looked up from her day-old copy of the *Times* of London and studied the situation of the brothers.

"Have you lost a filling, Josef?"

"He has something in his mouth," said Thomas. "It's shiny."

"What do you have in your mouth, young man?" said the boys' mother, marking her place with a butter knife.

Josef stuck two fingers between his right cheek and upper right gum and pulled out a flat strip of metal, notched at one end: a tiny fork, no longer than Thomas's pinkie.

"What is that?" his mother asked him, looking as if she was going to be ill.

Josef shrugged. "A torque wrench," he said.

"What else?" said his father to his mother, with the unsubtle sarcasm that was itself a kind of subtlety, ensuring that he never appeared caught out by the frequently surprising behavior of his children. "Of course it's a torque wrench."

"Herr Kornblum said I should get used to it," Josef explained. "He said that when Houdini died, he was found to have worn away two sizable pockets in his cheeks."

Herr Dr. Kavalier returned to his *Tageblatt*. "An admirable aspiration," he said.

Josef had become interested in stage magic right around the time his hands had grown large enough to handle a deck of playing cards. Prague had a rich tradition of illusionists and sleight-of-hand artists, and it was not difficult for a boy with preoccupied and indulgent parents to find competent instruction. He had studied for a year with a Czech named Bozic who called himself Rango and specialized in card and coin manipulation, mentalism, and the picking of pockets. He could also cut a fly in half with a thrown three of diamonds. Soon Josef had learned the Rain of Silver, the Dissolving Kreutzer, the Count Erno pass, and rudiments of the Dead Grandfather, but when it was brought to the attention of Josef's parents that Rango had once been jailed for replacing the jewelry and money of his audiences with paste and blank paper, the boy was duly removed from his tutelage.

The phantom aces and queens, showers of silver korunas, and purloined wristwatches that had been Rango's stock in trade were fine for mere amusement. And for Josef, the long hours spent standing in front of the lavatory mirror, practicing the palmings, passes, slips, and sleights that made it possible to seem to hurl a coin into the right ear, through the brainpan, and out the left ear of a chum or relative, or to pop the knave of hearts into the handkerchief of a pretty girl, required a masturbatory intensity of concentration that became almost more pleasurable for him than the trick itself. But then a patient had referred his father to Bernard Kornblum, and everything changed. Under Kornblum's tutelage, Josef began to learn the rigorous trade of the *Ausbrecher* from the lips of one of its masters. At the age of fourteen, he had decided to consecrate himself to a life of timely escape.

Kornblum was an "eastern" Jew, bone-thin, with a bushy red beard he tied up in a black silk net before every performance. "It distracts them," he said, meaning his audiences, whom he viewed with the veteran performer's admixture of wonder and disdain. Since he worked with a minimum of patter, finding other means of distracting spectators was always an important consideration. "If I could work without the pants on," he said, "I would go naked." His forehead was immense, his fingers long and dexterous but inelegant with knobby joints; his cheeks, even on May mornings, looked rubbed and peeling, as though chafed by polar winds. Kornblum was among the few eastern Jews whom Josef had ever encountered. There were Jewish refugees from Poland and Russia in his parents' circle, but these were polished, "Europeanized" doctors and musicians from large cities who spoke French and German. Kornblum, whose German was awkward and Czech nonexistent, had been born in a shtetl outside of Vilna and had spent most of his life wandering the provinces of imperial Russia, playing the odeons, barns, and market squares of a thousand small towns and villages. He wore suits of an outdated, pigeon-breasted, Valentino cut. Because his diet consisted in large part of tinned fish—anchovies, smelts, sardines, tunny—his breath often carried a rank marine tang. Although a staunch atheist, he nonetheless kept kosher, avoided work on Saturday, and kept a steel engraving of the Temple Mount on the east wall of his room. Until recently, Josef, then fourteen, had given very little thought to the question of his own Jewishness. He believed—it was enshrined in the Czech constitution—that Jews were merely one of the numerous ethnic minorities making up the young nation of which Josef was proud to be a son. The coming of Kornblum, with his Baltic smell, his shopworn good manners, his Yiddish, made a strong impression on Josef.

Twice a week that spring and summer and well into the autumn, Josef went to Kornblum's room on the top floor of a sagging house on Maisel Street, in the Josefov, to be chained to the radiator or tied hand and foot with long coils of thick hempen rope. Kornblum did not at first give him the slightest guidance on how to escape from these constraints.

"You will pay attention," he said, on the afternoon of Josef's first lesson, as he shackled Josef to a bentwood chair. "I assure you of this. Also you will get used to the feeling of the chain. The chain is your silk pajamas now. It is your mother's loving arms."

Apart from this chair, an iron bedstead, a wardrobe, and the picture of Jerusalem on the east wall, next to the lone window, the room was almost bare. The only beautiful object was a Chinese trunk carved from some kind of tropical wood, as red as raw liver, with thick brass hinges, and a pair of fanciful brass locks in the form of stylized peacocks. The locks opened by a system of tiny levers and springs concealed in the jade eyespots of each peacock's seven tail feathers. The magician pushed the fourteen jade buttons in a certain order that seemed to change each time he went to open the chest.

For the first few sessions, Kornblum merely showed Josef different kinds of locks that he took out, one by one, from the chest; locks used to secure manacles, mailboxes, and ladies' diaries; warded and pin-tumbler door locks; sturdy padlocks; and combination locks taken from strongboxes and safes. Wordlessly, he would take each of the locks apart, using a screwdriver, then reassemble them. Toward the end of the hour, still without freeing Josef, he talked about the rudiments of breath control. At last, in the final minutes of the lesson, he would unchain the boy, only to stuff him into a plain pine box. He would sit on the closed lid, drinking tea and glancing at his pocket watch, until the lesson was over.

"If you are a claustrophobe," Kornblum explained, "we must detect this now, and not when you lie in chains at the bottom of the Moldau, strapped inside a postman's bag, with all your family and neighbors waiting for you to swim out."

At the start of the second month, he introduced the pick and the torque wrench, and set about applying these wonderful tools to each of the various sample locks he kept in the chest. His touch was deft and, though he was well past sixty, his hands steady. He would pick the locks, and then, for Josef's further edification, take them apart and pick them again with the works exposed. The locks, whether new or antique, English, German, Chinese, or American, did not resist his tinkerings for more than a few seconds. He had, in addition, amassed a small library of thick, dusty volumes, many illegal or banned, some of them imprinted with the seal of the Bolsheviks' dreaded Cheka, in which were listed, in infinite columns of minuscule type, the combination formulae, by lot number, for thousands of the combination locks manufactured in Europe since 1900.

For weeks, Josef pleaded with Kornblum to be allowed to handle a pick himself. Contrary to instructions, he had been working over the locks at home with a hat pin and a spoke from a bicycle wheel, with occasional success.

"Very well," said Kornblum at last. Handing Josef his pick and a torque wrench, he led him to the door of his room, in which he had himself installed a fine new Rätsel seven-pin lock. Then he unknotted his necktie and used it to blindfold Josef. "To see inside the lock, you don't use your eyes."

Josef knelt down in darkness and felt for the brass-plated knob. The door was cold against his cheek. When at last Kornblum removed the blindfold and motioned for Josef to climb into the coffin, Josef had picked the Rätsel three times, the last in under ten minutes.

On the day before Josef caused a disturbance at the breakfast table, after months of nauseous breathing drills that made his head tingle and of practice that left the joints of his fingers aching, he had walked into Kornblum's room and held out his wrists, as usual, to be cuffed and bound. Kornblum startled him with a rare smile. He handed Josef a small black leather pouch. Unrolling it, Josef found the tiny torque wrench and a set of steel picks, some no longer than the wrench, some twice as long with smooth wooden handles. None was thicker than a broom straw. Their tips had been cut and bent into all manner of cunning moons, diamonds, and tildes.

"I made these," said Kornblum. "They will be reliable."

"For me? You made these for me?"

"This is what we will now determine," Kornblum said. He pointed to the bed, where he had laid out a pair of brand-new German handcuffs and his best American Yale locks. "Chain me to the chair."

Kornblum allowed himself to be bound to the legs of his chair with a length of heavy chain; other chains secured the chair to the radiator, and the radiator to his neck. His hands were also cuffed—in front of his body, so that he could smoke. Without a word of advice or complaint from Kornblum, Josef got the handcuffs and all but one of the locks off in the first hour. But the last lock, a one-pound 1927 Yale Dreadnought, with sixteen pins and drivers, frustrated his efforts. Josef sweated and cursed under his breath, in Czech, so as not to offend his master. Kornblum lit another Sobranie.

"The pins have voices," he reminded Josef at last. "The pick is a tiny telephone wire. The tips of your fingers have ears."

Josef took a deep breath, slid the pick that was tipped with a small squiggle into the plug of the lock, and again applied the wrench. Quickly, he stroked the tip of the pick back and forth across the pins, feeling each one give in its turn, gauging the resistance of the drivers and springs. Each lock had its own point of equilibrium between torque and friction; if you turned too hard, the plug would jam; too softly, and the pins wouldn't catch properly. With sixteen-pin columns, finding the point of equilibrium was entirely a matter of intuition and style. Josef closed his eyes. He heard the wire of the pick humming in his fingertips.

With a satisfying metallic gurgle, the lock sprang open. Kornblum nodded, stood up, stretched.

"You may keep the tools," he said.

However slow the progress of the lessons with Herr Kornblum had seemed to Josef, it had come ten times slower for Thomas Kavalier. The endless tinkering with locks and knots that Thomas had covertly witnessed, night after night, in the faint lamplight of the bedroom the boys shared, was far less interesting to him than Josef's interest in coin tricks and card magic had been.

Thomas Masaryk Kavalier was an animated gnome of a boy with a thick black thatch of hair. When he was a very young boy, the musical chromosome of his mother's family had made itself plain in him. At three, he regaled dinner guests with long, stormy arias, sung in a complicated gibberish Italian. During a family holiday at Lugano, when he was eight, he was discovered to have picked up enough actual Italian from his perusal of favorite libretti to be able to converse with hotel waiters. Constantly called upon to perform in his brother's productions, pose for his sketches, and vouch for his lies, he had developed a theatrical flair. In a ruled notebook, he had recently written the first lines of the libretto for an opera, *Houdini,* set in fabulous Chicago. He was hampered in this project by the fact that he had never seen an escape artist perform. In his imagination, Houdini's deeds were far grander than anything even the former Mr. Erich Weiss himself could have conceived: leaps in suits of armor from flaming airplanes over Africa, and escapes from hollow balls launched into sharks' dens by undersea cannons. The sudden entrance of Josef, at breakfast that morning, into territory once actually occupied by the great Houdini, marked a great day in Thomas's childhood.

After their parents had left—the mother for her office on Narodny; the father to catch a train for Brno, where he had been called in to consult on the mayor's giantess daughter—Thomas would not leave Josef alone about Houdini and his cheeks.

"Could he have fit a two-koruna piece?" he wanted to know. He lay on his bed, on his belly, watching as Josef returned the torque wrench to its special wallet.

"Yes, but it's hard to imagine why he might have wanted to."

"What about a box of matches?"

"I suppose so."

"How would they have stayed dry?"

"Perhaps he could have wrapped them in oilcloth."

Thomas probed his cheek with the tip of his tongue. He shuddered. "What other things does Herr Kornblum want you to put in there?"

"I'm learning to be an escape artist, not a valise," Josef said irritably.

"Are you going to get to do a real escape now?"

"I'm closer today than I was yesterday."

"And then you'll be able to join the Hofzinser Club?"

"We'll see."

"What are the requirements?"

"You just have to be invited."

"Do you have to have cheated death?"

Josef rolled his eyes, sorry he had ever told Thomas about the Hofzinser. It was a private men's club, housed in a former inn on one of the Stare Mesto's most crooked and crepuscular streets, which combined the functions of canteen, benevolent society, craft guild, and rehearsal hall for the performing magicians of Bohemia. Herr Kornblum took his supper there nearly every night. It was apparent to Josef that the club was not only the sole source of companionship and talk for his taciturn teacher but also a veritable Hall of Wonders, a living repository for the accumulated lore of centuries of sleight and illusion in a city that had produced some of history's greatest charlatans, conjurors, and fakirs. Josef badly wanted to be invited to join. This desire had, in fact, become the secret focus of every spare thought (a role soon afterward to be usurped by the governess, Miss Dorothea Horne). Part of the reason he was so irritated by Thomas's persistent questioning was that his little brother had guessed at the constant preeminence of the Hofzinser Club in Josef's thoughts. Thomas's own mind was filled with Byzantine, houris-and-candied-figs visions of men in cutaway coats and pasha pants walking around inside the beetle-browed, half-timbered hotel on Stupartskà with their upper torsos separated from their lower, summoning leopards and lyrebirds out of the air.

"I'm sure when the time comes, I will receive my invitation."

"When you're twenty-one?"

"Perhaps."

"But if you did something to show them . . ."

This echoed the secret trend of Josef's own thoughts. He swung himself around on his bed, leaned forward, and looked at Thomas. "Such as?"

"If you showed them how you can get out of chains, and open locks, and hold your breath, and untie ropes. . . ."

"All that's easy stuff. A fellow can learn such tricks in prison."

"Well, if you did something really grand, then ... something to amaze them."

"An escape."

"We could throw you out of an airplane tied to a chair, with the parachute tied to another chair, falling through the air. Like this." Thomas scrambled up from his bed and went over to his small desk, took out the blue notebook in which he was composing *Houdini,* and opened it to a back page, where he had sketched the scene. Here was Houdini in a dinner jacket, hurtling from a crooked airplane in company with a parachute, two chairs, a table, and a tea set, all trailing scrawls of velocity. The magician had a smile on his face as he poured tea for the parachute. He seemed to think he had all the time in the world.

"This is idiotic," Josef said. "What do I know about parachutes? Who's going to let me jump out of an airplane?"

Thomas blushed. "How childish of me," he said.

"Never mind," said Josef. He stood up. "Weren't you playing with Papa's old things just now, his medical-school things?"

"Right here," Thomas said. He threw himself on the floor and rolled under the bed. A moment later, a small wooden crate emerged, covered in dust-furred spider silk, its lid hinged on crooked loops of wire.

Josef knelt and lifted the lid, revealing odd bits of apparatus and scientific supplies that had survived their father's medical education. Adrift in a surf of ancient excelsior were a broken Erlenmeyer flask, a glass pear-shaped tube with a penny-head stopper, a pair of crucible tongs, the leather-clad box that contained the remains of a portable Zeiss microscope (long since rendered inoperable by Josef, who had once attempted to use it to get a better look at Pola Negri's loins in a blurry bathing photo torn from a newspaper), and a few odd items.

"Thomas?"

"It's nice under here. I'm not a claustrophobe. I could stay under here for weeks."

"Wasn't there ..." Josef dug deep into the rustling pile of shavings. "Didn't we used to have—"

"What?" Thomas slid out from under the bed.

Josef held up a long, glinting glass wand and brandished it as Korn-blum himself might have done. "A thermometer," he said.

"What for? Whose temperature are you going to take?"

"The river's," Josef said.

At four o'clock on the morning of Friday, September 27, 1935, the temperature of the water of the River Moldau, black as a church bell and ringing against the stone embankment at the north end of Kampa Island, stood at 22.2° on the Celsius scale. The night was moonless, and a fog lay over the river like an arras drawn across by a conjuror's hand. A sharp wind rattled the seedpods in the bare limbs of the island's aca-cias. The Kavalier brothers had come prepared for cold weather. Josef had dressed them in wool from head to toe, with two pairs of socks each. In the pack he wore on his back, he carried a piece of rope, a strand of chain, the thermometer, half a veal sausage, a padlock, and a change of clothes with two extra pairs of socks for himself. He also car-ried a portable oil brazier, borrowed from a school friend whose family went in for alpinism. Although he did not plan to spend much time in the water—no longer, he calculated, than a minute and twenty-seven seconds—he had been practicing in a bathtub filled with cold water, and he knew that, even in the steam-heated comfort of the bathroom at home, it took several minutes to rid oneself of the chill.

In all his life, Thomas Kavalier had never been up so early. He had never seen the streets of Prague so empty, the housefronts so sunken in gloom, like a row of lanterns with the wicks snuffed. The corners he knew, the shops, the carved lions on a balustrade he passed daily on his way to school, looked strange and momentous. Light spread in a feeble vapor from the streetlamps, and the corners were flooded in shadow. He kept imagining that he would turn around and see their father chas-ing after them in his dressing gown and slippers. Josef walked quickly, and Thomas had to hurry to keep up with him. Cold air burned his cheeks. They stopped several times, for reasons that were never clear to Thomas, to lurk in a doorway, or shelter behind the swelling fender of a parked Skoda. They passed the open side door of a bakery, and Thomas was briefly overwhelmed by whiteness: a tiled white wall, a pale man dressed all in white, a cloud of flour roiling over a shining white mountain of dough. To Thomas's astonishment, there were all manner of people about at this hour, tradesmen, cabdrivers, two drunken men singing, even a woman crossing the Charles Bridge in a long black coat, smoking and muttering to herself. And policemen. They were obliged to sneak past two en route to Kampa. Thomas was a contentedly law-abiding child, with fond feelings toward policemen. He was also afraid of them. His notion of prisons and jails had been keenly influenced by reading Dumas, and he had not the slightest doubt that little boys would, without compunction, be interred in them.

He began to be sorry to have come along. He wished he had never come up with the idea of having Josef prove his mettle to the members of the Hofzinser Club. It was not that he doubted his brother's ability. This never would have occurred to him. He was just afraid: of the night, the shadows, and the darkness, of policemen, his father's temper, spiders, robbers, drunks, ladies in overcoats, and especially, this morning, of the river, darker than anything else in Prague.

Josef, for his part, was afraid only of being stopped. Not caught; there could be nothing illegal, he reasoned, about tying yourself up and then trying to swim out of a laundry bag. He didn't imagine the police or his parents would look favorably on the idea—he supposed he might even be prosecuted for swimming in the river out of season—but he was not afraid of punishment. He just did not want anything to prevent him from practicing his escape. He was on a tight schedule. Yesterday he had mailed an invitation to the president of the Hofzinser Club:

The honored members of the Hofzinser Club
are cordially invited
to witness another astounding feat of autoliberation
by that prodigy of escapistry
CAVALIERI
at Charles Bridge
Sunday, 29 September 1935
at half past four in the morning.

He was pleased with the wording, but it left him only two more days to get ready. For the past two weeks, he had been picking locks with his hands immersed in a sinkful of cold water, and wriggling free of his

ropes and loosing his chains in the bathtub. Tonight he would try the
"feat of autoliberation" from the shore of Kampa. Then, two days later,
if all went well, he would have Thomas push him over the railing of the
Charles Bridge. He had absolutely no doubt that he would be able to
pull off the trick. Holding his breath for a minute and a half posed no
difficulty for him. Thanks to Kornblum's training, he could go for nearly
twice that time without drawing a breath. Twenty-two degrees Celsius
was colder than the water in the pipes at home, but again, he was not
planning to stay in it for long. A razor blade, for cutting the laundry
sack, was safely concealed between layers of the sole of his left shoe,
and Kornblum's tension wrench and a miniature pick Josef had made
from the wire bristle of a street sweeper's push broom were housed so
comfortably in his cheeks that he was barely conscious of their presence. Such considerations as the impact of his head on the water or on
one of the stone piers of the bridge, his paralyzing stage fright in front
of that eminent audience, or helplessly sinking did not intrude upon his
idée fixe.

"I'm ready," he said, handing the thermometer to his little brother. It
was an icicle in Thomas's hand. "Let's get me into the bag."

He picked up the laundry sack they had pilfered from their housekeeper's closet, held it open, and stepped into the wide mouth of the bag
as though into a pair of trousers. Then he took the length of chain
Thomas offered him and wrapped it between and around his ankles
several times before linking the ends with a heavy Rätsel he had bought
from an ironmonger. Next he held out his wrists to Thomas, who, as he
had been instructed, bound them together with the rope and tied it
tightly in a hitch and a pair of square knots. Josef crouched, and
Thomas cinched the sack over his head. "On Sunday we'll have you put
chains and locks on the cord," Josef said, his voice muffled in a way that
disturbed his brother.

"But then how will you get out?" The boy's hands trembled. He
pulled his woolen gloves back on.

"They'll be just for effect. I'm not coming out that way." The bag suddenly ballooned, and Thomas took a step backward. Inside the sack,
Josef was bent forward, reaching out with both arms extended, seeking
the ground. The bag toppled over. "Oh!"

"What happened?"

"I'm fine. Roll me into the water."

Thomas looked at the misshapen bundle at his feet. It looked too small to contain his brother.

"No," he said, to his surprise.

"Thomas, please. You're my assistant."

"No, I'm not. I'm not even in the invitation."

"I'm sorry about that," said Josef. "I forgot." He waited. "Thomas, I sincerely and wholeheartedly apologize for my thoughtlessness."

"All right."

"Now roll me."

"I'm afraid." Thomas knelt down and started to uncinch the sack. He knew he was betraying his brother's trust and the spirit of the mission, and it pained him to do so, but it couldn't be helped. "You have to come out of there this minute."

"I'll be fine," said Josef. "Thomas." Lying on his back, peering out through the suddenly reopened mouth of the sack, Josef shook his head. "You're being ridiculous. Come on, tie it back up. What about the Hofzinser Club, eh? Don't you want me to take you to dinner there?"

"But..."

"But what?"

"The sack is too small."

"What?"

"It's so dark out... it's too dark out, Josef."

"Thomas, what are you talking about? *Come on, Tommy Boy*," he added in English. This was the name Miss Horne called him. "Dinner at the Hofzinser Club. Belly dancers. Turkish delight. All alone, without Mother and Father."

"Yes, but—"

"Do it."

"Josef! Is your mouth bleeding?"

"God damn it, Thomas, tie up the goddamned sack!"

Thomas recoiled. Quickly, he bent and cinched the sack, and rolled his brother into the river. The splash startled him, and he burst into tears. A wide oval of ripples spread across the surface of the water. For a frantic instant, Thomas paced back and forth on the embankment, still hearing the explosion of water. The cuffs of his trousers were drenched and cold water seeped in around the tongues of his shoes. He had thrown his own brother into the river, drowned him like a litter of kittens.

The next thing Thomas knew, he was on the Charles Bridge, running past the bridge's statues, headed for home, for the police station, for the jail cell into which he would now gladly have thrown himself. But as he was passing Saint Christopher, he thought he heard something. He darted to the bridge parapet and peered over. He could just make out the alpinist's rucksack on the embankment, the faint glow of the brazier. The surface of the river was unbroken.

Thomas ran back to the stairway that led back down to the island. As he passed the round bollard at the stair head, the slap of hard marble against his palm seemed to exhort him to brave the black water. He scrambled down the stone stairs two at a time, tore across the empty square, slid down the embankment, and fell headlong into the Moldau.

"Josef!" he called, just before his mouth filled with water.

All this while Josef, blind, trussed, and stupid with cold, was madly holding his breath as, one by one, the elements of his trick went awry. When he had held out his hands to Thomas, he had crossed his wrists at the bony knobs, flattening their soft inner sides against each other after he was tied, but the rope seemed to have contracted in the water, consuming this half inch of wriggling room, and in a panic that he had never thought possible, he felt almost a full minute slip away before he could free his hands. This triumph calmed him somewhat. He fished the wrench and pick from his mouth and, holding them carefully, reached down through the darkness for the chain around his legs. Kornblum had warned him against the tight grip of the amateur picklock, but he was shocked when the tension wrench twisted like the stem of a top and spun out of his fingers. He wasted fifteen seconds groping after it and then required another twenty or thirty to slip the pick into the lock. His fingertips were deafened by the cold, and it was only by some random vibration in the wire that he managed to hit the pins, set the drivers, and twist the plug of the lock. This same numbness served him much better when, reaching for the razor in his shoe, he sliced open the tip of his right index finger. Though he could see nothing, he could taste a thread of blood in that dark humming stuff around him.

Three and a half minutes after he had tumbled into the river, kicking his feet in their heavy shoes and two pairs of socks, he burst to the surface. Only Kornblum's breathing exercises and a miracle of habit had kept him from exhaling every last atom of oxygen in his lungs in the instant that he hit the water. Gasping now, he clambered up the embankment and crawled on his hands and knees toward the hissing brazier. The smell of coal oil was like the odor of hot bread, of warm summer pavement. He sucked up deep barrelfuls of air. The world seemed to pour in through his lungs: spidery trees, fog, the flickering lamps strung along the bridge, a light burning in Kepler's old tower in the Klementinum. Abruptly, he was sick, and spat up something bitter and shameful and hot. He wiped his lips with the sleeve of his wet wool shirt, and felt a little better. Then he realized that his brother had disappeared. Shivering, he stood up, his clothes hanging heavy as chain mail, and saw Thomas in the shadow of the bridge, beneath the carved figure of Bruncvik, chopping clumsily at the water, paddling, gasping, drowning.

Josef went back in. The water was as cold as before, but he did not seem to feel it. As he swam, he felt something fingering him, plucking at his legs, trying to snatch him under. It was only the earth's gravity, or the swift Moldau current, but at the time, Josef imagined that he was being pawed at by the same foul stuff he had spat onto the sand.

When Thomas saw Josef splashing toward him, he promptly burst into tears.

"Keep crying," Josef said, reasoning that breathing was the essential thing and that weeping was in part a kind of respiration. "That's good."

Josef got an arm around his brother's waist, then tried to drag them, Thomas and his ponderous self, back toward the Kampa embankment. As they splashed and wrestled in the middle of the river, they kept talking, though neither could remember later what the subject of the discussion had been. Whatever it was, it struck them both afterward as having been something calm and leisurely, like the murmurs between them that sometimes preceded sleep. At a certain point, Josef realized that his limbs felt warm now, even hot, and that he was drowning. His last conscious perception was of Bernard Kornblum cutting through the water toward them, his bushy beard tied up in a hair net.

Josef came to an hour later in his bed at home. It took two more days for Thomas to revive; for most of that time, no one, least of all his doctor parents, expected that he would. He was never quite the same afterward. He could not bear cold weather, and he suffered from a lifelong snuffle. Also, perhaps because of damage to his ears, he lost his taste for music; the libretto for *Houdini* was abandoned.

The magic lessons were broken off—at the request of Bernard Kornblum. Throughout the difficult weeks that followed the escapade, Kornblum was a model of correctness and concern, bringing toys and games for Thomas, interceding on Josef's behalf with the Kavaliers, shouldering all the blame himself. The Doctors Kavalier believed their sons when they said that Kornblum had had nothing to do with the incident, and since he had saved the boys from drowning, they were more than willing to forgive. Josef was so penitent and chastened that they even would have been willing to allow his continued studies with the impoverished old magician, who could certainly not afford to lose a pupil. But Kornblum told them that his time with Josef had come to an end. He had never had so naturally gifted a student, but his own discipline—which was really an escape artist's sole possession—had not been passed along. He didn't tell them what he now privately believed: that Josef was one of those unfortunate boys who become escape artists not to prove the superior machinery of their bodies against outlandish contrivances and the laws of physics, but for dangerously metaphorical reasons. Such men feel imprisoned by invisible chains—walled in, sewn up in layers of batting. For them, the final feat of autoliberation was all too foreseeable.

Kornblum was, nevertheless, unable to resist offering that final criticism to his erstwhile pupil on his performance that night. "Never worry about what you are escaping *from*," he said. "Reserve your anxieties for what you are escaping *to*."

Two weeks after Josef's disaster, with Thomas recovered, Kornblum called at the flat off the Graben to escort the Kavalier brothers to dinner at the Hofzinser Club. It proved to be a quite ordinary place, with a cramped, dimly lit dining room that smelled of liver and onions. There was a small library filled with moldering volumes on deception and forgery. In the lounge, an electric fire cast a negligible glow over scattered armchairs covered in worn velour and a few potted palms and dusty rubber trees. An old waiter named Max made some ancient hard candies fall out of his handkerchief into Thomas's lap. They tasted of burned coffee. The magicians, for their part, barely glanced up from their chessboards and silent hands of bridge. Where the knights and rooks were missing, they used spent rifle cartridges and stacks of pre-war kreuzers; their playing cards were devastated by years of crimps, breaks, and palmings at the hands of bygone cardsharps. Since neither Kornblum nor Josef possessed any conversational skills, it fell upon Thomas to carry the burden of talk at the table, which he dutifully did until one of the members, an old necromancer dining alone at the next table, told him to shut up. At nine o'clock, as promised, Kornblum brought the boys home.

THE **PAIR** of young German professors spelunking with their electric torches in the rafters of the Old-New Synagogue, or Altneuschul, had, as it happened, gone away disappointed; for the attic under the stair-stepped gables of the old Gothic synagogue was a cenotaph. Around the turn of the last century, Prague's city fathers had determined to "sanitize" the ancient ghetto. During a moment when the fate of the Altneuschul had appeared uncertain, the members of the secret circle had arranged for their charge to be moved from its ancient berth, under a cairn of decommissioned prayer books in the synagogue's attic, to a room in a nearby apartment block, newly constructed by a member of the circle who, in public life, was a successful speculator in real estate. After this burst of uncommon activity, however, the ghetto-bred inertia and disorganization of the circle reasserted itself. The move, supposed to have been only temporary, somehow was never undone, even after it became clear that the Altneuschul would be spared. A few years later, the old yeshiva in whose library a record of the transfer was stored fell under the wrecking ball, and the log containing the record was lost. As a result, the circle was able to provide Kornblum with only a partial address for the Golem, the actual number of the apartment in which it was concealed having been forgotten or come into dispute. The embarrassing fact was that none of the current members of the circle could remember having laid eyes on the Golem since early 1917.

"Then why move it again?" Josef asked his old teacher, as they stood outside the art nouveau building, long since faded and smudged with thumbprints of soot, to which they had been referred. Josef gave a nervous tug at his false beard, which was making his chin itch. He was also wearing a mustache and a wig, all ginger in color and of good quality, and a pair of heavy round tortoiseshell spectacles. Consulting his image in Kornblum's glass that morning, he had struck himself, in the Harris tweeds purchased for his trip to America, as looking quite convincingly Scottish. It was less clear to him why passing as a Scotsman in the streets of Prague was likely to divert people's attention from his and Kornblum's quest. As with many novices at the art of disguise, he could not have felt more conspicuous if he were naked or wearing a sandwich board printed with his name and intentions.

He looked up and down Nicholasgasse, his heart smacking against his ribs like a bumblebee at a window. In the ten minutes it had taken them to walk here from Kornblum's room, Josef had passed his mother three times, or rather had passed three unknown women whose momentary resemblance to his mother had taken his breath away. He was reminded of the previous summer (following one of the episodes he imagined to have broken his young heart) when, every time he set out for school, for the German Lawn Tennis Club under Charles Bridge, for swimming at the Militär- und Civilschwimmschule, the constant possibility of encountering a certain Fraulein Felix had rendered every street corner and doorway a potential theater of shame and humiliation. Only now *he* was the betrayer of the hopes of another. He had no doubt that his mother, when he passed her, would be able to see right through the false whiskers. "If even *they* can't find it, who could?"

"I am sure they could find it," Kornblum said. He had trimmed his own beard, rinsing out the crackle of coppery red which, Josef had been shocked to discover, he had been using for years. He wore rimless glasses and a wide-brimmed black hat that shadowed his face, and he leaned realistically on a malacca cane. Kornblum had produced the disguises from the depths of his marvelous Chinese trunk, but said that they had come originally from the estate of Harry Houdini, who made frequent, expert use of disguise in his lifelong crusade to gull and expose false mediums. "I suppose the fear is that they will be soon be"— he flourished his handkerchief and then coughed into it—"*obliged* to try."

Kornblum explained to the building superintendent, giving a pair of false names and brandishing credentials and bona fides whose source Josef was never able to determine, that they had been sent by the Jewish Council (a public organization unrelated to, though in some cases co-constituent with, the secret Golem circle) to survey the building, as part of a program to keep track of the movements of Jews into and within Prague. There was, in fact, such a program, undertaken semi-voluntarily and with the earnest dread that characterized all of the Jewish Council's dealings with the Reichsprotektorat. The Jews of Bohemia, Moravia, and the Sudeten were being concentrated in the city, while Prague's own Jews were being forced out of their old homes and into segregated neighborhoods, with two and three families often crowding into a single flat. The resulting turmoil made it difficult for the Jewish Council to supply the protectorate with the accurate information it constantly demanded; hence the need for a census. The superintendent of the building in which the Golem slept, which had been designated by the protectorate for habitation by Jews, found nothing to question in their story or documents, and let them in without hesitation.

Starting at the top and working their way down all five floors to the ground, Josef and Kornblum knocked on every door in the building and flashed their credentials, then carefully took down names and relationships. With so many people packed into each flat, and so many lately thrown out of work, it was the rare door that went unanswered in the middle of the day. In some of the flats, strict concords had been worked out among the disparate occupants, or else there was a happy mesh of temperament that maintained order, civility, and cleanliness. But for the most part, the families seemed not to have moved in together so much as to have collided, with an impact that hurled schoolbooks, magazines, hosiery, pipes, shoes, journals, candlesticks, knickknacks, mufflers, dressmaker's dummies, crockery, and framed photographs in all directions, scattering them across rooms that had the provisional air of an auctioneer's warehouse. In many apartments, there was a wild duplication and reduplication of furnishings: sofas ranked like church pews, enough jumbled dining chairs to stock a large café, a jungle growth of chandeliers dangling from ceilings, groves of torchères, clocks that sat side by side by side on a mantel, disputing the hour. Conflicts, in the nature of border wars, had inevitably broken out. Laundry was hung to demarcate lines of conflict and truce. Dueling wireless sets

were tuned to different stations, the volumes turned up in hostile incre-
ments. In such circumstances, the scalding of a pan of milk, the frying
of a kipper, the neglect of a fouled nappy, could possess incalculable
strategic value. There were tales of families reduced to angry silence,
communicating by means of hostile notes; three times, Kornblum's
simple request for the relationships among occupants resulted in bitter
shouting over degrees of cousinage or testamentary disputes that in one
case nearly led to a punch being thrown. Circumspect questioning of
husbands, wives, great-uncles, and grandmothers brought forth no
mention of a mysterious lodger, or of a door that was permanently shut.

When, after four hours of tedious and depressing make-believe, Mr.
Krumm and Mr. Rosenblatt, representatives of the Census Committee of
the Jewish Council of Prague, had knocked at every flat in the building,
there were still three unaccounted for—all, as it turned out, on the
fourth floor. But Josef thought he sensed futility—though he doubted
his teacher ever would have admitted to it—in the old man's stoop.

"Maybe," Josef began, and then, after a brief struggle, let himself
continue the thought, "maybe we ought to give up."

He was exhausted by their charade, and as they came out onto the
sidewalk again, crowded with a late-afternoon traffic of schoolchildren,
clerks, and tradesmen, housekeepers carrying market bags and
wrapped parcels of meat, all of them headed for home, he was aware
that his fear of being discovered, unmasked, recognized by his disappointed parents, had been replaced by an acute longing to see them
again. At any moment he expected—yearned—to hear his mother calling his name, to feel the moist brush stroke of his father's mustache
against his cheek. There was a residuum of summer in the watery blue
sky, in the floral smell issuing from the bare throats of passing women.
In the last day, posters had gone up advertising a new film starring Emil
Jannings, the great German actor and friend of the Reich, for whom
Josef felt a guilty admiration. Surely there was time to regroup, consider the situation in the bosom of his family, and prepare a less lunatic
strategy. The idea that his previous plan of escape, by the conventional
means of passports and visas and bribes, could somehow be revived
and put into play started a seductive whispering in his heart.

"You may of course do so," Kornblum said, resting on his cane with a fatigue that seemed less feigned than it had that morning. "I haven't the liberty. Even if I do not send *you*, my prior obligation remains."

"I was just thinking that perhaps I gave up on my other plan too soon."

Kornblum nodded but said nothing, and the silence so counterbalanced the nod as to cancel it out.

"That isn't the choice, is it?" Josef said after a moment. "Between your way and the other way. If I'm really going to go, I have to go your way, don't I? Don't I?"

Kornblum shrugged, but his eyes were not involved in the gesture. They were drawn at the corners, glittering with concern. "In my professional opinion," he said.

Few things in the world carried more weight for Josef than that.

"Then there *is* no choice," he said. "They spent everything they had." He accepted the cigarette the old man offered. "What am I saying—'if I'm going'?" He spat a flake of tobacco at the ground. "I have to go."

"What you have to do, my boy," Kornblum said, "is to try to remember that you are already gone."

They went to the Eldorado Café and sat, nursing butter and egg sandwiches, two glasses of Herbert water, and the better part of a pack of Letkas. Every fifteen minutes, Kornblum consulted his wristwatch, the intervals so regular and precise as to render the gesture superfluous. After two hours they paid their check, made a stop in the men's room to empty their bladders and adjust their getups, then returned to Nicholasgasse 26. Very quickly they accounted for two of the three mystery flats, 40 and 41, discovering that the first, a tiny two-room, belonged to an elderly lady who had been taking a nap the last time the ersatz census takers came to call; and that the second, according to the same old woman, was rented to a family named Zweig or Zwang who had gone to a funeral in Zuerau or Zilina. The woman's alphabetic confusion seemed to be part of a more global uncertainty—she came to the door in her nightgown and one sock, and addressed Kornblum for no obvious reason as Herr Kapitan—encompassing, among many other points of doubt, Apartment 42, the third unaccounted-for flat, about whose occupant or occupants she was unable to provide any information at all. Repeated knocking on the door to 42 over the next hour brought no one.

The mystery deepened when they returned to the neighbors in 43, the last of the floor's four flats. Earlier that afternoon, Kornblum and Josef had spoken to the head of this household: two families, the wives and fourteen children of brothers, brought together in four rooms. They were religious Jews. As before, the elder brother came to the door. He was a heavyset man in skullcap and fringes, with a great beard, black and bushy, that looked much more false to Josef than his own. The brother would consent to speak to them only through a four-inch gap, athwart a length of brass chain, as if admitting them might contaminate his home or expose the women and children to untoward influences. But his bulk could not prevent the escape of children's shrieks and laughter, women's voices, the smell of stewing carrots and of onions half-melting in a pan of fat.

"What do you want with that—?" the man said after Kornblum inquired about Apartment 42. He seemed to have second thoughts about the noun he was going to employ, and broke off. "I have nothing to do with that."

"That?" Josef said, unable to contain himself, though Kornblum had enjoined him to play the role of silent partner. "That *what*?"

"I have nothing to say." The man's long face—he was a jewel cutter, with sad, exophthalmic blue eyes—seemed to ripple with disgust. "As far as I'm concerned, that apartment is empty. I pay no attention. I couldn't tell you the first thing. If you'll excuse me."

He slammed the door. Josef and Kornblum looked at each other.

"It's forty-two," Josef said as they climbed into the rattling lift.

"We shall find out," Kornblum said. "I wonder."

On their way back to his room, they passed an ash can and into it Kornblum tossed the clipped packet of flimsy on which he and Josef had named and numbered the occupants of the building. Before they had gone a dozen steps, however, Kornblum stopped, turned, and went back. With a practiced gesture, he pushed up his sleeve and reached into the mouth of the rusting drum. His face took on a pinched, stoic blankness as he groped about in the unknown offal that filled the can. After a moment, he brought out the list, now stained with a nasty green blotch. The packet was at least two centimeters thick. With a jerk of his sinewy arms, Kornblum ripped it cleanly in half. He gathered the halves together and tore them into quarters, then tore the gathered quarters into eighths. His mien remained neutral, but with each division and reassembly the wad of paper grew thicker, the force required to tear it correspondingly increased, and Josef sensed a mounting anger in Kornblum as he ripped to smithereens the inventory, by name and age, of every Jew who lived at Nicholasgasse 26. Then, with a gelid showman's smile, he rained the scraps of paper down into the waste-basket, like coins in the famous Shower of Gold illusion.

"Contemptible," he said, but Josef was not sure, then or afterward, whom or what he was talking about—the ruse itself, the occupiers who made it plausible, the Jews who had submitted to it without question, or himself for having perpetrated it.

Well past midnight, after a dinner of hard cheese, tinned smelts, and pimientos, and an evening passed in triangulating the divergent news from the Rundesfunk, Radio Moscow, and the BBC, Kornblum and Josef returned to Nicholasgasse. The extravagant front doors, thick plate glass on an iron frame worked in the form of drooping lilies, were locked, but naturally this presented Kornblum with no difficulty. In just under a minute, they were inside and headed up the stairs to the fourth floor, their rubber-soled shoes silent on the worn carpeting. The sconce lights were on mechanical timers, and had long since turned off for the night. As they proceeded, a unanimous silence seeped from the walls of the stairwell and hallways, as stifling as a smell. Josef felt his way, hesitating, listening for the whisper of his teacher's trousers, but Kornblum moved confidently in darkness. He didn't stop until he reached the door of 42. He struck a light, then gripped the door handle and knelt, using the handle to steady himself. He passed the lighter to Josef. It was hot against the palm. It grew hotter still as Josef kept it burning so that Kornblum could get the string of his pick-wallet untied. When he had unrolled the little wallet, Kornblum looked up at Josef with a question in his eyes, a teacherly amalgam of doubt and encouragement. He tapped the picks with his fingertips. Josef nodded and let the light go out. Kornblum's hand felt for Josef's. Josef took it and helped the old man to his feet with an audible creaking of bones. Then he passed back the lighter and knelt down himself, to see if he still knew how to work over a door.

There was a pair of locks, one mounted on the latch and a second set

higher up—a deadbolt. Josef selected a pick tipped with a bent parenthesis and, with a twitch of the torsion wrench, made short work of the
lower lock, a cheap three-pin affair. But the deadbolt gave him trouble.
He teased and tickled the pins, sought out their resonant frequencies as
if the pick were an antenna connected to the trembling inductor of his
hand. But there was no signal; his fingers had gone dead. He grew first
impatient, then embarrassed, huffing and blowing through his teeth.
When he let loose with a hissed *Scheiss,* Kornblum laid a heavy hand on
his shoulder, then struck another light. Josef hung his head, slowly
stood up, and handed Kornblum the pick. In the instant before the
flame of the lighter was again extinguished, he was humbled by the
lack of consolation in Kornblum's expression. When he was sealed up
in a coffin, in a container car on the platform in Vilna, he was going to
have to do a better job.

Seconds after Josef handed over the pick, they were inside Apartment 42. Kornblum closed the door softly behind them and switched on
the light. They just had time to remark on the unlikely decision someone had made to decorate the Golem's quarters in a profusion of Louis
XV chairs, tiger skins, and ormolu candelabra when a low, curt, irre-
sistible voice said, "Hands up, gents."

The speaker was a woman of about fifty, dressed in a green sateen
housecoat and matching green mules. Two younger women stood behind her, wearing hard expressions and ornate kimonos, but the
woman in green was the one holding the gun. After a moment, an elderly man emerged from the hallway at the women's back, in stocking
feet, his shirttails flapping around him, his broom-straw legs pale and
knobby. His seamed, potato-nosed face was strangely familiar to Josef.

"Max," Kornblum said, his face and voice betraying surprise for the
first time since Josef had known him. It was then that Josef recognized,
in the half-naked old man, the candy-producing magical waiter from
his and Thomas's lone night at the Hofzinser Club years before. A lineal
descendant, as it later turned out, of the Golem's maker, Rabbi Judah
Loew ben Bezalel, and the man who had first brought Kornblum to the
attention of the secret circle, old Max Loeb took in the scene before him,
narrowing his eyes, trying to place this graybeard in a slouch hat with a
commanding stage-trained voice.

"Kornblum?" he guessed finally, and his worried expression changed quickly to one of pity and amusement. He shook his head and signaled to the woman in green that she could put down her gun. "I can promise you this, Kornblum, you aren't going to find it here," he said, and then added, with a sour smile, "I've been poking around this apartment for years."

Early the next morning, Josef and Kornblum met in the kitchen of Apartment 42. Here they were served coffee in scalloped Herend cups by Trudi, the youngest of the three prostitutes. She was an ample girl, plain and intelligent, studying to be a nurse. After relieving Josef of the burden of his innocence the previous night, in a procedure that required less time than it now took her to brew a pot of coffee, Trudi had pulled on her cherry-pink kimono and gone out to the parlor to study a text on phlebotomy, leaving Josef to the warmth of her goose-down counterpane, the lilac smell of her nape and cheek lingering on the cool pillow, the perfumed darkness of her bedroom, the shame of his contentment.

When Kornblum walked into the kitchen that morning, his eyes and Josef's sought and avoided each other's, and their conversation was monosyllabic; while Trudi was still in the kitchen, they barely drew a breath. It was not that Kornblum regretted having corrupted his young pupil. He had been frequenting prostitutes for decades and held liberal views on the utility and good sense of sexual commerce. Their berths had been more comfortable and far more fragrant than either would have found in Kornblum's cramped room, with its single cot and its clanging pipes. Nevertheless, he was embarrassed, and from the guilty arc of Josef's shoulders and the evasiveness of his gaze, Kornblum inferred that the young man felt the same.

The apartment's kitchen was redolent of good coffee and *eau de lilas.* Wan October sunshine came through the curtain on the window and worked a needlepoint of shadow across the clean pine surface of the table. Trudi was an admirable girl, and the ancient, abused hinges of Kornblum's battered frame seemed to have regained an elastic hum in the embrace of his own partner, Madame Willi—the wielder of the gun.

"Good morning," Kornblum muttered.

Josef blushed deeply. He opened his mouth to speak, but a spasm of coughing seemed to seize him, and his reply was broken and scattered on the air. They had wasted a night on pleasure at a time when so much seemed to depend on haste and self-sacrifice.

Moral discomfort notwithstanding, it was from Trudi that Josef derived a valuable piece of information.

"She heard some kids talking," he told Kornblum after the girl, leaning down to plant a brief, coffee-scented kiss on Josef's cheek, had padded out of the kitchen and down the hall, to regain her disorderly bed. "There is a window in which no one ever sees a face."

"The *children*," Kornblum said, with a curt shake of his head. "Of course." He looked disgusted with himself for having neglected this obvious source of surprising information. "On what floor is this mysterious window?"

"She didn't know."

"On which side of the building?"

"Again, she didn't know. I thought we could find a child and ask it."

Kornblum gave his head a shake. He took another puff on his Letka, tapped it, turned it over, studied the tiny airplane symbol that was printed on the paper. Abruptly, he stood up and started to go through the kitchen drawers, working his way around the cabinets until he came up with a pair of scissors. He carried the scissors into the gilded parlor, where he began opening and closing cabinets. With gentle, precise movements, he went through the drawers of an ornate sideboard in the dining room. At last, in a table in the front hall, he found a box of notepaper, heavy sheets of rag tinted a soft robin's-egg blue. He returned to the kitchen with paper and scissors and sat down again.

"We tell the people we forgot something," he said, folding a sheet of the stationery in half and cutting it, without hesitation, his hand steady and sure. With a half-dozen strokes, he had snipped the three-pointed outline of a paper boat, the sort that children fold from pieces of newspaper. "We say they have to put one of these in every window. To show they have been counted."

"A boat," Josef said. "A boat?"

"Not a boat," Kornblum said. He put the scissors down, opened the cropped piece of paper at the center pleat, and held up a small blue Star of David.

Josef shivered at the sight of it, chilled by the plausibility of this imaginary directive. "They won't do it," he said, watching as Kornblum pressed the little star against the kitchen windowpane. "They won't comply."

"I would like to hope that you're right, young man," Kornblum said. "But we very much need you to be wrong."

Within two hours, every household in the building had spangled its windows in blue. By means of this base stratagem, the room that contained the Golem of Prague was rediscovered. It was on the top floor of Nicholasgasse 26, at the back; its lone window overlooked the rear courtyard. A generation of children at play had, like sky-gazing shepherds in ancient fields, perfected a natural history of the windows that looked down like stars upon them; in its perpetual vacancy, this window, like a retrograde planetoid, had attracted attention and fired imaginations. It also turned out to be the only simple means of ingress for the old escape artist and his protégé. There was, or rather there had once been, a doorway, but it had been plastered and papered over, no doubt at the time of the Golem's installment in the room. Since the roof was easily accessible via the main stair, Kornblum felt that it would attract less notice if they lowered themselves, under the cover of darkness, on ropes and came in through the window than if they tried to cut their way in through the door.

Once again they returned to the building after midnight—the third night of Josef's shadow-existence in the city. This time they came dressed in somber suits and derby hats, carrying vaguely medical black bags, all supplied by a member of the secret circle who ran a mortuary. In this funereal garb, Josef lowered himself, hand under leather-gloved hand, down the rope to the ledge of the Golem's window. He dropped much faster than he intended, nearly to the level of the window on the floor below, then managed to arrest his fall with a sudden jerk that seemed to wrench his shoulder from its socket. He looked up and, in the gloom, could just distinguish the outline of Kornblum's head, the expression as unreadable as the fists clutching the other end of the rope. Josef let out a soft sigh between his clenched teeth and pulled himself back up to the Golem's window.

It was latched, but Kornblum had provided him with a length of stout wire. Josef dangled, ankles snaked around the end of the rope, clinging to it with one hand while, with the other, he jabbed the wire up into the gap between the upper, outer sash and the lower, inner one. His cheek scraped against brick, his shoulder burned, but Josef's only thought was a prayer that this time he should not fail. Finally, just as the pain in his shoulder joint was beginning to intrude on the purity of his desperation, Josef succeeded in popping the latch. He fingered the lower sash, eased it up, and swung himself into the room. He stood panting, working his shoulder in circles. A moment later, there was a creaking of rope or old bones, a soft gasp, and then Kornblum's long narrow legs kicked in through the open window. The magician turned on his torch and scanned the room until he found a lightbulb socket, dangling on a looped cord from the ceiling. He bent to reach into his mortician's bag, took out a lightbulb, and handed it to Josef, who went up on tiptoe to screw it in.

The casket in which the Golem of Prague had been laid was the simple pine box prescribed by Jewish law, but wide as a door and long enough to hold two adolescent boys head to toe. It rested across the backs of a pair of stout sawhorses in the center of an empty room. After more than thirty years, the floor of the Golem's room looked new; free of dust, glossy, and smooth. The white paint on the walls was spotless and still carried a sting of fresh emulsion. Hitherto, Josef had been inclined to discount the weirdness in Kornblum's plan of escape, but now, in the presence of this enormous coffin, in this timeless room, he felt an uneasy prickling creep across his neck and shoulders. Kornblum, too, approached the casket with visible diffidence, extending toward its rough pine lid a hand that hesitated a moment before touching. Cautiously he circled the casket, feeling out the nail heads, counting them, inspecting their condition and the condition of the hinges, and of the screws that held the hinges in place.

"All right," he said softly, with a nod, clearly trying to hearten himself as much as Josef. "Let us continue with the remainder of the plan."

The remainder of Kornblum's plan, at whose midpoint they had now arrived, was this:

First, using the ropes, they would convey the casket out of the window, onto the roof, and thence, posing as undertakers, down the stairs and out of the building. At the funeral home, in a room that had been reserved for them, they would prepare the Golem for shipment by rail to Lithuania. They would begin by gaffing the casket, which involved drawing the nails from one side and replacing them with nails that had been trimmed short, leaving a nub just long enough to fix the gaffed side to the rest of the box. That way, when the time came, Josef would be able, without much difficulty, to kick his way out. Applying the sacred principle of misdirection, they would next equip the coffin with an "inspection panel," making a cut across its lid about a third of the way from the end that held the head and equipping this upper third with a latch, so that it could, like the top half of a Dutch door, be opened separately from the lower. This would afford a good view of the dead Golem's face and chest, but not of the portion of the coffin in which Josef would crouch. After that, they would label the casket, following all the complicated regulations and procedures and affixing the elaborate forms necessary for the transshipment of human remains. Forged death certificates and other required papers would have been left for them, properly concealed, in the mortuary's workroom. After the coffin was prepared and documented, they would load it into a hearse and drive it to the train station. While riding in the back of the hearse, Josef was to climb into the coffin alongside the Golem, pulling shut the gaffed panel after him. At the station, Kornblum would check to see that the coffin appeared sealed and would consign it to the care of the porters, who would load it onto the train. When the coffin arrived in Lithuania, Josef, at his earliest opportunity, would kick aside the gaffed panel, roll free, and discover what fate awaited him on the Baltic shore.

Now that they were confronted with the actual materials of the trick, however—as was so often the case—Kornblum encountered two problems.

"It's a giant," Kornblum said, with a shake of his head, speaking in a tense whisper. With his miniature crowbar, he had pried loose the nails along one side of the coffin's top and lifted the lid on its creaking, galvanized-tin hinges. He stood peering at the pitiable slab of lifeless and innocent clay. "And it's naked."

"It is very big."

"We'll never get it through the window. And if we do, we'll never get it dressed."

"Why do we have to dress it? It has those cloths, the Jewish scarves," Josef said, pointing to the tallises in which the Golem had been wrapped. They were tattered and stained, and yet gave off no odor of corruption. The only smell Josef could detect arising from the swarthy flesh of the Golem was one too faint to name, acrid and green, that he was only later to identify as the sweet stench, on a summer afternoon in the dog days, of the Moldau. "Aren't Jews supposed to be buried naked?"

"That is precisely the point," Kornblum said. He explained that, according to a recent promulgation, it was illegal to transport even a dead Jew out of the country without direct authority of Reichsprotektor von Neurath. "We must practice the tricks of our trade." He smiled thinly, nodding to the black mortician's bags. "Rouge his cheeks and lips. Fit that dome of his with a convincing wig. Someone will look inside the coffin, and when he does, we want him to see a dead *goyische* giant." He closed his eyes as if envisioning what he wanted the authorities to see, should they order the coffin to be opened. "Preferably in a very nice suit."

"The most beautiful suits I ever saw," said Josef, "belonged to a dead giant."

Kornblum studied him, sensing an implication in the words that he was unable to catch.

"Alois Hora. He was over two meters tall."

"From the Circus Zeletny?" Kornblum said. " 'The Mountain'?"

"He wore suits made in England, on Savile Row. Enormous things."

"Yes, yes, I remember," Kornblum said, nodding. "I used to see him quite often at the Café Continental. Beautiful suits," he agreed.

"I think—" Josef began. He hesitated. He said, "I know where I can find one."

It was not at all uncommon in this era for a doctor who treated glandular cases to maintain a wardrobe of wonders, stocked with underlinens the size of horse blankets, homburgs no bigger than berry bowls, and all manner of varied prodigies of haberdashery and the shoemaker's last. These items, which Josef's father had acquired or been given over the years, were kept in a cabinet in his office at the hospital, with the laudable but self-defeating intention of preventing their becoming objects of morbid curiosity to his children. No visit to their father at his place of work was ever complete without the boys at least making an attempt to persuade Dr. Kavalier to let them see the belt, fat and coiling as an anaconda, of the giant Vaclav Sroubek, or the digitalis-blossom slippers of tiny Miss Petra Frantisek. But after the doctor had been dismissed from his position at the hospital, along with the rest of the Jews on the faculty, the wardrobe of wonders had come home and its contents, in sealed packing boxes, stuffed into a closet in his study. Josef was certain that he would find some of Alois Hora's suits among them.

And so, after living for three days in Prague as a shadow, it was as a shadow that he finally went home. It was well past curfew, and the streets were deserted but for a few long, flag-fendered sedans with impenetrable black windows and, once, a lorry loaded with gray-coated boys carrying guns. Josef went slowly and carefully, inserting himself into doorways, ducking behind a parked car or bench when he heard the clank of gears, or when the fork of passing headlights jabbed at the housefronts, the awnings, the cobbles in the street. In his coat pocket, he carried the picks Kornblum had thought he would need for the job, but when Josef got to the service door of the building off the Graben he found that, as was not uncommonly the case, it had been left propped open with a tin can, probably by some housekeeper taking unauthorized leave, or by a vagabond husband.

Josef met no one in the back hall or on the stairs. There was no baby whimpering for a bottle, no faint air of Weber from a late-night radio, no elderly smoker intent on the nightly business of coughing up his lungs. Although the ceiling lights and wall sconces were lit, the collective slumber of the building seemed even more profound than that of Nicholasgasse 26. Josef found this stillness disturbing. He felt the same prickle on his nape, the creeping of his flesh, that he had felt on entering the Golem's empty room.

As he slunk down the hall, he noticed that someone had discarded a pile of clothes on the carpet outside the door of his family's home. For a preconscious instant, his heart leaped at the thought that, by some dreamlike means, one of the suits he sought had somehow been abandoned there. Then Josef saw that it was not a mere heap of clothing but one actually inhabited by a body—someone drunk, or passed out, or expired in the hallway. A girl, he thought, one of his mother's patients. It was rare, but not unheard of, for an analysand, tossed by tides of transference and desublimation, to seek the safety of Dr. Kavalier's doorstep or, by contrast, inflamed with the special hatred of countertransference, to leave herself there in some desperate condition, as a cruel prank, like a paper sack of dog turds set afire.

But the clothes belonged to Josef himself, and the body inside them was Thomas's. The boy lay on his side, knees drawn to his chest, head pillowed on an arm that reached toward the door, fingers spread with an air of lingering intention, as if he had fallen asleep with a hand on the doorknob, then subsided to the floor. He had on a pair of trousers, charcoal corduroy, shiny at the knee, and a bulky cable sweater, with a large hole under the arm and a permanent Czechoslovakia-shaped ghost of bicycle grease on the yoke, which Josef knew his brother liked to put on whenever he was feeling ill or friendless. From the collar of the sweater protruded the piped lapels of a pajama top. The cuffs of the pajama bottoms poked out from the legs of the borrowed pants. Thomas's right cheek was flattened against his outstretched arm, and his breath rattled, regular and clamorous, through his permanently rheumy nose. Josef smiled and started to kneel down beside Thomas to wake him, and tease him, and help him back to bed. Then he remembered that he was not permitted—could not permit himself—to make his presence known. He could not ask Thomas to lie to their parents, nor did he really trust him to do so in any sustained manner. He backed away, trying to think what could have happened and how best to proceed. How had Thomas gotten himself locked out? Was this who had left the service door propped open downstairs? What could have prompted him to risk being out so late when, as everyone knew, a girl in Vinorhady, not much older than Thomas, had just a few weeks before sneaked outside to look for her lost dog and been shot, in a gloomy alley, for violating curfew? There had been official expressions of regret from von Neurath over the incident, but no promise that such a thing would not happen again. If Josef could somehow manage to wake his brother undetected—say by throwing a five-haleru piece at his head from around the corner of the hallway—would Thomas ring to be let in? Or would he be too ashamed, and choose to continue to pass the night in the chilly, dark hall, on the floor? And how would he, Josef, possibly be able to get to the giant's clothes with his brother lying asleep in the doorway or else with the whole household awakened and in an uproar over the boy's waywardness?

These speculations were cut short when Josef stepped on something that crunched, at once soft and rigid, under his heel. His heart seized, and he looked down, dancing backward in disgust, to see not a burst mouse but the leather wallet of lock picks that had once been his reward from Bernard Kornblum. Thomas's eyes fluttered, and he snuffled, and Josef waited, wincing, to see if his brother would sink back into sleep. Thomas sat up abruptly. With the back of his arm he wiped the spittle from his lips, blinked, and gave a short sigh.

"Oh, dear," he said, looking sleepily unsurprised to find his Brooklyn-bound brother crouched beside him, three days after he was supposed to have departed, in the hallway of their building in the heart of Prague. Thomas opened his mouth to speak again, but Josef covered it with the flat of his hand and pressed a finger to his own lips. He shook his head and pointed at the door.

When Thomas cast his eyes in the direction of the door to their flat, he finally seemed to awaken. His mouth narrowed to a pout, as if he had something sour on his tongue. His thick black eyebrows piled up over his nose. He shook his head and again attempted to say something, and again Josef covered his mouth, less gently this time. Josef picked up his old pick-wallet, which he had not seen in months, perhaps years, and which he had supposed, when he gave the matter any thought at all, to be lost. The lock on the Kavaliers' door was one that, in another era, Josef had successfully picked many times. He got them inside now with little difficulty, and stepped into the front hall, grateful for its familiar smell of pipe smoke and paper-whites, for the distant hum of the electric icebox. Then he stepped into the living room and saw that the sofa and piano had been draped in quilts. The fish tank stood empty of fish and drained of water. The box orange in its putti-crusted terra-cotta pot was gone. Crates stood piled in the center of the room.

"They moved?" he said, in the softest whisper he could manage.

"To Dlouha eleven," Thomas said, in a normal tone. "This morning."

"They moved," Josef said, unable now to raise his voice, though there was no one to hear them, no one to alert or disturb.

"It's a *vile* place. The Katzes are *vile* people."

"The Katzes?" There were cousins of his mother, for whom she had never cared much, who went by this name. "Viktor and Renata?"

Thomas nodded. "And the Mucus Twins." He gave a vast roll of his eyes. "And their *vile* parakeet. They taught it to say 'Up your bum, Thomas.' " He sniffed, snickered when his brother did, and then, with another slow agglomeration of his eyebrows, began to discharge a series of coughing sobs, careful and choked, as if they were painful to let out. Josef took him into his arms, stiffly, and thought suddenly how long it had been since he had heard the sound of Thomas freely crying, a sound that had once been as common in the house as the teakettle whistle or the scratch of their father's match. The weight of Thomas on his knee was unwieldy, his shape awkward and unembraceable; he seemed to have grown from a boy to a youth in just the last three days.

"There's a beastly aunt," Thomas said, "and a moronic brother-in-law due tomorrow from Frydlant. I wanted to come back here. Just for tonight. Only I couldn't work the lock."

"I understand," Josef said, understanding only that, until now, until this moment, his heart had never been broken. "You were born in this flat."

Thomas nodded.

"What a day that was," Josef said, trying to cheer the boy. "I was never so disappointed in my life."

Thomas smiled politely. "Almost the whole building moved," he said, sliding off of Josef's knee. "Only the Kravniks and the Policeks and the Zlatnys are allowed to stay." He wiped at his cheek with a forearm.

"Don't get snot on my sweater," Josef said, knocking his brother's arm to one side.

"You left it."

"I might send for it."

"Why aren't you gone?" Thomas said. "What happened to your ship?"

"There have been difficulties. But I should be on my way tonight. You mustn't tell Mother and Father that you saw me."

"You aren't going to see them?"

The question, the plaintive rasp in Thomas's voice as he asked it, pained Josef. He shook his head. "I just had to dash back here to get something."

"Dash back from where?"

Josef ignored the question. "Is everything still here?"

"Except for some clothes, and some kitchen things. And my tennis racket. And my butterflies. And your wireless." This was a twenty-tube set, built into a kind of heavy valise of oiled pine, that Josef had constructed from parts, amateur radio having succeeded illusion and preceded modern art in the cycle of Josef's passions, as Houdini and then Marconi had given way to Paul Klee and Josef's enrollment at the Academy of Fine Arts. "Mother carried it on her lap in the tram. She said listening to it was like listening to your voice, and she would rather have your voice to remember you than your photograph, even."

"And then she said that I never photograph well, anyway."

"Yes, she did, as a matter of fact. The wagon is coming here tomorrow morning for the rest of our things. I'm going to ride with the driver. I'm going to hold the reins. What is it you need? What did you come back for?"

"Wait here," Josef said. He had already revealed too much; Kornblum was going to be very displeased.

He went down the hall to their father's study, checking to make sure that Thomas did not follow, and doing his best to ignore the piled crates, the open doors that ought at this hour to have been long shut, the rolled carpets, the forlorn knocking of his shoe heels along the bare wooden floors. In his father's office, the desk and bookcases had been wrapped in quilted blankets and tied with leather straps, the pictures and curtains taken down. The boxes that contained the uncanny clothing of endocrine freaks had been dragged from the closet and stacked, conveniently, just by the door. Each bore a pasted-on label, carefully printed in his father's strong, regular hand, that gave a precise accounting of the contents of the crate:

DRESSES (5)—MARTINKA
HAT (STRAW)—ROTHMAN
CHRISTENING GOWN—SROUBEK

For some reason, the sight of these labels touched Josef. The writing was as legible as if it had been typeset, each letter shod and gloved with serifs, the parentheses neatly crimped, the wavy hyphens like stylized bolts of lightning. The labels had been lettered lovingly; his father had always expressed that emotion best through troubling with details. In this fatherly taking of pains—in this stubbornness, persistence, orderliness, patience, and calm—Josef had always taken comfort. Here Dr. Kavalier seemed to have composed, on his crates of strange mementos, a series of messages in the very alphabet of imperturbability itself. The labels seemed evidence of all the qualities his father and family were going to require to survive the ordeal to which Josef was abandoning them. With his father in charge, the Kavaliers and the Katzes would doubtless manage to form one of those rare households in which decency and order prevailed. With patience and calm, persistence and stoicism, good handwriting and careful labeling, they would meet persecution, indignity, and hardship head-on.

But then, staring at the label on one crate, which read

SWORD-CANE—DLUBECK
SHOE TREE—HORA
SUITS (3)—HORA
ASSORTED HANDKERCHIEFS (6)—HORA

Josef felt a bloom of dread in his belly, and all at once he was certain that it was not going to matter one iota how his father and the others behaved. Orderly or chaotic, well inventoried and civil or jumbled and squabbling, the Jews of Prague were dust on the boots of the Germans, to be whisked off with an indiscriminate broom. Stoicism and an eye for detail would avail them nothing. In later years, when he remembered this moment, Josef would be tempted to think that he had suffered a premonition, looking at those mucilage-caked labels, of the horror to come. At the time it was a simpler matter. The hair stood up on the back of his neck with a prickling discharge of ions. His heart pulsed in the hollow of his throat as if someone had pressed there with a thumb. And he felt, for an instant, that he was admiring the penmanship of someone who had died.

"What's that?" Thomas said, when Josef returned to the parlor with one of Hora's extra-large garment bags slung over his shoulder. "What happened? What's wrong?"

"Nothing," said Josef. "Look, Thomas, I have to go. I'm sorry."

"I *know.*" Thomas sounded almost irritated. He sat down cross-legged on the floor. "I'm going to spend the night."

"No, Thomas, I don't think—"

"You don't get to say," Thomas said. "You aren't here anymore, re-member?"

The words echoed Kornblum's sound advice, but somehow they chilled Josef. He could not shake the feeling—reportedly common among ghosts—that it was not he but those he haunted whose lives were devoid of matter, sense, future.

"Perhaps you're right," he said after a moment. "You oughtn't to be out in the streets at night, anyway. It's too dangerous."

A hand on each of Thomas's shoulders, Josef steered his brother back to the room they had shared for the last eleven years. With some blankets and a slipless pillow that he found in a trunk, he made up a bed on the floor. Then he dug around in some other crates until he found an old children's alarm clock, a bear's face eared with a pair of brass bells, which he wound and set for five-thirty.

"You have to be back there by six," he said, "or they'll miss you."

Thomas nodded and climbed between the blankets of the makeshift bed. "I wish I could go with you," he said.

"I know," Josef said. He brushed the hair from Thomas's forehead. "So do I. But you'll be joining me soon enough."

"Do you promise?"

"I will make sure of it," Josef said. "I won't rest until I'm meeting your ship in the harbor of New York City."

"On that island they have," Thomas said, his eyelids fluttering. "With the Statue of Liberation."

"I promise," Josef said.

"Swear."

"I swear."

"Swear by the River Styx."

"I swear it," Josef said, "by the River Styx."

Then he leaned down and, to the surprise of both of them, kissed his brother on the lips. It was the first such kiss between them since the younger had been an infant and the elder a doting boy in knee pants.

"Goodbye, Josef," said Thomas.

When Josef returned to Nicholasgasse, he found that Kornblum had, with typical resourcefulness, solved the problem of the Golem's extrication. Into the thin panel of gypsum that had been used to fill the door frame at the time when the Golem was installed, Kornblum, employing some unspeakable implement of the mortuary trade, had cut a rectangle, at floor level, just large enough to accommodate the casket end-on. The obverse of the gypsum panel, out in the hall, was covered in the faded Jugendstil paper, a pattern of tall interlocking poppies, that decorated all the hallways of the building. Kornblum had been careful to cut through this thin outer hide on only three of his rectangle's four sides, leaving at its top a hinge of intact wallpaper. Thus he had formed a serviceable trapdoor.

"What if someone notices?" Josef said after he had finished inspecting Kornblum's work.

This gave rise to another of Kornblum's impromptu and slightly cynical maxims. "People notice only what you tell them to notice," he said. "And then only if you remind them."

They dressed the Golem in the suit that had belonged to the giant Alois Hora. This was hard work, as the Golem was relatively inflexible. It was not as rigid as one might have imagined, given its nature and composition. Its cold clay flesh seemed to give slightly under the pressure of fingertips, and a narrow range of motion, perhaps the faintest memory of play, inhered in the elbow of the right arm, the arm it would have used, as the legend records, to touch the mezuzah on its maker's doorway every evening when it returned from its labors, bringing its Scripture-kissed fingers to its lips. The Golem's knees and ankles, however, were more or less petrified. Furthermore, its hands and feet were poorly proportioned, as is often the case with the work of amateur artists, and much too large for its body. The enormous feet got snagged in the trouser legs, so that getting the pants on was particularly difficult. Finally, Josef had to reach into the coffin and grasp the Golem around the waist, elevating its lower body several inches, before Kornblum could tug the trousers over the feet, up the legs, and around the Golem's rather sizable buttocks. They had decided not to bother with underwear, but for the sake of anatomical verisimilitude—in a display of the thoroughness that had characterized his career on the stage—Kornblum tore one of the old tallises in two (kissing it first), gave a series of twists to one of the halves, and tucked the resulting artifact up between the Golem's legs, into the crotch, where there was only a smooth void of clay.

"Maybe it was supposed to be a female," Josef suggested as he watched Kornblum zip the Golem's fly.

"Not even the Maharal could make a woman out of clay," Kornblum said. "For that you need a rib." He stood back, considering the Golem. He gave a tug on one lapel of the jacket and smoothed the billowing pleats of the trousers front. "This is a very nice suit."

It was one of the last Alois Hora had taken delivery of before his death, when his body had been wasted by Marfan's syndrome, and thus a perfect fit for the Golem, which was not so large as the Mountain in his prime. Of excellent English worsted, gray and tan, shot with a burgundy thread, it easily could have been subdivided into a suit for Josef and another for Kornblum, with enough left over, as the magician remarked, for a waistcoat apiece. The shirt was of fine white twill, with mother-of-pearl buttons, and the necktie of burgundy silk, with an embossed pattern of cabbage roses, slightly flamboyant, as Hora had liked his ties. There were no shoes—Josef had forgotten to search for a pair, and in any case none would have been large enough—but if the lower regions of the casket's interior were ever inspected, the trick would fail anyway, shoes or no.

Once it was dressed, its cheeks rouged, its smooth head bewigged, its forehead and eyelids fitted with the tiny eyebrow and eyelash hairpieces employed by gentile morticians in the case of facial burning or certain depilatory diseases, the Golem looked, with its dull grayish complexion the color of boiled mutton, indisputably dead and passably human. There was only the faintest trace of the human handprint on its forehead, from which, centuries before, the name of God had been rubbed away. Now they only had to slide it through the trapdoor and follow it out of the room.

This proved easy enough; as Josef had remarked when he lifted it to get the trousers on, the Golem weighed far less than its bulk and nature would have suggested. To Josef, it felt as if they were struggling, down the hallway, down the stairs, and out the front door of Nicholasgasse 26, with a substantial pine box and a large suit of clothes, and little besides.

" '*Mach' bida lo nafsho*,' " Kornblum said, quoting Midrash, when Josef remarked on the lightness of their load. " 'His soul is a burden unto him.' This is nothing, this." He nodded toward the lid of the coffin. "Just an empty jar. If you were not in there, I would have been obliged to weight it down with sandbags."

The trip out of the building and back to the mortuary in the borrowed Skoda hearse—Kornblum had learned to drive in 1908, he said, taught by Franz Hofzinser's great pupil Hans Kreutzler—came off without incident or an encounter with the authorities. The only person who saw them carrying the coffin out of the building, an insomniac out-of-work engineer named Pilzen, was told that old Mr. Lazarus in 42 had finally died after a long illness. When Mrs. Pilzen came by the flat the next afternoon with a plate of egg cookies in hand, she found a wizened old gentleman and three charming if somewhat improper women in black kimonos, sitting on low stools, with torn ribbons pinned to their clothes and the mirrors covered, a set of conditions that proved bemusing to the clientele of Madame Willi's establishment over the next seven days, some of whom were unnerved and some excited by the blasphemy of making love in a house of the dead.

Seventeen hours after he climbed into the coffin to lie with the empty vessel that once had been animate with the condensed hopes of Jewish Prague, Josef's train approached the town of Oshmyany, on the border between Poland and Lithuania. The two national railway systems employed different gauges of track, and there was to be a sixty-minute delay as passengers and freight were shifted from the gleaming black Soviet-built express of Polish subjugation to the huffing, Czarist-era local of a tenuous Baltic liberty. The big *Iosef Stalin*–class locomotive eased all but silently into its berth and uttered a surprisingly sensitive, even rueful, sigh. Slowly, for the most part, as if unwilling to draw attention to themselves by an untoward display of eagerness or nerves, the passengers, a good many young men of an age with Josef Kavalier, dressed in the belted coats, knickers, and broad hats of Chasidim, stepped down onto the platform and moved in an orderly way toward the emigration and customs officers who waited, along with a representative of the local Gestapo bureau, in a room overheated by a roaring pot-bellied stove. The railway porters, a sad crew of spavined old men and weaklings, few of whom looked capable of carrying a hatbox, let alone the coffin of a giant, rolled back the doors of the car in which the Golem and its stowaway companion rode, and squinted doubtfully at the burden they were now expected to unload and carry twenty-five meters to a waiting Lithuanian boxcar.

Inside the coffin, Josef lay insensible. He had fainted with an excruciating, at times almost pleasurable, slowness over a period of some eight or ten hours, as the rocking of the train, the lack of oxygen, the deficit of sleep and surfeit of nervous upset he had accumulated over the past week, the diminished circulation of his blood, and a strange, soporific emanation from the Golem itself that seemed connected to its high-summer, rank-river smell, all conspired to overcome the severe pain in his hips and back, the cramping of his leg and arm muscles, the near-impossibility of urination, the tingling, at times almost jolting, numbness of his legs and feet, the growling of his stomach, and the dread, wonder, and uncertainty of the voyage on which he had embarked. When they took the coffin from the train, he did not waken, though his dream took on an urgent but inconclusive tinge of peril. He did not come to his senses until a beautiful jet of cold fir-green air singed his nostrils, lighting his slumber with an intensity matched only by the pale shaft of sunlight that penetrated his prison when the "inspection panel" was abruptly thrown open.

Once more it was Kornblum's instruction that saved Josef from losing everything in the first instant. In the first dazzling panic that followed the opening of the panel, when Josef wanted to cry out in pain, rapture, and fear, the word "Oshmyany" seemed to lie cold and rational between his fingers, like a pick that was going, in the end, to free him. Kornblum, whose encyclopedic knowledge of the railroads of this part of Europe was in a few short years to receive a dreadful appendix, had coached him thoroughly, as they worked to gaff the coffin, on the stages and particulars of his journey. He felt the jostle of men's arms, the sway of their hips as they carried the coffin, and this, together with the odor of northern forest and a susurrant snippet of Polish, resolved at the last possible instant into a consciousness of where he was and what must be happening to him. The porters themselves had opened the coffin as they carried it from the Polish train to the Lithuanian. He could hear, and vaguely understand, that they were marveling both at the deadness and giantness of their charge. Then Josef's teeth came together with a sharp porcelain chiming as the coffin was dropped. Josef kept silent and prayed that the impact didn't pop the gaffed nails and send him tumbling out. He hoped that he had been thrown thus into the new box-car, but feared that it was only impact with the station floor that had filled his mouth with blood from his bitten tongue. The light shrank and winked out, and he exhaled, safe in the airless, eternal dark; then the light blazed again.

"What is this? Who is this?" said a German voice.

"A giant, Herr Lieutenant. A dead giant."

"A dead Lithuanian giant." Josef heard a rattle of paper. The German officer was leafing through the sheaf of forged documents that Kornblum had affixed to the outside of the coffin. "Named Kervelis Hailonidas. Died in Prague the night before last. Ugly bastard."

"Giants are always ugly, Lieutenant," said one of the porters in German. There was general agreement from the other porters, with some supporting cases offered into evidence.

"Great God," said the German officer, "but it's a crime to bury a suit like that in a dirty old hole in the ground. Here, you. Get a crowbar. Open that coffin."

Kornblum had provided Josef with an empty Mosel bottle, into which he was, at rare intervals, to insert the tip of his penis and, sparingly, relieve his bladder. But there was no time to maneuver it into place as the porters began to kick and scrape at the seams of the giant coffin. The inseam of Josef's trousers burned and then went instantly cold.

"There is no crowbar, Herr Lieutenant," one of the porters said. "We will chop it open with an ax."

Josef struggled against a wild panic that scratched like an animal at his rib cage.

"Ah, no," the German officer said with a laugh. "Forget it. I'm tall, all right, but I'm not that tall." After a moment, the darkness of the coffin was restored. "Carry on, men."

There was a pause, and then, with a jerk, Josef and the Golem were lifted again.

"And he's ugly, too," said one of the men, in a voice just audible to Josef, "but he's not *that* ugly."

Some twenty-seven hours later, Josef staggered, dazed, blinking, limping, bent, asphyxiated, and smelling of stale urine, into the sun-tattered grayness of an autumn morning in Lithuania. He watched from behind a soot-blackened pillar of the Vilna station as the two dour-looking confederates of the secret circle claimed the curious, giant coffin from Prague. Then he hobbled around to the house of Kornblum's brother-in-law, on Pylimo Street, where he was received kindly with food, a hot bath, and a narrow cot in the kitchen. It was while staying here, trying to arrange for passage to New York out of Priekule, that he first heard of a Dutch consul in Kovno who was madly issuing visas to Curaçao, in league with a Japanese official who would grant rights of transit via the Empire of Japan to any Jew bound for the Dutch colony. Two days later he was on the Trans-Siberian Express; a week later he reached Vladivostok, and thence sailed for Kobe. From Kobe he shipped to San Francisco, where he wired his aunt in Brooklyn for money for the bus to New York. It was on the steamer carrying him through the Golden Gate that he happened to reach down into the hole in the lining of the right pocket of his overcoat and discover the envelope that his brother had solemnly handed to him almost a month before. It contained a single piece of paper, which Thomas had hastily stuffed into it that morning as they all were leaving the house together for the last time, by way or in lieu of expressing the feelings of love, fear, and hopefulness that his brother's escape inspired. It was the drawing of Harry Houdini, taking a calm cup of tea in the middle of the sky, that Thomas had made in his notebook during his abortive career as a librettist. Josef studied it, feeling as he sailed toward freedom as if he weighed nothing at all, as if every precious burden had been lifted from him.

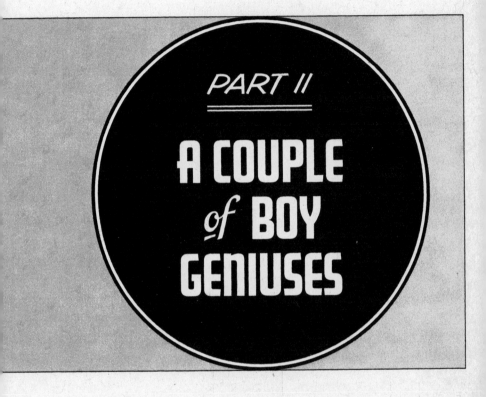

PART II

A COUPLE
of BOY
GENIUSES

WHEN THE ALARM CLOCK went off at six-thirty that Friday, Sammy awoke to find that Sky City, a chromium cocktail tray stocked with moderne bottles, shakers, and swizzle sticks, was under massive attack. In the skies around the floating hometown of D'Artagnan Jones, the strapping blond hero of Sammy's *Pimpernel of the Planets* comic strip, flapped five bat-winged demons, horns carefully whorled like whelks, muscles feathered in with a fine brush. A giant, stubbly spider with the eyes of a woman dangled on a hairy thread from the gleaming underside of Sky City. Other demons with goat legs and baboon faces, brandishing sabers, clambered down ladders and swung in on ropes from the deck of a fantastic caravel with a painstakingly rendered rigging of aerials and vanes. In command of these sinister forces, hunched over the drawing table, wearing only black kneesocks clocked with red lozenges, and swaddled in a baggy pair of off-white Czechoslovakian underpants, sat Josef Kavalier, scratching away with one of Sammy's best pens.

Sammy slid down to the foot of his bed to peer over his cousin's shoulder. "What the hell are you doing to my page?" he said.

The captain of the demonic invasion force, absorbed in his deployment and tipped dangerously back on the tall stool, was caught by surprise. He jumped, and the stool tipped, but he caught hold of the table's edge and neatly righted himself, then reached out just in time to catch the bottle of ink before it, too, could tip over. He was quick.

"I am sorry," Josef said. "I was very careful to don't harm your drawings. See." He lifted an overlaid sheet from the ambitious, *Prince Valiant*–style full-page panel Sammy had been working on, and the five noisome bat-demons disappeared. "I used separate papers for everything." He peeled away the baboon-faced demon raiders and lifted the paper spider by the end of her thread. With a few quick motions of his long-fingered hands, the hellish siege of Sky City was lifted.

"Holy cow!" said Sammy. He clapped his cousin on his freckled shoulder. "Christ, look at this! Let me see those things." He took the kidney-shaped sheet that Josef Kavalier had filled with slavering coal-eyed horned demons and cut to overlay Sammy's own drawing. The proportions of the muscular demons were perfect, their poses animated and plausible, the inkwork mannered but strong-lined. The style was far more sophisticated than Sammy's, which, while confident and plain and occasionally bold, was never anything more than cartooning. "You really can *draw*."

"I was two years studying at the Academy of Fine Arts. In Prague."

"The Academy of Fine Arts." Sammy's boss, Sheldon Anapol, was impressed by men with fancy educations. The ravishing, impossible scheme that had been tormenting Sammy's imagination for months seemed all at once to have a shot at getting off the ground. "Okay, you can draw monsters. What about cars? Buildings?" he asked, faking an employerly monotone, trying to conceal his excitement.

"Of course."

"Your anatomy seems not bad at all."

"It's a fascination for me."

"Can you draw the sound of a fart?"

"Sorry?"

"At Empire they put out a whole bunch of items that make farting sounds. A fart, you know what that means?" Sammy clapped the cupped palm of one hand to the opposite armpit and pumped his arm, squirting out a battery of curt, wet blasts. His cousin, eyes wide, got the idea. "Naturally, we can't say it outright in the ads. We have to say something like 'The Whoopee Hat Liner emits a sound more easily imagined than described.' So you really have to get it across in the drawing."

"I see," said Josef. He seemed to take up the challenge. "I would draw a breathing of wind." He scratched five quick horizontal lines on a scrap of paper. "Then I would put such small things, so." He sprinkled his staff with stars and curlicues and broken musical notation.

"Nice," said Sammy. "Josef, I tell you what. I'm going to try to do better than just get you a job drawing the Gravmonica Friction-Powered Mouth Organ, all right? I'm going to get us into the big money."

"The big money," Josef said, looking suddenly hungry and gaunt. "That would be good of you, Sammy. I need some of the very big money. Yes, all right."

Sammy was startled by the avidity in his cousin's face. Then he realized what the money was wanted for, which made him feel a little afraid. It was hard enough being a disappointment to himself and Ethel without having to worry about four starving Jews in Czechoslovakia. But he managed to discount the tremor of doubt and reached out his hand. "All right," he said. "Shake, Josef."

Josef put forth his hand, then pulled back. He put on what he must have thought was an American accent, a weird kind of British cowboy twang, and screwed his features into a would-be James Cagney wiseguy squint. "Call me Joe," he said.

"Joe Kavalier."

"Sam Klayman."

They started to shake again, then Sammy withdrew his own hand.

"Actually," he said, feeling himself blush, "my professional name is Clay."

"Clay?"

"Yeah. I, uh, I just think it sounds more professional."

Joe nodded. "Sam Clay," he said.

"Joe Kavalier."

They shook hands.

"Boys!" called Mrs. Klayman from the kitchen. "Breakfast."

"Just don't say anything about any of this to my mother," Sammy said. "And don't tell her I'm changing my name."

They went out to the laminate table in the kitchen and sat down in two of the padded chrome chairs. Bubbie, who had never met any of her Czech progeny, was sitting beside Joe, ignoring him completely. She had encountered, for better or worse, so many human beings since 1846 that she seemed to have lost the inclination, perhaps even the ability, to acknowledge faces or events that dated from any time after the

Great War, when she had performed the incomparable feat of leaving Lemberg, the city of her birth, at the age of seventy, to come to America with the youngest of her eleven children. Sammy had never felt himself to be anything more, in Bubbie's eyes, than a kind of vaguely beloved shadow from which the familiar features of dozens of earlier children and grandchildren, some of them dead sixty years, peered out. She was a large, boneless woman who draped herself like an old blanket over the chairs of the apartment, staring for hours with her gray eyes at ghosts, figments, recollections, and dust caught in oblique sunbeams, her arms streaked and pocked like relief maps of vast planets, her massive calves stuffed like forcemeat into lung-colored support hose. She was quixotically vain about her appearance and spent an hour each morning making up her face.

"Eat," Ethel snapped, depositing in front of Joe a stack of black rectangles and a pool of yellow mucilage that she felt obliged to identify for him as toast and eggs. He popped a forkful into his mouth and chewed it with a circumspect expression behind which Sammy thought he detected a hint of genuine disgust.

Sammy performed the rapid series of operations—which combined elements of the folding of wet laundry, the shoveling of damp ashes, and the swallowing of a secret map on the point of capture by enemy troops—that passed, in his mother's kitchen, for eating. Then he stood up, wiped his lips with the back of his hand, and pulled on his good wool blazer. "Come on, Joe, we gotta go." He leaned down to embed a kiss in Bubbie's suede cheek.

Joe dropped his spoon and, in the course of retrieving it, bumped his head on the table, hard. Bubbie cried out, and a minor commotion of silverware and chair-scraping ensued. Then Joe stood up, too, and delicately wiped his lips with his paper napkin. He smoothed it out when he finished and laid it on his empty plate.

"Delicious," he said. "Thank you."

"Here," Ethel said, taking a neat tweed suit, on a hanger, from the back of a kitchen chair. "I pressed your suit and took the spots off your shirt."

"Thank you, Aunt."

Ethel put her arm around Joe's hips and gave him a proud squeeze. "This one knows how to draw a lizard, that I can tell you."

Sammy flushed. This was a reference to the peculiar difficulties Sammy had run into, the month before, with the Live Chameleon item ("Wear it on your lapel to amaze and impress!") that Empire had recently added to their line. An apparently congenital lack of skill with reptiles was compounded by the fact that he had no idea what kind of reptile twenty-five cents sent to Empire Novelty would buy, since there were, in fact, no Live Chameleons in stock, and would not be until Shelly Anapol saw how many orders, if any, came in. Sammy had spent two nights poring over encyclopedias and library books, drawing hundreds of lizards, thin and fat, Old World and New, horned and hooded, and had ended up with something that looked a little like a flattened, bald squirrel. It was his sole failure since taking on the draftsmanship chores at Empire, but his mother, naturally, seemed to regard it as a signal one.

"He won't have to draw any lizards, or cheap cameras, or any of that other dreck they sell," said Sammy, and then added, forgetting the warning he had given Joe, "not if Anapol goes in for my plan."

"What plan?" His mother narrowed her eyes.

"Comic books," yelled Sammy, right to her face.

"Comic books!" She rolled her eyes.

" 'Comic books'?" said Joe. "What are these?"

"Trash," said Ethel.

"What do you know about it?" Sammy said, taking hold of Joe's arm. It was almost seven o'clock. Anapol docked your pay if you came in after eight. "There's good money in comic books. I know a kid, Jerry Glovsky—" He pulled Joe toward the hallway that led to the foyer and the front door, knowing exactly what his mother was going to say next.

"Jerry Glovsky," she said. "A fine example. He's retarded. His parents are first cousins."

"Don't listen to her, Joe. I know what I'm talking about."

"He doesn't want to waste his time on any idiotic comic books."

"*It's not your business,*" Sammy hissed, "what he does. Is it?"

This, as Sammy had known it would, shut her right up. The question of something being one's business or not held a central position in the ethics of Ethel Klayman, whose major tenet was the supreme importance of minding one's own. Gossips, busybodies, and kibitzers were the fiends of her personal demonology. She was universally at odds with the neighbors, and suspicious, to the point of paranoia, of all visiting doctors, salesmen, municipal employees, synagogue committeemen, and tradespeople.

She turned now and looked at her nephew. "You want to draw comic books?" she asked him.

Joe stood there, head down, a shoulder against the door frame. While Sammy and Ethel argued, he had been affecting to study in polite embarrassment the low-pile, mustard-brown carpeting, but now he looked up, and it was Sammy's turn to feel embarrassed. His cousin looked him up and down, with an expression that was both appraising and admonitory.

"Yes, Aunt," he said. "I do. Only I have one question. What is a comic book?"

Sammy reached into his portfolio, pulled out a creased, well-thumbed copy of the latest issue of *Action Comics*, and handed it to his cousin.

In 1939 the American comic book, like the beavers and cockroaches of prehistory, was larger and, in its cumbersome way, more splendid than its modern descendant. It aspired to the dimensions of a slick magazine and to the thickness of a pulp, offering sixty-four pages of gaudy bulk (including the cover) for its ideal price of one thin dime. While the quality of its interior illustrations was generally execrable at best, its covers pretended to some of the skill and design of the slick, and to the brio of the pulp magazine. The comic book cover, in those early days, was a poster advertising a dream-movie, with a running time of two seconds, that flickered to life in the mind and unreeled in splendor just before one opened to the stapled packet of coarse paper inside and the lights came up. The covers were often hand-painted, rather than merely inked and colored, by men with solid reputations in the business, journeyman illustrators who could pull off accurate lab girls in chains and languid, detailed jungle jaguars and muscularly correct male bodies whose feet seemed really to carry their weight. Held in the hand, hefted, those early numbers of *Wonder* and *Detective*, with their chromatic crew of pirates, Hindu poisoners, and snap-brim avengers, their abundant typography at once stylish and crude, seem even today to promise adventure of a light but thoroughly nourishing variety. All too often, however, the scene depicted on the label bore no relation to the thin soup of material contained within. Inside the covers—whence today there wafts an inevitable flea-market smell of rot and nostalgia—the comic book of 1939 was, artistically and morphologically, in a far more primitive state. As with all mongrel art forms and pidgin languages, there was, in the beginning, a necessary, highly fertile period of genetic and grammatical confusion. Men who had been reading newspaper comic strips and pulp magazines for most of their lives, many of them young and inexperienced with the pencil, the ink brush, and the cruel time constraints of piecework, struggled to see beyond the strict spatial requirements of the newspaper strip, on the one hand, and the sheer overheated wordiness of the pulp on the other.

From the beginning, there was a tendency among educators, psychologists, and the general public to view the comic book as merely a debased offspring of the newspaper comic strip, then in the full flower of its since-faded glory, read by presidents and Pullman porters, a proud American cousin, in indigenous vitality and grace, of baseball and jazz. Some of the opprobrium and sense of embarrassment that would forever after attach itself to the comic book form was due to the way it at first inevitably suffered, even at its best, by comparison with the mannered splendor of Burne Hogarth, Alex Raymond, Hal Foster, and the other kings of funny-page draftsmanship, with the finely tuned humor and adultish irony of *Li'l Abner*, *Krazy Kat*, *Abbie 'n' Slats*, with the steady, metrical storytelling of Gould and Gray and *Gasoline Alley*, or with the dizzying, never surpassed interplay of verbal and visual narrative in the work of Milton Caniff.

At first, and until very recently in 1939, comic books had in fact been nothing more than reprint digests of the more popular strips, uprooted from their newspaper homes and forced, not without violence and scissoring, between a pair of cheap glossy covers. The strips' measured, three-to-four-panel pacing, with Friday cliffhangers and Monday recapitulations, suffered in the more spacious confines of the "funny book," and what felt stately, thrilling, or hilarious when doled out in spoonfuls on a daily basis seemed a jerky, repetitive, static, and unnecessarily protracted business in the pages of, say, *More Fun* (1937), the first comic book that Sammy Klayman ever bought. Partly for this reason, but also to avoid paying the established syndicates for the reprint rights, the early publishers of comic books began to experiment with original content, hiring artists or packagers of artists to create their own characters and strips. These artists, if experienced, were not generally successful or talented; if they had talent, they lacked experience. Those in the latter category were mostly immigrants or immigrants' children, or country boys right off the bus. They had dreams but, given their last names and lack of connections, no real chance of succeeding in the lofty world of *Saturday Evening Post* covers and ads for Mazda lightbulbs. Many of them, it must be said, could not even draw a realistic picture of the admittedly complicated bodily appendage with which they hoped to make their livings.

The drop-off in quality that followed the original-content revolution was immediate and precipitous. Lines grew tentative, poses awkward, compositions static, backgrounds nonexistent. Feet, notoriously difficult to draw in realistic depth, all but disappeared from the panels, and noses were reduced to the simplest variations on the twenty-second letter of the alphabet. Horses resembled barrel-chested, spindly dogs, and automobiles were carefully effaced with speed lines to disguise the fact that they lacked doors, were never drawn to scale, and all looked the same. Pretty women, as a requisite arrow in every boy cartoonist's quiver, fared somewhat better, but the men tended to stand around in wrinkleless suits that looked stamped from stovepipe tin and in hats that appeared to weigh more than the automobiles, ill at ease, big-chinned, punching one another in their check-mark noses. Circus strong men, giant Hindu manservants, and breechclouted jungle lords invariably sported fanciful musculature, eyeceps and octoceps and beltoids, and abdomens like fifteen racked pool balls. Knees and elbows bent at painful, double-jointed angles. The color was murky at best, and at worst there was hardly any color at all. Sometimes everything was just two tones of red, or two of blue. But most of all, comic books suffered not from insufficient artwork—for there was considerable vitality here, too, and a collective Depression-born urge toward self-improvement, and even the occasional talented hard-luck competent pencilman—but from a bad case of the carbon copies. Everything was a version, sometimes hardly altered at all, of a newspaper strip or a pulp-radio hero. Radio's Green Hornet spawned various colors of wasp, beetle, and bee; the Shadow was himself shadowed by a legion of suit-wearing, felt-hatted, lama-trained vigilantes; every villainess was a thinly disguised Dragon Lady. Consequently, the comic book, almost immediately upon its invention, or soon thereafter, began to languish, lacking purpose or distinction. There was nothing here one could not find done better, or cheaper, somewhere else (and on the radio one could have it for free).

Then, in June 1938, Superman appeared. He had been mailed to the offices of National Periodical Publications from Cleveland, by a couple of Jewish boys who had imbued him with the power of a hundred men, of a distant world, and of the full measure of their bespectacled adolescent hopefulness and desperation. The artist, Joe Shuster, while technically just barely apt, seemed to understand from the first that the big rectangular page of the comic book offered possibilities for pacing and composition that were mostly unavailable in the newspapers; he joined three panels vertically into one to display the full parabolic zest of one of Superman's patented skyscraper-hops (the Man of Steel could not, at this point in his career, properly fly), and he chose his angles and arranged his figures with a certain cinematic flair. The writer, Jerome Siegel, had forged, through the smelting intensity of his fanatical love and compendious knowledge of the pulps and their antecedents, a magical alloy of several previous characters and archetypes from Samson to Doc Savage, one with its own unique properties of tensility, hardness, and luster. Though he had been conceived originally as a newspaper hero, Superman was born in the pages of a comic book, where he thrived, and after this miraculous parturition, the form finally began to emerge from its transitional funk, and to articulate a purpose for itself in the marketplace of ten-cent dreams: to express the lust for power and the gaudy sartorial taste of a race of powerless people with no leave to dress themselves. Comic books were Kid Stuff, pure and true, and they arrived at precisely the moment when the kids of America began, after ten years of terrible hardship, to find their pockets burdened with the occasional superfluous dime.

"That's a comic book," said Sammy.

"Big money you say," Joe said, looking more doubtful than he had all morning.

"Fifty dollars a week. Maybe more."

"Fifty dollars!" said Ethel, her usual tone of disbelief modified, it seemed to Sammy, by a wrinkle of uncertainty, as if the very patent outrageousness of the claim might be a guarantee of its veracity.

"Forty at least."

Ethel folded her arms and stood there, chewing on her lower lip. Then she nodded. "I have to find you a better tie," she said to Joe. She turned and went back into the apartment.

"Hey, Sam Clay," Joe whispered, producing the neat little bundle, wrapped in a paper napkin, in which he had secreted his uneaten breakfast. He held it up with a little smile. "Where I can throw this?"

THE OFFICES of the Empire Novelty Company, Inc., were on the fourth floor of the Kramler Building, in a hard-luck stretch of Twenty-fifth Street near Madison Square. A fourteen-story office block faced with stone the color of a stained shirt collar, its windows bearded with soot, ornamented with a smattering of moderne zigzags, the Kramler stood out as a lone gesture of commercial hopefulness in a block filled with low brick "taxpayers" (minimal structures generating just enough in rent to pay property taxes on the land they occupied), boarded-up woolens showrooms, and the moldering headquarters of benevolent societies that ministered to dwindling and scattered populations of immigrants from countries no longer on the map. It had been dedicated in late 1929, then repossessed by the lien-holding bank when the developer leaped from the window of his office on the fourteenth floor. In the ten years since, it had managed to attract a small but varied number of tenants, among them a publisher of sexy pulp magazines; a distributor of hairpieces, false beards, male corsets, and elevator shoes; and the East Coast booking agents for a third-rate midwestern circus; all of them attracted, as Shelly Anapol had been, by the cut-rate rents and a collegial atmosphere of rascality.

Despite the air of failure and disrepute that permeated the neighborhood, Sheldon P. Anapol—whose brother-in-law Jack Ashkenazy owned Racy Publications, Inc., on the Kramler's seventh floor—was a talented businessman, likable and cruel. He had gone to work for Hyman Lazar, the founder of Empire Novelty, in 1914, at the age of twenty, as a penniless traveling salesman, and fifteen years later had saved enough to buy the company out from under Lazar when the latter ran afoul of his creditors. The combination of a hard-won cynicism, low overhead, an unstintingly shoddy product line, and the American boy's unassuageable hunger for midget radios, X-ray spectacles, and joy buzzers had enabled Anapol not only to survive the Depression but to keep his two daughters in private school and to support or, as he liked to put it, invoking unconscious imagery of battleships and Cunard liners, to "float" his immense and expensive wife.

As with all great salesmen, Anapol's past comprehended tragedy and disappointment. He was an orphan of pogrom and typhus, raised by unfeeling relations. His physical bulk, inherited from generations of slab-jawed, lumbering Anapols, had for much of his early life rendered him the butt of jokes and the object of women's scorn. As a young man, he had played the violin well enough to hope for a musical career, until a hasty marriage and the subsequent upkeep on his two dreadnought daughters, Belle and Candace, forced him into a life of commercial traveling. All of this left him hardened, battered, rumpled, and addicted to the making of money, but not, somehow, embittered. He had always been welcome, during his days on the road, in the lonely shops of the dealers in jokes and novelties, men who were often in their third or fourth line of work and almost universally broken, after years of guessing and disaster, of the ability to know what was amusing and what was not. The unambiguously comical sight of Anapol, with his vast, unbuttoned suits and mismatched socks, his sad violinist's eyes, modeling a blond horsehair wig or demonstrating a dentifrice that turned the teeth of victims black, had been the keystone of many a big sale in Wilkes-Barre or Pittsfield.

In the last decade, however, he had traveled no farther than Riverdale; and over the past year, following an intensification in his perennial "difficulties" with his wife, Anapol had rarely even left the Kramler Building. He had a bed and nightstand brought in from Macy's, and he slept in his office, behind an old crewelwork coverlet draped over a length of clothesline. Sammy had received his first raise the previous fall when he found an empty pushboy's clothes rack idling on Seventh Avenue one night and rolled it across town to serve as Anapol's clothes closet. Anapol, who had read widely in the literature of sales and was in fact eternally at work on a treatise-cum-autobiography he referred to sometimes as *The Science of Opportunity* and other times, more ruefully, as *Sorrow in My Sample Case,* not only preached initiative but rewarded it, an ethos on which Sammy now pinned all his hopes.

"So talk," said Anapol. He was wearing, as usual at this early hour, only socks, garters, and a pair of brightly patterned boxer shorts wide enough to qualify, Sammy thought, as a mural. He was bent over a tiny sink at the back of his office, shaving his face. He had been up, as every morning, since before dawn, settling on a move in one of the chess games he played by mail with men in Cincinnati, Fresno, and Zagreb; writing to other solitary lovers of Szymanowski whom he had organized into an international appreciation society; penning ill-concealed threats to particularly recalcitrant debtors in his creaky, vivid, half-grammatical prose in which there were hints of Jehovah and George Raft; and composing his daily letter to Maura Zell, his mistress, who was a chorine in the road company of *Pearls of Broadway.* He always waited until eight o'clock to begin his toilet, and seemed to set great store in the effect his half-naked imperial person had on his employees as they filed in for work. "What's this idea of yours?"

"Let me ask you this first, Mr. Anapol," Sammy said. He was standing, clutching his portfolio, on the threadbare oval of Chinese carpet that covered most of the wooden floor of Anapol's office, a large room set off from the desks of Mavis Magid, Anapol's secretary, and the five shipping, inventory, and account clerks by partitions of veneered presswood and glass. A hat rack, side chairs, and rolltop desk were all secondhand, scavenged in 1933 from the offices of a neighboring life-insurance company that went belly-up, and trucked on dollies down the hall to their present location. "What are they charging you over at National for the back cover of *Action Comics* this month?"

"No, let me ask *you* a question," Anapol said. He stepped back from the mirror and tried, as he did every morning, to induce a few long strands of hair to lie flat across the bald top of his head. He had said nothing so far about Sammy's portfolio, which Sammy had never before had the courage to show him. "Who is that kid sitting out there?"

Anapol did not turn around, and he hadn't taken his eyes from the tiny shaving mirror since Sammy had come into the room, but he could see Joe in the mirror. Joe and Sammy were sitting back to back, separated by the glass and wood partition that divided Anapol's office from the rest of his empire. Sammy craned around to get a look at his cousin. There was a pine drawing board on Joe's lap, a sketchpad, and some pencils. On the chair beside him lay a cheap pasteboard portfolio they had bought in a five-and-dime on Broadway. The idea was for Joe to fill it quickly with exciting sketches of muscular heroes while Sammy pitched his idea to Anapol and played for time. "You'll have to work fast," he had told Joe, and Joe had assured him that in ten minutes he would have assembled an entire pantheon of crime-fighters in tights. But then on the way in, as Sammy was talking up Mavis Magid, Joe had wasted precious minutes rummaging through the shipment of Amazing Midget Radios whose arrival yesterday morning from Japan had sent Anapol into a rage; the whole shipment was defective and, even by his relaxed standards, unsaleable.

"That's my cousin Joe," said Sammy, sneaking another glance over his shoulder. Joe was bent over his work, staring at his fingers and craning his head slowly from left to right, as if some invisible force beam from his eyes were dragging the tip of the pencil across the page. He was sketching in the bulge of a mighty shoulder that was connected to a thick left arm. Other than this arm and a number of faint, cryptic guidelines, there was nothing on the page. "My mother's nephew."

"He's a foreigner? Where's he from?"

"Prague. How did you know?"

"The haircut."

Anapol stepped over to the pushboy's rack and took a pair of trousers from their hanger.

"He just got here last night," Sammy said.

"And he's looking for a job."

"Well, naturally—"

"I hope, Sammy, that you told him I have no jobs for anybody."

"Actually . . . I may have misled him a little on that score, boss."

Again Anapol nodded, as another of his unerring snap judgments was confirmed. Sammy's left leg started to twitch. It was the worst-lamed of the two and the first to weaken when he was nervous or about to be caught in a lie.

"And all this has something to do," Anapol said, "with how much they charge me over at National for the back cover of *Action Comics*."

"Or *Detective*."

Anapol frowned. He lifted his arms and then disappeared into a huge linen undershirt that did not exactly look freshly laundered. Sammy checked Joe's work. A massive frame had begun to emerge, a squarish head, a thick, almost tubular chest. While confidently rendered, the figure had something bulky about it. The legs were mighty and booted, but the boots were stout workman's boots, laced prosaically up the front. Sammy's leg began to shake a little harder now. Anapol's head reemerged from his undershirt. He tucked it over his furred walrus belly and down into his trousers. He was still frowning. He lifted his suspenders up over his shoulders and let them snap into place. Then, his eyes fixed on the back of Joe's head, he went over to his desk and flicked a switch.

"I need Murray," he said into the speaker. "It's a slow week," he added to Sammy. "That's the only reason I'm indulging you this way."

"I understand," said Sammy.

"Sit down."

Sammy sat and rested the portfolio against his legs, relieved to set it down. It was stuffed almost to bursting with his own sketches, concepts, prototypes, and finished pages.

Mavis Magid got Murray Edelman on the phone. The advertising manager for Empire Novelty told him, as Sammy had known he would because he voluntarily worked extra hours in Edelman's department every week, absorbing what he could of the old man's skewed and exclamatory slant on the advertising game, that National was charging almost seven times the going rate for the space on the back cover of its bestselling titles—the August issue of *Action*, the last for which there were figures, had sold close to a million and a half copies. There was, according to Murray, one reason and one reason alone for the skyrocketing sales of certain titles in the still relatively inchoate comic book market.

"*Superman*," said Anapol when he hung up the phone, with the tone of someone ordering an unknown dish in an outlandish restaurant. He started to pace behind his desk, hands clasped behind his back.

"Think of how much product we could sell if we had our *own* Superman," Sammy heard himself saying. "We can call them *Joy Buzzer Comics. Whoopie Cushion Comics.* Think of how much you'll save on advertising. Think—"

"Enough," said Anapol. He stopped pacing and flicked the switch on his telephone console again. The cast of his face had altered, taking on a taut, faintly squeamish expression Sammy could recognize, after a year in his employ, as the repressed foreconsciousness of money. His voice was a hoarse whisper. "I need Jack," he said.

Mavis placed a call upstairs to the offices of Racy Publications, Inc., home of *Racy Police Stories, Racy Western,* and *Racy Romance.* Jack Ashkenazy was summoned to the phone. He confirmed what Murray Edelman had already said. Every pulp and magazine publisher in New York had taken notice of the explosive sales of National's *Action Comics* and its caped and booted star.

"Yeah?" Anapol said. "*Yeah?* You are? Any luck?"

He took the receiver from his ear and stuffed it under his left armpit.

"They've been looking around for a Superman of their own upstairs," he told Sammy.

Sammy jumped out of his chair.

"We can get him one, boss," he said. "We can have him his very own Superman by Monday morning. But just between you and me," he added, trying to sound like his great hero, John Garfield, tough and suave at the same time, the street boy ready to wear fancy suits and go where the big money was, "I'd advise you to keep a little piece of this for yourself."

Anapol laughed. "Oh, you would, would you?" he said. He shook his head. "I'll bear that in mind." He kept the receiver tucked under his arm and took a cigarette from the box on his desk. He lit it and inhaled, mulling things over, his big jaw tensed and bulging. Then he rescued the receiver and blew smoke into the mouthpiece.

"Maybe you'd better come down here, Jack," he said. He hung up again and nodded in Joe Kavalier's direction. "Is that your artist?"

"We both are," said Sammy. "Artists, I mean." He decided to match Anapol's dubiety with a burst of self-confidence he was rapidly inducing himself to feel. He went over to the partition and rapped, with a flourish, on the glass. Joe turned, startled, from his work. Sammy, not wanting to endanger his own display of confidence, didn't let himself look too closely at what Joe had done. At least the whole page seemed to have been filled in.

"May I—?" he said to Anapol, gesturing toward the door.

"Might as well get him in here."

Sammy signaled for Joe to come in, a ringmaster welcoming a famous aerialist into the spotlight. Joe stood up, gathering the portfolio and his stray pencils, then sidled into Anapol's office, sketchpad clutched to his chest, in his baggy tweed suit, with his hungry face and borrowed tie, his expression at once guarded and touchingly eager to please. He was looking at the owner of Empire Novelty as if all the big money Sammy had promised had been packed into the swollen carapace of Sheldon Anapol and would, at the slightest prick or tap, come pouring out in an uncontrollable green torrent.

"Hello, young man," said Anapol. "I'm told you can draw."

"Yes, sir!" Joe said, in a voice that sounded oddly strangled, startling them all.

"Give it here." Sammy reached for the pad and found, to his surprise, that he couldn't pry it loose. For an instant, he was afraid that his cousin had done something so abominable that he was afraid to show it. Then he caught a glimpse of the upper left corner of Joe's drawing, where a fat moon peered from behind a crooked tower, a crooked bat flapping across its face, and he saw that, on the contrary, his cousin simply couldn't let go.

"Joe," he said softly.

"I need a little more time with it," Joe said, handing the pad to Sammy.

Anapol came around from behind his desk, lodged the burning cigarette in a corner of his mouth, and took the pad from Sammy. "Look at that!" he said.

In the drawing it was midnight, in a cobblestone alley crosshatched with menacing shadows. There were evocative suggestions of tiled roofs, leaded windows, icy puddles on the ground. Out of the shadows and into the light of the bat-scarred moon strode a tall, brawny man. His frame was as sturdy and thick as his hobnailed boots. For costume he wore a tunic with deep creases, a heavy belt, and a big, shapeless stocking hat like something out of Rembrandt. The man's features, though regular and handsome, looked frozen, and his intrepid gaze was empty. There were four Hebrew characters etched into his forehead.

"Is that the *Golem*?" said Anapol. "My new Superman is the Golem?"

"I didn't—the conceit is new for me," Joe said, his English stiffening up on him. "I just drawed the first thing I could think of that resembled ... To me, this Superman is ... maybe ... only an American Golem." He looked for support to Sammy. "Is that right?"

"Huh?" said Sammy, struggling to conceal his dismay. "Yeah, sure, but, Joe ... the Golem is ... well ... *Jewish*."

Anapol rubbed his heavy chin, looking at the drawing. He pointed to the portfolio. "Let me see what else you got in there."

"He had to leave all his work back in Prague," Sammy put in quickly, as Joe untied the ribbon of the portfolio. "He just started throwing together some new stuff this morning."

"Well, he isn't fast," Anapol said when he saw that Joe's portfolio was empty. "He has talent, anyone can see that, but . . ." The look of doubtfulness returned to his face.

"Joe," cried Sammy. "Tell him where you studied!"

"The Academy of Fine Art, in Prague," said Joe.

Anapol stopped rubbing his chin. "The Academy of Fine Art?"

"What is that? Who are these guys? What's going on in here?" Jack Ashkenazy burst into the office without warning or a knock. He had all his hair, and was a much snappier dresser than his brother-in-law, favoring checked vests and two-tone shoes. Because he had prospered, in a Kramler Building kind of way, more easily than Anapol, he had not been forced to develop the older man's rumpled salesman's charm, but he shared Anapol's avidity for unburdening America's youth of the oppressive national mantle of tedium, ten cents at a time. He plucked the cigar from his mouth and yanked the sketchpad out of Anapol's hands.

"Beauteeful," he said. "The head is too big."

"The head is too big?" said Anapol. "That's all you can say?"

"The body's too heavy. Looks like he's made out of stone."

"He *is* made out of stone, you idiot, he's a golem."

"Clay, actually," said Joe. He coughed. "I can do something more lighter."

"He can do anything you want," said Sammy.

"Anything," Joe agreed. His eyes widened as an inspiration seemed to strike, and he turned to Sammy. "Maybe I ought to show them my fart."

"He's only ever read one comic book," Sammy said, ignoring this suggestion. "But I've read them all, boss. I've read every issue of *Action*. I've studied this stuff. I know how it's done. Look." He picked up his own portfolio and untied the strings. It was a cheap pasteboard number from Woolworth's, like Joe's, but battered, scraped, and carefully dented. You couldn't sit around in some art director's waiting room with a brand-new-looking portfolio. Everyone would know you were a tyro. Sammy had spent an entire afternoon last fall hitting his with a hammer, walking across it in a pair of his mother's heels, spilling coffee on it. Unfortunately, since purchasing it he had managed to land only two cartoons, one in a completely humor-free magazine called *Laff* and the other in *Belle-Views,* house organ of the psychiatric ward where his mother worked.

"I can do it all," he boasted, pulling out a fistful of sample pages and passing them around. What he meant, more precisely, was that he could steal it all.

"It isn't half bad," Anapol said.

"It ain't beauteeful, either," said Ashkenazy.

Sammy glared at Ashkenazy, not because Ashkenazy had insulted his work—no one was ever more aware of his own artistic limitations than Sam Clay—but because Sammy felt that he was standing on the border of something wonderful, a land where wild cataracts of money and the racing river of his own imagination would, at last, lift his makeshift little raft and carry it out to the boundless freedom of the open sea. Jack Ashkenazy, whose watery eyes could easily, Sammy imagined, be stabbed out with the letter opener on Anapol's desk, was threatening to get in his way. Anapol caught the look of visionary murder in Sammy's eyes and took a chance on it.

"What say we let these boys go home over the weekend and try to come up with a Superman for us." He fixed Sammy with a hard look. "Our own kind of a Superman, naturally."

"Of course."

"How long is a Superman story?"

"Probably twelve pages."

"I want a character and a twelve-page story by Monday."

"We're going to need a lot more than that," said Ashkenazy. "They got typically five or six characters in there. You know, a spy. A private eye. A shadowy avenger of the helpless. An evil Chinaman. These two can't come up with all that themselves *and* draw it. I got artists, Shelly. I got George Deasey."

"No!" said Sammy. George Deasey was the editor in chief of Racy Publications. He was a tyrannical, ill-tempered old newspaperman who filled the Kramler Building's elevators with the exacerbated smell of rye. "It's mine. Ours, me and Joe. Boss, I can handle it."

"Absolutely, boss," said Joe.

Anapol grinned. "Get a load of this guy," he said. "You just get me a Superman," he went on, putting a placating hand on Sammy's shoulder. "Then we'll see about what you can handle or not. All right, Jack?"

Ashkenazy twisted his usually genial features into a grimace. "I have to tell you, Shelly. I got serious doubts. I'm going to have to say—"

"The radios," Joe said. "The little radios outside."

"Aw, forget the damn radios, Joe, will you?" Sammy said.

"What, the midgets?" Anapol said.

Joe nodded. "They are just wrong in the wires. All in the same way. One little wire is not, hmm. So." He kissed the tip of one index finger with the other. "Stuck together to the resistance."

"You mean to the *resistor*?"

"Okay."

"You know from radios?" Anapol narrowed his eyes doubtfully. "You're saying you could fix them?"

"Oh, assuredly, boss. It is simple to me."

"How much is it going to cost?"

"Not anything. Some few pence for the— I do not know the word." He angled his fingers into the form of a pistol. "*Weichlöte*. You must to melt it."

"Solder? A soldering gun?"

"Okay. But perhaps I can to borrow that."

"Just a few pence, huh?"

"Maybe one penny for the radio, each radio."

"That's cutting it pretty close to my cost."

"But okay, I don't charge to do the work."

Sammy looked at his cousin, amazed and only a little put out at his having shanghaied the negotiation. He saw Anapol raise a meaningful eyebrow at his brother-in-law, promising or threatening something.

At last Jack Ashkenazy nodded. "There's just one thing," he said. He put a hand on Joe's arm, restraining him before he could sidle out of the office, with his blank-eyed Golem and his empty portfolio. "This is a comic book we're talking about, okay? Half bad is maybe better than beauteeful."

3

THE FIRST OFFICIAL MEETING of their partnership was convened outside the Kramler Building, in a nimbus compounded of the boys' exhalations and of subterranean steam purling up from a grate in the pavement.

"This is good," Joe said.

"I know."

"He said *yes*," Joe reminded his cousin, who stood patting idly with one hand at the front of his overcoat and a panicked expression on his face, as though worried that he had left something important behind in Anapol's office.

"Yes, he did. He said yes."

"Sammy." Joe reached out and grabbed Sammy's wandering hand, arresting it in its search of his pockets and collar and tie. "This is *good*."

"Yes, this is good, god damn it. I just hope to God we can *do* it."

Joe let go of Sammy's hand, shocked by this expression of sudden doubt. He had been completely taken in by Sammy's bold application of the Science of Opportunity. The whole morning, the rattling ride through the flickering darkness under the East River, the updraft of Klaxons and rising office blocks that had carried them out of the sub-way station, the ten thousand men and women who immediately sur-rounded them, the ringing telephones and gum-snapping chitchat of the clerks and secretaries in Sheldon Anapol's office, the sly and har-ried bulk of Anapol himself, the talk of sales figures and competition and cashing in big, all this had conformed so closely to Joe's movie-derived notions of life in America that if an airplane were now to land on Twenty-fifth Street and disgorge a dozen bathing-suit-clad Fairies of Democracy come to award him the presidency of General Motors, a contract with Warner Bros., and a penthouse on Fifth Avenue with a swimming pool in the living room, he would have greeted this, too, with the same dreamlike unsurprise. It had not occurred to him until now to consider that his cousin's display of bold entrepreneurial confidence might have been entirely bluff, that it was 8°C and he had neither hat nor gloves, that his stomach was as empty as his billfold, and that he and Sammy were nothing more than a couple of callow young men in thrall to a rash and dubious promise.

"But I have belief in you," Joe said. "I trust you."

"That's good to hear."

"I mean it."

"I wish I knew why."

"Because," said Joe. "I don't have any choice."

"Oh ho."

"I need money," Joe said, and then tried adding, "god *damn* it."

"Money." The word seemed to have a restorative effect on Sammy, snapping him out of his daze. "Right. Okay. First of all, we need horses."

"Horses?"

"Arms. Guys."

"Artists."

"How about we just call them 'guys' for right now?"

"Do you know where we can find some?"

Sammy thought for a moment. "I believe I do," he said. "Come on."

They set off in a direction that Joe decided was probably west. As they walked Sammy seemed to get lost quickly in his own reflections. Joe tried to imagine the train of his cousin's thoughts, but the particulars of the task at hand were not clear to him, and after a while he gave up and just kept pace. Sammy's gait was deliberate and crooked, and Joe found it a challenge to keep from getting ahead. There was a humming sound everywhere that he attributed first to the circulation of his own blood in his ears before he realized that it was the sound produced by Twenty-fifth Street itself, by a hundred sewing machines in a sweatshop overhead, exhaust grilles at the back of a warehouse, the trains rolling deep beneath the black surface of the street. Joe gave up trying to think like, trust, or believe in his cousin and just walked, head abuzz, toward the Hudson River, stunned by the novelty of exile.

"Who is he?" Sammy said at last, as they were crossing a broad street which a sign identified, improbably somehow, as Sixth Avenue. Sixth Avenue! The Hudson River!

"Who is he," Joe said.

"Who is he, and what does he do?"

"He flies."

Sammy shook his head. "Superman flies."

"So ours does not?"

"I just think I'd . . ."

"To be original."

"If we can. Try to do it without flying, at least. No flying, no strength of a hundred men, no bulletproof skin."

"Okay," Joe said. The humming seemed to recede a little. "And some others, they do what?"

"Well, Batman—"

"He flies, like a bat."

"No, he doesn't fly."

"But he is blind."

"No, he only dresses like a bat. He has no batlike qualities at all. He uses his fists."

"That sounds dull."

"Actually, it's spooky. You'd like it."

"Maybe another animal."

"Uh, well, yeah. Okay. A hawk. Hawkman."

"Hawk, yes, okay. But that one must fly."

"Yeah, you're right. Scratch the bird family. The, uh, the Fox. The Shark."

"A swimming one."

"Maybe a swimming one. Actually, no, I know a guy works in the Chesler shop, he said they're already doing a guy who swims. For Timely."

"A lion?"

"Lion. The Lion. Lionman."

"He could be strong. He roars very loud."

"He has a super roar."

"It strikes fear."

"It breaks dishes."

"The bad guys go deaf."

They laughed. Joe stopped laughing.

"I think we have to be serious," he said.

"You're right," said Sammy. "The Lion, I don't know. Lions are lazy. How about the Tiger. Tigerman. No, no. Tigers are killers. Shit. Let's see."

They began to go through the rolls of the animal kingdom, concentrating naturally on the predators: Catman, Wolfman, the Owl, the Panther, the Black Bear. They considered the primates: the Monkey, Gorillaman, the Gibbon, the Ape, the Mandrill with his multicolored wonder ass that he used to bedazzle opponents.

"Be serious," Joe chided again.

"I'm sorry, I'm sorry. Look, forget animals. Everybody's going to be thinking of animals. In two months, I'm telling you, by the time our guy hits the stands, there's going to be guys running around dressed like every damn animal in the zoo. Birds. Bugs. Underwater guys. And I'll bet you anything there's going to be five guys who are really strong, and invulnerable, and can fly."

"If he goes as fast as the light," Joe suggested.

"Yeah, I guess it's good to be fast."

"Or if he can make a thing burn up. If he can—listen! If he can, you know. Shoot the fire, with his eyes!"

"His eyeballs would melt."

"Then with his hands. Or, yes, he turns into a fire!"

"Timely's doing that already, too. They got the fire guy and the water guy."

"He turns into *ice*. He makes the ice everywhere."

"Crushed or cubes?"

"Not good?"

Sammy shook his head. "Ice," he said. "I don't see a lot of stories in ice."

"He turns into electricity?" Joe tried. "He turns into acid?"

"He turns into gravy. He turns into an enormous hat. Look, stop. Stop. Just stop."

They stopped in the middle of the sidewalk, between Sixth and Seventh avenues, and that was when Sam Clay experienced a moment of global vision, one which he would afterward come to view as the one undeniable brush against the diaphanous, dollar-colored hem of the Angel of New York to be vouchsafed to him in his lifetime.

"This is not the question," he said. "If he's like a cat or a spider or a fucking wolverine, if he's huge, if he's tiny, if he can shoot flames or ice or death rays or Vat 69, if he turns into fire or water or stone or India rubber. He could be a Martian, he could be a ghost, he could be a god or a demon or a wizard or monster. Okay? It doesn't *matter*, because right now, see, at this very moment, we have a bandwagon rolling, I'm telling you. Every little skinny guy like me in New York who believes there's life on Alpha Centauri and got the shit kicked out of him in school and can smell a dollar is out there right this minute trying to jump onto it, walking around with a pencil in his shirt pocket, saying, 'He's like a falcon, no, he's like a tornado, no, he's like a goddamned wiener dog.' Okay?"

"Okay."

"And no matter what we come up with, and how we dress him, some other character with the same shtick, with the same style of boots and the same little doodad on his chest, is already out there, or is coming out tomorrow, or is going to be knocked off from our guy inside a week and a half."

Joe listened patiently, awaiting the point of this peroration, but Sammy seemed to have lost the thread. Joe followed his cousin's gaze along the sidewalk but saw only a pair of what looked to be British sailors lighting their cigarettes off a single shielded match.

"So . . ." Sammy said. "So . . ."

"So that is not the question," Joe prompted.

"That's what I'm saying."

"Continue."

They kept walking.

"How? is not the question. What? is not the question," Sammy said.

"The question is why."

"The question is *why*."

"Why," Joe repeated.

"Why is he doing it?"

"Doing what?"

"Dressing up like a monkey or an ice cube or a can of fucking corn."

"To fight the crime, isn't it?"

"Well, yes, to fight crime. To fight evil. But that's all any of these guys are doing. That's as far as they ever go. They just . . . you know, it's the right thing to do, so they do it. How interesting is that?"

"I see."

"Only Batman, you know . . . see, yeah, that's good. That's what makes Batman good, and not dull at all, even though he's just a guy who dresses up like a bat and beats people up."

"What is the reason for Batman? The why?"

"His parents were killed, see? In cold blood. Right in front of his eyes, when he was a kid. By a robber."

"It's revenge."

"That's *interesting*," Sammy said. "See?"

"And he was driven mad."

"Well . . ."

"And that's why he puts on the bat's clothes."

"Actually, they don't go so far as to say that," Sammy said. "But I guess it's there between the lines."

"So, we need to figure out what is the why."

" 'What is the why,' " Sammy agreed.

"Flattop."

Joe looked up and saw a young man standing in front of them. He was short-waisted and plump, and his face, except for a pair of big black spectacles, was swaddled and all but invisible in an elaborate confection of scarf and hat and earflaps.

"Julius," Sammy said. "This is Joe. Joe, this is a friend from the neighborhood, Julie Glovsky."

Joe held out his hand. Julie studied it a moment, then extended his own small hand. He had on a black woolen greatcoat, a fur-lined leather cap with mammoth earflaps, and too-short green corduroy trousers.

"This guy's brother is the one I told you about," Sammy told Joe. "Making good money in comics. What are you doing here?"

Somewhere deep within his wrappings, Julie Glovsky shrugged. "I need to see my brother."

"Isn't that remarkable, we need to see him, too."

"Yeah? Why's that?" Julie Glovsky shuddered. "Only tell me fast before my nuts fall off."

"Would that be from cold or, you know, atrophy?"

"Funny."

"I am funny."

"Unfortunately not in the sense of 'humorous.' "

"Funny," Sammy said.

"I am funny. What's your idea?"

"Why don't you come to work for me?"

"For you? Doing what? Selling shoestrings? We still got a box of them at my house. My mom uses them to sew up chickens."

"Not shoelaces. My boss, you know, Sheldon Anapol?"

"How would I know him?"

"Nevertheless, he is my boss. He's going into business with his brother-in-law, Jack Ashkenazy, who you also do not know, but who publishes *Racy Science, Racy Combat*, et cetera. They're going to do comic books, see, and they're looking for talent."

"What?" Julie poked his tortoise face out from the shadows of its woolen shell. "Do you think they might hire *me*?"

"They will if I tell them to," said Sammy. "Seeing as how I'm the art director in chief."

Joe looked at Sammy and raised an eyebrow. Sammy shrugged.

"Joe and I, here, we're putting together the first title right now. It's going to be all adventure heroes. All in costumes," he said, extemporizing now. "You know, like Superman. Batman. The Blue Beetle. That type of thing."

"Tights, like."

"That's it. Tights. Masks. Big muscles. It's going to be called *Masked Man Comics*," he continued. "Joe and I've got the lead feature all taken care of, but we need backup stuff. Think you could come up with something?"

"Shit, Flattop, yes. You bet."

"What about your brother?"

"Sure, he's always looking for more work. They got him doing *Romeo Rabbit* for thirty dollars a week."

"Okay, then, he's hired, too. You're both hired, on one condition."

"What's that?"

"We need a place to work," said Sammy.

"Come on then," said Julie. "I guess we can work at the Rathole." He leaned toward Sammy as they started off, lowering his voice. The tall skinny kid with the big nose had fallen a few steps behind them to light a cigarette. "Who the hell *is* that guy?"

"This?" Sammy said. He took hold of the kid's elbow and tugged him forward as though bringing him out onstage to take a deserved bow. He reached up to grab a handful of the kid's hair and gave it a tug, just kind of rocking his head from side to side while holding on to his hair, grinning at him. Had Joe been a young woman, Julie Glovsky might almost have been inclined to think that Sammy was sweet on her. "This is my *partner*."

SAMMY WAS THIRTEEN when his father, the Mighty Molecule, came home. The Wertz vaudeville circuit had folded that spring, a victim of Hollywood, the Depression, mismanagement, bad weather, shoddy talent, philistinism, and a number of other scourges and furies whose names Sammy's father would invoke, with incantatory rage, in the course of the long walks they took together that summer. At one time or another he assigned blame for his sudden joblessness, with no great coherence or logic, to bankers, unions, bosses, Clark Gable, Catholics, Protestants, theater owners, sister acts, poodle acts, monkey acts, Irish tenors, English Canadians, French Canadians, and Mr. Hugo Wertz himself.

"Hell with 'em," he would invariably finish, with a sweeping gesture that, in the dusk of a Brooklyn July, was limned by the luminous arc of his cigar. "The Molecule one day says 'fuck you' to the all of them."

The free and careless use of obscenity, like the cigars, the lyrical rage, the fondness for explosive gestures, the bad grammar, and the habit of referring to himself in the third person were wonderful to Sammy; until that summer of 1935, he had possessed few memories or distinct impressions of his father. And any of the above qualities (among several others his father possessed) would, Sammy thought, have given his mother reason enough to banish the Molecule from their home for a dozen years. It was only with the greatest reluctance and the direct intervention of Rabbi Baitz that she had agreed to let the man back in the house. And yet Sammy understood, from the moment of his father's reappearance, that only dire necessity could ever have induced the Genius of Physical Culture to return to his wife and child. For the last dozen years he had wandered, "free as a goddamn bird in the bush," among the mysterious northern towns of the Wertz circuit, from Augusta, Maine, to Vancouver, British Columbia. An almost pathological antsiness, combined with the air of wistful longing that filled the Molecule's simian face, petite and intelligent, when he spoke of his time on the road, made it clear to his son that as soon as the opportunity presented itself, he would be on his way again.

Professor Alphonse von Clay, the Mighty Molecule (born Alter Klayman in Drakop, a village in the countryside east of Minsk), had abandoned his wife and son soon after Sammy's birth, though every week thereafter he sent a money order in the amount of twenty-five dollars. Sammy came to know him only from the embittered narratives of Ethel Klayman and from the odd, mendacious clipping or newspaper photo the Molecule would send along, torn from the variety page of the Helena *Tribune,* or the Kenosha *Gazette,* or the Calgary *Bulletin,* and stuffed, with a sprinkling of cigar ash, into an envelope embossed with the imprint of a drinking glass and the name of some demi-fleabag hotel. Sammy would let these accumulate in a blue velvet shoe bag that he placed under his pillow before he went to sleep each night. He dreamed often and intensely of the tiny, thick-muscled man with the gondolier mustachios who could lift a bank safe over his head and beat a draft horse in a tug-of-war. The plaudits and honors described by the clippings, and the names of the monarchs of Europe and the Near East who had supposedly bestowed them, changed over the years, but the essential false facts of the Mighty Molecule's biography remained the same: ten lonely years studying ancient Greek texts in the dusty libraries of the Old World; hours of painful exercises performed daily since the age of five, a dietary regimen consisting only of fresh legumes, seafoods, and fruits, all eaten raw; a lifetime devoted to the careful cultivation of pure, healthy, lamblike thoughts and to total abstention from insalubrious and immoral behaviors.

Over the years, Sammy managed to wring from his mother scant, priceless drops of factual information about his father. He knew that the Molecule, who derived his stage name from the circumstance of his standing, in calf-high gold lamé buskins, just under five feet two inches tall, had been imprisoned by the Czar in 1911, in the same cell as a politically minded circus strong man from Odessa known as Freight Train

Belz. Sammy knew that it was Belz, an anarcho-syndicalist, and not the ancient sages of Greece, who had schooled his father's body and taught him to abstain from alcohol, meat, and gambling, if not pussy and cigars. And he knew that it was in Kurtzburg's Saloon on the Lower East Side in 1919 that his mother had fallen in love with Alter Klayman, newly arrived in this country and working as an iceman and freelance mover of pianos.

Miss Kavalier was almost thirty when she married. She was four inches shorter than her diminutive husband, sinewy, grim-jawed, her eyes the pale gray of rainwater pooled in a dish left on the window ledge. She wore her black hair pulled into an unrelenting bun. It was impossible for Sammy to imagine his mother as she must have been that summer of 1919, an aging girl upended and borne aloft on a sudden erotic gust, transfixed by the vein-rippled arms of the jaunty homunculus who carried winking hundred-pound blocks of ice into the gloom of her cousin Lev Kurtzburg's saloon on Ludlow Street. Not that Ethel was unfeeling—on the contrary, she could be, in her way, a passionate woman subject to transports of maudlin nostalgia, easily outraged, sunk by bad news, hard luck, or doctor's bills into deep, black crevasses of despair.

"Take me with you," Sammy said to his father one evening after dinner, as they were strolling down Pitkin Avenue, on their way out to New Lots or Canarsie or wherever the Molecule's vagabond urges inclined him that night. Like a horse, Sammy had noticed, the Molecule almost never sat down. He cased any room he entered, pacing first up and down, then back and forth, checking behind the curtains, probing the corners with his gaze or the toe of a shoe, testing out the cushions in the chair or sofa with a measured bounce, then springing back onto his feet. If compelled to stand in one place for any reason, he would rock back and forth like someone who needed to urinate, worrying the dimes in his pocket. He never slept more than four hours a night, and even then, according to Sammy's mother, with inquietude, thrashing and gasping and crying out in his sleep. And he seemed incapable of staying in any one place for longer than an hour or two at a time. Though it enraged and humiliated him, the process of looking for work, crisscrossing lower Manhattan and Times Square, haunting the offices of booking agents and circuit managers, suited him well enough. On the days when he stayed in Brooklyn and hung around the apartment, he drove everyone else to distraction with his pacing and rocking and hourly trips to the store for cigars, pens, a *Racing Form*, half a roast chicken—anything. In the course of their post-prandial wanderings, father and son ranged far and sat little. They explored the eastern boroughs as far as Kew Gardens and East New York. They took the ferry from the Bush Terminal out to Staten Island, where they hiked out of St. George to Todt Hill, returning well after midnight. When, rarely, they hopped a trolley or caught a train, they would stand, even if the car was empty; on the Staten Island Ferry, the Molecule prowled the decks like a character out of Conrad, uneasily watching the horizon. From time to time in the course of a walk, they might pause in a cigar shop or at a drugstore, where the Molecule would order a celery tonic for himself and a glass of milk for the boy and, disdaining the chrome stool with its Naugahyde seat, would down his Cel-Ray standing up. And once, on Flatbush Avenue, they had gone into a movie theater where *The Lives of a Bengal Lancer* was playing, but they stayed only for the newsreel before heading back out to the street. The only directions the Molecule disliked to venture were to Coney Island, in whose most evil sideshows he had long ago suffered unspecified torments, and to Manhattan. He had his fill of it during the day, he said, and what was more, the presence on that island of the Palace Theatre, the pinnacle and holy shrine of Vaudeville, was viewed as a reproach by the touchy and grudge-cherishing Molecule, who never had, and never would, tread its storied boards.

"You can't leave me with her. It isn't healthy for a boy my age to be with a woman like that."

The Molecule stopped and turned to face his son. He was dressed, as always, in one of the three black suits that he owned, pressed and shiny with wear at the elbows. Though, like the others, it had been tailored to fit him, it nonetheless strained to encompass his physique. His back and shoulders were as broad as the grille of a truck, his arms as thick as the thighs of an ordinary man, and his thighs, when pressed together, rivaled his chest in girth. His waist looked oddly fragile, like the throat of an egg timer. He wore his hair cropped close and an anachronistic handlebar mustache. In his publicity photographs, where he often posed shirtless or in a skintight leotard, he appeared smooth as a polished ingot, but in street clothes he had an unwieldy, comical air and, with the dark hair poking out at his cuffs and collar, he looked like nothing so much as a pants-wearing ape, in a cartoon satirizing some all too human vanity.

"Listen to me, Sam." The Molecule seemed taken aback by his son's request, almost as though it dovetailed with his own thinking or, the thought crossed Sammy's mind, he had been caught on the verge of skipping town. "Nothing makes me happier than I take you with me," he continued, with the maddening vagueness his ill grammar permitted. He smoothed Sammy's hair back with a heavy palm. "But then again, Jesus, what a crazy fucking idea."

Sammy started to argue, but his father raised a hand. There was more to be said, and in the balance of his speech Sammy sensed or imagined a faint glimmer of hope. He knew that he had chosen a particularly auspicious night to make his plea. That afternoon, his parents had quarreled over dinner—literally. Ethel scorned the Molecule's dietary regimen, claiming not only that the eating of raw vegetables had none of the positive effects her husband attributed to it but also that, every chance the man got, he was sneaking off around the corner to dine in secret on steak and veal chops and french-fried potatoes. That afternoon, Sammy's father had returned to the apartment on Sackman Street (this was in the days before the move to Flatbush) from his afternoon of job hunting with a bag full of Italian squash. He dumped them out with a wink and a grin onto the kitchen table, like a haul of stolen goods. Sammy had never seen anything like these vegetables. They were cool and smooth and rubbed against one another with a rubbery squeak. You could see right where they had been cut from the vine. Their sliced-off stems, woody and hexagonal, implied a leafy green tangle that seemed to fill the kitchen along with their faint scent of dirt. The Molecule snapped one of the squashes in two and held its bright pale flesh up to Sammy's nose. Then he popped one in his mouth and crunched it, smiling and winking at Sammy as he chewed.

"Good for your legs," he had said, walking out of the kitchen to shower away the failures of the day.

Sammy's mother boiled the squash until it was a mass of gray strings.

When the Molecule saw what she had done, there were sharp and bitter words. Then the Molecule had grabbed brusquely for his son, like a man reaching for his hat, and dragged Sammy out of the house and into the heat of the evening. They had been walking since six. The sun had long since gone down, and the sky to the west was a hazy moiré of purple and orange and pale gray-blue. They were walking along Avenue Z, dangerously close to the forbidden precincts of the Molecule's early sideshow disasters.

"I don't think you got the picture what's it like out there for me," he said as they walked along. "You think it's like a circus in the pictures. All the clowns and the dwarf and the fat lady sitting around a nice big fire eating goulash and singing songs with an accordion."

"I don't think that," Sammy said, though there was stunning accuracy in this assessment.

"If I did to take you with me—and I am just saying now if—you will have to work very hard," the Molecule said. "They will only accept you if you can work."

"I can work," Sammy said, holding out an arm toward his father. "Look at that."

"Yeh," the Molecule said. He felt very carefully up and down the stout arms of his son, very much in the way Sammy had fingered the zucchini squash that afternoon. "You have arms that are not bad. But your legs are not so good."

"Well, jeez, I mean, I had polio, Pop, what do you want?"

"I know you had polio." The Molecule stopped again. He frowned, and in his face Sammy saw anger and regret and something else that looked almost like wishfulness. He stepped on his cigar end, and stretched, and shook himself a little, as if trying to shrug out of the constricting nets that his wife and son had thrown across his back. "What a fucking day I have. Holy shit."

"What?" Sammy said. "Hey, where are you going?"

"I need to think," his father said. "I need to think about what you are asking me."

"Okay," Sammy said. His father had started walking again, taking a right on Nostrand Avenue, striding along on his thick little legs with Sammy struggling to keep up, until he came to a peculiar building, Arabic in style, or maybe it was supposed to look Moroccan. It stood in the middle of the block, between a locksmith's stall and a weedy yard stacked with blank headstones. Two skinny towers, topped with pointy dollops of peeling plaster, reached into the Brooklyn sky at either corner of the roof. It was windowless, and its broad expanse was clad, with weary elaboration, in a mosaic of small square tiles, fly-abdomen blue and a soapy gray that once must have been white. Many of the tiles were missing, chipped, or picked or tumbled loose. The doorway was a wide, blue-tiled arch. In spite of its forlorn appearance and hokum Coney Island air of the Mysterious East, there was something captivating about it. It reminded Sammy of the city of domes and minarets that you could just get a glimpse of, faint and illusory, behind the writing on the front of a pack of Chesterfields. Alongside the arched doorway, in letters of white tile bordered in blue, was written BRIGHTON GRAND HAMMAM.

"What's a ham-mam?" Sammy said as they went in. His nose was immediately assaulted by a pungent odor of pine, by the smell of scorched ironing, damp laundry, and something deeper underneath it all, a human smell, salty and foul.

"It's a shvitz," the Molecule said. "You know what a shvitz is?"

Sammy nodded.

"When it's time for thinking," said the Molecule, "I like to have a shvitz."

"Oh."

"I hate thinking."

"Yeah," said Sammy. "Me too."

They checked their clothes in the dressing room, in a tall black iron locker that creaked and fastened shut with the loud clang of a torture instrument. Then they went slapping down a long tiled corridor into the main steam room of the Brighton hammam. Their footsteps echoed as if they were inside a fairly large room. It was painfully hot, and Sammy felt that he couldn't fill his lungs with sufficient air. He wanted to run back out to the relative cool of the Brooklyn evening, but he crept along, feeling his way through the billowing garments of steam, a hand on his father's bare back. They climbed onto a low tiled bench and sat back, and Sammy felt each tile as a burning square against his skin. It was very hard to see, but from time to time a rogue current of air, or the vagaries of the invisible, wheezing, steam-producing machinery, would produce a break in the cover, and he could see that they were indeed inside a grand space, ribbed with porcelain groins, set with white and blue faience that was cracked in places, sweating and yellowed with age. As far as he could see, there were no other men or boys in the room with them, but he couldn't be sure, and he felt obscurely afraid of an unknown face or naked limb suddenly looming out of the murk.

They sat for a long time, saying nothing, and at some point Sammy realized, first, that his body was producing veritable torrents of sweat with an abandon it had never before in his life displayed, and, second, that all along he had been imagining his existence in vaudeville: carrying an armload of spangled costumes down a long dark corridor of the Royal Theatre in Racine, Wisconsin, past a practice room where a piano tinkled and out the back door to the waiting van on a Saturday in midsummer, the deep midwestern night rich with june bugs and gasoline and roses, the smell of the costumes fusty but animated by the sweat and makeup of the chorus girls who had just vacated them, envisioning and inhaling and hearing all this with the vividness of a dream, though he was, as far as he could tell, wide-awake.

Then his father said, "I know you had polio." Sammy was surprised; his father sounded extremely angry, as though ashamed that he had been sitting there all this time when he was supposed to be relaxing, working himself into a rage. "I was there. I finded you on the steps of the building. You were pass out."

"You were there? When I got polio?"

"I was there."

"I don't remember that."

"You were a baby."

"I was four."

"So, you were four. You don't remember."

"I would remember that."

"I was there. I carried you into the room we had."

"In Brownsville, this was." Sammy could not keep the skepticism out of his tone.

"I was there, god damn it."

As if blown by a gust of anger, the curtain of steam that hung between Sammy and his father parted suddenly, and he saw, for the first time really, the great brown spectacle of his naked father. None of the carefully posed studio photographs had prepared him for the sight. His father glistened, massive, savagely furred. The muscles in his arms and shoulders were like dents and wheel ruts in an expanse of packed brown earth. The root systems of an ancient tree seemed to furcate and furrow the surface of his thighs, and where his skin was not covered in dark hair, it was strangely rippled with wild webs of some kind of tissue just beneath the skin. His penis lay in the shadow of his thighs like a short length of thick twisted rope. Sammy stared at it, then realized he was staring. He looked away, and his heart jumped. There was a man there with them. He was sitting, a yellow towel across his lap, on the other side of the room. He was a dark-haired, swarthy young man with a single long eyebrow and a perfectly smooth chest. His eyes met Sammy's for a moment, then slid away, then back. It was as if a tunnel of clear air had opened between them. Sammy looked back at his father, his stomach awash in an acid of embarrassment, confusion, and arousal. Somehow the hirsute magnificence of him was too much. So he just looked down at the towel draped across his own two broomstick legs.

"You were so heavy to carry," his father said, "I thought you have to be dead. Only also you were so hot against the hand. The doctor came and we put ice on you and when you woke up you couldn't walk anymore. And then when you come back from the hospital I started taking you and I took you around, I carried you and I dragged you and I made you walk. Until your knees were scraped and bruised, I made you walk. Until you cried. First holding on to me, then on to the crutches, then not with crutches. All by yourself."

"Jeez," Sammy said. "I mean, huh. Mom never told me any of this."

"What a wonder."

"I honestly don't remember."

"God is merciful," the Molecule said dryly; he didn't believe in God, as his son well knew. "You hated every minute. You just as good hated me."

"But Mom lied."

"I am shocked."

"She always told me you left when I was just a little baby."

"I did. But I came back. I am there when you come sick. Then I stay and teach you to help you walk."

"And then you left again."

The Molecule appeared to choose to ignore this observation. "That's why I try to walk you around so much now," he said. "To make your legs strong."

This possible second motive for their walks—after his father's inherent restlessness—had occurred to Sammy before. He was flattered, and believed in his father, and in the potency of long walks.

"So you'll take me?" he said. "When you go?"

Still the Molecule hesitated. "What about your mother?"

"Are you kidding? She can't wait to get rid of me. She hates having me around as much as she hates having you."

At this the Molecule smiled. From all outward appearances, the renewed presence of her husband in her household was nothing but an annoyance to Ethel, or worse—a betrayal of principles. She criticized his habits, his clothing, his diet, his reading material, and his speech. Whenever he tried to escape the fetters of his awkward, obscene English and speak with his wife in the Yiddish in which both were fluent, she ignored him, pretended not to hear, or simply snapped, "You're in America. Talk American." Both in his presence and behind his back, she berated him for his coarseness, his long-winded stories of his vaudeville career and his childhood in the Pale of Settlement. She told him that he snored too loudly, laughed too loudly, simply lived too loudly, beyond the limit of tolerance of civilized beings. Her entire discourse with him appeared to consist solely of animadversion and invective. And yet the previous night, and every night since his return, she had invited him, in a voice that trembled with girlish shame, into her bed and allowed him to enjoy her. At forty-five, she was not very different than she had been at thirty, lean, ropy, and smooth, with skin the color of almond hulls and a neat soft tangle of ink-black hair between her legs, which he liked to grab hold of and pull until she cried out. She was a woman of appetite who had gone without the companionship of a man for a decade, and on his unexpected return she granted him access to even those parts and uses of her that in their early life she had been inclined to keep to herself. And when they were finished, she would lie beside him in the darkness of the tiny room she had partitioned from the kitchen by a beaded curtain, and stroke his great hairy chest, and repeat into his ear in a low whisper all the old endearments and professions of her beholdenness to him. At night, in the dark, she did not hate to have him around. It was this thought that had made him smile.

"Don't be so sure of it," he said.

"I don't care, Pop. I want to leave," said Sammy. "Damn it, I just want to get away."

"All right," said his father. "I promise that I will take you when I go."

The next morning, when Sammy woke up, his father had gone. He had found an engagement on the old Carlos circuit, in the Southwest, said his note, where he spent the rest of his career playing hot, dusty theaters from Kingman as far south as Monterrey. Though Sammy continued to receive cards and clippings, the Mighty Molecule never again passed within a thousand miles of New York City. One night, about a year before Joe Kavalier's arrival, a telegram had come with word that, at a fairground outside Galveston, under the rear wheels of a Deere tractor he was attempting to upend, Alter Klayman had been crushed, and with him Sammy's fondest hope, in the act of escaping from his life, of working with a partner.

5

THE TWO UPPERMOST FLOORS of a certain ancient red row house in the West Twenties, in the ten years before it was pulled down along with all of its neighbors to make way for a gigantic, step-gabled apartment block called Patroon Town, were a notorious tomb for the hopes of cartoonists. Of all the many dozens of young John Helds and Tad Dorgans who had shown up, bearing fragrant, graduation-gift portfolios, mail-order diplomas from cartoonists' schools, and the proud badge of ink under a ragged thumbnail, to seek lodging under its rotted timbers, only one, a one-legged kid from New Haven named Alfred Caplin, had gone on to meet with the kind of success they had all believed they would find—and the father of the Shmoo had spent only two nights there before moving on to better lodgings across town.

The landlady, a Mrs. Waczukowski, was the widow of a gagman for the Hearst syndicate who had signed his strips "Wacky" and on his death had left her only the building, an unconcealed disdain for all cartoonists veteran or new, and her considerable share of their mutual drinking problem. Originally, there had been six separate bedrooms on the top two stories, but over the years these had been recombined into a kind of ad hoc duplex with three bedrooms, a large studio, a living room in which there was usually an extra cartoonist or two lodged on a pair of cast-off sofas, and what was referred to, generally without irony, as the kitchen: a former maid's room equipped with a hot plate, a pantry made from a steel supply cabinet stolen from Polyclinic Hospital, and a wooden shelf affixed with brackets to the ledge outside the window, on which, in the cool months, milk, eggs, and bacon could be kept.

Jerry Glovsky had moved in about six months earlier, and since then Sammy, in the company of his friend and neighbor Julie Glovsky, Jerry's younger brother, had visited the apartment several times. Though he was largely ignorant of the details of the apartment's past, Sammy had been sensitive to its thick-layered cigar-smoke allure of male fellowship, of years of hard work and sorrow in the service of absurd and glorious black-and-white visions. At the present time there were two other "permanent" occupants, Marty Gold and Davy O'Dowd, both of whom, like the elder Glovsky, shed sweat for Moe Shiflet, a.k.a. Moe Skinflint, a "packager" of original strips who sold his material, usually of poor quality, to the established syndicates and, more recently, to publishers of comic books. The place always seemed filled with ink-smirched young men, drinking, smoking, lying around with their naked big toes protruding from the tips of their socks. In the whole city of New York, there was no more logical hiring hall for the sort of laborers Sammy required to lay the cornerstone of the cheap and fantastic cathedral that would be his life's work.

There was nobody home—nobody conscious, at any rate. The three young men pounded on the door until Mrs. Waczukowsi, her hair tied up in pink paper knots and a robe pulled around her shoulders, at last dragged herself up from the first floor and told them to scram.

"Just another minute, madam," said Sammy, "and we shall trouble you no more."

"We have left some valuable antiquities in there," Julie said, in the same clench-jawed Mr. Peanut accent.

Sammy winked, and the two young men smiled at her with as many of their teeth as they could expose until finally she turned, consigning them all to hell with the eloquent back of her hand, and retreated down the stairs.

Sammy turned to Julie. "So where is Jerry?"

"Beats me."

"Shit, Julius, we've got to get in there. Where is everybody else?"

"Maybe they went with him."

"Don't you have a key?"

"Do I live here?"

"Maybe we could get in the window."

"Five stories up?"

"Damn it!" Sammy gave the door a feeble kick. "It's past noon and we haven't drawn a line! Christ." They would have to go back to the Kramler Building and ask to work at the rutted tables in the offices of Racy Publications, a course that would inevitably bring them within the baleful circumference of George Deasey's gaze.

Joe was kneeling by the door, running his fingers up and down the jamb, fingering the knob.

"What are you doing, Joe?"

"I could get us in, only I leave behind my tools."

"What tools?"

"I can pick the locks," he said. "I was trained to, to what, to get out of things. Boxes. Ropes. Chains." He stood up and pointed to his chest. "*Ausbrecher*. Outbreaker. No, what it is? 'Escape artist.' "

"You are a trained escape artist."

Joe nodded.

"You."

"Like Houdini."

"Meaning you can get *out* of things," Sammy said. "So you can get us *in*?"

"Normally. In, out, it's only the same thing in the other direction. But sadly, I left my tools in the Flat Bush." He pulled a small penknife from his pocket and began to probe the lock with its thin blade.

"Hold on," Julie said. "Wait a second, Houdini. Sammy. I don't think we ought to go breaking in—"

"Are you sure you know what you're doing?" Sammy said.

"You're right," Joe said. "We're in a hurry." He put the knife away and started back down the stairs. Sammy and Julie went after him.

In the street, Joe pulled himself up onto the newel that topped the right-hand baluster of the front steps, a chipped cement sphere onto which some long-vanished tenant had inked a cruel caricature of the querulous lunar face of the late Mr. Waczukowski. He pulled off his jacket and threw it to Sammy.

"Joe, what are you doing?"

Joe didn't answer. He perched for a moment atop the pop-eyed newel, his long feet side by side in their rubber-soled oxfords, and studied the retractable iron ladder of the fire escape. He pulled a cigarette from his shirt pocket and cupped a match. He let out a thoughtful cloud of smoke, then fit the cigarette between his teeth and rubbed his hands together. Then he sprang from the top of Mr. Waczukowski's head, reaching out. The fire escape rang against the impact of his palms, and the ladder sagged and with a rusted groan slid slowly downward, six woozy inches, a foot, a foot and a half, before jamming, leaving Joe to dangle five feet off the pavement. Joe chinned himself, trying to loosen it, and swung his legs back and forth; but it stayed latched.

"Come on, Joe," said Sammy. "That won't work."

"You'll break your neck," said Julie.

Joe let go of the ladder with his right hand, snatched a puff from his cigarette, then replaced it. Then he took hold of the ladder again and swung himself, throwing his entire body into it, with each swing describing an increasingly wider arc. The ladder rattled and chimed against the fire escape. Suddenly he folded himself in half, let go of the ladder completely, and allowed his momentum to jackknife him out, up and over, onto the bottom platform of the fire escape, where he landed on his feet. It was a completely gratuitous performance, done purely for effect or for the thrill of it; he easily could have pulled himself up the ladder hand over hand. He easily could have broken his neck. He paused for a moment on the landing, flicking ash from the end of his cigarette.

At that instant, the steady northerly wind that had been harrying the clouds over New York City all day succeeded at last in scattering them, sweeping clear over Chelsea a patch of wispy blue. A shaft of yellow sunlight slanted down, twisting with ribbons of vapor and smoke, a drizzling ribbon of honey, a seam of yellow quartz marbling the featureless gray granite of the afternoon. The windows of the old red row house pooled with light, then spilled over. Lit thus from behind by a brimming window, Josef Kavalier seemed to shine, to incandesce.

"Look at him," said Sammy. "Look what he can do."

Over the years, reminiscing for friends or journalists or, still later, the reverent editors of fan magazines, Sammy would devise and relate all manner of origin stories, fanciful and mundane and often conflicting, but it was out of a conjunction of desire, the buried memory of his father, and the chance illumination of a row-house window, that the Escapist was born. As he watched Joe stand, blazing, on the fire escape, Sammy felt an ache in his chest that turned out to be, as so often occurs when memory and desire conjoin with a transient effect of weather, the pang of creation. The desire he felt, watching Joe, was unquestionably physical, but in the sense that Sammy wanted to inhabit the body of his cousin, not possess it. It was, in part, a longing—common enough among the inventors of heroes—to be someone else; to be more than the result of two hundred regimens and scenarios and self-improvement campaigns that always ran afoul of his perennial inability to locate an actual self to be improved. Joe Kavalier had an air of competence, of faith in his own abilities, that Sammy, by means of constant effort over the whole of his life, had finally learned only how to fake.

At the same time, as he watched the reckless exercise of Joe's long, cavalier frame, the display of strength for its own sake and for the love of display, the stirring of passion was inevitably shadowed, or fed, or entwined by the memory of his father. We have the idea that our hearts, once broken, scar over with an indestructible tissue that prevents their ever breaking again in quite the same place; but as Sammy watched Joe, he felt the heartbreak of that day in 1935 when the Mighty Molecule had gone away for good.

"Remarkable," Julie said dryly, in a voice that suggested there was something funny, and not in the sense of humorous, about the expression on his old friend's face. "Now if only he could draw."

"He can draw," said Sammy.

Joe ran clanking up the steps of the fire escape to the fourth-floor window, threw up the sash, and fell headfirst into the room. A moment later there was an impossibly musical Fay Wray scream from the apartment.

"Huh," Julie said. "The guy might do all right in the cartoon business."

A GIRL WITH WILD BROWN RINGLETS, looking like she was going to cry, came barreling into the stairwell. She was wearing a man's herringbone overcoat. Joe stood in the middle of the apartment, his head hung at a comically sheepish angle, rubbing at the back of his neck. Sammy just had time to notice that the girl was carrying a pair of black engineer boots in one hand and a knot of black hose in the other before she brushed past Julie Glovsky, almost sending him over the banister, and went thumping bare-legged down the stairs. In her immediate wake, the three young men stood there looking at one another, stunned, like cynics in the wake of an irrefutable miracle.

"Who was that?" Sammy said, stroking his cheek where she had brushed against him with her perfume and her alpaca scarf. "I think she might have been beautiful."

"She was." Joe went to a battered horsehide chair and picked up a large satchel lying on it. "I think she forgot this." It was black leather, with heavy black straps and complicated clasps of black metal. "Her purse."

"That isn't a *purse*," said Julie, looking nervously around the living room, reckoning up the damage they had already done. He scowled at Sammy as if sensing another one of his friend's harebrained schemes already beginning to fall apart. "That's probably my brother's. You'd better put it down."

"Is Jerry transporting secret documents all of a sudden?" Sammy took the bag from Joe. "Suddenly he's Peter Lorre?" He undid the clasps and lifted the heavy flap.

"No!" said Joe. He lunged to snatch the bag, but Sammy yanked it away. "It's not nice," Joe chided him, trying to reach around and grab it. "We should respect her privacies."

"This *couldn't* be hers," said Sammy. And yet he found in the black courier's pouch a pricey-looking tortoiseshell compact, a much-folded pamphlet entitled "Why Modern Ceramics Is the People's Art," a lipstick (Helena Rubinstein's Andalucia), an enameled gold pillbox, and a wallet with two twenties and a ten. Several calling cards in her wallet gave her name, somewhat extravagantly, as Rosa Luxemburg Saks, and reported that she was employed in the art department at *Life* magazine.

"I don't think she was wearing any panties," said Sammy.

Julie was too moved by this revelation to speak.

"She wasn't," said Joe. They looked at him. "I came in through the window and she was sleeping there." He pointed to Jerry's bedroom. "In the bed. You heard her scream, yes? She put on her dress and her coat."

"You saw her," said Julie.

"Yes."

"She was naked."

"Quite naked."

"I'll bet you couldn't draw it." Julie pulled off his sweater. It was the color of Wheatena, and underneath it he wore another, identical sweater. Julie was always complaining that he felt cold, even in warm weather; in the wintertime he went around swelled to twice his normal bulk. Over the years, his mother, based only on knowledge gleaned from the pages of the Yiddish newspapers, had diagnosed him with several acute and chronic illnesses. Every morning she obliged him to swallow a variety of pills and tablets, eat a raw onion, and take a teaspoon each of Castoria and vitamin tonic. Julie himself was a great perpetrator of nudes, and was widely admired in Sammy's neighborhood for his unclothed renditions of Fritzi Ritz, Blondie Bumstead, and Daisy Mae, which he sold for a dime, or, for a quarter, of Dale Arden, whose lovely pubic display he rendered in luxuriant strokes generally agreed to be precisely those with which Alex Raymond himself would have endowed her, if public morals and the exigencies of interplanetary travel had permitted it.

"Of course I could draw it," said Joe. "But I would not."

"I'll give you a dollar if you draw me a picture of Rosa Saks lying naked in bed," said Julie.

Joe took Rosa's satchel from Sammy and sat down on the horsehide chair. He seemed to be balancing his material need against the desire he felt, as had Sammy, to hold on to a marvelous apparition and keep it for his own. At last he sighed and tossed the satchel to one side.

"Three dollars," he said.

Julie was not happy with this, but nonetheless he nodded. He pulled off another sweater. "Make it good," he said.

Joe knelt to grab a broken stub of Conte crayon lying on an overturned milk crate at his feet. He picked up an unopened overdue notice from the New York Public Library and pressed it flat against the milk crate. The long forefingers of his right hand, stained yellow at their tips, skated leisurely across the back of the envelope. His features grew animated, even comical: he squinted, pursed his lips and shifted them from side to side, grimaced. After a few minutes, and as abruptly as it had begun, his hand came to a stop, and his fingers kicked the crayon loose. He held up the envelope, wrinkling his forehead, as if considering the thing he had drawn and not simply the way he had drawn it. His expression grew soft and regretful. It was not too late, he seemed to be thinking, to tear up the envelope and keep the pretty vision all to himself. Then his face resumed its habitual mien, sleepy, unconcerned. He passed the envelope to Julie.

His short flight through the window had landed him on the floor of the bedroom, and Joe had chosen to draw Rosa Saks the way he'd first seen her, at eye level as he picked himself up from the floor, looking past a carved acorn that crowned the footboard of the bed. She was lying passed out on her belly, her sprawling right leg kicked free of the blankets and leaving exposed rather more than half of a big and fetching tuchis. Her right foot loomed large in the foreground, slender, toes curled. The lines of her bare and of her blanketed leg converged, at the ultimate vanishing point, in a coarse black bramble of shadow. In the distance of the picture, the hollows and long central valley of her back rose to a charcoal Niagara of hair that obscured all but the lower portion of her face, her lips parted, her jaw wide and perhaps a bit heavy. It was a four-by-nine-inch slice cut fresh from Joe's memory but, for all its immediacy, rendered in clean, unhurried lines, with a precision at once anatomical and emotional: you felt Joe's tenderness toward that curled little foot, that hollow back, that open, dreaming mouth drawing a last deep breath of unconsciousness. You wanted her to be able to go on sleeping, as long as you could watch.

"You didn't show her boobs!" said Julie.

"Not for three dollars," said Joe.

With grumbling and a great show of reluctance, Julie paid Joe off, then slid the envelope into the hip pocket of his overcoat, wedging it protectively into a copy of *Planet Stories*. When, fifty-three years later, he died, the drawing of Rosa Saks naked and asleep was found among his effects, in a Barracini's candy box, with a souvenir yarmulke from his eldest son's bar mitzvah and a Norman Thomas button, and was erroneously exhibited, in a retrospective at the Cartoon Art Museum in San Francisco, as the work of the young Julius Glovsky. As for *Common Errors in Perspective Drawing*, the overdue library book, recent inquiries have revealed that it was returned, under a citywide amnesty program, in 1971.

IN THE IMMEMORIAL STYLE of young men under pressure, they decided to lie down for a while and waste time. They took their shoes off, rolled up their shirtsleeves, and loosened their neckties. They moved ashtrays around, swept stacks of magazines to the floor, put a record on, and generally acted as if they owned the place. They were in the room where the boy-genius artists kept their drawing tables and taborets, a room variously referred to by its occupants over the years as the Bullpen, the Pit, the Rathole, and Palooka Studios, the latter a name often applied to the entire apartment, to the building, occasionally to the neighborhood, and even, on grim, hungover, hacking mornings with a view out the bathroom window of a sunrise the color of bourbon and ash, to the whole damn stinking world. At some time in the last century, it had been an elegant lady's bedroom. There were still curvy brass gas fixtures and egg-and-dart moldings, but most of the moss-green moiré paper had been ripped down for drawing stock, leaving the walls covered only by a vast brown web of crazed glue. But in truth, Sammy and Joe scarcely took note of their surroundings. It was just the clearing in which they had come to pitch the tent of their imaginations. Sammy lay down on a spavined purple davenport; Joe, on the floor, was aware for a moment that he was lying on a sour-smelling oval braided rug, in an apartment recently vacated by a girl who had impressed him, in the few instants of their acquaintance, as the most beautiful he had ever seen in his life, in a building whose face he had scaled so that he could begin to produce comic books for a company that sold farting pillows, in Manhattan, New York, where he had come by way of Lithuania, Siberia, and Japan. Then a toilet flushed elsewhere in the apartment, and Sammy peeled his socks off with a happy sigh, and Joe's sense of the present strangeness of his life, of the yawning gap, the long, unretraceable path that separated him from his family, receded from his mind.

Every universe, our own included, begins in conversation. Every golem in the history of the world, from Rabbi Hanina's delectable goat to the river-clay Frankenstein of Rabbi Judah Loew ben Bezalel, was summoned into existence through language, through murmuring, recital, and kabbalistic chitchat—was, literally, talked into life. Kavalier and Clay—whose golem was to be formed of black lines and the four-color dots of the lithographer—lay down, lit the first of five dozen cigarettes they were to consume that afternoon, and started to talk. Carefully, with a certain rueful humor inspired in part by self-consciousness at his broken grammar, Joe told the story of his interrupted studies with the *Ausbrecher* Bernard Kornblum, and described the role his old teacher had played in his departure from Prague. He told Sammy merely that he had been smuggled out in a shipment of unspecified artifacts that Sammy pictured aloud as big Hebrew grimoires locked with golden clasps. Joe did not disabuse him of this picture. He was embarrassed now that, when asked for a lithe aerial Superman, he had drawn a stolid golem in a Phrygian cap, and felt that the less said from now on about golems, the better. Sammy was keen on the details of autoliberation, and full of questions. Was it true that you had to be double-jointed, that Houdini was a prodigy of reversible elbow and knee sockets? No, and no. Was it true that Houdini could dislocate his shoulders at will? According to Kornblum, no. Was it more important in the trade to be strong or dexterous? It required more finesse than dexterity, more endurance than strength. Did you generally cut, pick, or rig a way out? All three and more—you pried, you wriggled, you hacked, you kicked. Joe remembered some of the things Kornblum had told him of his career in show business, the hard conditions, the endless travel, the camaraderie of performers, the painstaking and ongoing transmission among magicians and illusionists of accumulated lore.

"My father was in vaudeville," Sammy said. "Show business."

"I know. I have heard from my father one time. He was a strong man, yes? He was very strong."

"He was the World's Strongest Jew," Sammy said.

"He is now . . ."

"He is now dead."

"I am sorry."

"He was a bastard," Sammy said.

"Oh."

"Not literally. That's just an expression. He was a schmuck. He left when I was a little kid and never came back."

"Ah."

"He was all muscle. No heart. He was like Superman without the Clark Kent."

"Is that why you don't want our guy"—he had adopted Sammy's term—"to be strong?"

"No! I just don't want our guy to be the same as everybody else's, you know?"

"My mistake," said Joe. He sensed, however, that he was right. He could hear the admiration in Sammy's voice even as he pronounced the late Mr. Klayman a bastard.

"What's your father like?" Sammy said.

"He is a good man. He is a doctor. He is not the most strongest Jew in the world, sadly."

"That's what they need over there," Sammy said. "Or, look at you, you got out. Maybe what they need is like a super-Kornblum. Hey." He stood up and began to pound his right hand into the palm of his left. "Ooh. Ooh, ooh. Okay. Hold on a minute." Now he pressed the heels of his hands against his temples. You could almost see the idea elbowing its way around the inside of his mind, like Athena in the cranium of Zeus. Joe sat up. He ran his mind back over the last half hour of conversation and, as if he were picking up a transmission direct from Sammy's brain, saw in his own mind the outlines, the dark contours, the balletic contortions, of a costumed hero whose power would be that of impossible and perpetual escape.* He was just envisioning or fore-

---

* The still-fresh memory of Harry Houdini in the American mind thirteen years after his death—of his myth, his mysterious abilities, his physique, his feats, his dedicated hunting down and exposure of frauds and cheats—is a neglected source of the superhero idea in general; an argument in its favor, as it were.

tasting or, strangely, remembering this dashing character when Sammy opened his eyes. His face was twisted and flushed with excitement. He looked very much as if, to employ one of his own expressions, his bowels were in an uproar.

"Okay," he said, "listen to this." He started to pace between the drawing tables, looking down at his feet, declaiming in a sharp, barking tenor that Joe recognized from the announcers on American radio. "To, uh, to all those who, uh, toil in the bonds of slavery—"

"Bonds?"

"Yeah." Sammy's cheeks reddened, and he dropped the radio voice. "Chains, like. Just listen. It's comics, all right?"

"All right."

He resumed his pacing and radio-announcer tone and continued to compose his historic series of exclamations.

"To all those who toil in the bonds of slavery and, uh, the, the shackles of oppression, he offers the hope of liberation and the promise of freedom!" His delivery grew more assured now. "Armed with superb physical and mental training, a crack team of assistants, and ancient wisdom, he roams the globe, performing amazing feats and coming to the aid of those who languish in tyranny's chains! He is"—he paused and threw Joe a helpless, gleeful glance, on the point of vanishing completely into his story now—"the Escapist!"

" 'The Escapist.' " Joe tried it out. It sounded magnificent to his unschooled ear—someone trustworthy and useful and strong. "He is an escape artist in a costume. Who fights crime."

"He doesn't just fight it. He *frees* the world of it. He *frees* people, see? He comes in the darkest hour. He watches from the shadows. Guided only by the light from—the light from—"

"His Golden Key."

"That's great!"

"I see," Joe said. The costume would be dark, dark blue, midnight blue, simple, functional, ornamented only with a skeleton-key emblem on the chest. Joe went over to one of the drawing tables and climbed onto the stool. He picked up a pencil and a sheet of paper and started to sketch rapidly, closing his inner eyelid and projecting against it, so to speak, the image of a lithe, acrobatic man who had just leaped into his mind, a man in the act of alighting, a gymnast dismounting the rings, his right heel about to meet the ground, his left leg raised and flexed at the knee, his arms thrown high, hands outspread, trying to get at the physics of the way a man moved, the give-and-take of sinews and muscle groups, to forge, in a way that no comic book artist yet had, an anatomical basis for grace and style.

"Wow," Sammy said. "Wow, Joe. That's good. That's beautiful."

"He is here to free the world," said Joe.

"Exactly."

"Permit me to ask a question to you."

"Ask me anything. I got it all up here." Sammy tapped his head in a cocky manner that reminded Joe almost painfully of Thomas; in the next minute, when Sammy heard Joe's question, he looked crestfallen in exactly the same way.

"What is the why?" said Joe.

Sammy nodded slowly, then stopped.

"The why," he said. "Shit."

"You said—"

"I know, I know. I know what I said. All right." He picked up his coat and grabbed the last package of cigarettes. "Let's take a walk," he said.

THE CURTAIN ITSELF is legendary: its dimensions, its weight, its darker-than-chocolate color, the Continental fineness of its stuff. It hangs in thick ripples like frosting poured from the proscenium arch of the most famous theater in the most celebrated block of the world's greatest city. Call it Empire City, home of the needle-tipped Excelsior Building, tallest ever built; home of the Statue of Liberation, on her island in the middle of Empire Bay, her sword raised in defiance to the tyrants of the world; and home also of the Empire Palace Theatre, whose fabled Black Curtain trembles now as, at stage right, the narrowest of fissures opens in the rich dark impasto of its velour. Through this narrow gap a boy peers out. His face, ordinarily a trusting blank surmounted by tousled yellow curls, is creased with worry. He is not measuring the numbers of the audience—the house is sold out, as it has been for every night of the current engagement. He is looking for someone or something that no one will discuss, that he has only inferred, for the unnamed person or thing whose advent or presence has been troubling the company all day.

Then a hand as massive and hard as an elk's horn, lashed by tough sinews to an arm like the limb of an oak, grabs the boy by the shoulder and drags him back into the wings.

"You know better, young man," says the giant, well over eight feet tall, to whom the massive hand belongs. He has the brow of an ape and the posture of a bear and the accent of a Viennese professor of medicine. He can rip open a steel drum like a can of tobacco, lift a train carriage by one corner, play the violin like Paganini, and calculate the velocity of asteroids and comets, one of which bears his name. His name is Alois Berg and the comet is called Berg's comet, but to the theatergoing public and to his friends he is usually just Big Al. "Come, there is a problem with the water tank."

Backstage, the instruments of torture and restraint stand in their proper places, looking both menacing and droll, ready for the stage-hands to drag, wheel, or hoist them out onto the storied boards of the Palace. There is a regulation, asylum-issue, strap-strewn lunatic's bed; a large, slender milk can of riveted iron; a medieval Catherine wheel; and an incongruous chrome suit rack, from which dangle on prosaic wire hangers a fantastic array of straitjackets, ropes, chains, and thick leather straps. And there is the water tank, a great oblong box of glass, dolphin-sized, standing on one end: a drowned telephone booth. The glass is inch-thick, tempered, and tamperproof. The seals are neat and watertight. The timbers that frame the glass are sturdy and reliable. The boy knows all this because he built the tank himself. He wears, we see now, a leather apron filled with tools. There is a pencil stuck behind his ear and a chalk string in his pocket. If there is a problem with the tank, he can fix it. He must fix it: curtain is in less than five minutes.

"What's the matter with it?" The boy—really he is almost a man—makes his way toward the tank with aplomb, heedless of the crutch under his arm, untroubled by the left leg that has been lame since he was an infant.

"It seems to be inert, my boy. Immobilized." Big Al goes to the tank and gives it a friendly shove. The thousand-pound box tips, and the water inside shivers and sloshes. He could move the tank onstage un-aided, but there are union rules, and greater showmanship in the five big stagehands that the feat requires. "In words of one syllable, stuck."

"Something's caught in this wheel here." The young man lowers himself down his crutch, hand under hand, lies on his back, and slides under a corner of the tank's heavy base. There is a rubber-tired wheel, mounted on a steel caster, at each corner. At one corner, something has lodged itself between tire and caster. The young man slips a screw-driver from his tool belt and starts to poke around.

"Al," comes his voice from under the tank. "What's the matter with him today?"

"Nothing, Tom," Big Al says. "He is merely tired. It's the last night of the engagement. And he is no longer as youthful as he once was."

They have been joined, silently, by a small, slender man in a turban. His face is ageless and brown, his eyes dark and sensitive. He has never joined any group, party, or discussion in any way other than silently. Stealth is in his nature. He is laconic and cautious and light on his feet. No one knows how old he is, or how many lives he lived before entering the employ of the Master of Escape. He can be a doctor, a pilot, a sailor, a chef. He is at home on every continent, conversant with the argot of policemen and thieves. There is no one better at bribing a prison guard before a jailbreak stunt to plant a key in a cell, or a reporter to inflate the number of minutes that the Master remained underwater during a bridge leap. He is called Omar, a name so patently corny that it, with the turban and the desert-brown skin, is widely believed by the public to be nothing more than atmosphere, a getup, part of the thrill-making shtick of Misterioso the Great. But if his origins and true name are doubtful, his dusky complexion is genuine. As for the turban, none outside the company know how vain he is about his receding hairline.

"Okay, then what's the matter with *you*," the young man persists. "You and Omar. You've been acting strange all day."

Omar and Big Al exchange looks. The revelation of secrets is more than anathema to them; it goes against their nature and training. They would be incapable of telling the boy, even if they wanted to.

"*Imagination,*" Omar says finally, decisively.

"Too many pulp novels," says Big Al.

"Tell me this, then." The young man, Tom Mayflower, slides out from under the tank, clutching a black leather button lost from a coat front or a sleeve, embossed with a curious symbol, like three interlinked ovals. "What's the Iron Chain?"

Big Al looks toward Omar again, but his comrade has already disappeared, as silently as he came. Though he knows that Omar has gone to warn the Master, still Big Al curses him for leaving him alone to answer or not answer this question. He takes the button, to whose eyelet a bit of thread still clings, and tucks it into the pocket of his giant waistcoat.

"Two minutes," he says, suddenly as terse as their turbaned friend. "Have you fixed it?"

"It's perfect," Tom says, accepting the great antler hand that Big Al offers, scrambling to his unsteady feet. "Like everything I do."

Later, he will remember this flip reply and regret it with a flush of shame. For the tank is not perfect, not at all.

At five minutes past eight o'clock, Tom knocks. There is a star on the door, and under it, painted on a strip of card, the words "Mr. Misterioso." Tom's uncle, Max Mayflower, has never missed a curtain before. Indeed, his entire act is timed to the half second, tailored and endlessly readjusted to suit the abilities and, increasingly, the limitations of its star. His unheard-of tardiness has caused Big Al to fall silent, and Omar to utter a string of oaths in a barbarous tongue. But neither has the nerve to disturb the man they call Master. It is Miss Plum Blossom, the costumer, who has pushed Tom toward the door. Naturally, the ageless Chinese seamstress is widely believed to be secretly in love with Max Mayflower. Naturally, she *is* secretly in love with him. There are even rumors about these two and the somewhat misty parentage of Tom Mayflower, but though he loves Miss Blossom and his uncle dearly, Tom takes these rumors for the idle gossip they are. Miss Blossom would never dare disturb the Master in his dressing room before a show either, but she knows that Tom may penetrate certain of the man's mysteries and humors in a way that no one else can. Behind him, she gives another gentle push at the small of his back.

"It's Tom," the young man says, getting no answer. And then takes the unprecedented liberty of opening the dressing-room door unbidden.

His uncle sits at his dressing table. His body has grown fibrous and tough, like a stalk that hardens as it withers. His wiry legs are already clad in the skintight dark blue stuff of his costume, but his upper torso remains bare and freckled, lightly traced with the dull orange wisps that are the sole reminders of the ginger thatch that once covered him. His flaming orange mane has become gray stubble. His hands are wildly veined, his fingers knobbed like bamboo. And yet, until tonight, Tom has never seen a trace in him—not in body, voice, or heart—of the triumph of age. Now he sags, half naked, his bare head gleaming in the lighted mirror like a memento mori.

"How's the house?" he says.

"Standing room only. Can't you hear them?"

"Yes," his uncle says. "I hear them."

Something, some weary edge of self-pity in the old man's tone, irritates Tom.

"You shouldn't take it for granted," he says. "I'd give anything to hear them cheering that way for me."

The old man sits up and looks at Tom. He nods. He reaches for his dark blue jersey and pulls it over his head, then tugs on the soft blue acrobat's boots made for him in Paris by the famous circus costumer Claireaux.

"You're right, of course," he says, clapping the boy on the shoulder. "Thank you for reminding me."

Then he ties on his mask, a kind of kerchief with eyeholes, which knots at the back and covers the entire upper half of his skull.

"You never know," he says as he starts out of the dressing room. "You may get your chance some day."

"Not likely," Tom says, though this is his deepest desire, and though he knows the secrets, the mechanisms, procedures, and eventualities of the escape trade as well as any man alive save one. "Not with this leg of mine."

"Stranger things have happened," the old man says. Tom stands there, watching in admiration the way the old man's back straightens as he walks out, the way his shoulders settle and his gait becomes springy, yet calm and controlled. Then Tom remembers the button he found lodged in the wheel of the water tank, and runs after his uncle to tell him. By the time he reaches the wings, however, the orchestra has already struck up the *Tannhäuser* overture, and Misterioso has strode, arms outspread, onto the stage.

Misterioso's act is continuous—from first bow till last, the performer does not leave the stage to change costume, not even after the drenching he receives during the Oriental Water Torture Trick. Entrances and exits imply flummery, substitutions, switcheroos. Like the tight costume that promises to betray any concealed tools, the constant presence of the performer is supposed to guarantee the purity and integrity of the act. Thus it causes considerable alarm in the company when—after the roar of applause that follows Misterioso's emergence, unchained, untied, unshackled, right side up, and still breathing, from the Oriental Water Torture tank—the performer staggers into the wings, hands pressed to a spreading stain, darker than water and sticky-looking, at his side. When, a moment later, the water tank is wheeled off by the five union stagehands, sharp-eyed Omar quickly discerns the drizzled trail of water it has left on the stage, which he traces back to a small—a perfect—hole in the glass of the front panel. A pale pink ribbon twists in the green water of the tank.

"Get off me," the old man says, staggering into his dressing room. He pushes free of Omar and Big Al. "Find him," he tells them, and they vanish into the theater. He turns to the stage manager. "Ring down the curtain. Tell the orchestra to play the waltz. Tom, come with me."

The young man follows his uncle into the dressing room and watches in astonishment and then horror as the old man strips away the damp jersey. His ribs are beaded with a lopsided star of blood. The wound beneath his left breast is small, but brimming like a cup.

"Take another one from the trunk," Max Mayflower says, and somehow the bullet hole gives even greater authority to his words than they would have ordinarily. "Put it on."

Immediately, Tom guesses the incredible demand that his uncle is about to place on him, and, in his fear and excitement and with *The Blue Danube* vamping endlessly in his ears, he does not attempt to argue or to apologize for not having fitted the tank he built with bulletproof glass, or even to ask his uncle who has shot him. He just gets dressed. He has tried on the costume before, of course, secretly. It takes him only a minute to do it now.

"You just have to do the coffin," his uncle tells him. "And then you're done."

"My leg," Tom says. "How am I supposed to?"

That is when his uncle hands him a small key, gold or gold-plated, old-fashioned and ornate. The key to a lady's diary or to a drawer in an important man's desk.

"Just keep it about you," Max Mayflower says. "You'll be all right."

Tom takes the key, but he doesn't feel anything right away. He just stands there, holding the key so tightly that it pulses against his palm, as he watches his beloved uncle bleed to death in the harsh light of the dressing room with the star on the door. The orchestra launches into their third assault on the waltz.

"The show must go on," his uncle says dryly, and so Tom goes, slipping the gold key into one of the thirty-nine pockets that Miss Blossom has concealed throughout the costume. It is not until he is actually stepping out onto the stage, to the frenzied derisive happy waltz-weary cheering of the audience, that he notices not only that he has left the crutch behind in the dressing room but that, for the first time in his life, he is walking without a limp.

Two Shriners in fezzes drape him with chains and help him into a heavy canvas mailbag. A lady from the suburbs cinches the neck of the mailbag and fixes the ends of the cord with a ham-sized padlock. Big Al lifts him as if lifting a swaddled babe and carries him tenderly to the coffin, which has been carefully inspected beforehand by the mayor of Empire City, its chief of police, and the head of its fire department, and pronounced tight as a drum. Now these same worthies, to the delight of the house, are given hammers and big twenty-penny nails. Gleefully, they seal Tom into the coffin. If anyone notices that Misterioso has, in the last ten minutes, put on twenty pounds and grown an inch, he or she keeps it to himself; what difference could it make, anyway, if it is not the same man? He will still have to contend with chains and nails and two solid inches of ash wood. And yet among the women in the audience, at least, there is an imperceptible shade of difference, a deepening or darkening, in the pitch of their admiration and fear. "Look at the shoulders on him," says one to another. "I never noticed."

Inside the thoroughly rigged coffin, which has been eased into an elaborate marble sarcophagus by means of a winch that was then used to lower the marble lid into place with a ringing tocsin of finality, Tom tries to banish images of bloody stars and bullet holes from his mind. He concentrates on the routine of the trick, the series of quick and patient stages that he knows so well; and, one by one, the necessary thoughts drive out the terrible ones. He frees himself of them. His mind, as he pries open the lid of the sarcophagus with the crowbar that has conveniently been taped to its underside, is peaceful and blank. When he steps into the spotlight, however, he is nearly upended by the applause, blown over, laved by it as by some great cleansing tide. All of his years of limping self-doubt are washed away. When he sees Omar signaling to him from the wings, his face even graver than usual, he is loath to surrender the moment.

"My curtain call!" he says as Omar leads him away. It is the second remark he will come to regret that day.

The man known professionally as Misterioso has long lived, in a detail borrowed without apologies from Gaston Leroux, in secret apartments under the Empire Palace Theatre. They are gloomy and sumptuous. There is a bedroom for everyone—Miss Blossom has her own chambers, naturally, on the opposite side of the apartment from the Master's—but when they are not traveling the world, the company prefers to hang around in the vast obligatory Organ Room, with its cathedral-like, eighty-pipe Helgenblatt, and it is here, twenty minutes after the bullet entered his rib cage and lodged near his heart, that Max Mayflower dies. Before doing so, however, he tells his ward, Tom Mayflower, the story of the golden key, in whose service—and not that of Thalia or Mammon—he and the others circled the globe a thousand times.

When he was a young man, he says, no older than Tom is now, he was a wastrel, a rounder, and a brat. A playboy, spoiled and fast. From his family's mansion on Nabob Avenue, he sallied night after night into the worst dives and fleshpots of Empire City. There were huge gambling losses, and then trouble with some very bad men. When they could not collect on their loans, these men instead kidnapped young Max and held him for a ransom so exorbitant that the revenue from it easily would have funded their secret intention, which was to gain control over all the crime and criminals in the United States of America. This would in turn enable them, they reasoned, to take over the country itself. The men abused Max violently and laughed at his pleas for mercy. The police and the federals searched for him everywhere but failed. Meanwhile, Max's father, the richest man in the state of which Empire City was the capital, weakened. He loved his profligate son. He wanted to have him back again. The day before the deadline for payment fell, he came to a decision. The next morning the *Eagle* newsboys hit the streets and exposed their veteran uvulas to the skies. "FAMILY TO PAY RANSOM!" they cried.

Now, imagine that somewhere, says Uncle Max, in one of the secret places of the world (Tom envisions a vague cross between a bodega and a mosque), a copy of the Empire City *Eagle* bearing this outrageous headline was crushed by an angry hand emerging from a well-tailored white linen sleeve. The owner of the hand and the linen suit would have been difficult to make out in the shadows. But his thoughts would be clear, his anger righteous, and from the lapel of his white suit there would have been dangling a little golden key.

Max, it turns out, was being held in an abandoned house on the outskirts of Empire City. Several times he tried to escape from his bonds, but could not loosen even one finger or toe. Twice a day he was unfettered enough to use the bathroom, and though several times he tried for the window, he could not manage even to get it unlatched. So after a few days he had sunk into the gray timeless hell of the prisoner. He dreamed without sleeping and slept with his eyes open. In one of his dreams, a shadowy man in a white linen suit came into his cell. Just walked right in through the door. He was pleasant and soothing and concerned. Locks, he said, pointing to the door of Max's cell, mean nothing to us. With a few seconds' work, he undid the ropes that bound Max to a chair and bid him to flee. He had a boat waiting, or a fast car, or an airplane—in his old age and with death so near, old Max Mayflower could no longer remember which. And then the man reminded Max, with a serious but suave and practiced air, that freedom was a debt that could be repaid only by purchasing the freedom of others. At that moment, one of Max's captors came into the room. He was waving a copy of the *Eagle* with the news of Max's father's capitulation, and until he saw the stranger in white he looked very happy indeed. Then he took out his gun and shot the stranger in the belly.

Max was enraged. Without reflecting, without a thought for his own safety, he rushed at the gangster and tried to wrestle away the gun. It rang like a bell in his bones, and the gangster fell to the floor. Max returned to the stranger and cradled his head in his lap. He asked him his name.

"I wish I could tell you," the stranger said. "But there are rules. Oh." He winced. "Look, I'm done for." He spoke in a peculiar accent, polished and British, with a strange western twang. "Take the key. Take it."

"Me? Take your key?"

"No, you don't seem likely, it's true. But I have no choice."

Max undid the pin from the man's lapel. From it dangled a little golden key, identical to the one that Max had given Tom a half hour before.

"Stop wasting your life," were the stranger's last words. "You have the key."

Max spent the next ten years in a fruitless search for the lock that the golden key would open. He consulted with the master locksmiths and ironmongers of the world. He buried himself in the lore of jailbreaks and fakirs, of sailor's knots and Arapaho bondage rituals. He scrutinized the works of Joseph Bramah, the greatest locksmith who ever lived. He sought out the advice of the rope-slipping spiritualists who pioneered the escape-artist trade and even studied, for a time, with Houdini himself. In the process, Max Mayflower became a master of self-liberation, but the search was a costly one. He ran through his father's fortune and, in the end, still had no idea how to use the gift that the stranger had given him. Still he pressed on, sustained without realizing it by the mystic powers of the key. At last, however, his poverty compelled him to seek work. He went into show business, breaking locks for money, and Misterioso was born.

It was while traveling through Canada in a two-bit sideshow that he had first met Professor Alois Berg. The professor lived, at the time, in a cage lined with offal, chained to the bars, in rags, gnawing on bones. He was pustulous and stank. He snarled at the paying public, children in particular, and on the side of his cage, in big red letters, was painted the come-on SEE THE OGRE! Like everyone else in the show, Max avoided the Ogre, despising him as the lowest of the freaks, until one fateful night when his insomnia was eased by an unexpected strain of Mendelssohn that came wafting across the soft Manitoba summer night. Max went in search of the source of the music and was led, to his astonishment, to the miserable iron wagon at the back of the fairgrounds. In the moonlight he read three short words: SEE THE OGRE! It was then that Max, who had never before in all this time considered the matter, realized that all men, no matter what their estate, were in possession of shining immortal souls. He determined then and there to purchase the Ogre's freedom from the owner of the sideshow, and did so with the sole valuable possession he retained.

"The key," Tom says. "The golden key."

Max Mayflower nods. "I struck the irons from his leg myself."

"Thank you," the Ogre says now, in the room under the stage of the Palace, his cheeks wet with tears.

"You've repaid your debt many times, old friend," Max Mayflower tells him, patting the great horny hand. Then he resumes his story. "As I pulled the iron cuff from his poor, inflamed ankle, a man stepped out of the shadows. Between the wagons," he says, his breath growing short now. "He was dressed in a white suit, and at first I thought it must be him. The same fellow. Even though I knew. That he was where. I'm about to go myself."

The man explained to Max that he had, at last and without meaning to, found the lock that could be opened by the little key of gold. He explained a number of things. He said that both he and the man who had saved Max from the kidnappers belonged to an ancient and secret society of men known as the League of the Golden Key. Such men roamed the world acting, always anonymously, to procure the freedom of others, whether physical or metaphysical, emotional or economic. In this work they were tirelessly checked by agents of the Iron Chain, whose goals were opposite and sinister. It was operatives of the Iron Chain who had kidnapped Max years before.

"And tonight," Tom says.

"Yes, my boy. And tonight it was them again. They have grown strong. Their old dream of ruling an entire nation has come to pass."

"Germany."

Max nods weakly and closes his eyes. The others gather close now, somber, heads bowed, to hear the rest of the tale.

The man, Max says, gave him a second golden key, and then, before returning to the shadows, charged him and the Ogre to carry on the work of liberation.

"And so we have done, have we not?" Max says.

Big Al nods, and, looking around at the sorrowing faces of the company, Tom realizes that each of them is here because he was liberated by Misterioso the Great. Omar was once the slave of a sultan in Africa; Miss Plum Blossom had toiled for years in the teeming dark sweatshops of Macao.

"What about me?" he says, almost to himself. But the old man opens his eyes.

"We found you in an orphanage in Central Europe. That was a cruel place. I only regret that at the time I could save so few of you." He coughs, and his spittle is flecked with blood. "I'm sorry," he says. "I meant to tell you all this. On your twenty-first birthday. But now. I charge you as I was charged. Don't waste your life. Don't allow your body's weakness to be a weakness of your spirit. Repay your debt of freedom. You have the key."

These are the Master's last words. Omar closes his eyes. Tom buries his face in his hands and weeps for a while, and when he looks up again he sees them all looking at him.

He calls Big Al, Omar, and Miss Blossom to gather around him, then raises the key high in the air and swears a sacred oath to devote himself to secretly fighting the evil forces of the Iron Chain, in Germany or wherever they raise their ugly heads, and to working for the liberation of all who toil in chains—as the Escapist. The sound of their raised voices carries up through the complicated antique ductwork of the grand old theater, rising and echoing through the pipes until it emerges through a grate in the sidewalk, where it can be heard clearly by a couple of young men who are walking past, their collars raised against the cold October night, dreaming their elaborate dream, wishing their wish, teasing their golem into life.

THEY HAD BEEN WALKING for hours, in and out of the streetlights, through intermittent rainfall, heedless, smoking and talking until their throats were sore. At last they seemed to run out of things to say and turned wordlessly for home, carrying the idea between them, walking along the trembling hem of reality that separated New York City from Empire City. It was late; they were hungry and tired and had smoked their last cigarette.

"What?" Sammy said. "What are you thinking?"

"I wish he was real," said Joe, suddenly ashamed of himself. Here he was, free in a way that his family could only dream of, and what was he doing with his freedom? Walking around talking and making up a lot of nonsense about someone who could liberate no one and nothing but smudgy black marks on a piece of cheap paper. What was the point of it? Of what use was walking and talking and smoking cigarettes?

"I bet," Sammy said. He put his hand on Joe's shoulder. "Joe, I bet you do."

They were at the corner of Sixth Avenue and Thirty-fourth Street, in a boisterous cloud of light and people, and Sammy said to hold on a minute. Joe stood there, hands in his pockets, helplessly ordering his thoughts with shameful felicity into the rows and columns of little boxes with which he planned to round out the first adventure of the Escapist: Tom Mayflower donning his late master's midnight-blue mask and costume, his chest hastily emblazoned by the skilled needle of Miss Plum Blossom with a snappy gold-key emblem. Tom tracking the Nazi spy back to his lair. A full page of rousing fisticuffs, then, after bullet-dodging, head-knocking, and collapsing beams, an explosion: the nest of Iron Chain vipers wiped out. And the last panel: the company gathered at the grave of Misterioso, Tom leaning again on the crutch that will provide him with his disguise. And the ghostly face of the old man beaming down at them from the heavens.

"I got cigarettes." Sammy pulled several handfuls of cigarette packages from a brown paper bag. "I got gum." He held up several packs of Black Jack. "Do you like gum?"

Joe smiled. "I feel I must learn to."

"Yeah, you're in America now. We chew a lot of gum here."

"What are those?" Joe pointed to the newspaper he saw tucked under Sammy's arm.

Sammy looked serious.

"I just want to say something," he said. "And that is, we are going to kill with this. I mean, that's a good thing, kill. I can't explain how I know. It's just—it's like a feeling I've had all my life, but I don't know, when you showed up . . . I just knew. . . ." He shrugged and looked away. "Never mind. All I'm trying to say is, we are going to sell a million copies of this thing and make a pile of money, and you are going to be able to take that pile of money and pay what you need to pay to get your mother and father and brother and grandfather out of there and over here, where they will be safe. I—that's a promise. I'm sure of it, Joe."

Joe felt his heart swell with the longing to believe his cousin. He wiped at his eyes with the scratchy sleeve of the tweed jacket his mother had bought for him at the English Shop on the Graben.

"All right," he said.

"And in that sense, see, he really *will* be real. The Escapist. He will be doing what we're saying he can do."

"All *right*," Joe said. "*Ja ja,* I believe you." It made him impatient to be consoled, as if words of comfort lent greater credence to his fears. "We will kill."

"That's what I'm saying."

"What are those papers?"

Sammy winked and handed over a copy each of the issues for Friday, October 27, 1939, of the *New Yorker Staats-Zeitung und Herold* and of a Czech-language daily called *New Yorske Listy.*

"I thought maybe you'd find something in these," he said.

"Thank you," Joe said, moved, regretting the way he had snapped at Sam. "And, well, thank you for what you just said."

"That's nothing," said Sammy. "Wait till you hear my idea for the cover."

THE ACTUAL CURRENT OCCUPANTS of Palooka Studios, Jerry Glovsky, Marty Gold, and Davy O'Dowd, came home around ten, with half a roast chicken, a bottle of red wine, a bottle of seltzer, a carton of Pall Malls, and Frank Pantaleone. They walked in the front door boisterously quibbling, one of them imitating a muted trumpet; then they fell silent. They fell so quickly and completely silent, in fact, that one would have said they had been expecting intruders. Still, they were surprised to find, when they came upstairs, that Palooka Studios had been transformed, in a matter of hours, into the creative nerve center of Empire Comics. Jerry smacked Julie on the ear three times.

"What are you doing? Who said you could come in here? What is this shit?" He pushed Julie's head to one side and picked up the piece of board on which Julie had been penciling page two of the adventure he and Sammy had cooked up for Julie's own proud creation, a chilling tale of that Stalker of the Dark Places, that Foe of Evilness himself,

"*The Black Hat,*" said Jerry.

"I don't remember saying you could use my table. Or my ink." Marty Gold came over and snatched away the bottle of India ink into which Joe was about to dip his brush, then dragged his entire spattered taboret out of their reach, scattering a number of pens and pencils onto the rug, and completely discomposing himself. Marty was easily discomposed. He was dark, pudgy, sweated a lot, and was, Sammy had always thought, kind of a priss. But he could fake Caniff better than anyone, especially the way he handled blacks, throwing in slashes, patches, entire continents of black, far more freely than Sammy would ever have dared, and always signing his work with an extra-big letter O in Gold. "Or my brushes, for that matter."

He snatched at the brush in Joe's hand. A pea of ink fell onto the page Joe was inking, spoiling ten minutes' work on the fearsome devices arrayed backstage at the Empire Palace Theatre. Joe looked at Marty. He smiled. He drew the brush back out of Marty's reach, then presented it to him with a flourish. At the same time, he passed his other hand slowly across the hand that was holding the brush. The brush disappeared. Joe brandished his empty palms, looking surprised.

"How did you get in here?" Jerry said.

"Your girlfriend let us in," Sammy said. *"Rosa."*

"Rosa? Aw, she's not my girlfriend." It was stated not defensively but as a matter of fact. Jerry had been sixteen when Sammy first met him, and had already been dating three girls at a time. Such bounty was then still something of a novelty for him, and he had talked about them incessantly. Rosalyn, Dorothy, and Yetta: Sammy could still remember their names. The novelty had long since worn off; three was a dry spell now for Jerry. He was tall, with vulpine good looks, and wore his kinky, brilliantined hair combed into romantic swirls. He cultivated a reputation, without a great deal of encouragement from his friends, for having a fine sense of humor, to which he attributed, unconvincingly in Sammy's view, his incontestable success with women. He had a "bigfoot" comedy drawing style swiped, in about equal portions, from Segar and McManus, and Sammy wasn't entirely sure how well he'd do with straight adventure.

"If she's not your girlfriend," said Julie, "then why was she in your bed naked?"

"Shut up, Julie," Sammy said.

"You saw her in my bed naked?"

"Alas, no," said Sammy.

"I was just kidding," said Julie.

Joe said, "Do I smell chicken?"

"These are not bad," said Davy O'Dowd. He had close-cropped red hair and tiny green eyes, and was built like a jockey. He was from Hell's Kitchen, and had lost part of an ear in a fight when he was twelve; that was about all Sammy knew about him. The sight of the pink nubbin of his left ear always made Sammy a little sick, but Davy was proud of it. Lifting the sheet of tracing paper that covered each page, he stood perusing the five pages of "The Legend of the Golden Key" that Sammy and Joe had already completed. As he looked each page over, he passed it to Frank Pantaleone, who grunted. Davy said, "It's like a Superman-type thing."

"It's better than Superman." Sammy got down off his stool and went over to help them admire his work.

"Who inked this?" said Frank, tall, stooped, from Bensonhurst, sad-jowled, and already, though not yet twenty-two, losing his hair. In spite of, or perhaps in concert with, his hangdog appearance, he was a gifted draftsman who had won a citywide art prize in his senior year at Music and Art and had taken classes at Pratt. There were good teachers at Pratt, professional painters and illustrators, serious craftsmen; Frank thought about art, and of himself as an artist, the way Joe did. From time to time he got a job as a set painter on Broadway; his father was a big man in the stagehands' union. He had worked up an adventure strip of his own, *The Travels of Marco Polo*, a Sunday-only panel on which he lavished rich, Fosterian detail, and King Features was said to be interested. "Was it you?" he asked Joe. "This is good work. You did the pencils, too, didn't you? Klayman couldn't do this."

"I laid it out," Sammy said. "Joe didn't even know what a comic book was until this morning." Sammy pretended to be insulted, but he was so proud of Joe that, at this word of praise from Frank Pantaleone, he felt a little giddy.

"Joe Kavalier," said Joe, offering Frank his hand.

"My cousin. He just got in from Japan."

"Yeah? Well what did he do with my brush? That's a one-dollar red sable Windsor and Newton," said Marty. "Milton Caniff *gave* me that brush."

"So you have always claimed," said Frank. He studied the remaining pages, chewing on his puffy lower lip, his eyes cold and lively with more than mere professional interest. You could see he was thinking that, given a chance, he could do better. Sammy couldn't believe his luck. Yesterday his dream of publishing comic books had been merely that: a dream even less credible than the usual run of his imaginings. Today he had a pair of costumed heroes and a staff that might soon include a talent like Frank Pantaleone. "This is really not bad at all, Klayman."

"The Black . . . *Hat*," Jerry said again. He shook his head. "What is he, crime-fighter by night, haberdasher by day?"

"He's a wealthy playboy," said Joe gravely.

"Go draw your bunny," Julie said. "I'm getting paid seven-fifty a page. Isn't that right, Sam?"

"Absolutely."

"Seven-fifty!" Marty said. With mock servility, he scooted the taboret back toward Sammy and Joe and replaced the bottle of ink at Joe's elbow. "Please, Joe-*san*, use my ink."

"Who's paying that kind of money?" Jerry wanted to know. "Not Donenfeld. He wouldn't hire you."

"Donenfeld is going to be begging me to work for him," said Sammy, uncertain who Donenfeld was. He went on to explain the marvelous opportunity that awaited them all if only they chose to seize it. "Now, let's see." Sammy adopted his most serious expression, licked the point of a pencil, and scratched some quick calculations on a scrap of paper. "Plus the Black Hat and the Escapist, I need—thirty-six, forty-eight—three more twelve-page stories. That'll make sixty pages, plus the inside covers, plus the way I understand it we have to have two pages of just plain words." So that their products might qualify as magazines, and therefore be mailed second-class, comic book publishers made sure to toss in the minimum two pages of pure text required by postal law—usually in the form of a featherweight short story, written in sawdust prose. "Sixty-four. But, okay, here's the thing. Every character has to wear a mask. That's the gimmick. This comic book is going to be called *Masked Man*. That means no Chinamen, no private eyes, no two-fisted old sea dogs."

"All masks," said Marty. "Good gimmick."

"Empire, huh?" said Frank. "Frankly—"

"Frankly—frankly—frankly—frankly—frankly," they all chimed in. Frank said "frankly" a lot. They liked to call his attention to it.

"—I'm a little surprised," he continued, unruffled. "I'm surprised Jack Ashkenazy is paying seven-fifty a page. Are you sure that's what he said?"

"Sure, I'm sure. Plus, oh, yeah, how could I forget. We're putting Adolf Hitler on the cover. That's the other gimmick. And Joe here," he said, nodding at his cousin but looking at Frank, "is going to draw that one all by himself."

"I?" said Joe. "You want me to draw Hitler on the cover of the magazine?"

"Getting punched in the jaw, Joe." Sammy threw a big, slow punch at Marty Gold, stopping an inch shy of his chin. "Wham!"

"Let me see this," said Jerry. He took a page from Frank and lifted the tracing-paper flap. "He looks just like Superman."

"He does not."

"Hitler. Your villain is going to be Adolf Hitler." Jerry looked at Sammy, eyebrows lifted high, his amazement not entirely respectful.

"Just on the cover."

"No way are they going to go for that."

"Not Jack Ashkenazy," Frank agreed.

"What's so bad about Hitler?" said Davy. "Just kidding."

"Maybe you ought to call it *Racy Dictator*," said Marty.

"They'll go for it! Get out of here," Sammy cried, kicking them out of their own studio. "Give me those." Sammy grabbed the pages away from Jerry, clutched them to his chest, and climbed back onto his stool. "Fine, listen, all of you, do me a favor, all right? You don't want to be in on this, good, then stay out of it. It's all the same to me." He made a disdainful survey of the Rathole: John Garfield, living high in a big silk suit, taking a look around the cold-water flat where his goody-goody boyhood friend has ended up. "You probably already have more work than you can handle."

Jerry turned to Marty. "He's employing sarcasm."

"I noticed that."

"I'm not sure I could take being bossed around by this wiseass. I've been having problems with this wiseass for years."

"I can see how you might."

"If Tokyo Joe, here, will ink me," said Frank Pantaleone, "I'm in." Joe nodded his assent. "Then I'm in. Fra— To tell you the truth, I've been having a few ideas in this direction, anyway."

"Will you lend one to me?" said Davy. Frank shrugged. "Then I'm in, too."

"All right, all right," said Jerry at last, waving his hands in surrender. "You already took over the whole damned Pit anyway." He started back down the stairs. "I'll make us some coffee." He turned back and pointed a finger at Joe. "But stay away from my food. That's my chicken."

"And they can't sleep here, either," said Marty Gold.

"And you have to tell us how's come if you're from Japan, you could be Sammy's cousin and look like such a Jew," Davy O'Dowd said.

"We're in Japan," Sammy said. "We're everywhere."

"Jujitsu," Joe reminded him.

"Good point," said Davy O'Dowd.

FOR TWO DAYS, none of them slept. They drank Jerry's coffee until it was gone, then brought up cardboard trays of sour black stuff from the all-night Greek on Eighth Avenue, in blue-and-white paper cups. As promised, Jerry was cruel in his administration of the chicken, but another half was fetched, along with bags of sandwiches, hot dogs, apples, and doughnuts; they cleared the hospital-pantry of three cans of sardines, a can of spinach, a box of Wheaties, four bouillon cubes, and some old prunes. Joe's appetite was still stranded somewhere east of Kobe, but Sammy bought a loaf of bread that Joe spread with butter and devoured over the course of the weekend. They went through four cartons of cigarettes. They blared the radio, when the stations signed off they played records, and in the quiet moments between they drove one another mad with their humming. Those who had girlfriends broke dates.

It became clear fairly quickly that Sammy, deprived of his bible of clipped panels and swiped poses, was the least talented artist in the group. Within twelve hours of commencing his career as a comic book artist, he retired. He told Joe to go ahead and lay out the rest of the artwork for the Escapist story by himself, guided, if he needed a guide, by some of the issues of *Action* and *Detective* and *Wonder* that littered the floor of the Pit. Joe picked up a copy of *Detective* and began to leaf through it.

"So the idea for me is to draw very badly like these fellows."

"These guys aren't *trying* to draw bad, Joe. Some of what they do is okay. There's a guy, Craig Flessel, he's really pretty good. Try to keep an open mind. Look at this." Sammy grabbed a copy of *Action* and opened it to a page where Joe Shuster showed Superman freeing Lois Lane from the grasp of some big-shouldered crooks—war profiteers, as Sammy recalled. The backgrounds were reduced to their essence, hieroglyphs signifying laboratory, log cabin, craggy mountaintop. The chins were jutting, the musculature conventionalized, Lois's eyes plumed slits. "It's simple. It's stripped down. If you sat there and filled every panel with all your little bats and puddles and stained-glass windows, and drew in every muscle and every little tooth and based it on Michelangelo and cut your own ear off over it, *that* would be bad. The main thing is, you use pictures to tell a good story."

"The stories are good?"

"Sometimes the stories are good. Our story is really fucking good, if I do say so myself."

"Fucking," Joe said, letting it out slowly like a satisfying drag.

"Fucking what?"

Joe shrugged. "I was just saying it."

Sammy's real talents, it developed, lay elsewhere than in the pencil or brush. This became clear to everyone after Davy O'Dowd returned to the Pit from a brief conference with Frank over ideas for Davy's character. Frank was already wrapped up in his own idea, or lack thereof, working at the kitchen table and, in spite of his promise to Davy, could not be bothered. Davy came in from the kitchen scratching his head.

"My guy flies," said Davy O'Dowd. "That I know."

Joe shot a look at Sammy, who clapped a hand to his forehead.

"Oy," he said.

"What?"

"He flies, huh?"

"Something wrong with that? Frank says this is all about wishful figments."

"Huh?"

"Wishful figments. You know, like it's all what some little kid *wishes* he could do. Like for you, hey, you don't want to have a gimpy leg no more. So, boom, you give your guy a magic key and he can walk."

"Huh." Sammy had not chosen to look at the process of character creation in quite so stark a manner. He wondered what other wishes he might have subsumed unknowingly into the character of lame Tom Mayflower.

"I always wished I could fly," Davy said. "I guess a lot of guys must have wished that."

"It's a common fantasy, yeah."

"It seems to me that makes it something you can't have too many of," Jerry Glovsky put in.

"All right, then, so he can fly." Sammy looked at Joe. "Joe?"

Joe glanced up briefly from his work. *"Why."*

"Why?"

Sammy nodded. "Why can he fly? Why does he want to? And how come he uses his power of flight to fight crime? Why doesn't he just become the world's best second-story man?"

Davy rolled his eyes. "What is this, comic book catechism? I don't know."

"Take one thing at a time. How does he do it?"

"I don't know."

"Stop saying you don't know."

"He has big wings."

"Think of something else. A rocket pack? Antigravity boots? An autogyro hat? Mythological powers of the winds? Interstellar dust? Blood transfusion from a bee? Hydrogen in his veins?"

"Slow down, slow down," Davy said. "Jesus, Sam."

"I'm good at this shit. Are you scared?"

"Just embarrassed for you."

"Take a number. Okay, it's a fluid. An antigravity fluid in his veins, he has this little machine he wears on his chest that pumps the stuff into him."

"He does."

"Yeah, he needs the stuff to stay alive, see? The flying part is just a, like an unexpected side benefit. He's a scientist. A doctor. He was working on some kind of, say, artificial blood. For the battlefield, you know. Synth-O-Blood, it's called. Maybe it's, shit, I don't know, maybe it's made out of ground-up iron meteorites from outer space. Because blood is iron-based. Whatever. But then some criminal types, no, some enemy spies, they break into his laboratory and try to steal it. When he won't let them, they shoot him and his girl and leave them for dead. It's too late for the girl, okay, how sad, but our guy manages to get himself hooked up to this pump thing just before he dies. I mean, he *does* die, medically speaking, but this stuff, this liquid meteorite, it brings him back from the very brink. And when he comes to—"

"He can fly!" Davy looked happily around the room.

"He can fly, and he goes after the spies that killed his girl, and now he can really do what he always wanted to, which was help the forces of democracy and peace. But he can never forget that he has a weakness, that without his Synth-O-Blood pump, he's a dead man. He can never stop being . . . being . . . " Sammy snapped his fingers, searching for a name.

"Almost Dead Flying Guy," suggested Jerry.

"Blood Man," said Julie.

"The Swift," Marty Gold said. "Fastest bird in the world."

"I draw really nice wings," said Davy O'Dowd. "Nice and feathery."

"Oh, all right, damn it," Sammy said. "They can just be there for show. We'll call him the Swift."

"I like it."

"He can never stop being the Swift," Sammy said. "Not for one goddamned minute of the day." He stopped and rubbed his mouth with the back of his hand. His throat was sore and his lips were dry and he felt as if he had been talking for a week. Jerry, Marty, and Davy all looked at one another, and then Jerry got down from his stool and went into his bedroom. When he came out, he was carrying an old Remington typewriter.

"When you're done with Davy's, do mine," he said.

Jerry did manage to slip out for an hour, late Saturday, to return Rosa Saks's purse to her, and then again on Sunday afternoon, for two hours, returning with the crooked mark on his neck of the teeth of a girl named Mae. As for Frank Pantaleone, he disappeared sometime around midnight on Friday and eventually turned up fully dressed in the empty bathtub, behind the shower curtain, drawing board against his knees. When he finished a page, he would bellow out, "Boy!" and Sammy would run it upstairs to Joe, who did not look up from the shining trail of his brush until just before two o'clock on Monday morning.

"Beauteeful," said Sammy. He had been finished with his scripts for several hours but had stayed awake, drinking coffee until his eyeballs quivered, so that Joe would have company while he finished the cover he had designed. This was the first word either had said for at least an hour. "Let's go see if there's anything left to eat."

Joe climbed down from his stool and carried the cover over to the foot-high pile of illustration board and tracing paper that would be the first issue of their comic book. He hitched up his trousers, worked his head around a few times on the creaky pivot of his neck, and followed Sammy over to the kitchen. Here they found and proceeded to devour a light supper consisting of the thrice-picked-over demi-carcass of a by now quite hoary chicken, nine soda crackers, one sardine, some milk, as well as a yellow doorstop of adamantine cheese they found wedged, under the milk bottle, between the slats of the shelf outside the window. Frank Pantaleone and Julie Glovsky had long since gone home to Brooklyn; Jerry, Davy, and Marty were asleep in their rooms. The cousins chewed their snack in silence. Joe stared out the window onto the blasted backyard, black with ice. His heavy-lidded eyes were ringed with deep shadows. He pressed his high forehead against the cold glass of the window.

"Where am I?" he said.

"In New York City," said Sammy.

"New York City." He thought it over. "New York City, U.S.A." He closed his eyes. "That is not possible."

"You all right?" Sammy put his hand on Joe's shoulder. "Joe Kavalier."

"Sam Clay."

Sammy smiled. Once again, as when he had first enclosed the pair of newly minted American names in a neat inked rectangle of partnership on page 1 of the Escapist's debut, Sammy's belly suffused with an uncomfortable warmth, and he felt his cheeks color. It was not merely the blush of pride, nor of the unacknowledged delight he took in thus emblematizing his growing attachment to Joe; he was also moved by a grief, half affectionate, half ashamed, for the loss of Professor von Clay that he had never before allowed himself to feel. He gave Joe's shoulder a squeeze.

"We've done something great, Joe, do you realize that?"

"Big money," said Joe. His eyes opened.

"That's right," said Sammy. "Big money."

"Now I remember."

In addition to the Escapist and the Black Hat, their book now boasted the opening adventure, inked and lettered by Marty Gold, in the career of a third hero, Jerry Glovsky's Snowman, essentially the Green Hornet in a blue-and-white union suit, complete with a Korean houseboy, a gun that fired "freezing gas," and a roadster that Sammy's text described as "ice-blue like the Snowman's evil-detecting eyes." Jerry had managed to rein in his bigfoot style, letting it emerge usefully in the rendering of Fan, the bucktoothed but hard-fighting houseboy, and of the Snowman's slavering, claw-fingered, bemonocled adversary, the dreaded Obsidian Hand. They also had Davy O'Dowd's first installment of the Swift, with his lush, silky Alex Raymond wings, and Radio Wave, drawn by Frank Pantaleone and inked by Joe Kavalier with, Sammy was forced to admit, mixed results. This was Sammy's own fault. He had yielded, in the creation of Radio Wave, to Frank's experience and prowess with a pencil, not daring to offer him assistance in the development or plotting of the strip. This act of deference resulted in a dazzlingly drawn, tastefully costumed, sumptuously muscled, and beautifully inked hero with no meddling girlfriend, quarrelsome sidekick, ironic secret identity, bumbling police commissioner, Achilles' heel, corps of secret allies, or personal quest for revenge; only the hastily explained, well-rendered, and dubious ability to transmit himself through the air "on the invisible rails of the airwaves," and leap unexpectedly from the grille of a Philco into the hideout of a gang of jazz-loving jewel thieves. It was soon apparent to Sammy that once they were wise to him, all the crooks in Radio Wave's hometown need simply turn off their radios in order to thrive unmolested, but by the time he had a chance to look the thing over, Joe had already inked half of it.

Julie had done a nice job on his Hat story, illustrating one of Sammy's retooled, custom-fitted Shadow plots in a flat, slightly cartoony style not too different from that of Superman's Joe Shuster, only with better buildings and cars; and Sammy was satisfied with the Escapist adventure, though Joe's layouts were, to be honest, a little static and overly pretty, and then rushed and even scratchy-looking at the very end.

But the undisputed glory of the thing was the cover. It was not a drawing but a painting, executed in tempera on heavy stock, in a polished illustrator's style, at once idealized and highly realistic, that reminded Sammy of James Montgomery Flagg but which Joe had actually derived, he said, from a German illustrator named Kley. Unlike the great anti-Nazi covers to come, there was no hullabaloo of tanks or burning airplanes, no helmeted minions or screaming females. There were just the two principals, the Escapist and Hitler, on a neoclassical platform draped with Nazi flags against a blue sky. It had taken Joe only a few minutes to get the Escapist's pose right—legs spread, big right fist arcing across the page to deliver an immortal haymaker—and hours to paint in the highlights and shadows that made the image seem so real. The dark blue fabric of the Escapist's costume was creased with palpable pleats and wrinkles, and his hair—they had decided to do the kerchief as a mask that left the hair exposed—glinted like gold and at the same time looked messy and windblown. His musculature was lean and understated, believable, and the veins in his arm rippled with the strain of the blow. As for Hitler, he came flying at you backward, right-crossed clean out of the painting, head thrown back, forelock a-splash, arms flailing, jaw trailing a long red streamer of teeth. The violence of the image was startling, beautiful, strange. It stirred mysterious feelings in the viewer, of hatred gratified, of cringing fear transmuted into smashing retribution, which few artists working in America, in the fall of 1939, could have tapped so easily and effectively as Josef Kavalier.

Joe nodded and squeezed Sammy's hand in return. "You're right," he said. "Maybe we done something good."

Joe leaned against the wall of the kitchenette, then slid down until he hit the floor. Sammy sat down next to him and handed him the last saltine. Joe took it but, instead of eating it, began snapping off tiny pieces of cracker and tossing them out into the greater Pit. His nose in profile was a billowing sail; his hair descended in exhausted coils over his forehead. He seemed to be a million miles away, and Sammy imagined that he was wistfully recalling some part of his homeland, some marvel he had seen long ago, an advertising jingle for pomade, a dancing chicken in a gimcrack museum, his father's ear-whiskers, the lace hem of his mother's slip. All at once, like the paper flower inside one of Empire Novelty's Instant Miracle Garden capsules, the consciousness of everything his cousin had left behind bloomed in Sammy's heart, bleeding dye.

Then Joe said, half to himself, "Yes, I would like to see again that Rosa Saks."

Sammy laughed. Joe looked at him, too tired to inquire, and Sammy was too tired to explain. Another few minutes passed in silence. Sammy's chin dropped down onto his chest. After bobbing there for a moment, his head bounced up again and he snapped open his eyes.

"Was that the first woman you ever saw naked?"

"No," said Joe. "I drew models at the art school."

"Right."

"Have you seen?"

There was more implicit in this question, naturally, than the mere *observation* of a woman without her clothes. Sammy had long ago prepared a detailed account of the loss of his virginity, the moving tale of an encounter under the boardwalk with Roberta Blum on her last night in New York City, the eve of her departure for college, but he found he lacked the energy to recount it. So he just said, "No."

When Marty Gold wandered upstairs an hour later, in search of a desperate glass of milk to counteract the effects of the coffee he had drunk, he found the cousins asleep on the floor of the kitchenette, half in and half out of each other's arms. Sleepless, ulcerated, Marty was in a very ill mood, and it is to his lasting credit that, instead of throwing a fit at their having violated his prohibition on sleeping in the apartment, he threw an army blanket over Joe and Sammy, one that had returned with the Waczukowski son from Ypres, and warmed the five toes of Al Capp. Then he brought in the bottle of milk from the windowsill and carried it with him back to bed.

MONDAY DAWNED as the most beautiful morning in the history of New York City. The sky was as blue as the ribbon on a prize-winning lamb. Atop the Chrysler Building, the streamlined gargoyles gleamed like a horn section. Many of the island's 6,011 apple trees were heavy with fruit. There was an agrarian tinge of apples and horse dung in the air. Sammy whistled "Frenesi" all the way across town and into the lobby of the Kramler Building. As he whistled, he entertained a fantasy in which he featured, some scant years hence, as the owner of Clay Publications, Inc., putting out fifty titles a month, pulp to highbrow, with a staff of two hundred and three floors in Rockefeller Center. He bought Ethel and Bubbie a house out on Long Island, way out in the sticks, with a vegetable garden. He hired a nurse for Bubbie, someone to bathe her and sit with her and mash her pills up in a banana. Someone to give his mother a break. The nurse was a stocky, clean-cut fellow named Steve. He played football on Saturdays with his brothers and their friends. He wore a leather helmet and a sweatshirt that said ARMY. On Saturdays, Sammy left his polished granite and chromium office and took the train out to visit them, feasting in his private dining car on turtle meat, the most abominated and unclean of all, which the Mighty Molecule had once sampled in Richmond and never to his dying day forgotten. Sammy hung his hat on the wall of the charming, sunny Long Island cottage, kissed his mother and grandmother, and invited Steve to play hearts and have a cigar. Yes, on this last beautiful morning of his life as Sammy Klayman, he was feeling dangerously optimistic.

"Did you bring me a Superman?" Anapol said without preamble when Sammy and Joe walked into his office.

"Wait till you see," said Sammy.

Anapol made room on his desk. They opened the portfolios one after another, and piled on the pages.

"How much did you do?" Anapol said, lifting an eyebrow.

"We did a whole book," said Sammy. "Boss, allow me to present to you"—he deepened his voice and flourished his hands in the direction of the pile—"the debut issue of Empire Comics' premier title, *Masked–*"

"*Empire* Comics."

"Yeah, I was thinking."

"Not Racy."

"Maybe it's better."

Anapol fingered his Gibraltar chin. "Empire Comics."

"And their premier title . . ." Sammy lifted the sheet of tracing paper on Joe's painting. *"Masked Man Comics."*

"I thought it was going to be called *Joy Buzzer* or *Whoopee Cushion.*"

"Is that what you want to call it?"

"I want to sell novelties," said Anapol. "I want to move radios."

"*Radio Comics,* then."

"*Amazing Midget Radio Comics,*" Joe said, clearly under the impression that it sounded very fine.

"I like it," Anapol said. He put on his glasses and leaned down to examine the cover. "He's a blond. All right. He's hitting someone. That's good. What's his name?"

"His name's the Escapist."

"The Escapist." He frowned. "He's hitting Hitler."

"How about that."

Anapol grunted. He picked up the first page, read the first two panels of the story, then scanned the rest. Quickly, he scanned the next two pages. Then he gave up.

"You know I have no patience with nonsense," said the Northeast's leading wholesaler of chattering windup mandibles. He put the pages aside. "I don't like it. I don't get it."

"What do you mean? How can you not get it? He's a superhuman escape artist. No cuffs can hold him. No lock is secure. Coming to the rescue of those who toil in the chains of tyranny and injustice. Houdini, but mixed with Robin Hood and a little bit of Albert Schweitzer."

"I can see you have a knack for this," said Anapol, "by the way. I'm not saying that's a good thing." His large, woebegone features drew tight, and he looked as if his breakfast were repeating on him. He smells money, thought Sammy. "On Friday, Jack talked to his distributor, Seaboard News. Turns out Seaboard's looking for a Superman, too. And we're not the first ones they've heard from." He hit the switch that buzzed his secretary. "I want Jack." He picked up the phone. "Everybody's trying to get in on this costumed-character thing. We've got to jump on it before the bubble goes pop."

"I already have seven guys lined up, boss," said Sammy. "Including Frank Pantaleone, who just sold a strip to King Features." This was nearly true. "And Joe here. You see what kind of work he can do. How about that cover?"

"Punching Adolf Hitler," Anapol said, inclining his head doubtfully. "I just don't know about that. Hello, Jack? Yeah. That's right. Okay." He hung up. "I don't see Superman getting mixed up in politics. Not that I personally would mind seeing somebody clean Hitler's clock."

"That's the point, boss," said Sammy. "Lots of people wouldn't mind. When they see this—"

Anapol waved the controversy away. "I don't know, I don't know. Sit down. Stop talking. Why can't you be a nice, quiet kid like your cousin here?"

"You asked me . . ."

"And now I'm asking you to stop. That's why a radio has a switch. Here." He pulled open a drawer in his desk and took out his humidor. "You did good. Have a cigar." Sammy and Joe each took one, and Anapol set fire to the twenty-cent lonsdales with the silver Zippo that had been presented to him as a token of gratitude by general subscription of the International Szymanowski Society. "Sit down." They sat down. "We'll see what George thinks."

Sammy leaned back, letting out one vainglorious swallowtail cloud of blue smoke. Then he sat forward. "George? George who? Not George Deasey?"

"No, George Jessel. What do you think, of course George Deasey. He's the editor, isn't he?"

"But I thought . . . you said—" Sammy's protest was interrupted by a fit of severe coughing. He stood up, leaned on Anapol's desk, and tried to fight down the spasm of his lungs. Joe patted him on the back. "Mr. Anapol—I thought I was going to be the editor."

"I never said that." Anapol sat down, the springs of his chair creaking like the hull of an imperiled ship. His sitting down was a bad sign; Anapol did business only on his feet. "I'm not going to do that. Jack's not going to do that. George Deasey has been in the business for thirty years. He's smart. Unlike you or I, he went to college. To *Columbia* College, Sammy. He knows writers, he knows artists, he meets deadlines, and he doesn't waste money. Jack trusts him."

It is easy to say, at this remove, that Sammy ought to have seen this coming. In fact, he was shocked. He had trusted Anapol, respected him. Anapol was the first successful man Sammy had ever known personally. He was as dedicated to his work, as tireless a wanderer, as imperious, as remote from his family as Sammy's father, and to be betrayed by him, too, came as a terrible blow. Day after day, Sammy had listened to Anapol's lectures about taking the initiative, and the Science of Opportunity, and as these jibed with his own notions of how the world functioned, Sammy had believed. He didn't think it would be possible to show more initiative, or seize an opportunity more scientifically, than he had in the last three days. Sammy wanted to argue, but once deprived of their central pillar of Enterprise Rewarded, the arguments in favor of making him editor, and not the unquestionably qualified and proven George Deasey, struck him, abruptly, as ludicrous. So he sat back down. His cigar had gone out.

A moment later, wearing a corn-colored jacket over green velour pants and an orange-and-green-plaid tie, Jack Ashkenazy came in, followed by George Deasey, who, as ever, appeared to be in a testy mood. He was, as Anapol had mentioned, a graduate of Columbia, class of 1912. Over the course of his career, George Debevoise Deasey had published symbolist poetry in the *Seven Arts*, covered Latin America and the Philippines as a correspondent for the *American* and the Los Angeles *Examiner*, and written over a hundred and fifty pulpwood novels under his and a dozen other names, including, before he was made editor in chief of all their titles, more than sixty adventures of Racy's biggest seller, the Shadow-like Gray Goblin, star of *Racy Police Stories.* Yet he took no pride or true satisfaction in these or any of his other experiences and achievements, because when he was nineteen, his brother Malcolm, whom he idolized, had married Oneida Shaw, the love of Deasey's life, and taken her down to a rubber farm in Brazil, where they both died of amoebic dysentery. The bitter memory of this tragic episode, while long since corrupted by time and crumbled to an ashy gray powder in his breast, had outwardly hardened into a well-known if not exactly beloved set of mannerisms and behaviors, among them heavy drinking, prodigious work habits, an all-encompassing cynicism, and an editorial style based firmly on ruthless adherence to deadlines and on the surprise administration, irregular and devastating as the impact of meteors from space, of the scabrous and literate tongue-lashings with which he regularly flensed his quavering staff. A tall, corpulent man who wore horn-rimmed glasses and a drooping ginger mustache, he still dressed in the stiff-collared shirts and high-button waistcoats of his generation of literary men. He professed to despise the pulps and never lost an opportunity to ridicule himself for earning his living by them, but all the same he took the work seriously, and his novels, each of them composed in two or three weeks, were written with verve and an erudite touch.

"So it's to be comic books, now, is it?" he said to Anapol as they shook hands. "The devolution of American culture takes another great step forward." He took his pipe from his hip pocket.

"Sammy Klayman and his cousin Joe Kavalier," Anapol said. He put a hand on Sammy's shoulder. "Sammy, here, is pretty much responsible for this whole thing. Aren't you, Sammy?"

Sammy had the shakes. His teeth were chattering. He wanted to pick up something heavy and spray Anapol's brains across his blotter. He wanted to run weeping from the room. He just stood there, staring at Anapol until the big man looked away.

"You boys sure you want to work for me?" said Deasey. Before they could answer, he gave a nasty little chuckle and shook his head. He held a match to the bowl of his pipe and took six small sips of cherry smoke. "Well, let's have a look."

"Sit down, George, please," said Anapol, his normal saturnine hauteur giving way, as usual, in the proximity of a gentile with a diploma to arrant toadyism. "I think the boys here did a very nice job." Deasey sat down and dragged the pile of pages toward his right side. Ashkenazy pressed in close behind to peer over Deasey's shoulder. As Deasey lifted the protective sheet of tracing paper on the cover art, Sammy glanced over at Joe. His cousin was sitting stiffly in his chair, hands in his lap, watching the editor's face. Deasey's air of ruined integrity and confidence in his own judgments had made an impression on Joe.

"Who did this cover?" Deasey looked at the signature, then over the tops of his round glasses at Joe. "Kavalier, is that you?"

Joe got to his feet, literally holding his hat in his hand, and extended the other to Deasey.

"Josef Kavalier," Joe said. "How do you do."

"I'm fine, Mr. Kavalier." They shook. "And you're hired."

"Thank you," Joe said. He sat back down and smiled. He was just happy to get the job. He had no idea what Sammy was going through, the humiliation he was undergoing. All of his boasting to his mother! His strutting around Julie and the others! How in God's name would he ever be able to face Frank Pantaleone again?

Deasey set the cover art to his left, reached for the first page, and started to read. When he finished, he put it under Joe's cover and took the next page. He didn't look up again until the entire pile was on his left side and he had read through to the end.

"You put this together, son?" He smiled at Sammy. "You know, don't you, that this is pure trash. Superman is pure trash, too, of course. Batman, the Blue Beetle. The whole menagerie."

"You're right," said Sammy through his teeth. "Trash sells."

"By God, it does," said Deasey. "I can testify to that personally."

"Is it *all* trash, George?" said Ashkenazy. "I like that guy that comes out of the radio." He turned to Sammy. "How'd you come up with that?"

"Trash I don't mind," said Anapol. "Is it the same kind of trash as Superman, that's what I want to know."

"Might I confer with you gentlemen in private?" said Deasey.

"Excuse us, boys," Anapol said.

Sammy and Joe went and sat in the chairs outside Anapol's office.

Sammy tried to listen through the glass. Deasey could be heard murmuring gravely but indecipherably. Sometimes Anapol interrupted him with a question. After a few minutes, Ashkenazy came out, winked at Sammy and Joe, and left the Empire offices. When he came back a few minutes later, he was carrying a thin rattling sheaf of paper. It looked like a legal contract. Sammy's left leg started to twitch. Ashkenazy stopped in front of the door to Anapol's office and gestured grandly for them to enter.

"Gentlemen?" he said.

Sammy and Joe followed him in.

"We want to buy the Escapist," said Anapol. "We'll pay you a hundred and fifty dollars for the rights."

Joe looked at Sammy, eyebrows raised. Big money.

"What else?" said Sammy, though he had been hoping for a hundred at most.

"The other characters, the backups, we'll pay eighty-five dollars for the lot of them," Anapol continued. Seeing Sammy's face fall a little, he added, "It would have been twenty dollars apiece, but Jack felt that Mr. Radio was worth a little extra."

"That's just for the rights, kid," said Ashkenazy. "We'll also take you both on, Sammy for seventy-five dollars a week and Joe at six dollars a page. George wants you for an assistant, Sam. Says he sees real potential in you."

"You certainly know your trash," Deasey said.

"Plus we'll pay Joe, here, twenty dollars for every cover he does. And for all your pals and associates, five dollars a page."

"Though of course I'll have to meet them first," said Deasey.

"That's not enough," said Sammy. "I told them the page rate would be eight dollars."

"Eight dollars!" said Ashkenazy. "I wouldn't pay eight dollars to John Steinback."

"We'll pay five," said Anapol gently. "And we want a new cover."

"You do," Sammy said. "I see."

"This hitting Hitler thing, Sammy, it makes us nervous."

"What? What is this?" Joe's attention had wandered a little during the financial discussions—he had heard one hundred and fifty dollars, six dollars a page, twenty per cover. Those numbers sounded very good to him. But now he thought he had just heard Sheldon Anapol declaring that he would not use the cover in which Hitler got his jaw broken. Nothing that Joe had painted had ever satisfied him more. The composition was natural and simple and modern; the two figures, the circular dais, the blue and white badge of the sky. The figures had weight and mass; the foreshortening of Hitler's outflying body was daring and a little off, but in a way that was somehow convincing. The draping of the clothes was right; the Escapist's uniform looked like a uniform, like jersey cloth bunched in places but tight-fitting, and not merely blue-colored flesh. But most of all, the pleasure that Joe derived from administering this brutal beating was intense and durable and strangely redemptive. At odd moments over the past few days, he had consoled himself with the thought that somehow a copy of this comic book might eventually make its way to Berlin and cross the desk of Hitler himself, that he would look at the painting into which Joe had channeled all his pent-up rage and rub his jaw, and check with his tongue for a missing tooth.

"We're not in a war with Germany," Ashkenazy said, shaking his finger at Sammy. "It's illegal to make fun of a king, or a president, or somebody like that, if you're not at war with them. We could get sued."

"May I suggest that you keep Germany in the story if you change the name and don't call them Germans. Or Nazis," said Deasey. "But you'll have to figure out a different kind of image for the cover. If not, I can give it to Pickering or Clemm or one of my other regular cover artists."

Sammy looked over at Joe, who stood looking down, nodding his head a little bit, as if he should have known all along that it would come to something like this. When he looked up again, however, his face was composed, his voice measured and calm.

"I like the cover," he said.

"Joe," said Sammy. "Just think about it a minute. We can figure something else out. Something just as good. I know it's important to you. It's important to me, too. I think it ought to be important to these gentlemen, too, and frankly I'm a little ashamed of them right now"—he shot

Anapol a dirty look—"but just think about it a minute. That's all I'm say-ing."

"I do not need to do that, Sam. I will not agree to the other cover, no matter."

Sammy nodded, then turned back to Sheldon Anapol. He closed his eyes, very tight, as though about to jump into a swiftly moving ice-choked stream. His faith in himself had been shaken. He didn't know what was right, or whose welfare he ought to consider. Would it be helping Joe if they walked out over this? If they stayed and compro-mised, would it be hurting him? Would it be helping the Kavaliers in Prague? He opened his eyes and looked straight at Anapol.

"We can't do it," said Sammy, though it cost him great effort. "No, I'm sorry, that has to be the cover." He appealed to Deasey. "Mr. Deasey, that cover is dynamite and you know it."

"Who wants dynamite?" said Ashkenazy. "Dynamite blows up. A guy could lose a finger."

"We're not changing the cover, boss," Sammy said, and then, bring-ing to bear all his powers of dissimulated pluck and false bravado, he picked up one of the portfolios and began filling it with pieces of illus-tration board. He did not allow himself to think about what he was doing. "The Escapist fights evil." He tied the portfolio shut and handed it to Joe, still without looking at his cousin's face. He picked up another portfolio. "Hitler is evil."

"Calm down, young man," said Anapol. "Jack, maybe we can push the page rate for the others up to six, *nu?* Six dollars a page, Sammy. And eight for your cousin here. Come, Mr. Kavalier, *eight dollars a page!* Don't be foolish."

Sammy handed the second portfolio to Joe and started on the third.

"They aren't all *your* characters, don't forget," said George Deasey. "Maybe your friends would see things differently."

"Come on, Joe," said Sammy. "You heard what he said before. Every publisher in town wants in on this thing. We'll be all right."

They turned and walked out to the elevator.

"Six and a half!" called Anapol. "Hey, what about my *radios?*"

Joe looked back over his shoulder, then at Sammy, who had settled his snub features into an impassive mask. Sammy pushed the DOWN button with a determined jab of his finger. Joe inclined his head toward his cousin.

"Sammy, is this a trick?" he whispered. "Or are we serious?"

Sammy thought it over. The elevator chimed. The operator threw open the door.

"You tell me," Sammy said.

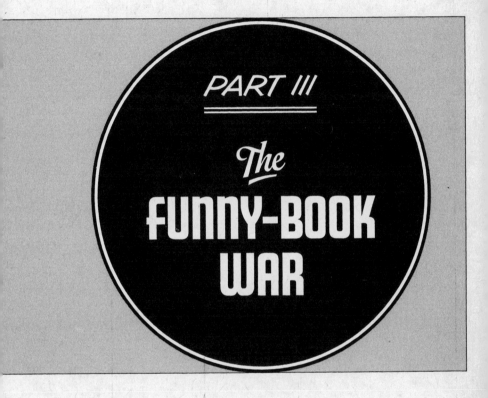

PART III

The

FUNNY-BOOK
WAR

HIS EARS STILL RINGING with artillery shells, screaming rockets, and the clattering *ack-ack* of Gene Krupa from the Crosley in a corner of the studio, Joe Kavalier laid down his brush and closed his eyes. He had been drawing, painting, smoking cigarettes, and nothing else for much of the past seven days. He clapped a hand to the back of his neck and engaged the bones that supported his battle-blown head in a few slow rotations. The vertebrae clicked and creaked. The joints of his hand throbbed, and the ghost of a brush notched his index finger. Each time he took a breath, he could feel a hard little billiard of nicotine and phlegm rattling around in his lungs. It was six o'clock on a Monday morning in October 1940. He had just won the Second World War, and he was feeling pretty good about it.

He slid off of his stool and went to look down on the autumn morning through the windows of the Kramler Building. Steam purled from the orifices of the street. A crew of a half-dozen workers in tan canvas coveralls, with peaked white caps perched atop their heads, used a water hose and long disheveled brooms to sluice a grimy tide down the gutters toward the storm drains at the corner of Broadway. Joe threw open the rattling sash of the window and poked his head out. It looked like it was going to be a fine day. The sky in the east was a bright Superman blue. There was a dank Octoberish smell of rain in the air with a faint acrid tang from a vinegar works along the East River, seven blocks away. To Joe, at that moment, it was the smell of victory. New York never looks more beautiful than to a young man who has just pulled off something he knows is going to knock them dead.

Over the course of the last week, in the guise of the Escapist, Master of Elusion, Joe had flown to Europe (in a midnight-blue autogyro), stormed the towered *Schloss* of the nefarious Steel Gauntlet, freed Plum Blossom from its deep dungeon, defeated the Gauntlet in protracted two-fisted combat, been captured by the Gauntlet's henchmen and dragged off to Berlin, where he was strapped to a bizarre multiple guillotine that would have sliced him like a hard-boiled egg while the Führer himself smugly looked on. Naturally, patiently, indomitably, he had worked his way loose of his riveted steel bonds and hurled himself at the throat of the dictator. At this point—with twenty pages to go until the Charles Atlas ad on the inside back cover—an entire Wehrmacht division had come between the Escapist's fingers and that gravely desired larynx. Over the course of the next eighteen pages, in panels that crowded, jostled, piled one on top of the other, and threatened to burst the margins of the page, the Wehrmacht, the Luftwaffe, and the Escapist had duked it out. With the Steel Gauntlet out of the picture, it was a fair fight. On the very last page, in a transcendent moment in the history of wishful figments, the Escapist had captured Adolf Hitler and dragged him before a world tribunal. Head finally bowed in defeat and shame, Hitler was sentenced to die for his crimes against humanity. The war was over; a universal era of peace was declared, the imprisoned and persecuted peoples of Europe—among them, implicitly and passionately, the Kavalier family of Prague—were free.

Joe leaned forward, the heels of his hands pressed against the windowsill and the lowermost edge of the sash digging into his back, and breathed in a cool vinegar whiff of the morning. He felt contented and hopeful and, in spite of having slept no more than four hours at a stretch in the last week, not in the least tired. He looked up and down the street. He was struck by a sudden sense of connectedness to it, of knowing where it led to. The map of the island—which looked to him like a man whose head was the Bronx, raising an arm in greeting—was vivid in his mind, flayed like an anatomical model to reveal its circulatory system of streets and avenues, of train, trolley, and bus routes.

When Marty Gold finished inking the pages that Joe had just completed, they would be strapped to the back of a motorcycle by the kid from Iroquois Color and carried along Broadway, down past Madison Square and Union Square and Wanamaker's, to the Iroquois plant on Lafayette Street. There, one of four kindly, middle-aged women, two of whom were named Florence, would guess with surprising violence and aplomb at the proper coloration for the mashed noses, the burning Dorniers, the Steel Gauntlet's diesel-driven suit of armor, and all the other things that Joe had drawn and Marty had inked. The big Heidelberg cameras with rotating three-color lenses would photograph the colored pages, and the negatives, one cyan, one magenta, one yellow, would be screened by the squinting old Italian engraver, Mr. Petto, with his corny green celluloid visor. The resulting color halftones would be shipped uptown once more, along the ramifying arterials, to the huge loft building at West Forty-seventh and Eleventh, where men in square hats of folded newsprint labored at the great steam presses to publish the news of Joe's rapturous hatred of the German Reich, so that it could be borne once more into the streets of New York, this time in the form of folded and stapled comic books, lashed with twine into a thousand little bundles that would be hauled by the vans of Seaboard News to the newsstands and candy stores of the city, to the outermost edges of its boroughs and beyond, where they would be hung up like laundry or marriage banns from wire display racks.

It was not that Joe felt at home in New York. That was something he never would have allowed himself to feel. But he was very grateful to his headquarters in exile. New York City had led him, after all, to his calling, to this great, mad new American art form. She had laid at his feet the printing presses and lithography cameras and delivery vans that allowed him to fight, if not a genuine war, then a tolerable substitute. And she paid him handsomely for doing so: he already had seven thousand dollars—his family's ransom—in the bank.

Then the music program ended, and the newsreader for WEAF came on the radio to report the announcement, that morning, by the government of unoccupied France, that it had promulgated a series of statutes, modeled after the German Nuremberg Laws, that would enable it to "superintend," in the newsreader's odd formula, its population of Jews. This followed earlier reports, the newsreader reminded his listeners, that some French Jews—communists, mostly—were being transported to labor camps in Germany.

Joe fell back into the Empire offices, banging the crown of his head against the window frame. He went over to the radio, rubbing at the knot that began to swell on his head, and turned up the volume. But that was apparently all there was to say about the Jews of France. The rest of the war news concerned itself with air raids on Tobruk and on Kiel in Germany, and with the continued harassment by German U-boats of Allied and neutral shipping to Britain. Another three ships had been lost, among them an American tanker carrying a load of oil pressed from the seeds of Kansas sunflowers.

Joe was deflated. The surge of triumph he felt when he finished a story was always fleeting, and seemed to grow briefer with every job. This time it had lasted about a minute and a half before turning to shame and frustration. The Escapist was an impossible champion, ludicrous and above all *imaginary*, fighting a war that could never be won. His cheeks burned with embarrassment. He was wasting his time. "Idiot," he said, wiping at his eyes with the back of an arm.

Joe heard the groan of the Kramler's old elevator, the whistle and rattle of its cage door being rolled to one side. He saw that his shirt-sleeve was stained not only by tears but with coffee and smudges of graphite. The cuff was frayed and inky. He became aware of the grit and the clammy residue of sleeplessness on his skin. He was not sure how long it had been since his last shower.

"Look at this." It was Shelly Anapol. He had on a pale-gray shark-skin suit that Joe didn't recognize, as giant and gleaming as the lens of a lighthouse. His face was sunburned bright red, and the skin of his ears was peeling. Pale phantom sunglasses framed his mournful eyes, which somehow, this autumn morning, looked incrementally less so than usual. "I'd say you're here early if I didn't know that you never left."

"I just finished *Radio,*" Joe said glumly.

"So what's the matter?"

"It stinks."

"Don't tell me it stinks. I don't like to hear you talk like that."

"I know."

"You're too hard on yourself."

"Not really."

"Does it stink?"

"It is all baloney."

"Baloney is okay. Let me see." Anapol crossed the space that formerly had been occupied by the desks and file cabinets of the Empire Novelties shipping clerks, but which were now filled, to Anapol's oft-expressed surprise, with the drawing boards and worktables of Empire Comics, Inc.

The previous January, *Amazing Midget Radio Comics* had debuted with a sold-out print run of three hundred thousand.* On the cover of the issue now on the stand—destined to be the first of the Empire titles (there were currently three) to break the million mark in circulation—the words "Amazing" and "Midget," which had been shrinking each month until they were a vestigial ant-high smudge in the upper left-hand corner, had been dropped forever, and along with them the whole idea of promoting novelties through comics. In September, Anapol had found himself compelled by the implacable arguments of good sense to sell off the inventory and accounts of Empire Novelties, Inc., to Johnson-Smith Co., the country's largest dealer in cheap novelties. It was this epochal sale and its proceeds that had financed the two-week trip to Miami Beach from which Anapol had just returned, red-faced and shining like a dime. He had not taken a vacation, as he had informed everyone several times before his departure, in fourteen years.

"How was Florida?" Joe said.

Anapol shrugged. "I'll tell you what, they have a nice setup down there in Florida." He seemed reluctant to admit this, as if he had invested considerable effort over the years in running Florida down. "I like it there."

"What did you do?"

"Ate, mostly. I sat out on the veranda. I had my violin. One night I played pinochle with Walter Winchell."

"A good cardplayer?"

"You might think so, but I cleaned his clock for him."

---

* In 1998, the New York branch of Sotheby's offered a rare copy of *Amazing Midget Radio Comics* #1 in Very Good condition. The minimum bid was fixed at ten thousand dollars. Its staples were shiny, its corners sharp, its pages white as piano keys. The cover had a long transverse crease, but after more than half a century—three generations removed now from that jittery year in that brutal yet innocent city—the joy and rage incarnate in the knockout Kavalier punch still startled. It sold, after lively bidding, for $42,200.

"Huh."

"Yes, I was surprised, too."

Joe slid the stack of pages across to Anapol, and the publisher began to sort through them. He tended to take a greater interest in their content, and to show a slightly more discerning eye, than he had on his first exposure to comics. Anapol had never been a devotee of the funny papers, so it had taken him a while simply to learn how to *read* a comic book. Now he went through each one twice, first when it was in production and then again when it hit the stands, buying a copy on his way to his train and reading it all the way home to Riverdale.

"*Germany?*" he said, stopping at the first panel of the second page. "We're calling them *Germans* now? Did George okay that?"

"A lot of guys are also calling them Germans, sir," Joe said. "The Spy Smasher. The Human Torch. You are going to look like the idiot who does not."

"Oh, am I, now?" Anapol said, twisting up a corner of his mouth.

Joe nodded. In his first three appearances, the Escapist along with his eccentric company had toured a thinly fictionalized Europe, in which he wowed the Razi elites of Zothenia, Gothsylvania, Draconia, and other pseudonymous dark bastions of the Iron Chain, while secretly going about his real business of arranging jailbreaks for resistance leaders and captured British airmen, helping great scientists and thinkers out of the clutches of the evil dictator, Attila Haxoff, and freeing captives, missionaries, and prisoners of war. But Joe had soon seen that this was not going to be anywhere near enough—for the Allies or for him. On the cover of the fourth issue, readers were startled to see the Escapist lift an entire panzer over his head, upside down, and tumble a pile of Gothsylvanian soldiers from its hatch like a kid shaking pennies out of a pig.

Within the covers of *Radio Comics* #4, it was revealed that the League of the Golden Key, depicted for the first time in its "secret mountain sanctum at the roof of the world," had called, in this time of great urgency, for a rare convention of the scattered masters of the globe. There was a Chinese master, a Dutch master, a Polish master, a master in a fur hood who might perhaps have been a Lapp. The assembled masters seemed mostly to be elderly, even gnomelike men. All agreed that our guy, Tom Mayflower, though he was new at the game and still young, was fighting the hardest and accomplishing the most of any of them. It was therefore voted to declare him "an emergency CHAMPION OF FREEDOM." The power of Tom Mayflower's key was increased twentyfold. He found that he now could peel the skin from an airplane, lasso a submarine with a steel cable borrowed from a nearby bridge, or tie the obligatory superheroic love knot in a battery of antiaircraft guns. He also developed an improvement on the old Ching Ling Soo trick of catching bullets—the Escapist could catch artillery shells. It hurt, and he would be knocked flat, but he could do it, staggering to his feet afterward and saying something like "I'd like to see Gabby Hartnett do *that*!"

From that point on, it had been total war. The Escapist and his gang fought on land, at sea, in the skies of Fortress Europa, and the punishment taken by the minions of the Iron Chain grew operatically intense. It soon become clear to Sammy, however, that if Joe's monthly allotment of pages was not increased—if he was not kept fighting, round the clock—his cousin might be overcome by the imprisoning futility of his rage. Around this time, fortunately, the first complete circulation figures for *Radio Comics* #2 had come in at well in excess of half a million. Sammy immediately made the natural proposal of adding a second title to the line; Anapol and Ashkenazy, after the briefest of conferences, authorized the addition of two, to be called *Triumph Comics* and *The Monitor*. Sammy and Joe went for a series of long strolls, in and out of the streets of Manhattan and Empire City, talking and dreaming and walking in circles in the prescribed manner of golem makers. When they returned from the last of these arcane strolls, they had brought forth the Monitor, Mr. Machine Gun, and Dr. E. Pluribus Hewnham, the Scientific American, filling out both books with characters drawn by the now regular Empire stable: Gold, the Glovskys, Pantaleone. Both titles had, as Sammy had once predicted, killed; and Joe had soon found himself responsible every month for more than two hundred pages of art and wholesale imaginary slaughter on a scale that, many years later, could still horrify the good Dr. Fredric Wertham when he set about to probe at the violent foundations of the comics.

"Jesus Christ," Anapol said, wincing. He had reached the point, toward the end of the story, in which the Escapist went to work on the massed panzer divisions and storm troopers of the Wehrmacht. "Ouch."

"Yes."

Anapol pointed with a thick finger. "Is that a *bone* sticking out of the guy's arm?"

"It is meant to suggest this."

"Can we *show* a bone sticking out of a human arm?"

Joe shrugged. "I could erase it."

"Don't erase it, just . . . Jesus."

Anapol looked, as he generally did when he inspected Joe's work, as if he was going to be sick. Sammy had reassured Joe, however, that it was not disgust at the violence portrayed but at the awareness, always for some reason painful to Anapol, of how big the latest Escapist donnybrook was going to go over with the remarkably bloodthirsty children of America.

It was Joe's battle scenes—the type of panel or sequence known in the trade as a slugfest—that first got his work noticed, both in the business and by the boggled young manhood of America. These scenes have been described as wild, frenetic, violent, extreme, even Breughelian. There is smoke, fire, and lightning. There are thick flocks of bombers, spiky flotillas of battleships, gardens of blooming shell bursts. Up in one corner, a bombed-out castle looms stark on a hill. Down in another corner, a grenade is exploding in a henhouse as chickens and eggs go flying. Messerschmitts dive, finned torpedoes plow up the surf. And somewhere in the middle of it all struggles the Escapist, lashed with naval chain to the business end of a prescient Axis rocket bomb.

"One of these days you're going to go too far," Anapol said, shaking his head. He put the stack of Bristol board back together and started toward his office. "Somebody is going to get hurt."

"Somebody is getting hurt already," Joe reminded him.

"Well, not around here." Anapol unlocked his door and went in. Joe followed uninvited. He wanted Anapol to understand the importance of the fight, to succumb to the propaganda that he and Sammy were unabashedly churning out. If they could not move Americans to anger against Hitler, then Joe's existence, the mysterious freedom that had been granted to him and denied to so many others, had no meaning.

Anapol looked around at the meager furnishings of his office, the sagging shelves, the desk lamp with its cracked shade, as if he had never seen them before.

"This place *is* a dump," he said, nodding, as if agreeing with some inaudible critic, possibly, Joe thought, his wife. "I'm glad we're getting out of here."

"Did you hear about Vichy?" Joe said. "The laws they passed?"

Anapol set a paper bag down on his desk and opened it. He took out a net sack filled with oranges.

"No, I did not," he said. "Florida orange?"

"They are planning to restrict the Jews there."

"That's terrible," Anapol said, handing him an orange. Joe put it into the hip pocket of his trousers. "I still can't believe I'm going to be in the *Empire State Building*." His eyes developed a faraway glaze. "Empire Comics, Empire State Building, you see the connection?"

"As also they have such laws as these in Czechoslovakia."

"I know. They're animals. You're right. Tell me, what do you hear from your family?"

"The usual," Joe said. Envelopes bearing the strange Dlouha Street address arrived at a rate of about two a month, his mother's scratchy, baroque hand tattooed over with swastikas and eagles. There was often nothing at all in these letters in the way of news; they had been emptied of information by the censor. Joe was obliged to type his replies, because although on the comics page he had one of the steadiest lines in the business, when he sat down to write his brother—most of his letters were addressed to Thomas—his hand shook too violently to hold a pen. His missives were terse, as if to forestall the incoherence of emotion. In each one, he begged Thomas not to despair, assured him that he had not forgotten his promise, and that he was doing everything he could to get them all to New York. "Not anything is different."

"Look," Anapol said. "I won't stop you from cutting their goddamned heads off if that's what you want to do, as long as it sells enough comic books. You know that."

"I know."

"It's just . . . it makes me nervous."

The entire phenomenon of comic books, as it had turned out, made Anapol a little nervous. For fifteen years he'd broken his back traveling to the remote, humorless hinterlands of Pennsylvania and Massachusetts. He had slept little, flirted with bankruptcy, driven six hundred miles a day, eaten appalling food, developed an ulcer, neglected his daughters, and worked his ass off trying to get novelty dealers to laugh. Now, suddenly, having done nothing more than allow himself to be persuaded by someone he had hitherto considered a young maniac to put up seven thousand dollars he could just barely afford, he was rich. All of the tables and equations for calculating the nature of the world had been thrown into question. He had broken off his affair with Maura Zell, moved back in with his wife, attended High Holiday services for the first time in forty years.

"I'm worried about *you*, Kavalier," he went on. "I suppose it can only be healthy for you to get your killer instincts or what have you out of your system that way"—he gestured vaguely toward the studio room—"but I can't help thinking that in the long run it's only going to make you . . . make you . . ." He seemed to lose his train of thought. He had been rummaging inside the paper bag, taking out various other souvenirs of his trip. There was a conch shell with its lush pink lip. There was a grinning monkey head made out of two coconut halves. And there was a framed photograph of a house, the colors hand-tinted and garish. The house in the picture stood on a patch of vibrant emerald lawn. The sky behind it was lurid blue. It was a modernistic house, low and flat and pale gray, charming as a carton of eggs. Anapol stood the photograph on his desk, beside the pictures of his wife and daughters. The frame was sober, plain black enamel, as if to suggest that the picture it contained was a document of rare importance, a diploma or government license.

"What is that?" Joe said.

Anapol blinked, looking at the picture. "That is my house in Florida," he said, sounding tentative.

"I thought you went to a hotel."

Anapol nodded. He looked queasy and happy and doubtful all at the same time. "We did. The Delano."

"You bought a *house* there?"

"Apparently. It seems crazy to me now." He pointed to the picture. "That isn't even my house. There is no house. There's just a piece of muddy sand with string tied around it on little sticks. In the middle of Palm River, Florida. Only there is no Palm River, either."

"You went to Florida and bought a house."

"Why don't I like the way you keep repeating it? Why do I feel like you're accusing me of something? Are you saying I don't have a right to throw my money away on whatever I damn well feel like, Kavalier?"

"No, sir," Joe said. "I would not dream." He yawned, a deep, joint-tightening yawn that made his entire body shudder. He was exhausted, but the yawn that racked him was the product of his anger and not his fatigue. The only people winning the war that Joe had been fighting in the pages of Empire Comics since January were Sheldon Anapol and Jack Ashkenazy. Between them, they had pocketed something in the neighborhood, according to Sammy's guess, of six hundred thousand dollars. "Excuse me."

"That's right," Anapol said. "Go home. Get some sleep. You look like hell."

"I have an appointment," Joe said stiffly. He put on his hat and slung his jacket over his shoulder. "Goodbye."

UNDER ORDINARY CIRCUMSTANCES, the trip downtown to the German consulate discouraged Joe; today he found it difficult even to get himself on to the subway. He felt obscurely furious with Sheldon Anapol. He took a comic book out of the hip pocket of his jacket and tried to read. He had become a constant and careful consumer of comic books. By stalking the Fourth Avenue bookstalls, he had managed to acquire a copy of nearly every one that had been published in the past few years, acquiring also, while he was at it, stacks of old Sunday *New York Mirror*s so that he could study Burne Hogarth's vehement, precise, and painterly work in *Tarzan*. The same masturbatory intensity of concentration that Joe had once brought to the study of magic and wireless sets he now focused on the fledgling, bastard, wide-open art form into whose raffish embrace he had fallen. He noticed how strong the influence of movies was on artists like Joe Shuster and *Batman*'s Bob Kane, and began to experiment with a cinematic vocabulary: an extreme close-up, say, on the face of a terrified child or soldier, or a zoom shot, drawing ever closer, over the course of four panels, on the battlements and keep of a grim Zothenian redoubt. From Hogarth he learned to trouble over the emotional occasion, so to speak, of a panel, choosing carefully, among the infinitude of potential instants to arrest and depict, the one in which the characters' emotions were most extreme. And from reading the comic books that featured art by the great Louis Fine, like the one in his hands right now, Joe learned to view the comic book hero, in his formfitting costume, not as a pulp absurdity but as a celebration of the lyricism of the naked (albeit tinted) human form in motion. It was not *all* violence and retribution in the early stories of Kavalier & Clay; Joe's work also articulated the simple joy of unfettered movement, of the able body, in a way that captured the yearnings not only of his crippled cousin but of an entire generation of weaklings, stumblebums, and playground goats.

Today, however, he could not seem to focus on the copy of *Wonderworld Comics* that he had brought along. His thoughts veered between irritation with the giddiness, the indecency, of Anapol's sudden prosperity and dread of his appointment with the Adjutant for Minority Relocation at the German consulate on Whitehall Street. It was not the prosperity itself he resented, for that was a measure of his and Sammy's success, but rather the disproportionate share of it that was going to Anapol and Ashkenazy, when it was he and Sammy who had invented the Escapist and were doing all the work of bringing him to life. No, it was not even that. It was the impotence of the money, and of all the pent-up warlike fancies that had earned it, to do anything but elaborate the wardrobe and fatten the financial portfolios of the owners of Empire Comics that so frustrated and enraged him. And there was nothing guaranteed to emphasize his fundamental powerlessness more thoroughly than a morning spent with Adjutant Milde at the German consulate. There was no pursuit more disheartening than the immigration goose chase.

Whenever he found himself with an empty morning or a week between issues, Joe would put on a good suit, a sober tie, a neatly blocked hat, and set out as he had this morning, burdened by an ever swelling satchel of documents, to try to make headway in the case of the Kavaliers of Prague. He paid endless visits to the offices of HIAS, to the United Jewish Appeal for Refugees and Overseas Needs, to travel agents, to the New York office of the President's Action Committee, to the wonderfully polite Adjutant at the German consulate with whom he had an appointment for ten o'clock that morning. To a certain cross section of clerks in that city of rubber stamps, carbon paper, and spindles, he had become a familiar figure, a slender, tall twenty-year-old with nice manners and a rumpled suit, appearing in the middle of a stifling afternoon, looking painfully cheerful. He would doff his hat. The clerk or secretary—a woman, more often than not—pinned to a hard chair by a thousand cubic feet of smoky, rancid air that caught like batter in the blades of the ceiling fans, deafened by the thunder of file cabinets, dyspeptic, despairing, and bored, would look up and see that Joe's thick thatch of curls had been deformed by his headgear into a kind of glossy black hat, and smile.

"I come to be pesky once again," Joe would say, in his increasingly slang-deformed English, and then take from the breast pocket of his jacket a slim humidor filled with five fifteen-cent panatelas or, when the clerk was a woman, a folding paper fan patterned with pink flowers, or simply a pearly-cold bottle of Coca-Cola. And she would take the fan or the soda pop, and listen to his pleas, and want to help him very much. But there was little to be done. Every month, Joe's income increased, and every month, he managed to put more and more money away, only to find that there was nothing to spend it on. The bribes and bureaucratic lubrications of the first years of the protectorate were a thing of the past. At the same time, obtaining a United States visa, never an easy thing, had become nearly impossible. By last month, when his own permanent residency had been approved, he had accumulated and sent to the State Department seven affidavits from noted New York gland doctors and psychiatrists attesting to the fact that the three senior members of his family would be unique and valuable additions to the populace of his adopted country. With each passing month, however, the number of refugees making their way to America shrank, and the news from home grew darker and more fragmentary. There was word of relocations, resettlements; the Jews of Prague were all to be sent to Madagascar, to Terezin, to a vast autonomous reservation in Poland. And Joe found himself in receipt of three officially discouraging letters from the Undersecretary for Visas, and a polite suggestion that he make no further inquiries in this regard.

His sense of entrapment in the toils of bureaucracy, of being powerless to help or free his family, also found its way into the comics. For as the Escapist's powers were augmented, the restraints required to contain him, either by his enemies or (as happened more rarely now) by himself when he was performing, grew more elaborate, even baroque. There were gigantic razor-jawed bear traps, tanks filled with electric sharks. The Escapist was tied to immense gas rings into which his captors needed only to toss a stray cigar butt to incinerate him, strapped to four rumbling panzers pointed in the cardinal directions, chained to an iron cherry at the bottom of an immense steel tumbler into which a forty-ton frothing "milkshake" of fresh concrete was poured, hung from the spring-loaded firing pin of an immense cannon aimed at the capital of "Occupied Latvonia" so that if he freed himself, thousands of innocent citizens would die. The Escapist was laid, lashed and manacled, in the paths of threshing machines, pagan juggernauts, tidal waves, and swarms of giant prehistoric bees revived by the evil science of the Iron Chain. He was imprisoned in ice, in strangling vines, in cages of fire.

Now it seemed very warm in the subway car. The fan in the center of the ceiling was motionless. A bead of sweat splashed a panel in the story about the fire-spewing Flame, lean and balletic in the great Lou Fine style, that Joe had been pretending to read. He closed the comic book and stuck it back in his pocket. He began to feel that he could not breathe. He loosened his tie and walked down to the end of the car, where there was an open louver. A faint black ripple of breeze blew from the tunnel, but it was sour and unrefreshing. At the Union Square station, a seat became available and Joe took it. He sat back and closed his eyes. He could not seem to rid his mind of the phrase *superintend its population of Jews.* All of his greatest fears for his family's safety seemed to lie folded within the bland envelope of that first word. Over the past year, his family had had their bank accounts frozen. They had been forced out of the public parks of Prague, out of the sleeping and dining cars of the state railways, out of the public schools and universities. They could no longer even ride the streetcars. Lately the regulations had grown more complex. Perhaps in an effort to expose the telltale badge of a yarmulke, Jews were now forbidden to wear caps. They were not allowed to carry knapsacks. They were not permitted to eat onions or garlic; also banned was the eating of apples, cheese, or carp.

Joe reached into his pocket and took out the orange that Anapol had given him. It was big and smooth and perfectly spherical, and oranger than anything Joe had ever seen. No doubt it would have seemed a prodigy in Prague, monstrous and illicit. He held it to his nose and inhaled, trying to find some kind of cheer or comfort in the bright volatile oils of its skin. But instead, he felt only panic. His breath was shallow and labored. The sour tunnel smell pouring in through the open louver seemed to drive away everything else. All at once, the shark of dread that never deserted its patrol of Joe's innards rose to the surface. *You cannot save them*, said a voice very close to his ear. He turned around. There was no one.

He found himself looking at the back page of the newspaper, a *Times*, that was being read by the man in the seat beside him, and his eye alighted on the shipping column. The *Rotterdam*, he saw, was due in port at eight A.M.—twenty minutes from now.

Joe had often entertained fantasies of the day he would go to greet his family as they disembarked from the *Rotterdam* or the *Nieuw Amsterdam*. He knew that the Holland America docks were across the river, in Hoboken. You had to ride the ferry to get there. When the train pulled into the Eighth Street station, Joe got off.

He walked along Eighth Street, over to Christopher, then to the river, threading his way like a pickpocket through the crowds just off the ferryboats from New Jersey: taut-jawed men in stiff hats and suits and obsidian shoes, newspapers pinned under their arms; brusque, brick-lipped, hard-heeled women in floral dresses. They stampeded down the ramps and onto Christopher and then scattered like raindrops blown across a window. Jostled, excusing himself, offering his apologies as he stumbled against them, half overwhelmed by the acrid miasma of cigar smoke and violent coughing they brought with them from the other shore, Joe nearly gave up and turned back.

But then he arrived at the huge, peeling shed that served the Delaware, Lackawanna, and Western Railroad ferries on the Manhattan side. It was a grand old barn whose high central gable was improbably endowed with the lilting pediment of a Chinese pagoda. The people disembarking here from New Jersey retained a faint air of wind and adventure, hats askew, neckties disarranged. The smell of the Hudson River that filled the building stirred memories of the Moldau. The ferryboats themselves amused Joe. They were wide craft, low-slung, upcurving at either end like dented hats, trailing pompous billows of black smoke from their solemn funnels. The pair of big wheelhouses on either side of the boats sent Joe's imagination drifting down the bear-haunted Mississippi to New Orleans.

He stood on the foredeck, hat in hand, squinting into the haze as the terminus of the DL&W and the low red roofline of Hoboken drew nearer. He breathed in coal smoke and a whiff of salt, wide-awake and flush now with the optimism of transit. The color of the water shifted in bands that ran from verdigris to cold coffee. The river was as crowded as the city itself: garbage scows piled high, swarming with gulls; tankers pumped full of petroleum, kerosene, or linseed oil; anonymous black cargo ships and, in the distance, at once thrilling and terrible, the magnificent steamship of the Holland America Line on the arm of its proud tugboat escort, lofty, remote. Behind Joe lay the jumble, at once regular and random, of Manhattan, strung like the roadbed of a bridge between the high suspending piers of midtown and Wall Street.

At a certain point about halfway through the crossing, he was taunted by a hopeful apparition. The mad spires of Ellis Island and the graceful tower of the New Jersey Central terminus came into conjunction, merging to form a kind of crooked red crown. It was, for a moment, as if Prague herself were floating there, right off the docks of Jersey City, in a shimmer of autumn haze, not even two miles away.

He knew that the chances of his family's suddenly appearing, unheralded and intact, at the top of the *Rotterdam*'s gangway were nil. But as he walked along River Street in Hoboken, past raw bars and cheap sailors' hotels, to the Eighth Street pier, with all of the other people come to greet their arriving beloveds, he found he could not prevent a tiny flame from kindling in his chest. When he reached the pier, there seemed to be hundreds of men, women, and children shouting and embracing and milling around. There was a bright line of taxis, and there were black limousines. Porters rumbled around with their hand trucks, yelling out "Porter!" with opéra-bouffe gusto. The elegant black-and-white ship, all 24,170 tons of it, loomed like a mountain in a dinner jacket.

Joe watched as several families reunited. Few of them seemed to have been separated by a mere whim to travel. They came from the countries of the war. He heard people speaking German, French, Yiddish, Polish, Russian, even Czech. Two men whose relation Joe could not quite figure out, but whom he finally decided must be brothers, went past him, arms around each other's necks, one man saying to the other in Czech, with joyful solicitude, "First thing we do is get you filthy stinking drunk, you poor bastard!" From time to time, Joe's attention would be diverted by the spectacle of a couple kissing or by some vaguely governmental-looking men shaking hands, but for the most part he watched the families. It was an incredibly cheering sight; he wondered that he had never thought of coming over to meet the *Rotterdam* before. He felt left out, and deeply envious of them, but what he felt most was the radiant ache of happiness that attended their reunions. It was like a noseful of wine that he could not drink; yet it intoxicated him.

As he watched the people emerging from under the striped awning of the gangway, he was surprised to see Dr. Emil Kavalier. His father appeared in the parting between two old women, squinting nearsightedly through the mica-chip lenses of his eyeglasses, head tilted ever so slightly backward, scanning the faces, looking for one in particular, it was Joe's, yes, he started this way, his face broke into a smile. He was enveloped in a large blond woman and her timber-wolf coat. It was not his father at all. The smile, if not the woman, was all wrong. The man saw Joe staring at him, and as he and his paramour moved past, he tipped his hat and nodded in a way that was once again eerily identical to the manner of Joe's dad. The forlorn trill of a purser's whistle sent a shiver down Joe's spine.

On his return to the city, although he was late for his meeting, he walked from Christopher Street to the Battery. He was snuffling, and his ears burned with cold, but the sunshine felt warm. He had shaken off his attack of panic from the train, the despair that had been brought on by the report from Vichy and his resentment of Anapol's prosperity. He bought a banana from a fruit stand, and then another several blocks farther down. He had always been passionately fond of bananas; they were the sole indulgence of his own sudden affluence. By the time he arrived at the German consulate on Whitehall Street, he was ten minutes late, but he thought it would be all right. It was only a matter of paperwork, and no doubt the secretary would be able to handle the problem herself. Joe might not even need to see the Adjutant.

The thought was appealing. The Adjutant, Herr Milde, was a polite and genial man who seemed to make a point of—indeed, he seemed to enjoy—wasting Joe's time. While he would never make promises or predictions, and never seemed to be in possession of information that had any but the most remote pertinence to the situation of the Kavalier family, he steadfastly, even pedantically refused to rule out the possibility that Joe's family might any day be granted their exit visas and permitted to leave. "Such things are always possible," he would affirm, though he never gave any examples. Milde's cruelty made it impossible for Joe finally to do that which his head counseled and his heart opposed: give up hope of his family's ever getting out until Hitler was defeated.

"It's quite all right," Fraulein Tulpe said when Joe walked into Milde's office. It was in the farthest corner of the consulate, which occupied a middle story of a drab neoclassical office block near the Bowling Green, at the back, between the agricultural desk and the men's lavatory. Milde's secretary was a sullen young woman with tortoiseshell glasses and straw-colored hair. She, too, was unfailingly polite with Joe in a way that, in her case, seemed intended to convey gentle distaste. "He isn't back from breakfast yet."

Joe nodded and sat down beside the watercooler. It sent a derisive belch of comment wobbling up into its reservoir.

"A late breakfast," he said, a little uncertainly. Her gaze seemed to fixate on him more than usual. He gazed down at his wrinkled trousers, the semipermanent bend in his necktie, the ink blotches on his cuffs. His hair felt lank and clammy. No doubt he smelled. For a moment he was acutely sorry that he had not stopped at Palooka Studios to shower on his way downtown, instead of wasting an hour on a foolish cruise to Hoboken. Then he thought, the hell with her. Let her smell my high Jewish smell.

"It is a farewell breakfast," she said, returning to her typewriter.

"Who is leaving?"

At that moment Herr Milde returned. He was a broad, athletic-looking man with a heroic chin and a receding hairline. He had stern, handsome features marred only when his upper lip lifted to reveal a set of big yellow equine teeth.

"*I* am," he said. "Among others. Sorry to keep you waiting, Herr Kavalier."

"You are returning to Germany?" Joe said.

"I have been transferred to Holland," he said. "I sail Thursday on the *Rotterdam*."

They went into his office. Milde showed Joe to one of two steel-legged chairs and offered a cigarette, which Joe declined. He lit one of his own instead. It was a petty gesture, but it gave Joe satisfaction. If Milde remarked it, he did not let on. He folded his hands on his desk blotter and hunched over them, leaning forward a little bit, as if eager to help Joe in any way. It was part of his policy of cruelty.

"I trust you are well?" he said.

Joe nodded.

"And your family?"

"As well as can be expected."

"I am gratified to hear it."

They sat there a moment. Joe waited for the latest bit of mummery and stage business from the Adjutant. Whatever it was, he could bear it today. He had witnessed, on the pier in Hoboken, as people something like his own had found themselves rejoined on the other side of the world. The trick could still be done. He had seen it with his own eyes.

"Now, if you please," Milde said, a little curtly. "I have a busy schedule and I am getting off to a late start."

"By all means," Joe said.

"What did you wish to speak to me about?"

Joe was thrown into confusion. "What did *I* wish?" he said. "You telephoned *me*."

Now it was Herr Milde's turn to look confused. "Did I?"

"Fraulein Tulpe did. She said you had found some problem in the paperwork for my brother. Thomas Masaryk Kavalier." He inserted the middle name as a patriotic gesture.

"Ah, yes," Milde nodded, frowning. It was clear he had no idea what Joe was talking about. He reached for the ranked dossiers waiting in a wire rack on his desk and found Joe's. He paged through it for a few minutes with an air of great diligence, flipping back and forth amid the crinkly sheets of onionskin it contained. He shook his head and clucked his tongue. "I'm sorry," he said, lifting the file to replace it in the rack. "I can't seem to find any reference to— Hello."

A piece of pale yellow paper that looked as if it might have been torn from a teletype machine fell out. Milde picked it up. He appeared to make his way very slowly through its contents, forehead furrowed, as if they presented an argument that was difficult to follow.

"Well, well," he said. "This is regrettable. I don't— It appears that your father has died."

Joe laughed. For the briefest instant, he thought that Milde was making a joke. But Milde had never made a joke before in Joe's hearing, and Joe saw that he was not kidding now. His throat tightened. He felt his eyes burning. If he had been alone, he would have broken down, but he was not alone, and he would rather have died himself than allow Milde to see him cry. He looked down at his lap, clamping down on his emotions and setting his jaw.

"I just had a letter . . ." he said weakly, his tongue thick amid his teeth. "My mother said nothing. . . ."

"When was the letter posted?"

"Nearly a month ago."

"Your father has been dead for only three weeks. It says here that the cause was pneumonia. Here."

Milde passed the ragged sheet of soft yellow paper across the desk to Joe. It had been torn from a much longer list of the dead. The name KAVALIER EMIL DR was one of nineteen, beginning with Eisenberg and running alphabetically through to Kogan, each of them followed by a terse notation of age and date and cause of death. It appeared to be a partial list of the Jews who had died in Prague or environs during the months of August and September. Joe's father's name had been circled in pencil.

"Why . . . ?" Joe could not seem to sort out the knot of questions interfering with his thoughts. "Why was I not informed?" he managed finally.

"I have no idea how that piece of paper, which I have never seen before, even found its way into your dossier," Milde said. "It's perfectly mysterious. Bureaucracy is a mysterious force." He seemed to realize that humorous remarks might not be appropriate at this time. He coughed. "It is regrettable, as I said."

"It may be an error," Joe said. It must be, he thought, for I saw him only this afternoon, in Hoboken! "A case of mistaken identity."

"Such things are always possible," Milde said. He stood up and extended a condolent hand. "I shall write a memorandum to my successor about your father's case. I will see that inquiries are made."

"You are most kind," Joe said, rising slowly from his chair. He felt a flush of gratitude to Herr Milde. Inquiries would be made. He had at least managed to obtain that much for his family. Someone now would take an interest, if only to this extent, in their case. "Goodbye, Herr Milde."

"Goodbye, Herr Kavalier."

Afterward, Joe found he had no memory of how he got out of Milde's office, along the warren of corridors, down the elevator, into the lobby. He wandered up Broadway for a block before it occurred to him to wonder where he was going. He went into a saloon and telephoned the office. Sammy was in. He started in about Joe's pages in grandiloquent terms, but when he perceived the silence on Joe's end, he ran out of steam and asked, "What?"

"I come from the consulate," Joe said. The telephone was old-fashioned, with a speaking tube and a cylindrical earpiece. There had been one like it in the kitchen of the house off the Graben. "They had some bad news for me." Joe told him how, quite by accident, he had learned that his father was dead.

"Could there be a mistake?"

"No," Joe said. He was thinking more clearly now. He was a little shaky, but it seemed to him that his thoughts were clear. His gratitude toward Adjutant Milde had turned once again to anger. "I'm sure it is not a mistake."

"Where are you?" Sammy said.

"Where am I?" Joe looked around and realized for the first time that he was in a saloon on Broadway, down at the toe of the city. "Where am I." It was not a question the second time he said it. "I'm on my way to Canada."

"No," he heard Sammy say, as he hung the receiver back on its hook. He went over to the bar. "I wonder if you can help me?" he said to the bartender.

The bartender was an elderly man with a shining pate and big rheumy blue eyes. He had been trying to explain to one of his customers, when Joe interrupted him, how to work the abacus he used to figure tabs. The customer looked glad of the interruption.

"Montreal, Canada," the bartender repeated, when Joe told him where he wanted to go. "I believe you want to leave from Grand Central Station."

The customer agreed with this. He said Joe wanted to take the Adirondack.

"What do you want to go there for?" he said. "If you don't mind my being so nosy?"

"I'm going to enlist in the R.A.F.," Joe said.

"Are you?"

"Yes. Yes, I'm tired of waiting."

"Attaboy," said the customer.

"They speak French up there," the bartender said. "Watch out."

3

JOE DID NOT STOP at home to pack a bag. He did not want to risk running into someone who would try to talk him out of his plan. Anyway, there was nothing he needed that he could not buy in a drugstore or find in a bus-station vending machine; his passport and visa he carried with him at all times. The Royal Air Force would dress and shoe and feed him.

He distracted himself for a while on the train by worrying about his interview with the recruiters. Would his resident-alien status in the United States be an impediment to his enlisting in the R.A.F.? Would they find some unknown flaw in his body? He had heard of guys being rejected for having flat feet and bad eyesight. If the air force didn't take him, he would join the Royal Navy. If he was not deemed fit for the navy, then he would take his chances in the infantry.

By Croton-on-Hudson, however, his spirits began to flag. He tried to cheer himself with thoughts of dropping bombs on Kiel or Tobruk, but his fantasies struck him as uncomfortably reminiscent of his slugfests in the pages of *Radio, Triumph,* and *The Monitor.* In the end, neither fretting nor bravado could distract him any longer from the thought that he was fatherless.

He and his father had in their jocular, gingerly fashion loved each other, but now that his father was dead, Joe felt only regret. It was not just the usual regret over things left unsaid, thanks unexpressed and apologies withheld. Joe did not yet regret the lost future opportunities for expatiation on favorite shared subjects, such as film directors (they revered Buster Keaton) or breeds of dogs. Such regrets would come only belatedly, a few days after, when he made the realization that death really did mean that you were never going to see the dead person ever again. What he regretted most of all just now was simply that he had not been there when it happened; that he had left to his mother, grandfather, and brother the awful business of watching his father die.

Emil Kavalier, like many doctors, had always been a terrible patient. He refused to acknowledge that he could fall prey to an illness, and had never taken a sick day in his life. When laid low by a grippe, he would suck mentholated pastilles, consume copious amounts of chicken broth, and go about his business. Joe could not even *imagine* him sick. How had he died? In a hospital? At home? Joe pictured him lying in a heavy scrolled bed in the middle of a jumbled apartment like the ones he had seen in the building where the Golem had been hidden.

What would become of his mother, grandfather, and brother? Their names might have appeared already on some other list of deaths that no one had bothered to report to him. Was pneumonia contagious? No, he felt fairly certain it was not. But it could be brought on by ill health and misery. If his father had been vulnerable to something like that, what kind of shape must Thomas be in? He imagined that the little food or medicine they possessed went to Thomas before it went to anyone else. Perhaps his father had sacrificed his health for the sake of Thomas's. Had his entire family died? How would he ever find out?

By the time the Adirondack pulled into Albany that afternoon, Joe's adventure into the unknown of war had come to seem one unknown too many for him to bear. He had convinced himself that it was far more likely that both his mother and Thomas were still alive. And if this was so, then they required rescue no less than they had before. He could not abandon them further by running off and trying, like the Escapist, single-handedly to end the war. It was imperative for him to remain focused on the possible. At least—it was a cruel thought, but he could not prevent himself from thinking it—there would now be one visa fewer to try to wrest from the Reich.

He got down from the train at Union Station in Albany and stood on the platform, getting in the way of people who were boarding. A man with round rimless spectacles brushed past, and Joe remembered the man on the *Rotterdam*'s gangway whom he had mistaken for his father. In retrospect, it seemed like an omen.

The conductor urged Joe to make up his mind; he was holding up the train. Joe wavered. All his doubts were counterbalanced by a powerful urge to kill German soldiers.

Joe let the train go without him, then suffered sharp stabs of regret and self-reproach. He stood outside by the taxi stand. He could get in a cab and order the driver to take him to Troy. If he missed the train at Troy, then he could have the driver take him straight on to Montreal. He had plenty of money in his wallet.

Five hours later, Joe was back in New York City. He had suffered through seven changes of mind on the way down the Hudson. He had spent the entire trip back in the train's club car, and he was much the worse for drink. He stumbled out in the evening. A cold front seemed to have moved in. The air burned his nostrils, and his eyes felt raw. He wandered up Fifth Avenue and then went into a Longchamps and ordered himself whiskey and soda. Then he went once again to the phone.

It took Sammy half an hour to get there; by that time, Joe was drunk enough, if not yet quite filthy stinking. Sammy walked into Longchamps' boisterous bar, pulled Joe off his stool, and caught him in his arms. Joe tried, but this time he could not stop himself. His weeping sounded to his own ears like sad, hoarse laughter. None of the people in the bar knew what to make of him. Sammy guided him to a booth at the back of the barroom and handed Joe his handkerchief. After Joe had swallowed the rest of his sobs, he told Sammy the little he knew.

"Could there be some mistake?" Sammy said.

"Such things are always possible," Joe said bitterly.

"Oh, Jesus," Sammy said. He had ordered two bottles of Ruppert's and was staring down at the neck of his. He was not a drinker and had not taken even a sip. "I hate to tell my mother this."

"Your poor mother," Joe said. "And my poor mother." The thought of his mother a widow started him crying all over again. Sammy came around from the other side of the table and slid into the booth alongside him. Then they just sat there for a while. Joe thought back to that morning, when he had stuck his head out into the day and felt as powerful as the Escapist, surging with the mystic Tibetan energies of his rage.

"Useless," he said.

"What is?"

"I am."

"Joe, don't say that."

"I'm worthless," Joe said. He felt that he must leave the bar. He did not want to sit around drinking and crying anymore. He wanted to do something. He would find something that could be done. He grabbed Sammy by the sleeve and shoulder of his peacoat and gave him a push, nearly knocking him out of the booth.

"Out," he said. "Let's go."

"Where are we going?" Sammy said, rising to his feet.

"I don't know," Joe said. "Work. I'm going to work."

"But you just—all right," Sammy said, looking into Joe's face. "Maybe that isn't a bad idea." They left Longchamps and went down into the cool, foul gloom of the subway.

On the southbound platform, a few feet from the cousins, stood a dark, glowering gentleman—reading the cut of his topcoat, or some indefinable emission radiating from his chin or eyes or haircut, Joe felt certain that he was German. This man was giving them the fish-eye. Even Sammy had to agree afterward that the man had been giving them the fish-eye. He was a German right out of a panel by Joe Kavalier, massive, handsome in a prognathous, lupine way, wearing a beautiful suit. As the wait for the train dragged on, Joe decided that he did not like what he considered to be the superior manner in which the theoretically German man was looking at him. He considered a number of possible styles, in German and in English, of expressing his feelings about the man and his fish-eye. Finally opting for a more universal statement, he spat, as if casually, onto the platform between him and the man. Public spitting was common enough at the time in that city of smokers, and the gesture might have remained safely ambiguous if Joe's missile had not overshot its mark. Spittle frosted the tip of the man's shoe.

Sammy said, "Did you just spit at that man?"

"What?" said Joe. He was a little surprised himself. "Eh, yes."

"He didn't mean it, mister," Sammy told the man. "He's just a little upset right now."

"Then he makes the apology," the man suggested not unreasonably.

His accent was thick and unquestionably German. He waited for his apology with the air of one accustomed to receiving apologies when he asked for them. He took a step closer to Joe. He was younger than Joe had thought at first, and even more imposing. He looked as if he could more than handle himself in a fight.

"Oh, my God," Sammy said in an undertone. "Joe, I think that man is Max Schmeling."

There were other people waiting for the train, and they had taken an interest. They started to argue about whether the man whose shoes Joe had spat on was or was not Schmeling, the Black Bull of the Uhlan, former heavyweight champion of the world.

"I'm sorry," Joe mumbled, sort of meaning it.

"What was that?" said the man, cupping a hand to his ear.

"Go to hell," Joe said, this time with greater sincerity.

"Shit-head," the man said, taking care with his English. With pugilistic quickness, he crowded Joe against an iron pillar, crooked an arm around Joe's neck, and gave him a swift punch in the stomach. Joe's breath deserted his body in a single hard gust and he pitched forward, striking his chin on the concrete platform. His eyeballs seemed to clang in their sockets. He felt as if someone had opened an umbrella inside his rib cage. He waited, flopped on his belly, unblinking as a fish, to see if he would ever again be able to draw a breath. Then he let out a long, low moan, a little at a time, testing the muscles of his diaphragm. "Wow," he said finally. Sammy knelt beside him and helped him to one knee. Joe gulped up big lopsided gouts of air. The German man turned to the other people on the platform, one arm raised in challenge or, perhaps, it seemed to Joe, in appeal. Everyone had seen Joe spit on his shoe, hadn't they? Then the big man turned and stalked off, way down to the far end of the platform. The train came, and the people all got on it, and that was the end of that. When they got back to Palooka Studios, Sammy, at Joe's request, said nothing about Joe's father. But he did tell everyone that Joe had gotten his ass kicked by Max Schmeling. Joe received their ironic congratulations. He was informed that he was lucky Schmeling had pulled his punch.

"Next time I see that guy," Joe said, to his surprise, "I am going to hit him back."

Joe never did encounter Max Schmeling, or his doppelgänger, again. In any case, there is good reason to believe that Schmeling was not in New York at all but in Poland, having been drafted into the Wehrmacht and sent to the front as punishment for his defeat by Joe Louis in 1938.

THERE COULD NOT HAVE BEEN more than a couple of thousand German citizens in New York at that time, but in the following two weeks, wherever Joe went in the city, he managed to run across at least one. He seemed to have acquired, as Sammy remarked, a superpower of his own: he had become a magnet for Germans. He found them in elevators, on buses, in Gimbel's and at Longchamps restaurants. At first he would just watch them, or eavesdrop, sizing them up as good Germans or evil ones with sweeping certainty even if they were just talking about the rain or the taste of their tea, but it wasn't long before he began to approach them and attempt to engage them in conversation that was · menacingly bland and suggestive. Often enough, his advances were met with a certain amount of resistance.

"*Woher kommen Sie?*" he asked a man he met buying a pound of steak at the butcher on Eighth Avenue, around the corner from Palooka Studios. "*Schwabenland?*"

The man nodded warily. "Stuttgart," he said.

"How is everything back there?" He could feel the note of intimidation creeping into his voice, of menacing innuendo. "Is everybody all right?"

The man shrugged, blushing, and made a mute appeal to the butcher with a raised eyebrow.

"Is there a problem?" the butcher asked Joe. Joe said that indeed there was not. But when he walked out of the butcher shop with his lamb chops, he felt strangely pleased with himself for having discomfited the man. He supposed that he ought to be ashamed of this feeling. He believed that on some level he was. But he could not seem to keep himself from remembering with pleasure the furtive look and the flushed cheeks when he had addressed the man in his own language.

The following day, a Saturday—this was about a week after Joe had learned of his father's death—Sammy took him to see a Brooklyn Dodgers football game. The idea was to get Joe out into the air and cheer him up a little. Sammy was partial to football, and seemed to have a particular fondness for the Dodgers' star back, Ace Parker. Joe had seen English rugby played in Prague, and once he decided there was no great difference between it and American football, he gave up trying to pay attention to the game and just sat smoking and drinking beer in the sharp raw breeze. Ebbets Field had a faintly ramshackle air that reminded him of a drawing in a comic strip—*Popeye* or *Toonerville Trolley*. Pigeons wheeled in the dark spaces of the grandstands. There was a smell of hair oil and beer and a fainter one of whiskey. The men in the crowd passed flasks and muttered comically violent sentiments.

After a while, Joe realized two things. The first was that he was quite drunk. The second was that, two rows behind him and up a little to his left, there sat a pair of German men. They were drinking beer from big paper cups, grinning, fair, stolid-looking men, brothers perhaps. They kept up an excited commentary and, on the whole, seemed to be enjoying the game, though they did not seem to understand it any better than Joe. They cheered whenever a fumble was recovered, regardless of who recovered it.

"Just ignore them," Sammy warned him, chary of his cousin's aggressive good luck in turning up Germans.

"They are looking at me," Joe said, fairly certain that this was so.

"They are not."

"They are looking over here."

"Joe."

Joe kept glancing back over his shoulder, forcing himself into their consciousness, their experience of the game—practically into their laps. Presently, even in their drunken state, they became aware of his attention. A certain amount of scowling and leering ensued. One of the brothers—they had to be brothers—had a crooked nose and a scarred ear indicating that he was not unfamiliar with the use of his fists. At last, toward the end of the third quarter, Joe overheard what he was quite certain was an anti-Semitic remark pass from the man who looked like a boxer to his brother or chum. It sounded to Joe as if the man had said, "Jew bastard." Joe stood up. He clambered over the back of his seat. The row behind him was full, and in the course of clearing it, he elbowed one of his neighbors in the ear. He tumbled into the Germans' row, nearly losing his balance. The Germans laughed, and the arm of a seat jabbed Joe in the side sharply, but he scrambled to his feet and, without a word, knocked the boxer's hat off his head. It fell into a clotted puddle of spilled beer and a rubble of peanuts at the other man's feet. The man with the cauliflower ear looked very surprised, and then astonished when Joe grabbed hold of his shirt collar. Joe yanked so hard that three buttons popped loose and shot off in all directions with audible whizzing sounds. But the man had a long reach, and he managed to get a hand around the back of Joe's neck. He pulled Joe to him and, at the same time, with the other hand connected his fist to the side of Joe's skull. While Joe was thus held, bent over the seat with his nose smashed against the man's left knee, the brother pummeled Joe's back over and over as if he were driving nails into a plank with two hammers. Before Sammy and some of the men sitting in the seats around them could pull the two Germans off, they had closed Joe's right eye for him, chipped a tooth, bruised his rib cage, and ruined a new suit. Then an usher came and threw Joe and Sammy out of Ebbets Field. They went quietly, Joe holding a paper cup of ice to the tender orbit of his eye. The pain was keen. There was an odor of urinals along the ramp leading down to the gates of the ballpark, a masculine smell, bitter and bracing.

"What are you doing?" Sammy asked him. "Are you crazy?"

"I'm sorry," Joe said. "I thought he said something."

"Why are you smiling, god damn it?"

"I don't know."

That night, when he and Sammy went to dinner at Ethel Klayman's, he bent down to pick up the napkin he had dropped, and when he sat up again, there was a bright exclamation mark of blood on his cheek.

"You need sutures," said his aunt in her most inarguable tone.

Joe protested. He had given out to his friends that he was afraid of needles and doctors, but the truth was that he felt edified by the wound to his head. It was not that he felt he deserved the pain so much as that it suited him. No matter how well he cleaned the cut, how tightly he compressed it, how thick the bandage he applied, within an hour or so, the first telltale freckle of red would have reappeared. It was like the memory of home, a tribute to his father's stoical denial of illness, injury, or pain.

"It's going to be fine," he said.

His aunt took hold of his elbow with her five-pronged iron grapple and sat him down on the lid of the toilet in the bathroom. She had Sammy fetch a bottle of slivovitz that had been left behind by a friend of her late husband in 1935 and not touched since. Then she crooked his head under her left arm and sewed him up. The thread was dark blue, exactly the color of the Escapist's uniform.

"Don't go looking for trouble," she begged him as she worked the long thin needle into his skin. "You'll be getting plenty of trouble soon enough."

After that, Joe went looking for trouble. For no good reason, he started going up, every day, to Yorkville, where there were numerous German beer halls, German restaurants, German social clubs, and German-Americans. Most of the time, he merely skulked around for a while and returned home from these forays without incident, but sometimes one thing led to another. The ethnic neighborhoods of New York have always been alert to the incursions of intemperate strangers. He got himself punched in the stomach yet again, on East Ninetieth Street, waiting for a bus, by a man who did not take kindly to the sneer that Joe armed himself with whenever he ventured uptown. Hanging around a candy store one afternoon, Joe attracted the attention of some little neighborhood boys, one of whom, for reasons having nothing to do with politics or racial theories, shot him in the back of the head with a big wet oyster of a spitball. These boys were all regular readers of the Escapist, and admirers of Joe Kavalier's work. If they had known who it was, they would probably have felt very sorry for peashooting him. But they just didn't like the way Joe looked. They had observed, with the ruthless acuity of boys, that there was something funny about Joe Kavalier, about his rumpled suit, his air of banked and smoldering testiness, the curly strands standing up from his imperfectly slicked-back hair like an exploded clockworks. He looked like a patsy for pranksters and practical jokers. He looked like a man who was looking for trouble.

It must be said at this point that a very large number of German New Yorkers were vehemently opposed to Hitler and the Nazis. They wrote outraged letters to the editors of the major dailies, condemning Allied and American inaction after the Anschluss and the annexation of the Sudetenland. They joined anti-fascist leagues, brawled with brownshirts—Joe was far from the only young man who went out into the streets of New York that autumn spoiling for a fight—and vigorously supported the president and his policies when they took action against Hitler and his war. Nevertheless, there was a fair number of New York Germans who took open pride in the accomplishments, civil, cultural, sporting, and military, of the Third Reich. Among these was a smaller group that was regularly active in various patriotic, nationalistic, generally racist, and sometimes violent organizations sympathetic to the aims of the homeland. Joe frequently returned from Yorkville with anti-Jewish newspapers and tracts that he read through from front to back, stomach tight with fury, then stuffed into one of three peach crates that he used for a filing cabinet. (The other two held his letters from home and his comic books.)

One day, as he was haunting the streets of Yorkville, Joe noticed a sign painted in the window of a second-floor office:

ARYAN-AMERICAN LEAGUE

Standing there, staring up at the window, Joe underwent a dark fantasy of running up to that office and bursting into that warren of snakes, feet flying right up at you out of the panel as jagged splinters of the door shot in all directions. He saw himself wading into a roiling tangle of brownshirts, fists and boots and elbows, and finding, in that violent surf of men, triumph, or if not that then atonement, retribution, or deliverance. He watched the window for nearly half an hour, trying to catch a glimpse of an actual party member. No one entered the building or walked in front of the second-floor window. Joe soon gave up and went home.

Inevitably, he went back to Yorkville. There was a *konditorei* called Haussman's across the street from the headquarters of the AAL, and from a table by the window Joe had a good view of the door to the building's lobby and of the window. He ordered a slice of the house's excellent Sacher torte and a cup of coffee that was unusually drinkable for New York, and waited. Another slice and two cups later there was still no sign of any Aryan-American at work. He paid his tab and crossed the street. The building's directory, as he had already observed, listed an optometrist, an accountant, a publisher, and the AAL, but none of these concerns appeared to have any patients, clients, or employees. The building—it was called the Kuhn Building—was a graveyard. When he climbed the stairs to the second floor, the door to the AAL offices was locked. Gray daylight through the frosted glass of the door suggested that there were no lamps turned on inside. Joe tried the knob. Then he got down on one knee to examine the lock. It was a Chubb, old and solid, but if he'd had his tools, it would have presented no problem. Unfortunately, his picks and wrench were in a drawer beside his bed down at Palooka Studios. He felt around in his pockets and found a mechanical pencil whose metal pocket clip, attached to the shaft with a two-pronged collar, would serve well enough, suitably deformed, as a tension wrench. But there was still the matter of a pick. He went back downstairs and walked around the block until he found a child's bicycle chained to a window grate on East Eighty-eighth Street. It looked like a new bike, sugary red, its chrome parts bright as mirrors and its tires glossy and stubbled. He waited for a moment to make sure that no one was coming. Then he grasped the shiny handlebars and, with savage jabs of the heel of his shoe at the bike's front wheel, managed to spring loose a spoke. He wiggled it free of the wheel rim and then ran back to the corner of Eighty-seventh and York. Using an iron railing as a crimping form and the sidewalk itself as a rough file, he was able to fashion a serviceable pick from the thin strong wire of the spoke.

When he got back up to the offices of the Aryan-American League, he knocked on the scarred oak frame of the door. There was no reply. He hitched up his trousers, knelt down, put his forehead to the door, and set to work. The crude tools, lack of practice, and pulsation of his own excitement in his arteries and joints made the work more difficult than it ought to have been. He took off his jacket. He rolled up his sleeves. He tipped his hat into his hands and set it on the floor beside him. Finally he opened his collar and yanked his tie to one side. He cursed and sweated and listened so avidly for the sound of the door opening downstairs that he could not hear the lock through his fingers. It took him nearly an hour to get inside.

When he did, he found not the elaborate laboratory or manufactory of fascism he had been expecting but a wooden desk, a chair, a lamp, a typewriter, and a tall oak filing cabinet. The venetian blinds were dusty and crooked, and missing slats. The wooden floor was bare and spotted with cigarette burns. The telephone, when Joe lifted the receiver, was dead. On one wall was a framed color lithograph of the Führer in a romantic mood, chin held at a poetic angle, an alpine breeze stirring his dark forelock. Against another wall stood a shelf piled high with various publications, in English and in German, whose titles alluded to the aims and predictions of National Socialism and the pan-German dream.

Joe went over and stood behind the desk. He pulled out the chair and sat down. The blotter was lost amid a blizzard of notes and memoranda, some typed, some scrawled in a minute and angular hand.

> *hypnosis used on FT can prove it*
> *FT and haschisshin old man of mountain further study*
> *FT master swordsman*

There were bus transfers, candy wrappers, a ticket stub from the Polo Grounds. There was a copy of a book called *Thuggee.* There were numerous newspaper clippings and articles that had been torn from *Photoplay* and *Modern Screen.* All of the magazine articles, Joe noticed, seemed to be concerned with the film star Franchot Tone. And larded throughout the layers of rubbish and cryptic notations were dozens of comic books: *Superman, Marvel Mystery, Flash, Whiz, Shield-Wizard*— as well as, Joe could hardly fail to notice, the latest issues of *Radio, Triumph,* and *The Monitor.* In spots, the drifts of paper grew positively mountainous. Paper clips, tacks, and pen nibs were scattered everywhere, like conventional features on a map. A jagged palisade of pencils bristled from an empty Savarin coffee can. Joe reached out and, with two quick sweeps of his arms, sent everything tumbling. The thumbtacks made a pattering sound as they hit the floor.

Joe went through the drawers. In one he found a statement from New York Telephone promising, reliably as it had turned out, to disconnect service if the AAL account continued unpaid; a typed manuscript; and, inexplicably, the menu from the recent wedding reception, at the Hotel Trevi, of Bruce and Marilyn Horowitz. Joe yanked out the drawer and tipped it over. The manuscript split into halves that sprawled like a dropped deck of cards. Joe picked up a page and read it. It appeared to be science fiction. Someone named Rex Mundy was taking aim with his ray pistol at the suppurating hide of a hideous Zid. Someone named Krystal DeHaven was dangling upside down from a chain above the yawning maw of a hungry tork.

He crumpled the page and resumed his raid on the desk drawers. One contained a framed photograph of Franchot Tone, in the lower left corner of which, tucked into the gap between the glass and the inner edge of the picture frame, was a panel that Joe recognized at once as having been cut from the pages of *Radio Comics* #1. It was a close-up shot of old Max Mayflower as a young man, rich and devil-may-care. His expression was dreamy, his cheeks were dimpled, and in the word balloon he was saying, "Oh, what do I care? The important thing is *having fun.*" Joe noticed that the angle of Max's head, a certain wryness in his expression, and his chiseled nose were very similar, indeed identical, to those of Franchot Tone in the publicity photo. It was a resemblance that no one had ever noticed or remarked on before. Tone was not an actor whose work or face were especially familiar to Joe, but now, as he studied the slender, melancholy long face in the glossy photograph—it was signed *To Carl with all the best wishes of Franchot Tone*—he wondered if he could have unconsciously modeled the character on Tone.

In the last, bottom-right drawer, at the back, there was a small, leather-bound diary. On its flyleaf was an inscription dated Christmas 1939. *To Carl, someplace to put his brilliant thoughts in order, with love, Ruth.* For its first fifty pages or so the diary carried on a tiny and furious handwritten argument, the burden of which—insofar as Joe could make it out—seemed to be that Franchot Tone was a member of a secret league of assassins, funded by the company run by Tone's father, American Carborundum, who were bent on eliminating Adolf Hitler. The revelation stopped mid-sentence, and the remaining pages of the diary were taken up by several hundred variations on the words "Carl Ebling," signed in an encyclopedia of styles from florid to scratchy, over and over again. Joe opened the diary to its center, gripped each half, and tore it down the spine into two pieces.

When he had finished with the desk, Joe went over to the bookcase. Coolly, methodically, he sent the stacks of books and pamphlets fluttering to the floor. He was afraid that if he allowed himself to feel anything, it would be neither rage nor satisfaction but merely pity for the mad, dusty nullity of Carl Ebling's one-man league. So he proceeded without feeling anything, hands numb, emotions pinched like a nerve. He lifted the picture of Hitler from its hook, and it hit with a tinkle. Proceeding next to the file cabinet, he drew out the top drawer, A–D, upended it, and shook its contents loose, like the Escapist emptying soldiers from the turret of a tank. He yanked out E–J, and was about to send its contents spilling down atop the mound of A–D when he noticed the legend typed on the index tab of one of the very first files in the drawer: "Empire Comics, Inc."

The rather swollen folder contained all ten issues of *Radio Comics* that had so far appeared; affixed by a paper clip to the first issue were some twenty-five sheets of onionskin, densely typed. It was a report, in the form of a memorandum to All League Members, from Carl Ebling, President of the New York Chapter, AAL. The subject of the memorandum was, of all things, the superpowered escape artist known as the Escapist. Joe sat down in the chair, lit a cigarette, and started to read. In the opening paragraph of Carl Ebling's memorandum, the costumed hero, his publisher, and his creators, the "Jew cartoonists" Joe Kavalier and Sam Clay, were all identified as threats to the reputations, dignity, and ambitions of German nationalism in America. Carl Ebling had read an article in the *Saturday Evening Post** detailing the success and burgeoning circulation of Empire's comic book line, and he expounded briefly on the negative effects such crass anti-German propaganda would have on the minds of those in whose hands rested the future of the Saxon peoples—America's children. Next he drew his readers' hy-

---

* "Fighting Fascism in His Underwear," issue of August 17, 1940.

pothetical attention to the remarkable resemblance between the character of Max Mayflower, the original Misterioso, and the secret Allied agent Franchot Tone. After this, however, the sense of critical purpose seemed to abandon the author. In the paragraphs that followed, and for the remainder of the memorandum, Ebling contented himself—there was no better way of putting it—with summarizing and describing the adventures of the Escapist, from the first issue detailing his origins through the most recent issue to hit the newsstands. Ebling's summaries were, on the whole, careful and accurate. But the striking thing was the way, as he went along, month by month adding another entry to his dossier on Empire, Ebling's tone of dismissive scorn and outrage moderated and then vanished altogether. By the fourth issue, he had stopped larding his descriptions with terms like "outrageous" and "offensive"; meanwhile, the entries grew longer and more detailed, breaking down at times into panel-by-panel recitations of the action in the books. The final summary, of the most recent issue, was four pages long and so devoid of judgmental language as to be completely neutral. In the last sentence, Ebling seemed to realize how far he had strayed from his original project, and appended with unpunctuated haste that implied a certain shamefaced recovery of purpose, "Of course all this is the usual Jewish warmongering propiganda [*sic*]." But it was plain to Joe that there was no real purpose being served by the Ebling memorandum except the exegesis, the precisely annotated recording, of ten months of pure enjoyment. Carl Ebling was, in spite of himself, a fan.

Joe had received letters from readers over the past months, boys and girls—mostly boys—scattered all over the United States from Las Cruces to LaCrosse, but these were usually limited to rather simple expressions of appreciation and requests for signed pinups of the Escapist, enough that Joe had evolved a standard pinup pose, which at first he drew each time by hand but had recently had photostatted, complete with his signature, to save time. Reading the Ebling memorandum marked the first time that Joe became aware of the possibility of an adult readership for his work, and the degree of Ebling's passion, his scholarly enthusiasm replete with footnotes, thematic analyses, and lists of dramatis personae, however reluctant and shamed, touched him strangely. He was aware—he could not deny it—of a desire to meet

Ebling. He looked around at the havoc he had created in the poor, sad offices of the Aryan-American League and felt a momentary pang of remorse.

Then, abruptly, it was his turn to feel ashamed, not only for having extended, however momentarily, the consideration of his sympathy to a Nazi, but for having produced work that appealed to such a man. Joe Kavalier was not the only early creator of comic books to perceive the mirror-image fascism inherent in his anti-fascist superman—Will Eisner, another Jew cartoonist, quite deliberately dressed his Allied-hero Blackhawks in uniforms modeled on the elegant death's-head garb of the Waffen SS. But Joe was perhaps the first to feel the shame of glorifying, in the name of democracy and freedom, the vengeful brutality of a very strong man. For months he had been assuring himself, and listening to Sammy's assurances, that they were hastening, by their make-believe hammering at Haxoff or Hynkel or Hassler or Hitler, the intervention of the United States into the war in Europe. Now it occurred to Joe to wonder if all they had been doing, all along, was indulging their own worst impulses and assuring the creation of another generation of men who revered only strength and domination.

He never knew afterward whether he failed to hear the sounds of Carl Ebling entering the building, climbing the stairs, and fingering the violated knob of the door because he was so lost in thought, or because Ebling walked with a light tread, or if the man had sensed an intruder and hoped to catch him unaware. In any case, it was not until the hinges squealed that Joe looked up to find an older, pastier version of Franchot Tone, the weak chin weaker, the recessive hairline farther along in its flight. He was zipped into a ratty gray parka, standing in the doorway of the Aryan-American League. He was holding a fat black sap in his hand.

"Who the hell are you?" The accent was not the elegant Tone drawl but something more or less local. "How did you get in here?"

"The name is Mayflower," Joe said. "Tom Mayflower."

"Who? Mayflower? That's—" His gaze lighted on the fat Empire file. His mouth opened, then shut again.

Joe closed the file and rose slowly to his feet. Keeping his eyes on Ebling's hands, he began to circle sideways around the desk.

"I was just leaving," Joe said.

Ebling nodded and narrowed his eyes. He looked frail, consumptive perhaps, a man in his late thirties or forties, his skin pale and freckled. He blinked and swallowed repeatedly. Joe took advantage of what he perceived to be an irresolute nature and made a dash for the door. Ebling caught him on the back of the head with the blackjack. Joe's skull rang like a coppery bell, and his knees buckled, and Ebling hit him again. Joe caught hold of the doorway, then turned, and another blow caught his chin. The pain swept away the last of the shame and remorse that had been muddling his thinking, and he was aware of a fast freshet of anger in his heart. He lunged at Ebling and caught hold of the arm that swung the sap, yanking it so hard that there was a pop of the joint. Ebling cried out, and Joe swung him by his arm and threw him up against the wall. Ebling's head struck the corner of the shelf on which the Nazi literature had been piled, and he dropped like an empty pair of trousers to the floor.

In the aftermath of his first victory, Joe hoped—he never forgot this wild, evil hope—that the man was dead. He stood breathing and swallowing, ears ringing, over Ebling and wished the twisted soul from his body. But no, there was the breath, lifting and lowering the fragile frame of the American Nazi. The sight of this involuntary, rabbitlike motion stanched the flow of Joe's anger. He went back to the desk and gathered up his jacket, cigarettes, and matches. He was about to leave when he saw the Empire Comics file, with a corner of the Ebling memorandum poking out of the top. He opened the folder, tugged the memorandum free of its clip, and flipped it over. On the back of the last page, using his mechanical pencil, he drew a quick sketch of the Escapist in the standard pose he had developed for pinups: the Master of Escape smiling, arms outstretched, the sundered halves of a pair of handcuffs braceleting his wrists.

To my pal Carl Ebling, he wrote across the bottom in big cheerful American cursive script. *Lots of luck, The Escapist.*

SHORTLY AFTER THREE on the afternoon of Friday, October 25, 1940 (according to both his journal and the statement that he made to police), James Haworth Love, majority shareholder and chairman of the board of Oneonta Mills, was sitting with Alfred E. Smith, president-for-life of the Empire State Building Corporation, in the latter's souvenir-cluttered office on the thirty-second floor of the world's tallest building, when the building manager entered "ashen-faced and looking," as the industrialist put it in his private account of the day's events, "quite as if he were going to be ill." After a careful sideways glance at Love, the building manager, Chapin L. Brown, informed his boss that they had themselves a tricky situation down on twenty-five.

Alfred Emanuel Smith—trounced by Herbert Hoover in his 1928 bid for the White House—had been a political crony and business associate of Love's ever since his days as governor of New York. Love was in Smith's office that afternoon, in fact, to enlist Smith as the front man for a syndicate hoping to revive Gustav Lindenthal's old dream of a Hudson River Bridge, eight hundred feet tall and two hundred feet wide, at Fifty-seventh Street, its eastern approaches to be constructed on a large parcel of West Side real estate that had recently come into Love's possession. Smith and Love were by no means confidants—James Love made do without confidants, as far as Smith could tell—but the textile magnate was a man of almost legendary reticence, even secretiveness, well known for keeping his own counsel. With a confidential nod toward his guest, meant to signal his implicit trust in Mr. Love's discretion and good judgment, Smith said he supposed that Brown had better just go ahead and spill it. Brown nodded in turn to Mr. Love, clamped his hands onto his hips as if to steady himself, and let out a brief sigh which seemed intended to express both incredulity and pique.

"We may have a bomb in the building," he said.

At three o'clock, he went on, a man who claimed to represent a group of American Nazis—Brown pronounced it "nazzies"—had telephoned to say, in a handkerchief-muffled false baritone, that he had hidden, somewhere in the offices of the tenants on the twenty-fifth floor, a powerful explosive device. The bomb was set to detonate, the caller had claimed, at three-thirty, killing everyone in its vicinity, and possibly doing harm to the fabric of the celebrated building itself.

In his police statement, Mr. Love reported that His Honor took the news as gravely as it was delivered, though, as he noted in his journal, no amount of anxiety could have induced a pallor in that rubicund face.

"Have you called M'Naughton?" Smith said. His gravelly voice was soft and his demeanor calm, but there was a strangled quality, as of anger suppressed, in his tone, and his brown eyes, which tended to have the slightly sorrowful cast common among convivial men, bulged from his jowly old-baby's face. Captain M'Naughton was the chief of the building's private fire battalion. Brown nodded. "Harley?" This was the captain of the building's private police force. Brown nodded again.

"They're evacuating the floor," he said. "M'Naughton's boys are in there now, looking for the goddamned thing."

"Call Harley and say I'm coming down," Smith said. He was already on his feet and headed around his desk for the door. Smith was a native of the Lower East Side, a tough boy from the old Fourth Ward, and his feelings for the building of which he was, in the eyes of New York and the nation, the human symbol were intensely proprietary. He took one last backward glance at his office when they went out, as if just in case, Love thought, he would never see it again. It was crammed like an old attic with trophies and mementos of his career, which had taken him nearly to Washington but in the end had led him to reign over this (normally) far more harmonious kingdom in the sky. Smith sighed. Today marked the start of the final weekend in the grand two-year adventure of the New York World's Fair, whose official headquarters were in the Empire State Building, and a lavish banquet was on the schedule for tonight in the dining room of the Empire State Club, down on the twenty-first floor. Smith hated to see a lavish banquet spoiled for any reason. He shook his head regretfully. Then, settling his trademark brown derby on his head, he took his visitor's arm and led the way out to the elevator bank. Ten elevators served this floor, all locals running between twenty-five and forty-one.

"Twenty-five," Smith snapped to the operator as they got in. Bill Roy, Smith's bodyguard, came along to guard Smith's old Irish body. "Twenty-five," Smith repeated. He squinted at Mr. Brown. "The funny-book people?"

"Empire," said Mr. Brown. Then he added sourly, "Very funny."

At twenty-nine, the elevator slowed as if to stop, but the operator pressed a button, and the local, having received a kind of battlefield promotion to express, continued on its way down.

"What Empire?" Love wanted to know. "What funny books?"

"They call them comic books," said Mr. Brown. "The outfit's called Empire Comics. New tenants."

"Comic books." Love was a widower with no children of his own, but he had observed his nephews reading comic books a couple of summers back, up at Miskegunquit. At the time, he had taken note only of the charming scene: the two boys lying shirtless and barefoot, in a swinging hammock stretched between a pair of unblighted elms, in a dappled bend dexter of sunlight, their downy legs tangled together, the restless attention of each wholly absorbed in a crudely stapled smear of violent color labeled *Superman.* Love had followed the subsequent conquest by the strapping, tights-wearing hero of the newspapers, of cereal boxes, and lately of the Mutual Broadcasting System, and was not unknown to cast an eye toward Superman's funny-page adventures. "And what could Bundists possibly have against *them?*"

"Ever seen one of these funny books, Jim?" Smith said. "If I was a ten-year-old boy, I'd be amazed there was still any Nazis left over there in Germany, the way our friends here at Empire have been poundin' away at 'em."

The elevator doors opened onto the unnerving dreamlike spectacle of a hundred people moving in complete silence toward the stairs. Except for the occasional urgent, not especially polite, reminder from one of the dozens of building policemen swarming the elevator lobby that pushing and shoving was only going to get somebody a busted leg, the only sounds to be heard were the drumskin rumble of rubber boots and raincoats, the squeak and clatter of soles and heels, and the impatient tapping of umbrella tips on tile. As his party got off the elevator, James Love noticed that a big policeman, with a nod to Chapin Brown, stepped in behind them to block the doors. All of the elevators had been cordoned by blue-coated guards who stood rocking back on their heels, hands clasped behind their backs, a grim-faced, impenetrable line.

"Captain Harley thought we'd better get 'em out as a group and keep 'em all together," said Brown. "I tended to concur."

Al Smith nodded once. "No need to spook the whole building," he said. He glanced at his watch. "Not yet, at any rate."

Captain Harley now came hurrying over. He was a tall, broad Irishman with a scarred left eye socket, clenched like a fist around the white and blue bauble of the eye.

"You shouldn't be here, Governor," he said. He turned his angry eye on Love. "I gave orders to clear the floor. With all due respect, that means you, too, and your guest."

"Have you found the bomb, Harley, or haven't you?" said Smith.

Harley shook his head. "They're still in there poking around."

"And what are you going to do with all these people?" said Smith, watching as the last few stragglers, among them a stooped, sullen-looking, bespectacled young man who appeared to be swathed in four or five layers of clothing, were herded into the stairwell.

"We're taking them down to the station room—"

"Send all those good people on over to Nedick's. Buy them an orange drink on me. I don't want them milling around on the sidewalk blabber-mouthing." Smith lowered his voice to a conspiratorial whisper not entirely devoid, even under the circumstances, of congeniality. "In fact," he said. "No. I'll tell you what. Have one of your boys walk them all over to Keen's, all right, and tell Johnny, or whoever it is, to give everyone a drink and put it on Al Smith's tab."

Harley signaled to one of his men, and sent him after the evacuees.

"If you haven't found the thing in"— Smith checked his watch again—"ten minutes, I want you to clear out twenty-three, twenty-four, twenty-six, and twenty-seven, too. Send them to . . . I don't know, Stouffer's or someplace like that. You got it?"

"Yes, Governor. Tell you the truth, I was only going to give it five minutes before I evacuated the other floors."

"I have faith in M'Naughton," Smith said. "Take ten."

"All right, now there's only one more problem, Your Honor," Captain Harley went on, working a meaty hand first over his lips, then across the whole lower half of his face, leaving a mottled flush. It was the frustrated gesture of a big man fighting a natural inclination to snap something in half. "I was working on it when I heard you come down."

"What is it?"

"There's one of 'em won't come out."

"Won't come out?"

"A Mr. Joe Kavalier. Foreign kid. Can't be more than twenty."

"Why won't this fellow come out?" said Al Smith. "What's the matter with him?"

"He says he has too much work to do."

Love snorted, then averted his face so as not to offend the policeman or his host with his amusement.

"Well, of all the— Carry him out, then," Smith said. "Whether he likes it or not."

"I'd love to, Your Honor. Unfortunately . . ." Harley hesitated, and mauled his jowls a little more with his big hand. "Mr. Kavalier has seen fit to handcuff his self to his drawing table. At the ankle, to be exact."

This time Mr. Love contrived to cover his laughter with a spasm of coughing.

"What?" Smith closed his eyes for a moment, then opened them. "How the hell did he manage that? Where did he get the handcuffs?"

Here Harley flushed deeply, and muttered a barely audible reply.

"What's that?" Smith said.

"They're mine, Your Honor," said Harley. "And to tell you the truth, I'm not really sure how he got ahold of them."

Love's coughing fit had by now become quite genuine. He was a three-pack-a-day man, and his lungs were in terrible shape. To prevent public embarrassment, he generally laughed as little as possible.

"I see," Smith said. "Well, then, Captain, get a couple of your biggest boys and carry out the goddamn table, too."

"It's, uh, well, it's built in, Your Honor. Bolted to the wall."

"*Then unbolt it!* Just get the stupid S.O.B. out of there! His damn pencil sharpener is probably booby-trapped!"

Harley signaled to a couple of his stoutest men.

"Wait a minute," Smith said. He checked his watch. "God damn it." He pushed his derby toward the back of his head, making himself look at once younger and more truculent. "Leave me have a word with this pup. What is his name again?"

"It's Kavalier with a K, Your Honor, only I don't see the use or the sense in letting you—"

"In all my eleven years as president of this building, Captain Harley, I have never once sent you or your men in to lay a hand on one of the tenants. This isn't some flophouse on the Bowery." He started toward the door of Empire Comics. "I hope we can afford to devote a minute to reason before we give Mr. Kavalier with a K the bum's rush."

"Mind if I come with you?" Love said. He had recovered from his spasm of mirth, though his pocket handkerchief now contained the evidence of something evil and brown inside him.

"I can't let you do that, Jim," Smith said. "It would be irresponsible."

"You have a wife and children to lose, Al. All I have is my money."

Smith looked at his old friend. Before Chapin Brown had rushed in to interrupt them with word of the bomb threat, they had been discussing not the Hudson River Bridge, a scheme that with Love's subsequent, abrupt retirement from public life came, once again, to nothing, but rather the man's strongly held and oft-aired views on the war that Britain was losing in Europe. A loyal Willkie man, James Love was among a small number of powerful industrialists in the country who had been actively in favor of American entry into the war almost from its beginning. Though he was the son and grandson of millionaires, he had been troubled all his life, much like the president of the United States, by wayward liberal impulses that, however fitful—the Love mills were all open shops—made him a natural anti-fascist. Also figuring into his views, undoubtedly, was the memory, handed down from millionaire to millionaire in Love's family, of the colossal and enduring prosperity that war and government contracts had brought to Oneonta Woolens during the Civil War. All of this was known, or more or less understood, by Al Smith, and led him to conclude that the thought of risking death at the hands of American Nazis held a certain appeal to someone who had been trying to get into the war, one way or another, for almost two years now. Then, too, the man had lost his famously beautiful wife to cancer back in '36 or '37; since that time, vague rumors had reached Smith's ear of profligate conduct that might suggest the be-havior of a man who had, in that tragedy, also lost his moorings, or at least his fear of death. What Smith did not know was that the one great and true friend of James Love's life, Gerhardt Frege, had been one of the first men to die—of internal injuries—at Dachau, shortly after the camp opened in 1933.* Smith did not suspect, and never would have imag-ined, that the animus James Love held against Nazis and their Ameri-can sympathizers was, at bottom, a personal matter. But there was an eagerness in the man's eyes that both worried Smith and touched him.

"We give it five minutes," Smith said. "Then I have Harley drag the bastard out by his suspenders."

The waiting room of Empire Comics was a cold expanse of marble and leather moderne, a black tundra frosted over with glass and chrome. The effect was huge and intimidating and coldly splendid, rather like its designer, Mrs. Sheldon Anapol, though neither Love nor Smith had any way, of course, of drawing this parallel. There was a long hemicircular reception desk opposite the entry, faced with black mar-ble and ribbed with Saturn's rings of glass, behind which three black-coated firemen, their faces concealed by heavy welder's masks, crouched, poking around carefully with broom handles. On the wall over the reception desk, there was a painting of a lithe masked giant in a dark blue union suit, his arms outspread in ecstatic embrace as he burst from a writhing nest of thick iron chains that entangled his loins, belly, and chest. On his chest, he wore the emblem of a stylized key.

---

* Frege, a socialist, an alpine skier, and, like Love, a Rhodes scholar (they had met at Trinity College), was stripped of his title as German national downhill champion and sentenced to Dachau for "soliciting an act of depravity" in the Munich *Bahnhof*.

Above his head arched foot-high letters proclaiming boldly THE ES-CAPIST! while at his feet a pair of firefighters crawled around on their hands and knees, searching the drawers and kneeholes of the reception desk for a bomb. The firemen, their visors glinting, looked up as Harley led Governor Smith and Mr. Love past. ·

"Find anything?" Smith said. One of the firemen, an elderly fellow whose helmet looked far too large for him, shook his head.

The comic book workshop, or whatever it was called, had none of the polish and gleam of the waiting room. The floor was concrete, painted light blue and littered with fag ends and crumpled carnations of drawing paper. The tables were a homely jumble of brand-new and semidecrepit, but there was full daylight on three sides, with spectacular if not quite breathtaking views of the hotel and newspaper towers of midtown, the green badge of Central Park, the battlements of New Jersey, and the dull metal glint of the East River, with a glimpse of the iron mantilla of the Queensboro Bridge. The windows were shut, and a pall of tobacco lay over the room. In a far corner, against a wall from which his built-in drawing table canted downward and out, hunched a pale young man, lean, rumpled, shirttails dangling, adding billowing yards of smoke to the pall. Al Smith signaled to Harley to leave them. "Five minutes," Harley said as he withdrew.

As soon as the police captain spoke, the young man whirled around on his stool. He squinted nearsightedly in the direction of Smith and Love as they approached, looking mildly annoyed. He was a good-looking Jewish kid, with large blue eyes, an aquiline nose, a strong chin.

"Young man," Smith said. "Mr. Kavalier, is it? I'm Al Smith. This is my friend Mr. Love."

"Joe," the young man said. His grip in Love's was firm and dry. Though he appeared to have been wearing his clothes rather too long, they were good enough clothes: a broadcloth shirt with a monogram stitched onto the breast pocket, a raw silk necktie, gray worsted trousers with a generous cuff. But he had the undernourished look of an immigrant, his deep-set eyes bruised and wary, the tips of his fingers stained yellow. The careful manicure of his nails had been ruined by ink. He looked ill rested, dog-tired, and—it was a surprising thought to Love, who was not a man especially sensitive to the feelings of others—sad. A less refined New Yorker probably would have asked him, *Where's the funeral?*

"Look here, young man," Smith said. "I've come to make a personal request. Now, I admire your dedication to your work here. But I'd like you just to do me a favor, a personal favor to me, you understand. Here it is. Come along now, and let me stand you to a drink. All right? We'll get this little problem cleared up, and then you'll be my guest at the club. Okay, kid? What do you say?"

If Joe Kavalier was impressed by this generous offer from one of the best-known, most beloved characters in contemporary American life, a man who once might have been president of the United States, he didn't show it. He merely looked amused, Love thought, and behind this amusement there were hints of irritation.

"I'd like to another time, maybe, thank you," he said, in an indeterminate Hapsburg accent. He reached for a stack of art board and took a fresh piece from the top. It appeared to the observant Love, who always took a ready interest in learning the secrets and methods of any kind of manufacturing or production, to have been preprinted with nine large square frames, in three tiers of three. "Only I have so much work."

"You're quite *attached* to your work, I can see that," Love said, catching the younger man's air of amused unconcern.

Joe Kavalier looked down at his feet, where a pair of metal cuffs linked his left ankle, in a gray sock with white and burgundy clocks, to one of the legs of his table. "I was not wanting to be interrupted, you know?" He tap-tap-tapped the end of his pencil against the piece of board. "So many little boxes to fill."

"Yes, all right, that's very admirable, son," Smith said, "but for gosh sakes, how much drawing will you be able to do when your arm is lying down on Thirty-third Street?"

The young man gazed around the studio, empty but for the smoke of his cigarette and a pair of grunting firemen, the buckles on their raincoats rattling as they clambered around the room.

"There isn't no bomb," he said.

"You think this thing's a hoax?" Love said.

Joe Kavalier nodded, then lowered his head to his work. He considered the page's first little box from one angle, then another. Then, rapidly, in a firm and certain manner and without stopping, he began to draw. In choosing the image he was now putting to paper, he didn't appear to be following the typewritten script lying stacked at his elbow. Perhaps he had committed it all to memory. Love craned his head to get a better look at what the kid was drawing. It seemed to be an airplane, one with the fierce-looking jambeaux of a Stuka. Yes, a Stuka in a streaking power dive. The detail was impressive. The plane had solidity and rivets. And yet there was something exaggerated in the backward sweep of the wings that suggested great speed and even a hint of falconish malevolence.

"Governor?" It was Harley. He sounded as if he was irritated with Al Smith now, too. "I got two men with a wrench ready and waiting."

"Just a moment," Love said, and then felt himself blush. It was Al Smith's decision, of course—it was Al Smith's building—but Love was impressed by the young man's good looks, his air of certainty with regard to the bomb's fraudulence; and he was fascinated, as always, by the sight of someone making something skillfully. He wasn't ready to leave either.

"You've got half a moment," Harley said, ducking out again. "With all due respect."

"Well, now, Joe," Smith said, checking his watch once again, looking and sounding more nervous than before. His tone grew patient and slightly condescending, and Love sensed that he was trying to be psychological. "If you won't evacuate, maybe you'll tell me why the Bund—would this be the Bund?"

"The Aryan-American League."

Smith looked at Love, who shook his head. "I don't believe I've ever heard of them," Smith said.

Joe Kavalier's mouth bunched up at one corner in a small, eloquent smirk, as if to suggest that this was hardly surprising.

"Why are these Aryans so upset with you people here? How did they come across these controversial drawings of yours? I wasn't aware that Nazis *read* comic books."

"All kinds of people are reading them," said Joe. "I get mail from all over the country. California. Illinois. From Canada, too."

"Really?" Love said. "How many of your comic books do you sell every month?"

"Jimmy—" Smith began, tapping the crystal of his wristwatch with a fat finger.

"We have three titles," the young man said. "Though now it's going to be five."

"And how many do you sell in a month?"

"Mr. Kavalier, this is fascinating stuff, but if you won't agree to come quietly I'm going to be obliged to—"

"Close to three million," Joe Kavalier said. "But they all get passed along at least once. They get traded for other ones, between the kids. So the number of people reading them, Sam—my partner, Sam Clay—says it's maybe two times how many we sell, or more."

"*Das ist bemerkenswert,*" said Love.

For the first time, Joe Kavalier looked surprised. "*Ja,* no kidding."

"And that fellow out there in the lobby, with the key on his chest. That your star attraction?"

"The Escapist. He is the world-greatest escape artist, no chains to hold him, sending him to liberate the enprisoned peoples in the world. It's good stuff." He smiled for the first time, a smile that was self-mocking but not quite enough to conceal his evident professional pride. "He is made up by my partner and me."

"I take it your partner had sense enough to evacuate," Smith said, returning them to the ostensible purpose of this conversation.

"He is with an appointment. And there isn't any bomb."

At that moment, just as Joe Kavalier said "bomb," there was a burst of clamor—*brrrang!*—right over their heads. James Love jumped and let go of his cigarette.

"All clear," Smith said, mopping his forehead with a hankie. "Well, thank God for that."

"Good heavens." There was ash all down Love's jacket, and he brushed it away, blushing.

"All clear!" called a husky voice. A moment later, the elderly fire-fighter stuck his head into the workroom. "It was just an old clock, your honor," he told Smith, looking at once relieved and disappointed. "In the desk of a Mister . . . Clay. Taped to a couple of dowels painted red."

"I knew it," said Joe softly, starting in on the second little box.

"Dynamite isn't even red," the old fireman said, walking off. "Not really."

"The guy reads too much comic books," Joe said.

"Governor Smith!"

They turned, and three men came into the workroom. One of them, balding and vast in every part and extremity, had the air of a high official in some disreputable labor union; the other, tall and merely pot-bellied, had thinning rusty hair, a football hero gone to seed. Behind the two big fellows stood a tiny, quarrelsome-looking young man, dressed in an outsize gray pinstriped suit with padded shoulders that were almost comical in their breadth. The little one immediately came over to the drawing table where Joe Kavalier was working. He nodded to Love, sizing him up, and put a hand on Kavalier's shoulder.

"Mr. Anapol, isn't it?" Smith said, shaking the fat man's hand. "We've had a little excitement around here."

"We were at lunch!" Anapol cried, coming to shake Al Smith's hand. "We came running back as soon as we heard! Governor, I'm so sorry for all the trouble we caused you. I guess maybe"—here he shot a look at Kavalier & Clay—"these two young hotheads have been taking things a little too far in our magazines."

"Maybe so," Love said. "But they're brave young men, and I congratulate them."

Anapol looked taken aback.

"Mr. Anapol, may I present an old friend, Mr. James Love. Mr. Love is—"

"Oneonta Mills!" Anapol said. "Mr. James Love! What a pleasure. I regret that we're obliged to meet under such—"

"Nonsense," Love said. "We've been having a fine time." He ignored the scowl this statement produced on Al Smith's puss. "Mr. Anapol, this may be neither the time nor the place for this. But my firm has just brought all of our various accounts together under one umbrella and placed them with Burns, Baggot & DeWinter," Love went on. "Perhaps you've heard of them."

"Of course," Anapol said. "The Knackfalder Trousers Man. The dancing nuts."

"They're smart boys, and one of the smart things they've been talking about is taking a fresh look at our radio accounts. I'd like to have some of their fellows sit down with you and Mr. Kavalier, here, and Mister—Clay, is it?—and talk about finding a way for Oneonta Mills to sponsor this Escaper of yours."

"Sponsor?"

"On the radio, boss," said the little one, catching on quickly. He jutted his chin and deepened his voice and clutched an imaginary microphone. "Oneonta Mills, makers of Ko-Zee-Tos brand thermal socks and undergarments, presents *The Amazing Adventures of the Escapist*!" He looked at Love. "That the idea?"

"Something like that," Love said. "Yes, I like that."

"The idea," said Anapol. "A radio show." He pressed a hand to his belly as if he was not feeling well. "It makes me a little nervous. With all due respect, and I don't say I'm not interested, but . . ."

"Well, think it over, Mr. Anapol. I suppose there must be other characters available, but I have a feeling this is the one for me. Let's say I'll telephone Jack Burns and make arrangements to have you sit down and talk about it this week," Love said. "That is, if you gentlemen are free."

"*I'm* free," Anapol said, recovering himself. "My partner, Jack Ashkenazy, will also, I am sure, be free. And this is our editor in chief, Mr. George Deasey."

Love shook Deasey's hand, recoiling at the smell of cloves covering the whiskey on his breath.

"But these young fellows over here," Anapol continued, "well, they do good work, as you've seen, and they're very good boys, if maybe a little bit excitable. But they're, how should I put it, they're the hired hands on this farm."

Sam Clay and Joe Kavalier exchanged a look in which Love saw the smoldering coals of a grudge.

"Moo," Sam Clay said, with a shrug of his enormous false shoulders.

"I'm going to need a statement from you, Mr. Anapol," Captain Harley said. "And from you, Governor, and your guest. It won't take long."

"What do you say we do it down at the club," Al Smith said. "I could use a drink."

At that moment a messenger in blue livery walked in, carrying a special-delivery letter.

"Sheldon Anapol?" he said.

"Here," Anapol said, signing for it. "George, stay here and see that things get settled down."

Deasey nodded. Anapol tipped the messenger and exited behind Al Smith. Love signaled to Smith that he would follow, then turned back to the two young men. Sam Clay stood, his shoulder against his partner's, looking a little woozy, as if he had been sandbagged. Then he went over to a low shelf in a corner of the room. He quickly gathered a stack of magazines and brought them to Love, looking the older man right in the eye.

"Maybe you'd like to get to know the character a little better," he said. "*Our* character."

" 'Ours' as in . . . ?"

" 'Ours' as in Joe and myself. The Escapist. Also the Monitor, the Four Freedoms, Mr. Machine Gun. All of Empire's leading sellers. Here. Joe, do you have— Yeah." He scrabbled around in the clutter under Joe Kavalier's table to find a sheet of stationery on whose elaborate letterhead a group of handsome, muscular men and boys lounged, relaxing on and about the letters, one wild-haired, hook-nosed boy perched atop the ampersand of the words "Kavalier & Clay." "I've always thought the Escapist would be perfect for radio."

"Well, I'm really not qualified to judge, Mr. Clay," Love said, not unkindly, taking the magazines and the sheet of paper. "To be perfectly honest, my only concern is whether or not he'll sell socks. But I will say"—and here his face took on an odd expression that Joe almost would have called a leer—"I do like what I've seen here today. Take care, boys."

He exited the workroom, troubled, but not unduly, by a pang of sympathy for Kavalier & Clay. Love saw how it was. These boys had come up with this Escapist character and then, in exchange for some token payment and the opportunity of seeing their names in print, signed away all the rights to Anapol and company. Now Anapol and company were prospering—enough to let a quarter of a floor in the Empire State Building, enough to exert an impressive mass-cultural influence over the vast American marketplace of children and know-nothings. And while, to judge from their attire, Messrs. Kavalier & Clay were sharing to some degree in the general prosperity, Sheldon Anapol had just made it apparent to both of them that the course of the river of money beside which they had pitched their camp had been diverted, and would henceforth flow no more around them. In his life as a business-man, Love had seen plenty of boy geniuses left deserted amid the bleached bones and cacti of their dreams. These two would, no doubt, have other brilliant ideas, and furthermore, no one was ever born smart in business. Love's feeling of pity, while sincere—and inspired in part by Joe's dark good looks and the quickness of spirit of the two young men—lasted no longer than it took for the elevator to deposit him in the richly paneled lobby of the Empire State Club. He did not imagine for a moment that he had just set in motion the wheels not of another minor midtown ruination but, very nearly, his own.

Back in the workroom—once again alive with chitchat and gum-snap and some shivery Hampton on the radio—George Deasey stood in the doorway to his office. He knit his ginger eyebrows and pursed his lips, looking uncharacteristically moved.

"Gentlemen," he said to Joe and Sammy. "A word."

He went into his office and, as was his wont, lay down in the middle of the floor and began to pick his teeth. He had been trampled by a fly-maddened cavalry horse while covering one of the U.S. Marine Corps' numerous attempts to capture A. C. Sandino, and on chill afternoons like this one, his back tended to stiffen up on him. His toothpick was solid gold, a legacy from his father, a former associate justice of the New York State Court of Appeals. "Close the door," he told Sam Clay after the boys came in. "I don't want anyone to hear what I'm going to say."

"Why not?" Sammy said, obediently shutting the door as he followed Joe in.

"Because it would cause me considerable pain if anyone should form the mistaken impression that I actually give a tinker's damn about you, Mr. Clay."

"Fat chance of that," said Sammy. He flopped into one of the two straight-backed chairs that flanked Deasey's enormous desk. If he was stung by the insult, he gave no sign of it. He had toughened under the constant administration of tiny mallet blows from Deasey. During their first months working for him, on days when Deasey had ridden Sammy particularly hard, Joe had often listened in the dark, pretending to be asleep, as Sammy lay clenched tight in the bed beside him, barking into his pillow. Deasey mocked his grammar. In restaurants, he made fun of Sammy's poor table manners, unsophisticated palate, and amazement with such simple things as sculpted butter pats and cold potato soup. He offered Sammy a chance to write a Gray Goblin novel for *Racy Police Stories,* sixty thousand words at half a cent a word; Sammy, sleeping two hours a night for a month, wrote three books, which Joe had read and enjoyed, only to have Deasey dissect one after another, each time with terse, bitter criticism that was infallibly accurate. In the end, however, he had bought all three.

"First of all," Deasey said, "Mr. Clay, where is *Strange Frigate?*"

"Halfway done," Sammy said. This was a fourth Goblin novel that Racy Publications, now operating very much in the shadow of its younger sibling but still turning a profit for Jack Ashkenazy, had commissioned from Sam Clay. Like all seventy-two of its predecessors in the series, it would be published, of course, under the house name of Harvey Slayton. Actually, as far as Joe knew, Sammy had not even started it yet. The title was one of two hundred and forty-five that George Deasey had dreamed up during a two-day bender in Key West in 1936 and had been working his way through ever since. *Strange Frigate* was number seventy-three on the list. "I'll have it for you by Monday."

"You must."

"I shall."

"Mr. Kavalier." Deasey had a sneaky way of lolling his head around toward you, one hand half-covering his face as if he were about to drop off for a catnap—an impression made all the stronger if he was, as now, stretched out on the floor. Then, suddenly, his drooping eyelids would snap open, and you would find yourself on the point of a sharp inquisitorial gaze. "Please reassure me that my suspicions of your involvement in this afternoon's charade are unfounded."

Joe struggled to meet Deasey's sleepy Torquemada stare. Of course he knew that the bomb threat had been made by Carl Ebling, in direct retaliation for his attack on the headquarters of the AAL two weeks before. Clearly, Ebling had been casing the Empire offices, tracking the move from the Kramler Building, observing the comings and goings of the employees, preparing his big red comic book bomb. Such fixity of purpose ought to have been, in spite of the harmlessness of today's reprisal, cause for alarm. Joe really ought to have told the police about Carl Ebling right away, and had the man arrested and jailed. And the prospect of the man's imprisonment, by rights, ought to have given him satisfaction. But why, instead, did it feel like surrender? It seemed to Joe that Ebling could have just as easily reported *him*, for breaking and entering, destruction of property, even assault, but instead had pursued his solitary and furtive course, engaging Joe—all right, the man was under the false impression that his antagonist was Sam Clay, Joe was somehow going to have to set him straight about that—in a private battle, a *concours à deux*. And Joe had *known*, somehow, from the moment Anapol's secretary took the call, with an illusionist's instinct for hooey, that the threat was a sham, the bomb a fiction. Ebling wanted to frighten Joe, to threaten him into calling off the comic book war that he found so offensive to the dignity of the Third Reich and the person of Adolf Hitler, and yet, at the same time, he was unwilling actually to annihilate the source of a pleasure that in his lonely *verbitterte* life must be all too rare. If the bomb had been real, Joe thought, I would naturally turn him in. It did not occur to him that if the bomb had been real he would now, quite possibly, be dead; that the next blow in their battle, if it were struck not by the impersonal force of the law but by Joe himself, might well reify the conflict in Ebling's unbalanced mind; and least of all, that he had begun to lose himself in a labyrinth of fantastical revenge whose bone-littered center lay ten thousand miles and three years away.

"Completely," Joe said. "I don't even know the guy."

"What guy is that?"

"What I said. I don't know him."

"I can smell it," Deasey said dubiously. "But I just can't figure it out."

"Mr. Deasey," Sammy said. "What did you want us for?"

"Yes. I wanted— God help me, I wanted to warn you."

Like a wreck being winched from the sea bottom, Deasey lumbered to his feet. He had been drinking since before lunch and, as he got himself upright, nearly fell over again. He went over to the window. The desk, a scarred, tiger-oak behemoth with fifty-two pigeonholes and twenty-four drawers, had followed him from his old office in the Kramler, its drawers stocked with fresh ribbons, blue pencils, pints of rye, black twists of Virginia shag, clean sheets of foolscap, aspirin, Sen-Sen, and sal hepatica. Deasey kept both it and his office spotless, uncluttered, and free of dust. This was the first time in his entire career that he had ever had an office all to himself. This—these fifty square feet of new carpet, blank paper, and inky black ribbons—was the mark and clear summation of what he had attained. He sighed. He slipped two fingers between the slats of the venetian blinds and let a wan slice of autumn light into the room.

"When they did the *Gray Goblin* on the DuMont network," he said. "You remember that, Mr. Clay?"

"Sure," Sammy said. "I used to listen sometimes."

"What about *Crack Carter*? Remember that one?"

"With the bullwhip?"

"Fighting evil amid the tumbleweeds. *Sharpe of the Mounties*?"

"Sure, absolutely. They all started in the pulps, is that it?"

"They have their common origin in a far more exclusive and decrepit locale than that," Deasey said.

Sammy and Joe looked at each other uncertainly. Deasey tapped his forehead with the tip of the toothpick.

"You were *Sharpe of the Mounties*?" Sammy asked.

Deasey nodded. "He started out in *Racy Adventure*."

"And Whiskey, the husky dog with whom he shares an almost uncanny bond?"

"That one ran for five years on NBC Blue," Deasey said. "I never made a dime." He turned from the window. "Now, boys, it's your turn in the barrel."

"They have to pay us something," Sammy said. "After all. I mean, it may not be in the contract—"

"It isn't."

"But Anapol isn't a thief. He's an honorable person."

Deasey pressed his lips together tightly and hoisted the corners. It took Joe a moment to realize that he was smiling.

"It's my experience that honorable people live by the contracts they sign," Deasey said at last. "And not a tittle more."

Sammy looked at Joe. "He isn't cheering me up," he said. "Is he cheering you up?"

The question of a radio program, indeed the entire exchange that had taken place with the slim, silver-haired man wearing the eager expression, had largely escaped Joe. He was still far less proficient in English than he pretended to be, particularly when the subject ran to sports, politics, or business. He had no idea how socks or barrels figured into the discussion.

"That man wants to make a show on the radio about the Escapist," Joe said, slowly, feeling slow, thick-witted, and obscurely abused by inscrutable men.

"He seemed at least to be interested in having his flacks explore the possibility," Deasey said.

"And if they do, you are saying that they will not have to pay us for it."

"I'm saying that."

"But of course they must."

"Not a dime."

"I want a look at that contract," Sammy said.

"Look all you want," Deasey said. "Look it up and down. Hire a lawyer and have him nose around in it. All the rights—radio, movies, books, tin whistles, Cracker Jack prizes—they all belong to Anapol and Ashkenazy. One hundred percent."

"I thought you said you wanted to warn us." Sammy looked annoyed. "It seems to me the time for a warning would have been about a year ago, when we put our names to that piece-of-shit-excuse-my-language contract."

Deasey nodded. "Fair enough," he said. He went to a glass-fronted lawyer's bookcase, stocked with a copy of every pulp magazine in which one of his novels had appeared, each bound in fine morocco and stamped soberly in gold characters RACY POLICEMAN or RACY ACE, with the issue number and date of publication and, beneath these, the uniform legend COMPLETE WORKS OF GEORGE DEASEY.* He stepped back and studied the books with, it seemed to Joe, a certain air of regret, though for what, exactly, Joe could not have said. "For what it's worth, here's the warning now. Or call it advice, if you like. You boys were powerless when you signed that contract last year. You aren't quite so powerless anymore. You've had a good run. You've come up with some good ideas that have sold well. You've begun to make a name for yourselves. Now, we could debate the merits of making a name for yourselves in a third-rate industry by cranking out nonsense for numbskulls, but what isn't in doubt is that there's money to be found in this game right now, and you two have shown a knack for dowsing it. Anapol knows it. He knows that, if you wanted to, you could probably walk over to Donenfeld or Arnold or Goodman and write yourself a much better deal to dream up nonsense over there. So that's my warning: stop handing this crap over to Anapol as if you owed it to him."

"Make him pay for it from now on. Make him give us a piece," Sammy said.

"You didn't hear it from me."

"But in the meantime—"

"You are screwed, gentlemen." He consulted his pocket watch. "Now get out. I have duds of my own to secrete about the premises before I—" He broke off and looked at Joe, then stared down at his watch as if trying to make up his mind about something. When he looked up again, his face had twisted in a false, almost sickeningly cheery, rictus. "The hell with it," he said. "I need a drink. Mr. Clay—"

"I know," Sammy said. "I have to finish *Strange Frigate*."

"No, Mr. Clay," Deasey said, awkwardly settling an arm over the shoulders of each of them and dragging them toward the door. "Tonight you are going to *sail* on it."

---

* This legendary library of self-mortification was lost, and widely considered apocryphal, until 1993, when one of its volumes, *Racy Attorney* #23, turned up at an IKEA store in Elizabeth, New Jersey, where it was mutely serving as a dignified-looking stage property on a floor-model "Hjörp" wall unit. It is signed by the author and bears the probably spurious but fascinating inscription *To my pal Dick Nixon.*

WHEN CARL EBLING looked in the *News* the next morning, he was disappointed to find not the slightest mention of a bomb scare at the Empire State Building, of the Aryan-American League, or of a fiendish (if for the time being sham) bomber who called himself—deriving the moniker from a shrouded villain who made scattered appearances in the pages of *Radio Comics* throughout the prewar years—the Saboteur. The last would have been pretty unlikely, since Ebling had, in his nervous haste to squirrel the device in the desk of his imagined nemesis Sam Clay, forgotten to leave the note that he had prepared specially and signed with his nom de guerre. When he checked all the other Saturday papers, once again he found not a word to connect him to anything that had gone on in the city the previous day. The whole matter had been hushed up.

The party thrown for Salvador Dalí that last Friday of the New York World's Fair got considerably more play. It rated twenty lines in Leonard Lyons's column, a mention in Ed Sullivan's, and an unsigned squib by E. J. Kahn in "Talk of the Town" the following week. It was also described in one of Auden's letters to Isherwood in L.A., and figured in the published memoirs of at least two mainstays of the Greenwich Village art scene.

The guests of honor, the satrap of Surrealism and his Russian wife, Gala, were in New York to close *The Dream of Venus*, an attraction, conceived and designed by Dalí, that had been among the wonders of the Fair's Amusement Area. Their host, a wealthy New Yorker named Longman Harkoo, was the proprietor of Les Organes du Facteur, a Surrealist art gallery and bookshop on Bleecker Street, inspired by the dreaming postman of Hauterives. Harkoo, who had sold more of Dalí's work than any other dealer in the world, and who was a sponsor of *The Dream of Venus*, had met George Deasey in school, at Collegiate, where the future Underminister of Agitprop for the Unconscious was two years ahead of the future Balzac of the Pulps; they had renewed their acquaintance in the late twenties, when Hearst had posted Deasey to Mexico City.

"Those Olmec heads," Deasey said in the cab on the way downtown. He had insisted on their taking a cab. "That was all he wanted to talk about. He tried to buy one. In fact, I once heard that he did buy it, and he's hidden it in the basement of his house."

"You used them in *The Pyramid of Skulls*," Sammy said. "Those big heads. There was a secret compartment in the left ear."

"It's bad enough you read them," Deasey said. Sammy had prepared for the composition of his first work as Harvey Slayton by immersing himself deeply in Deasey's oeuvre. "I find it incredibly sad, Clay, that you also remember the *titles*." Actually, he looked, Joe thought, quite flattered. He probably had never expected, at this point in a career that he so publicly accounted a failure, to encounter a genuine admirer of his work. He seemed to have discovered in himself a tenderness—unsuspected by no one more than he—for both of the cousins, but particularly for Sammy, who still viewed, as a springboard to literary renown, work that Deasey had long since concluded was only "a long, spiraling chute, greased with regular paychecks, to the Tartarus of pseudonymous hackdom." He had shown some of his old poems to Sammy, and the yellowed manuscript of a serious novel that he had never completed. Joe suspected that Deasey had intended these revelations to be warnings to Sammy, but his cousin had chosen to interpret them as proof that success in the pulpwoods was not incompatible with talent, and that he ought not to abandon his own novelistic dreams. "Where was I?"

"Mexico City," Joe said. "Heads."

"Thank you." Deasey took a pull from his flask. He drank an extremely cheap brand of rye called Brass Lamp. Sammy claimed that it was not rye at all but actual lamp oil, as Deasey was strongly nearsighted. "Yes, the mysterious Olmecs." Deasey returned the magic lamp to his breast pocket. "And Mr. Longman Harkoo."

Harkoo, Deasey said, was a Village eccentric of long standing, connected to the founders of one of the posh Fifth Avenue department stores. He was a widower—twice over—who lived in a queer house with a daughter from his first marriage. In addition to looking after the day-to-day affairs of his gallery, orchestrating his disputes with fellow members of the American Communist Party, and pulling off his celebrated fetes, he was also, in idle moments, writing a largely unpunctuated novel, already more than a thousand pages long, which described, in cellular detail, the process of his own birth. He had taken his unlikely name in the summer of 1924, while sharing a house at La Baule with André Breton, when a pale, hugely endowed figure calling himself the Long Man of Harkoo recurred five nights running in his dreams.

"Right here," Deasey called out to the driver, and the cab came to a stop in front of a row of indistinct modern apartment blocks. "Pay the fare, will you, Clay? I'm a little short."

Sammy scowled at Joe, who considered that his cousin really ought to have expected this. Deasey was a classic cadger of a certain type, at once offhand and peremptory. But Joe had discovered that Sammy was, in his own way, a classic tightwad. The entire concept of taxicabs seemed to strike Sammy as recherché and decadent, on a par with the eating of songbirds. Joe took a dollar from his wallet and passed it to the driver.

"Keep the change," he said.

The Harkoo house lay entirely hidden from the avenue, "like an emblem (heavy-handed at that) of suppressed nasty urges," as Auden put it in his letter to Isherwood, at the heart of a city block the whole of which subsequently passed into the hands of New York University, was razed, and now forms the site of the massive Levine School of Applied Meteorology. The solid rampart of row houses and apartment blocks that enclosed the Harkoo house and its grounds on all four sides could be breached only by way of a narrow ruelle that slipped unnoticed between two buildings and penetrated, through a tunnel of ailanthus trees, to the dark, leafy yard within.

The house, when they reached it, was a vest-pocket Oriental fantasy, a miniature Topkapi, hardly bigger than a firehouse, squeezed onto its tiny site. It curled like a sleeping cat around a central tower topped with a dome that resembled, among other items, a knob of garlic. Through skillful use of forced perspective and manipulation of scale, the house managed to look much bigger than it really was. Its luxurious coat of Virginia creeper, the gloom of its courtyard, and the artless jumble of its gables and spires gave the place an antique air, but it had in fact been completed in September 1930, around the time that Al Smith was laying the cornerstone for the Empire State Building. Like that structure, it was a kind of dream habitation, having, like the Long Man of Harkoo himself, originally appeared to Longman Harkoo in his sleep, giving him the excuse he had long sought to pull down the dull old Greek Revival house that had been the country home of his mother's family since the founding of Greenwich Village. *That* house had itself replaced a much earlier structure, dating to the first years of British dominion, in which—or so Harkoo claimed—a Dutch-Jewish forebear of his had entertained the devil during his 1682 tour of the colonies.

Joe noticed that Sammy was hanging back a little, looking up at the miniature tower, absently massaging the top of his left thigh, his face solemn and nervous in the light of the torches that flanked the door. In his gleaming pinstriped suit, he reminded Joe of their character the Monitor, armored for battle against perfidious foes. Suddenly Joe felt apprehensive, too. It had not quite sunk in until now, with all the talk of bombs and woolens and radio programs, that they had come downtown with Deasey to attend a *party*.

Neither of the cousins was much for parties. Though Sammy was mad for swing, he could not, of course, dance on his pipe-cleaner legs; his nerves killed his appetite, and at any rate, he was too self-conscious about his manners to eat anything; and he disliked the flavor of liquors and beer. Introduced into a cursed circle of jabber and jazz, he would drift helplessly behind a large plant. His brash and heedless gift of conversation, by means of which he had whipped up *Amazing Midget Radio Comics* and with it the whole idea of Empire, deserted him. Put him in front of a roomful of people at work and he would be impossible to shut up; work was not work for him. Parties were work. Women were work. At Palooka Studios, whenever there occurred the chance conjunction of girls and a bottle, Sammy simply vanished, like Mike Campbell's fortune, at first a little at a time, and then all at once.

Joe, on the other hand, had always been the boy for a party in Prague. He could do card tricks and hold his alcohol; he was an excellent dancer. In New York, however, all this seemed to have changed. He had too much work to do, and parties seemed a great waste of his time. The conversation came fast and slangy, and he had trouble following the gags and patter of the men and the sly double-talk of the ladies. He was vain enough to dislike it when something he said in all seriousness for some reason broke up a room. But the greatest obstacle he faced was that he did not feel that he ought—ever—to be enjoying himself socially. Even when he went to the movies, he did so in a purely professional capacity, studying them for ideas about light and imagery and pacing that he could borrow or adapt in his comic book work. Now he drew back alongside his cousin, looking up at the scowling torchlit face of the house, ready to run at the first signal from Sam.

"Mr. Deasey," Sammy said, "listen. I feel I've got to confess . . . I haven't even started *Strange Frigate* yet. Don't you think I better—"

"Yes," Joe said. "And I have the cover for *The Monitor*—"

"All you need is a drink, boys." Deasey looked greatly amused by their sudden qualms of conscience and courage. "That will make it go much easier when they pitch you both into the volcano. I presume you *are* virgins?" They scraped up the rough, clinker-brick front steps. Deasey turned, and all at once his face looked grave and admonitory. "Just don't let him *hug* you," he said.

THE PARTY HAD originally been planned for the pint-sized mansion's ballroom, but when that room was rendered uninhabitable by the noise from Salvador Dalí's breathing apparatus, everyone crowded into the library instead. Like all the rooms in the house, the library was diminutive, built to a three-quarter scale that gave visitors a disquieting sense of giantism. Sammy and Joe squeezed in behind Deasey to find the room packed to the point of immobility with Transcendental Symbolists, Purists, and Vitalists, copywriters in suits the color of new Studebakers, socialist banjo players, writers for *Mademoiselle*, experts on Yuggogheny cannibal cults and bird-worshipers of the Indochinese Highlands, composers of twelve-tone requiems and of slogans for Eas-O-Cran, the Original New England Laxative. The gramophone—and (of course) the bar—had been carried up to the library as well, and over the heads of the crammed-together guests there veered the notes of an Armstrong trumpet solo. Beneath this bright glaze of jazz and a frothy layer of conversation there was a low, heavy rumbling from the distant air compressor. Along with the smells of perfume and cigarettes, the air in the room had a faint motor-oil smell of the wharves.

"Hello, George." Harkoo fought his way toward them, a round, broad, not at all long man, with thinning coppery hair cropped close. "I was hoping you would show."

"Hello, Siggy." Deasey stiffened and offered his hand in a way that struck Joe as defensive or even protective, and then, in the next instant, the man he called Siggy had put a wrestling hold on him, in which seemed to be mingled affection and a desire to snap bones.

"Mr. Clay, Mr. Kavalier," Deasey said, fighting free of the embrace like Houdini jerking and thrashing his way out of a wet straitjacket. "May I—present—Longman Harkoo, known to those who prefer not to indulge him as Mr. Siegfried Saks."

Joe had an uneasy feeling, as if the name meant something to him, but he could not quite get hold of the connection. He searched his memory for "Siegfried Saks," shuffling through the cards, trying to pop the ace that he knew was in there somewhere.

"Welcome!" The former Mr. Saks let go of his old friend and turned smiling to the cousins; they each took a step back, but he just offered them his hand, with a mischievous twinkle in his mild blue eyes that seemed to suggest he subjected to his demonic hugs only those who least liked to be touched. At a time when an honorable place in the taxonomy of male elegance was still reserved for the genus Fat Man, Harkoo was a classic instance of the Mystic Potentate species, managing to look at once commanding, stylish, and ultramundane in a vast purple-and-brown caftan, heavily embroidered, that hung down almost to the tops of his Mexican sandals. The little toe of his horny right foot, Joe saw, was adorned with a garnet ring. A venerable Kodak Brownie hung from an Indian-beaded strap around his neck.

"Sorry about all that *racket* downstairs," he said with a hint of weariness.

"Is it really him?" Sammy said. "Inside that thing?"

"It really is. I've tried to coax him out of it. I told him it was a *marvelous* idea in the, you know, the abstract, but in *practice. . . .* But he's a terribly stubborn man. I've never known a genius who was not."

The doorman had pointed Dalí out to them when they came in, standing in the ballroom, just off the front hall. He was wearing a deep-sea diving costume, complete with rubberized canvas coverall and globular brass helmet. A striking woman whom Deasey identified as Gala Dalí stood loyally by her husband's side in the middle of the empty room, along with two or three other people too stubborn, too sycophantic, or perhaps simply too deaf to mind the intolerable coughing hum of the large gasoline-powered air pump, to which the Master was connected by a length of rubber hose. They were all yelling at the top of their lungs. "No one at the party," as Kahn wrote in *The New Yorker,* was ill-mannered enough to ask Dalí what he intended by this get-up. Most took it to be either an allusion to the tenebrous benthos of the human unconscious or else to "The Dream of Venus," which as everyone knows featured a school of live girls dressed up as mermaids swimming around half-naked in a tank. In any case Dalí would not, in all likelihood, have been able to hear the question through the diving helmet.

"But never mind," Harkoo continued cheerily, "we're all quite cozy in here. Welcome, welcome. Comic books, is it? *Marvelous* stuff. Love it. Regular reader. Positively a devotee."

Sammy beamed. Harkoo slipped the camera from around his neck and handed it to Joe. "I'd be very honored if you would take my picture," he said.

"Please? I'm sorry?"

"Take a picture of me. With the camera." He looked at Deasey. "Does he speak English?"

"He has his own brand. Mr. Kavalier is from Prague."

"Very good! Yes, you must! I have a marked deficit of Czech impressions."

Deasey nodded to Joe, who raised the camera's viewfinder to his left eye and framed Longman Harkoo's big, cracked-baby face. Harkoo settled his jowls and eyebrows into a sober, nearly blank expression, but his eyes gleamed with pleasure. Joe had never in his life made anyone so happy so easily.

"How do I focus it?" Joe asked him, lowering the camera.

"Oh, don't bother about that. Just look at me and push the little lever. Your mind will do the rest."

"My mind." Joe snapped a photo of his host, then handed the camera back to him. "The camera is . . ." He searched for the word in English. "Telepathic."

"All cameras are," his host said mildly. "I have been photographed now by seven thousand one hundred and . . . eighteen . . . people, all with this camera, and I assure you that no two portraits are alike." He handed the camera to Sammy, and his features, as if stamped from a machine, once more settled into the same corpulent happy mask. Sammy snapped the lever. "What possible other explanation can there be for this endless variation but interference by waves emanating from the photographer's own mind?"

Joe did not know how to reply to this, but he saw that a reply was expected, and as the intensity of his host's expectation increased, he realized somewhat belatedly what that reply must be.

"None," he said finally.

Longman Harkoo looked extremely pleased. He put one arm across Sammy's shoulders and the other across Joe's and, with a good deal of shoving and apologizing, managed to take them on a tour of their immediate neighbors, introducing them to painters and writers and various holders of cocktails, furnishing each, without even appearing to stop to organize his thoughts, with a miniature curriculum vitae that touched on the high points of their oeuvres, sex lives, or family connections.

"... her sister is married to a Roosevelt, don't ask me which one ... you must have seen his *Art and Agon* ... she's standing right under one of her ex-husband's paintings ... he was publicly slapped by Siquieros ..."

Most of the names were unfamiliar to Joe, but he did recognize Raymond Scott, a composer who had recently hit it big with a series of whimsical, cacophonous, breakneck pseudo-jazz pop tunes. Just the other day, when Joe stopped in at Hippodrome Radio, they had been playing his new record, *Yesterthoughts and Stranger*, over the store PA. Scott was feeding a steady diet of Louis Armstrong platters to the portable RCA while explaining what he had meant when he referred to Satchmo as the Einstein of the blues. As the notes fluttered out of the fabric-covered loudspeaker, he would point at them, as if to illustrate what he was saying, and even tried to snatch at one with his hands. He kept turning the volume up, the better to compete with the less important conversations taking place all around him. Over there, under the saguaro cactus, was the girl painter Loren MacIver, whose luminous canvases Joe had admired at the Paul Matisse gallery. Tall, overly thin by Joe's lights, but with a New York kind of beauty—sharp, tense, stylish—she was chatting with a tall, striking Aryan beauty who was holding a tiny baby to her breast. "Miss Uta Hagen," Harkoo explained. "She's married to José Ferrer, he's around here someplace. They're doing *Charley's Aunt.*"

The women offered their hands. MacIver's eyes were kohled, her lips painted a surprising shade of cocoa.

"These gentlemen make comic books," Harkoo told them. "The adventures of a fellow named the Escaper. Wears a union suit. Big muscles. Vapid expression."

"The Escapist," said Loren MacIver. Her face lit up. "Oh, I *like* him."

"You do?" said Sammy and Joe together.

"A man in a mask, who likes to be tied up with ropes?" Miss Hagen laughed. "Sounds racy."

"It's quite surreal," Harkoo said.

"That's good, right?" Sammy said to Joe in a whisper. Joe nodded. "Just checking."

They made their way past several more curricula vitae holding cocktails, as well as a number of actual Surrealists, like raisins studded in a pudding. For the most part these seemed to be a remarkably serious, even sober bunch of fellows. They wore dark suits with waistcoats and solid neckties. Most of them seemed to be Americans—Peter Blume, Edwin Dickinson, a shy, courtly fellow named Joseph Cornell—who shared an air of steel-rimmed, Yankee probity that surrounded like a suburb their inner Pandemonium. Joe tried to keep all the names straight, but he was still not sure who Charley was or what was being done by Uta Hagen to his aunt.

At the far end of the library, a number of men had gathered into a tight, jostling ring around a very pretty, very young woman who was talking at what must have been the top of her lungs. Joe could not really understand what she was telling them, but it appeared to be a story that reflected poorly on her own judgment—she was blushing and grinning at the same time—and it unquestionably ended with the word "fuck." She tugged on the word, drawing it out to several times its usual length. She wound it all the way around her in two or three big loops and reveled in it as if it were a luxuriant shawl.

"*Fuuuuuuuck.*"

The men around her burst out laughing, and she blushed even more deeply. She had on a loose, sleeveless kind of smock, and you could see the flush reaching all the way down past her shoulders to the tops of her arms. Then she looked up, and her eyes met Joe's.

"Saks," Joe said, producing the card at last. "Rosa Luxemburg Saks."

"Nah," Sammy said. "Is it?"

8

IT WAS FASCINATING to see her face again after so long. Although Joe had never forgotten the girl whom he had surprised that morning in Jerry Glovsky's bedroom, he saw that, in his nocturnal reimaginings of the moment, he had badly misremembered her. He never would have recalled her forehead as so capacious and high, her chin as so delicately pointed. In fact, her face would have seemed overlong were it not counterbalanced by an extravagant flying buttress of a nose. Her rather small lips were set in a bright red hyphen that curved downward just enough at one corner to allow itself to be read as a smirk of amusement, from which she herself was not exempted, at the surrounding tableau of human vanity. And yet in her eyes there was something unreadable, something that did not want to be read, the determined blankness that in predator animals conceals hostile calculation, and in prey forms part of an overwhelming effort to seem to have disappeared.

The men around her had parted reluctantly as Harkoo, providing blocking for Joe and Sammy like a back for the latter's beloved Dodgers, shoehorned them into the circle.

"We've met," Rosa said. It was almost a question. She had a strong, deep, droll, masculine voice, turned up to a point that verged on speaker-rattling, as if she were daring everyone around her to listen and to judge. But then maybe, Joe thought, she was just very drunk. There was a glass of something amber in her hand. In any case, her voice went well, somehow, with her dramatic features and the wild mass of brown woolen loops, constrained here and there by a desperate bobby pin, that constituted her hairstyle. She gave his hand a squeeze that partook of the same bold intentions as her voice, a businessman's shake, dry and curt and forceful. And yet he noticed that she was, if any-thing, blushing more obviously than ever. The delicate skin over her clavicles was mottled.

"I don't believe so," said Joe. He coughed, partly to cover his discom-fiture, partly to camouflage the suave rejoinder he had just been fed by the prompter crouching by the footlights of his desire, and partly be-cause his throat had gone bone-dry. He felt a weird urge to lean down—she was a small woman, the top of whose head barely reached his collarbone—and kiss her on the mouth, in front of everyone, as he might have done in a dream, with that long optimistic descent across the distance between their lips enduring for minutes, hours, centuries. How *surreal* would that be? Instead, he reached into his pocket and took out his cigarettes. "Someone like you I would absolutely remember," he said.

"Oh, good God," said one of the men beside her in disgust.

The young woman to whom he was lying produced a smile which—Joe couldn't tell—might have been either flattered or appalled. Her smile was a surprisingly broad and toothy achievement for a mouth that in contemplation had been compacted into such a tiny pout.

"Huh," said Sammy. He, at least, sounded impressed by Joe's suavity.

Longman Harkoo said, "That's our cue." He put his arm once more around Sammy's shoulder. "Let's get you a drink, shall we?"

"Oh, I don't— I'm not—" Sammy reached out to Joe as Harkoo led him away, as though worried that their host was about to drag him off to the promised volcano. Joe watched him go with a cold heart. Then he held the pack of Pall Malls out to Rosa. She tugged a cigarette free and put it to her lips. She took a long drag. Joe felt constrained to point out that the cigarette was not lit.

"Oh," she said. She snorted. "I'm such an idiot."

"Rosa," chided one of the men standing beside her, "you don't smoke!"

"I just took it up," Rosa said.

There was a muffled groan, then the cloud of men around her seemed to dissolve. She took no notice. She inclined toward Joe and peered up, curving her hand around his and the flame of the match. Her eyes shone, an indeterminate color between champagne and the green of a dollar. Joe felt feverish and a little dizzy, and the cool talcum smell of Shalimar she gave off was like a guardrail he could lean against. They had drawn very close together, and now, as he tried and failed to prevent himself from thinking of her lying naked and facedown on Jerry Glovsky's bed, her broad downy backside with its dark furrow, the alluvial hollow of her spine, she took a step backward and studied him.

"You're *sure* we haven't met."

"Fairly."

"Where are you from?"

"Prague."

"You're Czech."

He nodded.

"A Jew?"

He nodded again.

"How long have you been here?"

"One year," he said, and then, the realization filling him with wonder and chagrin, "one year *today.*"

"Did you come with your family?"

"Alone," he said. "I left them there." Unbidden, there flashed in his mind's eye the image of his father, or the ghost of his father, striding down the gangplank of the *Rotterdam,* arms outstretched. Tears stung his eyes, and a ghostly hand seemed to clutch at his throat. Joe coughed once and batted at the smoke from his cigarette, as if it were irritating him. "My father has recently died."

She shook her head, looking sorrowful and outraged and, he thought, entirely lovely. As his glibness had departed him, so a more earnest nature seemed to feel greater liberty to confess itself in her.

"I'm really sorry for you," she said. "My heart goes out to them."

"It's not so bad," Joe said. "It will be all right."

"You know we're getting into this war," she declared. She wasn't blushing now. The brass-voiced party girl of a moment before, telling a story on herself that ended in an oath, seemed to have vanished. "We have to, and we will. Roosevelt will arrange it. He's working toward it now. We won't let them win."

"No," Joe said, though Rosa's views were hardly typical of her countrymen, most of whom felt that the events in Europe were an embroilment to be avoided at any price. "I believe . . ." He found himself, to his mild surprise, unable to finish the sentence. She reached out and took his arm.

"What I'm saying is just, I don't know. I guess 'don't despair,' " she said. "I really, really do mean that, Joe."

At her words, the touch of her hand, her pronouncing of his short blank American name devoid of all freight and family associations, Joe was overcome with a flood of gratitude so powerful that it frightened him, because it seemed to reflect in its grandeur and force just how little hope he really had left. He pulled away.

"Thank you," he said stiffly.

She let her hand fall, dismayed at having offended him. "I'm sorry," she said again. She lifted an eyebrow, quizzical, bold, and on the verge, he thought, of recognizing him. Joe averted his eyes, his heart in his throat, thinking that if she were able to recollect him and the circumstances of their first meeting, his chances with her would be ruined. Her eyes got very big, and her throat, her cheeks, her ears were flooded with the bright heart's blood of humiliation. Joe could see her making an effort not to look away.

Just then a series of sharp metallic sounds cut the air, as if someone had thrust a spanner into the blades of a giant fan. The room fell silent, and everyone stood listening as the harsh chopping sounds ceased and were followed by an oscillating mechanical whine. A woman screamed, her musical horror carrying all the way up from the ballroom on the ground floor. Everyone turned to the door of the library.

"Help!" came a cry from downstairs, a man's hoarse voice. "He's drowning!"

SALVADOR DALÍ lay on his back in the middle of the ballroom floor, smacking ineffectually at the helmet of his diving suit with his gloved hands. His wife knelt beside him, working fiercely at a wingnut that kept the helmet bolted to the brass collar of the suit. A vein bulged in her forehead. A heavy lump of black onyx that she wore at the end of a thick gold chain kept clapping against the bell of the diving helmet.

"*Il devient bleu*," she observed in a calm panic. Two of the guests ran to Dalí's side. One of them—it was the composer, Scott—brushed Señora Dalí's hands away and took hold of the wings of the nut. Longman Harkoo barreled across the room, showing surprising alacrity for one of his girth. He began to slap at the whining air pump with the sole of his sandaled right foot.

"It's jammed! It's overloaded! Oh, what's the matter with this thing!"

"He's not getting any oxygen!" offered someone.

"Get that helmet off him!" another suggested.

"What the fuck do you think I'm trying to do!" shouted the composer.

"Stop shouting!" cried Harkoo. He pushed Scott out of the way now, grabbed the wingnut in his meaty fingers, and threw all of his bulk and momentum into a single great twist. The nut turned. He grinned. The nut turned again, and the grin faded. The nut turned, and turned, and turned again, never loosening; it had become fused to the bolt.

Joe stood in the doorway beside Rosa, watching, and as the nut turned helplessly in her father's fingers, she took hold of Joe's arm with both hands, without seeming to notice that she was doing so, and squeezed. The plea for his help implicit in the gesture thrilled and alarmed him. He reached into his pocket and took out the Victorinox knife that had been a gift from Thomas on his seventeenth birthday.

"What are you doing?" she said, letting go of him.

He didn't answer. He walked quickly across the room and knelt down beside Gala Dalí, whose armpits smelled oddly of fennel seed. After ascertaining that Salvador Dalí was indeed beginning to turn blue, Joe opened the screwdriver blade of the knife. He jammed it into the slot on the bolt head to hold the bolt steady. Then he worked the nut. Through the wire grid of the face plate, his eyes met Dalí's, abulge with terror and asphyxia. A stream of muffled Spanish rattled against the far side of the inch-thick glass. As near as Joe could tell—his Spanish was poor—Dalí was calling abjectly for the intercession of the Holy Mother of God. The bolt held. Joe bit down hard on his lip and twisted until his fingers felt that they would split at the tips. There was a snap, and the nut began to protest and grow warm. Then, slowly, it gave. Fourteen seconds later, with a loud Dom Pérignon pop, Joe yanked the helmet off.

Dalí gave great sobbing gasps as they helped him out of his suit. New York, though lucrative, was in many ways a dangerous place for him: in the spring of 1938, he had made all the papers by falling through a display window at Bonwit Teller. A glass of water was brought; he sat up and drained it. The left brachium of his famous mustache had wilted. He asked for a cigarette. Joe gave him one and held a match to it. Dalí inhaled deeply, coughed, picked a flake of tobacco from his lip. Then he nodded to Joe.

"*Jeune homme, vous avez sauvé une vie de très grand valeur,*" he said.

"*Je le sais bien, maître,*" said Joe.

He felt a heavy hand on his shoulder. It was Longman Harkoo.

He was beaming, fairly rocking up and down in his sandals at the turn things had taken. The near death of a world-famous painter in a diving accident, in a Greenwich Village drawing room, contributed an unimpeachable Surrealist luster to the party.

"Hot stuff," he said.

Then the party seemed to close its fingers around Joe, treasuring him in its palm. He was a hero.* People gathered around, tossing handfuls of hyperbolic adjectives and coarse expostulations at his head, holding their pale tin-pan faces up to his as if to catch a splash of his rattling-jackpot moment of glory. Sammy managed to swim or shoulder his way through the people slapping and grabbing at Joe, and gave him a hug. George Deasey brought him a drink that was bright and cold as metal in his mouth. Joe nodded slowly, without speaking, accepting their tributes and acclaim with the sullen, abstracted air of a victorious athlete, breathing deep. It was nothing to him: noise, smoke, jostling, a confusion of perfumes and hair oils, a throb of pain in his right hand. He looked around the room, rising on tiptoe to see over the waxy tops of men's heads, peering through the dense foliage of the plumes on women's hats, searching Rosa out. All his self-denial, his Escapist purity of intentions, were forgotten in the flush of triumph and a sense of calm very like that which pervaded him after he had taken a beating. It seemed to him that his fortunes, his life, the entire apparatus of his sense of self were concentrated only on the question of what Rosa Saks would think of him now.

"She fairly bounded across the room to him," as E. J. Kahn would afterward describe it—referring in his item to Rosa (whom he knew slightly) only as "a fetching Village art maiden"—and then, after managing to reach him, she seemed to grow suddenly shy.

"What did he say to you?" she wanted to know. "Dalí."

" 'Thank you,' " said Joe.

"That's all?"

"He called me *'jeune homme.'* "

"I thought I heard you speaking French," she said, hugging herself to still a tremor of unmistakable, almost maternal pride. Joe, seeing his exploit so richly rewarded by the flush in her cheeks and her un-

* Two weeks after Kahn's piece appeared in *The New Yorker*, giving some particulars of Josef Kavalier and of his family's plight, Kahn forwarded to Joe a check for twelve dollars, one for ten, and a letter from a Mrs. F. Bernhard of East Ninety-sixth Street, offering to feed him a home-cooked meal of schnitzel and knödelen. It is probable that Joe never took her up on the offer. Records indicate, however, that the checks were cashed.

wavering regard, stood there scratching at the side of his nose with the thumb of his right hand, embarrassed by the ease of his success, like a fighter who mats his opponent nineteen seconds into the first round.

"I know who you are," she said, coloring again. "I mean, I . . . remember you now."

"I remember you, too," he said, hoping it did not sound salacious.

"How would you . . . I'd like you to see my paintings," she said. "If you want to, I mean. I have a—a studio upstairs."

Joe hesitated. From the time of his arrival in New York City, he had never permitted himself to speak to a woman for pleasure. It was not an easy thing to do in English, and anyway, he had not come here to flirt with girls. He didn't have time for it, and furthermore, he did not feel that he was entitled to such pleasures, or to the commitments that they would inevitably entail. He felt—it was not an articulated feeling, but it was powerful and, in its way, a comfort to him—that he could justify his own liberty only to the degree that he employed it to earn the freedom of the family he had left behind. His life in America was a conditional thing, provisional, unencumbered with personal connections beyond his friendship and partnership with Sammy Clay.

"I—"

At this very moment, Joe's attention was diverted by the sound of someone, somewhere in the drawing room, talking in German. He turned and searched among the faces and the blare of conversation until he found the lips that were moving in time to the elegant Teutonic syllables he was hearing. They were fleshy, sensual lips, in a severe way, downturned at the corners in a somehow intelligent frown, a frown of keen judgment and bitter good sense. The frowner was a trim, fit man in a black turtleneck sweater and corduroy trousers, rather chinless but with a high forehead and a large, dignified German nose. His hair was fine and fair, and his bright black eyes held a puckish gleam that belied the grave frown. There was great enthusiasm in the eyes, pleasure in the subject of his discourse. He was talking, as far as Joe could tell, about the Negro dance team the Nicholas Brothers.

Joe felt the familiar exultation, the epinephrine flame that burned away doubt and confusion and left only a pure, clear, colorless vapor of rage. He took a deep breath and turned his back on the man.*

"I would love to see your work," he said.

---

* It was probably just as well. The man was Max Ernst, not merely an artist whose work Joe admired but a committed anti-fascist, public enemy of the Nazis, and fellow exile.

THE PITCH of the staircase was steep and the treads narrow. There were three stories above the ground floor, and she took him all the way to the top. It got darker and spookier as they climbed. The walls on either side of the stairs were hung with hundreds of framed portraits of her father, carefully fit together like tiles to cover every inch of available space. In each of them, as far as Joe could tell from a hasty inspection, the subject wore the same goofy suppressing-a-fart expression, and if there was any significant difference among them, apart from the fact that some people were evidently more adept at telepathically focusing a lens than others, it was lost on Joe. As they made their way up through the increasing gloom, Joe seemed to steer only according to the light shed by the action of her palm against his wrist, by the low steady flow of voltage through the conducting medium of their sweat. He stumbled like a drunken man and laughed as she hurried him along. He was vaguely aware of the ache in his hand, but he ignored it. As they turned the landing to the top floor, a strand of her hair caught in the corner of his mouth, and for an instant he crunched it between his teeth.

She took him into a small room in the middle of the house, which curved queerly where it backed up against the central tower. In addition to her tiny, girlish white iron bed, a small dresser, and a nightstand, she had crowded in an easel, a photo enlarger, two bookcases, a drawing table, and a thousand and one other items piled atop one another, strewn about, and jammed together with remarkable industry and abandon.

"This is your *studio*?" Joe said.

A smaller blush this time, at the tips of her ears.

"Also my bedroom," she said. "But I wasn't going to ask you to come up to *that.*"

There was something unmistakably exultant about the mess that Rosa had made. Her bedroom-studio was at once the canvas, journal, museum, and midden of her life. She did not "decorate" it; she infused it. Sometime around four o'clock that morning, for example, half-disentangled from the tulle of a dream, she had reached for the chewed stub of a Ticonderoga she kept by her bed for this purpose. When, just after dawn, she awoke, she found a scrap of loose-leaf paper in her left hand, scrawled with the cryptic legend "lampedusa." She had run to the unabridged on its lonely lectern in the library, where she learned this was the name of a small island in the Mediterranean Sea, between Malta and Tunisia. Then she had returned to her room, taken a big thumbtack with an enameled red head from an El Producto box she kept on her supremely "cluttered-up" desk, and tacked the scrap of paper to the eastern wall of her room, where it overlapped a photograph, torn from the pages of *Life*, of Ambassador Joseph Kennedy's handsome eldest son, tousled and wearing a Choate cardigan. The scrap joined a reproduction of a portrait of Arthur Rimbaud at seventeen, dreaming with chin in palm; the entire text of her only play, a Jarry-influenced one-act called *Homunculus Uncle;* plates, sliced from art books, of a detail from Bosch that depicted a woman being pursued by an animate celery, of Edvard Munch's *Madonna*, of several Picasso "blue" paintings, and of Klee's *Cosmic Flora;* Ignatius Donnelly's map of Atlantis, traced; a grotesquely vibrant full-color photo, also courtesy of *Life*, of four cheerful strips of bacon; a spavined dead locust, forelegs arrested in an attitude of pleading; as well as some three hundred other scraps of paper bearing the numinous vocabulary of her dreams, a puzzling lexicon that included "grampus," "ullage," "parbuckle," and some entirely fictitious words, such as "luben" and "salactor." Socks, blouses, skirts, tights, and twisted underpants lay strewn across teetering piles of books and phonograph albums, the floor was thick with paint-soaked rags and chromo-chaotic cardboard palettes, canvases stacked four deep stood against the walls. She had discovered the surrealistic potential of food, about which she had rather pioneeringly complicated emotions, and everywhere lay portraits of broccoli stalks, cabbage heads, tangerines, turnip greens, mushrooms, beets—big, colorful, drunken tableaux that reminded Joe of Robert Delaunay.

When they walked into the room, Rosa went over to the phonograph and switched it on. When the needle hit the groove, the scratches on the disk popped and crackled like a burning log. Then the air was filled with a festive wheeze of violins.

"Schubert," said Joe, rocking on his heels. "*The Trout.*"

"*The Trout*'s my favorite," Rosa said.

"Me too."

"Look out."

Something hit him in the face, something soft and alive. Joe brushed at his mouth and came away with a small black moth. It had electric-blue transverse bands on its belly. He shuddered.

Rosa said, "Moths."

"Moths more than one?"

She nodded and pointed to the bed.

Joe noticed now that there were a fair number of moths in the room, most of them small and brown and unremarkable, scattered on the blankets of the narrow bed, flecking the walls, sleeping in the folds of the curtains.

"It's an annoyance," she said. "They're all over the upstairs of the house. Nobody's really sure why. Sit down."

He found a moth-free spot on the bed and sat down.

"Apparently there were moths all through the last house, too," she said. She knelt down before him. "And in the one before that. That was the one where the murder happened. What's the matter with your finger?"

"It's sore. From when I was turning the screw."

"It looks dislocated."

His right index finger was curled a little to one side, in a queer parenthetical crook.

"Give me your hand. Come on, it's all right. I was almost a nurse once."

He gave her his hand, sensing the thin strong rod of obdurate competence that was the armature of her artsy Village style. She turned his hand over and over, probed delicately with the tips of her own fingers at the joints and skin.

"Doesn't it hurt?"

"Actually," he said. The pain, now that he attended to it, was fairly sharp.

"I can fix it."

"You really are a nurse? I thought you worked at *Life* the magazine." She shook her head.

"No, I'm really not a nurse," she said briskly, as if skipping over some incident or emotion she preferred to keep to herself. "It was just something I—pursued." She gave an explanatory sigh as if tired of her own tale. "I wanted to be a nurse in Spain. You know. In the war. I volunteered. I had a post in a hospital run by the A.C.P. in Madrid, but I . . . hey." She let his hand fall. "How did you know . . ."

"I saw your business card."

"My— Oh." He was rewarded with a full new flush. "Yes, it's such a bad habit," she went on, resuming her big stage voice though there was no crowd to overhear the performance, "leaving things in men's bedrooms."

Joe wasn't, in Sammy's phrase, buying any of that. He would have been willing to bet not only that having left her purse behind in Jerry Glovsky's room had mortified Rosa Luxemburg Saks but that her habits did not even encompass the regular visiting of men's bedrooms.

"This is going to hurt," she promised him.

"Badly?"

"Horribly, but only for a second."

"All right."

She looked at him, steadily, and licked her lips, and he had just noticed that the pale brown irises of her eyes were flecked with green and gold when abruptly she twisted his hand one way and his finger the other, and, crazing his arm to the elbow with instantaneous veins of lightning and fire, set the joint back into place.

"Wow."

"Hurt?"

He shook his head, but there were tears rolling down his cheeks.

"Anyway," she said. "I had a ticket from New York to Cartagena on the *Bernardo*. On March twenty-fifth, 1939. On the twenty-third, my stepmother died very suddenly. My father was devastated. I postponed sailing for a week. On the thirty-first, the Falangists took Madrid."

Joe remembered the Fall of Madrid. It had come two weeks after the fall, uncapitalized, disregarded, of Prague.

"You were disappointed?"

"Crushed." She cocked her head to one side, as if listening to the echo of the word she had just uttered. She gave her head a decisive shake. A curl slipped free of its pin and tumbled down the side of her face. She brushed it irritably to one side. "You want to know something? Honestly, I was relieved. What a coward, huh?"

"I don't think so."

"Oh, yes. I am. A big coward. That's why I just keep daring myself to do things I'm afraid of doing."

He had a notion. "Such things like?"

"Like bringing you up here to my room."

This was unquestionably the moment to kiss her. Now he was the coward. He leaned over and started to flip with his good hand through a stack of paintings by the bed. "Very good," he said after a moment. Her brushwork seemed hasty and impatient, but her portraits—the term "still life" did not suffice—of produce, canned foods, and the occasional trotter or lamb chop were at once whimsical, worshipful, and horrifying, and managed to suggest their subjects perfectly without wasting too much time on the details. Her line was very strong; she could draw as well as he, perhaps better. But she took no pains with her work. The paint was streaked, blotchy, studded with dirt and bristles; the edges of paintings often were left ragged and blank; where she couldn't get something quite right, she just blotted it out with furious, petulant strokes. "I can almost to smell them. What murder?"

"Huh?"

"You said there was a murder."

"Oh, yes. Caddie Horslip. She was a socialite or a debutante or—they hung my great-granduncle for it. Moses Espinoza. It was a huge sensation at the time, back in the eighteen-sixties, I think." She noticed that she was still holding his hand. She let it go. "There. Good as new. Have you got a cigarette?"

He lit one for her. She continued to kneel in front of him, and there was something about it that aroused him. It made him feel like a wounded soldier, making time in a field hospital with his pretty American nurse.

"He was a lepidopterist, Moses," she said.

"A—?"

"He studied moths."

"Oh."

"He knocked her out with ether and killed her with a pin. Or at least that's what my father says. He's probably lying. I made a dreambook about it."

"A pin," he said. "Ouch." He waggled his finger. "It's good, I think. You fixed it."

"Hey, how about that."

"Thank you, Rosa."

"You're welcome, Joe. Joe. You don't make a very convincing Joe."

"Not yet," he said. He flexed his hand, turned it over, studied it. "Am I going to be able to draw?"

"I don't know, can you draw now?"

"I'm not bad. What's a dreambook?"

She set the burning cigarette down on a phonograph record that lay on the floor beside her and went to her desk. "Would you like to see one?"

Joe bent over and picked up the cigarette, holding it upright between the very tips of his fingers as though it were a stick of burning dynamite. It had melted a small divot into the second movement of Mendelssohn's *Octet*.

"Here, this is one. I can't seem to find the Caddie Horslip."

"Really?" he said dryly. "What a surprise."

"Don't be smart, it's unattractive in a man."

He handed the cigarette to her and took from her a large, clothbound book, black with a red spine. It was an accounts ledger, swollen to twice its normal thickness, like a book left out in the rain, from all the things pasted into it. When he turned to the first page, he found the words "Airplane Dream #13" written in an odd, careful hand like a scattering of spindly twigs.

"Numbered," he said. "It's like a comic book."

"Well, there are just so many. I'd lose track."

"Airplane Dream #13" told the story, more or less, of a dream Rosa had had about the end of the world. There were no human beings left but her, and she had found herself flying in a pink seaplane to an island inhabited by sentient lemurs. There seemed to be a lot more to it—there was a kind of graphic "sound track" constructed around images relating to Peter Tchaikovsky and his works, and of course abundant food imagery—but this was, as far as Joe could tell, the gist. The story was told entirely through collage, with pictures clipped from magazines and books. There were images from anatomy texts, an exploded musculature of the human leg, a pictorial explanation of peristalsis. She had found an old history of India, and many of the lemurs of her dream-apocalypse had the heads and calm, horizontal gazes of Hindu princes and goddesses. A seafood cookbook, rich with color photographs of boiled crustacea and poached whole fish with jellied stares, had been thoroughly mined. Sometimes she inscribed text across the pictures, none of which made a good deal of sense to him; a few pages consisted almost entirely of her brambly writing, illuminated, as it were, with collage. There were some penciled-in drawings and diagrams, and an elaborate system of cartoonish marginalia like the creatures found loitering at the edges of pages in medieval books. Joe started to read sitting down in her desk chair, but before long, without noticing, he had risen to his feet and started pacing around the room. He stepped on a moth without noticing.

"These must take hours," he said.

"Hours."

"How many have you done?"

She pointed to a painted chest at the foot of her bed. "A lot."

"It is beautiful. Exciting."

He sat down on the bed and finished reading, and then she asked him about what he did. Joe permitted himself, for the first time in a year, to consider himself, under the pressure of her interest in him and what he did, an artist. He described the hours he had put into his covers, lavishing detail on the flanges and fins of a death-wave generator, distorting and exaggerating his perspectives with mathematic precision, dressing up Sammy and Julie and the others and taking test photographs to get his poses right, painting luscious plumes of fire that, when printed, seemed to burn the slick ink and paper of the cover itself. He told her about his experiments with a film vocabulary, his sense of the emotional moment of a panel, and of the infinitely expandable and contractible interstice of time that lay between the panels of a comic book page. Sitting on Rosa's moth-littered bed, he felt a resurgence of all the aches and inspirations of those days when his life had revolved around nothing but Art, when snow fell like the opening piano notes of the Emperor Concerto, and feeling horny reminded him of a passage from Nietzsche, and a thick red-streaked dollop of crimson paint in an otherwise uninteresting Velázquez made him hungry for a piece of rare meat.

At some point, he noticed that she was looking at him with a strange air of expectancy, or dread, and he stopped. "What is it?"

"Lampedusa," she said.

"What's that? Lampedusa?"

Her eyes widened as she waited, in expectancy or dread. She nodded.

"You mean the island?"

"Oh!" She threw her arms around his neck, and he fell backward on the bed. Moths scattered. The sateen coverlet brushed against his cheek like a moth's wing.

"Hey!" said Joe. Then she settled her mouth on his and left it there, lips parted, whispering an unintelligible dreambook sentence.

"Hello? Hey! Joe, you up here?"

Joe sat up. "Shit."

"Is that your brother?"

"My cousin Sam. My partner. In here, Sam," he said.

Sammy stuck his head in the door of the bedroom.

"Oh, hi," he said. "Jeez, I'm sorry. I was just—"

"She's a nurse," Joe said, feeling oddly culpable, as if he had somehow betrayed Sammy and must excuse his presence here. He held up his repaired hand. "She fixed it."

"That's great, uh, hi. Sam Clay."

"Rosa Saks."

"Listen, Joe, I was uh—I was just wondering if you were ready to leave this—excuse me, Miss, I know you live here and all—creepy place."

Joe could see that something had upset Sammy.

"What is it?"

"The kitchen . . ."

"The kitchen?"

"It's *black*."

Rosa laughed. "True," she said.

"I don't know. I just—I just want to get home, you know. Get to work on that thing. The uh, sorry. Forget about it. I'll see you."

He turned and started out. In Joe's absence, he had undergone a strange experience. He had wandered through the ballroom and a small conservatory behind it and into the mansion's kitchen, where the walls and floor were covered in gleaming black tile and the countertops coated with black enamel. There were a fair number of people crowded in there as well, and, hoping to find a place where he could be alone for just a moment and perhaps use the toilet, he had turned into a large butler's pantry. Here he had come upon the unlikely sight of two men, each wearing, with the overdetermination of a dream, a necktie and a mustache, embracing, their mustaches interlocked in a way that had reminded Sammy, for some reason, of the way his mother used to fit his comb into the bristles of the brush on top of his dresser when he was a kid.

Sammy had backed quickly out of the kitchen and come looking for Joe; he felt that he wanted to leave, right away. He knew about homosexuality, of course, as an *idea*, without ever having really connected it to human emotion; certainly never to any emotion of his own. It had never occurred to him that two men, even homosexual men, might kiss in that way. He had assumed, to the degree he had ever permitted himself to give it any thought it all, that the whole thing must be a matter of blow jobs in dark alleyways or the foul practices of love-starved British sailors. But those men with the neckties and mustaches—they had been kissing the way people kissed in the movies, with care and vigor and just a hint of showiness. One fellow had caressed the other's cheek.

Sammy rummaged through the riot of furs and overcoats draped on hooks in the front hall until he located his own. He settled his hat on his head and went out. He stopped and lingered on the top step. His thoughts were disordered and strange to him. He was appallingly jealous; it was like a heavy round stone had lodged in the center of his chest, but he could not have said for sure whether he was jealous of Joe or of Rosa Luxemburg Saks. At the same time, he was glad for his cousin. It was marvelous that in this big town he had managed to rediscover, a year later, the girl with the miraculous behind. Perhaps she would be able, as Sammy had not, to find a way to distract Joe at least a little from his evident project of getting his clock cleaned by every last German in the city of New York. He turned and looked back at the doorman, a raffish-looking fellow in a greasy gray jacket who leaned against the front door, smoking a cigarette. What had so rattled Sammy about the scene he had witnessed? What was he afraid of? Why was he running away?

"Forget something?" said the doorman.

Sammy shrugged. He turned and went back into the house. Not entirely sure of what he was doing, he forced himself to walk back through the ballroom that was, now that Dalí had abandoned his diving costume, filled with happy and confident people who knew what they wanted and whom they loved, and into the black-tiled kitchen. A group of people were standing around the stove arguing about the proper way to make Turkish coffee, but the two men in the pantry had gone, leaving no trace of their presence. Had he imagined the whole thing? Was such a kiss really possible?

"Is he a fairy?" Rosa was, at that moment, asking Joe. They were still sitting on her bed, holding hands.

Joe was at first shocked by this suggestion, and then suddenly not. "Why would you say that?" he said.

She shrugged. "He has the feel," she said.

"Hmm," Joe said. "I don't know. He is—" He shrugged. "A good boy."

"Are you a good boy?"

"No," Joe said.

He leaned forward to kiss her again. They bumped teeth, and it made him weirdly aware of all the bones in his head. Her tongue was milk and salt, an oyster in his mouth. She put her hands on his shoulders, and he could feel her getting ready to push him away, and then after a moment she did.

"I'm worried about him," she said. "He looked a little lost. You should go after him."

"He will be fine."

"Joe," she said.

"Oh." She wanted him, he understood, to leave. They had taken it as far as she was prepared to go now. It was not what he expected from a foulmouthed flower of bohemia, but he had a feeling there was both more and less to her than that. "Okay," he said. "Yes. I—I have work to do, too."

"Good," Rosa said. "Go work. Will you call me?"

"May I?"

"UNiversity 4-3212," she said. "Here." She got up and went over to her drawing table and scrawled the number on a sheet of paper, then tore it off and handed it to Joe. "Get whoever it is to absolutely *promise* to take a message because they're horribly unreliable around here about that kind of thing. Wait a minute." She wrote out another number. "This is my number at work. I work at *Life*, in the art department. And this is my number at the T.R.A. I'm there three afternoons a week and on Saturdays. I'll be there tomorrow."

"The tea array?"

"Transatlantic Rescue Agency. I'm a volunteer secretary there. It's a small operation on this end. Shoestring. Really it's just me and Mr. Hoffman. Oh, he is a wonderful man, Joe. He has a boat, he bought it himself, and he's working right now to get as many Jewish children out of Europe as the boat can fit."

"Children," Joe said.

"Yes. What are—is there—do you have children—in your family? Back in—"

"Where is it?" Joe said. "The T.A.R.?"

Rosa wrote out an address on Union Square.

"I would like to see you there tomorrow," Joe said. "Would that perhaps be possible?"

WE HAVE ONE SHIP," said Hermann Hoffman. He was dimpled and plump, with a trim Vandyke, bags under his eyes that had an air of permanence, and a shiny black hairpiece almost aggressive in its patent falsity. His office at the Transatlantic Rescue Agency overlooked the iron-black trees and rusty foliage of Union Square. He had spent twenty times on his gray worsted suit what Joe, whose economy grew more draconian as his income increased, had spent on his own. With the precision of someone cutting a deck of cards, Hoffman drew three brown cigarettes from a pack that featured a gilt pharaoh and dealt one to Joe, one to Rosa, and one to himself. His nails were clipped and pearly, and his brand of cigarette, Thoth-Amon, imported from Egypt, was excellent. Joe could not imagine why such a man would wear a toupee that looked as if it had been ordered from the back cover of *Radio Comics.* "One ship, twenty-two thousand dollars, and half a million children." Hoffman smiled. It was, on his face, an expression of defeat.

Joe glanced at Rosa, who raised an eyebrow. She had warned him that Hoffman and his agency, struggling to achieve the impossible, operated on the perpetual brink of failure. In order to avoid having his heart broken, she said, her boss adopted the manner of an inveterate pessimist. She nodded, once, urging Joe to speak.

"I understand," said Joe. "I knew, of course—"

"It's a very nice ship," Hoffman continued. "She was called the *Lioness,* but we've renamed her the *Ark of Miriam.* Not large, but extremely well maintained. We bought her from Cunard, which had her on the Haiphong-to-Shanghai run. That's a picture of her." He pointed to a tinted photograph on the wall behind Joe. A trim liner, its plimsoll colored bold red, steamed across a bottle-green sea under a heliotrope sky. It was a very large photograph, in a platinum frame. Hermann Hoffman regarded it lovingly. "She was originally built for the P&O Company in 1893. A good deal of our initial endowment went toward her purchase and refitting, which, due to our emphasis on hygiene and humane treatment, proved to be quite costly." Another hangdog smile. "Most of the remainder went into the bank accounts and mattresses of various German officers and functionaries. After we take out pay for the crew and documentation, I don't honestly know how much we'll be able to accomplish with the little we have left. We may not be able to underwrite passage for half the children we have already arranged to bring over. It's going to cost us more than a thousand dollars per child."

"I understand," Joe said. "If I may say, I—" Joe looked at Rosa again. She had, overnight, worked a thorough transformation on herself. Joe was amazed. It was as though she had set out to eradicate every trace of the moth girl. She had on a Black Watch kilt, dark hose, and a plain white blouse buttoned at the wrists and collar. Her lips were bare, and she had ironed her flyaway hair into two frizzy pleats parted down the middle. She had even put on a pair of glasses. Joe was taken aback by the change, but found the presence of the caterpillar girl reassuring. If he had walked into the outer office of the T.R.A. and found a wild-haired portraitist of vegetables, he might have been a little dubious about the agency's credentials. He was not sure which of the two poses, moth or caterpillar, was the less sincere, but either way, he was grateful to her now.

"Mr. Kavalier has money, Mr. Hoffman," Rosa said. "He can afford to underwrite his brother's passage himself."

"I'm happy for you, Mr. Kavalier, but tell me. We have space on *Miriam* for three hundred and twenty-four. Our agents in Europe have already arranged for the transit of three hundred and twenty-four German, French, Czech, and Austrian children, with a waiting list that is considerably longer than that. Should one of them be left behind to make room for your brother?"

"No, sir."

"Is that what you propose we do?"

"No, sir." Joe shifted in his chair miserably. Couldn't he think of anything better to say to this man than *No, sir,* over and over again like a child being shown the error of his ways? His brother's fate might well be settled in this room. And it all depended on him. If he was, to Hoffman, in any way insufficiently . . . something, the *Ark of Miriam* would sail from Portsmouth without Thomas Kavalier. He stole another look at Rosa. It's all right, her face told him. Just tell him. Talk to him.

"I understand there may be room in the sick bay," Joe said.

Now Hoffman shot a look at Rosa. "Well, ye-es. In the best of circumstances, perhaps. But suppose there is an outbreak of measles, or some kind of accident?"

"He is a very small boy," Joe said. "For his age. He would not occupy very much space."

"They are *all* small, Mr. Kavalier," Hoffman said. "If I could safely pack in three hundred more of them, I would."

"Yes, but who would *pay* for them?" Rosa burst out. She was getting impatient. She pointed her finger at Hoffman. Joe noticed a streak of aubergine paint on the palm of her hand. "You say that three hundred and twenty-four have been cleared for passage, but you know that right now we can't pay for more than two hundred and fifty."

Hoffman sat back in his chair and stared at her in what Joe hoped was only mock horror.

Rosa covered her mouth. "Sorry," she said. "I'll be quiet."

Hoffman turned to Joe. "Watch out when she points that finger at you, Mr. Kavalier."

"Yes, sir."

"She's right. We are short of funds around here. The right adverb, I believe, is 'chronically.' "

"This is what I was thinking," Joe said. "What if I paid for another child *beside* to my brother?"

Hoffman sat forward, chin in palm. "I'm listening," he said.

"It's possible that I most likely can arrange to pay the fare for two or perhaps three others."

"Indeed?" Hoffman said. "And just what is it you do, Mr. Kavalier? Some kind of artist, is that it?"

"Yes, sir," Joe said. "I work in comic books."

"He's very talented," Rosa said, though last night she had admitted to

Joe that she had never looked between the covers of a comic book in her life. "And very well paid."

Hoffman smiled. He had been concerned for some time at the apparent lack in his young secretary's life of a suitable male companion.

"Comic books," he said. "That's all I hear about, Superman, Batman. My son, Maurice, is a regular reader." Hoffman reached for a picture frame on his desk and turned it around, revealing the face of a smaller version of himself, bags under the eyes and all. "He's having his bar mitzvah in a month."

"Congratulations," Joe said.

"Which comic book do you draw? Do you draw *Superman*?"

"No, but I know a guy, a young man, who does. I work at Empire Comics, sir. We do the Escapist. Also, maybe your son knows them, the Monitor, Mr. Machine Gun. I draw a lot of it. I make about two hundred dollars a week." He wondered if he ought to have brought along his pay stubs or some other kind of financial documentation. "I usually manage to save all of this but perhaps twenty-five."

"My goodness," Hoffman said. He looked over at Rosa, whose face also betrayed a fair amount of surprise. "We're in the wrong line of work, dear."

"It seems that way, boss," she said.

"The Escapist," Hoffman continued. "I think maybe I've seen that, but I'm not sure—"

"He is an escape artist. A performing magician."

"A performing magician?"

"That's correct."

"Do you know anything about magic?"

There was a whetted edge to the question. It was more than a friendly inquiry, though Joe could not imagine why.

"I have studied it," Joe said. "In Prague. I studied with Bernard Kornblum."

"Bernard Kornblum!" Hoffman said. "Kornblum!" His expression softened. "I saw him once."

"You saw Kornblum?" Joe turned to Rosa. "That's astonishing."

"I'm completely astonished," Rosa said. "Was it in Königsberg, sir?"

"It was in Königsberg."

"When you were a boy."

He nodded. "When I was a boy. I was quite an amateur magician my-self at one time. Still dabble from time to time. Now let me see." He wag-gled his fingers, then wiped his hands on an invisible napkin. His cigarette was gone. "Voilà." He rolled his heavy-lidded eyes to the ceil-ing and plucked the cigarette from thin air. "Et voilà." The cigarette slipped from his fingers and fell onto his jacket, left a streak of ash on his lapel, then dropped to the floor. Hoffman cursed. He pushed his chair back, clapped a hand onto his head, and, with a grunt, bent over to pick up the cigarette. When he sat up again, the warp of his wig seemed to have come free of the weft. Coarse black hairs stood up all over his head, wavering like a pile of iron filings drawn toward a distant but powerful magnet. "I'm terribly out of practice, I'm afraid." He patted down his hairpiece. "Are you any good?"

Kornblum had disdained patter as unworthy of the true master, and now Joe rose, wordlessly, and took off his jacket. He shot his cuffs and casually presented his empty hands for Hermann Hoffman's inspection. He was aware that he was taking a certain risk. Close work had never been his forte. He hoped that his index finger was all right.

"How is your finger?" Rosa whispered.

"Fine," said Joe. "May I trouble you for your cigarette lighter?" he asked Hoffman. "I'll only need it for a moment."

"But of course," said Hoffman. He handed his gold lighter to Joe.

"And another cigarette, I'm afraid."

Hoffman complied, watching Joe carefully. Joe stepped back from the desk, fit the cigarette to his lips, lit it, and inhaled deeply. Then he held up the lighter between the thumb and forefinger of his right hand and blew out a long blue jet of smoke. The lighter vanished. Joe took another deep drag and held it, and pinched his nose, and comically bugged out his eyes. The brown Thoth-Amon vanished. He opened his mouth and breathed out slowly. The smoke had vanished, too.

"Sorry," said Joe. "Clumsy of me."

"Very nice. Where is the lighter?"

"Here is the smoke."

Joe raised his left hand in a fist, drew it across his face, and then opened his hand like a flower. A teased knot of smoke floated out. Joe smiled. Then he picked up his jacket, hanging from the back of his chair, and took out his own cigarette case. He opened the case and revealed the Egyptian cigarette snug inside it, like a brown egg in a carton full of whites. It was still burning. He leaned forward and rolled the burning end in the ashtray on Hoffman's desk until it went out. As he straightened, he put the cigarette back into his mouth and snapped his fingers in front of the extinguished coal. The lighter reappeared. He scratched up a new flame and relit the cigarette. "Ah," he said, as if settling into a warm bath, exhaling.

Rosa applauded. "How did you do it?" she said.

"Maybe I'll tell you one day," Joe said.

"Oh, no, don't do that," Hoffman said. "I'll tell you what, Mr. Kavalier. If you will agree to underwrite, let us say *two* children, in addition to your brother, then we will start working on your brother's case, and do what we can to find room on *Miriam* for him."

"Thank you, sir." Joe turned to Rosa. Once again she looked all business. She nodded. He had done well. "That's very—"

"But first I have a favor to ask of you."

"What's that? Anything."

Hoffman nodded toward the picture of Maurice.

"If I were a wealthy man, Mr. Kavalier, I would finance this entire venture out of my own pocket. As it is, nearly every spare penny I have goes to the agency. I'm not sure if you're aware of this, or what it was like in Prague, but here in New York, bar mitzvahs are not cheap. In the circle my wife and I move in, they can be quite lavish. It's deplorable, but there it is. A photographer, caterers, the ballroom at the Hotel Trevi. It's costing me an arm and a leg."

Joe nodded slowly and glanced at Rosa. Was Hoffman really asking him to help pay for his son's reception?

"Do you have any idea," Hoffman said, "what it's going to cost me to hire a magician?" A cigarette appeared between the fingers of his right hand. It was, Joe noticed, still burning—it was the one he had dropped on the floor a few minutes before. Joe was certain he had seen Hoffman pick it up and snuff it in the ashtray. On further consideration, he was somewhat less certain. "I wonder if you might consider working something up?"

"I—I will be happy to."

"Excellent," Hoffman said.

They went out of his office. Rosa closed the door and grinned at him, her eyes wide. "How about that?"

"Thank you," he said. "Thank you very much, Rosa."

"I'm going to start a file for him right now." She went over to her desk, sat down, and took a printed form from a tray on the desk. "Tell me how to spell his name. Kavalier."

"With a K."

"Kavalier with a K. Thomas. Is that with an h, or—?"

"With an h. I want to see you," he said. "I want to take you to dinner."

"I'd like that," she said without looking up. "Middle name?"

WHEN HE WALKED OUTSIDE again, the sky was shining like a nickel and the air was filled with the smell of sugared nuts. He bought a bag, and it was hot in the hip pocket of his twelve-dollar suit. He walked across the street to the square. Thomas was coming to America! He had a date for dinner!

Crossing the park, he found himself puzzling over the secret of Hoffman's cigarette trick. Where had he concealed the holder from which he stole the burning cigarette? What kind of holder could keep a cigarette burning for so long? He was halfway across the square before he had the answer—the toupee.

Just as he passed the statue of George Washington, he noticed a small group of people up ahead, gathered around one of the long green benches to his right. Joe, supposing that someone on the park bench must be handing out slices of the latest grim confection from the battlefields and capitals of Europe, plucked a cashew from the bag, tossed it into the air, threw back his head and caught the nut, and kept on walking. As he passed the little knot of murmuring people, however, he saw that they all seemed to be looking not at the bench but at the tall slim maple rising up just behind it, in a lacy iron cage. Some of the people, he saw, were smiling. An older woman in a checked wool coat took a dancing little backward step away, hand pressed to her chest, laughing in embarrassment at her alarm. There must, Joe thought, be some kind of animal on the tree, a mouse or a monkey or a monitor lizard escaped from the Central Park Zoo. He went over to the bench and, when no one would make room for him, pushed up on the tips of his toes to see.

A surprising fact about the magician Bernard Kornblum, Joe remembered, was that he believed in magic. Not in the so-called magic of candles, pentagrams, and bat wings. Not in the kitchen enchantments of Slavic grandmothers with their herbiaries and parings from the little toe of a blind virgin tied up in a goatskin bag. Not in astrology, theosophy, chiromancy, dowsing rods, séances, weeping statues, werewolves, wonders, or miracles. All these Kornblum had regarded as fakery far different—far more destructive—than the brand of illusion he practiced, whose success, after all, increased in direct proportion to his audiences' constant, keen awareness that, in spite of all the vigilance they could bring to bear, they were being deceived. What bewitched Bernard Kornblum, on the contrary, was the impersonal magic of life, when he read in a magazine about a fish that could disguise itself as any one of seven different varieties of sea bottom, or when he learned from a newsreel that scientists had discovered a dying star that emitted radiation on a wavelength whose value in megacycles approximated π. In the realm of human affairs, this type of enchantment was often, though not always, a sadder business—sometimes beautiful, sometimes cruel. Here its stock-in-trade was ironies, coincidences, and the only true portents: those that revealed themselves, unmistakable and impossible to ignore, in retrospect.

There was, on the slender bole of the youthful maple tree in its cage on the west side of Union Square, an enormous moth. It rested, papillating its wings with a certain languor like a lady fanning herself, iridescent green with a yellowish undershimmer, as big as that languid lady's silk clutch. Its wings lay spread flat and when, every so often, they pulsed, the woman in the checked coat would squeal, to the amusement of the others gathered around, and jump back.

"What is this moth?" Joe asked the man beside him.

"Guy here says it's called a luna." The man nodded toward a stout, bankerish-looking fellow in a tyrolean hat with a moth-green feather, standing nearer to the tree and the moth than any of them.

"That's right," the portly man said in an oddly wistful voice. "A luna moth. We used to see them from time to time when I was a kid. In Mount Morris Park." He reached out his pudgy hand, in its yellow pigskin glove, toward the beating blue heart of his childhood memory.

"Rosa," Joe said, under his breath. Then, like an ambiguous trope of hopefulness, the luna moth took wing with an audible rustle, tumbled upward into the open sky, and staggered off in the general direction of the Flatiron Building.

SO MUCH HAS BEEN WRITTEN and sung about the bright lights and ballrooms of Empire City—that dazzling town!—about her nightclubs and jazz joints, her avenues of neon and chrome, and her swank hotels, their rooftop tea gardens strung in the summertime with paper lanterns. On this steely autumn afternoon, however, our destination is a place a long way from the horns and the hoohah. Tonight we are going down, under the ground, to a room that lies far beneath the high heels and the jackhammers, lower than the rats and the legendary alligators, lower even than the bones of Algonquins and dire wolves—to Office 99, a small, neat cubicle, airless and white, at the end of a corridor in the third subbasement of the Empire City Public Library. Here, at a desk that lies deeper in the earth than even the subway tracks, sits young Miss Judy Dark, Under-Assistant Cataloguer of Decommissioned Volumes. The nameplate on her desk so identifies her. She is a thin, pale thing, in a plain gray suit, and life is clearly passing her by. Twice a week a man with skin the color of boiled newspaper comes by her office to cart away the books that she has officially pronounced dead. Every ten minutes or so her walls are shaken by the thunder of the uptown local racing overhead.

On this particular autumn night, only the prospect of another solitary evening lies before her. She will fry her chop and read herself to sleep, no doubt with a tale of wizardry and romance. Then, in dreams that strike even her as trite, Miss Dark will go adventuring in chain mail and silk. Tomorrow morning she will wake up alone, and do it all again.

Poor Judy Dark! Poor little librarians of the world, those girls, secretly lovely, their looks marred forever by the cruelty of a pair of big black eyeglasses!

Judy packs her satchel and turns out her light, not forgetting to take her umbrella from its hook. She is a kind of human umbrella, folded, with her strap snapped tight. She walks down the long corridor and accidentally steps into a huge puddle; whenever it rains, Subbasement 3 begins to leak. Her feet are soaked to the ankles. Shoes squeaking, she gets into the elevator. Like a diver, she rises slowly to the surface of the city. Turning up her collar, she heads for the front door of the library. Tonight, as every night, she is the last to leave.

There is a policeman by the front doors. He is there to help guard the book.

"Good night, Miss," the policeman says as he unlocks the heavy bronze door for her. He is a big-shouldered, knuckle-chinned fellow with a twinkle in his eye because her shoes are squeaking.

"Good night." Miss Dark is mortified by the sound of her feet.

"The name's O'Hara." He has thick, shining hair, glossy as a squirt of black paint.

"Judy Dark."

"Well, Miss Dark, I have just one question."

"Yes, Officer O'Hara?"

"What's it take to get a smile out of you?"

A dozen smart retorts spring to her lips but she says nothing. She tries fervently to fix a frown on her lips but to her dismay cannot prevent herself from smiling. O'Hara takes advantage of her confusion to keep her there talking for a moment longer.

"Did you have a chance to see the book in all the confusion today, Miss Dark? Would you like me to show it to you?"

"I saw it," she says.

"And what did you think?"

"It's lovely."

"*Lovely,*" he tries. "Is it, now?"

She nods, not meeting his gaze, and steps out into the evening. It is raining, of course. The umbrella now does what its owner has never been able to manage, and Miss Dark goes home. She fries her veal chop and turns on the radio. She eats her dinner and wonders why she lied to the policeman. She has not, in fact, been to see the Book of Lo, though she is dying to see it. She meant to go on her lunch break, but the crowd around its case was too big. She wonders what the book *is,* if not lovely.

The Book of Lo was the sacred book of the ancient and mysterious Cimmerians. Last year—as was widely reported at the time—this legendary text, long since given up for lost, turned up in the back room of an old wine cellar downtown. It is the oldest book in the world, three hundred ancient pages, in a leather case encrusted with rubies, diamonds, and emeralds, devoted to the strange particulars of the worship of the great Cimmerian moth goddess, Lo. Today it went on display in the grand exhibition hall of the Public Library, behind bulletproof glass. Half the city, it seemed, came to get a look. Miss Dark, driven away by the pushing crowds, returned to Office 99 without having gotten so much as a glimpse of it and ate her lunch at her desk. Now, looking up from her empty plate, at the walls of her empty apartment, she feels a sharp inward bite of regret. She ought to have taken the policeman up on his offer. Maybe, she thinks, it isn't too late. She puts on her hat and coat and a pair of dry shoes and heads back out into the night. She will tell Officer O'Hara, when she gets there, that there is work she has forgotten to do.

But when she gets there, Officer O'Hara seems to have abandoned his post, and what's more, he has left the front door unlocked. Curious, and vaguely annoyed—suppose someone really should try to steal the Book of Lo?—she wanders into the exhibit hall. There, on the black marble expanse of the floor, men in black masks stand around the fallen body of Officer O'Hara. Miss Dark ducks behind a convenient arras. She thrills with horror as the men—an apelike trio in stevedore sweaters and newsdealer caps—use a diamond-tipped can opener to slice the lid from the glass case and so relieve Empire City of its book. Hastily they stuff the book into a sack. Now: what about O'Hara? One of the thieves knows for sure, he says, that the copper made him; he and O'Hara grew up on the same block, way back when. Maybe they had better just do the poor sap in.

This is too much for the Under-Assistant Cataloguer of Decommissioned Volumes. She rushes into the echoing hall with a vague plan to frighten or at the very least distract the men from their evil work. Or perhaps she can lead them away by drawing their attention to herself. Taking advantage of the momentary confusion created by her appearance and her cry of "NOOOOOO!" she snatches up the sack with the sacred Book of Lo inside and runs out of the gallery. The thieves, having recovered their presence of mind, give chase now, guns drawn, curses streaming from their lips in mad torrents of printer's marks and random punctuation.

Miss Dark, terrified but not so that it prevents her from entertaining the ironic thought that for the first time in her life she knows what it feels like to have men chasing after her, heads for the safest place she knows: her neat, square hole underground. She cannot afford to wait for the elevator. Running headlong down the fire stairs she is struck by the odd feeling that the Book of Lo has come to pulsing life in her arms; but no, that's just the reverberation of her own pounding heart.

They catch her in the long corridor of Subbasement 3. She turns, a gun glints, then sprouts a bright white flower. But the shot, in that dark, cramped corridor, goes wild. It ricochets, knitting a wild web of velocity trails across the corridor before settling, finally, into the meat of a conduit in the ceiling. The pipe snaps in half, and out of it tumbles a live power line, like a snake falling from a tree onto a piglet. It lands in the very puddle that earlier ruined Miss Dark's shoes. Now many watts of power course through her slender frame, and through the circuitry of gems and gold wire on the leather case of the Book of Lo. A flash turns everything white but the black roentgen skeleton of Miss Judy Dark, and she utters a somewhat unladylike cry of "YE-OOOW!"

"Nice shot," says one of the thieves. They lift the book from her slack grip and make off with it to the surface world, leaving Miss Judy Dark for dead.

Which she very well may be. She flies, hair streaming, upward through a spiral column of smoke and light. The first thing we notice about her may not be, surprisingly, that she appears to be flying in the nude, the zones of her modesty artfully veiled by the coils of the astral helix. No, what we notice first is that she appears to have grown an immense pair of swallowtailed moth's wings. They are a pale greenish-white and have a translucent quality; they might even, like Wonder Woman's airplane, be visibly invisible, at once ghostly and solid. All around her, outside the column spiraling infinitely upward, reality dissolves into dream-landscapes and wild geometric prodigies. Chessboards dissolve, parabolas bend themselves into asterisks, whorls, and pinwheels. Mysterious hieroglyphs stream past like sparks from a roman candle. Miss Dark, her great phantom wings steadily flapping, takes it all strangely in stride—for, dead or alive, there is no question that Judy Dark, that human umbrella, has, at long last, opened to the sky.

Finally, in the immeasurable and timeless distance, she makes out something that has the appearance of solidity, a smudge of stony gray, wavering. As she draws nearer, she glimpses a flash of silver, a ghostly stand of cypress, the plinth and columns of a temple, rough-hewn, pyramidal, at once Druidic and Babylonian, and withal vaguely reminiscent of the great institution in whose bowels she has for so long dreamed away her days. It looms ever larger, and then the spiral finally unravels around her and gives out, depositing her, clothed now only in the clasp of her wings, on the temple's threshold. The great doors, cast from solid silver and ornamented with crescent moons, creak as they slowly open inward to admit her. With a final glance back toward the shattered chrysalis of her old life, she steps through the portal and into a high chamber. Here, in a weird radiance cast by the tails of a thousand writhing glowworms, sits on a barbarous throne a raven-haired giantess with immense green wings, sensuously furred antennae, and a sharp expression. She is, quite obviously, the Cimmerian moth goddess, Lo. We know it before she even opens her rowanberry mouth.

"You?" the goddess says, her feelers wilting in evident dismay. "*You* are the one the book has chosen? You are to be the next Mistress of the Night?"

Miss Dark—wreathed discreetly now in curling tufts of dry-ice smoke—concedes that it seems unlikely. Only now we notice, perhaps for the first time, that our Judy is no longer wearing her glasses. Her unpinned hair strays around her face with Linda Darnell abandon. And all at once the idea of her being a Mistress of the Night—whatever that may mean—is somehow less difficult to swallow.

"Know that before my homeland, great Cimmeria, was plunged into eternal darkness," the goddess explains, "it was ruled by women." Ah, she reminisces, her face wistful, her eyes brimming, and that was a paradise! All were happy in the Queendom of Cimmeria, peaceful, contented—the men in particular. Then one shrivel-hearted malcontent, Nanok, schooled himself in the ways of bloodshed and black magic, and set himself upon an obsidian throne. He sent his armies of demons into battle against the peace-loving Cimmerians; the outcome was foreordained. Men took over the world, Lo was banished to the nether kingdoms, and the Queendom of Cimmeria was plunged into its legendary perpetual night. "And since Cimmeria fell into eternal darkness," Lo says, "men have been making a hash of things. War, famine, slavery. Things got so bad after a while that I felt obliged to send help. A champion, out of the land of darkness, to fly in darkness but always to seek the light. A *woman warrior* with power enough to help right the world's many wrongs."

Unfortunately, the goddess continues, her power is not what it once was. She is able to underwrite, as it were, only one Mistress of the Night at a time. The previous incarnation having at last, after a thousand years, grown too old, the moth goddess has sent forth her sacred book to find a new girl worthy of donning the witchy green wings of the great luna moth.

"I confess I did have someone a little more . . . sturdy . . . in mind," Lo says. "But I suppose that you will have to do. Go now." She waves her ancient slender hand and draws the outline of a moon in the air between herself and Judy. "Return to the mortal realm, and haunt the night in which evil so often goes prowling. You now possess all the mystic power of ancient Cimmeria."

"If you say so," Judy says. "But, well . . ."

"Yes? What is it?"

"I really think I'll need some *clothes*."

The goddess, a serious old girl, cannot suppress the faint pale crescent of a smile. "You will find, Judy Dark, that you have only to imagine something to make it so."

"Gee whiz!"

"Take care—there is no force more powerful than that of an unbridled imagination."

"Yes. I mean, yes, mistress."

"Usually the girls come up with something involving boots. I don't know why." She shrugs, then outspreads the mighty span of her wings. "Now go, and remember, if ever you should need me, you have only to come to me in your dreams."

Worlds and aeons hence, in a dilapidated old tenement along the river, two of the thieves set to work with chisel and tongs on the gems in the ancient book's case. In a chair, in a corner, bound and gagged, Officer O'Hara sits slumped. It is still raining, there is a chill in the air, and the third thief is trying to start a fire in an old black potbellied stove.

"Here," says the first thief as he reaches to tear a sheaf of pages from the Book of Lo. "I'll bet this old thing'll burn real nice."

There is a silken rustle, like a billowing ball gown or an immense, soft pair of wings. They look up and see a giant shadow flit in through the window.

"It's a bat!" says a thief.

"It's a bird!" says another.

"It's a *lady*!" says the third, no fool, starting to run for the door.

The lady turns, eyes flashing. The garment she has imagined for herself is iridescent green, part Merry Widow, part Norman Bel Geddes, tricked out with fins and vanes and laced, with evident complexity, up the front. Her lower parts, in their tight green underpants, are barely covered by the merest suggestion of a skirt, her nine miles of leg are enmeshed in black fishnet, and the heels on her ankle boots are stingingly high. She wears a purple cowl, topped with a pair of lushly furred antennae, that covers her eyes and nose but leaves her black curls free to tumble around her bare shoulders. And from her back bloom, no longer ghostly but green as leaves, a pair of great swallowtailed moth's wings, each jeweled with a staring blind eye.

"That's right, little mouse," she cries to the man headed for the door. "Run!"

She extends her arm. Bright green light ripples from her outspread fingers and enmeshes the thief before he can reach the door. There is an unpleasant crackling sound, a snapping of twigs and pinecones, as an entire skeleton of human bones is compressed rapidly into a very small skin; then silence; then a tiny thin squeak.

"Holy cats!" the moth woman says.

"She turned Louie into a mouse!" cries the first thief. Now he is running, too.

"Freeze!" Green light leaps again, and with a crunching even more sickening than before the atoms and fibers of the thief's body are rearranged and simplified into cold blue crystals of ice. He stands gleaming like a man of diamond. The corners of his fedora glint. "Oops," the moth woman mumbles. "Goodness me!"

"What kind of a dolly are you?" the remaining thief demands. "What are you trying to do to us?"

"I just want to give you a hot time, big boy," she says, and at once the man bursts into flames of such intensity that they melt his erstwhile confederate to a shallow puddle on the floor. The mouse, its tail singed and smoking, dives for the safety of the nearest floorboard.

"Guess I still have a little bit to learn," muses the newly minted Mistress of the Night. She unties the policeman, who has begun, in all the excitement, to revive. He opens his eyes in time to see a scantily clad woman with enormous green wings jump into the sky. For a while to come he will tell himself, and half believe, that what he saw was the last apparition of a fading dream. It is not until he gets home, and goes to examine his battered handsome mug in the mirror, that he finds, on his cheek, the red butterfly imprint of her lips.

DEASEY, as they had known he would, objected to the latest bit of degeneracy from Kavalier & Clay.

"I can't allow this to happen to my country," he said. "Things are bad enough already."

Sammy and Joe were not caught unprepared. "She's not showing anything any kid can't see at Jones Beach" was the line that they had decided on. Sammy gave it.

Joe said, "Just like at Jones Beach." He had never been to Jones Beach.

The morning was gloomy, and as usual in cool weather, Deasey lay spread out on the floor like an old bearskin. Now he pulled himself carefully up to a sitting position, his considerable bulk shifting audibly on his arthritic joints.

"Let me have another look," he said.

Sammy handed him the sheet of Bristol board with the character design for Luna Moth, "the first sex object," in Jules Feiffer's memorable phrase, "created expressly for consumption by little boys." It was a pinup. A woman with the legs of Dolores Del Rio, black witchy hair, and breasts each the size of her head. Her face was long, her chin pointed, and her mouth a bright red hyphen, downturned at one corner in a saucy little smirk. The pair of furry antennae hung at playful angles, as if tasting the viewer's desire.

The golden toothpick waggled up and down. "Your usual wasted effort, Mr. Kavalier, my condolences."

"Thank you."

"That means you think it could be a hit," said Sammy.

"It's very difficult to fail at pornography," said Deasey. He gazed out beyond the river at the sere brown cliffs of New Jersey and allowed himself to recall a winter afternoon twelve years before, on a cool, sunny terrace overlooking Puerto Concepción and the Sea of Cortez, when he had sat down at the keys of his portable Royal and begun work on a great and tragic novel, about the love between two brothers and a woman who died. Although the novel was long since abandoned, the typewriter was on his desk even now, page 232 of *Death Wears a Black Sarong* rolled around its platen. Surely, Deasey thought, that *fonda,* that terrace, that heartbreaking sky, that novel—they were all still there, waiting for him. He had only to make his way back.

"Mr. Deasey?" said Joe.

Deasey left off looking out at the expanse of sandstone sky and rusty palisade and went over to his desk. He picked up the phone.

"Fuck it," he said. "We'll leave it up to Anapol. I have a feeling they may be looking for a new kind of character, anyway."

"Why's that?" Sammy said.

Deasey looked at Sammy and then at Joe. There was something he wanted to tell them. "Why is what?"

"Why might Shelly and Jack be looking for a new kind of character?"

"I never said that. Let's call him. Get me Mr. Anapol," he said into the phone.

"What about Ashkenazy?" said Joe. "What will he say?"

Deasey said, "Do you seriously have any doubts?"

BEAUTEEFUL." Ashkenazy sighed. "Look at those . . . those . . ."

"They're called knockers," said Anapol.

"*Look at them!* Which one of you thought this up?" said Ashkenazy. He looked at Joe with one eye while he kept the other on Luna Moth. Affluence had brought with it an entire panoply of new suits, striped and checked and boldly herringboned, madly checkered three-piece numbers, each of them the color of a different variety of squash, from butternut to Italian green. The fabrics were rich woolens and cashmeres, the cuts jazzy and loose, so that he no longer looked like a racetrack tout, with his chewed cigar end and his thumbs in his waistcoat. Now he looked like a big-time gangster with a fix in on the third at Belmont. "I bet it was you, Kavalier."

Joe looked at Sammy. "We did it together," he said. "Sammy and I. Mostly Sammy. I just said something about a moth."

"Aw, now don't be modest, Joe," Sammy said, stepping over to pat Joe on the shoulder. "He pretty much slapped the whole thing together himself."

The practice of magic, which Joe had resumed in front of the mirror in Jerry Glovsky's bedroom immediately after meeting with Hermann Hoffman, also seemed to have played a role in her parturition. It was true, however, that Sammy, for some time, had been digging around for a female superbeing. The addition of sex to the costumed-hero concept was a natural and, apart from a few minor efforts at other companies— the Sorceress of Zoom, the Woman in Red—yet to be attempted. Sammy had been toying with ideas for a cat-woman, a bird-woman, a mythological Amazon (all of them soon to be tried elsewhere), and a lady boxer named Kid Vixen when Joe had proposed his secret tribute to the girl from Greenwich Village. The idea of a moth-woman was also, in its way, a natural. National had another huge hit on its hands with Batman in *Detective Comics,* and the appeal of a nocturnal character, one who derived her power from the light of the moon, was evident.

"I don't know," said Shelly Anapol. "It makes me a little nervous." He took from his partner, and held with the tips of his fingers, the painting of Luna Moth, which Joe had invested with all the hopefulness and desire that Rosa, admittedly in person a somewhat less buxom creature, had stirred in him—he had worked most of the time with an erection. Anapol pushed aside a letter that lay open on his desk blotter and dropped the painting there, as if it were extremely hot or had been dipped in carbolic. "Those are very large breasts, boys."

"We know it, Mr. Anapol," said Sammy.

"But a moth, I don't know, it's not a popular insect. Why can't she be a butterfly? There must be some good names there. Red, uh, what? Red Dot . . . Bluewing . . . Pearly . . . I don't know."

"She can't be a *butterfly,*" said Sammy. "She's the Mistress of the *Night.*"

"That's another thing: we can't say 'mistress.' Already I'm getting fifty letters a week from priests and ministers. A rabbi from Schenectady. Luna Moth. Luna Moth." The look of incipient nausea had come into his eyes and slack jaw. They were going to make themselves a pile with this.

"George, you think this is a good idea?"

"Oh, it's drivel, Mr. Anapol," Deasey said brightly. "Extremely pure."

Anapol nodded. "You haven't been wrong yet," he said. He picked up the letter that he had pushed aside, scanned it quickly, then put it back down. "Jack?"

"They got nothing like it," Ashkenazy said.

Anapol turned to Sammy. "It's settled, then. Call Pantaleone, the Glovskys, whoever you need to fill in the rest of the book. What the hell, make 'em all dollies. Maybe we could call it *All Doll.* Huh? Huh? *All Doll.* That's new. Is that new?"

"I never heard of anything like it."

"Let *them* infringe on us for a change. Yeah, good, get the kids in here, George, and get them started on this. I want something by Monday."

"Here we go again," said Sammy. "There's just one thing, Mr. Anapol."

Ashkenazy and Anapol looked at him. You could see they knew what was coming. Sammy glanced at Deasey, remembering the speech the editor had made on Friday night, hoping to find some encouragement. Deasey was watching intently, his face expressionless but pale, his forehead beaded with perspiration.

"Uh-oh," Anapol said. "Here it comes."

"We want in on the Escapist radio program, that's first."

"That's *first?*"

"Second is, you agree that this character, Luna Moth, is half ours. Fifty percent to Empire Comics, fifty percent to Kavalier & Clay. We get half of the merchandising, half the radio program if there is one. Half of everything. Otherwise we take her, and our services, elsewhere."

Anapol half turned his head toward his partner. "You were right," he said.

"And we want raises, too," Sammy said, with another glance at Deasey, deciding, now that the subject seemed to be open for discussion, to press it as far as he could.

"Another two hundred dollars a week," Joe said. The *Ark of Miriam* was scheduled to sail in the early spring of next year. At that rate, if he put away an additional two hundred a week, he would be able to underwrite four, five, perhaps half a dozen passages more than he had promised.

"*Two hundred dollars a week!*" Anapol shouted.

Deasey chuckled and shook his head. He seemed genuinely tickled.

"And, uh, yeah, the same for Mr. Deasey, here, too," said Sammy. "He's going to have a lot more to do."

"You can't *negotiate* for me, Mr. Clay," Deasey said dryly. "I'm management."

"Oh."

"But I do thank you."

All at once Anapol looked very tired. What with phony bombs and millionaires and threatening letters from famous attorneys hand-delivered by messengers, he had not slept well since Friday. Last night he had tossed and turned for hours, while beside him Mrs. Anapol growled at him to lie still.

"Shark!" she had called him. "Shark, be still." She called him "shark" because she had read in Frank Buck's column that this animal literally could not stop moving or it would die. "What's the matter with you, my God, it's like trying to sleep with a cement mixer in the bed."

I almost got blown up! he wanted to tell her for the one hundredth time. He had decided to say nothing about the cheap-novelty bomb in the Empire offices, as he had said nothing about the threatening letters that had been trickling in steadily ever since Kavalier & Clay had declared unilateral war on the Axis.

"I'm going to lose my shirt," he had said instead.

"So you'll lose your shirt," his wife said.

"It's a goddamn very nice shirt I'm going to lose. Do you know how much money there is in radio? With the pins, the pencils, the cereal boxes. We're not just looking at novelties, you know. This is Escapist pajamas. Bath towels. Board games. Soft drinks."

"They won't take it away."

"They're going to try."

"So let them try. In the meantime, you get on the radio, and I have a chance to meet an important and cultivated man like James Love. I saw him in the newsreel once. He looks just like John Barrymore."

"He does look like John Barrymore."

"So what's the matter with you? Why can't you ever *enjoy* anything you get?"

Anapol shifted a little in bed and produced the latest entry in an encyclopedic display of groaning. As was the case every night since Empire had made the move to the Empire State Building, his knees ached, his back was sore, and there was a sharp crick in the side of his neck. His beautiful black-marble office was so spacious and high-ceilinged that it made him uncomfortable. He couldn't get used to having so much room. As a result, he had a tendency to sit hunched all day, balled up in his chair, as if to simulate the paradoxically comforting effects of more cramped and uncomfortable quarters. It gave him a pain.

"Sammy Klayman," she said finally.

"Sammy," he agreed.

"So then don't cut him out."

"I have to cut him out."

"And why is that."

"Because cutting him in would set what your brother calls 'a dangerous president.' "

"Because."

" 'Because.' Because those two signed a contract. A perfectly legal, standard industry contract. They signed all their rights to the character away, now and forever. They're just not entitled."

"So it would be against the law, you're saying," his wife said with her usual light ironic touch, "for you to give them a piece of the radio money."

A fly came into the room. Anapol, wearing green silk pajamas with black piping, got out of bed. He turned on the bedside light and pulled on his dressing jacket. He took a copy of *Modern Screen* with Dolores Del Rio's picture on the cover, rolled it up, and greased the fly against the window. He cleaned up the mess, took off his dressing jacket, climbed back into bed, and turned out the light.

"No," he said, "it would not be against the goddamn law."

"Good," Mrs. Anapol had said. "I don't want you breaking any laws. A jury hears that you're in the comic book business, they'll lock you away in Sing Sing just like that." Then she rolled over and settled in for the night. Anapol had groaned and flopped and drunk three glasses of Bromo-Seltzer, until at last he hit on the general outlines of a plan that eased the pangs of a modest but genuine conscience and allayed his anxieties about the mounting ire that Kavalier & Clay's war appeared to be drawing down on Empire Comics. He had not had time to run it past his brother-in-law, but he knew that Jack would go along.

"So," he said now. "You can have in on the radio show. Assuming there is a radio show. We'll give you credit, all right, something like, what, 'Oneonta Woolens, et cetera, presents *The Adventures of the Escapist,* based on the character by Joe Kavalier and Sam Clay appearing every month in the pages of et cetera.' Plus, for every episode that airs, let's say you two receive a payment. A royalty. Call it fifty dollars per show."

"Two hundred," Sammy said.

"One."

"One fifty."

"*One.* Come on, that's three hundred a week. You're looking at possibly fifteen grand a year to split between you."

Sammy looked at Joe, who nodded. "Okay."

"Smart boy. All right, as for Miss Moth here. Fifty percent is out of the question. You have no right to any part of her. You boys came up with her as employees of Empire Comics, on our payroll. She's ours. We have the law on our side here, I know, because I have spoken to my attorney, Sid Foehn of Harmattan, Foehn & Buran, about this very subject in the past. The way he explained it to me, it's just like they do at the Bell Laboratories. Any invention a guy comes up with there, no matter who thought it up or how long they worked on it, even if they did it all by themselves, it doesn't matter, as long as they were employed there, it belongs to the laboratory."

"Don't cheat us, Mr. Anapol," Joe put in abruptly. Everyone looked shocked. Joe had misjudged the force of the word "cheat" in English. He thought it merely meant to treat someone unfairly, without any necessary implication of evil intent.

"I would never *cheat* you boys," said Anapol, looking profoundly hurt. He took out his handkerchief and blew his nose. "Excuse me. Coming down with a cold. Let me finish, all right? Fifty percent is, like I say, we'd be crazy and foolish and stupid to go along with that, and you can't threaten me with taking this dolly to somebody else because, like I say, you made her up on my payroll and she's mine. Talk to a lawyer of your own if you want. But, look, let's avoid confrontation, why don't we? In recognition of the fine track record you two have so far, coming up with this stuff, and just to show you boys, you know, that we appreciate what you've done for us, we'd be willing to cut you in on this Moth deal to the tune of what—"

He looked at Ashkenazy, who shrugged elaborately.

"Four?" he croaked.

"Call it five," Anapol said. "Five percent."

"Five percent!" Sammy said, looking as though Anapol's meaty hand had slapped him.

"Five percent!" said Joe.

"To split between you."

"What!" Sammy leapt from his chair.

"Sammy." Joe had never seen his cousin so red in the face. He tried to remember if he had ever seen him lose his temper at all. "Sammy, five percent, even so, this could be talking about the hundreds of thousands of dollars." How many ships could be fitted out, for that, and filled with the lost children of the world? With enough money, it might not matter if the doors of all the world's nations were closed—a very rich man could afford to buy some island somewhere, empty and temperate, and build the damned children a country of their own. "Maybe the millions someday."

"But five percent, Joe. Five percent of something we created one hundred percent!"

"And owe to Jack and me one hundred percent," said Anapol. "You know, it wasn't so long ago a hundred dollars sounded like a lot of money to you boys, as I recall."

"Sure, sure," said Joe. "Okay, look, Mr. Anapol, I'm sorry for what I said about cheating. I think you are being very much square."

"Thank you," Anapol said.

"Sammy?"

Sammy sighed. "Okay. I'm in."

"Hold on a minute," Anapol said. "I'm not done. You get your radio royalty. And the credit I mentioned. And the raises. Hell, we'll raise George's pay, too, and happy to do it." Deasey tipped an imaginary hat to Anapol. "And cut you two in for five percent of the Moth character. There's just one condition."

"What is it?" Sammy asked warily.

"We can't have any more nonsense around here like we had on Friday. I've always thought you were taking this Nazi business too far, but we were making money and I didn't think I could really complain. But now we're putting a stop to it. Right, Jack?"

"Lay off the Nazis for a while, boys," Ashkenazy said. "Let Marty Goodman get the bomb threats." This was the publisher of Timely Periodicals, home of the Human Torch and the Submariner, both of whom were giving the Empire heroes a run for the money now in the anti-fascist sweepstakes. "All right?"

"What does this mean, 'lay off'?" Joe said. "You mean no fighting the Nazis at all?"

"Not a one."

Now it was Joe's turn to rise from his chair. "Mr. Anapol—"

"No, now listen, you two know I bear no goodwill toward Hitler, and I'm sure eventually we're going to have to deal with him, et cetera. But bomb threats? Crazy maniacs that live right here in New York writing me letters saying they're going to stave in my big fat Jewish head? That I don't need."

"Mr. Anapol—" Joe felt the ground falling away under his feet.

"We've got plenty of problems right here at home, and I don't mean spies and saboteurs. Gangsters, crooked cops. I don't know. Jack?"

"Rats," said Ashkenazy. "Bugs."

"Let the Escapist and the rest of 'em take care of that sort of thing for a while."

"Boss—" Sammy said, seeing the blood drain from Joe's face.

"And what's more, I don't care what James Love feels personally, I know the Oneonta Woolens Company, the board of that company is a bunch of conservative, rock-rib Yankee gentlemen, and they are god-damned well not going to want to sponsor anything that's going to get them bombed, not to mention Mutual or NBC or whoever we end up taking this to."

"No one is going to get bombed!" Joe said.

"You were right once, young man," Anapol said. "That may be all the being right you get."

Sammy folded his thick arms across his broad chest, elbows out. "And so what if we don't agree to the condition?"

"Then you don't get any five percent of Luna Moth. You don't get the raise. You don't get a piece of the radio money."

"But we could still keep on doing our stuff. Joe and I could keep fight-ing those Nazis."

"Certainly," said Anapol. "I'm sure Marty Goodman would be more than happy to hire you two to lob grenades at Hermann Göring. But you'd be finished here."

"Boss," said Sammy, "don't do this."

Anapol shrugged. "Not up to me. It's up to you. You have an hour," he said. "I want to get this all squared away before we meet with the radio people, which we are doing over lunch today."

"I don't need an hour," Joe said. "The answer is no. Forget it. You are cowards, and you are weak, and no."

"Joe?" Sammy said, calming himself now, trying to take everything in. "You're sure?"

Joe nodded.

"That's it, then," said Sammy. He put his hand on the small of Joe's back, and they started out of the office.

"Mr. Kavalier," George Deasey said now, pulling himself up out of his chair. "Mr. Clay. A word. Excuse us, gentlemen?"

"Please, George," Anapol said, handing the editor the painting of Luna Moth. "Talk some sense into them."

Sammy and Joe followed Deasey out of Anapol's office and into the workroom.

"Gentlemen," Deasey said. "I apologize for this, but I feel another little speech coming on."

"There's no point," Sammy said.

"This one is aimed more at Mr. K., here, I think."

Joe lit a cigarette, blew out a long stream of smoke, looked away. He didn't want to hear it. He knew that he was being unreasonable. But for a year now, unreason—the steadfast and all-consuming persecution of a ridiculous, make-believe war against enemies he could not defeat, by a means that could never succeed—had offered the only possible salvation of his sanity. Let people be reasonable whose families were not held prisoner.

"There is only one sure means in life," Deasey said, "of ensuring that you are not ground into paste by disappointment, futility, and disillusion. And that is always to ensure, to the utmost of your ability, that you are doing it solely for the money."

Joe didn't say anything. Sammy laughed nervously. He was prepared to back Joe up, of course, but he wanted to make sure, insofar as you could ever be sure, that it was really the right thing to do. He was hungry to follow Deasey's advice—to follow any fatherly guidance that came his way—but at the same time, he hated the thought of conceding so decisively to the man's cynical view of everything.

"Because, Mr. K., when I look at the way you have our various costumed friends punching the lights out of Herr Hitler and his associates month after month, tying their artillery into pretzels and so forth, I sometimes get the feeling, well, that you may have, let's say, other ambitions for your work here."

"Of course I do," said Joe. "You know that."

"It makes me very sorry to hear," Deasey said. "This kind of work is a graveyard of every kind of ambition, Kavalier. Take my word for it. Whatever you may hope to accomplish, whether from the standpoint of art or out of . . . other considerations, you will fail. I have very little faith in the power of art, but I remember the flavor of that faith, if you will, from when I was your age; the taste of it on the back of my tongue. Out of respect for you and the graceful idiot I once was, I concede the point. But this." He nodded toward the drawing of Luna Moth, then expanded the gesture with a weary spiral of his hand to take in the offices of Empire Comics. "Powerless," he said. "Useless."

"I . . . I do not believe that," Joe said, feeling himself weaken as his own worst fears were given voice.

"Joe," Sammy said. "Think of what you could do with all the money they're talking about. Think of how many kids you could afford to bring over here. That's something *real*, Joe. Not just a comic book war. Not just getting a fat lip from some kraut in the IRT."

And that was the problem, Joe thought. Giving in to Anapol and Ashkenazy would mean admitting that everything he had done until now had been, in Deasey's phrase, powerless and useless. A waste of precious time. He wondered if it could possibly be simple vanity that made him want to refuse the offer. Then the image of Rosa came into his mind, sitting on her disordered bed, head cocked to one side, eyes wide, listening and nodding as he told her about his work. No, he thought. Regardless of what Deasey says, I believe in the power of my imagination. I believe—somehow, when saying this to the image of Rosa, it did not sound trite or overblown—in the power of my art.

"Yes, god damn it, I want the money," Joe said. "But I can't stop fighting now."

"Okay," Sammy said. He sighed and looked around the workroom with a slump in his shoulders and a valedictory expression on his face.

It was the end of the dream that had flickered into life a year ago, in the darkness of his bedroom in Brooklyn, with the scraping of a match and the sharing of a hand-rolled cigarette. "That's what we'll tell them, then." He started to walk back into Anapol's office.

Deasey reached out and took hold of his shoulder. "Just a minute, Clay," he said.

Sammy turned back. He had never seen the editor look so uncertain before.

"Oh, Jesus," Deasey said. "What am I doing?"

"What are you doing?" said Joe.

The editor reached into the breast pocket of his tweed jacket and took out a folded sheet of paper. "This was in my in box this morning."

"What is it?" Sammy said. "Who's it from?"

"Just read it," Deasey said.

It was a photostatted copy of a letter from the firm of Phillips, Nizer, Benjamin & Krim.

DEAR MESSRS. ASHKENAZY AND ANAPOL:

This letter is being written to you on behalf of National Periodical Publications, Inc. ("National"). National is the exclusive owner of all copyright, trademark, and other intellectual property rights in and to the comic book magazines "Action Comics" and "Superman" and the character of "Superman" featured therein. National has recently learned of your magazine, "Radio Comics," featuring the fictional character "The Escapist." This character represents a blatant attempt to copy the protected work of our client, namely the various series that feature the adventures of the fictional character known as "Superman," which our client has been publishing since June of 1938. As such, your character constitutes a blatant infringement of our client's copyrights, trademarks, and common-law rights. We hereby demand that you immediately cease and desist from any further publication of your comic book magazine "Radio," and that all existing copies of these comic books be destroyed with a letter verifying destruction signed by an officer of your corporation.

If you fail to cease and desist from such publication, or fail to submit such a verification letter within five days of this letter, National Periodical Publications, Inc., shall forthwith pursue all of its legal and equitable remedies, including seeking to enjoin your further publication of "Radio Comics." This letter is written without waiver of any of our client's rights and remedies, at law and in equity, all of which are hereby expressly reserved.

"But he's nothing *like* Superman," Sammy said when he had finished. Deasey gave him a baleful look, and Sammy realized he was missing the point. He tried to work his way through to what the point might be. There was clearly something about this letter that Deasey felt would be helpful to them, though he was unwilling to go so far as to tell them what it was. "But that doesn't matter, does it?"

"They've already beaten Victor Fox and Centaur on this," Deasey said. "They're going after Fawcett, too."

"I heard about this thing," Joe said. "They made Will Eisner go in there, Sammy, and he had to tell them that Victor Fox told him, 'Make me a Superman.' "

"Yeah, well, that's what Shelly said to me, too, remember? He said—oh. Oh."

"It's very likely," Deasey said steadily and slowly, as if speaking to an idiot, "that you will be deposed as a witness. I imagine your testimony could be damaging."

Sammy slapped Deasey's arm with the letter.

"Yeah," he said. "Yeah, hey, thanks, Mr. Deasey."

"What are you going to say?" Joe asked Sammy, as his cousin stared at the door to Anapol's office.

Sammy drew himself up and ran a hand across the top of his head.

"I guess I'm going to go in there and offer to perjure myself," he said.

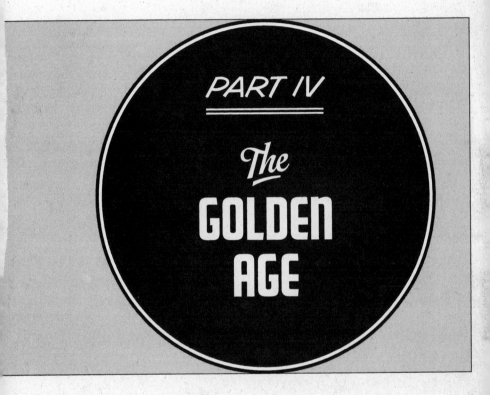

PART IV

The
GOLDEN
AGE

IN 1941, ITS BEST YEAR EVER, the partnership of Kavalier & Clay earned $59,832.27. Total revenues generated that year for Empire Comics, Inc.—from sales of all comic books featuring characters created either in whole or in part by Kavalier & Clay, sales of two hundred thousand copies apiece for each of two Whitman's Big Little Books featuring the Escapist, sales of Keys of Freedom, of key rings, pocket flashlights, coin banks, board games, rubber figurines, windup toys, and diverse other items of Escapism, as well as the proceeds from the licensing of the Escapist's dauntless puss to Chaffee Cereals for their Frosted Chaff-Os, and from the Escapist radio program that began broadcasting on NBC in April—though harder to calculate, came to something in the neighborhood of $12 to $15 million. Out of his twenty-nine thousand and change, Sammy gave a quarter to the government, then half of what remained to his mother to spend on herself and his grandmother.

On the leftovers, he lived like a king. He ate lox at breakfast every morning for seven weeks. He went to baseball games at Ebbets Field and sat in a box. He might spend as much as two dollars on dinner, and once, on a day when his legs were feeling tired, he rode seventeen blocks in a taxi. He had an entire week's worth of big, visible suits, five gray skyscrapers of pinstripe and worsted, made for himself at twenty-five dollars a pop. And he bought himself a Capehart Panamuse phonograph. It cost $645.00, nearly half as much as a new Cadillac Sixty-one. It was finished in a ridiculously beautiful Hepplewhite style, maple and birch inlaid with ash, and in the cousins' otherwise modern, rather spartan apartment—soon after taking up with Joe, Rosa had begun to lobby him to move out of the Chelsea Rathole—it stood out disturbingly.

It demanded that you play music on it and then maintain the respectful silence of a sinner being sermonized. Sammy loved it as he had never loved anything in his life. The sad flutter of Benny Goodman's clarinet came so poignantly through its deluxe "panamusical" loudspeakers that it could make Sammy cry. The Panamuse was fully automatic; it could store twenty records and play them, in any order, on both sides. The marvelous operations of the record-changing mechanism, in the manner of the time, were on proud display inside the cabinet, and new guests to the apartment, like visitors to the U.S. Mint, were always given a look at the works. Sammy was smitten for weeks, and yet every time he looked at the phonograph, he was racked with guilt and even horror over the cost. His mother would die without ever having learned of its existence.

The funny thing was that, after you threw in the large but still piddling sum Sammy spent every month on books, magazines, records, cigarettes, and amusements, and his half of the $110 monthly rent, there was still more money left over than Sammy knew what to do with. It piled up in his bank account, making him nervous.

"You should get married," Rosa liked to tell him.

Her name was not on the lease, but Rosa had become the apartment's third occupant, and in a very real sense its animating spirit. She had helped them find it (it was a new building on Fifth Avenue, just north of Washington Square), to furnish it, and, when she realized that she would never otherwise be able to share a bathroom with Sammy, to obtain the weekly services of a cleaning woman. At first she would just drop by once or twice a week, after work. She had quit her job at *Life* for a job retouching, in lurid hues, color pictures of prune-and-noodle casseroles, velvet crumb cakes, and bacon canapés for a publisher of cheap cookbooks that were given away as premiums in five-and-dimes. It was tedious work, and when things got really bad, Rosa liked to indulge minute Surrealist impulses. With an airbrush she would equip a pineapple in the background with a slick black tentacle, or conceal a tiny polar explorer in the frigid peaks of a meringue desert. The publisher's offices were on East Fifteenth, ten minutes from the apartment. Rosa would often come in at five with a bag full of unlikely roots and leaves and cook strange recipes that her father had acquired a taste for in his travels: *tagine, mole,* something green and slippery that she called *sleek.* In general these dishes tasted very good; and their exotic dress served to conceal fairly well, Sammy thought, her fairly retrograde approach to winning Joe's heart via the kitchen. She herself never took more than a bite of any of it.

"There's a girl at work," Rosa said at breakfast one morning, setting in front of Sammy a plate of eggs scrambled with Portuguese sausage. She was a frequent guest at breakfast, too, if "guest" was the proper term to apply to someone who shopped for the meal, prepared it, served it to you, and cleaned up when you were through. Their across-the-hall neighbors were visibly outraged by this waywardness, and the doorman's eyes would twinkle crudely as he held the door for her in the mornings. "Barbara Drazin. She's a dish. And she's looking. You should let me introduce you."

"College girl?"

"City."

"No thanks."

When Sammy looked up from the platter of pastry, which Rosa had as usual arranged with such photogenic artfulness that he was loath to disturb the cheese danish he had his eye on, he caught her giving Joe a look. It was a look he had seen them exchange before, whenever the subject of Sammy's love life came up, as when Rosa was around it tended rather too often to do.

"What?" he said.

"Nothing."

She spread her napkin in her lap, pointedly somehow, and Joe went on tinkering with some kind of spring-loaded card-passing contraption that was part of his act; he had another of his magic gigs tomorrow night, a bar mitzvah at the Pierre. Sammy snatched the cheese danish, collapsing Rosa's giveaway-cookbook pyramid.

"It's just," she continued, never requiring an actual rejoinder to sustain a conversation, "you always have an excuse."

"It's not an excuse," Sammy said. "It's a disqualification."

"And why are college girls disqualified? I forget."

"Because they make me feel dumb."

"But you aren't dumb. You are extremely well read, fairly well spoken, and you make your living by the pen or, in your case, the typewriter."

"I know this. It's not a rational feeling. And I can't stand stupid women. It's just, I guess I feel bad that I don't have a college education myself. And I'm embarrassed when they start asking me about what I do, and I have to tell them I write comic books, and then it's either 'Gee, aren't they awfully, well, *trashy*,' or else it's that patronizing '*Comic books!* I *adore* comic books!'—which is even worse."

"Barbara Drazin would never make you feel bad about what you do," Rosa said. "Besides, I told her you also wrote three novels."

"Oh my *God*," Sammy said.

"I'm sorry."

"Please, Rosa, how many times do I gotta ask you not to tell anybody that anymore, okay?"

"I'm *so* sorry. It's just that I—"

"For God's sake, those were *pulps*, I got paid by the *yard*. Why do you think they invented the *pseudonym*?"

"All right," said Rosa, "all right. I just think you ought to *meet* her."

"Thanks, but no thanks. I got too much work to do anyway."

"He's writing a novel," Joe said, peeling a Chiquita. He seemed to take a good deal of pleasure in the exchanges between his girlfriend and his best friend. His only contribution to the decor of the apartment had been the stack of wooden crates in which he kept his burgeoning collection of comic books. "In his spare time," he added, through a big white mouthful of banana. "A *real* one."

"Yeah, well," Sammy said, feeling himself blush. "At the rate I'm going, we'll all be sitting around in the old-age home reading it."

"I'll read it," Rosa said. "Sammy, I'd love to. I'm sure it's very good."

"It isn't. But thank you. You mean it?"

"Of course."

"Maybe," he said, for the first but by no means the final time in their long association, "when I get chapter one into shape."

When Sammy arrived at the Empire offices on that textbook April morning—tufted sky, daffodils swinging like a big band on every patch of green, love in the air, et cetera—he took the oft-revised first (and sole) chapter of *American Disillusionment* out of his bottom desk drawer, rolled a fresh sheet of paper into his typewriter, and tried to work, but the conversation with Rosa had left him uneasy. Why didn't he want to, at least, say, have a drink with a dish from City College? How did he even *know* that he didn't like dating college girls? It was like saying he didn't care for golf. He had a fairly good idea that it was not the game for him, but the fact was the closest he had ever been to a golf course was the peeling plaster windmills of the old Tom Thumb course at Coney Island. Why, for that matter, wasn't he jealous of Joe? Rosa was a great-looking girl, soft and powdery-smelling. While it was true that he found her remarkably easy to talk to, tease with, confide in, and let down his guard around, easier than he had ever found any other girl, he felt only the faintest itch for her. At times this absence of prurient feeling, so marked and plain to both of them that Rosa had no compunction about lounging around the apartment with her underpants covered only by the flapping tails of one of Joe's shirts, troubled Sammy, and he would try, lying in his bed at night, to imagine kissing her, stroking her thick dark curls, lifting those shirttails to reveal the pale belly beneath. But such chimeras invariably faded in the light of day. The real question was, why wasn't he more jealous of *Rosa*?

He was just happy to see his friend happy, he typed. It was an autobiographical novel, after all. *There was a hole in the man's life that no one person ever would have been able to fill.*

The phone rang. It was his mother.

"I have the night off," she said. "Why don't you bring him and we'll make Shabbes. He can bring that girlfriend of his, too."

"She's kind of picky about food," Sammy said. "What are you burning?"

"All right, so don't come."

"I'll be there."

"I don't want you."

"I'll be there. Ma?"

"What?"

"Ma?"

"What?"

"Ma?"

"What?"

"I love you."

"Big joker." She hung up.

He put *American Disillusionment* back in the drawer and started to work on the script for *Kid Vixen*, the crime-fighting female boxer feature, with art by Marty Gold, that he had put in as a backup for *All Doll*, along with the Glovsky brothers' *Venus McFury*, about a hard-boiled girl detective who was the reincarnation of one of the classical Erinyes, and Frank Pantaleone's *Greta Gatling*, a cowgirl strip. The first issue of *All Doll Comics* had sold out its entire run of half a million copies; #6 was in production now, and orders were extremely strong. Sammy had half of an idea for the latest *Vixen* story, involving a catfight between the Kid and a champion Nazi girl boxer whom he was thinking of calling Battling Brunhilde, but he could not seem to get his mind into it this morning. The funny thing was that, as hard as he had fought with Sheldon Anapol for them to be able to keep plugging away at the Nazis, fighting the funny-book war was getting tougher all the time; though futility was not an emotion Sammy was accustomed to experiencing, he had begun to be plagued by the same sense of inefficacy, of endless make-believe, that had troubled Joe from the first. Only there was nothing Sammy saw to do about it; he wasn't about to start picking fights at ball games.

He kept at the script, starting over three times, drinking Bromo-Seltzer through a straw to keep down the pang of dread that had begun to gnaw at his belly. Much as Sammy did love his mother, and craved her approval, five minutes of conversation with her was all it took to induce a matricidal rage in his breast. The large sums of money he gave over to her, though she was gratifyingly astonished by them and always managed, in her curt way, to thank him, proved nothing to her about anything. To get paid vast sums for wasting one's life, in her view, only added to the cosmic tallying of wastefulness. Most maddening of all to Sammy was the way that, in the face of the sudden influx of money, Ethel steadfastly refused to change any element of her life, except to shop for better cuts of meat, buy a new set of carving knives, and spend a relatively lavish amount on new underwear for Bubbie and herself.

The rest she socked away. She viewed each fat paycheck as the last, certain that eventually, as she put it, "the bubble gets popped." Each month that the comic book bubble not only continued to float but expanded exponentially just confirmed Ethel's belief that the world was insane and growing madder, so that when the pin finally went in, the pop would be all the more terrible. Yes, it was always loads of fun dropping in on old Ethel, to share in the revelry and good times, to banter and sing and sup on the delicious fruits of her kitchen. Bubbie would have baked one of her bitter, brittle Bubbie babkas that they all had to make a fuss over even though each tasted as if she had baked it in 1877 and then mislaid it in a drawer until yesterday.

The only bright prospect for the day was that he and Joe had also been invited to come down to the radio studio to meet the cast of *The Amazing Adventures of the Escapist*, in run-throughs for the debut next Monday afternoon. Hitherto, Burns, Baggot & DeWinter, the advertising agency, had not involved Sammy or Joe or any of the Empire people in the production, though Sammy had heard that several of the first few episodes were being adapted directly from the comic books. Once, Sammy had met the show's writers by chance, as they were coming out of Sardi's. They knew him from the unflattering drawing that had run in the *Saturday Evening Post*, and stopped him to say hello and shed the gentle luster of their scorn upon him. They all seemed to Sammy like college-boy types, with pipes and bow ties. Only one would admit to ever having read a comic book, and probably all of them considered the form beneath contempt. One had written previously for *Mr. Keen, Tracer of Lost Persons*, another for *Mrs. Wiggs of the Cabbage Patch*.

But there was to be a party on Monday after the first broadcast, to which Sammy and Joe were invited; and on this balmy Friday, they went over to Radio City to get a look, if that was the right way to put it, at the vocal embodiments of their characters.

"Shabbes dinner," Joe said, as they passed the Time-Life Building. Joe claimed to have once seen Ernest Hemingway coming out of it, and Sammy looked for the writer as they went by.

"I saw him, I tell you."

"Sure you did. Yes, Shabbes dinner. At my mother's. Bad food. House like an oven. You don't want to miss that."

"I have a date with Rosa," Joe said. "I think we're supposed to eat with her father at the house."

"You do that almost every night! Come on, Joe, don't make me go alone. I'll go mad, mad, I tell you."

"Rosa is right," Joe said.

"As usual, but this time about what?"

"You need a girl."

It was cool and dark in the lobby of the RCA Building. The soft knocking of shoe heels on stone floors and the somber, reassuring pomposity of the Sert and Brangwyn murals allowed Sammy to experience what he dimly recognized as tranquility for the first time all day. A chubby young fellow was waiting for them at the guard's desk, nibbling on a manicured finger. He introduced himself as Larry Sneed, assistant to the producer George Chandler, and showed them how to sign in and pin passes to their jackets.

"Mr. Chandler's really glad you could make it over," Sneed said over his shoulder.

"It was nice of him to invite us."

"Well, he's become quite a fan of your work."

"He reads it?"

"Oh, he studies it like the Bible."

They got out of the elevator, went down a stairwell and across a hall into another stairwell, this one gray cinder-block and iron stairs, then into a dingy white corridor, past the closed door of a studio with the ON AIR light illuminated, left, and into another studio. It was cool and smoky and dim. At one end of the big yellow room, three casually dressed groups of actors, holding scripts, were loitering around a trio of microphones. In the middle of the room, two men sat at a small table, listening. Pages of script lay everywhere, scattered on the ground and blown into drifts in the corners. There was a gunshot. Sammy was the only one in the room who jumped. He looked wildly around. Three men stood off to the left in the midst of an assortment of kitchen utensils, lumber, and scrap metal. One of them was holding a gun. They were all sweating profusely in spite of the air-conditioning.

"Ooh, got me!" cried Larry Sneed. He clutched his silk-fronted potbelly and spun around. "Ha ha ha." He pretended to laugh. The actor who was delivering his line stopped talking, and everyone turned to look. They seemed to welcome the distraction, Sammy thought, except for the director, who scowled. "Hi, folks, I'm sorry to interrupt you. Mr. Chandler, here's a couple of bright young fellows like me who want to meet our marvelous cast. Mr. Sam Clay and Mr. Joe Kavalier."

"Hello, boys," said one of the two men at the center table, rising from his chair. He was about the same age as Sammy's father would have been, but tall and refined, with a trim Vandyke and extra-big black glasses that made him look, Sammy thought, like a man of science. He shook their hands. "This is Mr. Cobb, our director." Cobb nodded. Like Chandler, he was wearing a suit and tie. "And this ragged bunch is our cast. Forgive their appearance, but they've been rehearsing all week." Chandler pointed to the actors around the microphones, anointing each one from a distance with a momentary dab of his finger as he gave the name and role. "That's Miss Verna Kaye, our Plum Blossom; Pat Moran, our Big Al; and Howard Fine as the evil Kommandant X. Over there may I present Miss Helen Portola, our Poison Rose; Ewell Conrad as Omar; Eddie Fontaine as Pedro; and our announcer, Mr. Bill Parris."

"But Poison Rose is dead," said Joe.

"We haven't killed her on the radio yet," said Chandler. "And that big, handsome fellow over there is our Escapist, Mr. Tracy Bacon."

Sammy was too distracted just then to notice Mr. Tracy Bacon.

"Pedro?" he said.

"The old Portuguese stagehand." Chandler nodded. "For comic relief. The sponsor felt we ought to lighten things up a little."

"Nize to mitts your ekwentinz," said Eddie Fontaine, with a tip of his imaginary Portuguese hat.

"And old Max Mayflower?" Sammy wanted to know. "And the man from the League of the Golden Key? You aren't having the League?"

"We tried it with the League, didn't we, Larry?"

"Yes, we did, Mr. Chandler."

"When you're debuting a series, it's better to get right down to business," said Cobb. "Skip the preliminaries."

"We take care of all that with the intro," Chandler explained. "Bill?"

"Armed with superb physical and mental training," Bill Parris began, "a crack team of assistants, and ancient wisdom, he roams the globe, performing amazing feats—"

The whole cast chimed in for the tag.

"And coming to the aid of those who languish in tyranny's chains!"

"This—is—the Escapist!"

Everyone laughed, except Joe, who clapped his hands. But for some reason, Sammy was irritated.

"And what about Tom Mayflower?" he persisted. "Who's going to be him?"

A cheerful, scratchy teenage voice rang out from the corner.

"I'm going to be Tom, Mr. Clay! And golly, I'm awful darn excited about it!"

That busted everybody up again. Tracy Bacon was looking right at Sammy, grinning, his cheeks flushed, mostly with pleasure, it seemed, at the astonished look on Sammy's face. Bacon was such a perfect Escapist that one would have thought he had been cast to play the role in a film, not on the air. He was well over six feet tall, broad-shouldered, with a dimple in his chin and glossy blond hair fitted to the top of his head like a polished brass plate. He wore an oxford shirt unbuttoned over a ribbed undershirt, blue jeans, and socks with no shoes. His muscles were not as large, perhaps, as the Escapist's, but they were distinctly visible. Clean-favored, thought Sammy, and imperially slim.

"Please, gentlemen, take a seat," said Chandler. "Larry, find them a place to sit down."

"That guy looks exactly like the Escapist," said Joe. "It gives me the creep."

"I know," said Sammy. "And he sounds just like Tom Mayflower."

They sat in the corner and watched the rehearsal. The script had been adapted—very freely—from Sammy's third Escapist story, which had introduced the character of Miss Plum Blossom's evil sister Poison Rose, a straight steal from Caniff's Dragon Lady whom Sammy, embarrassed by the blatancy of his theft, had killed off in *Radio* #4. In the Grand Opera House on the Bund in Shangpo, Rose had thrown herself between a bullet meant for Tom Mayflower and the pistol of a Razi agent with whom she had, until that moment, been allied. But the radio boys had revived her, and Sammy had to admit she certainly appeared to be well. Helen Portola was the only cast member not dressed casually, and in her bright green poplin dress she looked cool and refined and appetizing. When she growled her diabolical lines at the Escapist, whom she had rendered powerless with the stolen, legendary Eye of the Moon Opal, she looked at Tracy Bacon with accurate love in her eyes and made it sound like flirtation. Walter Winchell had already linked their names in his column.

On the whole, Sammy found it a depressing couple of hours. It was his first experience, though by no means his last, with having one of his creations appropriated and made to serve the purposes of another writer, and it upset him to such a degree that he was ashamed. It was all pretty much the same stuff—except for Pedro, of course—and yet somehow it was all totally different. It all seemed to have a lighter, more playful tone than in the comic books, no doubt in part because of the audible brilliance of Tracy Bacon's smile. The dialogue sounded a lot like the dialogue on *Mr. Keen, Tracer of Lost Persons.* This was logical, but somehow it, too, depressed Sammy. He had written dialogue as bad—although, at Deasey's suggestion, he had been studying the work of snappy dialogue writers like Irwin Shaw and Ben Hecht—but spoken aloud, it sounded worse. All the characters seemed to be slow on the uptake, vaguely retarded. Sammy shifted uncomfortably in his chair. Joe got lost in the proceedings for a while, but then abruptly seemed to snap out of it. He leaned over.

"Isn't this great?" he said. He was whispering now, which meant that he was up to something. He looked at his watch. "Shit, five o'clock. I have to go, gate."

"You have to go, 'gate'?"

"Yes, 'gate.' It's like 'man.' 'What's happening, gate?' 'Don't be late, gate.' You never say 'gate'?"

"No, that's something I never say," Sammy said. "Only Negroes say that, Joe. Ethel's expecting us around six."

"Yes, okay. Six."

"That's in an hour."

"Okay."

"You're coming, aren't you?" said Sammy.

Mr. Cobb turned around in his chair and scowled at them again. They covered their mouths. Joe nodded his head toward the door. Sammy got up and followed him out into the hall. Joe closed the heavy studio door and leaned his shoulder against it.

"Joe, you said you'd come."

"I was very careful not to say that."

"Well, I don't have the transcript handy, but that was how it sounded."

"Sammy, please. Don't make me. I don't *want* to go. I want to go out with my girl. I want to have fun." He blushed. Having fun was still a difficult thing for Joe to admit he was able to do. "It isn't my fault that you don't have anyone—"

The studio door burst open, throwing Joe back against the wall.

"Sorry!" said Tracy Bacon. He gingerly pulled back the door to see what had become of Joe. "Holy Eye of the Moon Opal, are you all right?"

"Yes, thank you," said Joe, rubbing his forehead.

"I was in such a damn hurry to get out here I didn't bother to look where I was going! I was afraid you two might have left before I got a chance to talk to Mr. Clay."

"Yes, talk! You talk," Joe said, patting Bacon on the shoulder. "Unfortunately, I have to go. Mr. Bacon, it was nice meeting you, you are a perfect Escapist I think."

"Well, thank *you*."

Joe drew himself up. "So," he said, pronouncing it in the German fashion. With Bacon interposed very carefully between them, he gave Sammy an awkward little wave and ducked around Bacon to make a dash for the end of the hall. Before reaching the stairwell, he stopped and turned back. He looked at Sammy right in the eyes, his expression grave and remorseful, as though he were on the verge of making a full confession of everything bad that he had ever done. Then he flashed his visitor's badge, Melvin Purvis–style, and was gone. And that, Sammy knew, was about as close as Joe Kavalier could get to an apology.

"So," said Bacon, "what's he so hot to trot about?"

"His girl," said Sammy. "Miss Rosa Luxemburg Saks."

"I see." Bacon had a little bit of a southern accent. "She a foreigner, too?"

"Yeah, she is," Sammy said. "She's from Greenwich Village."

"I've heard of it."

"It's a pretty backward place."

"Is it."

"The people are little more than savages."

"I hear they eat dogs there."

"Rosa can do amazing things with dog."

When this burst of somewhat labored bantering flagged, they were embarrassed. Sammy rubbed at the back of his neck. For some reason, he was a little afraid of Tracy Bacon. He decided that Bacon was playing with him, condescending to him. Big, radiant, confident fellows with string-bass voices always made him feel acutely how puny, dark, and Jewish he was, a goofy little curlicue of ink stamped on a sheet of splintery paper.

"You had something to ask me?" Sammy said coldly.

"Yes, I wanted—look here." He punched Sammy on the shoulder. Not painfully, but not gently, either. Not always knowing his own strength was eventually to become, thanks to Tracy Bacon, one of the Escapist's characteristic traits. "Ordinarily I wouldn't do something like this, but when I got a look at you and saw you weren't any older than I am, maybe even younger—how old are you?"

"Safely in my twenties," Sammy said.

"I'm twenty-four," said Bacon. "Last week."

"Happy birthday."

"Mr. Clay—"

"Sammy."

"Tracy."

Bacon's grip was firm and dry, and he pumped Sammy's hand up and down half a dozen times.

"Sammy, I don't know if you could tell it or not," Bacon said, "but I'm having a little problem in there—"

The door opened again, and the other actors started to file out. Helen Portola sidled up to Bacon, took hold of his arm, and gazed up at him in the ardent manner Walter Winchell had alluded to. She could see that he had something on his mind and turned inquiringly to Sammy. She smiled, but Sammy thought he saw a waver of anxiety in her big green eyes.

"Trace? We're all going over to Sardi's."

"Save me a seat, all right, gorgeous?" said Bacon. He gave her shoulder a squeeze. "Turns out Mr. Clay and I have a mutual friend. We're just doing a little catching up."

Sammy was amazed by the ease and naturalness of Bacon's lie. Helen Portola looked Sammy over very carefully and coldly, as if trying to calculate what possible human could be the link between him and Tracy Bacon. Then she kissed Bacon on the cheek and, not without a show of reluctance, left. Sammy must have looked puzzled.

"Oh, I'm an awful liar," Bacon said airily. "Now, come on, let me buy you a drink, and I'll explain."

"Jeez," said Sammy, "I'd like to, but—"

Bacon actually took hold of Sammy by the elbow—gently enough—and put his arm around him, steering him down to the end of the hall by a fire door. He lowered his voice to a conspiratorial rasp.

"Sammy, I'm going to confess something to you." He paused, as if to give Sammy a moment to feel grateful for being taken into his confidence. Sammy was almost—almost—too taken aback to comply. "I'm in way over my head here. I'm no actor! I studied civil engineering in school. Two months ago I was swabbing out the mess on a cargo freighter. All right, I have an ideal voice for radio." He composed his features, his fair eyebrows and rather girlish mouth, into a stern, fatherly mien. "That isn't enough, and I know it. You can't get by in this business on natural ability alone." He looked so pleased by the harsh line he had taken with himself that all trace of it vanished at once. "This is my first big part. I want to be very, very good. If you could give me any, you know . . ."

"Insights?"

"Exactly!" He smacked Sammy on the chest with the palm of his right hand. "That's it! I was hoping we could sit down, see, and I could buy you a drink, and you could just talk to me a little bit about the Escapist. I'm not having any problems with Tom Mayflower."

"No, you seem to have him down pretty good."

"Well, I *am* Tom Mayflower, Mr. Clay, and that's the explanation for that. But the Escapist, jeez, I don't know. He just . . . he seems to take everything so damn *seriously.*"

"Well, Mr. Bacon, he has serious problems to deal with . . ." Sammy began, grimacing at his own pretension. He felt he ought to be glad for this chance Bacon was offering him to gain some small influence over the direction of the radio program, but instead he found that he was more afraid of Tracy Bacon than before. Sammy came from a land of intense, uninterruptable, and energetic speakers, and he was used to being harangued, but he had never before felt himself so addressed, with such a direct appeal, made not merely to his ears but to his eyes. No one who looked like Tracy Bacon had ever, to his memory, spoken to him at all. The lithe, knicker-clad golden halfback atop the football trophy, stiff-arming every obstacle in his path, was not a type stamped out in any great profusion by Brownsville, Flatbush, or the Manual Arts High School. Sammy had encountered one or two of these pink-skinned, cardigan-wearing, cultivated lunks with schoolboy haircuts during his brief dips into the world of Rosa Saks, but he had certainly never been addressed by one—or even acknowledged. "The world today has a lot of serious problems." God, he sounded like a school principal! He ought just to shut up. "I really can't," he said. He looked at his watch. It was nearly ten past five. "I'll be late for a dinner date."

"At five on a Friday night?" Bacon switched on his fifty-amp smile. "Sounds swank."

"You can't even begin to imagine," said Sammy.

WHERE IS the actual flat bush?" Bacon said as they came up out of the subway. He stopped and looked across the avenue at the entrance to Prospect Park. "Do they keep it in there?"

"Actually, they move it around," said Sammy. They'd had two drinks apiece, but for some reason, Sammy didn't feel in the least intoxicated. He wondered if fear forestalled the effects of alcohol. He wondered if he were more afraid of Tracy Bacon or of showing up for dinner at Ethel's late, reeking of gin, and with the world's largest piece of trayf in tow. In the subway station, he had bought a roll of Sen-Sen and eaten four. "It's on wheels." He gave a pull on the sleeve of Bacon's blue blazer. "Come on, we're late."

"Are we?" Bacon arched an eyebrow. "You hadn't mentioned it."

"You don't even know me," said Sammy. "How can you presume to razz me?"

As he buzzed for 2-B—he had misplaced his key—he realized that he must be very, very drunk. It was the only possible explanation for what he was about to do. He wasn't sure exactly when the invitation had been extended, or at what point it became clear to Sammy that Bacon had accepted it. In the bar at the St. Regis, under the jovial gaze of Parrish's *King Cole,* their conversation had veered so quickly from Bacon's difficulties with the character of the Escapist that Sammy could not remember now what wisdom, if any, he had been able to offer on that score. Almost at once, it seemed, Bacon had launched, unprompted, into a recitation (one that, while practiced, obviously still held great interest for him) of his upbringing, education, and travels, an extravagant tale—he had lived in Texas, California, the Philippines, Puerto Rico, Hawaii, and, most recently, Seattle; his father was a brigadier general, his mother was a titled Englishwoman; he had sailed on a merchant ship; he had broken horses on Oahu; he had attended a boarding school where he played hockey and lacrosse and boxed a little—which, paradoxically, he himself claimed to view as sadly lacking in some fundamental underpinning of sense or purpose. All the while, Sammy's own upbringing and education and his travels from Pitkin Avenue to Surf Avenue, alerting him to the unmistakable smell of bullshit, had been at war with his native weakness for romance. As he sat and listened, with the ointment flavor of gin in his mouth, at once envious and unable to shake the echo of Bacon's blithe avowal—"I'm such an awful liar"— there seemed to emerge, in spite of Bacon's good looks and his actor pals and his cool gin-and-tonic of a girlfriend, and regardless of the truth or falsehood of the claims he was making, an unmistakable portrait that Sammy was surprised to find he recognized: Tracy Bacon was lonely. He lived in a hotel and ate his meals in restaurants. His actor pals took him and his tale at face value not because they were credulous, but because it was less effort to do so. And now, with an unerring instinct, he had sniffed out the loneliness in Sammy. Bacon's presence at Sammy's side now, waiting for an answer from 2-B, was testimony to this. It didn't occur to Sammy that Bacon was just drunk and twenty-one (not twenty-four) and making everything up as he went along.

"That is the most angry-sounding door buzz I've ever heard," Bacon said when it finally came.

Sammy held the lobby door for him. "That was actually the voice of my mother," he said. "There's a little wax cylinder in there."

"You're just trying to scare me," Bacon said.

They climbed the steps that had wearied Sammy's legs for so many years now. Sammy knocked. "Stand back," he said.

"Stop it now."

"Watch your fingers. Ma!"

"Look who it is."

"Don't look so excited."

"Where's your cousin?"

"They already had plans. Ma, I brought a friend. This is Mr. Tracy Bacon. He's going to be playing the Escapist. On the radio."

"Look out you don't bump your head" was the first thing Ethel said to Bacon. Then "My goodness." She smiled and held out her hand, and Sammy saw that she was impressed. Tracy Bacon made quite an impression. She stepped back to get a better look and stood there like one of the tourists Sammy waded through on his way in and out of work every day. "You're very good-looking." It just missed sounding like a wholehearted compliment; there might have been some comment intended on the deceptiveness of attractive packages.

"Thank you, Mrs. Clay," said Bacon.

Sammy winced.

"That isn't my name," Ethel said, but not unkindly. She looked at Sammy. "I never cared for that name. Well, come in, sit down, I made too much, oh well. Dinner was ready once already, and you missed the candles, I'm sorry to say, but we can't postpone sundown even for big-shot comic book writers."

"I heard they changed that rule," said Sammy.

"You smell like Sen-Sen."

"I had a little drink," he said.

"Oh, you had a drink. That's good."

"What? I can have a drink if I want."

"Of course you can have a drink. I have a bottle of slivovitz someplace. Would you like me to get it out? You can drink the whole bottle if you want."

Sammy whirled around and made a face at Bacon: What'd I tell you? They followed Ethel into the living room. The electric fan was going in the window but, in accordance with Ethel's personal theories of hygiene and thermodynamics, faced outward, so as to draw the warm air out of the room, leaving an entirely theoretical zone of coolness behind. Bubbie was already on her feet, a big confused grin on her face, her spectacles glinting. She was wearing a loose cotton dress printed with scarlet poppies.

"Mom," said Ethel, in English, "this is a friend of Sammy's. Mr. Bacon. He's an actor on the radio."

Bubbie nodded and grabbed hold of Bacon's hand. "Oh, yes, how are you?" she said in Yiddish. She seemed to recognize Tracy Bacon at once, which was odd, since she had not seemed to recognize anyone in years.

It was never clear afterward who she thought Bacon was. She shook his hand vigorously with both of hers.

For some reason, the sight of Bubbie shaking Bacon's large pink hand made Ethel laugh. "Sit down, sit down," she said. "Ma, let go of him." She looked at Sammy. "Sit down." Sammy started to sit down. "What, I don't get a kiss from you anymore, Mr. Sam Clay?"

Sammy kissed his mother.

"Ma, you're hurting me! Ouch!"

She let go.

"I'd like to break your neck," she said. She seemed to be in a very good mood. "I'll get dinner on the table."

"Careful with the shovel."

"Funny."

"Is that how you talk to your mother?" said Bacon.

"Oh, I like your new friend," said Ethel. She took hold of his arm and gave his huge right biceps a pat. She looked supremely vindicated. The shock on Bacon's face appeared to be genuine. "This young man loves his mother."

"Boy, do I," said Bacon. "Can I help you in the kitchen, Mrs., uh—"

"It's Klayman. K-L-A-Y-M-A-N. Period."

"Mrs. Klayman. I have a lot of experience peeling potatoes, or whatever you might need me to do."

Now it was Ethel's turn to look shocked.

"Oh . . . no, it's already fixed. I'm just reheating everything again."

Sammy wanted to point out that reheating everything several times in order to remove as much flavor as possible was an integral part of Ethel's culinary technique, but he held his tongue. Bacon had embarrassed him.

"You wouldn't fit in my kitchen," Ethel said. "Sit down."

Bacon followed her into the kitchen. Sammy had yet to see his "new friend" take no for an answer. In spite of his height and his swimmer's shoulders, it was not a confidence in his own abilities that seemed to direct Tracy Bacon so much as an assuredness of being welcome wherever he went. He was golden and beautiful, and he knew how to peel a potato. To Sammy's surprise, Ethel let Bacon follow.

"I can never reach that bowl up there," he heard her say. "The one with the toucan."

"So, Bubbie," Sammy said. "How are you?"

"Fine, darling," she said. "I'm fine. How are you?"

"Come sit down." He tried to steer her into the other yellow chair. She pushed him away.

"Go. I want to stand. All day I'm sit."

From the kitchen Sammy could hear—could hardly miss—the cheerful thumping of Bacon's voice, with its lyric upper register. Like Sammy's, the constant barrage of chatter Bacon maintained seemed designed to impress and to charm, with a key difference: Bacon was impressive and charming. Ethel's burned-sugar laugh came drifting out of the kitchen. Sammy tried to hear what Bacon was saying to her.

"So what did you do today, Bubbie?" he said, flopping on the couch. "Belmont's open. Did you go out to the track?"

"Yes, yes," Bubbie said agreeably. "I went to the races."

"Did you win any money?"

"Oh, yes."

You were never sure with Bubbie whether you were really teasing her or not.

"Josef sends you a kiss," he said in Yiddish.

"I'm glad," Bubbie said in English. "And how is Samuel?"

"Samuel? Oh, he's fine," Sammy said.

"She kicked me out." Bacon emerged from the kitchen wearing a little dishwashing apron patterned with pale blue soap bubbles. "I guess I was getting in the way."

"Oh, you don't want to do that," Sammy said. "I got in the way of a dinner roll once and required nine stitches."

"Funny," said Ethel, stepping into the living room. She untied her apron and threw it at Sammy. "Come and eat."

Dinner was a fur muff, a dozen clothespins, and some old dish towels boiled up with carrots. The fact that the meal was served with a bottle of prepared horseradish enabled Sammy to conclude that it was intended to pass for braised short ribs of beef—flanken. Many of Ethel's specialties arrived thus encoded by condiments. Tracy Bacon took three helpings. He cleaned his plate with a piece of challah. His cheeks were rosy with the intensity of his pleasure in the meal. It was either that or the horseradish.

"Whew!" he said, laying down his napkin at last. "Mrs. K., I never had better in my life."

"Yes, but better what?" Sammy said.

"Did you get enough to eat?" Ethel said. She looked pleased but, it seemed to Sammy, a little taken aback.

"Did you save room for my babka?" Bubbie said.

"I *always* save room for dessert, Mrs. Kavalier," Bacon said. He turned to Sammy. "Is babka dessert?"

"An eternal question among my people," Sammy said. "There are some who argue that it's actually a kind of very small hassock."

Ethel got up to make coffee. Bacon stood up and started to clear away the dishes.

"Enough already," Sammy said, pushing him back down into his chair. "You're making me look very bad here." He gathered up the dirty plates and utensils and carried them into the tiny kitchen.

"Don't stack them," his mother said by way of thanks. "It gets the bottoms dirty."

"I'm just trying to be helpful."

"Your kind of help is worse than no help." She set the percolator on the ring and turned on the gas. "Stand back," she said, striking a match. She must have been lighting gas stoves for thirty years, but each time it was as if entering a burning building. She ran water in the sink and slid the dishes in. Steam rose from the bubbles of Lux; the dishwater must of course be antibacterially hot. "He looks just like Josef draws him," she said.

"Doesn't he, though."

"Is everything all right with your cousin?"

Sammy guessed that her feelings were hurt. "He really wanted to come, Ma," he said. "But it was short notice, you know?"

"It doesn't make any difference to me."

"I'm just saying."

"Is there news? What does the man at the agency say?"

"Hoffman says the kids are still in Portugal."

"With the nuns." As a girl, during the first war, Ethel had been sheltered briefly by Orthodox nuns. They had treated her with a kindness that she had never forgotten, and Sammy knew that she would have preferred her little nephew to remain with these Portuguese Carmelites, in the relative safety of a Lisbon orphanage, rather than to set off across a submarine-haunted ocean in a thirdhand steamer with a rickety name. But the nuns were apparently under pressure from the Catholic Church in Portugal not to make harboring Jewish children from Central Europe a permanent thing.

"The boat is on its way over there now," Sammy said. "To get them. It got itself into one of these convoy things, you know, with five U.S. Navy destroyers. Thomas ought to be here in a month, Joe said."

"A month. Here." His mother handed him a dishtowel and a dish. "Dry."

"Yeah, so Joe's happy about that. He seems happy with Rosa, too. He's not working those crazy hours like he used to anymore. We're making enough money now that I was able to talk him into dropping all the books he was working on but three.* I had to hire *five* guys to replace him."

"I'm glad he's settling down. He was getting wild before. Fighting. Getting hurt on purpose."

"The thing is, I think he likes it here," Sammy said. "I wouldn't·be surprised if he decided to stay, even after the war's over."

"*Kayn ayn hora,*" his mother said. "Let's hope he has a choice."

"That's a cheerful thought."

"I don't know this girl very well. But she seemed . . ." She hesitated, unwilling to go so far as to bestow actual praise on Rosa. "I got the feeling she has a good head on her shoulders." The previous month, Joe and Rosa had taken Ethel to see *Here Comes Mr. Jordan;* Ethel was partial to Robert Montgomery. "He could do much worse."

"Yeah," Sammy said. "Rosa's all right."

Then, for a minute, he just dried the dishes and forks she passed to him and set them, under his mother's scrutiny, in the rack. There was

---

* *Radio, All Doll,* and *Freedom.*

no sound but the squeak of the dishtowel, the chiming of the dishes, and the steady trickling of hot water into the sink. Bacon and Bubbie seemed, in the dining room, to have run out of things to say to each other. It was one of those prolonged silences that meant, Ethel always used to say, that somewhere an idiot had just been born.

"*I'd* like to meet someone, you know," Sammy said at last. "I mean, I've been thinking. Just recently. Meet someone nice."

His mother shut off the tap and pulled the stopper from the drain. Her hands were bright red from the scalding water.

"I'd like that, too," she said. She opened another drawer and took out the box of waxed paper. She tore off a piece, spread it on the zinc counter, and took a dish from the rack.

"So how was he?" she asked him, setting the dish upside down on the sheet of waxed paper.

"Who's that?"

She nodded toward the dining room. "That one." She folded the ends of the sheet of paper up over the dish and smoothed them down. "At the rehearsal today."

"He was all right," Sammy said. "He was good. Yeah, I think he'll do fine."

"Will he?" she said, and, lifting the wrapped dish, she looked him in the eye for the first time all evening.

Though it would recur often enough in his memory in later years, he would never know exactly what she had meant by that look.

THE FOLLOWING DAY, a wealthy young New Yorker named Leon Douglas Saks followed in the footsteps of his grandfathers and was called before the Torah to become a bar mitzvah. He was a second cousin of Rosa's, and although she had never met the boy, she managed without too much trouble to wangle an invitation to the reception at the Pierre as the date of one of the entertainers on the bill, the performing magician known as the Amazing Cavalieri.

When she woke from a post-coital nap that Saturday afternoon, in her bedroom under the eaves, the Amazing Cavalieri was standing in front of her scarf-draped mirror, looking with remarkable interest at his own naked reflection. Rosa pulled a pillow over her head and lay very still so that she could watch him watching himself. She could smell the trace of his breath in her own exhalations, the indeterminate but distinctive flavor of his lips, somewhere between maple and smoke. At first, as she watched him, she thought that he was engaging in rank self-admiration, and since she considered his lack of vanity about his appearance—his ink-stained shirtfronts, rumpled jackets, and ragged trouser cuffs—to be itself a kind of vanity, one for which she loved him, she was amused. She wondered if he could see how much weight he had added to his long, spare frame over the last several months. When they had first started going out, he was so absorbed by his work that he rarely took time for meals, existing quite mysteriously on coffee and bananas, but as Rosa herself, to her considerable satisfaction, had begun to absorb Joe more and more, he had become a regular guest at her father's dinner table, where there were never fewer than five courses and three different varieties of wine. His ribs no longer stuck out, and his skinny little-boy's behind had taken on a manlier heft. It was as if, she thought, he had been engaged in a process of transferring himself from Czechoslovakia to America, from Prague to New York, a little at a time, and every day there was more of him on this side of the ocean. She wondered if this could be what he was looking at now—this evidence of his irrefutable existence here, on this shore, in this bedroom, as her Joe. For a while she lay staring at the gloved knuckles of his spine, the stippled pale stone of his shoulders. Presently, however, she became aware of the way he kept narrowing and widening his blue eyes, tightening them at the corners and then opening them into a pop-eyed stare, over and over again. As he did so he moved his lips constantly, engaging in some kind of patter or incantation. From time to time he gestured broadly, flourishing his fingers around a handful of empty air, pointing proudly at some invisible wonderful thing.

Finally she couldn't stand it anymore and threw off the pillow.

"What the hell are you doing?"

He jumped and knocked his cigarette from the ashtray on her dressing table. He retrieved it, brushing ash from the carpet, then came over and sat on the bed. "How long were you watching?"

"An hour," she lied.

He nodded. Had he really been standing there like that for an hour, giving himself the evil eye and marveling at nothing?

"You looked like you were trying to hypnotize yourself or something."

"I guess I was. I guess I'm a little nervous," he said. As he spent night after night in the company of inveterate and literate talkers, his English had improved considerably. "Performing in front of your family. Your father." Rosa's father had not appeared at a Saks family event in years, but he was attending the reception tonight just to see Joe perform. He had been invited to the religious portion of the proceedings that morning, too, at B'nai Jeshurun, but God forbid. He hadn't been inside a synagogue, he calculated, since 1899. "Right now he thinks I'm the best magician in New York," Joe continued. "Because he's never seen me. After tonight, maybe he'll think I'm a palooka."

"He'll love you," she said. She was touched to see that her father's opinion meant so much to him. She interpreted it as further evidence of his belonging to her. "Don't worry."

"Mm-hmm," he said. "You already think I'm a palooka."

"Not me," she said, running a hand up his thigh and taking hold of his penis, which at once began to show renewed interest in her. "I know you're magic."

She had seen his act twice now. The truth was that Joe was a talented but careless performer, liable to bite off more than he could chew. He had renewed his career, as promised, with the Hoffman reception at the Hotel Trevi the previous November, and had gotten off to a rather shaky start when—forgetting the disdain in which his teacher Bernard Korn-blum had held such "mechanisms," and succumbing to his fatal weakness, from which he suffered all his life, for acts of daring and the beau geste—he became hopelessly entangled in the Emperor's Dragon, an elaborate set-piece trick that he had purchased, on credit, from Louis Tannen's Magic Shop. It was a hoary bit of mock-Chinese flummery from the heyday of Ching Ling Foo, in which a silk "dragon" in a brass cage was made to breathe fire, then lay a number of colored eggs, each presented to the inspection of a witness for signs of seams or apertures before it was cracked with a silver wand, disgorging some personal item belonging to a member of the audience who, up to this point, had not been aware of his watch's or lighter's disappearance from his or her person. Picking pockets had never been Joe's great strength, how-ever, and he was long out of practice. In the Trevi's lobby, before the show, there was an unpleasant incident with the bar mitzvah boy's aunt Ida, involving her beaded handbag, which had to be hastily smoothed over by Hermann Hoffman; and, during the performance, Joe singed off his own right eyebrow. He had moved quickly into cards and coins after that, and here his renewed training and the native gifts of his fingers served him well. He caused half-dollars and queens to behave in bizarre ways, endowed them with sentience and emotions, transformed them into kinds of weather, raising storms of aces and calling down nickel lightning from the sky. After Joe finished his act, young Maurice Hoffman brought over a friend who was having his own bar mitzvah in two weeks and had determined to impel his parents to hire Joe for the affair. More bookings followed: all at once Joe discovered that he had become the fashionable entertainer among the wealthy, male Jewish adolescents of the Upper West Side, many of them, of course, loyal read-ers of Empire comic books. They didn't seem to care that from time to time an ace dropped from his watchband or that he misread their minds. They adored him, and he accepted their adoration. In fact, he seemed actively to seek out the company of thirteen-year-old boys, not so much because it gratified his ego, Rosa thought, as because he longed to see his brother again so badly. And because their company— respectful, sardonic, willing to be awed, stubborn in their desire to get to the bottom of each trick—seemed to promise good things for Thomas on his arrival: friends of raucous intelligence, at once innocent and hard-edged, homely or handsome but uniformly well dressed, their faces free of all shadow save those of acne or an incipient beard. These were boys who lived free of the fear of invasion, occupation, cruel and arbitrary laws. With Rosa's encouragement, Joe began, tentatively at first and then with great ardor, to envision the transformation of his brother into an American boy.

Sometimes, when he was making arrangements with the parents beforehand, the name of Houdini came up, and Joe would be asked if he might (naturally with a commensurate increase in his fee) perform an escape; but here he drew the line.

"I escaped from Prague," he would say, looking down at his bare wrists as if for the reddened trace of a manacle. "I think maybe that is enough."

Here the parents, exchanging looks with Rosa, would invariably agree and write him out a check for a hundred dollars. It had never seemed to occur to Joe that the reason for his sudden popularity on the West Side bar mitzvah circuit was neither the erratic skill of his prestigious digits, nor the unwavering fervor of his young fans, but rather the sympathy those parents felt for a homeless Jewish boy who had somehow managed to get out from under the shadow of the billowing black flag that was unfurling across Europe, and who was known to donate his entire fee to the Transatlantic Rescue Agency.

"I'm not getting any better," he said now, watching abstractly as he expanded in her hand. "Really, it's embarrassing. At Tannen's they all make fun of me."

"You're much better than you used to be," she said, and then added, with just a hint of self-servingness: "Everything's much better, isn't it?"

"Much better," he said, moving a little in her grasp. "Yes. Much."

When she first met him, he had been such a forlorn, solitary figure, bruised and broken from all his street fighting, with the little fireplug, Sammy Clay, his lone prop and associate. Now he had friends, down at that magic shop of his, and in the New York art world. He had changed; she had changed him. In the pages of *Radio Comics*—Rosa was now a loyal reader—he and the Escapist continued to fight the forces of the Iron Chain, in battles that were increasingly grotesque and ornate. But the sad futility of the struggle, which Joe had sensed so early in his run on the magazine and which had been immediately apparent to Rosa, seemed to have begun to overtake the ingenuity of his pen. Month after month, the Escapist ground the armies of evil into paste, and yet here they were in the spring of 1941 and Adolf Hitler's empire was more extensive than Bonaparte's. In the pages of *Triumph*, the Four Freedoms* attained the orgasmically impossible goal of killing Hitler, only to learn in the next issue that their victim had been merely a mechanical double. Though Joe kept fighting, Rosa could see that his heart had gone out of the mayhem. It was in the pages of *All Doll*, in realms far from Zothenia or Prague, that Joe's art now blossomed.

Luna Moth was a creature of the night, of the Other World, of mystic regions where evil worked by means of spells and curses instead of bullets, torpedoes, or shells. Luna fought in the wonderworld against specters and demons, and defended all us unsuspecting dreamers against attack from the dark realms of sleep. Twice now she had flapped into battle against slavering Elder Creatures readying vast interdimensional armadas of demons, and while it was easy enough to see such plots as allegories of paranoia, invasion, and world war, and Joe's work here as a continuation of the internecine conflict of *Radio* and *Triumph*, the art Joe turned in for *Luna Moth* was very different from his work on the other books. Rosa's father, with his eye for native

---

* The Freedoms, whose sales, during the war years, came to rival those of the Escapist himself, were four teenage boys, Kid Einstein, Knuckleduster (known affectionately as "Knuck") O'Toole, Tommy Gunn, and Mumbles, a reformed gang of "Dead-End Hooligans" who had abandoned street fighting and pinked derbies in favor of the Axis menace and matching suits of tricolor long underwear.

American sources of the Surrealist idea, had introduced Joe to the work of Winsor McKay. The urban dreamscapes, the dizzying perspectives, the playful tone, and the bizarre metamorphoses and juxtapositions of *Little Nemo in Slumberland* all quickly found their way into Joe's pages for *Luna Moth*. Suddenly the standard three tiers of quadrangular panels became a prison from which he had to escape. They hampered his efforts to convey the dislocated and non-Euclidean dream spaces in which Luna Moth fought. He sliced up his panels, stretched and distorted them, cut them into wedges and strips. He experimented with benday dots, cross-hatching, woodcut effects, and even crude collage.* Through this bravura landscape of twilight flew a wisecracking, powerful young woman with immense breasts, fairy wings, and furry antennae. The strip lay poised on the needle-sharp fulcrum between the marvelous and the vulgar that was, to Rosa, the balancing point of Surrealism itself. She could see Joe, in each new issue, contending with the conventions and clichés of Sammy's more than usually literate stories, working his way toward some kind of breakthrough in his art. And she was determined to be there when he did. She had a feeling that she was going to be the only one to notice or appreciate it when it happened; to her, Joe had that authentic air of the solitary bricoleur, the potterer of genius, like the Facteur Cheval or that strange and diffident other Joe, Mr. Cornell, striking out toward the sublime in a vessel constructed of the commonplace, the neglected, the despised. Being there, supporting him in whatever way she could, at that moment of embarkation and on all the brilliant journey that would follow, had become a key element, along with helping him bring over his brother, and binding her to him and to America with unbreakable bonds, in her mission of love. As for the practice of her own art, that had always been less a matter of mission than of long, moody habit, a way of snatching at her emotions and ideas as they flitted past and pinning them, as it were, to canvas before they could elude her gaze. In the end, it would take far less time for the

---

* Thirty years later, when this work was first reprinted, *The Weird Worlds of Luna Moth* (Nostalgia Press, 1970; second edition, Pure Imagination, 1996) quickly became a head-shop bestseller.

world, or at least that small portion of the world that read and thought about comic books, to acclaim Joe's genius than it took for anyone—least of all Rosa—to acknowledge her own.

"I'd better start getting ready," he said, though he did not move, and she redoubled her grip on his penis.

"What are you planning to do with this?" she asked him. "Maybe you could work it into your act. I could paint a little face on it."

"I don't work with puppets."

There was a knock on the door. She let go of him, and he clambered over her to get underneath the coverlet, too.

"Yes?" she called.

"Open up! I have a little gift for the Amazing." It was her father. Rosa got up and pulled on a bathrobe. Then she picked up the cigarette that Joe had left burning on her dresser and went over to the door.

Her father stood in the hall, dressed for the reception in an enormous three-piece cocoa-brown seersucker suit, and carrying a canvas garment bag over one arm. He peered in curiously at Joe, who had sat up in bed, the blanket pulled up just high enough to cover himself. The question of this not being a convenient time to interrupt the young lovers, or of whether perhaps he ought to come back later, did not occur to her father. He just barreled right into her room.

"Josef," he said, raising the garment bag. "We have noticed that every time you perform, you're obliged to rent your tuxedo." Her father was inclined to the imperial "we" when he felt he was being particularly magnanimous. "It seemed to us you really ought to have one of your own." He unzipped the bag. "I had it made," he said.

The jacket was the color of the sky over Prague Castle on a clear winter night. The trousers were also a glossy, coal-dark blue, piped with a bright gold stripe. And affixed to one of the satiny black lapels was a small golden pin in the shape of a skeleton key.

"I sort of thought," her father said. "In honor of you-know-who." He reached into the pocket of the jacket and pulled out a domino mask of the same black satin as the jacket lapels, with long ties of black ribbon. "It couldn't hurt to add a little bit of mystery to the act."

Rosa was as surprised as Joe. She was smiling so hard that her ears started to hurt a little. "Joe," she said, "look what he did."

"Thank you," Joe said, "I—" He made a show of wanting to stand up, trapped in the bed by his nakedness.

"For God's sake, toss him a towel," her father drawled. "So he can thank us properly."

Joe climbed down from the bed, pulling the coverlet up around him. He knotted it around his waist and then took the blue tuxedo from Rosa's father. A rather clumsy embrace followed, then her father brought out a flask and, after a bit of hopeless rummaging through the chaos of Rosa's room, managed to find a glass that was only slightly smudged with lipstick prints.

"To the Amazing Cavalieri," he said, raising the pink-tinged glass of whiskey. "Whom—dare I say it?"

"Dare it," Rosa said, feeling herself blushing mightily.

"I'll just say that, in a family as small as this, there is most certainly room for one more." He drank.

Rosa was watching Joe's face, feeling almost drunk on the happiness of the moment, and so she saw the look of pain that flickered across it at these words.

"I already have a family," he said quietly.

"Oh, yes . . . Joe, for heaven's sake, I know that. I just—"

"I'm sorry," Joe said immediately. "That was very rude of me. Thank you so much, for everything. For this." He held up the tuxedo. "For your kindness. For Rosa."

He had nearly saved the moment, and they allowed him to think that he had. But her father fled the bedroom within the minute, and Rosa and her Joe were left alone, on the bed, naked, staring at the empty blue suit.

4

THE LAST LETTER that Joe was ever to receive from his mother, mailed from the Ostrovni Street post office, as the laws required, between the hours of one and three in the afternoon, read as follows (the black marks trace the brusque transit of the censor's pen across the text):

My dear son,

It is a puzzle worthy of the best psychiatrist that a human life can be so utterly void and at the same time filled to bursting with hope. With Thomas gone we have nothing to live for, it seems, but the knowledge that he is on his way to be with you in that fortunate nation which has already so kindly received you in its bosom.

We are all as well as can be expected given Tante Lou's fits of pique ["Tante Lou" was family code for the Nazi government of Prague]. Your grandfather has lost most of the hearing in his left ear due to an infection, and some of the use of his right ear as well. So now he dwells in a realm of shouted conversations and serene imperviousness to argument. The latter is a valuable skill to possess around our Dear Friends [i.e., the Katz family, with whom the Kavaliers shared their two-room flat], and indeed I am at times inclined to believe that Papa is simply pretending to be deaf, or at least that he arranged to become so on purpose. My wrist has not quite healed—it never may in the absence of ███████ diet—and is quite useless in poor weather but we have lately had a stretch of fine days, and I have continued to work on my *Reinterpretation of*

*Dreams** though paper [? smudged] is ███████████ bother, and I am obliged to soak my old typewriter ribbons in ███.

Please, Josef, do not continue to trouble yourself or waste your time attempting to win for us what you have, with the help of your friends, been able to attain for your brother. It is enough; more than enough. Your late father, as you know, suffered from chronic optimism, but it is clear to me and to anyone not foolish or addled by deafness that we ████████ and that the present state of affairs will be as permanent as any of us shall require. You must make a life for yourself there, with your brother, and turn your thoughts from us and from ██████.

I have not had word from you for three months, and while I am certain that you continue to write faithfully I take this silence however unintentional as a suggestion. In all likelihood this letter will not find you but if you are reading this, then please. Listen to me. I want you to forget us, Josef, to leave us behind once and for all. It is not in your nature to do so, but you must. They say that ghosts find it painful to haunt the living, and I am tormented by the idea that our tedious existence should dim or impair your enjoyment of your own young life. That the reverse situation should obtain is fair and proper, and you cannot imagine how I delight in picturing you standing on some bright, busy street corner in that city of freedom and swing music. But for you to waste another moment in worrying about us in this city of ███████████! No.

I shall not write again unless I have news of which you cannot fairly be deprived. Until then you must know, dear one, that you are in my thoughts every instant of my waking life and in my (clinically quite uninteresting) dreams as well.

Fondly,

Mother

This letter was in the hip pocket of Joe's new tuxedo as he entered the cream-and-gold Grand Ballroom of the Pierre. He had been carrying it around with him—unopened and unread—for days now. When-

* Lost.

ever he paused to consider this behavior he found it quite shocking; but he never paused for very long. The burst of guilt that lit up the radiant nerves of his solar plexus when he handled or suddenly remembered the unopened letter was every bit as intense, he was sure, as whatever he would feel upon tearing its fragile seal and letting out the usual gray compound of bad dreams and pigeon feathers and soot. Every evening he took out the letter, without looking at it, and set it on his dresser. In the morning he transferred it to the pocket of the next day's trousers. It would not be accurate to say that it weighed there like a stone, encumbering his progress through the city of freedom and swing, or that it caught like a bone in his throat. He was twenty years old, and he had fallen in love with Rosa Saks, in the wild scholastic manner of twenty-year-old men, seeing, in the tiniest minutiae, evidence of the systematic perfection of the whole and proof of a benign creation. He loved, for example, her hair in all the forms it took on her body: the down on her lip, the fuzz on her buttocks, the recurrent brown feelers her eyebrows sent toward each other in between tweezings, the coarse pubic ruff that she had allowed him to shave into the outline of a moth's wings, the thick smoke-fragrant curls of her head. When she worked on a canvas in her top-floor room, she had a habit, when pondering, of standing storklike on her left foot and lovingly massaging it with the big toe, its toenail painted aubergine, of the right. Somehow this shade of purple and the echo of contemplative childish masturbation in the way she rubbed at her ankle struck him every time as not merely adorable but profound. The two dozen commonplace childhood photographs—snowsuit, pony, tennis racket, looming fender of a Dodge—were an inexhaustible source of wonder for him, at her having existed before he met her, and of sadness for his possessing nothing of the ten million minutes of that black-and-white scallop-edged existence save these few proofs. Only the embattled standards of a fundamentally restrained and sensible character prevented him from nattering constantly, to friends and strangers alike, about the capers she put in chicken salad (it was how her late mother had made it), the pile of dream words that accumulated by her bedside night after night, the lily-of-the-valley smell of her hand soap, et cetera. His portrayals of Judy Dark, in her up-to-the-minute gowns and bathing costumes cribbed from *Vogue,* and of her winged alter ego

in streamlined bra and panties, grew ever more libidinous and daring—
as if Luna Moth had received from the secret councils of Sex Itself an
augmentation of powers like that granted to the Escapist at the outbreak
of war—until she verged, in certain panels that took on a sacred and
totemic significance for the boys of America, on total nakedness.

Thus, just as his mother begged him (though he did not know it), Joe
had turned his thoughts from Prague, his family, the war. Every golden
age is as much a matter of disregard as of felicity. It was only when he
was settling into the back of a taxicab, or reaching for his wallet, or
brushing against a chair, that there came the crinkling of paper; the
flutter of a wing; the ghostly foolscap whisper from home; and for a moment he would hang his head in shame.

"What is it?" Rosa said.

He had taken off the cutaway jacket, with the key pinned to its lapel,
in order to drape it over the back of a chair, and as he did so the letter
had rustled in its envelope.

"Nothing," he said. "Okay, sit there. I have to get to work."

This was his third time playing the Pierre, and he knew its charac-
teristics fairly well, but he always liked to take ten minutes to reconnoi-
ter or reacquaint himself with the room. He went up onto the low
bandstand, at the back of which there were three tall panels faced with
gilded mirrors. They had to be detached and lugged, one at a time,
down the steps and around to a side of the room where they would not
betray the secrets of his magician's table. He dialed the five rheostats to
a medium setting, so that the light of five massive chandeliers would
not reveal his black silk threads or expose the false bottom of a pitcher.
The crystal chandeliers had been draped for the occasion with some
green crepey stuff that was supposed to represent seaweed: the theme
of tonight's reception was, according to the printed programs laid
across each gleaming plate, Neptune's Kingdom. There were weird
purple stalagmites jutting up from the carpet all around the room, to
the right of the bandstand leaned the prow and bosomy figurehead, in
papier-mâché, of a sunken galleon buried in real sand, and in the center of it all yawned a giant opalescent clamshell from which Joe sincerely hoped Leon Douglas Saks was not planning to emerge. From the
ceiling hung two mannequins with scallops covering their waxen

breasts, and the sequined tails of hake and halibut where their legs ought to have been. Heavy fishing nets beaded with wooden floats hung from the walls, each filled with a catch of rubber starfish and lobster.

"You really look like you know what you're doing," Rosa said, watching him dismantle the mirrors and adjust the lights.

"That is the greatest of Cavalieri's illusions."

"You also look very handsome."

"Thank you."

"So are we going to have one of these things one day?"

"We are too old," he said, not quite paying attention. Then he caught on. "Oh," he said. "Well."

"I suppose we might have girls."

"A girl can have them, too, now. Somebody told me this. Then it's called a boss mitzvah."

"Which do you prefer?"

"Bas mitzvah. Bas or boss, I'm not really sure."

"Joe?"

"I don't know, Rosa," he said. He sensed that he should stop what he was doing and go over to her, but something about the topic irritated him and he felt himself closing up inside. "I can't be sure I want to have children at all."

The playfulness had left her manner. "That's okay, Joe," she said. "I'm not sure I do either."

"I mean, is this really the time or the kind of world that we want a child to be born, is all the thing."

"Yeah, yeah, yeah," she said. "Forget it." She blushed and smoothed out her skirt. "Those purple rocks look *so* familiar."

"I think so, too."

"I can't believe this room," she said. "I've never really, you know, dipped into the Talmud or anything like that, but it's hard to imagine that they were leaping out of giant clamshells back in Tarshish or wherever."

"So long as they did not *eat* the clams," Joe said.

"Did you have one of these?"

"No, I did not. I considered it. But no. We were not religious."

"Uh-huh."

"Are," he said. "Are not." He looked stricken. He stood up straight and flexed his fingers a few times. "We *are* not religious."

"No, we aren't either."

He walked back over to the chair where he had hung his jacket. He reached into the pocket and took out the letter in its pale-blue envelope and held it, looking at it.

"Why are you carrying that around?" Rosa said. "Did you open it? What does it say?"

There were voices; the ballroom doors burst open and the musicians came in, followed by one of the white-jacketed hotel waiters, pushing a cart. The musicians climbed up onto the bandstand and began opening their cases. Joe had worked with some of them before, and they nodded to one another, and Joe accepted their whistles and teasing about his .new clothes. Joe replaced the envelope, then put his jacket back on. He shot his cuffs, smoothed back his hair, and tied on the silken mask. When the musicians saw that, they burst into applause.

"Well?" he said, turning to Rosa. "What do you think?"

"Very mysterious," Rosa said. "Indeed."

There was a strange, strangled cry by the door, and Joe turned in time to see the white-jacketed waiter dash out of the ballroom.

THE STEEL GAUNTLET, Kapitan Evil, the Panzer, Siegfried, Swastika Man, the Four Horsemen, and Wotan the Wicked all confine their nefarious operations, by and large, to the battlefields of Europe and North Africa, but the Saboteur, King of Infiltration, Vandal Supreme, lives right in Empire City—in a secret redoubt, disguised as a crumbling tenement, in Hell's Kitchen. That is what makes him so effective and feared. He is an American citizen, an ordinary man from a farm in small-town America. By day he works as a humble unknown in one of the anonymous trades of the city. By night he creeps forth from his Lair, with his big black bag of dirty tricks, and makes war on the infrastructure of the city and the nation. He is every bit the dark obverse of the Escapist, as skilled at worming his way into something as the Escapist is at fighting his way out. As the Escapist's power has increased, so has the Saboteur's, until the latter can walk through walls, leap thirty feet straight up, and befog men's minds so that he may pass unseen among them.

On one wall of the command room in his Lair there is a giant electrical map of the United States. On it, military bases are marked with a blue light, munitions plants with a yellow, shipyards with a green. After the Saboteur strikes, the lightbulb for that target, whatever its original hue, turns an evil shade of red. The Saboteur is fond of declaring that he will not rest until the entire nation is alight with blood-red bulbs. On another wall hangs the Videoscope, by means of which the Saboteur keeps in constant contact with his network of agents and operatives throughout the country. There is a laboratory, in which the Saboteur devises sinister new kinds of explosives, and a machine shop in which he crafts the novelty bombs—the Exploding Seagull, the Exploding

Derby Hat, the Exploding Pine Tree—for which he is known and re-
viled. There are also a fully equipped gymnasium, a library filled with
all the most advanced texts on science and world domination, and a
posh paneled bedroom with a canopy bed that the Saboteur (implicitly)
shares with Renata von Voom, the Spy Queen, his girlfriend and a
founding member of the United Snakes. It is in the Saboteur's well-
appointed Lair that the Snakes hold their regular meetings. Ah, the raucous and jolly gatherings, over rare sweetmeats and good lager, of the
United Snakes of America! They sit around the gleaming obsidian table,
the Fifth Columnist, Mr. Fear, Benedict Arnold, Junior, the Spy Queen,
and he, regaling one another with tales of the havoc, hate, and destruction they have sown over the past week, laughing like the maniacs they
are, and plotting out new courses of action for the future. Ah, the terror
they will cause! Ah, the subnormals, mixed bloods, and inferior races
they will string up by their mongrel necks! Ah, Renata, in her slick
black trench coat and gleaming hip boots!

One Saturday afternoon, after a particularly boisterous convocation
of the Snakes, the Saboteur wakes in his sumptuous chambers and pre-
pares to leave the Lair for the menial job that is a cover for his subver-
sive activities. He peels off his night-black action suit and hangs it from
a hook in his armory, alongside its six duplicates. His symbol, a crimson crowbar, is outlined in silver on the chest. Is there a smell of beer
and sausages on the shoulder of the costume, and of Mexican cigars?
He will have to send it out to be cleaned. The Saboteur is particular
about such things; he cannot abide dirt or filth or disorder, unless it be
the mess, the splendid entropy of a fire, an explosion, or a train wreck.
Having removed his costume, he pulls on a pair of black trousers piped
in black. He runs a damp comb through his thinning colorless hair and
shaves his babyish pink face. Then he puts on a boiled white shirt, at-
taches the collar, ties on a black bow tie, and takes down a white dinner
jacket. It has just come back from the cleaners and hangs in a crinkly
paper bag. He slings it over his shoulder and then exits, not without regret, the clean and cavernous armory. Next he goes into his laboratory
and picks up the disassembled parts of the Exploding Trident, cleverly
concealed inside of a pink cake box from a Ninth Avenue bakery. With
the box under his arm and the jacket over his shoulder, he turns and

waves goodbye to Renata, who lies, gazing lazily at him through half-lowered long-lashed lids, under the portrait of the Führer, in the great oak bed.

"Knock 'em dead, Big Boy," she says in her vermouth voice, as he lets himself out through the Lair's air lock and enters the grit, filth, and foul atmosphere, ripe with the stench of immigrants and Negroes and mongrels, of Empire City. He does not reply to her languid farewell; he is on the job, all business now.

He hops a bus across town to Fifth Avenue, then another to ride the twenty blocks uptown. Ordinarily he dislikes taking the bus, but he is late already, and if you are late, they take it out of your pay. His rent on the Lair is cheap, but his pay is low enough without being docked again for lateness. He knows he can not afford to lose another job; his sister Ruth has already warned him that she will not "prop him up." Absurd that the Saboteur should have to trouble with such mundane concerns, but these are the sacrifices entailed by maintaining a secret identity—look at all the headaches and trouble that Lois Lane, for example, makes for Clark Kent.

He arrives ten minutes late—that's fifty cents, five Te Amos, lost—and, when he gets there, finds that they have already begun to set up the ballroom for the affair. The swish decorator is busy bossing around his employees, getting them to hang the fishnets, assemble the cardboard shipwreck, and roll in the big rubber rock formations that were salvaged, so Mr. Dawson, the ballroom manager, has told him, from that *Dream of Venus* girlie show on the midway at the World's Fair. The Saboteur is well informed on the particulars of this evening's reception, for it is the one he has chosen to make the scene of his greatest exploit to date.

The Pierre is a popular venue for the wedding and bar mitzvah receptions of the rich Jews of the city, as the Saboteur discovered shortly after taking the job. Almost every week, they crowd in like pigs to a trough and throw their money around (they just come right up to the pimply kid-of-the-week, for God's sake, and stuff packets of cash into his cummerbund!) and get drunk and dance their tedious dances to the music of their whining violins. While it galls him to have to serve and wait upon such people, the Saboteur has known from the first that this secret identity will afford him, in due course, the opportunity to strike a terrible blow. For months he bided his time, improving his skills, under the guidance of a drunken old anarcho-syndicalist named Fiordaliso, as a bomb constructor, reading Feuchtwangler and Spengler (and *Radio Comics*), watching for his moment. Then, at a bar mitzvah one night last winter, the Amazing Cavalieri appeared on the bill, passing cigarettes through handkerchiefs and making flowers bloom in his boutonniere, and turned out to be none other than Joe Kavalier. (The Saboteur had long since rectified his misapprehension that it was the Sam Clay half of the team who had been responsible both for the destruction of the AAL offices and for the autographed sketch of the Escapist, which now hung from a dartboard in the gymnasium at the Lair.) The Saboteur was too astonished to act at the time, but he began to sense then that his moment might soon be at hand. For weeks after that night, he chatted up Mr. Dawson and, through him, monitored the programs for upcoming events, watching the big schedule book for a reappearance of the Amazing Cavalieri. And tonight is the night. When he arrived at work, it was with the intention of showing Joe Kavalier that while Carl Henry Ebling may be a shiftless bumbler and pamphleteer, the Saboteur is not one to be trifled with, and his memory is long. At the same time, he would be removing with masterly precision whatever other mongrels happened to be standing in the young Jew's vicinity. Yes, he would have been contented with just that. How surprising, disturbing, marvelous, strange it is, then, to roll into the Grand Ballroom, pushing the service cart that conceals the Exploding Trident, and discover that the performing magician hired for the Saks bar mitzvah is not some moonlighting scribbler but the Escapist himself, the Saboteur's dark idol, his opposite number, masked and fully costumed and wearing in his lapel the symbol of his cursed League.

At that moment, the sheet of paper on which the contours of Carl Ebling's mind have been drawn is like a map that has been folded and carelessly refolded too many times. The reverse shows through; the poles meet; at the heart of a ramifying gray grid of city streets lies an expanse of virgin blue sea.

Was there ever a moment when Superman lingered a second too long in his timid Kent aspect and suffered a fatal hesitation? Did the Escapist ever forget to clasp his talisman and stumble on crippled legs into the fray? The Saboteur tries to remain calm, but the stuttering doormat with whom he must share his existence is a bundle of nerves and, like a fool, goes running out of the room.

He stands in the foyer outside the ballroom, leaning against a wall, his cheek pressed against the soft, cool flocked wallpaper. He lights a cigarette, inhales deeply, calms himself. There is no call for panic; he is the King of Infiltration, and he knows what to do. He stubs out the cigarette in the sand of a nearby ashtray, and takes hold of the cart once again. This time, when he enters the ballroom, he has the presence of mind to keep his head down, to avoid being recognized by the Escapist.

"Sorry, folks," he murmurs. He pushes the cart across to the far side of the stage, by the shivered timbers of the sunken ship. It has a squeaky wheel, and he feels certain that he must be attracting the attention of the musicians on the bandstand, of the magician and his big-nose girl. But when he looks back, they are absorbed in their own preparations. She is a pretty enough girl, he supposes, and her black mannish overcoat reminds him with a twinge of the queen of his own desire. When he reaches the ship, he stops, crouches behind the cart, and opens the compartment in which hot plates of food are stored by the room-service waiters on their way up to rooms.

Until now the ballroom has been too crowded with decorators, waiters, and hotel staff, coming and going as they prepared the room for the event, for him to find the opportunity to assemble the parts of his Exploding Trident. Now he works quickly, screwing the length of thin pipe that contains the black powder and cut-up nails into a second length of pipe that is empty. This will be the shaft. At the dummy end, he affixes tines of stiff red cellophane, copped from a costume-shop devil-suit pitchfork, with a piece of masking tape. It looks a little suspicious, he knows, but fortunately, verisimilitude is not something people generally expect from a sea god's trident. He unrolls the six-inch strip of fuse that protrudes through a hole drilled in the thing's business end. Then he stands up and, checking to see that he is not being observed, edges over toward one of the fishnets tacked to the wall, filled with its catch of fake crustaceans. No one sees; his rich lifelong powers of invisibility remain his truest ally. Gingerly, he slides the trident down through the heavy mesh of the fishnet until the fuse end bumps the carpet. When the time comes—when the Escapist has begun his legendary act—the Saboteur will contrive to pass by here again. He will rest half a lighted Camel against a strand of the net, so that the unlit end touches the fuse. Then he will hie himself out of harm's way and wait. And five minutes after that, the mongrels of Empire City will begin to know something of the terror their mongrel brothers and sisters are undergoing halfway around the world.

The Saboteur pushes the cart back toward the ballroom doors. At the last moment, as he is passing the magician, he cannot prevent himself from raising his head and looking his adversary in the eye. If there is a flicker of recognition there, it is extinguished in an instant as the doors to the ballroom fly open and, laughing and shouting and crying out in their loud barnyard voices, the first of the guests arrive.

6

WHAT FOLLOWS IS the intended program for the performance given by the Amazing Cavalieri on the evening of April 12, 1941. A copy, printed by the performer himself using a "Printer's Devil" Genuine Junior Printing Press that he had dug out of the Empire Novelties stockroom just before the move from the Kramler Building, was handed out to every guest just prior to the show.

> The Wanderings of a Handkerchief.
> Magic Bananas.
> A Miniature Conflagration.
> Fly Away Home.
> Please Don't Eat the Pets.
> A Contagious Knot.
> Adrift in the Stream of Time.
> Ice and Fire.
> Where Have I Been?
> The Tail Has Lost Its Monkey.

Joe's self-consciousness about his English, and a suspicion of patter inherited from his great teacher, kept his performance swift and wordless. Frequently he was told, usually by the mother or an aunt of the bar mitzvah boy, that the show had been very nice, but would it kill him to smile a little now and then? Tonight was no exception. If anything, it seemed to those scattered guests at the Saks reception who had caught his act before, he was even more guarded, more workmanlike in his approach than usual. His movements and his pacing were neither too hasty nor too slow, and there were no—as had sometimes happened in the past—dropped cards or spilled pitchers of water. But he took no apparent pleasure in the marvelous feats he performed. One would have thought it meant nothing to him that he could produce a bowlful of goldfish from a tin of sardines, or pass a bunch of bananas one at a time through the skull of a thirteen-year-old boy. Rosa supposed that he was troubled by something he had read in that latest letter from home, and wished, as she had wished many times, that he was more willing to share with her his fears, his doubts, and whatever bad news there was from Prague.

Longman Harkoo, though he tried, was one of those people incapable, due to some abnormality of vision or comprehension, of following the movements of a magic act, the way some people go to baseball games and never manage to see the ball in flight; a towering home run is just ten thousand people craning their necks. He soon gave up trying to pay attention to the things that were supposed to be amazing him, and found himself watching the boy's eyes behind the black silk mask. They continually scanned the room—that in itself was impressive enough, that he could manipulate the cards and other props of his act without looking at his hands—and they seemed, Harkoo noticed, to follow in particular the movements of one of the waiters.

Joe had recognized Ebling at once, though it took him a while, amid the distractions of greeting his hosts and Rosa's family and of pulling dimes and matchsticks out of the bar mitzvah boy's nose, to place him. The Aryan seemed to have lost weight since their last encounter. Then, too, the sheer surprise of seeing Ebling again had interfered with his ability to identify him. He had given no thought to the man, or to his own war on the Germans of New York, in many weeks. He no longer went looking for trouble; after the bomb scare last fall, Joe felt he had bested Carl Ebling in their duel. The man simply seemed to have abandoned the field. Joe had gone back up to Yorkville once, to leave a calling card or a nyah-nyah-nyah on the Aryan-American League. The sign was no longer in the window, and when Joe broke into the office for a second time, he found it empty. The desks and the files had been moved out, the portrait of Hitler taken down, leaving not even a discolored square on the wall. There was nothing left but an old potato chip lying like a moth in the middle of the scarred wooden floor. Carl Ebling had disappeared, leaving no forwarding address.

Now here he was, working as a waiter at the Hotel Pierre, and clearly—Joe knew this as surely as he knew that the goldfish in his bowl were only hunks of carrot that he had carved with an apple knife—up to no good. As Ebling hurried back and forth across the ballroom with a tray on his shoulder, he kept looking up at Joe, not at the silks and golden hoops in his hand but at *him*, right into his face, with an expression that struggled to remain blank and anonymous but which was tinged at the corners with a flush of bitter mischief.

As Joe was about to begin A Contagious Knot, in which, with a puff of breath, the knot that he had tied in a silk scarf appeared to transfer itself along the row of ordinary silk scarves held up by volunteers from the audience, one after another before their very eyes, Joe smelled smoke. For an instant he thought it must be the lingering odor of A Miniature Conflagration, but on further exposure he knew that it was unquestionably tobacco—and something more, something acrid like burning hair. Then he noticed a thin plume of smoke coming from the side of the bandstand, down to his left, by the sunken ship. At once he dropped the scarf with its devilish knot and walked, swiftly but without appearing to panic, toward the smoke that was scribbling the air. His first thought was that someone had dropped a cigarette; then he felt a tickle of suspicion, and the face of Ebling flashed through his mind. And then he saw it all; the cylinder of ash burned down almost to the printed tip of the cigarette, the singed carpet, the length of grayish fuse, the length of steel pipe crudely disguised with some gaudy red cellophane. He stopped, turned, and went back to his table, where the bowl from Please Don't Eat the Pets still sat, filled with bright swimming bits of carrot.

There was some murmuring from the tables as he picked up the bowl.

"Excuse me," he said, "we seem to have a little fire."

As he went to pour the water onto the cigarette, he felt something large, heavy, and extremely hard smash into the small of his back. It felt a good deal like a human head. Joe went flying forward, and the goldfish bowl tumbled from his hands and shattered on the bandstand. Ebling climbed on top of Joe, clawing at his cheeks from behind, and as Joe tried to roll onto his back, he looked over and saw that the fuse was throwing a tiny shower of sparks. He gave up trying to roll and instead pushed upward on his hands and knees and proceeded to crawl, Ebling riding him, wild as an ape on the back of a pony, toward the pipe bomb. By now the people sitting closest to the bomb had taken note of the burning, and there was a general sense in the room that none of this was part of the show. A woman screamed, and then a lot of women were screaming, and Joe was lumbering forward with his rider ripping at his face and yanking on his ears. Ebling got his arms around Joe's throat and started to choke him. At that point, Joe ran out of bandstand. He lost his balance, and he and Ebling toppled over the side to the floor. Ebling rolled, tumbling against the outspread fishnet. It snapped loose from the wall, spilling a pile of rubber starfish and lobsters across him.

Ebling just had time to say "No." Then a sheet of heavy foil seemed to fall onto Joe's head, to wrap his face and throat and ears in crumpling steel. He was thrown backward, and something hot, a burning wire, was laid with a hiss across his forehead. There followed almost immediately an awful sound like a heavy club falling on a bag of tomatoes, and then an autumnal whiff of gunpowder.

"Oh, shit," Carl Ebling said, sitting up, blinking, licking his lips, blood on his forehead, blood in his hair, tiny red pawprints of blood all over his bright white jacket.

"What did you do?" Joe heard, or rather he felt, the words somewhere down in his throat. "Ebling, god damn it, what did you do?"

They were taken to Mt. Sinai Hospital. Joe's injuries were minor compared to Ebling's, and after he had been cleaned up, his facial wounds treated, and the laceration on his forehead butterflied shut, he was able to return, by popular demand, to the Grand Ballroom of the Pierre, where he was hailed and toasted and showered with money and praise.

As for Ebling, he was first charged only with unlawful possession of explosives; but this was later expanded to a charge of attempted murder. He was eventually indicted for a number of minor fires, synagogue vandalizings, phone-booth bombings, and even an attempted subway derailment the previous winter that had gotten a good deal of attention in the papers but, until the Saboteur confessed to it and to all of his other exploits, had gone unsolved.

Late that night, Rosa and her father helped Joe from the taxi to the curb and thence along the narrow lane up to the steps of the Harkoo house. His arms were draped across their shoulders and his feet seemed to glide two inches off the ground. He had not touched a drop all night, on orders from the emergency-room doctor at Mt. Sinai, but the morphine painkillers he had been given had finally taken their toll. Of that journey from the taxi to the curb, Joe was later to retain only the faint pleasant memory of Siggy Saks's kölnischwasser smell and of the coolness of Rosa's shoulder against his own abraded cheek. They dragged him up to the study and laid him out on the couch. Rosa unlaced his shoes, unbuttoned his trousers, helped him off with his shirt. She kissed his forehead, his cheeks, his chest, his belly, pulled a blanket up to his chin, and then kissed his lips. Rosa's father brushed Joe's hair back from his bandaged brow with a soft motherly hand. Then there was darkness, and the sound of their voices draining out of the room. Joe felt sleep gathering around him, coiling like smoke or cotton wool about his limbs, and he fought against it for a few minutes with an agreeable sense of struggle, as a child in a swimming pool might attempt to stand buoyed atop a football. Just as he surrendered to his opiate exhaustion, however, the echo of the bomb burst began to chime again in his ears, and he sat up, his heart pounding. He switched on a table lamp and went over to the low settee on which Rosa had laid his blue tuxedo, and lifted the jacket. In a strange slow panic, as if his hands were wrapped in layers of gauze, he felt around the pockets. He took the jacket by the tails and dangled it upside down, and shook it and shook it again. Out tumbled wads of cash, stacks of business cards and *cartes de visite,* silver dollars and subway tokens, cigarettes, his pocketknife, torn corners of his program scrawled with the addresses and phone numbers of the people he had saved. He turned the jacket and each of its ten pockets inside out. He fell to his knees and shuffled over and over through the pile of cards and dollars and torn scraps of program. It was like the classic magician's nightmare in which the dreamer riffles, with mounting dread, through a deck at once ordinary and infinite, looking for a queen of hearts or a seven of diamonds that somehow never turns up.

Early the next morning he returned, groggy and aching and halfmad with tinnitus, to the Pierre and made a thorough search of its ballroom. He inquired several times over the next week at Mt. Sinai Hospital, and contacted the lost-and-found office of the Hack Bureau.

Later, after the world had been torn in half, and the Amazing Cavalieri and his blue tuxedo were to be found only in the gilt-edged pages of deluxe photo albums on the coffee tables of the Upper West Side, Joe would sometimes find himself thinking about the pale-blue envelope from Prague. He would try to imagine its contents, wondering what news or sentiments or instructions it might have contained. It was at these times that he began to understand, after all those years of study and performance, of feats and wonders and surprises, the nature of magic. The magician seemed to promise that something torn to bits might be mended without a seam, that what had vanished might reappear, that a scattered handful of doves or dust might be reunited by a word, that a paper rose consumed by fire could be made to bloom from a pile of ash. But everyone knew that it was only an illusion. The true magic of this broken world lay in the ability of the things it contained to vanish, to become so thoroughly lost, that they might never have existed in the first place.

ONE OF THE STURDIEST PRECEPTS of the study of human delusion is that every golden age is either past or in the offing. The months preceding the Japanese attack on Pearl Harbor offer a rare exception to this axiom. During 1941, in the wake of that outburst of gaudy hopefulness, the World's Fair, a sizable portion of the citizens of New York City had the odd experience of feeling for the time in which they were living, at the very moment they were living in it, that strange blend of optimism and nostalgia which is the usual hallmark of the aetataureate delusion. The rest of the world was busy feeding itself, country by country, to the furnace, but while the city's newspapers and newsreels at the Trans-Lux were filled with ill portents, defeats, atrocities, and alarms, the general mentality of the New Yorker was not one of siege, panic, or grim resignation to fate but rather the toe-wiggling, tea-sipping contentment of a woman curled on a sofa, reading in front of a fire with cold rain rattling against the windows. The economy was experiencing a renewal not only of sensation but of perceptible movement in its limbs, Joe DiMaggio hit safely in fifty-six straight games, and the great big bands reached their suave and ecstatic acme in the hotel ballrooms and moth-lit summer pavilions of America.

Given the usual urge of those who believe themselves to have lived through a golden age to expatiate upon the subject at great length afterward, it is ironic that the April night on which Sammy felt most aware of the luster of his existence—the moment when, for the first time in his life, he was fully conscious of his own happiness—was a night that he would never discuss with anyone at all.

It was one o'clock on a Wednesday morning, and Sammy stood alone atop the city of New York, gazing in the direction of the storm clouds, both literal and figurative, that were piling up away to the east. Before coming on to his shift at ten o'clock, he had showered in the rough stall Al Smith had arranged to have built for the spotters, down in their quarters on the eighty-first floor, and changed into the loose twill trousers and faded blue oxford shirt that he kept in his locker there and wore three nights a week throughout the war, taking them home after his Friday shift to wash them in time for Monday's. For appearances' sake, he put his shoes back on for the quick trip up to the observatory, but when he got there he always took them off again. It was his habit, his conceit, and his strange comfort to prowl the sky of Manhattan Island, on the lookout for enemy bombers and aerial saboteurs, in his stocking feet. As he made his regular rounds of the eighty-sixth floor, clipboard in hand, heavy army-issue binoculars on a cord around his neck, he whistled to himself, unaware that he was doing so, a tune at once tuneless and involved.

It promised to be a typically quiet shift; night flights of an authorized nature were rare even in good weather, and tonight, with warnings of thundershowers and electrical storms blowing in, there would be even fewer airplanes in the sky than usual. Affixed to Sammy's clipboard, as always, was a typed list provided by the Army Interceptor Command, in whose service he was a volunteer, of the seven aircraft that had been cleared for transit across New York metropolitan airspace that night. All but two were military, and by eleven-thirty Sammy had already spotted six of them, on schedule and in position, and made the required notation of their passages in his log. The seventh was not expected until around five-thirty, just before his shift ended and he went back down to the spotters' quarters to catch a few hours' sleep before his day at Empire Comics began.

He made another circuit through the long chrome expanse of the observation-deck restaurant, which initially had been built as the baggage and ticket counter for a planned worldwide dirigible service that had never materialized, and had then spent the last two years of Prohibition as a tearoom. The passage through the bar was the only real perturbation Sammy had ever experienced in his career as a plane spotter, for the temptation of the gleaming spigots, coffee urns, and orderly rows of glasses and cups had to be counterbalanced against the eventual subsequent need, should he indulge his thirst, to urinate. Sammy was certain that if a fatal black line of Junkers was ever to appear in the skies over Brooklyn, it would unquestionably be while he was in the bathroom taking a leak. He was just on the point of helping himself to a few inches of seltzer from the elaborate chrome tap under the still-illuminated neon Ruppert's sign when he heard a dark rumble. For a moment he thought it must have been the approaching thunder, but then, in his memory, he heard again the mechanical hiss that had underlaid it. He put down his glass and ran to the bank of windows on the other side of the room. The darkness of a Manhattan night, even at this late hour, was far from absolute, and the radiant carpet of streets reaching as far as Westchester, Long Island, and the wilds of New Jersey cast an upward illumination so bright that the stealthiest intruder flying without landing lights would have had a difficult time concealing itself from Sammy's gaze, even without binoculars. There was nothing in the sky, however, but the great cloud of light.

The rumble grew louder and somehow smoother; the hiss modulated to a soft hum; from the center of the building, there was a faint clacking of gears and cams: the elevators. It was not a sound he was accustomed to hearing at this hour, in this place. The fellow who generally relieved him at six, an American Legionnaire and retired oysterman named Bill McWilliams, always took the stairs up from the quarters on eighty-one. Sammy walked toward the elevator bank, wondering if he ought to pick up the telephone that connected him to the office of the Army Interceptor Command in the telephone-company building down on Cortlandt Street. In the pages of *Radio Comics*, the groundwork for an invasion of New York City could be laid in just a few panels, one of which would unquestionably depict the braining with a blackjack of a hapless plane spotter by the gloved fist of an Axis saboteur. Sammy could see the jagged star of impact, the sprung letters spelling out KR-RACK!, the word balloon in which the poor fool was shown saying, "Say, you can't come in—*ohhh!*"

It was one of the express elevators from the lobby. Sammy checked his clipboard again. If anyone was expected—his supervisor, some other military type, some colonel of the Interceptor Command making an inspection—surely his night's orders would have noted it. But there was only, as he had known there would be, the same list of seven planes and flight plans, and a terse notation about the bad weather expected. Perhaps this was a surprise inspection. As Sammy looked down at his stocking feet, wiggling his nonregulation toes, his thoughts took another turn: maybe this visit was unannounced because something unforeseen had occurred. Perhaps someone was coming to tell Sammy that the country was at war with Germany, or even, somehow, that the war in Europe had ended, and it was time for him to go home.

There was a metallic shiver as the car drew up to the eighty-sixth floor, a rattle of cables. Sammy ran a damp hand through his hair. Locked in a bottom drawer of the guard station, he knew, there was a service .45, but Sammy had lost track of the key, and would not even have known, in any case, how to get the safety off. He raised his clipboard, ready to bring it down on the skull of the spy. The binoculars were heavier. He took them from his neck and prepared to swing them like a mace on their leather strap. The doors slid open.

"Is this Men's Sportswear?" said Tracy Bacon. He wore a tuxedo jacket, a white silk cravat stiff and glossy as meringue, and a mien that was grave but volatile, stretched thin over an underlying smirk, as if some kind of prank were under way. A brown paper shopping bag dangled from each hand. "Have you got anything in a gabardine?"

"Bacon, you can't—"

"I was just passing by," the actor said. "Thought I'd, you know, stop in."

"We're a thousand feet up!"

"Are we?"

"It's one o'clock in the morning."

"Is it?"

"This is a U.S. Army facility," Sammy went on, sounding self-important and knowing it, struggling to ascribe a reason to the giddy flush of guilt, so like exhilaration, that suffused him at the arrival of Tracy Bacon on the eighty-sixth floor. He was perilously happy to see his new friend. "Technically speaking. After hours, nobody's allowed in or out without clearance from Command."

"Yikes," said Bacon. The magnificent Otis machinery that enclosed him gave a sigh, as of impatience. Bacon took a step backward. "Then you absolutely do *not* want a Nazi spy like me hanging around. What was I *thinking*?" The elevator doors stuck out their black rubber tongues. Sammy watched the sundered halves of his own reflection reach toward each other in the brushed chrome panels of the doors. "*Auf wiedersehen.*"

Sammy thrust his hand through the doors. "Wait."

Bacon waited, looking at Sammy, one eyebrow raised in the challenging manner of an auctioneer about to bring his gavel down. His jacket was a charcoal silk cutaway, with piped lapels, and his broad chest was plated in the largest and whitest dickie Sammy had ever seen. In his formal attire, he seemed to beam down from a greater height than usual, certain as ever that in the end he would be, even a thousand feet up, at one in the morning, and contrary to military regulations, welcome. Even with the incongruous pair of shopping bags, or perhaps because of them, he looked impossibly comfortable in his monkey suit, shoulders pressed against the back wall of the elevator, legs crooked at the knee, the great right foot in its long black Lagonda of a shoe twisting ever so slightly on its toe tip. The elevator sighed again.

"Well," Sammy said, "seeing as how your father's a general . . ."

Sammy stepped aside, keeping a hand on the door that was struggling to close. Bacon hesitated a moment longer, as if daring Sammy to change his mind again. Then he pushed himself off the elevator wall and sauntered out. The doors closed. Sammy was in gross violation of the code.

"Only a brigadier," Bacon said. "You all right, Clay?"

"Fine, I'm fine, come in."

"That's the lowest, you know."

"What is?"

"Brigadier. It's the lowest grade of general they make."

"That must chafe."

"Eats him away. Wow." Bacon looked around the cool marble sweep of the observation floor's lobby, kept dim at night to cut down on reflection and permit better viewing through the great dark windows, and he squinted a little as he peered off into the glints and shadows of the bar on one hand and the long bank of windows on the other. "Wow!"

"Yeah, wow," Sammy said, suddenly feeling less exhilarated than awkward, even slightly afraid. What had he done? What was Bacon up to? What was the faintly acrid but not unpleasant smell that seemed to be emanating from the actor's direction? "So, uh. Welcome."

"This is great!" Bacon said. He strode toward the windows that looked out over the Hudson River, toward the black cliffs and neon billboards of New Jersey. There was something faintly lurching, Frankensteinian, in Bacon's gait, and Sammy followed him closely to make sure nothing got broken. Bacon pressed his face to the window, smashing his straight, slightly pointed nose flat against it with a vehemence that made Sammy's heart leap. The windows were made of thick tempered glass, but Tracy Bacon possessed that brand of glamorous stupidity—or so it would come to seem to Sammy—which acts as a charm against such technological safeguards. He would wriggle his way out onto a theater balcony that had been closed because it was on the verge of collapse, enter any stairway marked No Admittance, and, as Sammy would later learn, Bacon especially liked, when there was no one looking, to sneak from subway platforms down onto the tracks, penetrating some ways into the tunnels by the pale glow of his platinum cigarette lighter. It had been a terrible mistake letting him up here tonight. "I must say, I couldn't figure out why anybody in his right mind would want to sign himself up for this kind of work . . . unpaid . . . but now . . . you have all this to yourself, every night?"

"Three nights a week. Are you drunk?"

"What kind of question is that?" Bacon said, without elaborating whether he found the question offensive or merely superfluous, or both. "I came up here my first day in New York City," he continued, his breath fogging up the glass. "It was a lot different in the daylight. Kids running around. All that blue sky and steam out there. Pigeons. Boats. Flags."

"I've actually never been up here in the daytime. I mean, I've seen the sun come up. But I'm always gone long before they let the people in."

Bacon stepped back. A ghostly print of his skull lingered a moment on the window before evaporating. Then he slid down along the windows to the southeast corner, where, as at the three other corners of the observation floor, there was a coin-operated telescope. He stooped to peer through it. The shopping bags made a crinkling sound. Bacon seemed to have forgotten he was carrying them.

"This is really something," he said, squinting into the eyepiece. "You can see the Statue of Liberty." Unless you fed it a dime, of course, you could see nothing at all. "How about that, she sleeps in a hair net." He whirled around, the expression on his face at once innocent and reckless, for all the world like a toddler searching the nursery for something new to break.

"Mind if I look around?"

"Well . . ."

"This where you sit?"

Still carrying the bags, trailing a now-unmistakable odor of asparagus, Bacon walked over behind the broad podium that served during the day as a station for the guards who took tickets and gave informal tours of the celebrated panorama. This was where the Interceptor Command had installed the telephone that would, in the event of an aerial attack, connect Sammy immediately to Cortlandt Street. Sammy kept his lunch box here, his spare pencils, cigarettes, and extra log forms.

"I don't really sit. . . . Bacon, maybe you'd better not . . . no!"

Bacon had set down one of the bags and lifted the receiver of the emergency phone. "Hello, Fay? It's Kong. Listen, sweetheart—hey. It's ringing."

Sammy ran around behind the guard station, snatched the phone from his hand, and slammed it back into place.

"Sorry."

"Can I ask you something, Bacon?" said Sammy. "Besides not to touch anything, I mean?" He leaned against Bacon as against a stuck door, getting his shoulder into it, and dislodged him from behind the guard station. "What's in the bags?"

Bacon looked down at his left hand, a little surprised, then at the bag he had set beside him. He picked it up and then hefted the bags in Sammy's direction. Sammy caught a whiff of something buttery and winy and green, shallots maybe.

"Dinner!" Bacon said.

They went into the dark café, bristling with the upturned legs of chairs. The polished stone floor whispered against their feet. The chrome bands that ringed the long bar glinted at one end in the light from the lobby. The refrigerators hummed softly to themselves. The muted atmosphere of the bar seemed to dampen, or at least to still, Bacon's spirits somewhat. He spun two chairs floorward, and then, without a word, began to unpack his shopping bags. One bag, it turned out, contained three lidded silver platters, of the type that hotel waiters in the movies were always wheeling in on linen-draped carts. The other bag held two more of the platters and a small tureen drizzled with pale green soup. After Bacon had arranged the platters and tureen on the table, he took out a somewhat random fistful of forks, knives, and spoons, an ornate, heavy pattern, and a pair of cloth napkins somewhat soiled by juices and liquids that had escaped the various platters. He also took out a bottle of wine, a corkscrew, and two glasses, one of which had broken along the way.

"We'll have to share," he said. "Or I can just drink from the bottle."

"What, no baked Alaska?" said Sammy.

Bacon looked hurt. With a curt gesture, he lifted the lid on one of the platters, revealing a sad little puddle of brown-streaked white sugary ooze. "What do you take me for?"

"Sorry," Sammy said. They sat down to eat. There were quails stuffed with oysters, steamed asparagus in sauce hollandaise, a Macedonian salad, and dauphin potatoes. The pale soup was cream of watercress. Sammy could not quite bring himself to dismember one of the little bird bodies, but he picked out the stuffing and found it quite delicious. "What did you do?" said Sammy. "Order room service to go?" Bacon lived well beyond his means, according to him, at the Mayflower Hotel.

"Not exactly."

"It's good. Could be hotter."

"Salt?" Bacon reached into the shopping bag once more, took out a silver salt cellar of a design even more ornate than the flatware, and set it on the table. It was empty. "Oops." He leaned down again, peered into the bag, then lifted it up and tipped it, dipping one corner to the mouth of the salt cellar. A thin stream of lumpy salt poured down from the bag. "There. Good as new. So," he continued, gesturing to Sammy's clipboard and spotter's badge. "You just wanted to do your part, is that it? Help the Escapist in his unending fight against the Iron Chain and their Axis stooges?"

"A lot of people ask me that," Sammy said, sprinkling his potatoes with salt. "That's usually what I say."

"But you'll tell me the truth, won't you?" Bacon said, his voice mocking, but with just the slightest hint of an earnest plea.

"Well," Sammy said, flattered. "I just felt like I . . . *ought* to. I—I did something that I—I wasn't proud of. And when I got back from doing it, there was a small group of these volunteer spotters in the lobby, they were being given a tour, and I just kind of blended in with them. Before I really stopped to think about what I was doing."

"A guilty conscience."

Sammy nodded, although it was true that his stint as a plane spotter had also roughly coincided with the period when Joe began to spend more and more of his time with Rosa Saks, leaving Sammy alone with hours to kill nearly every night. "And don't ask me what was the thing I did, because I can't tell you."

"Okay, I won't," Bacon said with a shrug. He shoved a forkful of asparagus into his mouth.

"All right," said Sammy, "I'll tell you."

Bacon waggled his eyebrows. "Is it something kind of racy?"

"No." Sammy laughed. "No, I—I committed perjury. In a legal deposition. I told the lawyers for Superman that Shelly Anapol never asked me to copy their character. When he really just out-and-out had."

"My God!" Bacon said, looking perfectly aghast.

"Pretty bad, huh?"

"Hanging is too good for you."

Sammy saw then that Bacon had been teasing him. But he found that the memory of his uncomfortable and tedious afternoon in a conference room at Phillips, Nizer could still bring a flush of humiliation to his cheeks.

"Well, it was wrong," he said. "I had a good reason, but still. I guess I felt like I wanted to make up for it somehow."

"If that's the worst thing you ever did," Bacon said, shaking his head.

"So far," Sammy said. "I think it is."

Some unknown memory swam briefly into Bacon's eyes and saddened them. "Lucky you," he said.

"So, uh, where were you?" Sammy said, changing the subject. "Dressed like that. A party?"

"A little party. Very little."

"Where at?"

"Helen's. Today's her birthday."

"Helen Portola?"

"You forgot to say 'the lovely.' "

"The lovely Helen Portola?"

Bacon nodded, studying or affecting to study the thigh joint of one of his quail, as if there were a spot of blood that troubled him.

"Who was there?"

"I was there. The lovely Helen Portola was there."

"Just the two of you?"

He nodded again. He was so uncharacteristically terse on the subject that Sammy wondered if Bacon and Helen had quarreled. Sammy had little direct experience of actresses but shared in the conventional notion that by and large they possessed the sexual mores of estrous chinchillas. Surely if Helen Portola had invited her leading man to celebrate her birthday *à deux* in the privacy of her home, it was not because she expected the evening to end with her boyfriend out wandering around midtown with a couple of shopping bags full of tepid gourmet food.

"So how old is she?" said Sammy.

"Seventy-two, actually."

"Bacon."

"The old gal's remarkably well preserved."

"Bacon!"

"What's her secret? Liver, folks, and lots of it."

"Tracy!"

Bacon looked up from his food, pretending an innocent surprise.

"Yes, Clay?"

"What are you doing here?"

"What do you mean?"

Sammy gave him a hard look.

"Well, I didn't want to waste all this great food. Helen's cook went to a lot of trouble."

"Helen's cook?"

"Yes. I think you really ought to write her a little note."

"You mean, it was a *dinner* party?"

"Originally."

"Did you and Helen have a fight?"

Bacon nodded.

"A big one?"

He nodded again, looking genuinely miserable. "But it wasn't my fault," he said.

Sammy was dying to ask what they had fought about, but felt that they didn't know each other well enough for that. It did not occur to him that under similar circumstances, with anybody else, he would not have hesitated, in his best Brooklyn manner, to inquire. But Bacon enlightened him of his own accord.

"For some reason," Bacon continued, "she was under the misapprehension that I intended to propose marriage to her this evening. God knows who told her that."

"It was in Ed Sullivan," said Sammy. He had chanced upon the item in the *News* with an odd sense of regret; his friendship with Bacon had had so little room in which to flourish—the tiny area that marked the intersection of their separate worlds; and he sensed that it could not survive once Bacon had married his leading lady and gone off to Hollywood to be a star. "Yesterday morning."

"Oh, yeah." He gave his big handsome head a rueful shake.

"You saw it?"

"No, but I remember running into Ed Sullivan at Lindy's a couple of nights ago."

"Did you tell him you were going to ask Helen to marry you?"

"Could have."

"But you aren't."

"Didn't."

"And she got upset."

"Ran into her bedroom and slammed the door. Hit me first, actually."

"Good for her."

"Sucker punched me."

"Ouch." There was something exciting about this narrative to Sammy, or rather about the scene as he reconstructed it in his imagination. He felt that old stirring of desire he had often experienced, growing up to have . . . not Tracy Bacon, but rather his life, his build, his beautiful and temperamental girlfriend and the power to break her heart. When in fact what he had was a pair of binoculars, a clipboard, and the most solitary perch in the city three nights a week. "So then you took her food."

"Well, it was just sitting there."

"And brought it up here."

"Well, you were just sitting here."

The lull that this observation introduced into their talk was filled all of a sudden by a dark purple stirring in the sky all around them, a long, low summery sound, at once menacing and familiar. There was an answering murmur of bells from the stacked glasses on the bar.

"Jeez," Bacon said, getting up from the table. "Thunder."

He went over to the windows and looked out. Sammy rose and followed him.

"This way," he said, taking Bacon by the arm. "It's blowing in from the southeast."

They stood side by side, shoulders pressed together, watching the slow black zeppelin as it steamed in over New York, trailing long white guy wires of lightning. Thunder harried the building like a hound, brushing its crackling coat against the spandrels and mullions, snuffling at the windowpanes.

"It seems to like us." A feather of laughter fluttered in Bacon's voice. Sammy saw that he was afraid.

"Yeah," Sammy said. "We're its favorite." He lit a cigarette, and at the spark of his lighter, Bacon jumped. "Relax. They've been coming all month. They come all through the summer."

"Huh," Bacon said. He took a swallow from the bottle of Burgundy, then licked his lips. "And I am relaxed."

"Sorry."

"That stuff doesn't ever, you know, hit the building."

"Five times so far this year, I think it is."

"Oh my God."

"Relax."

"Shut up."

"They've recorded strokes that were more than twenty-two thousand amperes."

"Hitting this building."

"Ten million volts, or something like that."

"Jesus."

"Don't worry," Sammy said, "the whole building acts like one gigantic— Oh." Bacon's breath was sour with wine, but one sweet drop of the stuff lingered on his lips as he pressed his mouth against Sammy's. The stubble on their chins scraped with a soft electric rasp. Sammy was so taken by surprise that by the time his brain with its considerable store of Judeo-Christian prohibitions and attitudes could begin sending its harsh and condemnatory messages to the various relevant parts of his body, it was too late. He was already kissing Tracy Bacon back. They angled their bodies half toward each other. The bottle of wine clinked against the window glass. Sammy felt a tiny halo, a gemstone of heat burning his fingers. He let the cigarette drop to the floor. Then the sky just beyond the windows was veined with fire, and they heard a sizzle that sounded almost wet, like a droplet on a hot griddle, and then a thunderclap trapped them in the deep black caverns of its palms.

"Lightning rod," said Sammy, pulling away. As if in spite of all he had been told one evening last week by the bland and reassuring Dr. Karl B. MacEachron of General Electric, who had been studying the electrical atmospheric phenomena associated with the Empire State Building, from Saint Elmo's fire to reverse lightning that struck the sky, he was suddenly afraid. He took a step back from Tracy Bacon, stooped to retrieve his smoldering cigarette, and sought refuge by unconsciously adopting the dry manner of Dr. MacEachron himself. "The steel structure of the building attracts but then totally dissipates the discharge. . . ."

"I'm sorry," Bacon said.

"That's all right."

"I didn't mean to—wow, look at that."

Bacon pointed to the deserted promenade outside the windows.

Along its railings, a bright blue liquid, viscous and turbulent, seemed to flow. Sammy opened the door and reached out into the ozone-sharp darkness, and then Bacon came beside him again and put out his hand, too, and they stood there, for a moment, watching as sparks two inches long forked from the tips of their outstretched fingers.

MONG THE MAGICIANS who haunted Louis Tannen's Magic Shop was a group of amateurs known as the Warlocks, men with more or less literary careers who met twice a month at the bar of the Edison Hotel to baffle one another with drink, tall stories, and novel deceptions. The definition of "literary" had been stretched, in Joe's case, to include work in the comic book line, and it was through his membership in the Warlocks, another of whom was the great Walter B. Gibson, biographer of Houdini and inventor of the Shadow, that Joe had come to know Orson Welles, a semiregular attendee of the Edison confabulations. Welles was also, as it turned out, a friend of Tracy Bacon, whose first work in New York had been with the Mercury Theatre, playing the role of Algernon in Welles's radio production of *The Importance of Being Earnest.* Between Joe and Bacon, they had managed to get four tickets to the premiere of Welles's first film.

"So what's he like?" Sammy wanted to know.

"He's quite a guy," Rosa said. She had briefly met the tall, baby-faced actor one afternoon when she dropped by the Edison bar to meet Joe, and thought she had sensed in him a kindred spirit, a romantic, someone whose efforts to shock other people were, more than anything else, the expression of a kind of hopefulness about himself, of a desire to escape the confines of a decent respectable home. In high school, she and a friend had gone uptown to see the booming, voodooistic *Macbeth,* and she had loved it. "I really think he's a genius."

"You think everyone's a genius. You think this guy's a genius," Sammy said, jabbing Joe in the knee with a stubby forefinger.

"I don't think *you* are," she said sweetly.

"True genius is never recognized in its own time."

"Except by the one who has it," Bacon said. "Orson has no doubts on that score."

They were all headed uptown together, crammed into the back of a taxicab. Sammy and Rosa had taken the jump seats, and Rosa had a good grip on Sammy's arm. She had come from the offices of the T.R.A. and was dressed, with a dowdiness that pained her considerably, in a square-shouldered, belted brown tweed suit, of a vaguely military cut. She had been dressed like a schoolteacher the last time Orson Welles had seen her, too—the man was going to think that Joe Kavalier's girl-friend was about as fascinating as a sack of onions. Sammy had on one of his big, pinstriped leftovers from a George Raft film, Bacon the usual penguin suit—he took the part of man-about-town a bit too seriously for Rosa's taste, though, to his credit, that seemed to be just about the only thing he *did* take seriously. And Joe, of course, looked as if he had just fallen out of a hedge. There was white paint in his hair. It looked as though he had used the end of his necktie to blot an ink spill.

"He is a clever fellow," Joe said. "But not so good a magician."

"Is he really dating Dolores Del Rio?" Bacon said. "That's what I want to know."

"I wonder," Joe said, though he seemed completely uninterested in the question. He was feeling blue tonight, Rosa knew. Hoffman's ship, having finally reached Lisbon a few weeks previously, was to have reembarked for New York by now. But two days ago, a telegram had come from Mrs. Kurtzweil, the agent of the T.R.A. in Portugal. Three of the children had come down with measles; one of them was dead. Today they had received word that the entire convent of Nossa Senhora de Monte Carmelo had been put on an "absolute but indefinite quarantine" by the Portuguese authorities.

"I thought *you* were dating Dolores Del Rio, Bake," Sammy said. "That's what it said in Ed Sullivan."

"It was Lupe Velez."

"I mix those two up."

"Anyway, you know better than to believe what you read in the papers."

"Like, for instance, that Parnassus Pictures plans to bring funny-book strong man the Escapist to the silver screen in the person of noted radio star Mr. Tracy Bacon?"

"*Are* they?" Rosa said.

"It's only going to be one of those *serials*," Bacon said. "Parnassus. They're from hunger."

"Joe," Rosa said, "you didn't tell me."

"It doesn't make no difference to me," Joe said, still looking out at the neon-and-steam spectacle of Broadway scrolling past the windows of the cab. A woman walked by with what looked like the tails of at least nine little dead weasels dangling from her shoulders. "For Sammy and me we don't get a penny."

Sammy looked at Rosa and lifted a shoulder—*What's eating him?* Rosa gave Sammy's arm a squeeze. She hadn't had a chance to tell Sammy about the latest telegram from Lisbon.

"Maybe not on this end, Joe," Sammy continued, "but listen. Tracy here said that if he does get the role, he's going to put in a word for us with the studio. Tell them they ought to hire us to write the thing."

"It's only natural," Bacon said. " 'Course that probably damns the idea right there."

"We could move to *Hollywood*, Joe. That could *lead* to something. It could be the start of something really *legit*."

"Something legit." Joe nodded his head in a ponderous way, as if, upon reflection, Sammy had settled the question that had been troubling Joe all day. Then he went back to his window. "I know that's important to you."

"There it is," Bacon said. "The Palace."

"The Palace," Sammy said, an odd crease in his voice.

They pulled up in front of what was now known as the RKO Palace, once the summit and capital of American vaudeville, at the end of a line of cabs and hired cars. A colossal cutout of Orson Welles, looking wild-eyed and tousle-haired, loomed from the marquee. The whole front of the theater was riotous with flashbulbs and shouting, and there was a general impression of imminent catastrophe and red lipstick. Sammy had gone white as a sheet.

"Sam?" Rosa said. "You look like you saw a ghost."

"He's just worried we're going to make him pay the fare," said Bacon, reaching for his wallet.

Joe climbed out of the cab, settled his hat on his head, and held the door for Rosa. As she got out of the cab, she threw her arms around his neck. He lifted her from the ground, squeezing her tight, and took a long deep breath of her. She could feel the people around them staring, wondering who these two were, or thought they were. Joe's gray hat started to tumble off the back of his head, but he caught it with one hand, then set Rosa back down on the ground.

"He's going to be fine," she told him. "He already had measles. It's just a little delay, that's all."

She knew from bitter experience that Joe hated to be consoled, but to her surprise, when he set her down again, he was smiling. He looked around at the photographers, the crowd, the dazzling kliegs, the long black limousines at the curb, and she could see that it excited him. It *was* exciting, she thought.

"I know," he said. "He's going to be fine."

"We could end up in Hollywood ourselves one of these days," she said, urged to recklessness by his unexpected change of mood. "You, me, and Thomas. In a little bungalow in the Hollywood Hills."

"Thomas would love that," Joe said.

"The Palace." Sammy had joined them, and was gazing up at the six giant letters atop the brilliant marquee. He took a five-dollar bill out of his wallet. "Here you go, buddy boy," he said, handing it to Bacon. "The cab's on me."

GREAT STUFF, THE ESCAPIST," Orson Welles told Sammy. He
seemed vastly tall and surprisingly young, and he smelled like
Dolores Del Rio. In 1941 it was fashionable among certain smart
people to confess to a more than passing knowledge of Batman, or
Captain Marvel, or the Blue Beetle. "I don't like to miss a word."

"Thank you," said Sam.

This, though he never forgot and in later years embellished it, was
the extent of his interaction with Orson Welles, on that night or any
other. At the party afterward, at the Pennsylvania Roof, Joe danced with
Dolores Del Rio, and Rosa danced with handsome Joseph Cotten and
with Edward Everett Horton, the latter by far the better dancer of the
two. Tommy Dorsey's band was playing. Sammy sat and watched and
listened, eyes half-closed, aware, as were all devotees of big-band swing
in 1941, that it was his privilege to be alive at the very moment when
the practitioners of his favorite music were at the absolute peak of their
artistry and craft, a moment unsurpassed in this century for verve, ro-
manticism, polish, and a droll, tidy variety of soul. Joe and Dolores Del
Rio danced a fox-trot and then, naturally, a rumba. That was the extent
of Joe's interaction with Dolores Del Rio, though he and Orson Welles
continued to see each other from time to time at the bar of the Edison
Hotel.

More significant by far than anything else that happened to the
cousins on that first day of May 1941 was the movie they had come to
see.

In later years, in other hands, the Escapist was played for laughs.
Tastes changed, and writers grew bored, and all the straight plots had

been pretty well exhausted. Later writers and artists, with the connivance of George Deasey, turned the strip into a peculiar kind of inverted parody of the whole genre of the costumed hero. The Escapist's chin grew larger and more emphatically dimpled, and his muscles hypertrophied until he bulged, as his postwar arch-foe Dr. Magma memorably expressed it, "like a sack full of cats." Miss Plum Blossom's ever-ready needle was pressed into providing the Escapist with a Liberacean array of specialized crime-fighting togs, and Omar and Big Al began to grumble openly about the bills their boss piled up by his extravagant expenditures on supervehicles, superplanes, and even a "hand-carved ivory crutch" for Tom Mayflower to use on big date nights. The Escapist was quite vain; readers sometimes caught him stopping, on his way to fight evil, to check his reflection and comb his hair in a window or the mirror of a drugstore scale. In between acts of saving the earth from the evil Omnivores, in one of the late issues, #130 (March 1953), the Escapist works himself into quite a little lather as he attempts, with the help of a lisping decorator, to renovate the Keyhole, the secret sanctum under the boards of the Empire Palace. While he continued to defend the weak and champion the helpless as reliably as ever, the Escapist never seemed to take his adventures very seriously. He took vacations in Cuba, Hawaii, and Las Vegas, where he shared a stage at the Sands Hotel with none other than Wladziu Liberace himself. Sometimes, if he was in no particular hurry to get anywhere, he let Big Al take over the controls of the Keyjet and picked up a movie magazine that had his picture on its cover. The so-called Rube Goldberg plots—in which the Escapist, as bored as anyone by the dull routine of crime-busting, deliberately introduced obstacles and handicaps into his own efforts to thwart the large but finite variety of megalomaniacs, fiends, and rank hoodlums he fought in the years after the war, in order to make things more interesting for himself—became a trademark of the character: he would agree with himself beforehand, say, to dispatch some particular gang of criminals "barehanded," and to use his by now vastly augmented physical strength only if one of them uttered some random phrase like "ice water," and then, just after he was almost licked and the weather too cold for anyone ever to ask for a glass of ice water, the Escapist would hit on a way to arrange things so that inexorably the gang ended up in the back of a truck full of onions. He was a superpowerful, muscle-bound clown.

The Escapist who reigned among the giants of the earth in 1941 was a different kind of man. He was serious, sometimes to a fault. His face was lean, his mouth set, and his eyes, through the holes in his head-scarf, were like cold iron rivets. Though he was strong, he was far from invulnerable. He could be knocked cold, bludgeoned, drowned, burned, beaten, shot. And his missions were just that—his business, fundamentally, was one of salvation. The early stories, for all their anti-fascist fisticuffs and screaming Stukas, are stories of orphans threatened, peasants abused, poor factory workers turned into slavering zombies by their arms-producer bosses. Even after the Escapist went to war, he spent as much time sticking up for the innocent victims of Europe as he did taking divots out of battleships with his fists. He shielded refugees and kept bombs from landing on babies. Whenever he busted a Nazi spy ring at work right here in the U.S.A. (the Saboteur's, for example), he would deliver the speeches by which Sam Clay tried to help fight his cousin's war, saying, for example, as he broke open yet another screw-nosed "armored mole" full of lunkish Germans who had been trying to dig under Fort Knox, "I wonder what that head-in-the-sand crowd of war ostriches would say if they could see this!" In his combination of earnestness, social conscience, and willingness to scrap, he was a perfect hero for 1941, as America went about the rumbling, laborious process of backing itself into a horrible war.

And yet, in spite of the fact that he sold in the millions, and for a time ascended or sank into the general popular consciousness of America, if Sammy had never written and Joe had never drawn another issue after the spring of 1941, the Escapist no doubt would have faded from the national memory and imagination, as have the Cat-Man and Kitten, the Hangman, and the Black Terror, all of whose magazines sold nearly as well as the Escapist's at their peaks. The cultists—the collectors and fans—would not have shelled out appalling sums for, or written hundreds of thousands of donnish words devoted to, the early collaborations of Kavalier & Clay. If Sammy had never written another word after *Radio Comics* #18 (June 1941), he would have been remembered, if at all, by only the most fanatic devotees of comic books as the creator of a number of minor stars of the early forties. If Ebling's Exploding Trident had killed Joe Kavalier that evening at the Hotel Pierre, he would have been recalled, if at all, as a dazzling cover artist, the creator of energetic and painstaking battle scenes, and the inspired fantasist of *Luna Moth*, but not, as he is by some today, as one of the greatest innovators in the use of layout, of narrative strategies, in the history of comic book art. But in July 1941, *Radio* #19 hit the stands, and the nine million unsuspecting twelve-year-olds of America who wanted to grow up to be comic book men nearly fell over dead in amazement.

The reason was *Citizen Kane.* The cousins sat, with Rosa and Bacon between them, in the balcony of the dowdy Palace with its fancy-pants chandelier and a fresh poultice of velvet and gilding applied to its venerable old bones. The lights went down. Joe lit a cigarette. Sammy sat back and arranged his legs, which had a tendency to fall asleep at the movies. The picture came on. Joe noted that Orson Welles's was the only name above the title. The camera hopped that spiky iron fence, soared like a crow up that sinister, broken hillside with its monkeys and its gondolas and its miniature golf course and, knowing just what it was looking for, burst in through the window and zoomed right in on a pair of monstrous lips as they rasped out that ultimate word.

"This is going to be good," Joe said.

He was impressed—demolished—by it. When the lights came up, Sammy leaned forward and looked past Rosa at Joe, eager to see what he had thought of the film. Joe sat looking straight ahead, blinking, working it all out in his mind. All of the dissatisfactions he had felt in his practice of the art form he had stumbled across within a week of his arrival in America, the cheap conventions, the low expectations among publishers, readers, parents, and educators, the spatial constraints that he had been struggling against in the pages of *Luna Moth*, seemed capable of being completely overcome, exceeded, and escaped. The Amazing Cavalieri was going to break free, forever, of the nine little boxes.

"I want us to do something like *that*," he said.

This was precisely the thought that had occupied Sammy from the moment he caught on to the film's structure, when the mock-newsreel about Kane ended and the lights came up on the men who worked for the "March of Time" newsreel company in the film. But for Joe it had been the utterance of his sense of inspiration, of taking up a challenge, while for Sammy it had been more the expression of his envy of Welles, and of his despair at ever getting out of this lucrative swindle, with its cheap-novelty roots. After they got home from the Pennsylvania, the four of them sat up well into the night, drinking coffee, feeding records to the Panamuse, recollecting bits, shots, and lines of dialogue to one another. They could not get over the long upward tilt of the camera, through the machinery and shadows of the opera house, to the pair of stagehands holding their noses while Susan Alexander made her debut. They would never forget the way the camera had dived through the sky-light of the seedy nightclub to pounce on poor Susie in her ruin. They discussed the interlocking pieces of the jigsaw portrait of Kane, and argued about how anyone knew his dying word when no one appeared to be in the room to hear him whisper it. Joe struggled to express, to formulate, the revolution in his ambitions for the ragged-edged and stapled little art form to which their inclinations and luck had brought them. It was not just a matter, he told Sammy, of somehow adapting the bag of cinematic tricks so boldly displayed in the movie—extreme close-ups, odd angles, quirky arrangements of foreground and background; Joe and a few others had been dabbling with this sort of thing for some time. It was that *Citizen Kane* represented, more than any other movie Joe had ever seen, the total blending of narration and image that was—didn't Sammy see it?—the fundamental principle of comic book storytelling, and the irreducible nut of their partnership. Without the witty, potent dialogue and the puzzling shape of the story, the movie would have been merely an American version of the kind of brooding, shadow-filled Ufa-style expressionist stuff that Joe had grown up watching in Prague. Without the brooding shadows and bold adventurings of the camera, without the theatrical lighting and queasy angles, it would have been merely a clever movie about a rich bastard. It was more, much more, than any movie really needed to be. In this one crucial regard—its inextricable braiding of image and narrative—*Citizen Kane* was like a comic book.

"I don't know, Joe," Sammy said. "I'd like to think we could do something like that. But come on. This is just, I mean, we're talking about *comic books.*"

"Why do you look at it that way, Sammy?" Rosa said. "No medium is inherently better than any other." Belief in this dictum was almost a requirement for residence in her father's house. "It's all in what you do with it."

"No, that's not right. Comic books actually *are* inferior," Sammy said. "I really do believe that. It's—it's just built in to the material. We're talking about a bunch of guys—and a girl—who run around in their long johns punching people, all right? If the Parnassus people make this Escapist serial, believe me, it's not going to be any *Citizen Kane.* Not even Orson Welles could manage that."

"You're just making excuses, Clay," Bacon said, taking them all by surprise but no one more than Sammy, who had never heard his friend sound so serious. "It's not comic books that you think are inferior, it's *you.*"

Joe, sipping his coffee, looked politely away.

"Huh," Rosa said after a moment.

"Huh," Sammy agreed.

Sammy and Joe got in to the office at seven sharp, pink-cheeked, tingling from lack of sleep, coughing and sober and saying little. In a leather portfolio under his arm, Joe had the new pages he had laid out, along with Sammy's notes not only for "Kane Street," the first of the so-called modernist or prismatic Escapist stories, but also ideas for a dozen other stories that had come to Sammy, not just for the Escapist but for Luna Moth and the Monitor and the Four Freedoms, since last night. They went down the hall to find Anapol.

The publisher of Empire Comics had abandoned the vast chromium office that had so discomfited him and taken up residence in a large custodial closet, in which he'd had installed a desk, a chair, a portrait of the composer of *Songs of an Infatuated Muezzin,* and two telephones. Since the move, he claimed to be far more comfortable and reported that he slept much better at night. Sammy and Joe walked right up to the office-closet door. Once Anapol got in, there was really no room for anyone else. Anapol was writing a letter. He held up a finger to signal that he was in the middle of an important thought.

Sammy saw that he was writing on the letterhead of the Szymanowski society. *Dear Brother,* the letter began. Anapol's hand hovered while he read the line over, moving his fleshy purple lips. Then he looked up. He smiled grimly.

"Why do I suddenly want to hide my checkbook?" he said.

"Boss, we need to talk to you."

"I can see that."

"First of all." Sammy cleared his throat. "Everything we've done around here up to now, as good as it's been, and I don't know if you ever look at what the competition's doing but we've been better than most of them and as good as the best of them, all of that is nothing, okay, nothing, compared to what Joe and I have worked out for the Escapist from now on, though I'm not at liberty to divulge just what that will be. At the moment."

"That's first of all," said Anapol.

"Right."

Anapol nodded. "First of all, you should congratulate me." He sat back, hands clasped smugly over his belly, and waited for them to catch on.

"They bought it," Sammy said. "Parnassus."

"I heard from their lawyer last night. Production is to commence by the end of this year, if not sooner. The money is certainly not enormous—we're not talking M-G-M here—but it isn't bad. Not bad at all."

"Naturally we are obliged to ask you to give us half of it," Joe said.

"Naturally," Anapol agreed. He smiled. "Now tell me what it is that you two have worked out."

"Well, basically it's a whole new approach to this game. We saw—"

"What do we need with a whole new approach? The old approach has been working great."

"This is better."

"Better in this context can mean only one thing," Anapol said. "And that is more money. Is this new approach of yours going to make more money for me and my partner?"

Sammy looked at Joe. He was, in fact, still not entirely persuaded of this. But he was still feeling the sting of Bacon's accusation the night before. And what was more, he knew Shelly Anapol. Money was not—not always—the most important thing in the world to him. Once, years before, Anapol had cherished hopes of playing the violin in the New York Philharmonic, and there was a part of him, albeit deeply buried, that had never completely resigned itself to the life of a dealer in whoopee cushions. As Empire Comics' sales figures had climbed, and the towering black cyclones of money came blowing in out of the heartland, Anapol, out of this residual ambition and a perverted sense of guilt over the brainless ease with which colossal success had been achieved, had grown extremely touchy about the poor reputation of comic books among the Phi Beta Kappas and literary pooh-bahs whose opinions meant so much to him. He had even imposed upon Deasey to write letters to *The New York Times* and *The American Scholar,* to which he then signed his own name, protesting the unfair treatment he considered those publications had given his humble product in their pages.

"Lots," Sammy said. "Piles, boss."

"Show me."

They fetched the portfolio and tried to explain what it was they intended to do.

"Adults," Anapol said after a few minutes of listening. "You're talking about getting adults to read comic books."

The cousins looked at each other. They had not quite expressed or understood it that way before.

"I guess so," Sammy said.

"Yes," said Joe. "Adults with adult money."

Anapol nodded, stroking his chin. Sammy could see a relief flowing into his shoulders and the hinges of his jaw, unknotting them, sending Anapol tilting back in his big leather swivel chair with a grandeur and an ease not entirely free of the threat of metal fatigue and failing springs. Whether it was relief at having at last found a worthy basis for his commerce, or merely that he was comforted by the reassuring proximity of certain failure, Sammy could not be sure.

"Okay," Anapol said, reaching for his unfinished letter. "We'll give it a try. Get to work."

Joe started to walk away, but Sammy took hold of his arm and pulled him back. They stood. Anapol added another sentence to his letter, considered it, then looked up.

"Yes?"

"What about this not-enormous money from Parnassus?" Sammy said. "We got a piece of the radio show. You gave us a piece of the newspaper strip. I don't see why we—"

"Oh, for God's sake," Anapol said. "Don't even bother to finish, Mr. Clay, I've heard it all before."

Sammy grinned. "And?"

Anapol's smile grew cagey and very, very small. "I'm not averse. I can't speak for Jack, but I'll take it up with him and see if we can't work something out."

"A-all right," Sammy said, surprised and a little suspicious, sensing an imminent condition.

"Now," Anapol said, "see if you can guess what I'm about to say to you."

"They're putting Szymanowski on a bubblegum card?"

"Maybe you aren't aware of this," Anapol said, "but Parnassus Pictures does a very healthy business in Europe."

"I didn't know that."

"Yes. As a matter of fact, their second-biggest market after the domestic is, of all places—"

"Germany," said Joe.

"Naturally, they're a little concerned about the reputation you two have earned for this company, in your many imaginative ways, as antagonistic to the citizens and government of that nation of fanatical moviegoers. I had a long talk with Mr. Frank Singe, the studio head. He made it very clear—"

"Don't even bother to finish," Sammy said. He was disgusted. " 'We've heard it all before.' " He looked appealingly at Joe, willing him to speak up, to tell Anapol about his family and the indignities to which they were being exposed, the one hundred cruelties, gross and tiny, to which, with an almost medical regimentation, they were being subjected by the Reichsprotektorat. He was sure that Anapol would give in once again.

"All right," Joe said softly. "I will stop the fighting."

Anapol's eyebrows shot up in surprise.

"Joe?" Sammy said. He was shocked. "Joe, come on. What are you talking about. You can't give up! This—this is *censorship*. We're being censored! This is the very thing we're supposed to be standing up to. The Escapist would stand up to something like this."

"The Escapist is not a real person."

"Yeah, I *know* that. Christ."

"Sam," said Joe, his cheeks reddening. He put a hand on Sammy's arm. "I appreciate what you think you are doing. But I want to do *this* now." He tapped the portfolio. "I'm tired of fighting, maybe, for a little while. I fight, and I am fighting some more, and it just makes me have *less* hope, not more. I need to do something . . . something that will be *great*, you know, instead of trying always to be Good."

"Joe, I—" Sammy started to argue, but just as quickly gave up. "Fine," he said. "We'll lay off the Nazis. It won't be long anyway till we're in this war."

"And then I promise to give you the satisfaction of reminding me of my ignoble behavior here this morning," said Anapol. "As well as a share—something very modest, I assure you—in the small bounty that Hollywood is going to provide us with."

The cousins started away. Sammy looked back.

"What about the Japs?" he said.

THE SUDDEN SMALL EFFLORESCENCE of art, minor but
genuine, in the tawdry product line of what was then the fifth- or
sixth-largest comic book company in America has usually been
attributed to the potent spell of *Citizen Kane* acting on the renascent
aspirations of Joe Kavalier. But without the thematic ban imposed by
Sheldon Anapol at the behest of Parnassus Pictures—the censorship of
all story lines having to do with Nazis (Japs, too), warfare, saboteurs,
fifth columnists, and so on—which forced Sammy and Joe to a drastic
reconsideration of the raw materials of their stories, the magical run of
issues that commenced with *Radio Comics* #19 and finished when
Pearl Harbor caught up to the two-month Empire lead time in the
twenty-first issue of *Triumph Comics* (February 1942) looks pretty
unlikely. In eight issues apiece of *Radio, Triumph, All Doll,* and the
now-monthly *Escapist Adventures,* the emphasis is laid, for the first
time, not only on the superpowered characters—normally so enveloped
in their inevitable shrouds of bullets, torpedoes, poison gases,
hurricane winds, evil spells, and so forth, that the lineaments of their
personalities, if not of their deltoids and quadriceps, could hardly be
discerned—but also, almost radically for the comic book of the time, on
the ordinary people around them, whose own exploits, by the time
hostilities with Germany were formally engaged in the early months of
1942, had advanced so far into the foreground of each story that such
emphasis itself, on the everyday heroics of the "powerless," may be seen
to constitute, at least in hindsight, a kind of secret, and hence probably
ineffectual, propaganda. There were stories that dealt with the minutiae
of what Mr. Machine Gun, at home in the pages of *Triumph,* liked to call

"the hero biz," told not only from the point of view of the heroes but from those of various butlers, girlfriends, assistants, shoe-shine boys, doctors, and even the criminals. There was a story that followed the course of a handgun through the mean streets of Empire City, in which the Escapist appeared on only *two pages*. Another celebrated story told the tale of Luna Moth's girlhood, and filled in gaps in her biography, through a complicated series of flashbacks narrated by a group of unemployed witches' familiars, talking rats and cats and reptilian whatsits, in a "dark little hangout outside of Phantomville." And there was "Kane Street," focusing for sixty-four pages on one little street in Empire City as its denizens, hearing the terrible news that the Escapist lies near death in the hospital, recall in turn the way he has touched their lives and the lives of everyone in town (only to have it all turn out, in the end, as a cruel hoax perpetrated by the evil Crooked Man).

All of these forays into chopping up the elements of narrative, in mixing and isolating odd points of view, in stretching, as far as was possible in those days, under the constraints of a jaded editor and of publishers who cared chiefly for safe profit, the limits of comic book storytelling, all these exercises were, without question, raised far beyond the level of mere exercise by the unleashed inventiveness of Joe Kavalier's pencil. Joe, too, made a survey of the tools at hand, and found them more useful and interesting than he ever had before. But the daring use of perspective and shading, the radical placement of word balloons and captions and, above all, the integration of narrative and picture by means of artfully disarranged, dislocated panels that stretched, shrank, opened into circles, spread across two full pages, marched diagonally toward one corner of a page, unreeled themselves like the frames of a film—all these were made possible only by the full collaboration of writer and artist together.

Whether the delightful fruit of this collaboration came at a price; whether the thirty-two extra issues, the two thousand extra pages of Nazi-smashing obviated by Anapol's ban, might somehow, incrementally, have slid America into the war sooner; whether the advantage gained in time would have precipitated an earlier victory; whether that victory coming a day or a week or a month earlier would have sufficed to preserve a dozen or a hundred or a thousand more lives; such questions now can have only an academic poignancy, as both the ghosts and those haunted by them are dead.

At any rate, the circulation figures for the Kavalier & Clay titles increased steadily until, by the abrupt termination of the partnership, they had nearly doubled, though whether this amazing growth was due to the books' marked advance in sophistication and quality, or was simply a product of the general explosion in comic book sales that occurred in the months leading up to the entry of America into the war, is difficult to assess. Great ringing blizzards—blowing in from Hollywood, from radio, from Milton Bradley and Marx Toys, Hostess Cakes and (inevitably) the Yale Lock Company, but most of all from the change purses, dungaree pockets, and Genuine Latex Rubber Escapist Coin Banks of the nation—blanketed the offices on the twenty-fifth floor of the Empire State Building. It required shovels and snowplows and crews of men working around the clock to keep ahead of the staggering avalanche of money. Some of this snowfall ended up, in due course, in the bank account of Josef Kavalier, where it towered in fantastic drifts and was left that way, aloof and glinting, to cool the fever of exile from the day his family should arrive.

WHEN FRANK SINGE, the head of production for Parnassus Pictures, came through New York City that September, Bacon got Sammy in to see him at the Gotham Hotel. Bacon had kept Sammy up all night, writing out scenarios, and Sammy, bleary-eyed and poorly shaved, had three ready to show Singe the following afternoon. Singe, a big, barrel-chested man who smoked a ten-inch Davidoff *gigante,* said that he had two writers in mind already, but that he liked what Sammy had done in the comics, and he would take a look at his pages. He was not at all discouraging; it was clear that he was personally fond of Bacon, and furthermore, as he said himself, it was not like the other two guys up for the job were Kaufman and Hart. After twenty-five minutes of semi-distracted listening, he told Sammy and Bacon that he had a very important appointment to look at a pair of very long legs, and the interview was over. The pair walked down to the street with the mogul from Poverty Row and stepped out of the Gotham into the dwindling afternoon. The weather had been fine all day, and though the sun had already set, the sky overhead was still as blue as a gas flame, with a flickering hint of black carbon in the east.

"Well, thanks, Mr. Singe," Sammy said, shaking his hand. "I appreciate the time."

"The kid can do it, sir," Bacon said, reaching an arm around Sammy and shaking him a little. "The Escapist is his baby."

It was a cool evening, and in his dense, soft camel coat, with Bacon's arm around his shoulders, Sammy felt warm and content and prepared to believe that anything could happen. He was touched by the degree of Bacon's eagerness to have him come along to California, though he suspected it, too; he worried that Bacon was really just afraid of being out there all alone. It was between them now just as it had been with Joe, before Rosa; Sammy was always available, always willing to join in, keep up, hang in there, go out, and pick up the pieces after a fight. Sometimes Sammy feared that he was on his way to becoming a professional sidekick. As soon as Bacon had made new friends, or a new friend, in California, Sammy would be left alone with the unhappy souls, pale gaping goldfish, whom he had read about in *Day of the Locust.*

"Whatever you decide is fine by me, Mr. Singe," Sammy said. "To tell you the truth, I don't even know if I want to move to Los Angeles."

"Oh, don't start in on that again," Bacon said, with a big fake radio laugh. They shook hands with Singe, and he got into a cab.

"See you boys around," Singe said. There was an odd note in his voice, hovering somewhere between mockery and doubt. The cab pulled away from the curb, and he waved a little, leaving Sammy standing there under the arm of his boyfriend.

Bacon turned on him. "What'd you go and say that for, Clayboy?"

"Maybe it's true. Maybe I like it here."

Boyfriend. The word flew into Sammy's mind and careened blindly around it like a moth while Sammy chased after it with a broom in one hand and a handbook of lepidoptery in the other. It sounded like a wisecrack, acidulous, hard-bitten, italicized: Who's your *boyfriend,* Percy? Though Sammy now spent all his free time with Bacon, and had agreed in principle on their sharing a house in the event that they did go west, Sammy still refused to admit to himself—at that irrelevant, senatorial level of consciousness where the questions that desire has already answered are proposed and debated and tabled till later—that he was in love, or falling in love, with Tracy Bacon. It was not that he denied what he was feeling, or that the implications of the feeling had frightened him; well, he did, and they had, but Sammy had been in love with men nearly all his life, from his father to Nikola Tesla to John Garfield, whose snarl of derision echoed so clearly in his imagination, taunting Sammy: *Hey, pretty boy, who's your* boyfriend?

However clandestine and impossible an enterprise it might hitherto always have been or seemed, loving men came naturally to Sammy, like a gift of languages or an eye for four-leaf clovers; notions of denial and fear were, in a very real sense, superfluous. Yes, all right, so maybe he was in love with Tracy Bacon; so what? What did that prove? So maybe there had been further kissing, and some careful exploitation of shadows and stairwells and empty hallways; even John Garfield would have had to agree that their behavior since that night in the lightning storm, on the eighty-sixth floor, had been playful and masculine and essentially chaste. Sometimes in the back of a taxicab, their hands might steal toward each other across the leather banquette, and Sammy would feel his small, damp palm and bitten fingers absorbed into the deep, sober Presbyterian fastness of Tracy Bacon's grip.

The previous week, when they were at Brooks being fitted for new suits, standing side by side in their BVDs like a before-and-after advertisement for vitamin tonic, they had watched the salesman leave the fitting room, and the tailor turn his back, and then Bacon had reached out and grabbed a handful of the wool of Sammy's chest. He had fitted the hinge of his fingers into the notch of Sammy's breastbone, and run his palm down the flat slope of Sammy's belly, and then, hardening his blue eyes with an innocent Tom Mayflower twinkle, darted his hand into and out of the waistband of Sammy's briefs, like a cook testing a pot of hot water with a pinky. Sammy's cock retained, to this moment, a furtive memory of the imprint of that cool hand. As for kisses, there had been three more: one just outside the doorway of Bacon's hotel room as Sammy was dropping him home; one amid the dark latticework under the Third Avenue El at Fifty-first; and then the third and boldest, in a back row of the Broadway, at a showing of *Dumbo*, during the pink elephant bacchanal. For here was the novelty, the difference between the love that Sammy had felt for Tesla and Garfield and even for Joe Kavalier, and that which he felt for Tracy Bacon: it really did seem to be reciprocated. And these blossomings of desire, these entanglings of their fingers, these four nourishing kisses stolen from the overflowing standpipe of New York's indifference, were the inevitable product of that reciprocity. But did they mean that he, or Bacon, was a homosexual? Did they make Tracy Bacon Sammy's boyfriend?

"I don't care," Sammy said, aloud, to Mr. Frank Singe, New York, the world; and then, turning back to Bacon, "I don't care! I don't care if I get the job or not. I don't want to think about it, or Los Angeles, or you leaving, or any of it. I just want to live my life and be a good boy and have a nice time. That all right with you?"

"That's fine by me, sir," Bacon said, knotting his scarf against the chill. "How about we go do something?"

"What do you want to do?"

"I don't know. What's your favorite place ever? In the whole city, I mean."

"My favorite place ever in the whole city?"

"Right."

"Including the boroughs?"

"Don't tell me it's in Brooklyn. That's awfully disappointing."

"Not Brooklyn," Sammy said. "Queens."

"Worse still."

"Only it isn't there anymore, my favorite place. They closed it. Packed it up and rolled it right out of town."

"The Fair," Bacon said. He shook his head. "You and that Fair."

"You never went, did you?"

"*That's* your favorite place ever, huh?"

"Yeah, but—"

"All right, then." Bacon hailed a taxicab and opened the door for Sammy. Sammy stood there a moment, knowing that Bacon was about to get him into something he was not going to be able to get out of very easily. He just didn't know what.

"We're going to Queens," Bacon said to the driver. "To the World's Fair."

It was not until they had reached the Triborough Bridge that the driver, in a dry monotone, said, "I don't know how to tell you fellas this."

"Isn't there *anything* left?" Bacon said.

"Well, I seen in the papers they been arguing about what to do with the land, between the city and Mr. Moses and the Fair people. I guess some of it still might be there."

"We'll keep very low expectations," Bacon said. "How about that?"

"I'm comfortable with that," Sammy said.

Sammy had loved the Fair, visiting it three times in its first season of 1939, and until the end of his life, he kept one of the little buttons he had been given when he exited the General Motors pavilion, which said

I HAVE SEEN THE FUTURE. He had grown up in an era of great hopelessness, and to him and millions of his fellow city boys, the Fair and the world it foretold had possessed the force of a covenant, a promise of a better world to come, that he would later attempt to redeem in the potato fields of Long Island.

The cab left them off outside the LIRR station, and they wandered along the Fair's perimeter for a while, looking for a way in. But there was a high fence, and Sammy didn't think he could get over it.

"Here," Bacon said, crouching behind some shrubs and arching his back. "Climb on."

"I can't—I'll hurt you—"

"Come on, I'll be fine."

Sammy scrambled up onto Bacon's back, leaving a muddy footprint on his coat.

"I have mystically augmented strength, you know," Bacon said. "Oof."

Sammy tumbled and dangled and fell into the fairgrounds, landing on his ass. Bacon launched, hoisted, and dropped himself up, over, and down the fairground side of the fence. They were in.

The first thing Sammy's eye sought out were the monumental Mutt-and-Jeff structures, the soaring Trylon and its rotund chum the Perisphere, symbols of the Fair that for two years had been ubiquitous throughout the country, working their way onto restaurant menus, clock faces, matchbooks, neckties, handkerchiefs, playing cards, girls' sweaters, cocktail shakers, scarves, lighters, radio cabinets, et cetera, before disappearing as suddenly as they had flourished, like the totems of some discredited Millerite cult that briefly thrills and then bitterly disappoints its adherents with grand and terrible prophecies. He saw right away that the lowermost hundred feet or so of the Trylon was covered in scaffolding.

"They're taking the Trylon down," Sammy said. "Gee."

"Which one is the Trylon, now? The pointy one?"

"Yeah."

"I had no idea it was so tall."

"Taller than the Washington Monument."

"What is it made out of, granite or limestone or something?"

"Plaster of paris, I believe."

"We've been doing very well, haven't we? Not talking about my leaving for L.A."

"Are you thinking about it?"

"Not me. So the ball is the Perisphere?"

"That's right."

"Was there anything inside them?"

"Not in the Trylon. But yeah, inside the Perisphere they had this whole show. Democracity. It was like a scale model of the city of the future, and you sat in these little cars going all around the outside and looked down on it. It was all superhighways and garden suburbs. You just felt like you were soaring over it all in a zeppelin. They would make it like nighttime in there, and all the little buildings and streetlights would sort of light up and glow. It was great. I loved it."

"You don't say. I'd like to see that. I wonder if it's still in there, Sammy, what do you think?"

"I don't know," said Sammy, with a kind of wary thrill. By now he knew Bacon well enough to recognize the impulse, and its accompanying tone, that had sent his friend up to a military installation at the top of the Empire State Building at midnight with a gourmet meal in two shopping bags. "Probably not, Bake. I think—hey, wait for me."

Bacon was already on his way around the low circular wall that surrounded the immense pool, now drained and covered in a sodden-looking layer of burlap, in which the Perisphere once had swum. Sammy looked to see if there were any workmen still around, or guards, but they appeared to have the place to themselves. It made his heart ache to look around the vast expanse of the fairground that, not very long ago, had swarmed with flags and women's hats and people being whizzed around in jitneys, and see only a vista of mud and tarpaulins and blowing newspaper, broken up here and there by the spindly stump of a capped stanchion, a fire hydrant, or the bare trees that flanked the empty avenues and promenades. The candy-colored pavilions and exhibit halls, fitted out with Saturn rings, lightning bolts, shark's fins, golden grilles, and honeycombs, the Italian pavilion with its entire façade dissolving in a perpetual cascade of water, the gigantic cash register, the austere and sinuous temples of the Detroit gods, the fountains, the pylons and sundials, the statues of George Washington and Freedom of Speech and Truth Showing the Way to Freedom had been peeled, stripped, prized apart, knocked down, bulldozed into piles, loaded onto truck beds, dumped into barges, towed out past the mouth of the harbor, and sent to the bottom of the sea. It made him sad, not because he saw some instructive allegory or harsh sermon on the vanity of all human hopes and utopian imaginings in this translation of a bright summer dream into an immense mud puddle freezing over at the end of a September afternoon—he was too young to have such inklings—but because he had so loved the Fair, and seeing it this way, he felt in his heart what he had known all along, that, like childhood, the Fair was over, and he would never be able to visit again.

"Hey," Bacon called. "Clayboy. Over here."

Sammy looked around. There was no sign of Bacon. Sammy hurried, as quickly as he could, all the way around the low whitewashed wall with its rain stains and patchy skin of wet leaves, to the doors of the Trylon, which had led, via an imperial pair of escalators, into the heart of the magical egg. When the Fair was on, there was always a huge line of people coiling up to these big blue doors. Now there were only the scaffolding and a stack of planks. Some workman had forgotten the tin coffee-cup cap of his thermos. Sammy went over to the metal doors. They were heavily barred and padlocked with a thick chain. Sammy gave them a pull, and they did not budge in the least.

"I tried that," Bacon said. "Under here!"

The Perisphere was supported by a kind of tee, a ring of evenly spaced pillars joined to it at its antarctic circle, so to speak, all the way around. The idea had been for the great bone-white orb, its skin rippled with fine veins like a cigar wrapper, to look as if it were floating there, in the middle of the pool of water. Now that there was no water, you could see the pillars, and you could see Tracy Bacon, too, standing in the middle of them, directly under the Perisphere's south pole.

"Hey," Sammy said, rushing to the wall and leaning across its top. "What are you doing? That whole thing could come right down on top of you!"

Bacon looked at him, eyes wide, incredulous, and Sammy blushed; it was exactly what his mother would have said.

"There's a door," Bacon said, pointing straight up. Then he reached up over his head, and his hands went into the bottom of the Perisphere's hull. Bacon's head vanished next, his feet rose off the ground, and then he was gone.

Sammy got one leg over the wall, then the other, and lowered himself down into the pool bed. The damp burlap made squishing sounds under his shoes as he ran across the gently curved bottom of the basin toward the Perisphere. When he got underneath it, he looked up and saw a rectangular hatchway that looked as if Tracy Bacon might just have fit through it.

"Come on."

"It looks pretty dark in there, Bake."

A big hand emerged from the hatch, wavering, fingers flexing. Sammy reached for it, their palms crossed, and then Bacon pulled him bodily up into the darkness. Before he could begin to feel, or smell, or listen to the darkness, to Bacon and to the pounding of his own heart, the lights came on.

"Gee," Bacon said. "Look at that."

The systems that controlled the motion, sound, and lighting of Democracity and its companion exhibit, General Motors' Futurama, were quite literally the *dernier cri* of the art and ancient principles of clockwork machinery in the final ticking moments of the computerless world. Coordinating the elaborate sound track of voice and music, the motion of the cars, and the varying light-moods inside the Perisphere had required an array of gears, pulleys, levers, cams, springs, wheels, switches, relays, and belts that was sophisticated, complex, and sensitive to disruption. A mouse dropping, a sudden snap of cold, or the accumulated rumblings of ten thousand arriving and departing underground trains could throw the system out of whack and bring the ride to an abrupt halt, occasionally trapping fifty people inside. It was because of the need for frequent minor adjustments and repairs that there was a hatch in the Perisphere's underbelly. It led into an odd, bowl-shaped room. Where Bacon and Sammy came in, at the bottom of the bowl, there was a kind of corrugated steel platform. On one side of the platform, a series of cleats had been welded onto the inner frame of the sphere that reached, gradually, up along the inside of the bowl, toward the elaborate clockwork underside of Democracity.

Bacon took hold of one of the lower cleats of the ladder. "Think you can manage it?" he said.

"I'm not sure," Sammy said. "I really think—"

"You go first," Bacon said. "I'll give you a hand if you need it."

So Sammy and his bad legs climbed a hundred feet into the air. At the top, there was another hatch. Sammy poked his head through.

"It's dark," Sammy said. "Too bad. Okay, we better go."

"Just a minute," Bacon said. Sammy felt a sudden push from behind as Bacon took hold of his legs and more or less jackknifed him up into the cool, huge blackness. Something rough abraded Sammy's cheek, and then there was a creak and a series of rasping sounds as Bacon pulled himself up after. "Huh. You're right."

"Indeed." Sammy reached out along the ground, feeling for the hatch. "Good. You're crazy, Bake, you know that? You just won't take no for an answer. I—"

Sammy heard the metallic chirp of the hinge of a cigarette lighter, the scrape of its flint, and then a spark swelled magically and became the flickering face of Tracy Bacon.

"Now yours," he said.

Sammy lit his lighter. Together they managed to generate just enough light to see that they were camped far to one side of the display, in the middle of a wide, forested area half an inch high. Tracy stood up and started toward the center. Sammy followed him, protecting the flame. The surface of the floor beneath their feet was covered in a kind of rough, dry artificial moss that was meant to suggest vast rolling hills of trees. It made a crunching sound that echoed in the high empty dome. Every so often, though they tried to be careful, one of them stepped on a model farmhouse, or crushed the amusement district or central orphanage of a town of the future. Finally they reached the major city, at the very center of the diorama, which had been known as Centerville or Centerton or something equally imaginative. A single skyscraper rose from a cluster of smaller buildings. All the buildings looked streamlined and moderne, like a city on Mongo, or the Emerald

City in *The Wizard of Oz.* Bacon got down on one knee and brought his eyes level with the top of the lone tower.

"Huh," he said. He frowned, then lowered himself and leaned forward on one arm, slowly, taking care not to extinguish his flame, until he was lying flat on his belly along the ground. "Huh," he said again, grunting it this time. He lowered his chin to the ground. "Yeah. This is the way. I don't think I would have liked just floating over it near as much."

Sammy went over and stood beside Bacon for a moment. Then he eased himself down on the ground beside him. He folded an arm under his chest and, inclining his head slightly, squinted his eyes, trying to lose himself in the illusion of the model the way he used to lose himself in Futuria, back at his drawing board in Flatbush a million years before. He was a twentieth of an inch tall, zipping along an oceanic highway in his little antigravity Skyflivver, streaking past the silent faces of the aspiring silvery buildings. It was a perfect day in a perfect city. A double sunset flickered in the windows and threw shadows across the leafy squares of the city. His fingertips were on fire.

"Ow!" Sammy said, dropping his lighter. "Ouch!"

Bacon let his own flame go out. "You have to kind of pad it with your necktie, dopey," he said. He grabbed Sammy's hand. "This the one?"

"Yeah," Sammy said. "The first two fingers. Oh. Okay."

They lay there for a few seconds, in the dark, in the future, with Sammy's sore fingertips in Tracy Bacon's mouth, listening to the fabulous clockwork of their hearts and lungs, and loving each other.

12

ON THE LAST DAY of November, Joe had a letter from Thomas. In an execrable left-slanting hand, he announced, employing a sardonic tone that had not been present in his first letters from Lisbon, that the old tub—after a series of delays, reversals, mechanical failures, and governmental tergiversations, had finally been cleared— yet again—for departure, on the second of December. More than eight months had now passed since Thomas's journey from the Moldau to the Tagus. The boy had turned thirteen on a cot in the crowded refectory of the convent of Nossa Senhora de Monte Carmel, and in his letter he warned Joe that he suffered from a mysterious tendency to start rattling off paternosters and Hail Marys at the drop of a hat, and had become partial to wimples. He claimed to be afraid that Joe would not recognize him for the spots on his face and the "apparently permanent pubertal smudge on my upper lip that some have the temerity to call a mustache." When Joe had finished reading the letter, he kissed it and pressed it to his chest. He remembered the immigrant's fear of going unrecognized in a land of strangers, of being lost in the translation from there to here.

The following day Rosa came straight to the Empire offices from the T.R.A. and burst into tears in Joe's arms. She told Joe that Mr. Hoffman had, almost as an afterthought, placed a call that afternoon to the Washington offices of the President's Advisory Committee on Political Refugees, just to make certain that everything was in order. To his astonishment, he had been told by the chairman of the committee that it looked as though all of the children's visas were going to be revoked for reasons of "state security." The head of the State Department's visa section, Breckinridge Long, a man with, as the chairman carefully put it, "certain antipathies," had long since established a clear policy of refusing visas to Jewish refugees. Hoffman knew that perfectly well. But in this instance, he argued, the visas had already been issued, the ship was about to depart, and the "security risks" were three hundred and nineteen children! The chairman sympathized. He apologized. He expressed profound regret and embarrassment at this unfortunate turn of events. Then he hung up.

"I see" was Joe's only response when Rosa, perched on his high stool, had finished her tale. With one hand he stroked mechanically at the back of her head. With the other he spun the striker of his cigarette lighter, sparking it over and over again. Rosa was ashamed and confused. She felt that she ought to be comforting Joe, but here she was, in the middle of the Empire workroom, with a bunch of guys staring at her over their drawing boards, bawling into his shirtfront, while he stood patting her hair and saying, "There, there." His shoulders were tensed, his breathing shallow. She could feel the anger building inside him. Each time the lighter sparked, she flinched.

"Oh, honey," she said. "I wish there was something we could do. Someone we could turn to."

"Huh," Joe said, and then "Look here." He took hold of her shoulders and spun her around on the stool. On a low table next to his drawing board lay a stack of lettered but uninked comic book pages on big sheets of Bristol board. Joe shuffled through the stack of pages, passing them to her one by one. They presented a story that was narrated by the custodian at the Statue of Liberation, a tall, stooped man with a mop and a billed cap, drawn to look a lot like George Deasey. Apparently, the unfortunate fellow had a bone to pick with "that long-underwear bunch." He then went on to describe how, just that morning, he had watched in horror as Professor Percival "Smarty" Pantz, hapless know-it-all rival of Dr. E. Pluribus Hewnham, the Scientific American, performed an "electro-brain implantation procedure" on the Lady. The idea was to enlist the statue in the effort to keep the skies of Empire City clear of enemy planes and airships. "She'll be able to swat Messerschmitts like mosquitoes!" Pantz crowed. Instead, thanks to the usual miscalculation on the part of Dr. Pantz, she had, upon awakening, gone off striding across the bay toward Empire City, her spike-crowned electro-head filled with homicidal urges. Of course the Scientific American, employing a handy giant robot of his own manufacture that he quickly fitted out with an enormous Clark Gable mask, was able to lure her back to her pillar, and then neutralize her using "superdynamic electromagnets." But it all made, to the exasperation of the janitor-narrator, an awful mess. Not only the island but the entire seaport lay in shambles. His brother janitors and sanitation workers were already overburdened cleaning up after the donnybrooks in which the super-beings regularly indulged. How would they ever manage to clean up this latest?

At that moment, an airplane landed on Liberation Island, and a familiar figure in a broad-brimmed hat and belted topcoat climbed out, looking as if she meant business.

"That looks like Eleanor Roosevelt," said Rosa, pointing to the panel in which Joe had drawn a quite flattering version of the First Lady, waving from the top step of the plane's gangplank.

"She picks up a broom," Joe said. "And starts sweeping. Soon all the women in the town come out with their brooms. To help."

"Eleanor Roosevelt," Rosa said.

"I'm going to call her," Joe said, going to a telephone on a nearby desk.

"Okay."

"I wonder if she'll speak to me?" He picked up the receiver. "I should think she will. I get that picture from the things I read of her."

"No, Joe, I really don't think she will," Rosa said. "I'm sorry. I don't know how it was in Czechoslovakia, but here you can't just call up the president's wife and ask her for a favor."

"Oh," Joe said. He set the receiver back down and stared at his hand, his head bowed.

"But, oh, my God." She climbed down from the stool. "Joe!"

"What?"

"My father. He knows her slightly. They met doing something for the W.P.A."

"Is he allowed to call up the president's wife?"

"Yes, I believe he is. Get your hat, we're going home."

Longman Harkoo called the White House that afternoon and was told that the First Lady was in New York City. With some help from Joe Lash, whom he knew through his Red connections, Rosa's father managed to track down Mrs. Roosevelt, and received a brief appointment to visit her at her apartment on East Eleventh Street, not far from the Harkoo house. For fifteen minutes, over tea, Harkoo explained the predicament of the *Ark of Miriam* and its passengers. Mrs. Roosevelt, Rosa's father later reported, had seemed to become extremely angry, though all she said was that she would see what she could do.

The *Ark of Miriam,* her course smoothed by the invisible hand of Eleanor Roosevelt, set sail from Lisbon on the third of December.

The following day, Joe called Rosa and asked her if she could meet him on her lunch break at an address in the West Seventies. He wouldn't tell her why, only that he had something he wanted to give her.

"I have something for you, too," she said. It was a small painting that she had finished the night before. She wrapped it in paper, tied it with string, and carried it onto the train. Shortly afterward, she found herself standing in front of the Josephine, a fifteen-story pile of cool blue-tinged Vermont marble. It had pointed parapets and took up more than half of an entire block between West End Avenue and Broadway. The doorman was uniformed like a doomed hussar in the retreat from Smolensk, down to his trim waxed mustache. Joe was waiting for her when she walked up, his coat slung over his arm. It was a pretty day, cold and bright, the sky as blue as a Nash and cloudless but for one lost lamb overhead. It had been a long time since Rosa had been in this neighborhood. The walls of high apartment houses stretching far away to the north, which had struck her in the past as self-important and stuffily bourgeois, now had a sturdy, sober look to them. In the austere light of autumn, they looked like buildings filled with serious and thoughtful people working hard to accomplish valuable things. She wondered if perhaps she had had enough of Greenwich Village.

"What is this all about?" she said, taking Joe's arm.

"I just signed the lease," he said. "Come on up and see."

"A lease? You're moving out? You're moving *here*? Did you and Sammy have a fight?"

"No, of course not. I never fight with Sammy. I love Sammy."

"I know you do," she said. "You guys are a good team."

"It's first, well, he's moving to Los Angeles. Okay, he says for three months only to write the movie, but I bet you good money after the bad he will stay there when he goes. What's in the package?"

"A present," she said. "I guess you can hang it in your *new apartment*." She was a little put out that he had said nothing to her about a move, but that was the way he was about everything. When they had a date, he would never tell her where they were going or what they were going to do. It was not so much that he *refused* as that he managed to communicate he would prefer it if she didn't ask. "This *is* nice."

There was a marble fountain in the lobby, festooned with glinting Japanese carp, and an echoing interior courtyard of vaguely Moorish flavor. When the elevator door opened, with a deep and musical chime, a woman got out, followed by two small, adorable boys in matching blue woolen suits. Joe tipped his hat.

"This is for Thomas you're doing this," Rosa said, getting on the elevator. "Isn't it?"

"Ten," Joe said to the elevator man. "I just thought this might be a, well, a better neighborhood. You know, for me . . . for me to . . ."

"For you to raise him in."

He shook his head, smiling. "That sounds very strange."

"You are going to be like a father to him, you know," she said. And I could be like a mother. Just ask me, Joe, and I'll do it. It was on the tip of her tongue to say this, but she held back. What would she be saying if she did? That she wanted to marry him? For ten years, at least, since she was twelve or thirteen, Rosa had been declaring roundly to anyone who asked that she had no intention of getting married, ever, and that if she ever did, it would be when she was old and tired of life. When this declaration in its various forms had ceased to shock people sufficiently, she had taken to adding that the man she finally married would be no older than twenty-five. But lately she had been starting to experience strong, inarticulate feelings of longing, of a desire to be with Joe all the time, to inhabit his life and allow him to inhabit hers, to engage with him in some kind of joint enterprise, in a collaboration that would *be* their lives. She didn't suppose they needed to get married to do that, and she knew that she certainly ought not to *want* to. But did she? When her father had gone to see Mrs. Roosevelt, he had told the First Lady, explaining his connection to the matter, that one of the children on the ship was the brother of the young man his daughter was going to marry. Rosa had carefully neglected to pass that part of the story on to Joe. "I think it's very sweet of you. Sensible and sweet."

"There are good schools nearby. I have an interview for him at the Trinity School which I am told is excellent and takes Jews. Deasey said he would help me get him into Collegiate where he attended."

"Goodness, you've been making a lot of plans." She really ought to know better than to take offense at his secretiveness. Keeping things to himself was just his nature; she supposed it was what had drawn him to the practice of magic in the first place, with its tricks and secrets that must never be divulged.

"Well, I have a lot of time. It is eight months I have been waiting for this to happen. I've been doing a lot of thinking."

The elevator operator braked the car and hauled the door aside for them. He waited for them to step out. Joe was gazing at her with a strange, fixed look, and she thought, or perhaps she only wished, that she saw a glint of mischief there.

"Ten," said the operator.

"A lot of thinking," Joe repeated.

"Ten, sir," the elevator man said.

In the apartment there were views of New Jersey out the windows all along one side, gilded fixtures in the larger of the two bathrooms, and the parquetry of the floors was dizzying and mathematical. There were three bedrooms, and a library with shelves on three walls reaching from floor to ceiling; every room had at least one bookshelf built in. She visited all the rooms twice, unable to prevent herself, as she did so, from imagining a life in these elegant rooms, high over this cultivated swath of Manhattan with its Freudian psychoanalysts, first cellists, and appellate-court judges. They could all live here, she and Joe and Thomas, and maybe in time there would be another child, imperturbable and fat as a putto.

"Okay now, what do you have for me?" She couldn't refrain from asking anymore. She didn't see any obvious bulges in his pockets, but whatever it was might be concealed under the drape of his coat. Or it could be something very, very small. Was he about to propose to her? What was she going to say if he did?

"No," he said. "You first."

"It's a portrait," she said. "A portrait of you."

"Another one? I didn't sit for it."

"How odd," she said teasingly. She untied the wrapping and carried the painting over to the mantel.

She had done two previous portraits of Joe. He sat for the first in shirtsleeves and vest, sprawled in a leather chair in the dark-paneled parlor where they had first become acquainted. In the piece, his doffed jacket, with a curled newspaper in its hip pocket, hangs from the back of the chair, and he leans against the arm, his head with its long wolfhound face cocked a little to one side, the fingers of his right hand lightly pressed to his right temple. His legs are crossed at the knee, and he ignores a cigarette in the fingers of his left hand. Rosa's brush caught the rime of ash on his lapel, the missed button of his waistcoat, the tender, impatient, defiant expression in his eyes by means of which he is clearly trying to convey to the artist, telepathically, that he intends, in an hour or so, to fuck her. In the second portrait, Joe is shown working at the drawing table in his and Sammy's apartment. A piece of Bristol board lies before him, partly filled in with panels; careful examination reveals the discernible form, in one panel, of Luna Moth in flight. Joe is reaching with a long slender brush toward a bottle of ink on the taboret beside him. The table, which Joe had bought sixth- or seventh-hand shortly after his arrival in New York, is crusted and constellated with years of splattered paint. Joe's sleeves are rolled to the elbow and a few dark coils of hair dangle over his high forehead. The end of his necktie can be seen to lie precariously close to a fresh stroke of ink on the paper, and on his cheek he wears an adhesive bandage over some faint pink scratches. In this picture, his expression is serene and almost perfectly blank, his attention focused entirely on the bristles of the brush that he is about to dip into the bright black ink.

The third portrait of Joe Kavalier was the last painting Rosa ever made, and it differed from the first two in that it was not painted from life. It was executed with the same easy but accurate draftsmanship of all her work, but it was a fantasy. The style was simpler than in the other two portraits, approaching the cartoonish, slightly self-conscious naïveté of her food pictures. In this one, Joe is posed against an indeterminate background of pale rose, on an ornate carpet. He is naked. More surprisingly, he is entirely entangled, from head to toe, in heavy metal chains from which, like charms on a bracelet, dangle padlocks, cuffs, iron clasps, and manacles. His feet are shackled together with leg irons. The weight of all this metal bows him at the waist, but his head is held high, staring out at the viewer with a challenging expression. His long, muscular legs are straight, his feet spread as if he is ready to spring into action. The pose was borrowed from a photograph in a book about Harry Houdini, with the following crucial differences: unlike Houdini, who in the photo guarded his modesty with his manacled hands, Joe's genitals, with their forlorn expression, though heavily shadowed with fur, are plainly visible; the big lock in the middle of his chest is shaped like a human heart; and on his shoulder, in black overcoat and men's galoshes, sits the figure of the artist herself, holding a golden key.

"That's funny," he said. He reached into his trousers pocket. "This is what I have for you." He held out a fist to her, knuckles up. She turned the hand over and pried the fingers apart. On the palm of his hand lay a brass key. "I'm going to need help to do this," he said. "I hope with all my heart, Rosa, that you will want to help me."

"And what is this the key to?" she said, her voice sharper than she wanted it to be, knowing perfectly well that it was the key to this apartment, and that Joe was now asking her for the very thing she had been on the verge of asking for herself—that she be allowed to act as a mother, or at least a big sister, to Thomas Kavalier. She was disappointed in the same measure that she had been expecting a ring, and thrilled to the degree that she was horrified by her desire for one.

"Like in the painting," he said, in a kidding way, as if he could see she was upset, and was trying to figure out what tone to adopt with her. "The key to my heart."

She took the key and held it in her hand. It was warm from his pocket. "Thank you," she said. She was crying, bitterly and happily, ashamed of herself, thrilled to be able to really do something for him.

"I'm sorry," Joe said, taking the handkerchief from his jacket pocket.

"I wanted you to have a key, because . . . but I did the wrong thing." He gestured toward the painting. "I forget to say I love it. Rosa, I love it! It's incredible! It's a whole new thing for you."

She laughed, taking the hankie from him, and dabbed at her eyes. "No, Joe, it's not that," she said, though in fact the painting did represent a new direction for Rosa's work. It had been years since she had attempted to draw from her imagination. Her talent for capturing a likeness, a contour, her innate sense of shadow and weight, had biased her toward life drawing early on. Though she had worked partly from a photograph this time, the details of Joe's body and face were filled in from memory, a process she had found challenging and satisfying. You had to know your lover very well—to have spent a lot of time looking at him and touching him—to be able to paint his picture when he was not around. The inevitable mistakes and exaggerations she had made struck her now as proofs, artifacts, of the mysterious intercourse of memory and love. "No. Joe. Thank you for the key. I want it very much."

"I'm glad."

"And I'm happy to help in every way. Nothing would make me happier. But if you're saying you want to move in here . . . " She looked at him. Yes. He had been. "Well, I don't think I should. For Thomas. I don't think it would be right. He might not understand."

"No," he said. "I *was* thinking—but no. You're right, of course."

"But I will absolutely be here whenever you need me. As much as you need me." She blew her nose into his handkerchief. "As long as you need me."

"That's good," he said. "I think we may be talking about a very long time."

She held out the soiled handkerchief uncertainly, smiling a wincing little apologetic smile at the mess.

"It's fine. You keep it, darling."

"Thank you," she said, and this time burst unrestrainedly into a ridiculous, even bizarre, fit of uncontrollable sobbing. She knew perfectly well that the handkerchief was expressly intended for the comforting of women, and that Joe always kept another, reserved for his own personal use, tucked into the back pocket of his trousers.

MANY YEARS AFTERWARD, most of the aged boys at whose long-ago bar mitzvah receptions, in a vanished New York City, a young magician named Joe Kavalier had performed his brisk, lively, all but wordless act, could summon only fragmentary memories of the entertainer. Some of the men were able to recall a slender, quiet young man in a fancy blue cutaway who spoke accented English and seemed hardly older than they. Another, an avid reader of comic books, recalled that Joe Kavalier had invited him to drop by the Empire offices one day with his parents. Joe had given him a tour and sent him home with an armload of free comic books and a drawing, which he still had, of himself standing next to the Escapist. Yet another remembered that Joe worked with an entire menagerie of artificial animals: a collapsible fake-fur rabbit; goldfish carved from a carrot; a rather mangy stuffed parakeet that, to the surprise of spectators, remained perched on the magician's hand while its *cage* vanished into thin air. "I saw him cutting up the carrots in the men's room," this gentleman recalled. "In the bowl of water, they really did look like little fish." Stanley Konigsberg, however, whose bar mitzvah reception marked the last known appearance of the Amazing Cavalieri, retained for the rest of his life—like young Leon Douglas "Pipe Bomb" Saks—an ineradicable memory of our hero. An amateur magician himself, he had first seen Joe performing at the St. Regis for his classmate at Horace Mann, Roy Cohn, and had been impressed enough by Joe's natural movements, his solemnity, and his flawless presentations of the Miser's Dream, Rosini's Location, and the Stabbed Deck to insist that Joe be engaged to baffle his own relatives and schoolmates at the Hotel Trevi two months later. And if Mr. Konigsberg's youthful admiration, and the unfailing kindness shown him by its object, had not sufficed to preserve the Amazing Cavalieri in his memory for the next sixty years, then the singular performance Joe gave at the Hotel Trevi on the evening of December 6, 1941, undoubtedly would have been enough.

Joe arrived an hour before the reception began, as was his habit, to check the disposition of the Trevi's ballroom, salt a few aces and half-dollars, and go over the order of events with Manny Zehn, the bandleader whose fourteen Zehnsations, riotous in their mariachi shirts, were setting up on the bandstand behind them.

"How are they hanging?" said Joe, trying out an expression he had just heard in the subway on his way uptown. He pictured a row of pages from a calendar, hanging on a shiny string. He was young, he was making money hand over fist, and his little brother, after six months of quarantine, bureaucratic dithering, and those terrible days last week when it seemed that the State Department might, at the last moment, cancel all the children's entry visas, was on his way. Thomas would be here in three more days. Here, in New York City.

"Hey, kid," Zehn said, squinting a little mistrustfully at Joe, but finally shaking the hand Joe proffered. They had worked together twice before. "Where's your sombrero?"

"Sorry? I didn't—?"

"Our theme is 'South of the Border.' " Zehn reached behind his head and lifted a black sombrero embroidered with silver thread up onto his balding pate. He was a good-looking, portly man with a pencil mustache. "Sid?" The trombonist had been chatting up one of the waitresses, in a pink beribboned dress with Latin flounces. Sid turned around, an eyebrow arched. Manny Zehn raised his hands in the air and threw his head back. "Number three."

The trombonist nodded. "Hit it," he said to the band. The Zehnsations broke into a spirited bounce version of "The Mexican Hat Dance." They played four bars and then Manny Zehn cut his throat with a finger. "So where's your Mexican hat?"

"No one told me," said Joe. He smiled. "Beside to which I'm permitted only to use the topper," he added, pointing to the "loaded" silk hat on his head, which he had purchased secondhand at Louis Tannen's. "Or else maybe the Mexican magicians' union will complain."

592 · MICHAEL CHABON

Zehn narrowed his eyes again. "You're drunk," he said.

"Not at all."

"You're acting goofy."

"My brother is coming," said Joe, and then, just to see how it sounded, added, "and I am getting married. That is, I hope I am. I have decided I am going to ask her tonight."

Zehn blew his nose. "Mazel tov," he said, giving the blot on his handkerchief a chiromantic squint. "Only I thought you guys were experts at getting *out* of chains."

"Excuse me, Mr. Cavalieri?" said Stanley Konigsberg, appearing rather magically at Joe's side. "But that's what I wanted to ask you?"

"You can call me Joe."

"Joe. Sorry. Okay, I was wondering. Do you ever do escapes?"

"At one time," said Joe. "But I had to give it up." He frowned. "How long have you been standing there?"

"Don't worry, I won't tell anyone you hid a queen of hearts in the centerpiece of table seven," said Stanley. "If that's what you're worried about."

"I did not do any such thing," said Joe. He winked at Manny Zehn and, with a firm hand on Stanley's shoulder, steered the boy out of the ballroom and into the gilded corridor. Guests were taking off their coats, shaking the rain from their umbrellas.

"What kinds of things could you escape from?" Stanley wanted to know. "Chains? Ropes? Boxes? Trunks? Bags? Could you do it jumping off of a bridge? Or a building? What's so funny?"

"You remind me of someone," Joe said.

THAT SAME EVENING, Rosa shoved her paint box, a folded
canvas tarp, a yardstick, and a small stepladder into the back of a
taxi, and headed uptown to the apartment at the Josephine. The
echoing emptiness of the place, a tin-plate rattle in the ears, unnerved
her, and although with Joe's approval she had hastily called Macy's to
order a dining table and chairs, some basic kitchen things, and
bedroom furniture, there would be no time to furnish the rooms
properly before Thomas arrived. It occurred to her that, having gone
from the cramped jumble of a two-family flat on Dlouha Street, to the
provisional pandemonium of a convent refectory, to the packed-in-oil
tin of a stateroom on the *Ark of Miriam*, the boy might actually welcome a bit of space and emptiness, but all the same she wanted him to
feel that the place at which he had arrived, at long last, was home, or a
kind of home. She had tried to think of ways she could accomplish this.
She knew enough about thirteen-year-old boys to be fairly certain that
a plush bathrobe, a bouquet of flowers, or a ruffled canopy on the bed
was not going to do the trick. She thought that a dog or a kitten might
have been nice, but pets were not allowed in the building. She asked
Joe about his brother's favorite meal, color, book, song; but Joe had
proven quite ignorant of such preferences. Rosa was irritated with
him—she had said he was impossible—until she saw that he was, for
once, pained by his ignorance. It was the mark not of his usual
luftmensch obliviousness but of the chasm of strange separation that
had opened up between the brothers in the last two years. She apologized at once and went on trying to think what she could do for
Thomas, until finally she'd had the idea, which struck them both as a
nice one, of painting the blank expanse of his bedroom with a mural. It

was not just that she wanted Thomas to feel at home; she wanted him to like her—instantly, right away—and she hoped that the mural, whether it softened the edges of his arrival or not, would at the very least stand as an offer of friendship, as a hand extended in welcome from his American big sister. But intermingled with, secretly bubbling beneath, these other motives for the gesture was concealed a desire that had nothing to do with Thomas Kavalier. Rosa was *practicing*— beginning to dabble, on the walls of a boy's bedroom, with the idea of becoming a mother. This morning, her doctor had called to confirm the tale of a missed period and of a week of sudden squalls and unexpected flare-ups of emotion such as the one that had sent her into hysterics over the loan of an old pocket square. Thomas was going to be an uncle. That was how she had decided that she was going to put it to Joe.

When she got into the apartment, she first changed into a pair of dungarees and an old shirt of Joe's, and put her hair back with a ker-chief. Then she went into the bedroom that was going to be Thomas's and spread out the tarp on the floor. She had never painted a mural be-fore, but she had talked it over with her father, who had been involved in the fracas over the Rivera murals at Rockefeller Center and who knew many artists who had worked on murals for the W.P.A.

Rosa had wrestled for a long time with the proper subject. Charac-ters from nursery rhymes, wooden soldiers, fairies and frog princes and gingerbread houses, such motifs would be considered hopelessly puerile by a boy of thirteen. She considered doing a New York scene— tall buildings, taxicabs, traffic cops, the Camel sign blowing smoke rings toward the ceiling. Or perhaps some corny American montage, with redwood trees and cotton plants and lobsters. She wanted it to be sort of generally American, but also to relate in some way to the specific life Thomas was going to be leading here. Then she had started think-ing about Joe, and the kind of work that he did. She suspected that Thomas Kavalier was going to be learning a good deal of his English from the pages of Empire Comics. While she would not have felt com-fortable doing a mural that featured the Monitor, the Four Freedoms, or—God knew—Luna Moth, the idea of heroes, American heroes, in-trigued her. She went to the public library and checked out a big book, with impressive Rockwell Kent–style woodcuts, called *Heroes and Legends of the American People*. The larger-than-life figures of Paul Bunyan, John Henry, Pecos Bill, Mike Fink, and the rest—her favorite was the original man of steel, Joe Magarac—struck her as perfectly suited to the mural form, and not beneath the contempt of a boy to whom they would probably be largely unknown. What was more, Rosa had taken to thinking of Joe himself as a hero—he had paid, out of his own pocket, for fifteen of the children who were now steaming across the Atlantic. Though she would not put Joe into the mural, she decided to include an image of Harry Houdini, that immigrant boy from Central Europe, just to connect the theme of the mural that much more directly to Thomas's life.

She had made dozens of preliminary sketches and a two-by-three cartoon of the mural, which she now set about transferring, by means of a simple grid, to the largest of the room's walls. It was tricky work laying out the guidelines on the walls with the yardstick, first the horizontals, moving the stepladder across from left to right three feet at a hop, then the verticals, easy enough at the bottom but flirting more and more dangerously with wobbliness as she drew nearer to the top and was forced to go up on tiptoe. It required far more patience than she possessed, and several times she came close to abandoning the grid and just trying to sketch the thing out freehand on the wall. But she reminded herself that patience was a cardinal virtue in a mother—God knew her own mother had had little enough—and kept to her careful plan.

By ten o'clock, she had finished laying out the guidelines. Her shoulders ached, and her neck, and her knees, and she felt that before she started in on transferring the gridded cartoon to the wall she would go for a walk around the block, for a sandwich or a cigarette. She might run into Joe; he ought to be through with his show by now and on his way up to meet her. So she pulled on her coat and took the elevator back down to the lobby. She walked up to the corner of Seventy-ninth Street, where there was a late-night grocery.

Later, Rosa would imagine that, like a cat or a spirit camera trained on a dying person, she had seen her lost happiness at the instant of its passing. As she was paying for her Philip Morrises, she happened to glance down at the Sunday papers stacked in front of the counter, bulldog editions hot off the press. In the upper-right-hand corner of the *Herald* there was an extra, boxed in red. She read it five times, with all her heart and attention, but the tiny amount of information it conveyed never increased or—then or afterward—made any better sense. The ten lines of tentative, bland prose said only that a boat filled with refugees, many from Central Europe, most if not all of them believed to be Jewish children, was missing in the Atlantic off the Azores and believed lost. There was no mention, as there would not be for several more hours, of a U-boat, a forced evacuation, a sudden storm tearing in out of the northeast. Rosa stood there for a moment, her lungs filled with smoke, unable to exhale. Then she looked up at the storekeeper, who was watching her with interest. Evidently something quite engrossing was going on in her face. What should she do? Was he still at the Trevi? Was he on his way up to the Josephine, as they had planned? Had he heard the news?

She drifted out to the curb and fretted for a moment longer. Then she decided she had better just go back to the apartment and wait for him. She was sure that he would eventually come looking for her there, whether in ignorance or grief. Just as she was coming to this decision, however, a taxicab pulled up and let out an elderly couple in evening clothes. Rosa brushed past them and climbed into the back of the cab.

"The Trevi," she said.

She sat in a dark corner of the taxi. The light came and went, and in the mirror of her compact, her reflection was intermittently brave. She closed her eyes and tried to recite a snatch of Buddhist prayer her father had taught her, claiming it had a calming effect. It had little apparent impact on her father, and she wasn't even sure she had the words right. *Om mani padmi om.* Somehow it did make her feel calmer. She said it all the way from Seventy-ninth Street to the curb outside the Trevi. By the time she stepped out of the cab, she had pulled herself fairly together. She came into the severe marble reception hall, with its icy chandeliers, and went up to the desk to inquire. From the lobby came the somehow baleful laughter of the famous fountain.

"The magician was a friend of yours?" said the clerk with an unaccountably hostile air. "He cut out hours ago."

"Oh." It hit her like a blow. He was supposed to come up to the apartment after the performance. The fact that he had not done so meant that something terrible had happened to him. And in its wake, in possession of this knowledge, he had not wanted to see her. "Are they—is anyone—"

"There's the bar mitzvah boy now," the clerk said, pointing to a skinny little kid in a three-piece pink suit lolling on one of the watered silk couches in the lobby. "Why don't you ask him?"

Rosa went over, and the boy introduced himself as Stanley Konigsberg. Rosa told him she was looking for Joe, that she had some very bad news to give him. Oh, she had some wonderful news, too, but how would she ever be able to tell him? He would think she was trying to make some horrible equivalency, when it was only one of the monstrous coincidences of life.

"I think he already knows," Stanley Konigsberg said. He was a squat boy, small for his age, with crooked spectacles and coarse brown hair. The suit was incredible, trousers trimmed with white braid, pockets and buttonholes with white frogs, precisely the color of humiliation itself. "Is it about that boat that sank?"

"Yes," Rosa said. "His little brother was on it. A boy about your age."

"Jeez." He fidgeted with the end of his brown necktie, unable to make eye contact with Rosa. "That explains it, I guess."

That explains what, Rosa wanted to ask him, but she stuck to the more pressing question. "Do you know where he went?" she said.

"No, ma'am, I'm sorry. He just—"

"How long ago did he leave?"

"Oh, two hours at least. Maybe even more."

"Wait here," Rosa said. "Will you wait here, please?"

"I guess I kind of have to." He pointed to the doors of the Trevi's ballroom. "My parents aren't finished arguing."

Rosa went to a pay telephone and called Sammy and Joe's apartment, but there was no answer, and that was when she remembered that Sammy had gone out of town for the weekend with Tracy Bacon. To the Jersey shore, of all places. She was going to have to try to track him down. Next she had the operator call the superintendent of the Josephine, Mr. Dorsey. Mr. Dorsey grumbled and warned her not to make a habit of it, but when she told him it was urgent, he went up and checked the apartment for her. No, he said when he returned to the phone, there was nobody there, and no note. Rosa hung up and went back to Stanley Konigsberg.

"Tell me what happened," she said.

"Well, I mean, I guess he was upset, but nobody knew. I mean, everybody else was pretty upset when they heard. My uncle Mort works for the J.T.A. The Jewish Telegraphic Agency. It's a wire service."

"Yes."

"So he came in and told us the news, he heard it first."

"Did you see Joe leave, Stanley?" said Rosa.

"Well, yeah, I mean, yes, everybody did."

"And he seemed to be upset?"

Stanley nodded. "It was really quite strange," he said.

"What happened?" said Rosa. "What was strange?"

"It was all my fault," Stanley began. "I guess I was kind of nudzhing him, and he kept saying no, no, no, so then I went to my father and he said he'd give your friend another fifty dollars, and he still said no, so then I went to my mother." He winced. "After that, I guess he didn't really have any choice."

"Any choice about what?" Rosa said. She put her hand on Stanley's shoulder. "What did you want him to do?"

"I wanted him to do an escape," said Stanley, twitching as she touched him. "He said he knew how. Maybe he was just joking, I don't know. But he told my mother okay, he would. He said I was a nice kid and he would throw it in for no charge. But there was only about a half hour before he was supposed to go on, you know, so he had to rush it. He went down to the basement and got a big wooden packing crate that something, I think it was a filing cabinet, came in. And also a laundry bag. And a hammer and some nails. Then he went and talked for a while to the house detective, and he said no. My father had to go and give him fifty dollars, too. Then it was time for him, your friend, Joe, to go on. He did his show. He was really good. He did some card tricks, and some coin tricks, and he did some tricks with apparatuses. A little of everything, which is hard, which I know, see, because I'm a magician too, kind of. Most of them, when you see them . . . they have a specialty. Like I just do mostly stuff with cards. Then after maybe a half hour he, your friend, got us all to stand up, and we had to leave the ballroom, and he brought us down here. Over to that." He pointed to the fountain out in the lobby, an exact replica of the famous one in Rome, all tritons and seashells and blue-lit cataracts. "Everyone. I think it was on the way down that Uncle Lou must have told him about the ship, you know, sinking and all, 'cause when we got down here he looked, uh, I don't know. Like his mouth was kind of hanging crooked. And he kept putting his hand on my shoulder, like he was leaning on me. Then some waiters brought in the bag and the box. The hotel detective came over and put him in handcuffs. He got in the bag, and I got to tie it myself. We put him in the box, and I got to nail it shut. We dropped him into the fountain. He told us if he didn't come out in three minutes to come in after him."

"Oh my God," said Rosa.

Two minutes and fifty-eight seconds from the time of his immersion in the cool blue water of the Trevi's fountain, the two waiters, the house detective, and Mr. Konigsberg in his best suit went splashing in after Joe. They had been watching the crate for signs of movement, a telltale shuddering, a visible straining in the planks that made up the crate. But there was no motion at all. The crate lay inert, covered up to within an inch of its nailed-on lid, in water. When Mrs. Konigsberg began to scream, though there were still a few seconds to go until the deadline, the men went in. They rolled the crate up and out of the water, but in their haste they lost their grip on it, and it shattered against the floor. The laundry sack rolled out and flopped wildly on the floor like a gasping fish. Joe was thrashing around so much on the carpet that the house detective couldn't get the sack opened alone, and had to call on the other men to lend a hand. It took three of them to hold Joe down. When they peeled away the bag, his face was red as a fresh welt, but his lips were almost blue. His eyes rolled in their orbits, and he gagged and coughed as though fresh air were poison to him. They got him to his feet and the house detective removed the cuffs; when they were passed around afterward, it was plain they had not been tampered with. For a moment Joe wavered there, soaking wet, looking slowly across the two hundred faces ranged in an anxious and wondering ring around him. His face was twisted in an expression that most of the guests would later characterize as shame but that others, Stanley Konigsberg among them, saw as a terrible, inexplicable anger. Then, in a parody of the smooth courtliness he had exhibited toward them in the ballroom a bare twenty minutes before, he bowed deeply from the waist. His hair fell down over his face and then, as he snapped back upright, flung water across the bodice of Mrs. Konigsberg's silk dress, leaving spots that proved to be ineradicable.

"Thank you very much," he said. Then he dashed across the lobby, through the revolving doors, and out into the street, shoes squeaking every step of the way.

After Stanley had finished, Rosa went back to the telephone. If she was going to try to find Joe, she would need help, and the person whose help she most wanted was Sammy. She tried to think of who might be able to track him down. Then she picked up the phone and asked the operator if there was a listing for Klayman, in Flatbush.

"Yes? Who is this?" The voice was a woman's, deep, slightly accented. A little suspicious, perhaps, but not troubled.

"This is Rosa Saks, Mrs. Klayman. I hope you remember me."

"Of course, dear. How are you?" She had no idea.

"Mrs. Klayman. I don't know how to tell you this." All week she had been the slave to unpredictable torrents of sadness and rage, but from seeing that newspaper headline until now, she had remained remarkably calm, almost devoid of feeling apart from the urge to find Joe. Somehow the thought of poor, hardworking, sad-eyed Mrs. Klayman, in her tiny apartment in Flatbush, broke the ice. Rosa started to cry so hard that it was difficult for her to get the words out. At first Mrs. Klayman tried to soothe her, but as Rosa grew more incoherent, she lost her temper a little.

"Dear, you must calm down!" she snapped. "Take a deep breath, for God's sake."

"I'm sorry," Rosa said. She took a deep breath. "All right."

She related the little she knew. There was a long silence over there in Flatbush.

"Where is Josef?" Mrs. Klayman said finally, her voice calm and measured.

"I can't find him. I was hoping Sammy might—might help—"

"I'll find Sammy," Mrs. Klayman said. "You just go home. Back to your family's house. He may come there."

"He doesn't want to see me, I think," Rosa said. "I don't know why. Mrs. Klayman, I'm afraid he may try to kill himself! I think he already tried it once tonight."

"Don't talk crazy. We just have to wait," Mrs. Klayman said. "That's all we can really do."

When Rosa wandered outside to get another cab, there was a boy selling papers, tomorrow's *Journal-American*. This carried a more detailed, if not quite accurate, version of the sinking of the *Ark of Miriam*. A German U-boat assigned to one of the dreaded "wolf packs" that were tormenting Allied shipping in the Atlantic had set upon the innocent ship and sent it to the bottom with all hands.

This account, it later developed, was not quite true. When, after the war, he was put on trial for this and other crimes, the commander of *U-328,* an intelligent and cultivated career officer named Gottfried Halse, was able to produce ample evidence and testimony to prove that, in full accordance with Admiral Dönitz's "Prize Regulations," he had attacked the ship within ten miles of land—the island of Corvo in the Azores—and given ample warning to the captain of the *Ark of Miriam.* The evacuation had proceeded in an orderly fashion, and the transfer of all passengers to the lifeboats might have been effected safely and without incident if, immediately after the firing of the torpedoes, a storm had not appeared out of the northeast, overwhelming the boats so quickly that the crew of *U-328* had no time to help. It was only luck that had enabled Halse and his crew of forty to escape with their own lives. If he had known that the ship carried children, Halse was asked, a good many of them unable to swim, would he still have proceeded with the attack? Halse's reply is preserved in the transcript of his trial without comment or any notation as to whether his tone was one of irony, resignation, or sorrow.

"They were children," he said. "We were wolves."

W HEN THE LINE OF CARS pulled into the front drive of the
house, Ruth Ebling, the housekeeper, who was watching from
the great front porch as the chauffeur and Stubbs unloaded the
guests and their baggage, noticed the little Jew at once. He was so much
smaller and more spindly than the other men in the party—smaller,
indeed, than any of the rangy, slouching, sandy-haired types, with their
Brooks suits and their polished manners, who formed the usual
complement of Mr. Love's entertainments. Where the other fellows
emerged from the cars with the lithe step of adventurers come to plant
a conquering flag, the little Jewish boy scrambled out of the back of the
second car—a monstrous new bottle-green Cadillac Sixty-one—like a
man who had just fallen into a ditch. He looked as if he had spent the
past several hours not so much sitting alongside the other fellows in the
backseat as carelessly scattered in the spaces among them. He stood,
fumbling with a cigarette, blinking and pale, eyes watering in the stiff
wind, rumpled, vaguely misshapen, viewing the looming gables and
mad cheminations of Pawtaw with unconcealed mistrust. When he saw
Ruth watching him, he ducked his head and half-raised his hand in
greeting.

Ruth felt an uncharacteristic urge to avert her gaze. Instead, she
fixed him with the cold level stare, cheeks immobile, jaw set, which she
had heard Mr. Love refer to, when he thought her out of earshot, as her
"Otto von Bismarck look." An apologetic smile briefly creased the little
Jew's face.

Though he could not have known it (and never did learn for certain
just what went wrong that day), Sammy Clay's bad luck was to have arrived on the very afternoon when the bubbling motor of Ruth Ebling's

hostility toward Jews was being fueled not merely by the usual black compound of her brother's logical, omnivorous harangues and the silent precepts of her employer's social class. She was also burning a clear, volatile quart of shame blended with unrefined rage. The previous morning, in New York City, she had stood with her mother, her sister-in-law, and her uncle George, on the sidewalk outside the Tombs, watching as the bus carrying her remaining brother, Carl Henry, off to Sing Sing disappeared in a thick cloud of exhaust.

Carl Henry Ebling had pleaded guilty and been sentenced, by a judge named Cohn, to a term of twelve years for bombing the bar mitzvah reception of Leon Douglas Saks at the Pierre. Carl Henry, a fervent, dreamy, but never especially adroit or competent boy, had carried these traits with him into a passionate and shiftless manhood. But the formless and badly dented idealism with which he had returned from the battlefields of Belgium, curdling in the long indignity of the Depression, had taken on new shape and purpose after 1936, when a friend had invited him to join a Yorkville social organization, the Fatherland Club, which by the outbreak of war in Europe had transmogrified or splintered off—she had never been able to follow it—into the Aryan-American League. While Ruth had never entirely agreed with Carl Henry's views—Adolf Hitler made her nervous—or felt comfortable with her brother's having taken such an active role in his party's activities, she saw unquestionable nobility in his devotion to the cause of freeing the United States from the malevolent influence of Morgenthau and the rest of his cabal. And furthermore, it ought to have been as clear to the judge, to the prosecutor (Silverblatt), and to everyone as it was to Ruth herself that her brother, who had insisted, in spite of his lawyer's advice, on pleading guilty, and who much of the time seemed to be under the impression that he was a costumed villain in a comic book, was clearly out of his mind. He belonged in Islip, not Sing Sing. That the bomb her brother had made—in the shape of a trident, how could they not see the craziness in that?—had somehow managed to explode, injuring only him, Ruth blamed on the bad luck and fumbling nature that had never deserted her brother. As for the harsh sentence he had received, this she blamed, as did Carl Henry, not only on the workings of the Jewish Machine but, with an unwillingness that wrenched her heart, on her employer, Mr. James Haworth Love himself. James Love had, from the early thirties, been extremely vocal in his opposition to Charles Lindbergh, to the America Firsters, and above all to the German-American Bund and other pro-German groups in this country, which in speeches and newspaper editorials he typically characterized as "fifth columnists, spies, and saboteurs," attacks that had climaxed, at least in Ruth's view, with the prosecution and imprisonment of her brother. Thus was the dull dislike that Ruth ordinarily would have borne for Sammy made keen by her suppurating detestation of his host for the weekend, of the way Mr. James Haworth Love conducted his affairs, both political and social. Witnessing this relaxation of the ban, unarticulated yet absolute, on the presence of Jews at Pawtaw, hitherto among the few traditions of his parents and empire-building grandparents that Mr. Love had continued to respect, seeing it as a final proof of the man's shamelessness and debility, her heart rebelled. It would require only one further outrage to push Ruth into taking steps to alleviate the pressure that had been building in her breast for so long.

"Saw the smoke," Mr. Love barked. "Fires lit. Very good, Ruth. How are you?"

"I'm sure I'll live."

The men all trooped up the steps, tossing their bright empty greetings in her direction, complimenting her on her hair, the style of which had not altered since 1923, her color, the smells emanating from the kitchen. She greeted them politely, with something of her usual wary wryness, like a schoolteacher welcoming the return from vacation of a group of smart alecks and cutups, and told them, one by one, which rooms would be theirs and how they could find them if they didn't already know. The bedrooms had each been named by some early Love enthusiast after vanished local Indian tribes. One of the men, extraordinarily good-looking and with eyes the very color of the new Cadillac and a dimple in his chin, much taller and broader than any of the others, shook her hand and said that he had heard the most amazing things about her oyster stew. The spindly-legged Jew hung back, sheltering in the lee of the green-eyed giant. His only greeting to her was another crooked smile and a nervous cough.

"You'll be in Raritan," she told him, having held back especially for him this smallest and most cramped of the third-floor guest rooms, one with no porch and only a fragmentary view of the sea.

He looked almost fearful at this information, as if it were news of a grave responsibility she had placed upon him.

"Thank you, ma'am," he said.

Ruth would remember afterward that she was troubled by a brief, mild emotion that lay somewhere between affection and pity for the little snub-nosed Jewish boy; he seemed so out of place among all these tall and sporting daffodils. She had a hard time believing that he could really be one of them. She wondered if he had gotten here by some kind of mistake.

Ruth Ebling could not have known how nearly her speculations on Sam's status and position coincided with his own.

"Jesus," he said to Tracy Bacon, "what am I doing here?" He dropped his suitcase. It landed with a muffled thud on the thick carpet, one of several worn Oriental rugs with which the creaking floorboards of Raritan were patchworked. Tracy had already left his bags down in his second-floor room, which, in a striking access of precognition by that Indian-loving ancestor, had been designated Ramcock. He lay now across Sammy's iron bed on his back, legs raised and crossed at the knee, arms folded beneath his head, picking with a fingernail at the peeling white enamel of the bedstead. Like many big, well-built men, he was an inveterate layabout who disdained physical exertion except in brief Red Grange bursts of frantic grace. He furthermore detested standing upright, which made his radio work particularly obnoxious to him; and he loathed being obliged to sit up straight. His inherent ability to feel at ease wherever he went was coupled powerfully with a bone-deep laziness. Whenever he entered a room, no matter how formal the occasion, he generally sought out a place where he could at least put his feet up. "I'll bet I'm the first kike that's ever set foot in this joint."

"I don't think I'll take that bet."

Sammy went to the little window, each of its panes smudged with a thumbprint of frost, in the narrow dormer that overlooked the back lawn. He cranked it open, letting in a cool blast of brine and chimney smoke and the rumblings and fizzings of the sea. In the last quarter hour of the day, Dave Fellowes and John Pye were way down on the beach, tossing a football with a certain grim fervor, in dungarees and heavy sweatshirts but with their feet bare. John Pye was also a radio actor, the star of *Paging Dr. Maxwell,* and a friend of Bacon, who had introduced Pye to the sponsor of *The Adventures of the Escapist.* Fellowes ran the Manhattan office of a member of New York's congressional delegation. Sammy watched as Fellowes turned his back on Pye and took off down the beach, scattering white puffs of sand. Fellowes reached up, looking over his shoulder, and a short, accurate forward pass from Pye found his hands.

"This is so strange," said Sammy.

"Is it?"

"Yes."

"I guess it is," Bacon said. "I guess it must be."

"You wouldn't know."

"Well, I . . . maybe the reason I don't think so is that I always felt so strange, you know, before I found out that I wasn't the only one in the world—"

"That's not what I mean," Sammy said gently. He had not meant to sound argumentative. "That's not what feels strange to me, kid. Not because they're all a bunch of fairies, or because Mr. James Love the sock magnate is a fairy, or because you're a fairy or I'm a fairy."

"*If* you are," Bacon said with mock correctitude.

"If I am."

Bacon gazed at the ceiling, arms folded contentedly under his head. "Which you are."

"Which I might be."

In fact, the question of what a later generation would term Sammy's sexual orientation seemed, at least to the satisfaction of everyone who made up the party at Pawtaw on that first weekend of December 1941, to have largely been settled. In the weeks since their visit to the World's Fair and their lovemaking inside the dark globe of the Perisphere, Sammy had, along with his strapping young paramour, become a fixture in the circle of John Pye, considered at that time, and for long afterward in the mythos of gay New York, to be the most beautiful man in the city. At a spot in the East Fifties called the Blue Parrot, Sammy had experienced the novelty of seeing men doing the Texas Tommy and the Cinderella, close, in darkness, though his weak stems prevented him from joining in the fun. Tomorrow, as everyone knew, he and Tracy were leaving for the West Coast, to take up their new life together as scenarist and serial star.

"So what is strange, then?" said Tracy.

Sammy shook his head. "It's just, look at you. Look at them." He jerked a thumb toward the open window. "It's that they could all play the secret identity of a guy in tights. Your bored playboy, your gridiron hero, your crusading young district attorneys. Bruce Wayne. Jay Garrick. Lamont Cranston."

"Jay Garrick?"

"The Flash. Blond, muscles, nice teeth, a pipe."

"I would never smoke a pipe."

"This one went to Princeton, that one went to Harvard, the other one went to Oxford. . . ."

"Filthy habit."

Sammy wrinkled up his face to acknowledge that his attempts at rumination were being parried, then looked away. Down on the beach, Fellowes had tackled John Pye. They were rolling in the sand.

"A year ago, when I wanted to be around someone like you, I had to, you know, make you up. And now . . ." He looked across the broad, sere expanse of the lawn, past Pye and Fellowes. A signature of foam scrawled itself across the surface of the waves. How could he begin to say how happy he had been, this last month or so, in the radiant focus of Bacon's regard, how mistaken Bacon was in wasting that regard on him. No one as beautiful, as charming and poised and physically grand, as Bacon could possibly take an interest in him.

"If you're asking me if you can be my sidekick," Bacon said, "the answer's yes. We'll get you a mask of your own."

"Say, thanks."

"We'll call you, oh, how does 'Rusty' sound? Rusty or Dusty."

"Shut up."

"Actually, *Musty* would be more appropriate." When they were in bed together, Bacon was always sampling deep nostalgic drafts of Sammy's penis, claiming it gave off the precise odor of a pile of old tarpaulins in his grandfather's woodshed back in Muncie, Indiana. Once, the location of the shed had been given as Chillicothe, Illinois.

"I warn you. . . ." Sammy said, head inclined menacingly to one side, arms jutting out to execute a couple of judo chops, legs coiled to spring.

"Or, given the state of your linens, young man," Bacon said, raising his arms to his face, already cringing, "maybe we ought seriously to consider *Crusty.*"

"That does it," Sammy said, launching himself onto the bed. Bacon pretended to scream. Sammy scrambled on top of him and pinned his wrists to the bed. His face hung suspended twenty inches above Bacon's.

"Now I've got you," he said.

"Please," said Bacon. "I'm an orphan."

"This is what we used to do to wise guys in my neighborhood."

Sammy pursed his lips and allowed a long strand of saliva to dangle downward, tipped by a thick bubbled bead. The bubble lowered itself like a spider on its thread until it hung just over Bacon's face. Then Sammy reeled it back in. It had been years since he had last attempted the trick, and he was pleased to discover that his spittle retained its viscosity and he his pinpoint control of it.

"Ew," said Bacon. He thrashed his head from side to side and struggled under the weight of Sammy on his wrists, while Sammy dangled the silvery thread over him again. Then, abruptly, Bacon stopped struggling. He looked at Sammy, level, calm, and with a dangerous glint in his eye; of course he could have freed himself easily, if he so desired, from the puny grip of his lover. His look said so. He opened his mouth. The pearl of spit dangled. Sammy cut the thread. A minute later, they lay naked beneath the four piled blankets on the narrow bed, disporting themselves in the precise manner that Dr. Fredric Wertham, in his fatal book, would one day allege to be universal among costumed heroes and their "wards." They fell asleep holding each other, and were wakened by a smell, comforting and maternal, of boiled milk and salt water.

A number of fragmentary accounts survive of the events that transpired at Pawtaw on the sixth of December, 1941. The entry in James Love's journal for 6 December is characteristically terse. It notes that

Bob Perina had gained eighty-two yards for Princeton that afternoon, and gives details of the menu and highlights of conversation at dinner, with the rueful annotation "in rtrspct mr trivial than usl." The guests, as always, are identified by their initials: JP, DF, TB, SC, RP, DD, QT. The entry ends with the single word DISASTER. Only the absence of any entry at all for the following day, and the preoccupation of Monday's entry, when there was so much else going on in the world, with a visit to his attorney, give any further hint of what transpired. Roddy Parks, the composer, in an entry in his famous diary, supplies the name of another guest (his lover at the time, the photographer Donald Davis), and agrees with Love that the principal subjects of conversation at the table were a large exhibition of Fauvist paintings at the Marie Harriman Gallery, and the king of Belgium's surprise marriage. He also notes that the oyster stew was a failure and that Donald had remarked earlier in the afternoon that something seemed to be troubling the housekeeper, whom Parks calls Ruth Appling. His account of the raid is nearly as terse as Love's: "The police were called."

A check of the report filed by the Monmouth County sheriff supplies the name of the final guest that weekend, a Mr. Quentin Towle, as well as a rather more detailed account of events that evening, including some insight into the impetus that sent Ruth, at long last, to the telephone. "Miss Ebling," the report reads, "was exaspirated [*sic*] by the recent imprisonment of her brother Carl and happened in a bedroom to stumble upon a comic strip book of a type which she held responsible for many of the brother's mental problems. At this point, having identified the author of said comic strip book as one of the suspects, she determined to notify the authorities of the activities taking place in the house."

It is interesting to note that in spite of the emphasis, that night and during the course of the largely inconclusive legal proceedings that followed, on the role of the comic book in triggering Ruth Ebling's act of retribution, the only guest at Pawtaw that evening for whom there is no existing arrest record is the book's author.

Sammy got drunk at dinner for the first time in his life. Drunkenness came over him so slowly that at first he mistook it for the happiness of sexual fatigue. It had been a long day, one that had left a bodily imprint in his memory: the chill outside the Mayflower that morning as they waited for Mr. Love and his friends to pick them up; the elbow in his ribs, the roar and ashy smell of the Cadillac's heater, the sharp shaft of December air blowing in through the car window on the way down; the burn of a shot of rye he accepted from John Pye's flask; the lingering mark of Bacon's teeth and the imprint of his thumbs on Sammy's hips. As he sat at the dinner table, eating his stew and looking around him with an expression he knew, without anxiety, to be a stupid one, the day enveloped him in a pleasant confusion of aches and images like the one that overwhelms someone on the verge of sleep who has spent the entire day out of doors. He sank back into it and watched as the men around him unfurled the bright banners of their conversation. The wine was a '37 Puligny-Montrachet, from a case that had been the gift, Jimmy Love said, of Paul Reynaud.

"So, when are you two leaving?"

"Tomorrow," Bacon said. "Arriving Wednesday. I have an appearance. Someone from Republic is supposed to be coming on the train at Salt Lake City with my costume so it can be the Escapist who gets off in L.A."

There followed some prolonged teasing of Tracy Bacon on the subject of tight pants, veering amid general amusement into the question of codpieces. Love expressed his satisfaction that Bacon would be able to keep doing the Escapist on the radio, with the broadcast originating in Los Angeles. Sammy sank deeper into his Burgundy-fueled reverie. There was a faint disturbance in the air to his back, a murmur, a muffled cry.

"But won't they miss you at your cartoon factory?"

"What's that?" Sammy sat up straight in his chair. "I think someone's calling you, Mr. Love. I hear someone saying your—"

"I'm truly sorry to do this, Mr. Love," said a clear flat voice behind Sammy. "But I'm afraid you and your ladyfriends are under arrest."

A brief rout followed this announcement. The room filled with a bewildering variety of sheriff's deputies, policemen from Asbury Park, state highway patrolmen, newspaper reporters, and a couple of vacationing G-men from Philly who had been drinking in the Fly Trap, a roadhouse in Sea Bright favored by representatives of coastal New Jersey law enforcement, when the word went around that they were going to flush a fairy nest out at the beach house of one of the richest men in America. When they saw how large and powerfully built many of the fairies appeared to be, not to mention how surprisingly ordinary-looking, they suffered a moment of hesitation during which Quentin Towle managed to slip out. He was later caught on the county road. Only the two big men put up any resistance at all. John Pye had been raided before, twice, and he was tired of it. He knew that in the end it would cost him, but before he could be subdued, he managed to bloody the nose of one sheriff and break a bottle of Montrachet over the head of a second. He also smashed the camera of a photographer who sold to the Hearst papers, an act for which all of his friends were later grateful. Love, in particular, never forgot this service, and after Pye was killed in North Africa, where he had gone to drive an ambulance because the army would not take homosexuals, saw to it that Pye's mother and sisters were provided for. As for Tracy Bacon, he did not give the question of fighting or not fighting the police a moment's thought. Without revealing too much of the true history that he had so assiduously labored to erase and reconstitute, it can be said that Bacon had been falling afoul of the police since the age of nine, and defending himself with his fists since well before that. He waded into the writhing knot of nightsticks and broad-brimmed hats and cowering men, and began swinging. It took four men to subdue him, which they did with considerable brutality.

While Sammy, too drunk and confused to move, watched his lover and John Pye go down in a sea of tan shirts, he was engaged in a fierce struggle of his own. Someone had gotten hold of his legs and would not let go, no matter how hard Sammy kicked and flailed away at whoever it was. In the end, however, his attacker got the best of him, and Sammy found himself dragged down under the table.

"Idiot!" said Dave Fellowes, his eye closed and his nose bleeding from where Sammy had kicked him. "Get down."

He forced Sammy to crouch beside him under the table, and together they watched the boots and bodies thudding against the carpet from beneath the lacy hem of the tablecloth. It was in this ignoble position that they were found, five minutes later, when the two vacationing FBI agents, schooled in thoroughness, made a last sweep through the house.

"Your friends are all waiting for you," said one of them. He smiled at the other, who took hold of the collar of Fellowes's shirt and dragged him out from under the table.

"Be right there," said the other agent.

"I know you will," said the one who was taking Dave Fellowes away, with a harsh laugh.

The G-man, down on one knee, gazed in at Sammy with mock tenderness, as if trying to lure a recalcitrant child out of hiding.

"Come on, sweetheart," he said. "I won't hurt you."

The reality of the situation had begun to penetrate the fog of Sammy's drunkenness. What had he done? How could he possibly tell his mother that he had been arrested, and why? He closed his eyes, but when he did, he was tormented by a vision of Bacon going down under a tide of fists and boot heels.

"Where's Bacon?" he said. "What did you do to him?"

"The big fella? He'll be all right. More of a man than the rest of you. You his girlfriend?"

Sammy blushed.

"You're a lucky girl. He's a good-looking piece of beef."

Sammy felt a strange ripple in the air between him and the policeman. The room, the entire house, seemed to have gotten very quiet. If the cop was planning to arrest him, it seemed to Sammy as if he ought to have done it by now.

"Myself, I'm partial to darker types. Little guys."

"What?"

"I'm a federal agent, did you know that?"

Sammy shook his head.

"That's right. If I mention to those eager pie-hats out there that they ought to let you go, they will."

"Why would you do that?"

The G-man glanced over his shoulder slowly, almost in a parody of a man checking to see if the coast were clear, then scrambled in under the table with Sammy. He put Sammy's hand on the fly of his suit pants.

"Why indeed," said the G-man.

Ten minutes later, the pair of vacationing federal agents were re-united in the foyer of the house. Dave Fellowes and Sammy, pushed along in front of their respective champions, could hardly look at each other, let alone at Ruth Ebling, who was supervising the cleanup efforts of her staff. The bitter taste of Agent Wyche's semen was in Sammy's mouth, along with the putrid sweet flavor of his own rectum, and he would always remember the feeling of doom in his heart, a sense that he had turned some irrevocable corner and would shortly come face-to-face with a dark and certain fate.

"They've all gone," Ruth said, sounding surprised to see them. "You missed them."

"These two men are not suspects," Fellowes's agent said. "They're merely witnesses."

"We need to interrogate them further," said Agent Wyche, not bothering to disguise his amusement at his own implicit meaning. "Thank you, ma'am. We have our own vehicle."

Sammy managed to raise his head and saw that Ruth was looking at him curiously, with the same faint air of pity he thought he had spotted there earlier that afternoon.

"I just want to know this," she said. "How does it feel, Mr. Clay, to make your living preying off the weak-minded? That's the only thing I want to know."

Sammy sensed that he ought to know what she was talking about, and he was sure that under ordinary circumstances he would have. "I'm sorry, ma'am, I have no idea what—"

"A boy jumped off a building, I heard," she said. "Tied a tablecloth around his neck and—"

A telephone rang in a nearby room, and she stopped. She turned and went to answer it. Agent Wyche yanked Sammy's collar and dragged him to the door, and they went out into the burning cold night.

"Just a minute," came the housekeeper's voice from within. "There's a call for a Mr. Klayman. That *him*?"

Afterward, Sammy would often wonder what might have become of him, what alley or ditch his broken and violated body might have ended up in, if his mother had not telephoned the house at Pawtaw with the news that Thomas Kavalier had died. Agent Wyche and his colleague looked at each other, their expressions no longer quite professionally blank.

"Aw, shoot, Frank," said Fellowes's agent. "How 'bout that. It's his *mom.*"

When Sammy came out of the kitchen, Dave Fellowes stood slumped against the doorway, an arm over his red, damp face. The two G-men were gone; they had mothers of their own.

"I need to get back to the city right away," Sammy said.

Fellowes wiped at his face with his sleeve, then reached into his pocket and pulled out the key to his Buick.

Although the traffic was light, it took them nearly three hours to get back to New York. They did not say a word to each other from the moment Fellowes started the car until he dropped Sammy off in front of his apartment.

AFTER HE RAN OUT of the Hotel Trevi, Joe became merely one
of the 7,014 drowned men out stumbling through the streets of
New York that night. He carried a pint of rye that he had bought
in a bar on Fifty-eighth Street. His hair froze into icicles on his head and
his blue tuxedo turned to cold granite, but he felt nothing. He kept
walking, sipping from his bottle. The streets were alight with taxis, the
theaters were emptying, the windows of restaurants were haloed with
candlelight and the vapor of their patrons' breathing. He recalled with
shame the elation that had seized him as he walked to the subway
earlier that evening, the rattling ride underground with everyone
staring at the magician in their car, the general love of poodles and car
horns and the tooth marks of the Essex House on the face of the moon
that had suffused him as he walked in his top hat from the subway to
the Trevi. If he had not drowned an hour ago, he thought, the memory
of this vanished happiness might have been enough to make him hate
himself. Good thing I'm dead, he thought.

Somehow he ended up in Brooklyn. He rode the train all the way out
to Coney Island and then fell asleep and woke up in a place called
Gravesend, with a policeman's rough hand on his shoulder. Sometime
around two o'clock in the morning, more drunk than he had been since
the night he had appeared on the stairs in Bernard Kornblum's house
on Maisel Street, he showed up at 115 Ocean Avenue, at the door of
apartment 2-B.

Ethel answered the door almost immediately. She was fully dressed
and made up, and her hair was tied neatly in a bun. If she was at all surprised to see her nephew at her door, frozen stiff, bleary-eyed, in full
evening dress, she did not betray it. Without a word, she put her arm

around him and helped him to her kitchen table. She poured him a cup of coffee from a blue pot enameled with white flecks. It was dreadful, thin as the water in which he cleaned his brushes and sour as turned wine, but it was fresh and painfully hot. Its effect on him was devastating. As soon as it hit his throat, all the facts and contingencies he had held under the water, until it seemed to him that they had finally stopped struggling, now bobbed back up to the surface, and he knew that he was alive, and that his brother, Thomas, lay dead at the bottom of the Atlantic Ocean.

"We should turn on the radio" was all he could think of to say.

Ethel sat down across from him with her own cup of coffee. She took a handkerchief from the pocket of her black cardigan and handed it to him. "First cry," she said.

She gave him a gummy piece of honey cake and then, as she had on the night of his arrival, handed him a towel.

While he was showering, his grandmother shuffled into the bathroom, lifted the skirt of her nightgown, and, apparently unaware of Joe's presence, lowered her pale blue behind onto the pot.

"You don't listen to me, Yecheved," she said in Yiddish, calling him by his aunt's old-country name. "From the first day, I said I don't like this boat. Didn't I say it?"

Joe spoke English. "I'm sorry," he said.

His grandmother nodded and got off the toilet. Without a word, she turned out the light and shuffled back out. Joe finished his shower in darkness.

After he had warmed himself into an uncontrollable spasm of weeping, his aunt wrapped him in a bathrobe that had once been Sammy's father's, and led him to Sammy's old bed.

"All right," she said. "All right." She put a dry hand to his cheek and kept it there until he had stopped crying, and then until he stopped shaking, and then until he caught his stuttering breath. He lay still and snuffled. The hand on his cheek remained cool as brick.

He woke up a few hours later. It was still night outside the window, without a trace of morning. He ached in his joints and his chest, his lungs, burned as if he had been breathing smoke or poison. He felt hollow and flattened and quite unable to cry.

"She's coming," said his aunt. She was standing in the doorway to the room, outlined in wan blue light by the fixture over the kitchen sink. "I called her. She was out of her mind worrying."

Joe sat up, and rubbed his face, and nodded. He wanted nothing to do with Rosa, with Sammy, with his aunt or his parents or anyone who could tie him, through any bond of memory or affection or blood, to Thomas. But he was too tired to do anything about it, and he had, in any case, no idea of what he should do. His aunt found him some old clothes, and he dressed quickly in the polar light from the sink. The clothes were much too small, but they were dry and would do until he could change them. While they waited for Rosa, she made another pot of coffee, and they sat in silence, sipping at their cups. Three quarters of an hour later, with a trembling, all but invisible hint of blue light in the air, there was the sound of a car horn from the street below. He washed out his coffee cup, laid it in the drying rack, wiped his hands on the towel, and kissed his aunt goodbye.

Ethel hurried to the window, in time to see the girl step out of a taxicab. She threw her arms around him, and Joe held on to her for so long that Ethel found herself regretting, with an intensity that surprised her, that she had neglected to take her nephew into her arms. It seemed just then to be the worst mistake she had ever made in her life. She watched Joe and Rosa get into the taxi and drive away. Then she sat down in a chair, with its festive pattern of pineapples and bananas, and covered her face with her hands.

17

J OE AND R OSA crawled into her bed at six-thirty in the morning, and she held on to him until he fell asleep, lying there, the unknown mysterious product of their love growing in the space between them. Then she slept herself. When she woke, it was past two o'clock in the afternoon, and Joe was gone. She looked in the bathroom, then went downstairs to the black kitchen, where her father was standing with the most peculiar expression on his face.

"Where's Joe?" she said.

"He left."

"Left? Where did he go?"

"Well, he said something about enlisting in the navy," said her father. "But I don't imagine he'll be able to do that until tomorrow."

"The navy? What are you talking about?"

That was how she learned of the attack on the naval base at Pearl Harbor. According to her father, it was very likely that the United States would soon find itself at war with Germany, too. That was what Joe was banking on.

The doorbell played its weird tune, Raymond Scott's shortest composition, "Fanfare for the Fuller Brush Man." She ran to the door, certain that it was going to be Joe. It was Sammy; he looked as if he had been in a fight. There were abrasions on his cheek and a cut by his eye. Had he been fighting with Bacon? She knew that Sammy was supposed to have left with his friend for Los Angeles today—she and Joe had planned originally to go down to the train station and see them off. Had the two men quarreled? A guy of Bacon's size might be dangerous, though it was difficult to imagine him doing anything to hurt Sammy.

She noticed the frayed seam of the right sleeve of Sammy's shirt, where it met the shoulder.

"Your shirt is torn," she said.

"Yeah," he said. "I tore it. That's what you do when you're, you know. In mourning." Rosa had a dim memory of this custom from some long-ago funeral of a great-uncle. The widowed great-aunt had also covered all the mirrors in the house with dish towels, giving the place a disturbing air of having been blinded.

"Want to come in?" she said. "Joe's not here."

"Not really," Sammy said. "Yeah, I know. I saw him."

"You saw him?"

"He came by the apartment to get his things. I guess he woke me up. I guess I had kind of a rough night last night."

"Here," she said, sensing an odd note in his voice. She grabbed an old sweater of her father's from the hat stand, put it around her, and stepped out into the courtyard. It was good to get out into the cold air. She felt some order being restored to her thoughts. "Are you all right?" she said. She noticed that he winced when she touched him, as if his arm or his shoulder were sore. "What's the matter with your arm?"

"Nothing, I hurt it."

"How?"

"Playing football on the beach, how else?"

They sat down on the stone steps, side by side.

"Where is he now?"

"I don't know. He's gone. He left."

"What are you doing here, anyway?" she asked him. "Aren't you supposed to be on a train for Hollywood? Where's Bacon?"

"I told him to go ahead without me," Sammy said.

"Oh?"

He shrugged. "I never really wanted . . . I don't know. I think I got a little carried away with the whole thing."

That morning, at Penn Station, Sammy had said goodbye to Tracy Bacon, in the compartment that had been reserved for them both aboard the Broadway Limited.

"I don't understand," Bacon said. They were awkward and clumsy

with each other, in the closeness of the first-class compartment, a couple of men, one so intent on not touching the other, the second devoting
each movement and gesture to not being touched, that their careful
maintenance of a charged and shifting distance between them had itself
been a kind of bleak contact. "You didn't even get arrested. Jimmy's
lawyers are going to make the whole thing go away."

Sammy shook his head. They were sitting opposite each other on
the twin upholstered banquettes, which they would have, somewhere
around Fostoria that night, unfolded into a pair of beds.

"I just can't do it anymore, Bake," Sammy said. "It's just—I don't
want to be like this."

"You don't have a choice."

"I think I do."

Bacon had gotten up, then, and crossed the three feet of space between them, and sat down on the banquette beside Sammy.

"I don't believe that," he said, reaching for Sammy's hand. "Something like you and me is not a question of choosing or not choosing.
There's nothing you can do about it."

Sammy jerked his hand away. Regardless of what he felt for Bacon, it
was not worth the danger, the shame, the risk of arrest and opprobrium. Sammy felt, that morning, with his ribs bruised and a wan flavor of chlorine at the back of his mouth, that he would rather not love at
all than be punished for loving. He had no idea of how long his life
would one day seem to have gone on; how daily present the absence of
love would come to feel.

"Just watch me," he said.

In his haste to exit the compartment before Bacon could see him
break down, he had collided with an elderly woman making her way
down the corridor, and reopened the nasty cut over his eye.

"I'm glad you're still here," Rosa said now. "Sammy, listen to me. I
need help."

"I'll help you. What is it?"

"I think I need to get an abortion."

Sammy lit a cigarette and smoked half of it before he replied. "Joe is
the father," he said.

"Yes. Of course."

"And you told him and he said?"

"I didn't tell him. How could I tell him? Last night he tried to kill himself."

"He did?"

"I think he did."

"But Rosa, you know, he's joining the navy, he said."

"Right."

"He's just going to go off and enlist in the navy without knowing that you are pregnant with his baby."

"Also right."

"Even though you've known about this for . . ."

"Say a week."

"Why didn't you tell him? Really, I mean."

"I was afraid," said Rosa. "Really."

"Afraid that what? No, I know," he said. He sounded almost bitter about it. "That he would just tell you to get the thing. And not want to marry you."

"There you have it."

"And now you—"

"Just couldn't possibly ever, in a million years, tell him."

"Because he would certainly tell you—"

"Right. He wants to go kill them, Sam. I don't think anything I tell him could stop him now."

"So now you have to—"

"As I was trying to explain."

Sammy turned to look at her, his eyes bright, wild with an idea that Rosa grasped at once, in all its depths and particulars, in all the fear and hopelessness on which it fed.

"I get you," he said.

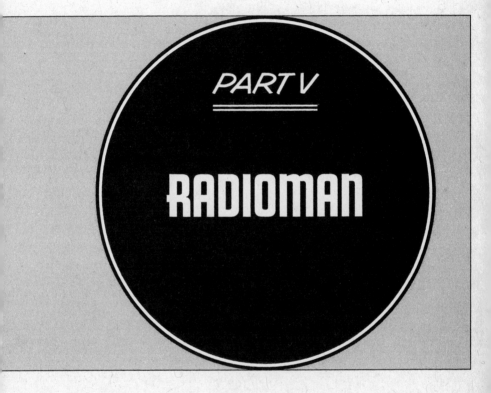

PART V

RADIOMAN

THE LOSER AT Lupe Velez was obliged to make his bed in the tunnels, out in the pandemonium of Dog-town. There were eighteen dogs, Alaskan malamutes for the most part, with a few odd Labrador and Greenland huskies and one unreliable skulker that was nearly all wolf. You took a sleeping bag and a blanket and, as often as not, a bottle of Old Grand-Dad, and bedded down in the frozen tunnel where, in spite of the snow floor and snow walls and ceiling of snow, the stench of urine, harness leather, and rancid, seal-greased black husky lip was surprisingly lively. They had started out with twenty-seven dogs, enough for two main teams and a team to spare, but four of them had been torn apart by their fellows out of some complex canine emotion composed of boredom, rivalry, and appalling high spirits; one had fallen into a bottomless hole in the ice; two had come down with something as mysterious as it was swift; one had been shot by the signalman, Gedman, for reasons that remained poorly understood; and Stengel, the true genius among the dogs, had wandered off into the fog one day when no one was looking and never come back. There were twenty-two men. They played poker, Parcheesi, chess, cribbage, hearts, go fish, geography, ghost, Ping-Pong, twenty questions, dime hockey, sock hockey, bottle-cap hockey, contract bridge, checkers, liar's dice, Monopoly, and Uncle Wiggily for cigarettes (they had as little use for money as for shovels and snow). They played to win exemption from the nasty work of chipping away with an ice chisel at the frozen ziggurat that mounted endlessly in the latrines, a pillar of turdsicles and of diarrhea plumes arrested by the cold into fantastic shapes out of Gaudí. Or they played (at chess in particular) for the treasured prize of reducing one another to little piles of ash and embers. But the winners at Lupe Velez won only the right to sleep in their bunks, warm and dry inside the Antarctic Waldorf, for one more night. It was a stupid, cruel, but at the same time forgiving game, and easy to play. There were always twenty-one winners at Lupe Velez and only one loser, and he had to go lie down with the dogs. Though in theory, given the essentially random and unskilled nature of play, they were all at an equal disadvantage, usually the one bedded down in the chaos and smell of the tunnels at the end of the evening, after a brisk inning of Lupe Velez, was Joe Kavalier. He was in there, tucked right into a crate alongside the dog called Oyster, the night that something went wrong with the Waldorf's stove.

Apart from the pilot Shannenhouse, there was not a man among them past the age of thirty-five (the first day the thermometer dipped below −20°F had occurred on the thirty-fifth birthday of their captain, Walter "Wahoo" Fleer, who marked the occasion by sprinting fifty yards from the Blubberteria to the Mess Hall, clad only in his mukluks), and three of the Seabees, Po, Mitchell, and Madden, were barely out of their teens, which probably went some way to explaining the essentially boy-ish stupidity of Lupe Velez. They would all be crammed into the Mess Hall, at once hours and weeks into the night, wasting time or doing something that pretended not to be wasting time or, in sober, intense bursts, being absorbed in some unavoidable and urgent business of re-pair, analysis, planning, or navy discipline, when somebody—often enough Gedman, though anyone could start a round—would call out the name of the star of *Mexican Spitfire* and *Honolulu Lu.* Immediately everyone in the room was obliged, according to the rules, to follow suit. Whoever was judged, by general determination of the players, to have uttered the critical words last (unless it was his turn on watch), spent that night (what they called night; it was all night) in Dog-town. If, through duty or good fortune, you chanced not to be in the room at the time, you were exempted. Play, except in the case of extreme tedium, was limited to one round per day. These were the rules of the game. Its origins were obscure, its conduct passionate. But for whatever reason, Joe could not seem to master it.

There were among the men a number of theories to account for this or, perhaps it would be more accurate to say, to account for Joe. Joe was a favorite with all the men, liked even by those who liked no one else, of which, as the winter night dragged on, there came to be more than a few. His sleight-of-hand and magic tricks were endlessly renewable sources of entertainment, particularly to the simpler-minded at Kelvinator Station. He was reliable, adept, resourceful, and industrious, but his accented and oddly skewed language softened the edges of his evident competence, the latter a quality that, in the other talented men of Kelvinator, could take on an aggressive, antagonistic sharpness. Furthermore, it was known, though Joe had said little about it, that he had, in some ways, a more personal stake than any of them in the outcome of the war. He was in many ways the man of mystery among them. Those who had known him since training days at Greenland Station spread the word that he never read his mail, that in his footlocker was a stack of unopened letters three inches thick. To men for whom correspondence was a kind of addiction, this made him the object of considerable awe.

Some said that Joe's weakness at Lupe Velez was due to his incomplete grasp of English, though the obvious rebuttal here was that several of the native speakers were considerably worse off in this regard than Joe. Others blamed the remote, dreamy aspect of his personality, as obvious to them as it had been to any of his friends in New York, even here in a place against which, it might be imagined, any lesser remoteness ought to have sunk into low relief. Then there were those who claimed that he just preferred the company of dogs. There was something to all of these explanations, though the last was the sole one that Joe would admit to.

He was generally fond of the dogs, but the one he had true feelings for was Oyster. Oyster was a gray-brown mongrel with the thick coat of an Eskimo dog, large ears inclined to undistinguished flopping, and a stout, baffled expression that suggested, said the dog men, a recent influence of Saint Bernard in his bloodlines. Earlier mistreatment with the lash during his first career in Alaska had blinded his left eye, leaving it the milky blue-white pearl that gave him his name. The very first time that Joe had been condemned to Dog-town for the night by a loss at Lupe Velez, he had noticed Oyster, way down in his niche at the very end of the sparkling tunnel, seeming to beckon to him, sitting up and laying his ears back in a pitiful way. The dogs were all desperately lonely for human companionship (they seemed to despise one another). But Joe had chosen to lie alone that night in a small bare patch at the door to a storeroom, away from the perpetual growling and muttering of the dogs.

Then, in mid-March, a food cache that they had neglected to get into the storehouse had been lost in the first great blizzard of the winter. Joe pitched in to help find it. He went on skis, for only the third time in his life, and soon was separated from the others in the party out searching for the lost ton of food. A sudden wind blew up, suspending him in an impenetrable gauze of snow dust. Blind and frantic, he had skied into a haycock and fallen, with a sound of chimes and splintering rafters, through the ice. It was Oyster, driven by ancestral Bernardine impulses, who had found him. After that, Joe and Oyster had become semiregular bedmates, according to the vagaries of Lupe Velez. Even when he slept in his bunk, Joe visited Oyster every day, bringing him hunks of bacon and ham and the dried apricots to which the dog was partial. Apart from the two dog men, Casper and Houk, who viewed the dogs as a coach viewed his linemen, as Diaghilev his corps, as Satan his devils, Joe was the only denizen of Kelvinator Station who did not find the animals merely an ill-smelling, loud, and perpetual source of annoyance.

It was only because he had lost so often at Lupe Velez and had, as a consequence, slept with the dog so many times, that Joe became aware, even deep in his own poisoned sleep, of an alteration in the usual pattern of Oyster's breathing.

The change, an absence of the dog's usual low, steady, grumbling wheeze, disturbed him. He stirred and woke just enough to become aware of an unfamiliar buzzing sound, faint and steady, in the dog tunnel. It droned on comfortingly for some time, and in his groggy state, Joe very nearly fell back into a slumber that undoubtedly would have been final. He sat up, slowly, on one arm. He could not seem to focus his thoughts, as if a gauzy curtain of snow dust hung and floated across the inside of his skull. He could not see very well, either, and he blinked and rubbed his eyes. After a moment it occurred to him that the sudden motion of his sitting up ought to have awakened at least his bedmate, who was always finely attuned to the least of Joe's movements; and yet Oyster slept on, silent, the rise and fall of his grizzled flank shallow and slow. That was when Joe realized that the buzz he had been contentedly listening to in the warmth of his sleeping bag for who knew how long was the chilly hum of the electric lights that were strung at intervals along the tunnels. It was a sound he had never heard, not once, in all his nights in Dog-town, because the ordinary wailing and termagancy of the dogs drowned it out. But now Dog-town was completely silent.

He reached out and slapped Oyster, gently, on the back of his head, then poked a finger into the soft flesh where his left foreleg met his body. The dog stirred, and Joe thought he might have whimpered softly, but he did not raise his head. His limbs were slack. Joe, feeling very wobbly, crawled out of the crate and went on his hands and knees across the tunnel to check on Forrestal, Casper's pure-breed malamute, who had succeeded lost Stengel as Dog King. He saw now why rubbing his eyes had done no good: the tunnel was full of fog, curling and billowing down from the Main Stem. Forrestal did not respond at all when Joe patted him, or poked him, or shook him hard, once. Joe lowered his ear to the animal's chest. There was no discernible heartbeat.

Quickly, now, Joe unhooked Oyster's collar from the chain whose other end was bolted into the wooden crate, picked up the dog, and carried him down the tunnel toward the Main Stem. He felt as if he was going to vomit, but he didn't know whether this was because there was something the matter with him, something that was going to kill him, too, or merely because to get to the end of the tunnel he had to walk past seventeen dogs lying dead in their carved-out niches. He was not thinking very clearly at all.

The Dog-town tunnel ran at right angles to the central tunnel of Kelvinator Station, and directly across from its mouth was the door of the Waldorf. The original plans had called for Dog-town to lie at some distance from the men's quarters, but they had run out of time here, too, and so been forced to shelter the dogs right at their doorstep, as it were, in a tunnel that had originally been dug for food storage. This door was supposed to be kept closed, to prevent the precious warmth of the stove from escaping the sleeping quarters, but as he approached it, struggling along with eighty-five pounds of dying dog in his arms, Joe saw that it stood open a few inches, prevented from closing by one of his own socks, which he must have dropped on his way out to Dog-town. He had been folding his clothes on his bunk that evening, as he later reconstructed, and the sock must have clung to his bedroll. A warm, flatulent breath of beer and unwashed woolen underwear came sighing into the tunnel from the Waldorf, melting the ice, filling the tunnel with ghostly clouds of condensation. Joe nudged the door open with his foot and stepped into the room. The air seemed unnaturally stuffy and far too warm, and as he stood there, listening for the usual congested snuffling of the men, his dizziness increased. The weight of the dog in his arms grew intolerable. Oyster fell from his arms and hit the plank floor with a thud. The sound made Joe gag. He stumbled to his left, wildly veering to avoid touching any of the bunks he walked between or the men lying in them, toward the light switch. No one protested or rolled away from the blaze of light.

Houk was dead; Mitchell was dead; Gedman was dead. That was as far as Joe got in his investigations before a sudden desperate understanding drove him to the ladder that led up through the hatch in the roof of the Waldorf and out onto the ice. Coatless, bareheaded, feet clad only in socks, he stumbled topside across the jagged skin of the snow. The cold jerked at his chest like a wire snare. It fell on him like a safe. It lapped eagerly at his unprotected feet and licked at his kneecaps. He took great breaths of that clean and wicked coldness, thanking it with every cell in his body. He heard his exhalations rustle like taffeta as they froze solid in the air around him. His blood filled with oxygen, quickening the nerves of his eyes, and the dark dull sky over his head seemed to thicken suddenly with stars. He reached an instant of bodily equipoise, during which the rapture of his survival to breathe and be burned by the wind perfectly balanced the agony of his exposure to it. Then the shivering took hold, in a single crippling shudder that racked his whole body, and he cried out, and fell to his knees on the ice.

Just before he pitched forward, he experienced a strange vision. He saw his old magic teacher, Bernard Kornblum, coming toward him through the blue darkness, his beard tied up in a hair net, carrying the bright glowing camp brazier that Joe and Thomas had once borrowed from a friend who went in for mountaineering. Kornblum knelt, rolled Joe over onto his back, and gazed down at him, his expression critical and amused.

"*Escapistry,*" he said, with his usual scorn.

J OE WOKE IN THE HANGAR to the smell of a burning cheroot and found himself gazing up at the oft-patched wing of the Condor.

"Lucky you," said Shannenhouse. He snapped shut his lighter and exhaled. He was sitting on a canvas folding stool beside Joe, legs spread wide in best cowboy manner. Shannenhouse was from a raw town called Tustin in California and cultivated cowboy habits that sat unlikely on his slight frame, with his professorial mien. He had fair thinning hair and rimless spectacles and hands that, while horny and scarred, remained delicate. He tried to be taciturn but was given to lecturing. He tried to be stern and friendless but was an inveterate kibitzer. He was the old man of Kelvinator Station, an eight-kills ace from the first war who had spent the twenties flying in the Sierras and in the Alaskan bush. He had enlisted after Pearl and was as disappointed as any of them by his assignment to Kelvinator. He had not seriously hoped to fight again, but he had been doing interesting work all his life and was looking for more. Since their arrival at Kelvinator—the official, classified name was Naval Station SD-A2(R)—the weather had been so bad that he had been up in the air only twice, once on a recon mission that was aborted after twenty minutes in the teeth of a blizzard, and once on an unauthorized, failed jaunt to try to find the base of the first Byrd expedition, or of the last Scott expedition, or of the first Amundsen expedition, or the site of *something* that had happened in this waste for which the adjective "godforsaken" appeared to have been coined. He was nominally a first lieutenant, but nobody stood on ceremony or rank at Kelvinator Station. They were all obedient to the dictates of survival, and no further discipline was really necessary. Joe himself was a radioman second-class, but nobody ever called him anything but Sparks, Dit, or, most often, Dopey.

The smoke of the cigar smelled very good to Joe. It had an unantarctic flavor of autumn and fire and dirt. There was something lurking inside him that the smell of the burning cheroot seemed to keep at bay. He reached for Shannenhouse's hand, raising an eyebrow. Shannenhouse passed the cheroot to Joe, and Joe sat up to take it in his teeth. He saw that he was tucked into a sleeping bag on the floor of the Hangar, his upper body propped on a pile of blankets. He leaned back on one elbow and took a long drag, inhaling the strong black stuff into his lungs. This was a mistake. His coughing spasm was long and racking, and the pain in his chest and head reminded him abruptly of the dead men and the dogs in the tunnels with their lungs full of some kind of agent or germ. He lay back down again, forehead stitched with sweat.

"Oh, shit," he said.

"Indeed," Shannenhouse said.

"Johnny, you can't go down in there, okay, you promise? They all—"

"Now you tell me."

Joe tried to sit up, scattering ash down the blankets. "You didn't go down in there?"

"You were not awake to warn me, remember?" Shannenhouse reclaimed his cigar as if in reproach, and shoved Joe back down to the floor. He gave his head a shake, trying to clear away a memory that clung. "Jesus. That." Normally his voice was fluting and animated by a scholarly verve, but now it came out cowboy flat, dry and flat as Joe imagined Tustin, California, to be. "That is the worst thing I have ever seen."

A good deal of Shannenhouse's talk over the months had been of awful things he had seen, tales rife with burning men, arterial fountains of blood spraying from the armless shoulders of fellows who strayed into the whirl of propellers, hunters half-devoured by bears dragging their stumps into camp in the morning.

"Oh, shit," Joe said again.

Shannenhouse nodded. "The worst thing I have ever seen."

"Johnny, I beg you not to say this again."

454 · MICHAEL CHABON

"Sorry, Joe."

"Where were *you*, anyway? Why didn't you . . ."

"I was out here." The Hangar, though buried in the snow of Marie Byrd Land like all the other buildings of Kelvinator Station, was not connected to the rest by tunnel, again because of the heavy weather that had come so viciously and early this year. "I had the watch, I came out here just to have a look at her." He jerked a thumb toward the aging Condor. "I do not know what Kelly thought he was doing, but the wire—"

"We have to raise Gitmo, we have to tell them."

"I tried to raise them," Shannenhouse said. "The radio is out. Could not raise shit."

Joe felt panic lurch up inside him now, as it had on the day he fell through the haycock, in a clatter of skis and bindings, the wind knocked from his lungs, mouth packed with snow, a cold blade of ice jabbing for his heart.

"The radio is out? Johnny, why is the radio out?" In his panic, the melodramatic notion, worthy of one of Sammy's plots, that Shannenhouse was a German spy and had killed them all streaked through his thoughts. *"What is going on?"*

"Relax, Dopey, all right? Please do not lose your shit." He passed the cheroot back to Joe.

"Johnny," Joe said, as calmly as he could, letting out smoke, "I feel that I am going to lose my shit."

"Look here, the fellows are dead and the radio is out, but there is no connection between the two. One has nothing to do with the other, like everything else in life. It was not some Nazi superweapon. Jesus Christ. It was the fucking stove."

"The stove?"

"It was carbon monoxide from Wayne." The Antarctic Waldorf was heated by a gasoline stove, affectionately known as Wayne because of the legend FT. WAYNE IRON WORKS INDIANA USA stamped on its side. The naming madness that came over men when they arrived here in the unmapped blankness seeped quickly into every corner of their lives. They named the radios, the latrine, they named their hangovers and cuts on their fingers. "I went up and checked the ventilators in the roof. Packed with snow. Same thing with Dog-town. I told Captain they were poorly made. Maybe I did not. The thought did occur to me at the time we were laying them in."

"They all died," Joe said, the statement rising at the end with just the faintest hopeful intimation of a doubt.

Shannenhouse nodded. "Everyone but you and your boyfriend, maybe I guess because you were lying at the very end of the tunnel from the door. Now, as far as the radio goes, who the fuck knows. Magnetism. Sunspots. It will come back."

"What do you mean, my boyfriend?"

"The mutt. Mussels."

"Oyster?"

Shannenhouse nodded again. "He is all right. I tied him up in the Mess Hall for the night."

"What?" Joe started to his feet, but Shannenhouse reached out and forced him back, not gently.

"Lie down, Dopey. I shut down the damn stove, I dug out the ventilators. Your dog will be all right."

So Joe lay down, and Shannenhouse leaned back against the wall of the Hangar and looked up at his airplane. They passed the cigar back and forth. In a little while, it was going to be time for them to discuss their chances, and plan for their survival until they could be rescued. They had food to last two dozen men two years, plenty of fuel for the generators. The Mess Hall would provide sleeping quarters suitably free of the spectacle of frozen corpses. Compared to the early heroes of the continent, starving and dying in their caribou-skin tents, gnawing a raw hunk of frozen seal, they were in clover. Even if the navy couldn't get a ship or a plane in until spring, they would have more than enough of what they needed to make it through. But somehow the idea that death had reached down through all that snow and ice into their tunnels and cozy rooms and in a single night—in an hour—killed all of their fellows and all but one of the dogs, made their survival, for all their ample provisions and matériel, seem less than assured.

Both of the men had felt all along, on certain evenings as they hurried from the transmitter tower or the Hangar back toward the hatch that led to safety and warmth, a stirring at the fringes of the station, a presence, something struggling to be born out of the winds, the darkness, the looming towers and jagged teeth of the ice. The hair on the back of the neck stood erect and you ran, in spite of yourself, ribs ringing with panic, certain as a child running up the cellar stairs that something very bad was after you. Antarctica was beautiful—even Joe, who loathed it with every fiber of his being as the symbol, the embodiment, the blank unmeaning heart of his impotence in this war, had felt the thrill and grandeur of the Ice. But it was trying, at every moment you remained on it, to kill you. They could not let their guard down for a moment; they had all known that from the start. Now it seemed to Joe and the pilot as if the evil intent of the place, the glittering ripples of dust gathering in the darkness, would find a way to get them no matter how warm their berth or full their bellies, no matter how many layers of wool and hide and fur they put between them and it. Survival, at that moment, seemed beyond the reach or agency of their plans.

"I don't like having the dogs in here, messing up my airplane," said Shannenhouse, studying the struts of the Condor's left wing with an approving frown. "You know that."

THE WINTER DROVE THEM MAD. It drove every man mad who had ever lived through it; there was only ever the question of degree. The sun disappeared, and you could not leave the tunnels, and everything and everyone you loved was ten thousand miles away. At best, a man suffered from strange lapses in judgment and perception, finding himself at the mirror about to comb his hair with a mechanical pencil, stepping into his undershirt, boiling up a pot of concentrated orange juice for tea. Most men felt a sudden blaze of recovery in their hearts at the first glimpse of a pale hem of sunlight on the horizon in mid-September. But there were stories, apocryphal, perhaps, but far from dubious, of men in past expeditions who sank so deeply into the drift of their own melancholy that they were lost forever. And few among the wives and families of the men who returned from a winter on the Ice would have said that what they got back was identical to what they had sent down there.

In the case of John Wesley Shannenhouse, the winter madness was merely a kind of modulation, a deepening of his long-standing involvement with his Curtiss-Wright AT-32. The Condor seaplane was ten years old, and had been hard used by the navy before finding her present billet. She had seen action and taken fire, hunting steamship pirates on the Yangtze in the mid-thirties. She had flown thousands of cargo runs in and out of Honduras, Cuba, Mexico, and Hawaii, and enough of the plane and her engines had been replaced over the years, according to the dictates of local expediency, parts shortages, and mechanics' ingenuity and neglect, from the tiniest bolts and wire clasps to one of the big Wright Cyclone engines and entire sections of the fuselage and wings, that it was a metaphysical question long pondered by Shannenhouse that winter whether she could fairly be said to be the same plane that had rolled out of Glenn Curtiss's plant in San Diego in 1934.

As the winter wore on, the question so vexed him—Joe was certainly well sick of it, and of Shannenhouse and his stinking cheroots—that he decided the only way to gain surcease would be to replace every replaceable part, making himself the guarantor of the Condor's identity. The navy had provided Kelly and Bloch, the dead mechanics, with an entire tractor-load of spare parts, and a machine shop equipped with a toolmaker's lathe, a milling machine, a drill press, an oxyacetylene welding outfit, a miniature blacksmith's shop, and eight different kinds of power saw from jig to joiner. Shannenhouse found that simply by dint of drinking sixty-five to eighty cups of coffee a day (with everyone dead, there was certainly no need to stint) he could reduce his sleep requirements to half their former seven hours, at least. When he did sleep, it was in the Condor, wrapped in several sleeping bags (it was cold in the Hangar). He moved in a dozen crates of canned food and took to cooking his meals in there, too, crouching over a Primus stove as if huddled out on the Ice.

First he rebuilt the engines, machining new parts where he found the originals worn or their replacements substandard or borrowed from some alien breed of plane. Then he went to work on the frame of the aircraft, milling new struts and ribs, replacing every screw and grommet. When Joe finally lost track of Shannenhouse's labors, the pilot had embarked on the long and difficult job of doping, repairing the airplane's canvas sheathing with a sickly-sweet bubbling compound he cooked up on the same stove he used to make his dinner. It was tough work for one man, but he refused Joe's halfhearted offer of help as if it had been a proposal that they share wives.

"Get your own airplane," he said. His beard stuck straight out from his chin, bristling and orange-blond and seven inches long. His eyes were pink and glittering from the dope, he was thickly covered in a reddish pelt of reindeer fur from his sleeping bag, and he stank more than any human Joe had ever smelled (though there would come worse), as if he had been dipped in some ungodly confection of Camembert and rancid gasoline brewed up in a spit-filled cuspidor. He punctuated this remark by hurling a crescent wrench, which missed Joe's head by two inches and gouged a deep hole out of the wall beside him. Joe quickly climbed back up through the hatch and went topside. He did not see Shannenhouse again for nearly three weeks.

He had his own madness to contend with.

Radio service at Naval Station SD-A2(R) had been restored seventeen hours after the Waldorf disaster. Joe did not sleep during that entire period, making a fresh attempt every ten minutes, and finally managed to raise Mission Command at Guantánamo Bay at 0700 GMT and inform them, transmitting in code, painfully slowly without Gedman there to assist him, that on April 10 every man at Kelvinator but Kavalier and Shannenhouse, and all the dogs but one, had been poisoned by carbon monoxide resulting from poor ventilation in quarters. The replies from Command were terse but reflected a certain amount of shock and confusion. A number of contradictory and impractical orders were issued and remanded. It took Command longer than it had Joe and Shannenhouse to realize that nothing could be done until September at the earliest. The dead men and dogs would keep perfectly well until then; putrefaction was an unknown phenomenon here. The Bay of Whales was frozen solid and impassable and would be for another three months, at least. In any case, Drake Passage, as Joe's own monitoring of short-burst transmissions to BdU had confirmed, was teeming with U-boats. There was no hope of being rescued by some passing whaler without the help of a military escort—the whalers and chasers had, by and large, abandoned the field by now—and even then, not until the barrier ice began to warm and fracture. At last, five days after Joe's first message, Command somewhat superfluously ordered them to sit tight and wait for spring. Joe was, in the meantime, to stay in regular radio contact and continue, so far as he was able, the primary mission (apart from the more elemental one of maintaining an American presence at the pole) of Kelvinator Station: to monitor the airwaves for U-boat transmissions, to transmit all intercepts back to Command, which would relay them to the cryptanalysts back in Washington, with their clacking electronic bombes, and finally to alert Command of any German movements toward the continent itself.

It was in the furtherance of this mission that Joe's sanity entered its period of hibernation. He became as inseparable from the radio as Shannenhouse from his Condor. And, again like Shannenhouse, he could not bring himself to inhabit the rooms that they had formerly shared with twenty other living, breathing men. Instead, Joe made the radio shack his principal lodgings, and although he continued to cook his meals in the Mess Hall, he carried them through the tunnels to the radio shack to eat them. His direction-finding observations, and intercepts of short-burst transmissions of the two German submarines then active in the region, were extensive and accurate, and in time, with some coaching from Command, he learned to handle the quirky and delicate navy code machine nearly as well as Gedman had.

But it was not just military and commercial shipping channels to which Joe tuned in. He listened through his powerful multiband Marconi CSR 9A set to anything and everything the three seventy-five-foot antenna towers could pull down out of the sky, at all hours of the day: AM, FM, shortwave, the amateur bands. It was a kind of ethereal fishing, sending out his line and seeing what he could catch, and how long he could hold on to it: a tango orchestra live from the banks of the Plate, stern biblical exegesis in Afrikaans, an inning and a half of a game between the Red Sox and the White Sox, a Brazilian soap opera, two lonely amateurs in Nebraska and Suriname droning on about their dogs. He listened for hours to the Morse code alarums of fishermen in squalls and merchant seamen beset by frigates, and once even caught the end of a broadcast of *The Amazing Adventures of the Escapist,* learning thus that Tracy Bacon was no longer playing the title role. Most of all, however, he followed the war. Depending on the hour, the tilt of the planet, the angle of the sun, the cosmic rays, the aurora australis, and the Heaviside layer, he was able to get anywhere from eighteen to thirty-six different news broadcasts every day, from all over the world, though naturally, like most of the world, he favored those of the BBC. The invasion of Europe was in full swing, and like so many others, he followed its fitful but steady progress with the help of a map that he tacked to the padded wall of the shack and studded with the colored pins of victory and setback. He listened to H. V. Kaltenborn, Walter Winchell, Edward R. Murrow, and, just as devotedly, to their mocking shadows, to the snide innuendos of Lord Haw-Haw, Patrick Kelly out of Japanese Shanghai, Mr. O.K., Mr. Guess Who, and to the throaty insinuations of Midge-at-the-Mike, whom he quite often thought of fucking. He would sit, awash in the aqueous burbling of his headphones, for twelve or fifteen hours at a time, getting up from the console only to use the latrine and to feed himself and Oyster.

It may be imagined that this ability to reach out so far and wide from the confines of his deep-buried polar tomb, his only company a half-blind dog, thirty-seven corpses human and animal, and a man in the grip of an idée fixe, might have served as a means of salvation for Joe, connected in his isolation and loneliness to the whole world. But in fact the cumulative effect, as day after day he at last doffed the headphones and lowered himself, stiff, head buzzing, onto the floor of the shack beside Oyster, was only, in the end, to emphasize and to mock him with the one connection he could not make. Just as, in his first months in New York, there had never been any mention in any of the eleven newspapers he bought every day, in any of three languages, about the well-being and disposition of the Kavalier family of Prague, there was now never anything on the radio that gave him any indication of how they might be faring. It was not merely that they were never personally mentioned—even at his most desperate, he didn't seriously imagine this possibility—but that he could never seem to get any information at all about the fate of the Jews of Czechoslovakia.

From time to time there were warnings and reports from escapees of camps in Germany, massacres in Poland, roundups and deportations and trials. But it was, from his admittedly remote and limited point of view, as if the Jews of his country, his Jews, his family, had been slipped unseen into some fold in the pin-bristling map of Europe. And increasingly, as the winter inched on and the darkness deepened around him, Joe began to brood, and the corrosion that had been worked on his inner wiring for so long by his inability to do anything to help or reach his mother and grandfather, the disappointment and anger he had been nursing for so long at the navy's having sent him to the fucking South Pole when all he had wanted to do was drop bombs on Germans and supplies on Czech partisans, began to coalesce into a genuine desperation.

Then one "evening" toward the end of July, Joe tuned in to a short-wave broadcast from the Reichsrundsfunk directed at Rhodesia, Uganda, and the rest of British Africa. It was an English-language documentary program cheerfully detailing the creation and flourishing of a marvelous place in the Czech Protectorate, a specially designed "preserve," as the narrator called it, for the Jews of that part of the Reich. It was called the Theresienstadt Model Ghetto. Joe had been through the town of Terezin once, on an outing with his Makabbi sporting group. Apparently, this town had been transformed from a dull Bohemian backwater into a happy, industrious, even cultivated place, of rose gardens, vocational schools, and a full symphony orchestra made up of what the narrator, who sounded like Emil Jannings trying to sound like Will Rogers, called "internees." There was a description of a typical musical evening at the preserve, into the midst of which, to Joe's horror and delight, floated the rich, disembodied tenor of his maternal grandfather, Franz Schonfeld. He was not identified by name, but there was no mistaking the faint whiskey undertones, nor for that matter the selection, "Der Erlkönig."

Joe struggled to make sense of what he had heard. The false tone of the program, the bad accent of the narrator, the obvious euphemisms, the unacknowledged truth underlying the blather about roses and violins—that all of these people had been torn from their homes and put in this place, against their will, because they were Jews—all these inclined him to a feeling of dread. The joy, spontaneous and unreasoning, that had come over him as he heard his little grandfather's sweet voice for the first time in five years subsided quickly under the swelling unease that was inspired in him by the idea of the old man singing Schubert in a prison town for an audience of captives. There had been no date given for the program, and as the evening went on and he mulled it over, Joe became more and more convinced that the pasteboard cheeriness and vocational training masked some dreadful reality, a witch's house made of candy and gingerbread to lure children and fatten them for the table.

The next night, trolling the frequencies around fifteen megacycles on the extremely off chance that there might be a sequel to the previous night's program, he stumbled onto a transmission in German, one so strong and clear that he suspected it at once of having a local origin. It was sandwiched carefully into an extremely thin interstice of band-width between the powerful BBC Asian Service and the equally power-ful A.F.R.N. South, and if you were not desperately searching for word of your family, you would have dialed past it without even knowing it was there. The voice was a man's, soft, high-pitched, educated, with a trace of Swabian accent and a distinct note of outrage barely suppressed. Conditions were terrible; the instruments were all either inoperable or unreliable; quarters were intolerably confined, morale low. Joe reached for a pencil and started to transcribe the man's philippic; he could not imagine what would have prompted the fellow to make his presence known in such an open fashion. Then, abruptly, with a sigh and a weary "Heil Hitler," the man signed off, leaving a burble of empty air-waves and a single, unavoidable conclusion: there were Germans on the Ice.

This had been a fear of the Allies ever since the Ritscher expedition of 1938–39, when that extremely thorough German scientist, lavishly equipped by the personal order of Hermann Göring, had arrived at the coast of Queen Maud Land in a catapult ship and hurled two excellent Dornier Wal seaplanes again and again into the unexplored hinterland of the Norwegian claim where, using aerial cameras, they had mapped over three hundred and fifty thousand square miles of territory (intro-ducing the art of photogrammetry to the Antarctic) and then pelted the whole thing with five thousand giant steel darts, specially crafted for the expedition, each one topped with an elegant swastika. The land was thus staked and claimed for Germany, and renamed New Schwabia. Initial difficulties with the Norwegians over this presumption had been neatly solved by the conquest of that country in 1940.

Joe put on his boots and parka and went out to tell Shannenhouse of his discovery. The night was windless and mild; the thermometer read 4°F. The stars swarmed in their strange arrangements, and there was a gaudy viridian ring around the low-hanging moon. Thin watery moon-light puddled over the Barrier without seeming to illuminate any part of it. Aside from the radio towers, and the chimneys jutting like the fins of killer whales from the snow, there was nothing to be seen in any direc-tion. The lupine mountains, the jutting pressure ridges like piles of giant bones, the vast tent city of peaked haycocks that lay to the east—he could see none of it. The German base could have lain not ten miles away across level ice, blazing like a carnival, and still remained invisible. When he was halfway to the Hangar, he stopped. The cessation of his crunching footsteps seemed to eliminate the very last sound from the world. The silence was so absolute that the inner processes of his cranium became first audible and then deafening. Surely a concealed German sniper could pick him out, even in this impenetrable gloom, just by hearing the storm-drain roaring of the veins in his ears, the hydraulic pistoning of his salivary glands. He hurried toward the hatch of the Hangar, crunching and stumbling. As he approached it, a breeze kicked up, carrying with it an acrid stench of blood and burning hair potent enough to make Joe gag. Shannenhouse had fired up the Blubberteria.

"Stay out," said Shannenhouse. "Get lost. Keep out. Go fuck your dog, you Jew, you bastard."

Joe was trapped halfway down the stairwell, not yet low enough to see into the Hangar. Every time he tried to get to the bottom, Shannenhouse threw something at his legs, a crankshaft, a dry cell.

"What you are doing?" Joe called to him. "What is this smell?"

Shannenhouse's odor had grown in the weeks since Joe's last encounter with him, slipping free of the confines of his body, absorbing further constituent smells of burned beans, fried wire, airplane dope, and, nearly drowning out all the others, freshly tanned seal.

"All the canvas I had was ruined," Shannenhouse said defensively and a little sadly. "It must have got wet on the trip down."

"You are covering the airplane in the skin of seals?"

"An airplane *is* a seal, dickhead. A seal that swims through the air."

"Yes, all right," Joe said. It is a well-known phenomenon that the Napoleons in the asylums of the world have little patience with one another's Austerlitzes and Marengos. "I just come to tell you one thing. Jerry is here. On the Ice. I heard him on the radio."

There was a long, expressive pause, though as to what emotion it expressed, Joe felt none too certain.

"Where?" Shannenhouse said at last.

"I'm not sure. He said something about the thirtieth meridian, but . . . I am not sure."

"Over there, though. Where they were before."

Joe nodded, although Shannenhouse couldn't see him.

"That is what, a thousand miles."

"At least."

"Fuck them, then. Did you raise Command?"

"No, Johnny, I did not. Not yet."

"Well, raise them, then. Christ, what the fuck is wrong with you."

He was right. Joe ought to have contacted Command the moment he finished transcribing the intercepted transmission. And once he had some idea of the nature and source of the transmission, his failure to do so was not only a breach of procedure, and a betrayal of an order—to preserve the continent from Nazi overtures—that had come directly from the president himself, but it also put him and Shannenhouse in potential danger. If Joe knew about them, they almost certainly knew about Joe. And yet, just as he had not reported Carl Ebling after the first bomb threat to Empire Comics, some impulse now prevented him from opening the channel to Cuba and making the report that duty obliged him to make.

"I don't know," Joe said. "I don't know what is the fuck wrong with me. I'm sorry."

"Good. Now get out."

Joe climbed back up the stairs and out into the mercury-blue night. As he started north, back toward the opening of the radio shack, something flickered in the middle of all the nothing, so tentatively that at first he thought it was an optic phenomenon akin to the effect of the silence on his ears, something bioelectric happening inside his eyeballs. No; there it was, the horizon, a dark seam, piped with an all but imaginary ribbon of pale gold. It was as faint as the glimmer of an idea that began to form, at that moment, in Joe's mind.

"Spring," said Joe. The cold air crumpled up the word like fish wrap.

When he got back to the radio shack, he dug out a broken portable shortwave that Radioman First Class Burnside had been planning to repair, plugged in the soldering iron, and, after a few hours' work, managed to fix up a set that he could dedicate exclusively to monitoring the transmissions of the German station, which, it transpired, was under the direct command of Göring's office, and referred to itself as Jotunheim. The man who made the transmissions was very careful about concealing them, and after the initial outburst that Joe had chanced upon, he limited himself to more spare and factual, but no less anxious, accounts of weather and atmospheric conditions; but with patience, Joe was able to locate and transcribe what he estimated to be around 65 percent of the traffic between Jotunheim and Berlin. He accumulated enough information to confirm the location at the thirtieth meridian, on the coast of Queen Maud Land, and to conclude that the bulk of their enterprise, at least so far, was of a purely observational and scientific character. In the course of two weeks of careful monitoring, he was able to reach a number of positive conclusions, and to listen as a drama unfolded.

The author of these hand-wringing transmissions was a geologist. He took an interest in questions of cloud formations and wind patterns, and he may also have been a meteorologist, but he was primarily a geologist. He was continually pestering Berlin with details of his plans for the spring, the schists and coal seams he intended to unearth. He had just two companions in Jotunheim. One was code-named Bouvard and the other Pecuchet. They had started out their season on the Ice at almost exactly the same time as their American counterparts, of whose existence they were fully aware, though they seemed to have no idea of the catastrophe that had struck Kelvinator Station. Their number had been reduced, too, but only by one, a radioman and Enigma operator who had suffered a nervous collapse and been taken away with the military party when the latter left for the winter; in spite of the risk of exposure without coded transmissions, the Ministry had seen no reason to force soldiers to winter over when there would be neither chance nor need of soldiering. The military party was due back on September 18, or as soon as they could get through the ice.

On the eleventh day following Joe's discovery of Jotunheim, for reasons that the Geologist, in the face of intense pressure and threats from the Ministry, refused to characterize as anything more than "unbecoming," "unsuitable," and "of an intimate nature," Pecuchet shot Bouvard and then turned his weapon fatally on himself. The message announcing the death of Bouvard three days later was filled with intimations of imminent doom that Joe recognized with a chill. The Geologist, too, had sensed that loitering presence in a veil of glittering dust at the fringes of his camp, waiting for its moment.

All this, for two weeks, Joe pieced together in secret and kept to himself. He told himself, each time he dialed in to what he came to call Radio Jotunheim, that he would listen just a little longer, accrue another bit of information, and then pass everything he had along to Command. Surely this was what spies generally did? Better to get it all, and then risk discovery in transmitting it, than tip off the Geologist and his friends before he had acquired the full picture. The shocking murder-suicide, which broke new ground for death on the continent, seemed to put a point on things, however, and Joe typed up a careful report that, conscious as ever of his English, he proofread several times. Then he sat in front of the console. While nothing would have pleased him more than to shoot this haughty-sounding, languid Geologist in the head, he had come to identify so strongly with his enemy that, as he prepared to reveal the man's existence to Command, he felt an odd reluctance, as if in doing so he would betray himself.

As he was attempting to make up his mind what to do with his report, the desire for revenge, for a final expiation of guilt and responsibility, that had been the sole animator of Joe's existence since the night of December 6, 1941, received the final impulse it required to doom the German Geologist.

The coming of spring had brought on another whaling season, and with it a fresh campaign of the undersea boats. *U-1421*, in particular, had been harassing traffic in Drake Passage, Allied and neutral, at a moment when shortages of the oil rendered from whales could mean the difference between victory and defeat in Europe for either side. Joe had been supplying Command with intercepts from *U-1421* for months, as well as providing directional information on the submarine's signals. But the South Atlantic D/F array had, until recently, been incomplete and provisional, and nothing had ever come of Joe's efforts. Tonight, however, as he picked up a burst of chatter on the DAQ huff-duff set that, even in its encrypted state, he could recognize as originating from

U-1421, there were two other listening posts tuned in as it made its report. When Joe supplied his readings on the signal from Kelvinator's HF/DF array in its cage atop the north aerial, a triangulation was performed at the Submarine Warfare Center in Washington. The resultant position, latitude and longitude, was supplied to the British navy, at which point an attack team was dispatched from the Falkland Islands. The corvettes and sub hunters found *U-1421*, chased it, and pelted it with hedgehogs and depth charges until nothing remained of it but an oily black squiggle scrawled on the water's surface.

Joe exulted in the sinking of *U-1421*, and in his role therein. He wallowed in it, even going so far as to permit himself to imagine that it might have been the boat that had sent the *Ark of Miriam* to the bottom of the Atlantic in 1941.

He trotted down along the tunnel to the Mess Hall and, for the first time in over two weeks, filled and turned on the snow melter, and took a shower. He fixed himself a plate of ham and powdered eggs, and broke out a new parka and pair of mukluks. On his way to the Hangar, he was obliged to pass the door to the Waldorf and the entrance of Dogtown. He shut his eyes and ran past. He did not notice that the dog crates were empty.

The sun, all of it, an entire dull red disk, hung a bare inch above the horizon. He watched it until his cheeks began to feel frostbitten. As it sank slowly back below the Barrier, a lovely salmon-and-violet sunset began to assemble itself. Then, as if to make certain Joe didn't miss the point, the sun rose for a second time, and set once more in a faded but still quite pretty flush of pink and lavender. He knew that this was only an optical illusion, brought on by distortions in the shape of the air, but he accepted it as an omen and an exhortation.

"Shannenhouse," he said. He had gone barreling down the steps without giving the pilot any warning and, as it turned out, had caught him during one of his rare periods of sleep. "Wake up, it's daytime! It's spring! Come on!"

Shannenhouse stumbled out of the plane, which glistened eerily in its tight glossy sheath of seal hides. "The sun?" he said. "Are you sure?"

"You just missed it, but it will be back in twenty hours."

A softness appeared in Shannenhouse's eyes that Joe recognized from their first days on the Ice long ago. "The sun," he said. Then, "What do you want?"

"I want to go kill Jerry."

Shannenhouse pursed his lips. His beard was a foot long now, his smell excoriating, probing, nearly sentient. "All right," he said.

"Can that plane fly or not?"

Joe started around the tail, over to the starboard side of the plane, where he noticed that the hides covering the front part of the fuselage were of a much lighter color and a different texture than those on the port side.

Stacked in a neat pyramid beside the plane, like cargo waiting to be loaded on board, sat the skulls of seventeen dogs.

WAHOO FLEER, their dead CO, had been at Little America with Richard Byrd in '33 and again in '40. When they went through his files, they found detailed plans and orders for transmontane Antarctic flights. In 1940 Captain Fleer himself had flown over part of the territory they would be crossing to kill the Geologist, over the Rockefeller Mountains, over the Edsel Fords, toward the shattered magnificent vacancy of Queen Maud Land. He had made carefully typed lists of the things a man ought to carry with him.

> 1 ice-chisel
> 1 pair of snow-shoes
> 1 roll toilet paper
> 2 handkerchiefs

The great anxiety of such a flight was the possibility of a forced land-ing. If they crashed, they would be alone and without hope of rescue at the magnetic center of nothingness itself. They would have to fight their way back to Kelvinator Station on foot, or press on ahead to Jotunheim. Captain Fleer had typed up lists of the emergency gear they would need in such an instance: tents, Primus stove, knives, saws, ax, rope, cram-pons. Sledges that they would have to drag themselves. Everything had to be considered for the weight it would add to the payload.

> Engine muff and blow-torch   4 lbs.
> 2 reindeer-fur sleeping-bags   18 lbs.
> Flare gun and eight cartridges   5 lbs.

The precision and order of Captain Fleer's instructions had a settling effect on their minds, as did the return of the sun, and the idea of killing one of the enemy. They resumed each other's company. Shannenhouse came in from the Hangar, and Joe moved his bedroll into the Mess Hall. They said nothing about their descent over the past three months into some ancient mammalian despair. Together they ransacked Wahoo Fleer's desk. They found a decoded tidbit from Command, received the previous autumn, passing along an unconfirmed report that there might or might not be a German installation on the Ice, code-named Jotunheim. They found a copy of the Book of Mormon, and a letter marked "In the Event of My Death," which they felt entitled, but could not bring themselves, to open.

Shannenhouse took a shower. This necessitated the melting of forty-five two-pound blocks of snow, which Joe, grunting and cursing in three languages, cut and shoveled, one by one, into the melter on the Mess Hall's roof, whose zinc maw, like the bell of a gramophone, broadcast the thin reedy voice of the pilot singing "Nearer My God to Thee." They spoke little, but their exchanges were amiable, and over the course of a week they resumed the air of comradely put-uponness that had been universal among the men before the Wayne disaster. It was as if they had forgotten that flying unsupported and alone across one thousand miles of storm-tossed pack and glacier to shoot a lonely German scientist had been their own idea.

"How would you feel about a nice ten- or twelve-hour stretch of, oh, say *shoveling snow*?" they would call to each other from their bunks in the morning, after they had spent the previous five days doing only that, as if some unfeeling superior had put them on shovel duty and they were just the unlucky stiffs who had to obey the order to dig out the Hangar and the tractor garage. In the evening, when they came aching, faces and fingers seared with cold, back into the tunnels, they filled the Mess Hall with cries of "Whiskey rations!" and "Steaks for the men!"

Once they had the snow tractor dug out, it required a full day of tinkering and heating various parts of its balky Kaiser engine to get it running again. They lost an entire day driving it thirty yards across level snow from the garage to the Hangar. They lost another day when the winch on the tractor failed, and the Condor, which they had managed to tow halfway up the snow ramp they'd crafted, snapped loose and went sledding back down into the Hangar, shearing off the tip of its left lower wing. This required another three days of repair, and then Shannenhouse came into the Mess Hall, where Joe had a Royal Canadian Mounted Police manual for 1912 open to the chapter entitled "Some Particulars of Sledge Maintenance," and was struggling to make sure the man-sledges were properly lashed. MAKE SURE SLEDGES PROPERLY LASHED was item 14 on Captain Fleer's Pre-Flight Checklist. Three languages did not suffice for his cursing needs.

"I'm out of dogs," Shannenhouse said. The new tip he had grafted on the Condor's wing needed to be covered and doped to the rest of the sheathing, otherwise the plane would not take off.

Joe looked at him, blinking, trying to take in his meaning. It was the twelfth of September. In another few days, perhaps, if it could break through the melting pack, a ship bringing soldiers and planes would be returning to Jotunheim, and if they had not managed to get aloft by then, their mission might have to be called off. That was part of Shannenhouse's meaning.

"You can't use the men," Joe said.

"I wasn't suggesting that," Shannenhouse said. "Though I would be lying, Dopey, if I said the thought hadn't occurred to me."

He stroked at his whiskers, looking at Joe; he still hadn't shaved his bearish red beard. His eyes rolled toward Joe's bunk, where Oyster lay sleeping.

"There's Mussels," he said.

They shot Oyster. Shannenhouse lured the not wholly unsuspecting dog topside with a slab of frozen porterhouse and then put a bullet point-blank between the good eye and the pearl. Joe couldn't bear to watch; he lay on his bunk fully dressed, zipped into his parka, and cried. All of Shannenhouse's former loutishness was gone; he respected Joe's grief at the sacrifice of the dog, and handled the grisly work of skinning and flensing and tanning himself. The next day Joe tried to forget about Oyster and to lose himself in vengeful thoughts and the stupendous tedium of adventure. He checked and rechecked their gear against Captain Fleer's lists. He found and removed the ice-hammer that had somehow fallen into the gearbox of the tractor's winch. He waxed the skis and checked the bindings. He dragged the sledges back in from the tunnels, undid them, and lashed them again the Mountie

way. He cooked steak and eggs for himself and Shannenhouse. He plucked the steaks from the salted pan, set them steaming on two big metal plates, and deglazed the pan with whiskey. He set the whiskey on fire and then blew the fire out. Shannenhouse came in stinking of processed flesh. He took the plate gratefully from Joe, his expression solemn.

"Just big enough," he said.

Joe took his plate, sat down at the captain's desk, and, hoping to absorb from the instrument some of the captain's thoroughness, typed the following statement:

> To those who will come searching for Lt John Wesley Shannenhouse (j.g.) and Radioman Second Class Joseph Kavalier:
>
> I apologize for our presence being elsewhere and probably in all truth dead.
>
> We have confirmed an establishment of a German military and scientific base located in the Queen Maud Land, also known as Neuschwabenland. This base is presently manned by one man only. (See, if you please, attached transcripts, intercepted radio transmissions A-RRR, 1.viii.44-2.ix.44.) As there are two of us the situation seems clear.

Here Joe stopped typing and sat chewing for a minute on a piece of steak. The situation was far from clear. The man they were going to kill had done nothing to harm either of them. He was not a soldier. It was unlikely that he had been involved in any but the most tangential, metaphysical of ways with the building of the witch's house in Terezin. He had had nothing to do with the storm that blew up out of the Azores or the torpedo that had blown a hole in the hull of the *Ark of Miriam*. But these things had, nonetheless, made Joe want to kill someone, and he did not know who else to kill.

> To those who quite reasonably inquire as to our motives or authorities in performing this mission,

He stopped typing again.

"Johnny," he said. "Why are you doing this?"

Shannenhouse looked up from a nine-month-old copy of *All Doll*. Cleaned up and bearded, he looked like one of the faces that had lined the main hall of Joe's old gymnasium, the portraits of past headmasters, stern and moral men untroubled by doubt.

"I came here to fly airplanes," he said.

let it be not doubtful that we thought only to serve our country (adopted in my case).

Please see to the care of the men in quarters who are dead and frozen.

Respectfully,
JOSEPH KAVALIER, Radioman Second Class.
September 12, 1944.

He pulled the sheet of paper out of the typewriter, then rolled it in again, and left it like that. Shannenhouse came over to read it, nodded once, and then went back out to the Hangar to see to the plane.

Joe lay down on his bunk and closed his eyes, but the sense of conclusiveness, of putting his affairs in order, which he had sought in typing up a final statement, eluded him. He lit a cigarette and took a deep draft of it, and tried to clear his mind and conscience so that he could face the next day and its duties untroubled by any scruple or distraction. When he had finished his smoke, he rolled over and tried to sleep, but the memory of Oyster's single trusting blue eye would not leave his mind. He turned, and tossed, and tried to lull himself to sleep, as Rosa had once instructed him to do, by imagining that he lay floating on a black raft, on a warm black lagoon, in the blackness of a moonless tropical night. There was nothing inside or outside of him but soft warm blackness. Presently he felt himself slipping toward sleep, pouring into it like sand racing toward the neck of an hourglass. In this twilit hypnogogic state he began to imagine—but it was stronger than a mere imagining, it was as if he were remembering the fact, believing it—that Oyster had been capable of speech, had possessed a sweet, calm, plaintive voice capable of expressing reason and passion and concern, and that he could not now get the dead dog's voice out of his ears. We had so much to say to each other, he thought. What a shame that I only real-

ized it now. Then in the instant before he went under, a sharp barking sounded in his inner ear and he sat bolt upright, his heart pounding. He realized that it was not the betrayed love of Oyster, but of someone far dearer and more lost to him, that haunted him now and prevented him from making peace with the possibility of his own death.

He crawled down to the foot of the bunk and opened his footlocker, and took out the thick sheaf of letters that he had received from Rosa after his enlistment at the end of 1941. The letters had followed him, irregularly but steadily, from basic training at Newport, Rhode Island, to the navy's polar training station at Thule, Greenland, to Guantánamo Bay, Cuba, where he had spent the fall of 1943 as the Kelvinator mission was assembled. After that, as no reply from their addressee was ever forthcoming, there had been no more letters. Her correspondence had been like the pumping of a heart into a severed artery, wild and incessant at first, then slowing with a kind of muscular reluctance to a stream that became a trickle and finally ceased; the heart had stopped.

Now he took out the penknife that had been a gift from Thomas, and that had once saved the life of Salvador Dalí, and slit open the first of the letters.

DEAR JOE,

I wish that we could at least have said goodbye to each other before you left New York. I think I understand why you ran away. I am sure that you must blame me for what happened. If I had not sent you to Hermann Hoffman, then your brother would not have been on that ship. I don't know what would have become of him in that case. And neither do you. But I accept and understand that you might hold me responsible. I suppose that I might have run away, too.

I know that you still love me. It's an article of faith for me that you do and that you always will. And it breaks my heart to think that we might never see or touch each other ever again. But what is even more painful to me is the thought—the certainty I have— that right now you are wishing that you and I had never met. If that is true, and I know it is, then I wish the same thing. Because knowing that you could feel that way about me makes all that we had seem like nothing at all. It was all wasted time. That is something I will never accept, even if it's true.

I don't know what is going to happen to you, to me, to the country or the world. And I don't expect you to answer this letter, because I can feel the door to you slamming in my face and I know that it's you slamming it shut. But I love you, Joe, with or without your consent. So that is how I plan to write to you—with or without your consent. If you don't want to hear from me, just throw away this and all the letters that follow it. For all I know these words themselves are lying at the bottom of the sea.

I have to go now. I love you.

ROSA

He read through the rest of them after that, proceeding in chronological order. In the second letter, she mentioned that Sammy had quit his job at Empire and gone to work for Burns, Baggot & DeWinter, the advertising agency that handled the Oneonta Woolens account. In the evenings, she said, he came home and worked on his novel. Then, in her fifth letter, Joe was startled to read that, in a civil ceremony on New Year's Day of 1942, Rosa had married Sammy. After that, there was a gap of three months, and she wrote to say that she and Sammy had bought a house in Midwood. Then there was another gap of a few months, and then in September 1942 she wrote with the news that she had given birth to a seven-pound, two-ounce son, and that, in honor of Joe's lost brother, they had named the baby Thomas. She called him Tommy. Subsequent letters gave news and details of little Tommy's first words, first steps, illnesses, and prodigies—at the age of fourteen months, he had drawn a recognizable circle with a pen. The scrap of paper place mat from Jack Dempsey's restaurant on which he had drawn it was included in the envelope. It was wobbly and poorly closed off, but it was, as Rosa said in the letter, as round as a baseball. There was a single photograph of the child, in undershirt and diaper, holding himself up against a table on which some comic books lay scattered. His head was big and luminous and pale as the moon, his expression at once wondering and hostile, as if the camera frightened him.

Had Joe read the letters from Rosa as they arrived, with gaps of weeks and months between them, he might have been deceived by the falsifying of the date of baby Thomas's birth, but read all at once—as a kind of continuous narrative—the letters betrayed just enough inconsistency in their accounting of months and milestones that Joe became suspicious, and his initial stab of jealousy and his deep puzzlement over Rosa's hasty marriage to Sammy gave way to a sad understanding. The letters were like fragments from a old-fashioned novel—they contained not only a mysterious birth and a questionable marriage, but a couple of deaths as well. In the spring of 1942, old Mrs. Kavalier had died, in her sleep, at the age of ninety-six. And then a letter from late summer of 1943, just after Joe's arrival in Cuba, reported the fate of Tracy Bacon. The actor had joined the Army Air Forces shortly after completing the second Escapist serial, *The Escapist and the Axis of Death,* and had been shipped to the Solomon Islands. In early June, the Liberator bomber of which Bacon was the copilot had been shot down during a raid on Rabaul. At the bottom of this letter, the last letter in the packet, there was a brief postscript from Sammy. *Hi buddy* was all it said.

Until now, Joe had told himself that he had buried his love for Rosa in the same deep hole in which he had laid his grief for his brother. She had been right: in the immediate aftermath of Thomas's death, he had blamed her, not merely for having introduced him to Hermann Hoffman and his cursed ship but also more vaguely and more crucially for having lured him into betraying the singleness of purpose—the dogged cultivation of a pure and unshakable anger—that had marked his first year of exile from Prague. He had all but abandoned the fight, allowed his thoughts to stray fatally from the battle, betrayed himself to the seductions of New York and Hollywood and Rosa Saks—and been punished for it. Although his need—indeed, his ability—to blame Rosa for all this had passed with time, his renewed resolve and his craving for revenge, which grew in intensity as it was frustrated again and again by the inscrutable plans of the U.S. Navy, so filled his heart that he believed his love to have been completely extinguished, as a great fire can put out a smaller one by starving it of oxygen and fuel. Now, as he returned the last letter to the packet, he was almost sick with longing for Mrs. Rosa Clay of Van Pelt Street, Midwood, Brooklyn.

Sammy had once told him about the capsule that had been buried at the World's Fair, in which typical items of that time and place—some nylon stockings, a copy of *Gone with the Wind*, a Mickey Mouse drinking cup—had been buried in the ground, to be recovered and marveled at by the people of some future gleaming New York. Now, as he read through these thousands of words that Rosa had written to him, and her raspy, plaintive voice sounded in his ear, his entombed memories of Rosa were hauled up as from a deep shaft within him. The lock on the capsule was breached, the hasps were thrown, the hatch opened, and with a ghostly whiff of lily of the valley and a fluttering of moths, he remembered—he allowed himself to enjoy a final time—the stickiness and weight of her thigh thrown over his belly in the middle of a hot August night, her breath against the top of his head and the pressure of her breast against his shoulder as she gave his hair a trim in the kitchen of his apartment on Fifth Avenue, the burble and glint of the *Trout* Quintet playing in the background as the smell of her cunt, rich and faintly smoky like cork, perfumed an idle hour in her father's house. He recalled the sweet illusion of hope that his love for her had brought him.

When he had finished the last letter, he slipped it back into its envelope. He went back to Wahoo Fleer's typewriter, pulled out the statement he had left, and laid it carefully on the desk. Then he rolled in a clean sheet and typed:

To be delivered to Mrs. Rosa Clay of Brooklyn U.S.A.

Dear Rosa,

It was not your fault; I do not blame you. Please forgive me for running away, and remember me with love as I remember you and our golden age. As for the child, who can only be our son, I wish

This time he could not think how to continue. He was astonished at the course that life could take, at the way things that had seemed once to concern him so much—indeed to revolve around him—could turn out to have nothing to do with him at all. The little boy's name, and his serious, wide-eyed stare in the photograph, jabbed at some place inside Joe that was so broken and raw that he felt it as a kind of mortal danger to consider the child for very long. Since he did not plan to return alive, one way or another, from the trip to Jotunheim, he told himself that the boy was much better off without him. He made up his mind then and there, sitting at the desk of the dead captain, that in the unlikely event his plan went awry and he should find himself somehow still living at war's end, he would never have anything to do with any of them, but in particular with this sober and fortunate American boy. He pulled the letter out of the typewriter and folded it into an envelope on which he typed the words "In the event also of my death." He laid his envelope under that in which Captain Fleer had made his final wishes known. He tied up the packet of letters and photographs from Rosa and fed them, in a single swallow, to Wayne. Then he picked up his sleeping bag and went out to the radio shack to see if he could tune in Radio Jotunheim.

5

SHANNENHOUSE SPENT A MINUTE considering the cloudless sky, the light wind from the southeast. They had had a weatherman, Brodie, but even when he had been alive, Shannenhouse had disdained his counsel, agreeing with his old friend Lincoln Ellsworth that no one could predict the weather in this place. As long as they could get the plane off the ground, they might as well go. He was complaining of bowel troubles, and Joe afterward said in his report that he noticed Shannenhouse looked a little pale, but attributed this to drink. They backed the tractor up to the ramp once again and hooked the plane to it. This time the winch performed correctly, and they got the plane up onto the surface. While Shannenhouse set to work heating the engines and readying the plane, Joe loaded on their gear. They closed up all the hatches on the buildings and took a look around at the place that had been their home for the last nine months.

"I will be glad to get out of here," Shannenhouse said. "I just wish we were going someplace different."

Joe went to the tip of the wing where Oyster was. In his haste, Shannenhouse had not done an especially good job, and the skin looked half-cured and hung a little loose and puckered over the frame. The entire airplane had a pied appearance, reddish-brown blotches of seal stitched against a background of silver-gray, as if it had been splashed with blood. Where the dog skins were, the plane looked bleached and sickly.

"Now or never, Dopey," said Shannenhouse. He pressed a hand to his side.

Thirty seconds later, they were bumping and scraping over ground as jagged and shining as rock candy, and then something seemed to cup its hand underneath and bear them up. Shannenhouse let out a cowboyish yip, a little shyly.

"Never going to know what hit him," he shouted over the basso profundo chorusing of the big twin Cyclones.

Joe said nothing. He never told Shannenhouse that the night before, just before he lay down in his sleeping bag, he had broken the fictitious invisible barrier that had hitherto been maintained between Kelvinator Station and Jotunheim, transmitting the following six words to the Geologist, in German plaintext, at one of the frequencies regularly used by Berlin to contact him:

WE ARE COMING TO GET YOU

He could never have prized apart to explain it to Shannenhouse the elf-knot of pity, remorse, and a desire to torment and terrify that had prompted this admonishment. In any case, it would have been superfluous to try, since on the third day of their journey, in a tent pitched on a plateau in the lee of the Eternity Mountains, Shannenhouse's appendix burst.

THE PIEBALD AIRPLANE, off-kilter, coughing, trailing a long
black thread from her port engine, hung in the sky for a moment
a hundred feet west of Jotunheim, as if her pilot doubted his eyes,
as if the glyph of huddled oblong mounds in the snow, the black barbell
of the radio tower, and the ice-stiffened crimson flag with its spider eye
were merely others in the long string of mirages, the phantom airplanes and fata morgana fairy castles, that had bewitched him in the
course of his halting and baffled flight. He paid for his moment of
hesitation: his remaining engine stalled. The plane dipped, jerked
upward, wobbled, then fell, in silence and with surprising slowness,
like a coin dropped into a jar of water. The plane hit the ground, and
with a whisper, the snow exploded. A great hood of glittering spray,
kicked up by the nose of the plane as it plowed along the ground,
billowed and drifted across the clearing. The sounds of splintering
timbers and steel bolts shearing away were caught up and muffled in
the roiling surf of snow. The silence deepened, broken only by a soft
teakettle ticking and the snap of fabric as a torn section of fuselage
sheathing flapped in the wind.

A few moments later, a head appeared over the top of the rugged furrow of ice and snow that the crash landing had piled up alongside the
airplane. It was hooded, the face concealed by a narrow circular ruff of
wolverine fur.

The German Geologist, whose name was Klaus Mecklenburg, and
who had been emerging from his solitary quarters to watch the skies
over Jotunheim at regular intervals of twenty minutes, raised his left
hand, the fingers of his reindeer-skin glove outspread. The greeting had
a somewhat incongruous appearance since, in his other hand, pointed

loosely but generally in the direction of the pilot's fur-trimmed head, he held a .45-caliber Walther service pistol. He had not slept at all in the five days since receiving the message that he had identified as originating from the American base in Marie Byrd Land, and had not slept well for nearly two months before that. He was drunk, jacked up on amphetamines, and suffering from the effects of a spastic colon. He kept the gun leveled at the man coming toward him over the ice, watching for other heads to appear, conscious of the tremor in his hand, aware that he might have time to get off only one or two shots before the others brought him down.

The American had halved the hundred meters that separated them before the Geologist began to wonder if he might not have been the only survivor of the crash. He came unsteadily, dragging his right leg behind him, the opening of his hood pointed straight ahead, as if without expectation of being followed or joined. He had pulled his arms down into his coat for warmth, and with the face invisible within the fur hole of the hood and the herky-jerk scarecrow gait, the sight of the sleeves flopping at the man's sides unnerved the Geologist. It was as if he were being stalked by a parka filled with bones, the ghost of some failed expedition. The Geologist raised the gun, extending his arm, and aimed directly for the vapor emerging from the center of the hood. The American stopped, and his parka began to crumple and squirm as he struggled to get his arms out. He had just thrust his hands through the cuffs of his sleeves, extending his arms in a gesture of protest or supplication, when the first shot hit him at the shoulder and spun him around.

Mecklenburg had shot at birds and squirrels as a boy but had never fired a pistol before, and his arm rang with pain, as if the cold had frozen his arm and the recoil shattered it. Quickly, before pain and fear and doubt of his actions could stop him, he squeezed off the rest of the clip. Only after he had emptied it did he realize that he had been firing with his eyes closed. When he opened them again, the American was standing directly in front of him. He pushed back the circle of fur, and his hair and eyebrows, moistened by the condensation of his breath inside the hood, began almost at once to rime over with frost. He was surprisingly young in spite of his beard, with an aquiline elegant face.

"I am very glad to be here," the American said in flawless German. He smiled. The smile caught for an instant as if on a sharp wire. There was a neat black hole in the shoulder of the parka. "The flight was difficult."

He pulled his right arm up inside the parka once more and felt around for a moment. When the hand reappeared, it was holding an automatic pistol. The American raised the gun up across his chest, as if to fire into the sky, and then his arm jerked. The Geologist took a step backward, then steeled himself, and threw himself onto the American, grabbing for the gun. As he did so, he realized that he had misinterpreted the situation, somehow, that the American had been in the act of tossing the pistol aside, that his unthreatening and even wistful air was not some elaborate ruse but merely the relief, dazed and unsteady, of someone who had survived an ordeal and was simply, as he had suggested, glad to be alive. Mecklenburg felt a sudden sharp regret for his behavior, for he was a peaceful and scholarly man who had always deplored violence, and one furthermore who liked and admired Americans, having known, in the course of his scientific career, a fair number of them. A gregarious man, he had nearly died of solitude in the last month, and now a boy had fallen out of the sky, an intelligent, able young man, one with whom he could discuss, in German no less, Louis Armstrong and Benny Goodman, and now Mecklenburg had shot at him—emptied his clip—in this place where the only hope for survival, as he had so long argued, was friendly cooperation among the nations.

A chime tuned to C-sharp sounded in his ear, and with an odd sense of relief he felt his tormented bowels empty into his trousers. The American caught him in his arms, looking startled and friendless and sad. The Geologist opened his mouth and felt the bubble of his saliva freeze against his lips. What a hypocrite I have been! he thought.

It took Joe nearly half an hour to drag the German across ten of the twenty meters that separated them from the hatch of Jotunheim. It was a terrible expense of strength and will, but he knew that he would find medical supplies inside the station, and he was determined to save the life of the man who, just five days before, he had set out across eight hundred miles of useless ice to kill. He needed benzoin, cotton wool, a hemostat, needle and thread. He needed morphia and blankets and the ruddy flame of a stout German stove. The shock and fragrance of life, steaming red life, given off by the trail of the German's blood in the snow was a reproach to Joe, the reproach of something beautiful and inestimable, like innocence, which he had been lured by the Ice into betraying. In seeking revenge, he had allied himself with the Ice, with the interminable white topography, with the sawteeth and crevasses of death. Nothing that had ever happened to him, not the shooting of Oyster, or the piteous muttering expiration of John Wesley Shannenhouse, or the death of his father, or internment of his mother and grandfather, not even the drowning of his beloved brother, had ever broken his heart quite as terribly as the realization, when he was halfway to the rimed zinc hatch of the German station, that he was hauling a corpse behind him.

INFORMAL GERMAN TERRITORIAL CLAIMS to the regions bordering the Weddell Sea had first been advanced in the wake of the Filchner expedition of 1911–13. Flying the eagle of the Hohenzollerns, the *Deutschland*, under the command of scientist and Arctic explorer Wilhelm Filchner, had sailed farther south into this grievous sea than any previous ship, battering its way through the semipermanent pack until it reached an immense, impassable palisade of barrier ice. The *Deutschland* then turned west and sailed for more than a hundred miles, finding no break or point of ingress in the sheer cliffs of the shelf that today bears Filchner's name; explorers invariably give their names to the places that haunt or kill them.

At last, with the end of the season only a few weeks away, they came upon a place, a fissure in the Barrier, where the level of the shelf dropped abruptly to no more than a few feet above sea level. A half-dozen ice anchors were quickly driven into the shore of this inlet, which the explorers named Kaiser Wilhelm II Bay, and crates unloaded for the construction of a winter base. They chose a site some three miles inland for the erection of the hut, to which they gave the rather too-grand name of Augustaburg, and prepared to hunker down in the southernmost German colony until spring. A series of severe tremors in the ice, some lasting nearly a minute, and the subsequent calving, witnessed by the awed and deafened crew of the *Deutschland*, of a colossal iceberg a few miles east of the ship, put an abrupt end to their plans. After an uneasy week spent wondering and arguing whether they were about to be set adrift, they abandoned camp, returned to ship, and sailed north for home. They were almost immediately beset, and spent the winter being chewed by the molars of the Weddell Sea before warmer weather thawed them out and sent them limping home.

It was in the base camp abandoned by this expedition that Joseph Kavalier, Radioman Second Class, was found by the navy icebreaker *William Dyer*. He had been in intermittent contact with the ship via a portable radio set, giving more or less accurate readings of his position. Commander Frank J. Kemp, skipper of the *Dyer*, noted in his log that the young man had been through considerable hardship in the last three weeks, surviving two long solo flights conducted with only limited skill as a pilot and a dying man for a navigator, a crash, a bullet wound to the shoulder, and a ten-mile hike, on a fractured ankle, to this ghost town of Augustaburg.

He had been living in this hut, noted Commander Kemp, on thirty-year-old tins of meat and biscuits, his only company the radio and a dead penguin, perfectly preserved. He was suffering from the effects of scurvy, frostbite, anemia, and a poorly healed flesh wound, which only the Antarctic uncongeniality to microbes had prevented from becoming infected, perhaps fatally; he had also, according to the ship's doctor who examined him, gone through two and a half thirty-year-old boxes of morphine. He said that he had set out alone across the ice from the German station, crawling the last part of the way, with no intention of getting anywhere at all, because he could not bear to be near the body of the man he had shot and killed, and had chanced upon Augustaburg just as the last of his strength was failing him. He was taken to the base at Guantánamo Bay, where he remained under psychiatric examination and investigation by a court-martial until shortly before V-E Day.

His claim to have killed the lone enemy occupant of a German Antarctic base some seventy-five miles to the east of the hut where he was found was investigated and confirmed, and in spite of certain questions raised by his behavior and his handling of the matter, Ensign Kavalier was awarded the Navy's Distinguished Service Cross.

In August 1977 a huge chunk of the Filchner Shelf, forty miles wide and twenty-five miles deep, calved off from the main body and drifted north as a giant iceberg into the Weddell Sea, carrying with it both the hut and the hidden remnants, some ten miles distant, of the German polar dream. This event put an abrupt end to tourism at Augustaburg. Filchner's Hut had become a required stop for the intrepid tourists who were just then beginning to brave the floe-choked waters of the Weddell Sea. The people would tramp in from out of the wind with their guide and respectfully examine the piles of empty tins with their quaint Edwardian-era labels, the abandoned charts and skis and rifles, the racks of unused beakers and test tubes, the frozen penguin, shot for examination but never dissected, standing eternal vigil under a portrait of the Kaiser. They might reflect on the endurance of this monument to a failure, or on the dignity and poignance that time can bring to human detritus, or they might merely wonder if the peas and gooseberries in the neat rows of cans on the shelves were still edible, and how they might taste. A few would linger a moment longer, puzzling over an enigmatic drawing that lay on the workbench, done in colored pencil, frozen solid and somewhat the worse from long-ago folding and refolding. Clearly the work of a child, it appeared to show a man in a dinner jacket falling from the belly of an airplane. Although the man's parachute was far beyond his reach, the man was smiling, and pouring a cup of tea from an elaborate plummeting tea service, as if oblivious of his predicament, or as if he thought he had all the time in the world before he would hit the ground.

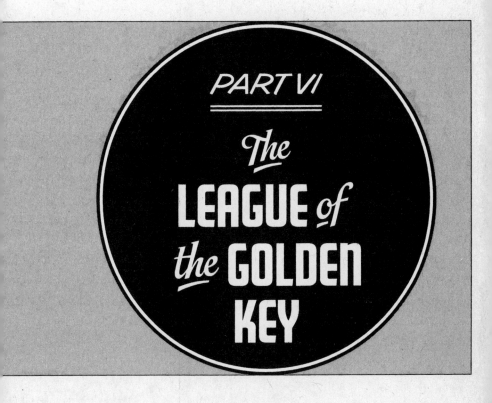

PART VI

The
LEAGUE of
the GOLDEN
KEY

WHEN SAMMY WENT IN to wake Tommy for school, he found the boy already up and modeling his eye patch in the bedroom mirror. The bedroom furniture, a set from Levitz—bed, dresser, the mirror, and a hutch with drawers—had a nautical theme: the back wall of the hutch was lined with a navigation chart for the Outer Banks, the brass drawer pulls shaped like pilot's wheels, the mirror trimmed in stout hawser rope. The eye patch did not look all that out of place. Tommy was trying different kinds of piratical scowls on himself.

"You're up?" Sammy said.

Tommy nearly jumped out of his skin; he had always been an easy child to startle. He yanked the patch up over his dark, tousled head and turned, blushing deeply. He was in possession of both his eyes; they were bright blue, with a slight puffiness of the lower lids. There was, in fact, nothing at all wrong with his vision. His brain was something of a puzzle to Sammy, but there wasn't any problem with his eyes.

"I don't know what happened," Tommy said. "I just somehow woke up."

He stuffed the eye patch into the pocket of his pajama top. The pajamas were patterned with red pinstripes and tiny blue escutcheons. Sammy was wearing a pair that had red escutcheons with blue pinstripes. That was Rosa's idea of fostering a sense of connection between father and son. As any two people who have ever dressed in matching pajamas will attest, it was surprisingly effective.

"That's unusual," Sammy said.

"I know."

"Usually I have to set off a charge of dynamite to get you up."

"That's true."

"You're like your mother that way." Rosa was still in bed, buried under an avalanche of pillows. She suffered from insomnia and rarely managed to fall asleep before three or four, but once she had gone under, it was nearly impossible to rouse her. It was Sammy's job to get Tommy out of the house on school mornings. "In fact, the only time you ever get yourself up early," Sammy continued, allowing a note of prosecutorial insinuation to enter his voice, "is for something like your birthday. Or when we're leaving for a trip."

"Or if I have to get a shot," Tommy said helpfully. "At the doctor."

"Or." Sammy had been hanging from the doorjamb, half in, half out of the room, but now he went over to stand behind Tommy. He was aware of an impulse to put his hand on the boy's shoulder, to let it lie there with the admonitory weight of a father's, but in the end, he just folded his arms and looked at the reflection of Tommy's serious face in the mirror. It pained Sammy to acknowledge it, but he was no longer comfortable around the boy whom, for the past twelve years, he had been obliged and delighted to call his son. Tommy had always been a tractable, moon-faced, watchful little boy, but lately, as his soft chestnut hair turned to black wire loops and his nose struck boldly out on its own, there began to gather around the features of his face some trouble that promised to develop into outright handsomeness. He was already taller than his mother, and nearly as tall as Sam. He took up greater mass and volume in the house, moved in unaccustomed ways, and gave off unfamiliar odors. Sammy found himself hanging back, giving ground, keeping out of Tommy's way. "You don't have something . . . *planned* for today?"

"No, Pop."

He was jocular. "No trips to the 'eye doctor'?"

"Ha," the boy said, wrinkling his freckled nose in a base simulation of amusement. "Okay, Pop."

"Okay, what?"

"Well, I'd better get dressed. I'm going to be late for school."

"Because if you were."

"I'm not."

"If you were, I would have to chain you to the bed. You realize that."

"I was only *playing* with an *eye patch.* Jeez."

"All right."

"I wasn't going to do anything bad." His voice put quotation marks around the last word.

"I'm glad to hear it," Sammy said. He didn't believe Tommy, but he tried to conceal his doubts. He didn't like to antagonize the boy. Sammy worked five long days a week in the city, and brought work home on the weekends. He could not bear to waste, in arguing, the brief hours he spent with Tommy. He wished that Rosa were awake, so that he could ask her what to do about the eye patch. He grabbed hold of Tommy's hair and, in an unconscious tribute to a favorite parental mannerism of his mother, vigorously shook Tommy's head from side to side. "A roomful of toys, you play with a ten-cent eye patch from Spiegelman's."

Sammy padded down the hall, scratching at his bottom, the bandy-legged captain of his own strange frigate, to make Tommy his lunch. It was a trim enough little tub, their house in Bloomtown. Its purchase had followed a string of ill-advised investments in the forties, among them the Clay Associates advertising firm, the Sam Clay School of Magazine Writing, and an apartment in Miami Beach for Sam's mother, in which she had died of a brain aneurysm after eleven days of retired discontentment, and which was then sold—six months after purchase—at a considerable loss. The last irreducible nut that remained from the palmy days at Empire Comics had been just enough for a down payment here in Bloomtown. And for a long time, Sammy had loved the house, the way a man was supposed to love his boat. It was the one tangible reminder of his brief success, and by far the best thing that had ever come of his money.

Bloomtown had been announced in 1948, with ads in *Life*, the *Saturday Evening Post*, and all the big New York papers. A fully functioning three-bedroom Cape Cod house, complete down to the ringing bottles of milk in the refrigerator, had been erected on the showroom floor of a former Cadillac dealership near Columbus Circle. The struggling young families of the Northeast—the white ones—were invited to visit the Bloomtown Idea Pavilion, tour the Bloomtown Home, and learn how an entire city of sixty thousand people was to be planted amid the potato fields west of Islip; a city of modest, affordable houses, each with its own yard and garage. An entire generation of young fathers and mothers raised in the narrow stairways and crowded rooms of the rust-

and-brick boroughs of New York, Sammy Clay among them, showed up to flick the model light switches, bounce on the model mattresses, and recline for just a moment in the pressed metal chaise longue on the cellophane lawn, tilting their chins upward to catch the imaginary rays of the suburban Long Island sun. They sighed, and felt that one of the deepest longings in their hearts might one day soon be answered. Their families were chaotic things, loud and distempered, fueled by anger and the exigencies of the wise-guy attitude, and since the same was true of New York City itself, it was hard not to believe that a patch of green grass and a rational floor plan might go a long way to soothing the jangling bundles of raw nerves they felt their families had become. Many, Sammy Clay once again among them, reached for their checkbooks and reserved one of the five hundred lots to be developed in the initial phase of construction.

For months afterward, Sammy carried around in his wallet a little card that had come with the packet of documents of sale and read simply:

THE CLAYS
127 LAVOISIER DRIVE
BLOOMTOWN, NEW YORK, U.S.A.

(All the streets in their neighborhood were to be named after eminent scientists and inventors.)

That feeling of pride had long since dissipated. Sammy no longer paid very much attention at all to his own Cape Cod, a Number Two or Penobscott model, with bay window and miniature-golf-sized widow's walk. He adopted the same policy with regard to it that he followed with his wife, his employment, and his love life. It was all habit. The rhythms of the commuter train, the school year, publishing schedules, summer vacations, and of his wife's steady calendar of moods had inured him to the charms and torments of his life. Only his relationship with Tommy, in spite of the recent light frost of irony and distance, remained unpredictable, alive. It was thick with regret and pleasure. When they did get an hour together, planning a universe on loose-leaf paper, or playing Ethan Allen's All-Star Baseball, it was invariably the happiest hour of Sammy's week.

When he walked into the kitchen, he was surprised to find Rosa sitting at the table with a cup of boiled water. On the surface of the water floated a canoe of sliced lemon.

"What's going on?" Sammy said, running water into the enameled coffeepot. "Everybody's up."

"Oh, I've been up all night," Rosa said brightly.

"Not a wink?"

"Not that I recall. My brain was going crazy."

"Get anything?"

Rosa had a lead story due for *Kiss Comics* in two days. She was the second-best illustrator of women in the business (he had to give the nod to Bob Powell) but a terrible procrastinator. He had long since given up trying to lecture her on her work habits. He was her boss in name only—they had settled that question years before, when Rosa first came to work for him, in a yearlong series of skirmishes. Now they were, more or less, a package. Whoever hired Sammy to edit his line of comics knew that he would be obtaining the valuable services of Rose Saxon (her professional name) as well.

"I have some ideas," she said in a guarded tone. All of Rosa's ideas sounded bad at first; she adapted them from a messy compound of her dreams, sensational newspaper articles, and things she picked up in women's magazines, and she was terrible at explaining them. It was always fascinating to see how they emerged under the teasing and topiary shapings of her pencil and brush.

"Something about the A-bomb?"

"How did you know?"

"I happened to be in the bedroom with you while you were talking out loud last night," he said. "Foolishly trying to sleep."

"Sorry."

Sammy broke a half-dozen eggs into a bowl, splashed them with milk, shook in pepper and salt. He rinsed one of the eggshells and tossed it into the coffeepot on the stove. Then he poured the eggs into a pan of foaming butter. Scrambled eggs was his only dish, but he was very good at it. You had to leave them alone; that turned out to be the secret. Most people stood there stirring them, but the way to do it was to let them sit for a minute or two over a low flame and bother them no more than half a dozen times. Sometimes, for variety, he threw in some chopped fried salami; that was how Tommy liked them.

"He was wearing the eye patch again," Sammy said, trying not to make it sound too important. "I saw him trying it on."

"Oh, God."

"He swore to me that he wasn't planning anything."

"Did you believe him?"

"I guess. I guess I chose to. Where's the salami?"

"I'll put it on my list. I'm going to the store today."

"You have to finish that story."

"And so I shall." She took a loud sip of her lemon water. "He's definitely up to something."

"You think." Sammy took down the peanut butter and got the grape jelly from the Frigidaire.

"I don't know, I just think he's been a little jumpy."

"He's always jumpy."

"I'd better walk him to school, as long as I'm up anyway." It was much easier for Rosa to govern her son than it was for Sammy. She didn't seem to give the question nearly as much thought. She believed that it was important to put trust in children, to hand over the reins to them from time to time, to let them decide things for themselves. But when, as frequently occurred, Tommy squandered that trust, she did not hesitate to clamp down. And Tommy never seemed to resent her heavy discipline in the way that he chafed under Sammy's lightest reproof. "You know, make sure he gets there."

"You can't walk me to school," Tommy said. He came into the kitchen, sat down before his plate, and stared at it, waiting for Sammy to pile it with eggs. "Mom, you can't possibly. I would die. I would absolutely die."

"He would die," Sammy told Rosa.

"Which would be very embarrassing for *me*," Rosa said. "Standing there next to a dead body in front of William Floyd Junior High."

"How about *I* walk him instead? It's only ten minutes out of my way." Sammy and Tommy generally said goodbye to each other at the front gate before setting off in opposite directions for the station and the junior high school, respectively. From second through sixth grade, they had parted with a handshake, but that custom, a minor beloved land-mark of Sammy's day for five years, had apparently been abandoned for good. Sammy was not sure why, or who had made the decision to aban-don it. "That way you can stay here and, you know, *draw my story.*"

"That might be a good idea."

Sammy gentled the steaming pudding of butter and eggs onto Tommy's plate. "Sorry," he said, "we're out of salami."

"It figures," Tommy said.

"I'll put it on my list," said Rosa.

They fell silent for a moment, Rosa in her chair behind her mug, and Sammy standing by the counter with a slice of bread in his hand, watching Tommy shovel it in. He was a trencherman, was Tom. The lit-tle stick of a boy had vanished under a mantle of muscle and fat; he was looking a little bit portly, in fact. After thirty-seven seconds, the eggs were gone. Tommy looked up from his plate.

"Why's everybody looking at me?" he said. "I didn't *do* anything."

Rosa and Sammy burst out laughing. Then Rosa stopped laughing, and focused on her son, always a little bit cross-eyed when she was making a point.

"Tom," she said. "You weren't planning to go into the city again?"

Tommy shook his head.

"Nevertheless," Sammy said, "I'll walk you."

"*Drive* me," Tommy said. "If you don't believe me."

"Why not?" Sammy said. If he took the car to the station, Rosa would not be able to drive to the grocery store, or to the beach, or to the library "for inspiration." She would be more likely to stay home and draw. "I might just take it all the way into the city. They opened a new lot around the corner from the office."

Rosa looked up, alarmed. "All the way into the *city?*" Even leaving their car, a 1951 Studebaker Champion, at the train station was not pro-tection enough. Rosa had been known to walk to the station to fetch it, just so that she would be able to drive around Long Island doing things that were not drawing romance comics.

"Just let me get dressed." Sammy handed the slice of bread to Rosa. "Here," he said, "you make his lunch."

BREAKFAST PALAVER at the Excelsior Cafeteria on Second Avenue, a favorite morning haunt of funny-book men, circa April 1954:

"It's a hoax."

"I just said that."

"Somebody's pulling Anapol's leg."

"Maybe it's *Anapol*."

"I wouldn't blame him if he did want to jump off the Empire State Building. I hear he's in all kinds of trouble over there."

"I'm in all kinds of trouble. Everybody is in all kinds of trouble. I challenge you to name me one house that isn't having problems. And it's only going to get worse."

"That's what you always say. Listen to you. Listen to this guy, he kills me. He's like a, a filling station of gloom. I spend ten minutes listening to him, I go away with a full tank of gloom, it lasts me all day."

"I'll tell you who's a fountain of gloom, Dr. Fredric Wertham. Have you read this book of his? What's it called? *How to Seduce an Innocent?*"

There was loud laughter at this. The men at the surrounding tables turned to look. The laughter had been a little too loud, certainly for the hour and the condition of their hangovers.

Dr. Fredric Wertham, a child psychiatrist with unimpeachable credentials and a well-earned sense of outrage, had for several years been trying to persuade the parents and legislators of America that the minds of American children were being deeply damaged by the reading of comic books. With the recent publication of the admirable, encyclopedic, and mistaken *Seduction of the Innocent*, Dr. Wertham's efforts had begun to bear real fruit; there had been calls for controls or outright bans, and in several southern and midwestern cities local governments had sponsored public comic book bonfires, onto which smiling mobs of American children with damaged minds had festively tossed their collections.

"No, I haven't read it. Have you read it?"

"I tried. It gives me a pain in the stomach."

"Has anybody read it?"

"Estes Kefauver has read it. Anybody get a summons yet?"

Now, word had it, the United States Senate was coming to town. Senator Kefauver of Tennessee and his Subcommittee on Juvenile Delinquency had determined to make a formal inquiry into the shocking charges leveled by Wertham in his book: that the reading of comic books led directly to antisocial behavior, drug addiction, sexual perversion, even rape and murder.

"That's it, maybe this *guy* got a summons. This guy on the Empire State. And that's why he's going to jump."

"You know who it just crossed my mind it could be. If it isn't a hoax, I mean. Hell, even if it is. In fact, if it's him, it definitely *is* a hoax."

"What is this, a game show? Tell us who he is."

"Joe Kavalier."

"Joe Kavalier, yes! That's exactly who I was thinking of."

"Joe Kavalier! Whatever happened to that guy?"

"I heard he's in Canada. Somebody saw him up there."

"Mort Meskin saw him at Niagara Falls."

"I heard it was Quebec."

"I heard it was Mort *Segal*, not Meskin. He took his honeymoon up there."

"I always liked him."

"He was a hell of an artist."

The half-dozen comics men gathered around a table at the back of the Excelsior that particular morning, with their bagels and soft-boiled eggs and steaming black coffee in cups with a red stripe around the rim—Stan Lee, Frank Pantaleone, Gil Kane, Bob Powell, Marty Gold, and Julie Glovsky—agreed that, before the war, Joe Kavalier had been one of the best in the business. They concurred that the treatment he and his partner had received at the hands of the Empire owners was deplorable, though hardly unique. Most could manage to supply a story, an instance of odd or eccentric behavior on Kavalier's part; but when these were added up, they did not, to any of the men, seem to predict something so rash and desperate as a death leap.

"What about that old *partner* of his," Lee said. "I ran into him here a couple of days ago. He looked pretty down in the mouth."

"Sammy Clay?"

"I don't know him very well. We've always been friendly. He never worked for us, but—"

"He's worked just about every place else."

"Anyway, the guy did not look good. And he barely gave me the time of day."

"He is not a happy man," Glovsky said. "Is old Sam. He is just not very happy over there at Pharaoh." Glovsky drew the violent *Mack Granite* feature for Pharaoh's *Brass Knuckle*.

"Frankly, he's never happy anywhere," Pantaleone said, and everyone agreed. They all knew Sammy's story, more or less. He had returned to the comic book business in 1947, covered in failure at everything else he had tried. His first defeat had been in the advertising game, at Burns, Baggot & DeWinter. He had managed to quit just before he was going to be asked to turn in his resignation. After that, he had tried going out on his own. When his advertising shop duly died a quiet and unremarked death, Sammy had found work in the magazine business, selling well-researched lies to *True* and *Yankee* and one miraculous short story to *Collier's*—it was about a crippled young boy's visit to a Coney Island steambath with his strong-man father, before the war—before settling into a deep and narrow groove at the third-tier magazine houses and what was left of the once-mighty pulps.

All along, there were regular offers from old funny-book friends, some of them seated around this table at the back of the Excelsior, which Sammy always refused. He was an epic novelist—that was a great thing to be, after the war—and though his literary career was not advancing as quickly as he would have liked, at least he could ensure that he was not moving backward. He swore, to anyone who would listen, and even on his mother's then-fresh grave, that he was never going back to comic books. Everybody who visited the Clays was taken to see some draft or other of his amorphous and wandering book. By day, he wrote articles on psittacosis and proustite for *Bird Lover* and *Gem and Tumbler*. He tried his hand at industrial writing, and had even written catalog copy for a seed company. The pay was mostly abysmal, the hours long, and Sammy was at the mercy of editors whose bitterness, as Sammy said, made George Deasey look like Deanna Durbin. Then, one day, he heard of an editor's job opening up at Gold Star, a now-forgotten publisher of comic books on Lafayette Street. The line was tattered and derivative, the circulation low, and the pay far from wonderful, but the position, if he took it, would at least give him authority and room to maneuver. Sammy's correspondence school for writers had enrolled only three pupils, one of whom lived in Guadalajara, Mexico, and spoke almost no English. Sammy had bills and debts and a family. When the Gold Star job came along, he had at last thrown in the towel on his old caterpillar dreams.

"No, you're right," Kane said. "He's never been happy anywhere."

Bob Powell leaned forward and lowered his voice. "I always thought he seemed a little bit—you know . . ."

"I have to agree with that," said Gold. "He's got that thing with the *sidekicks*. It's like an obsession with him. Have you noticed that? He takes over a character, first thing he does, no matter what, he gives the guy a little pal. After he came back to the business, he was at Gold Star doing the Phantom Stallion. All of a sudden the Stallion's hanging around with this kid, what was his name? Buck something."

"Buck Naked."

"Buckskin. The kid gunslinger. Then he goes to Olympic, and what, now the Lumberjack has Timber Lad. The Rectifier gets Little Mack the Boy Enforcer."

"The *Rect*ifier, that already sounds a little bit—"

"Then he comes to Pharaoh, all of a sudden it's the Argonaut and Jason. The Lone Wolf and Cubby. Christ, he even gave a sidekick to the *Lone* Wolf!"

"Yeah, but he's hired every one of you guys at one time or another, hasn't he?" Lee said. He looked at Marty Gold. "He's been very loyal to you over the years, Gold, God only knows why."

"Hey, shut up, already," said Kane. "That's him now coming through the door."

Sam Clay stepped into the moist, steam-table warmth of the Excelsior and was hailed from the table at the back. He nodded and waved, a little uncertainly, as if he didn't really care to join their party that morning. But after he had purchased his ticket for a cup of coffee and a doughnut he started toward them, head lowered a little in a bulldog way he had.

"Morning, Sam," Glovsky said.

"I drove in," he said. He was looking a little dazed. "It took *two hours.*"

"Seen the *Herald?*"

Clay shook his head.

"Looks like an old friend of yours is back in town."

"Yeah? Who would that be?"

"Tom Mayflower," Kane said, and everybody laughed, and then Kane went on to explain that someone signing himself "The Escapist" had, in this morning's *Herald-Tribune,* publicly announced his intention to jump from the Empire State Building at five o'clock that very afternoon.

Pantaleone dug around in the pile of newspaper in the center of the big table and found a *Herald-Tribune.* " 'Numerous grammatical and spelling errors,' " he read aloud, skimming quickly through the article, to which were devoted three column inches on page 2. " 'Threatened to expose the "unfair robberies and poor mistreatments of his finest artists by Mr. Sheldon Anapol." ' Huh. 'Mr. Anapol when reached refused to speculate publicly on the identity of the author. "It could be anyone," Mr. Anapol said. "We get a lot of nuts." ' Well," Pantaleone finished, shaking his head, "Joe Kavalier never struck me as any kind of nut. A little eccentric, maybe."

"Joe," Clay said wonderingly. "You guys think it's *Joe.*"

"Is he in town, Sam? Have you heard from him?"

"I haven't heard from Joe Kavalier since the war," Clay said. "It can't be him."

"I say it's a hoax," Lee said.

"The costume." Clay had begun to light a cigarette—he still had not sat down—but now he stopped with the flame halfway to the tip. "He'll want a costume."

"Who will?"

"The guy. If there really is a guy. He'll want a costume."

"He could make one."

"Yeah," Clay said. "Excuse me."

He turned, his cigarette still unlit in his fingers, and walked back toward the glass doors of the Excelsior.

"He just walked out of here with his meal ticket."

"He looked pretty upset," Julie Glovsky said. "You guys shouldn't have been teasing him."

He was already on his feet. He drained the last inch of coffee from his cup, then started after Sammy.

As fast as Sammy's pipe-stem legs could carry him, they headed over to the offices of Pharaoh Comics, in a loft on West Broadway, where Sammy was the editor in chief.

"What are you going to do?" Julie asked him. The fog that had lain over the city all morning had not lifted. Their breath issued from their mouths and seemed to be absorbed into the general gray gauziness of the morning.

"What do you mean? What can I do? Some kook wants to pretend he's the Escapist, he has a right."

"You don't think it's *him*?"

"Nah."

They rode up in the grinding iron cage of the elevator. When they walked into the offices, Sammy seemed to survey them with an ill-concealed shudder: the scarred cement floor, the bare white walls, the exposed, grease-blackened girders of the ceiling.

These were not the first headquarters of the company—those had been a suite of seven large rooms in the McGraw-Hill Building, all green lacquer and ivory Bakelite, with everything from the washroom fixtures to the team of buxom receptionists trimmed in chrome, and all of it paid for with the money Jack Ashkenazy had pocketed in 1943 when Sheldon Anapol had bought him out. Ashkenazy had next invested millions in a Canadian real estate venture predicated on his odd belief that, after the war, Canada and the United States would merge into one country. When, to his astonishment, this failed to pan out, he had gone back to the source of all his still-considerable wealth: the costumed hero. He had rented the gleaming offices on West Forty-second, hired away some of Empire's best writers and artists, and charged them with making a star out of a character of his own creation, the eponymous Pharaoh, a reincarnated Egyptian ruler, naturally, who sported an elaborate Tutankhamen headdress, metal armbands, and a loincloth made apparently of stiff cement, and went around thus, discreetly half-naked, foiling evil with the mystic power of his Scepter of Ra. The writers and artists had come up with a raft of even more unlikely heroes and heroines—Earthman (with his superhuman control over rocks and dirt), the Snowy Owl (with his "supersonic hoot"), and the Rolling Rose (with her shiny red skates)—to fill the pages of Pharaoh Comics' nine inaugural titles. Unfortunately, Jack Ashkenazy had bet heavily on the costumed superhero just as readers' interest in that genre was beginning to flag. The defeat of those actual world-devouring supervillains, Hitler and Tojo, along with their minions, had turned out to be as debilitating to the long-underwear hero trade as the war itself had been an abundant source of energy and plots; it proved to be hard for the cashiered captains and supersoldiers, on their return from tying Krupp artillery into half-hitches and swatting Zeros like midges over the Coral Sea, to muster the old pre-1941 fervor for busting up rings of car thieves, rescuing orphans, and exposing crooked fight promoters. At the same time, a new villain, the lawless bastard child of relativity and Satan, had appeared to cast its roiling fiery pall over even the mightiest of heroes, who could no longer be entirely assured that there would always be a world for them to save. The tastes of returning GIs, who had become hooked on the regular shipments of comic books provided them along with candy bars and cigarettes, turned to darker, more "adult-oriented" fare: true-crime comics had their vogue, followed by romances, horror tales, Westerns, science fiction; anything, in short, but masked men. Millions of unsold copies of *Pharaoh Comics* #1 and its eight companion titles came back from the distributors; after a year, none of the remaining six titles was making a profit. Ashkenazy, sensing catastrophe, had moved downtown, fired the expensive talent, and retrenched, overhauling his line through a program of cost-cutting and slavish imitation, transforming it into a modest success very like Racy Publications, the fourth-rate pulp-magazine house, home of retreads, copycats, and cheap imitations at which he had begun his career as a publisher in the lean Depression years before two foolish young men laid the Escapist in his lap. But his pride had never quite recovered from the blow, and it was generally felt that Pharaoh's failure, along with the Canadian debacle, had started him down the road to his decline and eventual death two years ago.

Sammy crossed the broad grimy expanse of the workroom to his office. Julie hesitated at the door before following him in. The prohibition against entering Sam Clay's office, except in the case of family emergency, was absolute and closely observed. He would admit no one if he was working, and he was always working. His bursts of fevered composition, during which he might knock out an entire year's worth of *Brass Knuckle* or *Weird Date* in a single night, were celebrated not only in the Pharaoh offices but throughout the small, collegial world of the New York comic book business. He unplugged his intercom, took the telephone off the hook, sometimes stuffed his ears with cotton paraffin gobbets of foam rubber.

He had typed stories for comic books for the past seven years: costumed hero, romance, horror, adventure, true-crime, science fiction and fantasy stories, Westerns, sea yarns, and Bible stories, a couple of issues of *Classics Illustrated*,* Sax Rohmer imitations, Walter Gibson imitations, H. Rider Haggard imitations, Rex Stout imitations, tales of both world wars, the Civil War, the Peloponnesian War, and the Napoleonic Wars; every genre but funny animals. Sammy drew the line at funny animals. The success in the trade of these dot-eyed, three-fingered imports from the world of animated cartoons, with their sawdusty gags and childish

---

* *Gargantua and Pantagruel*, and possibly *Vathek*.

antics, was one of the thousand little things to have broken Sammy Clay's heart. He was a furious, even romantic, typist, prone to crescendos, diminuendos, dense and barbed arpeggios, capable of ninety words a minute when under deadline or pleased with the direction his story was taking, and over the years his brain had become an instrument so thoroughly tuned to the generation of highly conventional, severely formalistic, eight-to-twelve-page miniature epics that he could, without great effort, write, talk, smoke, listen to a ball game, and keep an eye on the clock all at the same time. He had reduced two typewriters to molten piles of slag iron and springs since his return to comics, and when he went to bed at night his mind remained robotically engaged in its labor while he slept, so that his dreams were often laid out in panels and interrupted by surrealistic advertising, and when he woke up in the morning he would find that he had generated enough material for a full issue of one of his magazines.

Now he moved his latest Remington to one side. Julie Glovsky saw a little brass key lying in the center of a square patch of blotter that was free of ash and dust. Sammy took the key and went to a large wooden cabinet, dragged up from a defunct photographical processing lab on a lower floor of the building.

"You have an Escapist costume?" Julie said.

"Yeah."

"Where'd you get it?"

"From Tom Mayflower," Sammy said.

He rummaged around inside the cabinet until he came up with an oblong blue box stamped KING FAT HAND LAUNDRY in crooked black letters. On the side, in grease pencil, someone had, for some reason, written the word BACON. Sammy gave the box a shake, and something rattled dryly within; he looked puzzled. He pulled the box open, and a small yellow card, about the size of a matchbook, fluttered out and corkscrewed to the floor. Sammy stooped over, picked it up, and read the legend printed on its face in brightly colored ink. When he looked up, his face was pinched, his jaw set, but Julie caught an unmistakable glint of amusement in his eyes. Sammy handed Julie the card. It featured a drawing of two ornate, old-fashioned skeleton keys, one on either side of the following brief text:

Welcome, faithful Foe of Tyranny, to the
LEAGUE OF THE GOLDEN KEY!!!
This card bestows on

(print name above)

all the rights and duties
of a true-blue friend of Liberty and Humanity!

"It's him," Julie said. "Isn't it? He was here. He took it."

"How do you like that," said Sammy. "I haven't seen one of those in years."

AT LUNCHTIME, the police showed up. They were taking the letter to the *Herald* seriously, and the detective in charge had a few questions for Sammy about Joe.

Sammy told the detective, a man named Lieber, that he had not seen Joe Kavalier since the evening of December 14, 1941, at Pier 11, when Joe sailed for basic training in Newport, Rhode Island, aboard a Providence-bound packet boat called the *Comet*. Joe had never answered any of their letters. Then, toward the end of the war, Sammy's mother, as next of kin, had received a letter from the office of James Forrestal, the Secretary of the Navy. It said that Joe had been wounded or taken ill in the line of duty; the letter was vague about the nature of the injury and the theater of war. It said also that he had, for some time, been recuperating at Guantánamo Bay in Cuba, but that he was now being given a medical discharge and a commendation. In two days, he would be arriving at Newport News aboard the *Miskatonic*. Sammy had gone down to Virginia on a Greyhound bus to meet him and bring him home. But somehow or other, Joe had managed to escape.

"Escape?" Detective Lieber said. He was a young man, surprisingly young, a fair-haired Jew with pudgy hands, wearing a gray suit that looked expensive but not at all flashy.

"It was a talent he had," Sammy said.

At the time, Joe's vanishing had been a loss in some ways more genuine than that which death represents. He was not merely dead—and thus, in a sense, always locatable. No, they really had managed to *lose* him. He had gotten on the boat in Cuba; of this fact there was documentary evidence in the form of signatures and serial numbers on a medical transport record. But when the *Miskatonic* docked in Newport

News, Joe was no longer aboard. He had left a brief letter; though its contents were classified, one of the navy investigators had assured Sammy that it was not a suicide note. When Sammy returned from Virginia, after an interminable gray trip back up U.S. 1, he found their house in Midwood aflutter with bunting. Rosa had prepared a cake and a banner that welcomed Joe home. Ethel had bought a new dress and had her hair done, allowing the hairdresser to rinse out the gray. The three of them—Rosa, Ethel, and Tommy—were sitting in the living room, under the crepe-paper swags, crying. In the months that followed, they had generated all manner of wild and violent theories to explain what had happened to Joe, and pursued every lead and rumor. Because he had not been taken from them, they could not seem to let him go. Over the years, however, the intensity of Sammy's anger and of his shock over Joe's behavior had, inevitably, dwindled. The thought of his lost cousin was a sore one still; but it had, after all, been nearly nine years. "He was trained in Europe as an escape artist," he told Detective Lieber. "That's where we got the whole idea for the Escapist."

"I used to read it," Detective Lieber said. He coughed politely and looked around at the pages of art and framed covers of various Pharaoh titles that ornamented Sammy's office. On the wall behind Sammy hung the vastly blown-up image of a single frame, from a story that Rosa had done for *Frontier Comics*, the only superhero story that Rosa ever drew. It showed the Lone Wolf and Cubby, in tight coveralls of fringed buckskin and lupine headdresses, their arms around each other's shoulders. The blazing spokes of an Arizona sunrise reached out from behind them. Lone Wolf was saying, "WELL, PARDNER, IT LOOKS LIKE IT'S GOING TO BE A BEAUTIFUL DAY!" Rosa had done the enlargement herself and gotten it framed for Sammy's last birthday. You could see the lithography dots—they were as big as shirt buttons—and somehow the scale of the image gave it a surreal importance.*

"I'm afraid I'm not as familiar with what you do here," Detective Lieber said, eyeing the big Lone Wolf with a look of faint puzzlement.

---

* Sammy liked to tell a story about a hungry young artist named Roy Lichtenstein who had once wandered into his office at Pharaoh looking for a job. There is no evidence, however, that the story is true.

"Few people are," Sammy said.

"I'm sure it must be interesting."

"Don't be too sure."

Lieber shrugged. "Okay, so here's what I don't understand. Why would he *want* to 'escape,' as you put it? He just got out of the navy. He's been in some godforsaken place or other. From the sound of it, he's had it pretty tough. Why wouldn't he *want* to come home?"

Sammy didn't immediately reply. A possible answer had come to mind right away, but since it struck him as flippant, he held his tongue. Then he thought it over for a moment and saw that it might very well be the right answer to Detective Lieber's question.

"He didn't really have a home to come home to," Sammy said. "I guess maybe that's how it must have seemed to him."

"His family in Europe?"

"All dead. Every one of them, his mother, his father, his grandfather. His kid brother's boat was torpedoed. Just a little kid, a refugee."

"Jesus."

"It was not good."

"And you've *never* heard from your cousin since? Not even—"

"Not a postcard. And I've made a lot of inquiries, Detective. I hired private detectives. The navy conducted a full investigation. Nothing."

"Do you think— You must have considered the possibility that he might be dead?"

"He might be. My wife and I have discussed it over the years. But somehow I think— I just think that he isn't."

Lieber nodded and tucked his little notebook back into the hip pocket of his sharp gray suit.

"Thank you," he said. He stood and shook Sammy's hand. Sammy walked him out to the elevator.

"You look awfully young to be a detective," Sammy said. "If you don't mind my saying."

"Yes, but I have the heart of a seventy-year-old man," Lieber said.

"You're Jewish, if you don't mind me asking?"

"I don't mind."

"I didn't know they were making detectives out of Jews."

"They just started," Lieber said. "I'm kind of the prototype."

The elevator thudded into place, and Sammy dragged the rattling cage to one side.

Sammy's father-in-law stood there in a tweed suit. The jacket had epaulets, and there was enough tweed in it to clothe at least two grouse-hunting Scotsmen. Four or five years earlier, Longman Harkoo had delivered a series of lectures at the New School on the intimate relations between Catholicism and Surrealism, entitled "The Superego, the Ego, and the Holy Ghost." They had been desultory, mumbling, and sparsely attended, but since that time Siggy had abandoned his former caftans and magister's robes in favor of a more professorial attire. All of his enormous suits were made, badly, by the same Oxford tailor who ill-clothed the woolen flower of English academe.

"He's afraid you'll be angry with him," Saks said. "We told him you wouldn't be."

"You've seen him?"

"Oh, much more than see him." He smirked. "He's—"

"You've *seen* Joe, and you never said anything to me or Rosa?"

"Joe? You mean Joe *Kavalier?*" Saks looked dumbfounded. He opened his mouth and then closed it again. "Hmm," he said. Something seemed to be not quite adding up in his mind.

"This is my father-in-law, Mr. Harkoo," Sammy told Lieber. "Mr. Harkoo, this is Detective Lieber. I don't know if you've seen the *Herald* today, but there's—"

"Who's that behind you?" Lieber said, peering into the elevator, around the great dun bulk of Siggy Saks. The big man stepped deftly, and not without an air of happy anticipation, to one side, as though raising the curtain on a completed illusion. The bit of hocus-pocus produced an eleven-year-old boy named Thomas Edison Clay.

"I found him on the doorstep. Quite literally."

"God damn it, Tommy," Sammy said. "I walked you into the *building*. I saw you go into your *homeroom*. How did you get out?"

Tommy didn't say anything. He just stood looking down at the eye patch in his hands.

"Another escape artist," Detective Lieber said. "It must run in the family."

GREAT FEAT OF ENGINEERING is an object of perpetual interest to people bent on self-destruction. Since its completion, the Empire State Building, a gigantic shard of the Hoosier State torn from the mild limestone bosom of the Midwest and upended, on the site of the old Waldorf-Astoria, in the midst of the heaviest traffic in the world, had been a magnet for dislocated souls hoping to ensure the finality of their impact, or to mock the bold productions of human vanity. Since its opening almost twenty-three years earlier, a dozen people had attempted to leap from its ledges or its pinnacle to the street below; about half had managed the trick. None, however, had ever before given such clear and considerate warning of his intentions. For the building's private police and firefighting squadrons, working in concert with their municipal brethren, there had been ample time to post officers at all the street entrances and points of ingress, at the stairwell doors and elevator banks. The twenty-fifth floor, where the offices of Empire Comics were still to be found, swarmed with building cops in their big-shouldered brass and wool uniforms, with those old-fashioned peaked caps designed, legend had it, by the late Al Smith himself. Alerts had been issued to the building's fifteen thousand tenants, warning them to be on the lookout for a lean, hawk-faced madman, perhaps dressed in a dark blue union suit, or perhaps in a moth-eaten blue tuxedo with extravagant tails. Firefighters in canvas coveralls ringed the building on three sides, from Thirty-third Street, around Fifth Avenue, to Thirty-fourth. They peered up through fine German binoculars, scanning the infinite planes of Indiana rock for any emerging hand or foot. They were ready, insofar as readiness was possible. Should the madman actually make it through a window and out into the darkening stuff of the evening, their course of action was less clear. But they were hopeful.

"We'll get him before he goes," predicted Captain Harley, still in command of the building's police force after all these years, his blighted eye glittering brighter and more irascible than ever. "We'll get the poor dumb mud-turk."

The daily circulation of the New York *Herald-Tribune* in 1954 was four hundred and fifty thousand. Of these readers, some two hundred had been drawn, by the letter printed in their newspaper that morning, to stand in wondering clumps behind police lines, gazing up. They were mostly men in their twenties and thirties, in jackets and ties, shipping clerks, commercial draftsmen, clothing and textile whole-salers working their way up in their fathers' businesses. Many of them were employed in the neighborhood. They checked their watches and made the hard-bitten remarks of New Yorkers at the prospect of a suicide—"I wish he'd do it already, I got a date"—but they did not take their eyes from the sides of the building. They had grown up on the Escapist, or had discovered him and his adventures in a foxhole in Belgium or in a transport off Bougainville. In some of these men, the name Joe Kavalier stirred long-dormant memories of reckless, violent, beautiful release.

Then there were the passersby, the shoppers and office workers headed for home, drawn by the flashing lights and uniforms. Word of the promised entertainment had spread quickly among them. Where the flow of information flagged or was retarded by tight-lipped policemen, the small but voluble contingent of comic book men was on hand to fill in and embellish the details of Joe Kavalier's misfortunate career.

"I hear it's all a hoax," said Joe Simon, who, with his own partner, Jack Kirby, had created Captain America. The rights to Captain America had earned, and in the future would continue to earn, great sums for their owner, Timely Publications, one day to be better known as Marvel Comics. "I heard that from Stan."

By five-thirty, when no one had been found skulking in the building or had inched himself out onto a windblown sill, Captain Harley began to come to the same conclusion. He was standing with some of his men just in front of the Thirty-third Street entrance, chewing on the end of a briar pipe. For the eighth time, he took out a gold pocket watch and consulted its face. He snapped it shut and chuckled.

"It's a hoax," he said. "I knew it all along."

"More and more I'm inclined to agree," said Detective Lieber.

"Maybe his watch stopped," Sammy Clay said almost hopefully. Lieber got the feeling that if the threat did turn out to be a hoax, Clay was going to be disappointed.

"Tell me this," Lieber said to Clay. As a family member, the little writer—that was how Lieber thought of him—had been permitted within the police cordon. In the event that Joe Kavalier appeared, his cousin would be on hand for last-minute pleas and counsel. There was also the boy. Ordinary procedure would have barred children from such an event, but experience had taught Lieber, who had spent nine years as a patrolman in Brownsville, that every so often the face of a child, or even its voice over a telephone, could draw a person in from the ledge. "Before today, how many people knew this whole story about how you and your cousin were robbed and cheated and taken advantage of?"

"I resent that, Detective," said Sheldon Anapol. The big man had come down from the Empire offices at five o'clock precisely. He was wrapped in a long black overcoat, a tiny gray tyrolean cap roosting on his head like a pigeon, its feather troubled by the breeze. The day was turning cold and bitter now. The light was failing. "You don't know enough about this matter to pass judgment like that. There were contracts involved, copyrights. Not to mention the fact that, while they were working for us, both Mr. Kavalier and Mr. Clay made more money than almost anyone in the business."

"*I'm* sorry," Lieber said, unapologetically. He turned back to Sammy. "But you see my point."

Sammy shrugged, nodding, mouth pursed. He saw the detective's point.

"Not a hell of a lot before today. A few dozen guys in the business. A lot of them jokers, I have to admit. Some lawyers, probably. My wife."

"Well, now, look at this."

Lieber gestured toward the swelling crowd, pushed back to the opposite sidewalk, the streets blocked off and filled with honking cabs, the reporters and photographers, everyone looking up at the building around which the untold Escapist millions had coalesced for so many years. They had been told the names of the principal players, Sam Clay, Sheldon Anapol; they gestured and murmured and scowled at the publisher in his funereal coat. The sum of money out of which the team of Kavalier & Clay had been cheated by Empire Comics, though no one had ever actually sat down and calculated it, was widely current in the crowd, and growing by the moment.

"You can't buy this kind of publicity." Lieber's experience with suicides was fairly extensive. There was a very small set of them who chose to do away with themselves publicly, and, within this group, an even smaller subset who would provide an exact time and place in advance. Of these—and he could think of perhaps two in all the years since he got his badge in 1940—none was ever late for his appointment. "Mr. Anapol here"—he nodded to the publisher—"through no fault of his own, naturally, ends up looking like the bad guy."

"Character assassination," Anapol agreed. "That's what it amounts to."

Again Captain Harley of the building police snapped the watch shut, this time with greater finality. "I'm going to send my boys home," he said. "I don't think any of you have anything to worry about."

Lieber winked at the boy, a sullen, staring kid who, for the last forty-five minutes, had been standing in the lee of his vast grandfather with a finger in his mouth, looking as if he was going to vomit. When Lieber winked, the kid turned pale. The detective frowned. In his years as a beat cop on and off Pitkin Avenue, he had frightened children with a friendly wink or hello many times, but rarely one so old who did not have something on his conscience.

"I don't get it," said Sammy. "I mean, I see what you're saying. I thought the same thing. Maybe it *is* all just a stunt to get attention and he never had any intention of jumping at all. But then why did he steal the costume from my office?"

"Can you prove that *he* took the costume?" Lieber said. "Look, I don't know. Maybe he just got cold feet. Maybe he was run down by a pushcart or a taxicab. I'll check the hospitals, just in case."

He nodded to Captain Harley and agreed that it was time to pack up the show. Then he turned back to the boy. He didn't know exactly what he was going to say; the chain of reasons and possibilities lay still un-connected in his mind. It was just a fleeting policeman's impulse, a nose for trouble, that prompted his question. He was one of those men who couldn't help giving a squirrelly little kid a hard time.

"I hear you've been skipping school, young man, to come into our fair city and be a gadabout," he said.

The boy's eyes widened. He was good-looking, a little overfed but with thick black curls and big blue eyes that now grew even larger. The detective wasn't sure yet whether the boy was dreading punishment or longing for it. Usually, with solemn little reprobates of this sort, it was the latter.

"I don't want to catch you loose in my town again, you hear me? You stay out on Long Island where you belong."

He winked at the father now. Sam Clay laughed.

"Thank you, Detective," he said. He grabbed a fistful of his son's hair and shook the boy's head back and forth in a way that looked quite painful to Lieber. "He's become quite the forger, this one. Does his mother's signature on his excuses better than she can."

Lieber felt the links of the chain beginning to reach toward each other.

"Is that so?" he said. "Tell me, do you have one of these little master-pieces all ready to go for tomorrow?"

With three swift, mute nods of his head, the boy confessed that he did. Lieber held out his hand. The boy reached into his satchel and took out a manila folder. He opened it. A single leaf of good paper lay within, neatly typed and signed. He handed the paper over to Lieber. His move-ments were precise and preternaturally careful, almost showily so, and Lieber remembered that the boy's father believed his son had been sneaking into the city to hang out with stage magicians at Louis Tan-nen's Magic Shop. Lieber scanned the boy's note.

Dear Mr. Savarese,

Please excuse Tommy's absence from school yesterday. Once again as I told you previously I believe he required ophthalmo-logic type treatments from his specialist in the city.

Sincerely,

Mrs. Rosa Clay

"I'm afraid your boy was responsible for all this," Lieber said, passing the letter to the boy's father. "He wrote the letter to the *Herald-Tribune*."

"I had a feeling," the grandfather said. "I thought I recognized the style."

"What?" Sam Clay said. "What makes you say that?"

"Typewriters have personalities," said the boy in a small voice, looking down at his feet. "Like fingerprints."

"That is very often the case," Lieber agreed.

Sammy examined the note, then gave the boy a queer look. "Tommy, is this true?"

"Yes, sir."

"You mean nobody is going to jump?"

Tommy shook his head.

"You made up this whole thing yourself?"

He nodded.

"Well," said Lieber. "This is a serious thing you've done, son. I'm afraid you may have committed a crime." He looked at the father. "I'm sorry about your cousin," he said. "I know you were hoping he had come back."

"I was," Sammy said, surprised, either by the realization or by the fact that Lieber had guessed it. "You know, I guess I really was."

"He *has* come back!" The boy shouted this, and even Lieber jumped a little. "He's here."

"In New York?" the father said. The boy nodded. "Joe Kavalier is here in New York." Another nod. "Where? How do you know? Tommy, god damn it, where is your cousin Joe?"

The boy muttered something, his voice nearly inaudible. Then, to their surprise, he turned and walked into the building. He went over to the banks of express elevators and pressed the button for those that went all the way to the top.

5

I T ALL BEGAN—or had begun again—with the Ultimate Demon Wonder Box.

Last July 3, his eleventh birthday, Tommy's father had taken him to *The Story of Robin Hood* at the Criterion, to lunch at the Automat, and to visit a reproduction, at the Forty-second Street Library, of Sherlock Holmes's apartment, complete with unopened letters addressed to the sleuth, a curl-toed slipper filled with tobacco, the paw print of the Hound of the Baskervilles, and a stuffed Giant Rat of Sumatra. All of this was by Tommy's request, and in lieu of the usual birthday party. Tommy's one friend, Eugene Begelman, had moved to Florida at the end of fourth grade, and Tommy had had no desire to fill the Clays' living room with antsy, sullen, eye-rolling kids whose parents had forced them, out of politeness to his own, to attend. He was a solitary boy, unpopular with teachers and students alike. He still slept with a stuffed beaver named Bucky. But he was, at the same time, proud—even belligerent in defense—of his estrangement from the world of the normal, stupid, happy, enviable children of Bloomtown. The mystery of his real father, who—he had decided, deciphering the overheard hints and swiftly hushed remarks of his parents and his grandmother before her death—had been a soldier killed in Europe, was at once a source of amour propre and of bitter yearning, a grand opportunity that he had missed out on but that nevertheless could have befallen only him. He always sympathized with young people in novels whose parents had died or abandoned them (as much to help them fulfill their singular destinies as future Emperors or Pirate Kings, as out of the general grinding cruelty toward children of the world). There was no doubt in his mind that such a destiny awaited him, perhaps in the Martian colonies or the plutonium mines of the asteroid belt. Tommy was a little pudgy, and small for his age. He had been the target of some standard-issue cruelty over the years, but his taciturnity and his spectacularly average performance in school had earned him a certain measure of safe invisibility. Thus, over time, he had won the right to opt completely out of the usual theaters of juvenile strategy and angst—the playground coups, the permanent floating card-flipping games, the Halloween and pool and birthday parties. These interested him, but he forbade himself to care. If he could not see his health drunk in the huge oaken banquet room of a castle, filled with the smell of spit-roasted boar and venison, by tankard-clinking stalwart bowmen and adventurers, then a day in New York City with his father would have to do.

The crux, the key element of the celebration, was a stop at Louis Tannen's Magic Shop, on West Forty-second Street, to buy the birthday present that Tommy had requested: the Ultimate Demon Wonder Box. At $17.95, it represented considerable largesse on his parents' part, but they had been from the first remarkably indulgent of his recent interest in magic, as if it accorded with some secret itinerary they had charted out for him in their minds.

Eugene Begelman had started the whole magic business after his father returned from a business trip to Chicago with an oblong box in playing-card colors that contained, its label claimed, "everything necessary to AMAZE and ASTOUND your friends and turn YOU into the life of every party." Naturally, Tommy had affected to scorn such an agenda, but after Eugene briefly caused most of a hard-boiled egg to disappear, and nearly succeeded in pulling a rather limp artificial mouse out of a supposedly normal lady's stocking, Tommy had grown impatient. Such impatience—a tightening in his chest, a tapping of his feet, a feeling like the need to urinate—unbearable at times, always seemed to come over him whenever he came across something he could not figure out. He had borrowed the Al-A-Kazzam! Junior Magic Kit from Eugene and taken it home; over one weekend he had mastered every trick. Eugene said he could keep the kit.

Next, Tommy had gone to the library and discovered a hitherto unsuspected shelf of books on card tricks, coin tricks, tricks with silks and scarves and cigarettes. His hands were large for a boy his age, with long fingers, and he had a capacity for standing in front of the mirror with a quarter or a book of matches, repeating the same tiny flexings of his fingers over and over again, that surprised even him. It soothed him, practicing his palmings and fades.

It had not been long before he discovered Louis Tannen's. The greatest supplier of tricks and supplies on the Eastern seaboard, it was, in 1953, still the unofficial capital of professional conjuring in America, a kind of informal magicians' club where generations of silk-hat men, passing through town on their way north, south, or west to the vaudeville and burlesque houses, the nightclubs and variety theaters of the nation, had met to exchange information, to cadge money, and to dazzle one another with refinements too artistic and subtle to waste on an audience of elephant gapers and leerers at sawn-in-two ladies. The Ultimate Demon Wonder Box was one of Mr. Louis Tannen's signature tricks, a perennial bestseller that he personally guaranteed to reduce an audience—not, surely, of card-flipping, stickball-playing fifth graders but, Tommy imagined, of tuxedo-wearing types smoking long cigarettes on ocean liners, and women with gardenias in their hair—to a layer of baffled jelly on the floor. Its name alone was enough to render Tommy breathless with impatience.

At the back of the shop, Tommy had noticed on prior visits, were two doorways. One, painted green, led to the stockroom where the steel rings, trick birdcages, and false-bottomed trunks were kept. The other door, painted black, generally was kept closed, but sometimes a man would come in from the street, greet Louis Tannen or one of the salesmen, and pass through it, giving a glimpse of the world beyond; or else a man might come out, waving to whomever he was leaving behind, tucking five dollars into his pocket or shaking his head in wonderment over whatever miracle he had just witnessed. This was Tannen's famous back room. Tommy would have given anything—he would have forgone the Ultimate Demon Wonder Box, *The Story of Robin Hood*, Sherlock Holmes's Baker Street digs, and the Automat—just to be able to get a peek back there, and to watch the old pros brandish the puzzling flowers of their art. While Mr. Tannen himself was giving Tommy's father a demonstration of the Wonder Box, showing him that it was empty, feeding it seven scarves, then opening it to show him that it was still empty, a man wandered in, said, "Hello, Lou," and went on through to the back. As the door opened and closed, Tommy caught a glimpse of some magicians, in sweaters and suits, standing with their backs to him. They were watching another magician at work, a tall, slender guy with a large nose. The man with the large nose looked up, smiling at whatever little stunt he had just pulled off, his deep-set, heavy-lidded blue eyes unimpressed with himself. The other magicians swore in appreciation of the trick. The sad blue eyes met Tommy's. They widened. The door closed.

"Amazing," Sammy Clay said, taking out his wallet. "Worth every penny."

Mr. Tannen handed the box to Tommy, and he took it, his eyes still on the door. He had focused his thoughts into a sharp diamond beam and aimed them at the doorknob, willing it to turn. Nothing happened.

"Tommy?" Tommy looked up. His father was staring down at him. He looked irritated, and his voice had a tone of false good humor. "Do you have even an iota of desire left in your body for that thing?"

And he nodded, though his father had guessed the truth. He looked at the blue lacquered wooden box for which he had ached only last night with a fervor that kept him awake till past midnight. But knowing the secrets of the Ultimate Demon Wonder Box would never get him through the door to Tannen's back room, where travel-hardened men concocted private wonders for their own melancholy amusement. He looked from the Wonder Box to the black door. It remained closed. The Bug, he knew, would have made a break for it.

"It's great, Dad," Tommy said. "I love it. Thanks."

Three days later, on a Monday, Tommy stopped in at Spiegelman's Drugs to arrange the comic books. This was a service he provided at no charge and, so far as he knew, unbeknownst to Mr. Spiegelman. The week's new comics arrived on Monday, and by Thursday, particularly toward the end of the month, the long rows of wire racks along the wall at the back of the store were often a jumble of disordered and dog-eared titles. Every week, Tommy sorted and alphabetized, putting the Nationals with the Nationals, the E.C.s with the E.C.s, the Timelys with the Timelys, reuniting the estranged members of the Marvel Family, isolating the romance titles, which, though he tried to conceal this fact from his mother, he despised, in a bottom corner. Of course he reserved the centermost racks for the nineteen Pharaoh titles. He kept careful count over these, rejoicing when Spiegelman's sold out its order of *Brass Knuckle* in a week, feeling a mysterious pity and shame for his father when, for an entire month, all six copies of *Sea Yarns,* a personal favorite of Tommy's, languished unpurchased on Spiegelman's rack. He did all of his rearranging surreptitiously, under the guise of browsing. Whenever another kid came in, or Mr. Spiegelman walked by, Tommy quickly stuffed back whatever errant stack he was holding, any old way, and engaged in a transparent bit of innocent whistling. He further concealed his covert librarianship—which arose chiefly out of loyalty to his father but was also due to an innate dislike of messes—by spending a precious weekly dime on a comic book. This even though his father regularly brought him home big stacks of "the competition," including many titles that Spiegelman's didn't even carry.

Logically, if Tommy were throwing his money away, it ought to have been on one of the lesser-read Pharaohs, such as *Farm Stories* or the aforementioned nautical book. But when Tommy walked out of Spiegelman's every Thursday, it was with an Empire comic book in his hand. This was his small, dark act of disloyalty to his father: Tommy loved the Escapist. He admired his golden mane, his strict, at times obsessive, adherence to the rules of fair play, and the good-natured grin he wore at all times, even when taking it on the chin from Kommandant X (who had quite easily made the transition from Nazi to Commie), or from one of the giant henchmen of Poison Rose. The Escapist's murky origins, in the minds of his father and their lost cousin Joe, chimed obscurely in his imagination with his own. He would read the entire book on the way home from Spiegelman's, going slow, savoring it, aware of the scrape of his sneakers against the fresh-laid sidewalk, the bobbing progress of his body through the darkness that gathered around the outer margins of the pages as he turned them. Just before he turned the corner onto Lavoisier Drive, he would toss the comic book into the D'Abruzzios' trash can.

Those portions of his walk to and from school that were not taken up with his reading—in addition to comics, he devoured science fiction, sea stories, H. Rider Haggard, Edgar Rice Burroughs, John Buchan, and novels dealing with American or British history—or with detailed mental rehearsals of the full-evening magic shows by which he one day planned to dazzle the world, Tommy passed as scrappy Tommy Clay, All-American schoolboy, known to none as the Bug. The Bug was the name of his costumed crime-fighting alter ego, who had appeared one morning when Tommy was in the first grade, and whose adventures and increasingly involuted mythology he had privately been chronicling in his mind ever since. He had drawn several thick volumes' worth of Bug stories, although his artistic ability was incommensurate with the vivid scope of his mental imagery, and the resultant mess of graphite smudges and eraser crumbs always discouraged him. The Bug was a bug, an actual insect—a scarab beetle, in his current version— who had been caught, along with a human baby, in the blast from an atomic explosion. Somehow—Tommy was vague on this point—their natures had been mingled, and now the beetle's mind and spirit, armed with his beetle hardness and proportionate beetle strength, inhabited the four-foot-high body of a human boy who sat in the third row of Mr. Landauer's class, under a bust of Franklin D. Roosevelt. Sometimes he could avail himself, again rather vaguely, of the characteristic abilities—flight, stinging, silk-spinning—of other varieties of bug. It was always wrapped in the imaginary mantle, as it were, of the Bug that he performed his clandestine work at the Spiegelman's racks, feelers extended and tensed to detect the slightest tremor of the approach of Mr. Spiegelman, whom Tommy generally cast in this situation as the nefarious Steel Clamp, a charter member of the Bug's Rogue's Gallery.

That afternoon, as he was smoothing back the flagged corner of a copy of *Weird Date*, something surprising occurred. For the first time that he could remember, he felt an actual twinge in the Bug's keen antennae. Someone was watching him. He looked around. A man was standing there, half-hidden behind a rotating drum spangled with the lenses of fifty-cent reading glasses. The man snapped his face away and pretended that, all along, he had been looking at a tremble of pink and blue light on the back wall of the store. Tommy recognized him at once as the sad-eyed magician from Tannen's back room. He was not at all surprised to see the man there, in Spiegelman's Drugs in Bloomtown,

Long Island; this was something he always remembered afterward. He even felt—maybe this was a little surprising—glad to see the man. At Tannen's, the magician's appearance had struck Tommy as somehow pleasing. He had felt an inexplicable affection for the unruly mane of black curls, the lanky frame in a stained white suit, the large sympathetic eyes. Now Tommy perceived that this displaced sense of fondness had been merely the first stirring of recognition.

When the man realized that Tommy was staring at him, he gave up his pretense. For one instant he hung there, shoulders hunched, red-faced. He looked as if he were planning to flee; that was another thing Tommy remembered afterward. Then the man smiled.

"Hello there," he said. His voice was soft and faintly accented.

"Hello," said Tommy.

"I've always wondered what they keep in those jars." The man pointed to the front window of the store, where two glass vessels, baroque beakers with onion-dome lids, contained their perpetual gallons of clear fluid, tinted respectively pink and blue. The late-afternoon sun cut through them, casting the rippling pair of pastel shadows on the back wall.

"I asked Mr. Spiegelman that," Tommy said. "A couple times."

"What did he say?"

"That it's a mystery of his profession."

The man nodded solemnly. "One we must respect." He reached into his pocket and took out a package of Old Gold cigarettes. He lit one with a snap of his lighter and inhaled slowly, his eyes on Tommy, his expression troubled, as Tommy somehow expected it to be.

"I'm your cousin," the man said. "Josef Kavalier."

"I know," said Tommy. "I saw your picture."

The man nodded and took another drag on his cigarette.

"Are you coming over to our house?"

"Not today."

"Do you live in Canada?"

"No," said the man. "I don't live in Canada. I could tell you where I live, but if I do, you must promise not to reveal my whereabouts or identity to any persons. It's top secret."

There was a gritty scratch of leather sole against linoleum. Cousin

Joe glanced up and smiled a brittle adult smile, eyes shifting uneasily to one side.

"Tommy?" It was Mr. Spiegelman. He was staring curiously at Cousin Joe, not in an unfriendly way, but with an interest that Tommy recognized as distinctly unmercantile. "I don't believe I know your friend."

"This . . . is . . . Joe," Tommy said. "I . . . I know him." The intrusion of Mr. Spiegelman into the comic book aisle rattled him. The dreamlike sense of calm with which he had reencountered, in a Long Island pharmacy, the cousin who had disappeared from a military transport off the coast of Virginia eight years before, abandoned him. Joe Kavalier was the great silencer of adults in the Clay household; whenever Tommy entered a room and everyone stopped talking, he knew they had been discussing Cousin Joe. Naturally, he had pestered them mercilessly for information on this man of mystery. His father generally refused to talk about the early days of the partnership that had produced the Escapist—"All that stuff kind of depresses me, buddy," he would say— but he could sometimes be induced to speculate on Joe's current location, the path of his wanderings, the likelihood of his ever coming back. Such talk, however, made Tommy's father nervous. He would reach for his cigarettes, a newspaper, the switch of the radio: anything to cut the conversation short.

It was his mother who had provided Tommy with most of what he knew about Joe Kavalier. From her he had learned the full story of the Escapist's birth, of the vast fortunes that the owners of Empire Comics had made off the work of his father and his cousin. His mother worried about money. The lost bonanza that the Escapist would have represented to the family if they had not been cheated by Sheldon Anapol and Jack Ashkenazy haunted her. "They were robbed," she often said. Generally, she confined such statements to moments when mother and son were alone, but occasionally, when Tommy's father was around, she would drag up his sorry history in the comic book business, of which Cousin Joe had once formed a key part, to bolster some larger, more abstruse point about the state of their lives that Tommy, clinging fiercely to his childish understanding of things, every time managed to miss. His mother, as it happened, was in possession of all manner of interesting facts about Joe. She knew where he had gone to school in Prague, when and by what route he had come to America, the places he had lived in Manhattan. She knew which comic books he had drawn, and what Dolores Del Rio had said to him one spring night in 1941 ("You dance like my father"). Tommy's mother knew that Joe had been indifferent to music and partial to bananas.

Tommy had always taken the particularity, the enduring intensity, of his mother's memories of Joe as a matter of course, but then one afternoon the previous summer, at the beach, he had overheard Eugene's mother talking to another neighborhood woman. Tommy, feigning sleep on his towel, lay eavesdropping on the hushed conversation. It was hard to follow, but one phrase caught his ear and lodged there for many weeks afterward.

"She's been carrying a torch for him all these years," the other woman said to Helene Begelman. She was speaking, Tommy knew, of his mother. For some reason, he thought at once of the picture of Joe, dressed in a tuxedo and brandishing a straight flush, that his mother kept on the vanity she had built for herself in her bedroom closet, in a small silver frame. But the full meaning of this expression, "carrying a torch," remained opaque to Tommy for several more months, until one day, listening with his father to Frank Sinatra sing the intro to "Guess I'll Hang My Tears Out to Dry," its sense had become clear to him; at the same instant, he realized he had known all his life that his mother was in love with Cousin Joe. The information pleased him for some reason. It seemed to accord with certain ideas he had formed about what adult life was really like from perusing his mother's stories in *Heartache, Sweetheart,* and *Love Crazy.*

Still, Tommy didn't really know Cousin Joe at all, and he had to admit, seeing him through Mr. Spiegelman's eyes, that he looked kind of shady, loitering there in his wrinkled suit, several day's growth on his chin. The coils of his hair sprang upward from his head like excelsior. He had a pale, blinking aspect, as if he didn't get out into the light too often. It was going to be hard to explain him to Mr. Spiegelman without revealing that he was a relative. And why shouldn't he reveal this? Why shouldn't he tell everyone he knew—in particular his parents—that Cousin Joe had returned from his wanderings? This was big news. If it later emerged that he had kept this from his mother and father, he would certainly get into trouble.

"This is my—uh—" he stammered, seeing the look of mistrust in Mr. Spiegelman's mild blue eyes grow keener. "My—" He was just about to say "cousin," and was even considering prefixing it with the melodramatic novelty of "long-lost," when a far more interesting narrative possibility occurred to him: clearly Cousin Joe had come looking especially for him. There had been that moment when their eyes met across the counter at Louis Tannen's Magic Shop, and then, over the next few days, somehow or other, Joe had tracked Tommy down, observed his habits, even followed him around, waiting for the opportune moment. Whatever his reasons for concealing his return from the rest of the family, he had chosen to reveal himself to Tommy. It would be wrong and foolish, Tommy thought, not to respect that choice. The heroes of John Buchan's novels never blurted out the truth in these situations. For them, a word was always sufficient, and discretion was the better part of valor. The same sense of melodramatic cliché prevented him from considering the possibility that his parents knew all about Cousin's Joe's return and had merely, as was their habit with interesting news, kept it from him. "My magic teacher," he finished. "I told him I'd meet him here. The houses all look alike, you know."

"That is certainly true," Joe said.

"Magic teacher," said Mr. Spiegelman. "That's a new one to me."

"You have to have a teacher, Mr. Spiegelman," Tommy said. "All the great ones do." Then Tommy did something that surprised him. He reached out and took hold of his cousin's hand. "Well, come on, I'll show you the way. You just have to count the corners. The houses don't really all look alike. We have eight different models."

They started past the racks of comics. Tommy remembered that he had meant to pick up the Summer 1953 issue of *Escapist Adventures,* but he was afraid that to do so might offend or even anger his cousin. So Tommy just kept on going, pulling on Joe's hand. As they walked past it, Tommy glanced at the cover of *Escapist Adventures* #54, on which the Escapist, blindfolded and bound to a thick post with his hands behind his back, faced a grim-visaged firing squad. The signal to fire was about to be given by, of all people, Tom Mayflower, leaning on his crutch, one arm raised high, his face diabolical and crazed. "HOW CAN THIS BE?" the Escapist was crying out in an agonized, jagged word balloon. "I'M ABOUT TO BE EXECUTED BY MY OWN ALTER EGO!!!"

Tommy felt powerfully teased by this provocative illustration, even though he knew perfectly well that, in the end, when you read the story the situation on the cover would turn out to be a dream, a misunderstanding, an exaggeration, or even an outright lie. With his free hand, he stood fingering the dime in the pocket of his dungarees.

Cousin Joe gave his other hand a squeeze. "*Escapist Adventures*," he said, his tone light and mocking.

"I was just looking at it," said Tommy.

"Get it," Joe said. He plucked the four current Escapist titles from the rack. "Get them all. Go ahead." He waved at the wall, his gesture wild, his eyes flashing. "I'll buy you any ones you want."

It was hard to say why, but this extravagant offer frightened Tommy. He began to regret his buccaneering leap into the unknown plans of his first cousin once removed.

"No, thank you," he said. "My dad gets me them free. All except for the Empire ones."

"Of course," said Joe. He coughed into his balled fist, and his cheeks turned red. "Well then. Just the one."

"Ten cents," said Mr. Spiegelman, ringing it up at the cash register, still eyeing Joe carefully. He took the dime Joe offered him and then held out his hand.

"Hal Spiegelman," he said. "Mister . . ."

"Kornblum," said Cousin Joe.

They walked out of the store and stood on the sidewalk in front of Spiegelman's. This sidewalk, and the stores that fronted it, were the oldest built things in Bloomtown. They had been here since the twenties, when Mr. Irwin Bloom was still working in his father's Queens cement concern and there had been nothing around here but potato fields and this tiny village of Manticock, which Bloomtown had since overwhelmed and supplanted. Unlike the blinding fresh sidewalks of Mr. Irwin Bloom's utopia, this one was cracked, grayish, leopard-spotted by years of spat-out chewing gum, trimmed with a fur of Island weeds. There was no oceanic parking lot in front, as there was at Bloomtown

Plaza; State Road 24 rumbled right past. The storefronts were narrow, clad in clapboard, their cornices a ragged mess of telephone wires and power lines overgrown with Virginia creeper. Tommy wanted to say something about all this to his cousin Joe. He wished he could tell him how the churned-up sidewalk, the hectoring crows on the bare Virginia creeper, and the irritable buzzing of Mr. Spiegelman's neon sign made him feel a kind of premonitory sadness for adult life, as if Bloomtown, with its swimming pools, jungle gyms, lawns, and dazzling sidewalks, were the various and uniform sea of childhood itself, from which this senescent hunk of the village of Manticock protruded like a wayward dark island. He felt as if there were a thousand things he wanted to tell Cousin Joe, the history of their lives since his disappearance, the painful tragedy of Eugene Begelman's departure for Florida, the origin of the mysterious Bug. Tommy had never been successful at explaining himself to adults because of their calamitous heedlessness, but there was a look of forbearance in Cousin Joe's eyes that made him think it would be possible to tell this man things.

"I wish you could come over tonight," he said. "We're having Mexican chili."

"That sounds good. Your mother was always a very good cook."

"Come over." Suddenly, he felt that he would never be able to keep Joe's return a secret from his parents. The question of Joe's whereabouts had been a worry to them for Tommy's entire life. It would be unfair to hide the news from them. It would be wrong. What was more, he had an immediate sense, seeing his cousin for the first time, of the man's *belonging* to them. "You have to."

"But I can't." Every time a car went by, Joe turned to looked at it, peering into its interior. "I'm sorry. I came out here to see you, but now I have to go."

"Why?"

"Because I—because I am out of practice. Maybe next time I will come over to your house, but not now." He looked at his watch. "My train is in ten minutes."

He held out his hand to Tommy, and they shook, but then Tommy surprised himself and put his arms around Cousin Joe. The smell of ashes in the scratchy fabric of his jacket swelled Tommy's heart.

"Where are you going?" Tommy asked.

"I can't tell you. It would not be fair. I can't to ask you to keep my secrets for me. After I go, you should tell your parents that you saw me, okay? I don't mind. They won't be able to find me. But to be fair to you, I can't tell you where I go."

"I won't tell them," said Tommy. "I swear to God, honest, I won't."

Joe put his hands on Tommy's shoulders and pushed him back a little so that they could look at each other.

"You like magic, eh?"

Tommy nodded. Joe reached into his pocket and took out a deck of playing cards. They were a French brand of cards called Petit Fou. Tommy had an identical deck at home, which he had bought at Louis Tannen's. The continental cards were smaller in size, and thus easier for small hands to manipulate. The kings and queens had a lowering, woodcut air of medieval chicanery, as if they were out to rob you with their curving swords and pikes. Joe slid the cards out of their gaudy box and handed them to Tommy.

"What can you do?" he said. "Can you do a pass?"

Tommy shook his head, feeling his cheeks grow warm. Somehow, his cousin had managed to cut directly to the center of Tommy's weakness as a card manipulator.

"I'm no good at them," he said, shuffling morosely through the deck. "Whenever it says in a trick that you need to make a pass, I just skip that one."

"Passes are hard," Joe said. "Well, easy to do. But not easy to do well."

This was far from news to Tommy, who had devoted two futile weeks at the beginning of the summer to the spread, the half, the fan, and the Charlier pass, among others, but never had been able to finesse the various halves and quarters of the deck quickly enough to prevent the central deception of any pass—the invisible transposition of two or more portions of the deck—from being patent even to the least discerning eye, in Tommy's case that of his mother, who, during his final attempt before he abandoned the pass once and for all in disgust, had rolled her eyes and said, "Well, sure, if you're going to switch the halves like that."

Joe lifted Tommy's right hand, examined the knuckles, turned it over, and studied the palm, scrutinizing it like a palmist.

"I know I need to learn it," Tommy began, "but I—"

"They are a waste of your time," Joe said, letting go of the hand. "Don't bother until your hands are bigger."

"What?"

"Let me show you this." He took the deck of cards, opened them into a smooth, many-pleated fan, and offered Tommy his choice of them. Tommy glanced instantaneously at the three of clubs, then poked it resolutely back into the deck. He was intent on the movements of Joe's long digits, determined to spot the pass when it came. Joe opened his hands, palm upward. The deck seemed to tumble in two neat sections from the left to the right, in the proper order, and as Joe's fingers rippled with magicianly flair, there was a baffling suggestion of a further tumble, so brief as to leave Tommy questioning whether he had imagined it or been fooled into seeing more than was there by the artful anemone flutter of his cousin's fingers and thumbs. It seemed, on balance, as though nothing at all had happened to the cards beyond a simple lazy transfer from left hand to right. Then Tommy was holding a card in his hands. He turned it over. It was the three of clubs.

"Hey," Tommy said. "Wow."

"Did you see it?"

Tommy shook his head.

"You didn't see the pass?"

"No!" Tommy could not help feeling slightly irritated.

"Ah," Joe said, with a faint bass hint of theatricality in his voice, "but there was no pass. That is the False Pass."

" 'The False Pass.' "

"Easy to do, not so very hard to do well."

"But I didn't—"

"You were watching my fingers. Don't watch my fingers. My fingers are liars. I have taught them to tell pretty lies."

Tommy liked this. There was a sharp yank on the cord that kept his impatient heart tethered in his chest.

"Could you—?" Tommy began, then silenced himself.

"Here," said Joe. He walked behind Tommy and stood over him, arms reaching around, the way Tommy's father had once done when showing him how to knot a necktie. He notched the deck into Tommy's left hand, arranging his fingers, then took him slowly through the four simple motions, a series of flips and half-turns, that were all one needed to get the bottom of the deck onto the top, with the dividing line between portions, naturally, being the chosen card, invisibly marked with the tip of the tip of the left pinky. He stood behind Tommy, watching him imitate the movements, the vapor of his breath billowing steadily and bitter with tobacco around Tommy's head as the boy struggled to produce the effect. After the sixth try, though it was sloppy and slow, he could already sense that, in the end, he was going to get hold of it. He felt a softening in his belly, a feeling of happiness that was hollowed, somehow, with a small, vacant pocket, at its center, of loss. He laid his head back against his cousin's flat stomach and looked up at his inverted face. Joe's eyes looked bewildered, regretful, troubled; but Tommy had once read in a book on optical illusions that all faces looked sad when viewed upside down.

"Thank you," Tommy said.

Cousin Joe took a step backward, away from him, and Tommy lost his step and nearly fell over. He caught himself and turned to face his cousin.

"You really do have to know how to do a pass," Cousin Joe said. "Even if it's only a false one."

6

THE FOLLOWING MONDAY, Tommy went swimming at the Bloomtown Community Swimming Pool and Recreation Center, which had just reopened following a polio scare. When he came home on his bike, he found a letter waiting for him, in a long business envelope whose printed return address was Louis Tannen's Magic Shop. He did not often receive mail, and he felt his mother watching him as he opened it.

"They're offering you a job," she guessed. She stood by the kitchen counter, pencil poised over a grocery list that she was making out. Sometimes it took his mother as long as an hour and a half to compose a relatively simple shopping list. He had his father's stoical tendency toward bullet-biting, but his mother was never one to hasten a task that she despised. "Louis Tannen died and left you the shop in his will."

Tommy shook his head, unable to smile at her jokes. He was so excited that the sheet of foolscap, with its typed mishmash of grandiose and exotic terms, rattled in his hands. He knew that the letter was all part of the plan, but for an instant he forgot what the plan was. He was baffled with delight.

"So what is it?"

Boldly, his stomach twisting, Tommy thrust the sheet of paper toward her. She lifted to the bridge of her nose the reading glasses she wore on a silver chain around her neck. These were a recent development, one that his mother hated. She never actually settled the glasses onto her nose, but merely held them up before her eyes, as though she wanted to have as little to do with them as possible.

"Garden of Blooming Silks? Empire of Pennies? Haunted Fountain Pen?" She squinted a little as she read the last word.

"Tricks," Tommy said, pulling the paper back from her lest she study it too closely. "It's a price list."

"I see that," she said, eyeing him. "Pen is spelled wrong. Two N's."

"Hmm," Tommy said.

"How many tricks do you need, honey? We just got you that demonic box of yours."

"I know," he said. "It's just for wishing."

"Well, wish away," she said, lowering the glasses once more. "But don't take your coat off. We're going to the A&P."

"May I please stay home? I'm old enough."

"Not today."

"Please."

He saw that she was probably going to accede—they had been experimenting lately with leaving him by himself—and that the only thing giving her pause was her detestation of grocery shopping.

"You're going to make me go into the heart of darkness alone?"

He nodded.

"You'll be all right?"

He nodded again, afraid that if he said anything more, he would somehow give it all away. She hesitated a moment longer, then shrugged one shoulder, picked up her purse, and went out.

He sat, holding the paper and envelope in his hands, until he heard the muttering of the Studebaker's engine and the scrape of its rear bumper as she backed out of the driveway. Then he got up. He got the scissors from the kitchen drawer, went to the kitchen cupboard, and took out a box of Post Toasties cereal. He saw that his mother, as she always did, had left without the grocery list. It was written, he noticed, on the back of a strip torn from a page of artwork—it looked like it might have been from *Kiss*—that she had given up on. A pretty blond girl hid behind an old beached rowboat, spying on something that was making her cry. It was probably her doctor boyfriend kissing her best friend the nurse, or something like that.

Tommy carried the scissors and the cereal to his room. There was half an inch of mostly crumbs left in the wax-paper bag, and he munched them dutifully. As he had done every morning for the last week, he studied the text printed on the back panel of the box, which described the scientifically formulated merits of the cereal in sober tones and which he now knew by heart. When he was through, he balled up the bag and threw it into the wastebasket. He picked up the scissors and carefully cut the back panel off the box. He laid it flat on his desk. With a pencil and a ruler, he drew a box around every instance of the words "Post Toasties." Then he took the scissors and cut on the lines he had marked. He took the panel, with its eleven rectangular holes, and fit it over the purported list of magic tricks from Tannen's.

That was how he learned that he was to catch the 10:04 train at the Bloomtown LIRR station on December 3, wearing an eye patch that would be supplied, under cover of constituting part of a spurious trick called Pieces o' Eight, in a second letter from Joe. Tommy was to sit in the last car, at the back, transfer at Jamaica, disembark at Penn Station, then walk the two long blocks to, of all places, the Empire State Building. He was to ride the elevator to the seventy-second floor, go to Suite 7203, and rap out his initials on the door in Morse code. If he encountered some family friend or other adult who questioned him and his destination, he was to point to the eye patch and say, simply, "Ophthalmologist."

Every Thursday for the next seven months, Tommy followed the routine established by that first secret letter from Joe. He left the house at eight forty-five, like every day, and started walking toward William Floyd Junior High, where he was in the seventh grade. At the corner of Darwin Avenue, however, he turned left instead of right, slipped through the Marchettis' backyard, crossed Rutherford Drive, and then took his sweet time (unless it was raining) ambling across the half-built east side of Bloomtown toward the bland new cinder-block-and-steel structure that had replaced the old Manticock station. He spent the day with Cousin Joe, in his strange digs nine hundred feet above Fifth Avenue, and left at three o'clock. Then, again following Joe's original prescription, he stopped outside Reliant Office Supplies on Thirty-third Street and typed out an excuse to hand to the principal, Mr. Savarese, the next morning, on a piece of paper that Joe had already furnished with a perfect simulacrum of Rosa Clay's signature.

In the first months, Tommy loved everything about the trips into New York. The cloak-and-dagger protocols, the risk of capture, and the soar-

ing view from the windows of Joe's home could not have been better designed to appeal to the mind of an eleven-year-old boy who spent large
parts of every day pretending to pose as the secret identity of a superpowered humanoid insect. He loved, first of all, the ride into the city. As
with many lonely children, his problem was not solitude itself but that
he was never left free to enjoy it. There were always well-meaning
adults trying to jolly him, to improve and counsel him, to bribe and ca-
jole and bully him into making friends, speaking up, getting some fresh
air; teachers poking and wheedling with their facts and principles,
when all he really needed was to be handed a stack of textbooks and left
alone; and, worst of all, other children, who could not seem to play their
games without including him if they were cruel ones or, if their games
were innocent, pointedly keeping him out. Tommy's loneliness had
found a strangely happy expression in the pitch and rumble of the LIRR
trains, the stale breath of the heat blowers, the warm oatmeal smell of
cigarettes, the sere featureless prospect from the windows, the hours
given over entirely to himself, his book, and his imaginings. He also
loved the city itself. Coming to and leaving Cousin Joe's, he would gorge
himself on hot dogs and cafeteria pie, price cigarette lighters and snap-
brim hats in store windows, follow the pushboys with their rustling
racks of furs and trousers. There were sailors and prizefighters; there
were bums, sad and menacing, and ladies in piped jackets with dogs in
their handbags. Tommy would feel the sidewalks hum and shudder as
the trains rolled past beneath him. He heard men swearing and singing
opera. On a sunny day, his peripheral vision would be spangled with
light winking off the chrome headlights of taxicabs, the buckles on
ladies' shoes, the badges of policemen, the handles of pushcart lunch-
wagons, the bulldog ornaments on the hoods of irate moving vans. This
was Gotham City, Empire City, Metropolis. Its skies and rooftops were
alive with men in capes and costumes, on the lookout for wrongdoers,
saboteurs, and Communists. Tommy was the Bug, on solitary patrol in
New York City, soaring up from the underground like a cicada, hopping
on his mighty hind legs along Fifth Avenue in hot pursuit of Dr. Hate or
the Finagler, creeping unnoticed as an ant amid the hurrying black-
and-gray herds of briefcase-carrying humans, whose crude mammalian existences he had sworn to protect and defend, before at last

dropping in on the secret aerial lair of one of his fellow masked crime-fighters, whom he sometimes dubbed the Eagle but who went more generally, in Tommy's fancy, by the moniker Secretman.

Secretman lived in a two-room office suite with four windows that looked out toward Bloomtown and Greenland. He had a desk, a chair, a drafting table, a stool, an armchair, a floor lamp, a complicated multi-band radio array festooned with yards of rambling antenna, and a special little cabinet whose many shallow drawers were filled with pens, pencils, twisted tubes of paint, erasers. There was no telephone; nor was there any stove, icebox, or proper bed.

"It's illegal," Cousin Joe told Tommy, the first time he visited. "You're not allowed to live in an office building. That's why you can't tell anyone I'm here."

Even then, before he learned the depth and extent of Secretman's superhuman powers of self-concealment, Tommy did not entirely believe this explanation. He sensed from the first, though he could not have expressed it—at his age, both the name and the experience of grief were not so much foreign to as latent in him, and as yet undetected—that something was the matter with, or had happened to, Joe. But he was too thrilled with his cousin's style of life, and the opportunity it afforded, to think the problem over too carefully. He watched as Joe went to a door on the other side of the room and opened it. It was a supply closet. There were stacks of paper and bottles of ink and other supplies. There were also a folded cot, an electric hot plate, two boxes of clothes, a canvas garment bag, and a small porcelain sink.

"Isn't there a janitor?" Tommy asked him on the second trip, having given the question some consideration. "Or a guard?"

"The janitor comes at five minutes before midnight, and I make sure everything is all right before he gets here. The guard and I are old friends by now."

Joe answered all of Tommy's questions about the particulars of his life, and showed him all of the work he had done since leaving the comic book business. But he declined to tell Tommy how long he had been holed up in the Empire State Building, and why he stayed there, and for what reason he kept his return a secret. He would not say why he never left his rooms except to purchase those supplies that could not be delivered, often wearing a false beard and sunglasses, or to pay regular visits to Tannen's back room, or why, one afternoon in July, he had made an exception and gone all the way out to Long Island. These were the mysteries of Secretman. Such questions had occurred to Tommy, in any case, only in a fragmentary and inarticulate way. After the first two visits, and for a while thereafter, he just took the entire situation for granted. Joe taught him card tricks, coin tricks, bits with handkerchiefs and needles and thread. They ate sandwiches brought in from the coffee shop downstairs. They shook hands in greeting and farewell. And, month after month, Tommy kept Secretman's secrets, though they were always bubbling up on his lips and trying to escape.

Tommy was caught only twice before the day on which it all came out. The first time he attracted the attention of an LIRR conductor with nystagmus who soon plumbed the shallow surface of Tommy's cover story. Tommy spent much of November 1953, as a result, confined to his bedroom. But in school—he considered it part of his punishment that they continued to send him to school during the month he was grounded—he consulted with Sharon Simchas, who was nearly blind in one eye. He sent his cousin an explanatory letter in care of Louis Tannen. On the Thursday following the lifting of the punishment, he set off again for Manhattan, equipped this time with the name and address of Sharon's doctor, one of the doctor's business cards, and a plausible diagnosis of strabismus. The wobble-eyed ticket puncher, however, never reappeared.

The second time he was caught came a month before the leap of the Escapist. Tommy settled into his seat at the back of the last car and opened his copy of Walter B. Gibson's *Houdini on Magic.* Cousin Joe had given it to him the week before; it was signed by the author, the creator of the Shadow, with whom Joe still played cards from time to time. Tommy had his shoes off, his eye patch on, and half a pack of Black Jack in his mouth. He heard a clatter of heels and looked up in time to see his mother, in her sealskin coat, stumble into the train car, out of breath, mashing her best black hat down onto her head with one arm. She was at the opposite end of a relatively full car, and there was a tall man positioned directly in her line of sight. She sat down without noticing her son. This stroke of good fortune took a moment to sink in. He glanced down at the book in his lap. The dark gray wad of gum lay in a small pool of saliva on the left-hand page; it had fallen out of his mouth. He put it back in and lay down across the pair of seats in his row, his face hidden in the hood of his coat and behind the screen of his book. His sense of guilt was exacerbated by the knowledge that Harry Houdini had idolized his own mother and doubtless never would have deceived or hidden from her. At Elmont, the conductor came by to check his ticket, and Tommy scrabbled up onto one elbow. The conductor gave him a skeptical look, and though Tommy had never seen him before, he tapped the patch with a fingertip and tried to echo the nonchalance of Cousin Joe.

"Ophthalmologist," he said.

The conductor nodded and punched his ticket. Tommy lay back down.

At Jamaica, he waited until the car emptied completely, then dashed out onto the platform. He got to the train for Penn Station just as the doors were closing. There was no time for him to try to guess which car his mother might have boarded. The idea of waiting for a later train did not occur to him until several minutes later, when—soon after she let go of his earlobe—it was suggested to him by his mother.

He ran right into her, almost literally, smelling her perfume an instant before a hard corner of her imitation-tortoiseshell handbag poked him in the eye.

"Oh!"

"Ouch!"

He stumbled backward. She grabbed him by the hood of his coat and dragged him toward her, then, tightening her grip, actually raised him half an inch off the ground, like a magician brandishing by the ears the rabbit he was about to dematerialize. His legs kicked at the pedals of an invisible bicycle. Her cheeks were rouged, her eyelids lined with black paint like a Caniff girl's.

"What are you doing? Why aren't you in school?"

"Nothing," he said. "I'm just . . . I was just . . ."

He glanced around the car. Naturally, all of the other passengers were staring at them. His mother lifted him a little higher and brought her face close to his. The perfume blowing off her was called Ambush.

It sat on a mirrored tray on her dresser, under a mantle of dust. He could not remember the last time he had smelled it on her.

"I can't—" she began, but then she couldn't finish her sentence because she had started to laugh. "Take off that damned eye patch," she said. She lowered him to the floor of the train and lifted the patch. He blinked. She flicked the patch back over his eye. Keeping her grip on the hood of his Mighty Mac, she dragged him down to the end of the car and pushed him into a seat. He was sure she was going to yell at him now, but once more she surprised him by sitting down beside him and putting her arms around him. She rocked back and forth, holding him tight.

"Thank you," she said, her voice throaty and rough, the way it sounded the morning after a bridge night when she had gone through a pack of cigarettes. "Thank you."

She nuzzled his head and he felt that her cheeks were wet. He sat back.

"What's the matter, Mom?"

She snapped open her purse and took out a handkerchief.

"Everything," she said. "What's the matter with you? How come you keep doing this? You were going to Tannen's again?"

"No."

"Don't lie, Tommy," she said. "Don't make this worse than it already is."

"Okay."

"You can't do this. You can't just skip school whenever you want to and go to Tannen's Magic Shop. You're eleven years old. You aren't a hoodlum."

"I know."

The train shuddered and the brakes screeched. They were pulling into Pennsylvania Station now. Tommy stood up and waited for her to get up and drag him off the train, across the platform, back out to Jamaica, and then home. But she didn't move. She just sat there, checking her eyes in the mirror of her compact, shaking her head ruefully at the mess her tears had made.

"Mom?" he said.

She looked up.

"I don't see any reason to waste these clothes and this hat just because you would rather saw a lady in half than learn fractions," she said.

"You mean I'm not punished?"

"I thought we could spend the day in the city. The two of us. Eat at Schrafft's. Maybe see a show."

"So you aren't going to punish me?"

She shook her head, once, dismissively, as if the question bored her. Then she took hold of his hand. "I don't see any reason to tell your father about any of this, do you, Tommy?"

"No, ma'am."

"Your father has enough to worry about without this."

"Yes, ma'am."

"We'll just keep this whole little incident to ourselves."

He nodded, though there was an eager look in her eyes that made him uneasy. He felt a sudden mad desire to be grounded again. He sat down.

"But if you ever do this again," she added, "I'll take all of your cards and wands and all that other nonsense and toss them into the incinerator."

He sat back and relaxed a little. As she promised, they lunched at Schrafft's, she on stuffed peppers, he on a Monte Cristo sandwich. They spent an hour in Macy's and then took in *It Should Happen to You* at the Trans-Lux Fifty-second. They caught the 4:12 for home. Tommy was asleep by the time his father came in, and said nothing the next morning when he came in to wake him for school. The encounter on the train was scattered in the cracks in their family. Once, long afterward, he summoned up the courage to ask his mother what she had been doing on that inbound train, dressed in her fanciest clothes, but she had merely put a finger to her lips and gone on struggling over another of the lists she always left behind.

On the day that everything had changed, Tommy and Cousin Joe were sitting in the outer room of the offices of Kornblum Vanishing Creams, where there was a false receptionist's desk. Tommy was in the armchair, a big wingback covered in a rough fabric like burlap, pool-table green, legs dangling, drinking a can of cream soda. Joe was lying on the floor with his arms folded under his head. Neither of them had said anything for what felt to Tommy like several minutes. They often passed long periods of their visits without saying very much. Tommy would read his book, and Cousin Joe would work on the comic book that he had been drawing, he said, ever since taking up residence in the Empire State Building.

"How's your father?" Joe said abruptly.

"Fine," said Tommy.

"That's what you always say."

"I know."

"He is worried about this book by Dr. Wertham, I imagine? *The Seduction of the Innocents*?"

"Real worried. Some senators are coming from Washington."

Joe nodded. "Is he very busy?"

"He's always busy."

"How many titles is he putting out?"

"Why don't you ask him yourself?" Tommy said, with an unintended sharpness.

There was no reply for a moment. Joe took a long drag on his cigarette. "Maybe I will," he said. "Some of these days."

"I think you should. Everybody really misses you."

"Your father said that he misses me?"

"Well, no, but he does," Tommy said. Lately, he had begun to worry about Joe. In the months since his foray into the wilds of Long Island, he had by his own admission been leaving the building less and less frequently, as if Tommy's visits had become a substitute for regular experience of the external world. "Maybe you could come home with me, on the train. It's nice. There's an extra bed in my room."

"A 'trundle' bed."

"Yeah."

"Could I use your Brooklyn Dodgers bath towel?"

"Yeah, sure! I mean, if you wanted."

Joe nodded. "Maybe I will, some of these days," he said again.

"Why do you keep staying here?"

"Why do you keep asking me that?"

"Well, don't you—doesn't it bother you to be in the same building with them? With Empire Comics? If they treated you so bad and all?"

"It doesn't bother me at all. I like being near to them. To the Escapist. And you never know. Some of these days I could maybe bother *them*."

He sat up as he said this, rolling onto his knees brusquely.

"What do you mean?"

Joe waved the question away with his cigarette, obscuring it in a cloud of smoke. "Never mind."

"Tell me."

"Forget it."

"I hate it when people do that," said Tommy.

"Yeah," said Joe. "So do I." He dropped the cigarette on the bare cement floor and ground it under the toe of his rubber sandal. "To tell the truth, I've never quite figured out just what I'm going to do. I'd like to embarrass them somehow. Make that Shelly Anapol look bad. Maybe I will dress up as the Escapist and . . . jump off this building! I have only to figure out some way to make it look like I jumped and killed myself." He smiled thinly. "But, of course, without it actually killing myself."

"Could you do that? What if it didn't work and you were, like, smashed flat as a pancake on Thirty-fourth Street?"

"That would certainly embarrass them," Joe said. He patted his chest. "Where did I leave—ah."

That was the moment when everything had changed. Joe stepped toward his drawing table to get his pack of Old Golds and tripped over Tommy's satchel. He pitched forward, reaching for the air in front of him, but before he could catch hold of anything, his forehead, with a loud, disturbingly wooden knock, hit the corner of his drafting table. He uttered one broken syllable and then hit the ground, hard. Tommy sat, waiting for him to curse or roll over or burst into tears. Joe didn't move. He lay facedown with his long nose bent against the floor, hands splayed beside him, motionless and silent. Tommy scrambled out of the chair and went to his side. He grabbed one of his hands. It was still warm. He took hold of Joe's shoulders and pulled him, rocking him twice and then rolling him over like a log. There was a small cut on his forehead, beside the pale crescent-moon scar of an old wound. The cut looked deep, although there was only a small amount of blood. Joe's chest rose and fell, shallow but steady, and his breath came rattling through his nose. He was out cold.

"Cousin Joe," Tommy said, giving him a shake. "Hey. Wake up. Please."

He went into the other room and opened the tap. He wet a ragged washcloth with cool water and carried it back to Joe. Gently, he dabbed at the uninjured portion of Joe's forehead. Nothing happened. He lay the towel on Joe's face and rubbed it vigorously around. Still, Joe lay breathing. A constellation of concepts that were vague to Tommy, comas and trances and epileptic fits, now began to trouble him. He had no idea what to do for his cousin, how to revive or help him, and now the cut was beginning to bleed more freely. What should Tommy do? His impulse was to go for help, but he had sworn to Joe that he would never reveal his presence to anyone. Still, Joe was a tenant of the building, illegal or not. His name must appear on some lease or document. The management of the building knew he was here. Would they be able or willing to help?

Then Tommy remembered a field trip he had taken here, back in the second grade. There was a large infirmary—a miniature hospital, the tour guide had called it—on one of the lower floors. There had been a pretty young nurse in white hat and shoes. She would know what to do. Tommy stood up and started for the door. Then he turned to look back at Joe lying on the floor. What would they do, though, once they had revived him and bandaged his cut? Would they put him in jail for sleeping in his office night after night? Would they think he was some kind of nut? *Was* he some kind of nut? Would they lock him up in a "nutbin"?

Tommy's hand was on the knob, but he couldn't bring himself to turn it. He was paralyzed; he had no idea of what to do. And now, for the first time, he appreciated Joe's dilemma. It was not that he did not wish further contact with the world in general, and the Clays in particular. Maybe that was how it had started out for him, in those strange days after the war, when he came back from some kind of secret mission— this was what Tommy's mother had said—and found out that his mother had been put to death in the camps. Joe had run away, escaped without a trace, and come here to hide. But now he was ready to come home. The problem was that he didn't know how to do it. Tommy would never know how much effort it cost Joe to make that trip out to Long Island, how ardent his desire was to see the boy, speak to him, hear his thin reedy voice. But Tommy could see that Secretman was trapped in his Chamber of Secrets, and that the Bug was going to have to rescue him.

At that moment, Joe groaned and his eyes fluttered open. He touched a finger to his forehead and looked at the blood that came away. He sat up on one elbow, rolling toward Tommy by the door. The look on Tommy's face must have been easy to read.

"I'm fine," Joe said, his voice thick. "Get back in here."

Tommy let go of the doorknob.

"You see," Joe said, rising slowly to his feet, "goes to show you shouldn't smoke. It's bad for the health."

"Okay," Tommy said, marveling at the strange resolve that he had formed.

When he left Joe that afternoon, he went to the Smith-Corona typewriter that was chained to a podium in front of Reliant Office Supplies. He rolled out the sheet of typing paper that was there so that people could try out the machine. It featured its regular weekly fable, one sentence long, of the quick brown fox and the lazy dog, and exhorted him that now was the time for all good men to come to the aid of their country. He rolled in the usual piece of stationery, at the bottom of which Joe had forged his mother's name. "Dear Mr. Savarese," he typed, using the tips of his index fingers. Then he stopped. He rolled out the paper and set it to one side. He looked up at the polished black stone of the storefront. His reflection looked back at him. He went over to open the chrome-handled door and was immediately intercepted by a thin, white-haired man whose trousers were belted at the diaphragm. This man often watched Tommy from the doorway of his shop as the boy typed out his excuses, and every week, Tommy thought the man was going to tell him to get lost. At the threshold of the store, which he had never crossed before, he hesitated. In the man's stiffened shoulders and the backward cant of his head, Tommy recognized his own manner when faced with a big strange dog or other sharp-toothed animal.

"Whaddaya want, sonny?" the man said.

"How much is a sheet of paper?"

"I don't sell paper by the sheet."

"Oh."

"Run along now."

"Well, how much for a box, then?"

"A box of what?"

"Paper."

"What kind of paper? What for?"

"A letter."

"Business? Personal? This is for you? You're going to write a letter?"

"Yes, sir."

"Well, what kind of a letter is it?"

Tommy considered the question for a moment, seriously. He didn't want to get the wrong kind of paper.

"A death threat," he said at last.

For some reason, this cracked the man up. He went around behind the sales counter and bent down to open a drawer.

"Here," he said, handing Tommy a sheet of heavy tan paper as smooth and cool to the touch as marzipan. "My best twenty-five-pound cotton rag." He was still laughing. "Make sure you kill them good, all right?"

"Yes, sir," said Tommy. He went back out to the typewriter, rolled in the sheet of fancy paper, and in half an hour typed the message that would eventually draw a crowd to the sidewalk around the Empire State Building. This was not necessarily the outcome he anticipated. He didn't know exactly what he was hoping for as he pecked out his missive to the editor of the New York *Herald-Tribune*. He was just trying to help Cousin Joe find his way home. He wasn't sure what it would all lead to, or if his letter, though it sounded awfully official and realistic to his own ears, would even be believed. When he finished, he carefully withdrew it from the typewriter and went back into the shop.

"How much for an envelope?" he said.

WHEN THEY GOT OUT on seventy-two, the boy led them to the left, past the doorways of an import company and a wig manufacturer, to a door whose opaque glass light was painted with the words KORNBLUM VANISHING CREAMS, INC. The boy turned to look at them, an eyebrow raised, seeing, the captain thought, if they got the joke, although Lieber wasn't sure just what the joke was supposed to be. Then the boy knocked. There was no reply. He knocked again.

"Where is he?" he said.

"Captain Harley."

They turned. A second building cop, Rensie, had joined them. He put a finger to his nose as if he was about to impart some delicate or embarrassing information.

"What is it?" Harley said warily.

"Our boy is up there," Rensie said. "The leaper. Up on the o.d."

"What?" Lieber stared at the kid, more bewildered than he considered it competent for a detective to be.

"Costume?" Harley said.

Rensie nodded. "Nice blue one," he said. "Big nose. Skinny. It's him."

"How'd he get there?"

"We don't know, Captain. Swear to God, we were watching *everything.* We had a man on the stairs, and another on the elevators. I don't know how he got in there. He just kind of showed up."

"Come on," Lieber said, already moving for the elevators. "And bring your son," he told Sammy Clay; you had to bring a cleat to lash them to. The boy's face had gone blank and bloodless with what looked to Lieber like astonishment. Somehow his hoax had come true.

They stepped into the elevator, with its elaborate chevrons and rays of inlaid wood.

"He's on the parapet?," said Captain Harley. Rensie nodded.

"Wait a minute," said Sammy. "I'm confused."

Lieber allowed as how he was a tiny bit confused himself. He had thought that the mystery of the letter to the *Herald-Tribune* was solved: it was a harmless if inscrutable stunt, pulled by an eleven-year-old boy. No doubt, he thought, he had been fairly inscrutable himself at that age. The kid was looking for attention; he was trying to make a point that no one outside the family could possibly understand. Then, somehow, it had appeared that this long-lost cousin whom Lieber had assumed until that point to be a dead man, run down on the shoulder of some godforsaken road outside of Cat Butt, Wyoming, was actually holed up, somehow or other, in an office suite on the seventy-second floor of the Empire State. And now it looked as if the kid was not the author of the letter after all; the Escapist had kept his grim promise to the city of New York.

They had gone fourteen stories—special express all the way—when Rensie said in a small, unwilling voice, "There are orphans."

"There are *what*?"

"Orphans," said Clay. He had his arm crooked around his kid's neck in a fatherly display of reproof masquerading as solicitude. It was an embrace that said *Wait till I get you home.* "Why are there—?"

"Yes, Sergeant," Harley said. "Why are there?"

"Well, it didn't look like the, uh, the gentleman in the, uh, the blue suit was going to show," Rensie said. "And the little brats came all the way down from Watertown. Ten hours on a bus."

"An audience. Of little children," Harley said. "Perfect."

"What about you?" Lieber said to the boy. "You confused, too?"

The boy stared, then nodded slowly.

"You want to have your wits about you, Tom," Lieber said. "We need you to talk to this uncle of yours."

"First cousin," Clay said. He cleared his throat. "Once removed."

"Maybe you could talk to your first cousin once removed about those rubber bands," Rensie said. "That's a new one on me."

"Rubber bands," Captain Harley said. "And orphans." He rubbed at the wrecked half of his face. "I'm guessing there's also a nun?"

"A padre."

"Okay," said Captain Harley. "Well, that's something."

8

TWENTY-TWO ORPHANS from the Orphanage of St. Vincent de Paul huddled on the windswept roof of the city, a thousand feet up. Gray light was smeared across the sky like ointment on a bandage. The heavy steel zippers of the children's dark blue corduroy coats—donated by a Watertown department store the previous winter, along with the twenty-two chiming pairs of galoshes—were zipped tightly against the April chill. The children's two keepers, Father Martin and Miss Mary Catherine Macomb, circled the children like a couple of nipping sheepdogs, trying to cinch them with their voices and hands. Father Martin's eyes watered in the sharp breeze, and Miss Macomb's thick arms were stippled with gooseflesh. They were not excitable people, but things had gotten out of hand and they were shouting.

"Stay back!" Miss Macomb told the children, several hundred times.

"For pity's sake, man," Father Martin told the leaper, "come down."

There was something stunned in the faces of the children, blinking and tentative. The slow, dull, dark submarine of the lives in which they were the human cargo had abruptly surfaced. Their blood was filled with a kind of crippling nitrogen of wonder. Nobody was smiling or laughing, though with children, entertainment often seemed to be a grave business.

Atop the thick concrete parapet of the eighty-sixth floor, like a bright jagged hole punched in the clouds, balanced a smiling man in a mask and a gold-and-indigo suit. The suit clung to his lanky frame, dark blue with an iridescent glint of silk. He had on a pair of golden swim trunks, and on the front of his blue jersey was a thick golden appliqué, like the initial on a letterman's jacket, in the shape of a skeleton key. He wore a pair of soft gold boots, rather shapeless, with thin rubber soles. The trunks were nubbly and had a white streak on the seat, as if their wearer had once leaned against a freshly painted doorjamb. The tights were laddered and stretched out at the knees, the jersey sagged badly at the elbows, and the rubber soles of the flimsy boots were cracked and spotted with grease. His broad chest was girdled by a slender cord, studded with thousands of tiny knots, looped under his armpits, then stretched across the open-air promenade some twenty feet to the steel prong of an ornamental sun ray that jutted from the roof of the observation lounge. He gave the knotted cord a tug, and it twanged out a low D-flat.

He was putting on a show for them, for the children and for the policemen who had gathered at his feet, cursing and cajoling and begging him to climb down. He was promising a demonstration of human flight of the sort still routinely found, even in this diminished era of superheroism, in the pages of comic books.

"You will see," he cried. "A man can fly."

He demonstrated the strength of the elastic rope, woven out of eight separate strands, each strand made up of forty of the extra-long, extra-thick rubber bands he had picked up at Reliant Office Supplies. The policemen remained suspicious, but they were not sure what to believe. The midnight-blue costume, with its key symbol and its weird Hollywood sheen, affected their judgment. And then there was Joe's professional manner, still remarkably smooth and workmanlike after so many years of disuse. His confidence in his ability to pull off the trick of leaping from the roof, plunging to a maximum of 162 feet in the direction of the far-distant sidewalk, then reascending, tugged skyward by the enormous rubber band, to alight smiling at the feet of the policemen, appeared to be absolute.

"The children won't be able to see me flying," Joe said, the glint of misdirection in his eyes. "Let them come to the edge."

The children agreed, pressing forward. Horrified, Miss Macomb and Father Martin held them back.

"Joe!" It was Sammy. He and various policemen, uniformed and plainclothes, came stumbling in a confusion of waving arms out onto the windswept promenade. They were led by a wary-looking Tommy Clay.

When Joe saw the boy, his son, join the motley crowd that had con-vened on the observation deck to observe as a rash and imaginary promise was fulfilled, he suddenly remembered a remark that his teacher Bernard Kornblum had once made.

"Only love," the old magician had said, "could pick a nested pair of steel Bramah locks."

He had offered this observation toward the end of Joe's last regular visit to the house on Maisel Street, as he rubbed a dab of calendula oint-ment into the skin of his raw, peeling cheeks. Generally, Kornblum said very little during the final portion of every lesson, sitting on the lid of the plain pine box that he had bought from a local coffin maker, smok-ing and taking his ease with a copy of *Di Cajt* while, inside the box, Joe lay curled, roped and chained, permitting himself sawdust-flavored sips of life through his nostrils, and making terrible, minute exertions. Kornblum sat, his only commentary an occasional derisive blast of flat-ulence, waiting for the triple rap from within which signified that Joe had loosed himself from cuffs and chains, prized out the three sawn-off dummy screw heads in the left-hand hinge of the lid, and was ready to emerge. At times, however, if Joe was particularly dilatory, or if the temptation of a literally captive audience proved too great, Kornblum would begin to speak, in his coarse if agile German—always limiting himself, however, to shoptalk. He reminisced fondly about perfor-mances in which he had, through bad luck or foolishness, nearly been killed; or recalled, in apostolic and tedious detail, one of the three golden occasions on which he had been fortunate enough to catch the act of his prophet, Houdini. Only this once, just before Joe attempted his ill-fated plunge into the Moldau, had Kornblum's talk ever wandered from the path of professional retrospection into the shadowed, leafy margins of the personal.

He had been present, Kornblum said—his voice coming muffled through the inch of pine plank and the thin canvas sack in which Joe was cocooned—for what none but the closest confidants of the Hand-cuff King, and the few canny confreres who witnessed it, knew to be the hour when the great one failed. This was in London, Kornblum said, in 1906, at the Palladium, after Houdini had accepted a public challenge to free himself from a purportedly inescapable pair of handcuffs. The challenge had been made by the *Mirror* of London, which had discovered a locksmith in the north of England who, after a lifetime of tinkering, had devised a pair of manacles fitted with a lock so convoluted and thorny that no one, not even its necromantic inventor, could pick it. Kornblum described the manacles, two thick steel circlets inflexibly welded to a cylindrical shaft. Within this rigid shaft lay the sinister mechanism of the Manchester locksmith—and here a tone of awe, even horror, entered Kornblum's voice. It was a variation on the Bramah, a notoriously intransigent lock that could be opened—and even then with difficulty—only by a long, arcane, tubular key, intricately notched at one end. Devised by the Englishman Joseph Bramah in the 1760s, it had gone unpicked, inviolate, for over half a century until it was finally cracked. The lock that now confronted Houdini, on the stage of the Palladium, consisted of *two* Bramah tubes, one nested inside the other, and could be opened only by a bizarre double key that looked something like the collapsed halves of a telescope, one notched cylinder protruding from within another.

As five thousand cheering gentlemen and ladies, the young Kornblum among them, looked on, the Mysteriarch, in black cutaway and waistcoat, was fitted with the awful cuffs. Then, with a single, blank-faced, wordless nod to his wife, he retreated to his small cabinet to begin his impossible work. The orchestra struck up "Annie Laurie." Twenty minutes later, wild cheering broke out as the magician's head and shoulders emerged from the cabinet; but it turned out that Houdini wanted only to get a look at the cuffs, which still held him fast, in better light. He ducked back inside. The orchestra played the Overture to *Tales of Hoffmann*. Fifteen minutes later, the music died amid cheers as Houdini stepped from the cabinet. Kornblum hoped against hope that the master had succeeded, though he knew perfectly well that when the first, single-barreled Bramah was, after sixty years, finally picked, it had taken the successful lock-pick, an American master by the name of Hobbs, *two full days* of continuous effort. And now it turned out that Houdini, sweating, a queasy smile on his face, his collar snapped and dangling free at one end, had merely—oddly—come out to announce that, though his knees hurt from crouching in the cabinet, he was not yet ready to throw in the towel. The newspaper's representative, in the interests of good sportsmanship, allowed a cushion to be brought, and Houdini retreated to his cabinet once more.

When Houdini had been in the box for nearly an hour, Kornblum began to sense the approach of defeat. An audience, even one so firmly on the side of its hero, would wait only so long while the orchestra cycled, with an air of increasing desperation, through the standards and popular tunes of the day. Inside his cabinet, the veteran of five hundred houses and ten thousand turns could doubtless sense it, too, as the tide of hope and goodwill flowing from the galleries onto the stage began to ebb. In a daring display of showmanship, he emerged once again, this time to ask if the newspaper's man would consent to remove the cuffs long enough for the magician to take off his coat. Perhaps Houdini was hoping to learn something from watching as the cuffs were opened and then closed again; perhaps he had calculated that his request, after due consideration, would be refused. When the gentleman from the newspaper regretfully declined, to loud hisses and catcalls from the audience, Houdini pulled off a minor feat that was, in its way, among the finest bits of showmanship of his career. Wriggling and contorting himself, he managed to pluck from the pocket of his waistcoat a tiny penknife, then painstakingly transfer it to, and open it with, his teeth. He shrugged and twisted until he had worked his cutaway coat up over to the front of his head, where the knife, still clenched between his teeth, could slice it, in three great sawing rasps, in two. A confederate tore the sundered halves away. After viewing this display of pluck and panache, the audience was bound to him as if with bands of steel. And, Kornblum said, in the uproar, no one noticed the look that passed between the magician and his wife, that tiny, quiet woman who had stood to one side of the stage as the minutes passed, and the band played, and the audience watched the faint rippling of the cabinet's curtain.

After the magician had reinstalled himself, coatless now, in his dark box, Mrs. Houdini asked if she might not prevail upon the kindness and forbearance of their host for the evening to bring her husband a glass of water. It had been an hour, after all, and as anyone could see, the closeness of the cabinet and the difficulty of Houdini's exertions had taken a certain toll. The sporting spirit prevailed; a glass of water was brought, and Mrs. Houdini carried it to her husband. Five minutes later, Houdini stepped from the cabinet for the last time, brandishing the cuffs over his head like a loving cup. He was free. The crowd suffered a kind of painful, collective orgasm—a *"Krise,"* Kornblum called it—of delight and relief. Few remarked, as the magician was lifted onto the shoulders of the referees and notables on hand and carried through the theater, that his face was convulsed with tears of rage, not triumph, and that his blue eyes were incandescent with shame.

"It was in the glass of water," Joe guessed, when he had managed to free himself at last from the far simpler challenge of the canvas sack and a pair of German police cuffs gaffed with buckshot. "The key."

Kornblum, massaging the bands of raw skin at Joe's wrists with his special salve, nodded at first. Then he pursed his lips, thinking it over, and finally shook his head. He stopped rubbing at Joe's arms. He raised his head, and his eyes, as they did only rarely, met Joe's.

"It was Bess Houdini," he said. "She knew her husband's face. She could read the writing of failure in his eyes. She could go to the man from the newspaper. She could beg him, with the tears in her eyes and the blush on her bosom, to consider the ruin of her husband's career when put into the balance with nothing more on the other side than a good headline for the next morning's newspaper. She could carry a glass of water to her husband, with the small steps and the solemn face of the wife. It was not the key that freed him," he said. "It was the wife. There was no other way out. It was impossible, even for Houdini." He stood up. "Only love could pick a nested pair of steel Bramah locks." He wiped at his raw cheek with the back of his hand, on the verge, Joe felt, of sharing some parallel example of liberation from his own life.

"Have you—did you ever—?"

"That terminates the lesson for today," Kornblum said, snapping shut the lid of the box of ointment, and then managing to meet Joe's eyes again, not, this time, without a certain tenderness. "Now, go home."

Afterward, Joe found there was some reason to doubt Kornblum's account. The famous London *Mirror* handcuff challenge had taken place, he learned, at the Hippodrome, not the Palladium, and in 1904, not 1906. Many commentators, Joe's chum Walter B. Gibson among them, felt that the entire performance, including the pleas for light, water, time, a cushion, had been arranged beforehand between Houdini and the newspaper; some even went so far as to argue that Houdini himself had designed the cuffs, and that he had coolly whiled away his time of purported struggling in his cabinet, Kornblum-like, by reading the newspaper or by humming contentedly along with the orchestra down in the pit.

Nevertheless, when he saw Tommy step out onto the tallest rooftop in the city, wearing a small, horrified smile, Joe felt the passionate, if not the factual, truth behind Kornblum's dictum. He had returned to New York years before, with the intention of finding a way to reconnect, if possible, with the only family that remained to him in the world. Instead he had become immured, by fear and its majordomo, habit, in his cabinet of mysteries on the seventy-second floor of the Empire State Building, serenaded by a tirelessly vamping orchestra of air currents and violin winds, the trumpeting of foghorns and melancholy steamships, the plangent continuo of passing DC-3s. Like Harry Houdini, Joe had failed to get out of his self-created trap; but now the love of a boy had sprung him, and drawn him at last, blinking, before the footlights.

"It's a stunt!" cried an old blond trooper whom Joe recognized as Harley, chief of the building police force.

"It's a gimmick," said a thickset, younger man standing beside Sammy. A plainclothesman, by the look of him. "Is that what it is?"

"It's a great big pain in the ass," Harley said.

Joe was shocked to see how haggard Sammy's face had grown; he was pale as dough, and at thirty-two he seemed to have acquired at last the deep-set eyes of the Kavaliers. He had not changed much, and yet somehow he looked entirely different. Joe felt as if he were looking at a clever impostor. Then Rosa's father emerged from the observatory. With his dyed penny-red hair and the eternal youthfulness of cheek enjoyed by some fat men, he did not appear to have changed at all, though he was, for some reason, dressed like George Bernard Shaw.

"Hello, Mr. Saks," Joe said.

"Hello, Joe." Saks was relying, Joe noticed, on a silver-topped walking stick, in a way that suggested the cane was not (or not merely) an affectation. So that was one change. "How are you?"

"Fine, thank you," Joe said. "And you?"

"We are well," he said. He was the only person on the entire deck—children included—who looked entirely delighted by the sight of Joe Kavalier, standing on the high shoulder of the Empire State Building in a suit of blue long johns. "Still steeped in scandal and intrigue."

"I'm glad," Joe said. He smiled at Sammy. "You've put on weight?"

"A little. For Christ's sake, Joe. What are you doing standing up there?"

Joe turned his attention to the boy who had challenged him to do this, to stand here at the tip of the city in which he had been buried. Tommy's face was nearly expressionless, but it was riveted on Joe. He looked as if he was having a hard time believing what he saw. Joe shrugged elaborately.

"Didn't you read my letter?" he said to Sammy.

He threw out his arms behind him. Hitherto he had approached this stunt with the dry dispassion of an engineer, researching it, talking it over with the boys at Tannen's, studying Sidney Radner's secret monograph on Hardeen's abortive but thrilling Paris Bridge Leap of 1921.* Now, to his surprise, he found himself aching to fly.

"It said you were going to kill yourself," Sammy said. "It didn't say anything about doing a Human Yo-Yo act."

Joe lowered his arms; it was a good point. The problem, of course, was that Joe had not *written* the letter. Had he done so, he would not have promised, in all likelihood, to commit public suicide in a moth-eaten costume. He recognized the idea as his own, of course, filtered through the wildly elaborating imagination that, more than anything else—more than the boy's shock of black hair or delicate hands or guileless gaze, haunted by tenderness of heart and an air of perpetual disappointment—reminded Joe of his dead brother. But he had felt it necessary, in fulfilling the boy's challenge, to make a few adjustments here and there.

"The possibility of dying is small," Joe said, "but it is of course there."

"And it's just about the only way for you to avoid arrest, Mr. Kavalier," said the plainclothesman.

* *The Paris Bridge-Leap of 1921: A Memoir of Hardeen,* New York; privately printed, 1935. Now in the collection of Prof. Kenneth Silverman.

"I'll keep that in mind," Joe said. He threw his arms back again.

"Joe!" Sammy ventured a hesitant couple of inches toward Joe. "God damn it, you know damn well *the Escapist doesn't fly!*"

"That's what I said," said one of the orphans knowledgeably.

The policemen exchanged a look. They were getting ready to rush the parapet.

Joe stepped backward into the air. The cord sang, soaring to a high, bright C. The air around it seemed to shimmer, as with heat. There was a sharp twang, and they heard a brief, muffled smack like raw meat on a butcher block, a faint groan. The descent continued, the cord drawing thinner, the knots pulling farther apart, the note of elongation reaching into the dog frequencies. Then there was silence.

"Ow!" Captain Harley slapped the back of his head as if a bee had stung him. He looked up, then down, then jumped quickly to one side. Everybody looked at his feet. There, to one side, wobbly and distended, lay the elastic cord, tipped by the severed loop that had engirdled Joe Kavalier's chest.

All warnings and prohibitions were forgotten. The children and adults ran to the parapet, and those lucky or industrious enough to get themselves up onto it peered down at the man lying spread-eagled, a twisted letter K, on the projecting roof-ledge of the eighty-fourth floor.

The man lifted his head.

"I'm all right," he said. Then he lowered his head once more to the gray pebbled surface onto which he had fallen, and closed his eyes.

9

THE BEARERS CARRIED HIM DOWN to the subterranean
garage of the building, where an ambulance had been waiting
since four o'clock that afternoon. Sammy rode down with them in
the elevator, having left Tommy with his grandfather and the captain of
the building police, who would not permit the boy to ride along. Sammy
was a little hesitant about leaving Tommy, but it seemed crazy just
to let Joe be taken away again like that, not ten minutes after his
reappearance. Let the boy spend a few minutes in the hands of the
police; maybe it would do him good.

Every time Joe shut his eyes, the bearers told him rather curtly to
wake up. They were afraid that he might have a concussion.

"Wake up, Joe," Sammy told him.

"I am awake."

"How are you doing?"

"Fine," Joe said. He had bit his lip, and there was blood from it on his
cheek and shirt collar. It was the only blood that Sammy could see.
"How are you?"

Sammy nodded.

"I read *Weird Date* every month," Joe said. "It's very good writing,
Sam."

"Thanks," Sammy said. "Praise means so much when it comes from
a lunatic."

"*Sea Yarns* is also good."

"Think so?"

"I always learn something about boats or something."

"I do a lot of research." Sammy took out his handkerchief and dabbed
at the bloody spot on Joe's lip, remembering the days of Joe's war

against the Germans of New York. "It's all in my face, by the way," he said.

"What is?"

"The weight you mentioned. It's all in my face. I still swing the dumbbells every morning. Feel my arm."

Joe raised his arm, wincing a little, and gave Sammy's biceps a squeeze.

"Big," Joe said.

"You don't look so swell yourself, you know. In this ratty old getup."

Joe smiled. "I was hoping Anapol would see me in it. It was going to be like a bad dream coming true."

"I have a feeling a lot of his bad dreams are about to come true," Sammy said. "When did you take it, anyway?"

"Two nights ago. I'm sorry. I hope you don't mind. I realize that it . . . has sentimental value for you."

"It doesn't mean anything special to me."

Joe nodded, watching his face, and Sammy looked away.

"I'd like a cigarette," Joe said.

Sammy fished one out of his jacket and stuck it between Joe's lips.

"I'm sorry," Joe said.

"Are you?"

"About Tracy, I mean. I know it was a long time ago but I . . ."

"Yeah," Sammy said. "Everything was a long time ago."

"Everything I'm sorry about, anyway," Joe said.

10

THE VIEW OUT THE WINDOWS was pure cloud bank, a gray
woolen sock pulled down over the top of the building. On the
walls of Joe's strange apartment hung sketches of the head of a
rabbi, a man with fine features and a snowy white beard. The studies
were tacked up with pushpins, and they depicted this noble-looking
gentleman in a variety of moods: rapturous, commanding, afraid.
There were fat books on the tables and chairs; thick reference volumes
and tractates and dusty surveys: Joe had been doing a little research
himself. Sammy saw, stacked neatly in a corner, the wooden crates in
which Joe had always kept his comics—only there were ten times as
many as he remembered. Over the room lay the smell of long occupation by a solitary man: burned coffee, hard sausage, dirty linens.

"Welcome to the Bat Cave," Lieber said when Sammy came in.

"Actually," Longman Harkoo said, "it's apparently known as the
Chamber of Secrets."

"Is it?" Sammy said.

"Well, uh, that's what I call it," said Tommy, coloring. "But not really."

You came into the Chamber of Secrets from a small anteroom that
had been painstakingly decorated to simulate the reception area of a
small but going concern. It had a steel desk and typist's table, an armchair, a filing cabinet, a telephone, a hat stand. On the desk stood a
nameplate promising the daily presence behind it of a Miss Smyslenka,
and a vase of dried flowers, and a photograph of Miss Smyslenka's grinning baby, played by a six-month-old Thomas E. Clay. On the wall was
a large commercial painting of a sturdy-looking factory, luminous in
the rosy glow of a New Jersey morning, chimneys trailing pretty blue

smoke. KORNBLUM VANISHING CREAMS, read the engraved label affixed to the bottom of the frame, HO-HO-KUS, NEW JERSEY.

No one, not even Tommy, was quite sure how long Joe had been living in the Empire State Building, but it was clear that during this time he had been working very hard and reading a lot of comic books. On the floor stood ten piles of Bristol board, every sheet in each pile covered in neat panels of pencil drawings. At first Sammy was too overwhelmed by the sheer number of pages—there must have been four or five thousand—to look very closely at any of them, but he did notice that they seemed to be uninked. Joe had been working in a variety of gauges of lead, letting his pencils do the tricks of light and mass and shadow that were usually pulled off with ink.

In addition to the rabbis, there were studies of organ-grinders, soldiers in breastplates, a beautiful girl in a headscarf, in various attitudes and activities. There were buildings and carriages, street scenes. It didn't take Sammy long to recognize the spiky elaborate towers and crumbling archways of what must be Prague, lanes of queer houses huddled in the snow, a bridge of statues casting a broken moonlit shadow on a river, twisting alleyways. The characters, for the most part, appeared to be Jews, old-fashioned, black-garbed, drawn with all of Joe's usual fluidity and detail. The faces, Sammy noticed, were more specific, quirkier, uglier, than the lexicon of generic comic book mugs that Joe had learned and then exploited in all his old work. They were human faces, pinched, hungry, the eyes anticipating horror but hoping for something more. All except for one. One character, repeated over and over in the sketches on the walls, had barely any face at all, the conventional V's and hyphens of a comic physiognomy simplified to almost blank abstraction.

"The Golem," Sammy said.

"Apparently he was writing a novel," Lieber said.

"He was," Tommy said. "It's all about the Golem. Rabbi Judah Ben Beelzebub scratched the word 'truth' into his forehead and he came to life. And one time? In Prague? Joe saw the real Golem. His father had it in a closet in their house."

"It really does look marvelous," Longman said. "I can't wait to read it."

"A comic book novel," Sammy said. He thought of his own by-now legendary novel, *American Disillusionment,* that cyclone which, for years, had woven its erratic path across the flatlands of his imaginary life, always on the verge of grandeur or disintegration, picking up characters and plotlines like houses and livestock, tossing them aside and moving on. It had taken the form, at various times, of a bitter comedy, a stoical Hemingwayesque tragedy, a hard-nosed lesson in social anatomy like something by John O'Hara, a bare-knuckles urban *Huckleberry Finn.* It was the autobiography of a man who could not face himself, an elaborate system of evasion and lies unredeemed by the artistic virtue of self-betrayal. It had been two years now since his last crack at the thing, and until this very instant he would have sworn that his ancient ambitions to be something more than the hack scribbler of comic books for a fifth-rate house were as dead, as the saying went, as vaudeville. "My God."

"Come on, Mr. Clay," Lieber said. "You can ride over to the hospital with me."

"Why are you going to the hospital?" Sammy said, though he knew the answer.

"Well, I feel pretty strongly that I have to arrest him. I hope you understand."

"*Arrest* him?" Longman said. "What for?"

"Disturbing the peace, I suppose. Or maybe we'll get him for illegal habitation. I'm sure the building is going to want to press charges. I don't know. I'll figure it out on the way over."

Sammy saw his father-in-law's smirk shrink down to a hard little button, and his generally genial blue eyes went dead and glassy. It was an expression Sammy had seen before, on the floor of Longman's gallery,* when he was dealing with a painter who overvalued his own work or some lady with a title and most of a dead civet around her shoulders, who was better equipped with money than judgment. Rosa called it, in reference to her father's origins in retail, "his rug-merchant stare."

---

* Les Organes du Facteur moved to Fifty-seventh Street after the war, three doors down from Carnegie Hall, an inexorable journey uptown and into cultural irrelevance in the last moments before Surrealism was overwhelmed by the surging tribes of Action, Beat, and Pop.

"We'll see about that," Longman said, with deliberate indiscretion and a sideways look at Sammy. "Surrealism has agents at every level of the machinery of power. I sold a painting to the mayor's mother last week."

Your father-in-law is kind of a blowhard, said Detective Lieber's eyes. I know it, Sammy's replied.

"Excuse me." There was a new visitor to the offices of Kornblum Vanishing Creams. He was young, good-looking in a featureless governmental way, wearing a dark blue suit. In one hand he held a long white envelope.

"Sam Clay?" he said. "I'm looking for Mr. Sam Clay. I was told I might find him—"

"Here." Sammy came forward and took the envelope from the young man. "What's this?"

"That is a congressional subpoena." The young man nodded to Lieber, touching the brim of his hat with two fingers. "Sorry to disturb you gentlemen," he said.

Sammy stood for a moment, tap-tap-tapping the envelope against his hand.

"You better call Mom," said Tommy.

ROSE SAXON, the Queen of Romance Comics, was at her drawing board in the garage of her house in Bloomtown, New York, when her husband phoned from the city to say that, if it was all right with her, he would be bringing home the love of her life, whom she had all but given up for dead.

Miss Saxon was at work on the text of a new story, which she intended to begin laying out that night, after her son went to bed. It would be the lead story for the June issue of *Kiss Comics*. She planned to call it "The Bomb Destroyed My Marriage." The story would be based on an article that she had read in *Redbook* about the humorous difficulties of being married to a nuclear physicist employed by the government at a top-secret facility in the middle of the New Mexico desert. She was not writing so much as planning out her panels, one by one, at the typewriter. Over the years, Sammy's scripts had grown no less detailed but looser; he never bothered with telling an artist what to draw. Rosa couldn't operate that way; she hated working from Sammy's scripts. She needed to have everything figured out in advance—storyboarded, they called it in Hollywood—shot by shot, as it were. Her scripts were a tightly numbered series of master shots, the shooting scripts for ten-cent epics that, in their sparse elegance of design, elongated perspectives, and deep focus, somewhat resemble, as Robert C. Harvey has pointed out,* the films of Douglas Sirk. She worked at a bulky Smith-Corona, typing with such intense slowness that when her boss and husband called, she did not at first hear the ringing phone.

Rosa had gotten her start in comics soon after Sammy's return to the

* In his excellent *The Art of the Comic Book: An Aesthetic History.*

business, after the war. Upon taking over the editor's desk at Gold Star, Sammy's first move had been to clear out many of the subcompetents and alcoholics who littered the staff there. It was a bold and necessary step, but it left him with an acute shortage of artists, in particular of inkers.

Tommy had started kindergarten, and Rosa was just beginning to understand the true horror of her destiny, the arrant purposelessness of her life whenever her son was not around, one day when Sammy came home at lunch, harried and frantic, with an armload of Bristol board, a bottle of Higgins ink, and a bunch of #3 brushes, and begged Rosa to help him by doing what she could. She had stayed up all night with the pages—it was some dreadful Gold Star superhero strip, *The Human Grenade* or *The Phantom Stallion*—and had the job finished by the time Sammy left for work the next morning. The reign of the Queen had commenced.

Rose Saxon had emerged slowly, lending her ink brush at first only now and then, unsigned and uncredited, to a story or a cover that she would spread out on the dinette table in the kitchen. Rosa had always had a steady hand, a strong line, a good sense of shadow. It was work done in a kind of unreflective crisis mode—whenever Sammy was in a jam or shorthanded—but after a while, she realized that she had begun to crave intensely the days when Sammy had something for her to do.

Then one night, as they lay in bed, talking in the dark, Sammy told her that her brushwork already far exceeded that of the best people he could afford to hire at lowly Gold Star. He asked her if she had ever given any thought to penciling; to layouts; to actually writing and draw-ing comic book stories. He explained to her that Simon and Kirby were just then having considerable success with a new kind of feature they'd cooked up, based partly on teen features like *Archie* and *A Date with Judy* and partly on the old true-romance pulps (the last of the old pulp genres to be exhumed and given new life in the comics). It was called *Young Romance*. It was aimed at women, and the stories it told were centered on women. Women had been neglected until now as readers of comic books; it seemed to Sammy that they might enjoy one that had actually been *written and drawn* by one of their own. Rosa had accepted Sammy's proposal at once, with a flush of gratitude whose power was undiminished even now.

She knew what it had meant to Sammy to return to comics and take the editor's job at Gold Star. It was the one moment in the course of a long and interesting marriage when Sammy had stood on the point of following his cousin into the world of men who escaped. He had sworn, screamed, said hateful things to Rosa. He had blamed her for his penury and his debased condition and the interminable state of *American Disillusionment*. If there were not a wife and a child for him to support, *a child not even his own* . . . He had gone so far as to pack a suitcase, and walk out of the house. When he returned the next afternoon, it was as the editor in chief of Gold Star Publications, Inc. He allowed the world to wind him in the final set of chains, and climbed, once and for all, into the cabinet of mysteries that was the life of an ordinary man. He had stayed. Years later, Rosa found a ticket in a dresser drawer, dating from around that terrible time, for a seat in a second-class compartment on the Broadway Limited: yet another train to the coast that Sammy had not been on.

The night he offered her the chance to draw "a comic book for dollies," Rosa felt, Sammy had handed *her* a golden key, a skeleton key to her self, a way out of the tedium of her existence as a housewife and a mother, first in Midwood and now here in Bloomtown, soi-disant Capital of the American Dream. That enduring sense of gratitude to Sammy was one of the sustaining forces of their life together, something she could turn to and summon up, grip like Tom Mayflower gripping his talisman key, whenever things started to go wrong. And the truth was that their marriage had improved after she went to work for Sammy. It no longer seemed (to mistranslate) quite as blank. They became colleagues, coworkers, partners in an unequal but well-defined way that made it easier to avoid looking too closely at the locked cabinet at the heart of things.

The more immediate result of Sammy's offer had been *Working Gals*, "shocking but true tales from the fevered lives of career girls." It debuted in the back pages of *Spree Comics*, at the time the lowest-selling title put out by Gold Star. After three months of steadily increasing sales,

Sammy had moved *Working Gals* to the front of the book and allowed Rosa to sign it with her best-known pseudonym.* A few months after that, *Working Gals* was launched in its own title, and shortly thereafter, Gold Star, led by *three* "Rose Saxon Romance" books, began to show a profit for the first time since the heady early days of the war. Since then, as Sammy had moved on from Gold Star to editorships at Olympic Publications and now Pharaoh House, Rosa, in a tireless and (for the most part) financially successful campaign to portray the heart of that mythical creature, the American Girl, whom she despised and envied in equal measure, had filled the pages of *Heartache, Love Crazy, Lovesick, Sweetheart,* and now *Kiss* with all the force and frustration of a dozen years of lovelessness and longing.

After Sammy had hung up, Rosa stood for a moment holding the phone, trying to make sense of what she had just heard. Somehow—it was a little confusing—their truant son had managed to find the man who had fathered him. Joe Kavalier was being fetched back, alive, from his secret hideaway in the Empire State Building ("Just like Doc Savage," according to Sammy). And he was coming to sleep in her house.

She took clean linens from the built-in cupboard in the hall and carried them toward the couch on which, a few hours from now, Joe Kavalier would lay down his well-remembered, unimaginable body. Where the hallway met the living room, she passed a kind of star-shaped atomic squiggle with a mirror at its nucleus, and caught sight of her hair. She turned around, went into the bedroom she and Sammy shared, put down her fragrant armful of sheets, and yanked out the variety of junk, office supplies, and small bits of hardware she used to keep her hair out of her face when she was at home. She sat down on the bed, got up, went to her closet, and stood there, the sight of her wardrobe filling her with doubt and a mild sense of amusement that she recognized as, somewhat magically, Joe's. She had long since lost the sense of her dresses and skirts and blouses; they were rote phrases of rayon and cotton that she daily intoned. Now they struck her as, to a skirt, appallingly sensible and dull. She took off her sweatshirt and rolled dungarees. She lit a cigarette and walked into the kitchen in her

---

* Among some dozen she is believed to have employed over the years.

underpants and brassiere, the bramble of her loosed hair flapping around her head like a crown of plumes.

In the kitchen she took out a saucepan, melted half a cup of butter, and thickened it with flour to a paste. To the paste she added milk, a little at a time, then salt, pepper, and onion powder. She took her roux off the stove and started a pot of water for noodles. Then she went into the living room and put a record on the hi-fi. She had no idea what record it was. When the music began she did not listen, and when it finished she took no notice. It puzzled her to see that there were no sheets on the couch. Her hair was in her face. When flakes of ash had fallen into her roux, she now perceived, she had stirred them right in, as if they were dried bits of parsley. She had, however, forgotten to add the actual dried parsley. And for some reason, she was walking around in her bra.

"All right," she told herself. "And so what?" The sound of her voice calmed her and focused her thoughts. "He doesn't know from suburbia." She ground out her cigarette in an ashtray that was shaped like an eyebrow arched in surprise. "Get dressed."

She went back into the bedroom and put on a blue dress, knee-length, with a white waistband and a collar of dotted swiss. Various contradictory and insidious voices arose within her at this point to say that the dress made her look stout, hippy, matronly, that she ought to wear slacks. She ignored them. She brushed out her hair till it shot from her head in all directions like the mane of a dandelion, then brushed it back and tucked it up at the nape and fastened it there with a silver clasp. A dazed hesitancy returned to her manner over the question of makeup, but she settled quickly on lipstick alone, two plum streaks not especially well applied, and went out to the living room to make up the bed. The pot in the kitchen was boiling now, and she shook a rattling box of macaroni into the water. Then she began to shred into a mixing bowl a block of school-bus-yellow cheese. Macaroni and cheese. It seemed, as a dish, to exist at the very center of her sense of embarrassment over her life; but it was Tommy's favorite, and she felt an impulse to reward her son for the feat he had performed. And somehow she doubted that Joe—had he really been cooped up in an office in the Empire State Building since the nineteen-forties?—would be sensitive to the socioeconomic message inherent in the bubbling brown-and-gold square, in its white Corning casserole with the blue flower on the side.

After she had slid the casserole into the oven, she returned to the bedroom to put on a pair of stockings and blue pumps with white buckles that were covered in the same glossy fabric as the waistband of the dress.

They would be here in two hours. She went back to her table and sat down to work. It was the only sensible thing she could think of to do. Sorrow, irritation, doubt, anxiety, or any other turbulent emotion that might otherwise keep her from sleeping, eating, or, in extreme cases, speaking coherently or getting out of bed, would disappear almost completely when she was in the act of telling a story. Though she had not told as many as Sammy over the years, working, as she did, exclusively in the romance genre, she had told them perhaps with greater intensity. For Rosa (who, from the first, and uniquely among the few women then working in the business, had not only drawn but, thanks to the indulgence of her editor husband, also written nearly all of her own texts), telling the story of pretty Nancy Lambert—an ordinary American girl from a small island in Maine who put all her foolish trust in the unstable hands of handsome and brilliant Lowell Burns, socialite and nuclear physicist—was an act that absorbed not merely the whole of her attention and craft but of her senses and memories as well. Her thoughts were Nancy's thoughts. Her own fingers turned white at the knuckles when Nancy learned that Lowell had lied to her again. And little by little, as she peopled and developed the world she was building out of rows and columns of blocks on sheets of eleven-by-fifteen Bristol board, Nancy's past was transformed into her own. The velvet tongues of tame Maine deer had once licked her childish palms. The smoke from burning piles of autumn leaves, fireflies writing alphabets against the summer night sky, the sweet jets of salt steam escaping from baked clams, the creaking of winter ice on tree limbs, all of these sensations racked Rosa's heart with an almost unbearable nostalgia as, contemplating the horrific red bloom of the bomb that had become her Other Woman, she considered the possible destruction of everything she had ever known, from kindly Miss Pratt in the old island schoolhouse to the sight of her father's old dory among the lobster boats returning in the evening with the day's catch. At such moments, she did not invent her plots or design her characters; she remembered them. Her pages, though neglected by all but a few collectors, retain an imprint of the creator's faith in her creation, the beautiful madness that is rare enough in any art form, but in the comics business, with its enforced collaborations and tireless seeking-out of the lowest common denominator, all but unheard of.

All this is by way of explaining why Rosa, who had been stricken with panic and confusion at the telephone call from Sammy, gave so little thought to Josef Kavalier once she had sat down to work. Alone in her makeshift studio in the garage, she smoked, listened to Mahler and Fauré on WQXR, and dissolved herself in the travails and shapely contours of poor Nancy Lambert, as she would have on a day that included no reports of her son's wild truancy or revenants from the deepest-buried history of her heart. It was not until she heard the scrape of the Studebaker against the driveway that she even looked up from her work.

The macaroni and cheese turned out to be a superfluous gesture; Tommy was asleep by the time they got him home. Sammy struggled into the house with the boy in his arms.

"Did he have dinner?"

"He had a doughnut."

"That isn't dinner."

"He had a Coke."

He was deeply asleep, cheeks flushed, breath whistling through his teeth, mysteriously lost in an extra-large Police Athletic League sweatshirt.

"You broke your ribs," Rosa told Joe.

"No," Joe said. "Just a bad bruise." There was a fiery welt on his cheek, partially covered by a taped square of gauze. His nose looked luminous at the nostrils, as if it had recently been bleeding.

"Out of my way," Sammy said, through his teeth. "I don't want to drop him."

"Let me," Joe said.

"Your ribs—"

"Let me."

I want to see this, thought Rosa. In fact, there had been nothing in her life that she had ever wanted to see more.

"Why don't you let him?" she said to Sammy.

So Sammy, holding his breath, wincing in sympathy and wrinkling his brow, tipped the sleeping boy into Joe's arms. Joe's face tightened in pain, but he bore it and stood holding Tommy, gazing with alarming tenderness down at his face. Rosa and Sammy stood ardently watching Joe Kavalier look at his son. Then, at the same instant, they each seemed to notice that this was what the other was doing, and they blushed and smiled, awash in the currents of doubt and shame and contentment that animated all the proceedings of their jury-rigged family.

Joe cleared his throat, or perhaps he was grunting in pain.

They looked at him.

"Where is his room?" Joe said.

"Oh, sorry," said Rosa. "God. Are you all right?"

"I'm fine."

"It's this way."

She led him down the hall and into Tommy's bedroom. Joe laid the boy on top of the bedspread, which was patterned with colonial tavern signs and with curl-cornered proclamations printed in a bumpy Revolutionary War typeface. It had been quite some time since the duty and pleasure of undressing her son had fallen to Rosa. For several years, she had been wishing him, willing him, into maturity, independence, a general proficiency beyond his years, as if hoping to skip him like a stone across the treacherous pond of childhood, and now she was touched by a faint trace of the baby in him, in his pouting lips and the febrile sheen of his eyelids. She leaned over and untied his shoes, then pulled them off. His socks clung to his pale, perspired feet. Joe took the shoes and socks from her. Rosa unbuttoned Tommy's corduroy trousers and tugged them down his legs, then pulled up his shirt and the sweatshirt until his head and arms were a lost bundle within. She gave a kind of slow practiced tug, and the top portion of her boy popped free.

"Nicely done," Joe said.

Tommy had apparently been plied with ice cream and soda pop at the police station, to loosen his tongue. His face was going to have to be washed. Rosa went for a cloth. Joe followed her into the bathroom, carrying the shoes in one hand and the pair of socks, rolled into a neat ball, in the other.

"I have dinner in the oven."

"I'm very hungry."

"You didn't break a tooth or anything?"

"Luckily, no."

It was crazy; they were just talking. His voice sounded like his voice, orotund but with a slight bassoon reediness; the droll Hapsburg accent was still there, sounding doctoral and not quite genuine. Out in the living room, Sammy had turned over the record she'd put on earlier; Rosa recognized it now: Stan Kenton's *New Concepts of Artistry in Rhythm.* Joe followed her back into the bedroom, and Rosa scrubbed the sweet epoxy from Tommy's baby-boy lips and fingers. An unwrapped Charms Pop that he had plunged, half-sucked, into his pants pocket had mapped out a sticky continent on the smooth hairless hollow of his hip. Rosa wiped it away. Tommy muttered and winced throughout her attentions; once, his eyes shot open, filled with alarmed intelligence, and Rosa and Joe grimaced at each other: they had woken him up. But the boy closed his eyes again, and with Joe lifting and Rosa pulling, they got him into his pajamas. Joe hefted him, groaning again, as Rosa peeled back the covers of the bed. Then they tucked him in. Joe smoothed the hair back from Tommy's forehead.

"What a big boy," he said.

"He's almost twelve," Rosa said.

"Yes, I know."

She looked down at his hands, by his sides. He was still holding on to the pair of shoes.

"Are you hungry?" she said, keeping her voice low.

"I'm very hungry."

As they went out of the room Rosa turned to look at Tommy and had an impulse to go back, to get into his bed with him and just lie there for a while feeling that deep longing, that sense of missing him desperately, that came over her whenever she held him sleeping in her arms. She closed the door behind them.

"Let's eat," she said.

It wasn't until the three of them were seated around the dinette in the kitchen that she got her first good look at Joe. There was something denser about him now. His face seemed to have aged less than Sammy's or than, God knew, her own, and his expression, as he puzzled out the unfamiliar sights and smells of the cozy kitchen of their Penobscott, had something of the old bemused Joe that she remembered. Rosa had read about the Einsteinian traveler at the speed of light who returned after a trip that had taken a few years of his life to find everyone he knew and loved bent or moldering in the ground. It seemed to her as if Joe had returned like that, from somewhere distant and beautiful and unimaginably bleak.

As they ate, Sammy told Rosa the story of his day, from the time he had run into the boys at the Excelsior Cafeteria until the moment of Joe's leap into the void.

"You could have died," Rosa said in disgust, slapping gently at Joe's shoulder. "Very easily. *Rubber bands.*"

"The trick was performed with success by Theo Hardeen in 1921, from the Pont Alexandre III," Joe said. "The elastic band was specially prepared in that case, but I studied, and the conclusion was that my own was even stronger and more elastic."

"Only it *snapped*," Sammy said.

Joe shrugged. "I was wrong."

Rosa laughed.

"I don't say I wasn't wrong, I'm just saying I didn't think there was much chance I was going to die at all."

"Did you think there was any chance they were going to lock you up on Rikers Island?" Sammy said. "He got arrested."

"You got arrested?" said Rosa. "What for? 'Creating a public nuisance'?"

Joe made a face, at once embarrassed and annoyed. Then he helped himself to another shovelful of casserole.

"It was for squatting," Sammy said.

"It's not anything." Joe looked up from his plate. "I have been in a jail before."

Sammy turned to her. "He keeps saying things like that."

"Man of mystery."

"I find it very irritating."

"Did you make bail?" said Rosa.

"Your father helped me."

"My father? He was *helpful*?"

"Apparently the elder Mrs. Wagner owns two Magrittes," Sammy said. "The mayor's mother. The charges were dropped."

"Two *late* Magrittes," said Joe.

The telephone rang.

"I'll get it," Sammy said. He went to the phone. "Hello. Uh-huh. Which paper? I see. No, he won't talk to you. Because he would not be caught dead talking to a Hearst paper. No. No. No, that isn't true at all." Apparently, Sammy's desire to set the record straight was greater than his disdain for the New York *Journal-American*. He carried the receiver into the dining room; they had just had an extra-long cord put on so that it could reach the dining table Sammy used as a desk whenever he worked at home.

As Sammy began to harangue the reporter from the *Journal-American*, Joe put down his fork.

"Very good," he said. "I haven't eaten anything like this in so long I can't remember."

"Did you get enough?"

"No."

She served him another chunk from the dish.

"He missed you the most," she said. She nodded in the direction of the dining room, where Sammy was telling the reporter from the *Journal-American* how he and Joe had first come up with the idea for the Escapist, on a cold October night a million years ago. The day a boy had come tumbling in through the window of Jerry Glovsky's bedroom and landed, wondering, at her feet. "He hired private detectives to try to find you."

"One of them did find me," Joe said. "I paid him off." He took a bite, then another, then a third. "I missed *him*, too," he said finally. "But I used to always imagine that he was happy. When I would be sitting there at night sometimes thinking about him. I would read his comic books—I could always tell which ones were his—and then I would think, well, Sam is doing all right there. He must be happy." He washed down the last bite of his third helping with a swallow of seltzer water. "It's a very disappointment to me to find out that he is not."

"Isn't he?" Rosa said, not so much out of bad faith as from the enduring power of what a later generation would have termed her denial. "No. No, you're right, he really isn't."

"What about the book, the *Disillusioned American*? I have often thought of it, too, from time to time."

His English, she saw, had deteriorated during his years in the bush, or wherever he'd been.

"Well," Rosa said, "he finished it a couple of years ago. For the *fifth* time, actually, I think it was. And we sent it out. There were some nice responses, but."

"I see."

"Joe," she said. "What *was* the idea?"

"What was the idea of what? My jump?"

"Okay, let's start with that."

"I don't know. When I saw the letter in the newspaper, you know, I knew that Tommy wrote it. Who else could it be? And I just felt, well, since I am the one to mention to him about it . . . I wanted . . . I just wanted to have it be . . . *true* for him."

"But what were you trying to *accomplish*? Was the idea to *shame* Sheldon Anapol into giving you two more money, or . . . ?"

"No," Joe said. "I don't guess that was ever the idea."

She waited. He pushed his plate back and picked up her cigarettes. He lit two at once, then passed one to her, just the way he used to do, long, long ago.

"He doesn't know," he said after a moment, as if offering a rationale for his leap from the top of the Empire State Building, and although she didn't grasp it at once, for some reason the statement started her heart pounding in her chest. Was she keeping so many secrets, so many different kinds of guilty knowledge from the men in her life?

"Who doesn't know what?" she said. She reached, as if casually, to take an ashtray from the kitchen counter just behind Joe's head.

"Tommy. He doesn't know . . . what I know. About me. And him. That I—"

The ashtray—red and gold, stamped with the words EL MOROCCO in stylish gold script—fell to the kitchen floor and shattered into a dozen pieces.

"Shit!"

"It's all right, Rosa."

"No, it isn't! I dropped my El Morocco ashtray, god damn it." They met on their knees, in the middle of the kitchen floor, with the pieces of the broken dish between them.

"So all right," she said, as Joe started sweeping the shards together with the flat of his hand. "You know."

"I do now. I always thought so, but I—"

"You *always* thought so? Since when?"

"Since I heard about it. You wrote me, remember, in the navy, back in 1942, I think. There were pictures. I could tell."

"You have known since 1942 that you"—she lowered her voice to an angry whisper—"that you had a son, and you never—"

The rage that welled up suddenly felt dangerously satisfying, and she would have let it out, heedless of the consequences to her son, her husband, or their reputation in the neighborhood, but she was held back, at the very last possible moment, by the fiery blush in Joe's cheeks. He sat there, head bowed, stacking the pieces of the ashtray into a neat little cairn. Rosa got up and went to the broom closet for a dustpan and broom. She swept up the ashtray and sent the pieces jingling into the kitchen trash.

"You didn't tell him," she said at last.

He shook his bent head. He was still kneeling in the middle of the kitchen floor. "We always never spoke very much," he said.

"Why does that not surprise me?"

"And you never told him."

"Of course not," Rosa said. "As far as he knows, that"—she lowered her voice and nodded again toward the dining room—"is his father."

"This is not the case."

"What?"

"He told me that Sammy adopted him. He overheard this or some such thing. He has a number of interesting theories about his real father."

"He . . . did he ever . . . do you think he . . ?"

"At times I felt he might be leading up to asking me," Joe said. "But he never has."

She gave him her hand then, and he took it in his own. For an instant, his felt much drier and more callused than she remembered, and then it felt exactly the same. They sat back down at the kitchen table, in front of their plates of food.

"You still haven't said," she reminded him. "Why you did it. What was the point of it all?"

Sammy came back into the kitchen and hung up the phone, shaking his head at the profound journalistic darkness that he had just wasted ten minutes attempting to illuminate.

"That's what the guy was just asking me," he said. "What was the point of it?"

Rosa and Sammy turned to Joe, who regarded the inch of ash at the tip of his cigarette for a moment before tapping it into the palm of his hand.

"I guess this was the point," he said. "For me to come back. To end up sitting here with you, on Long Island, in this house, eating some noodles that Rosa made."

Sammy raised his eyebrows and let out a short sigh. Rosa shook her head. It seemed to be her destiny to live among men whose solutions were invariably more complicated or extreme than the problems they were intended to solve.

"Couldn't you have just *called*?" Rosa said. "I'm sure I would have invited you."

Joe shook his head, and the color returned to his cheeks. "I couldn't. So many times I wanted to. I would call you and hang up the phone. I would write letters but didn't send them. And the longer I waited, the harder it became to imagine. I just didn't know how to do it, you see? I didn't know what you would think of me. How you would feel about me."

"Christ, Joe, you fucking idiot," Sammy said. "We love you."

Joe put his hand on Sammy's shoulder and shrugged, nodding as if to say, yes, he had acted like an idiot. And that would be it for them, Rosa thought. Twelve years of nothing, a curt declaration, a shrug of apology, and those two would be as good as new. Rosa snorted a jet of smoke through her nostrils and shook her head. Joe and Sammy turned to her. They seemed to be expecting her to come up with a plan of action for them, a nice tight Rose Saxon script they could all follow, in which they would all get just the lines they wanted.

"Well?" she said. "What do we do now?"

The silence that ensued was long enough for three or four of Ethel Klayman's proverbial idiots to enter this woebegone world. Rosa could see a thousand possible replies working themselves through her husband's mind, and she wondered which one of them he was finally going to offer, but it was Joe who finally spoke up.

"Is there any dessert?" he said.

WITH A SHARPENED Ticonderoga tucked behind his ear and a fresh yellow lawyer's pad pressed to his chest, Sammy got into bed with her. He wore a pair of stiff cotton pajamas—these were white with a thin lime stripe and a diagonal pattern of gold stags' heads—to which clung a sweet steam whiff of her iron. Normally he folded into the envelope of their bed an olfactory transcript of his day in the city, a rich record of Vitalis, Pall Mall, German mustard, the sour imprint of his leather-backed office chair, the scorched quarter-inch membrane of coffee at the bottom of the company urn, but tonight he had showered, and his cheeks and throat had a stinging mint smell of Lifebuoy. He transferred his relatively slight bulk from the floor of the bedroom to the surface of the mattress with the usual recitative of grunts and sighs. At one time Rosa would have inquired as to whether there was some general or specific cause for these amazing performances, but there never was—his groaning was either some involuntary musical response to the effects of gravitation, like the "singing" of certain moisture-laden rocks that she had read about in *Ripley's,* produced by the first shafts of morning sun; or else it was just the inevitable nightly release, after fifteen hours spent ignoring and repressing them, of all the day's frustrations. She waited out the elaborate process by which he effected a comprehensive rearranging of the mucus in his lungs and throat. She felt him settle his legs and smooth the covers over them. At last she rolled over and sat up on one arm.

"Well?" she said.

Given everything that had happened that day, there were a lot of different possible answers to her question. Sammy might have said, "Apparently our son is not, after all, a little school-skipping, comic-book-corrupted delinquent right out of the most lurid chapters of *Seduction of the Innocent*." Or, for the thousandth time, with the usual admixture of wonder and hostility: "Your father is quite a character." Or—she dreaded and longed to hear it: "Well, you got him back."

But he just snuffled one last time and said, "I like it."

Rosa sat up a little bit more.

"Really?"

He nodded, folding his hands behind his head. "It's very disturbing," he continued, and she realized that she had known all along that this was the answer she was going to get, or rather that this would be the line he would probably choose to take in reply to her open-ended invitation to fill her with longing and dread. She was, as always, anxious for his opinion of her work, and grateful, too, that he wanted to reckon things between them, for just a little longer, by the old calendar, as rife with lacunae and miscalculations as it may have been. "It's like the Bomb really is the Other Woman."

"The Bomb is sexy."

"That's what's disturbing," Sammy said. "Actually, what's disturbing is that you could think such a thing."

"Look who's talking."

"You gave the Bomb a *figure*. A womanly shape."

"That comes right out of Tommy's *World Book*. I didn't make that up."

Sammy lit a cigarette and then stared at the match head until it burned down almost to the skin of his fingers. He shook it out.

"Is he out of his mind?" he said.

"Tommy or Joe?"

"He's been leading a *secret life* for the last ten years. I mean, but *really*. Disguises. Assumed names. He told me only a dozen people knew who he was. Nobody knew where he lived."

"Who knew?"

"A bunch of those magicians. That's where Tommy first saw him. In the back room at Tannen's."

"Louis Tannen's Magic Shop," she said. That explained the intensity of Tommy's attachment, which had always irritated her, to that shabby cabinet of trite tricks and flummery, which, the time she had visited it, had left her feeling depressed. *He seems quite obsessed with the place,* her father had once observed. She crept back now along the span of lies that Tommy had stretched across the last ten months. The carefully typed price lists, all fakes. Perhaps the interest in magic itself had all been faked. And the perfect simulacra of her signature, on those appalling excuse notes that Tommy concocted: of course it was Joe who had done them. Tommy's own signature was brambly and uncouth; his hand was still decidedly wobbly. Why hadn't it occurred to her before that the boy never could have produced such a forgery on his own? "They were pulling a giant sleight of hand on us. The eye patch was like, what did Joe used to call it?"

"Misdirection."

"A lie to cover a lie."

"I asked Joe about Orson Welles," Sammy said. "He knew."

She pointed to the pack of cigarettes, and Sammy handed her one. She was sitting up now, legs crossed, facing him. Her stomach hurt; that was nerves. Nerves, and the impact of years and years of accumulated fantasies collapsing all at once, toppling like a row of painted flats. She had imagined Joe not merely run down by passing trucks on a lonely road but drowned in remote Alaskan inlets, shot by Klansmen, tagged in a drawer in a midwestern morgue, killed in a jail riot, and in any number of various suicidal predicaments from hanging to defenestration. She could not help it. She had a catastrophic imagination; an air of imminent doom darkens much of even her sunniest work. She had guessed at the presence of violence in the story of Joe's disappearance (though she had mistakenly thought it lay at the end and not the beginning of the tale). One heard more and more of suicides—suffering from "survivor's guilt," as it was called—among the more fortunate relatives of those who had died in the camps. Whenever Rosa read or was told of such a case, she could not prevent herself from picturing Joe performing the same act, by the same means; usually it was pills or the horrible irony of gas. And every newspaper account of somebody's ill fate in the hinterlands—the man she had read about just yesterday tumbled from a sea cliff at the edge of San Francisco—she recast with Joe in the lead. Bear maulings, bee attacks, the plunge of a bus full of schoolchildren (he was at the wheel)—the memory of Joe underwent them all. No tragedy was too baroque or seemingly inapplicable for her to conceive of fitting Joe into it. And she had lived daily, for several years now, with the pain of knowing—*knowing*—all fantasy aside, that Joe really would never be coming home. But she could not seem to get hold, now, of the apparently simple idea that Joe Kavalier, secret life and all, was asleep on her couch, in her living room, under an old knit afghan of Ethel Klayman's.

"No," she said. "I don't think he's out of his mind. You know? I just don't know if there's a sane reaction to what he . . . what happened to his family. Is *your* reaction, and mine . . . you get up, you go to work, you have a catch in the yard with the kid on Sunday afternoon. How sane is that? Just to go on planting bulbs and drawing comic books and doing all the same old crap as if none of it had happened?"

"Good point," Sammy said, sounding profoundly uninterested in the question. He worked his legs up toward his chest and laid the legal pad against them. The pencil began to scratch. He was through with this conversation. As a rule, they tended to avoid questions like "How sane are we?" and "Do our lives have meaning?" The need for avoidance was acute and apparent to both of them.

"What is that?" she said.

"*Weird Planet.*" He did not lift his pencil from the pad. "Guy lands on a planet. Exploring the galaxy. Mapping the far fringes." While he spoke, he did not look at her, or interrupt the steady progress across the ruled lines of the tiny bold block letters he produced, regular and neat, as if he had a typewriter hand. He liked to talk through his plots for her, combing out into regular plaits what grew in wild tufts in his mind. "He finds a vast golden city. Like nothing he's ever seen. And he's seen it all. The beehive cities of Deneba. The lily-pad cities of Lyra. The people here are ten feet tall, beautiful golden humanoids. Let's say they have big wings. They welcome Spaceman Jones. They show him around. But something is on their minds. They're worried. They're afraid. There's one building, one immense palace he isn't allowed to see. One night our guy wakes up in his nice big bed, the entire city is shaking. He hears this terrible bellowing, raging like some immense monstrous beast. Screams. Strange electric flashes. It's all coming from the palace." He peeled the page he had filled, folded it over, plastered it down. Went on. "The next day everybody acts like nothing happened. They tell him he must have been dreaming. Naturally our guy has to find out. He's an explorer. It's his job. So he sneaks into this one huge, deserted palace and looks around. In the highest tower, a mile above the planet, he comes upon a giant. Twenty feet tall, huge wings, golden like the others but with ragged hair, big long beard. In chains. Giant atomic chains."

She waited while he waited for her to ask.

"And?" she said finally.

"We're in heaven, this planet," said Sam.

"I'm not sure I—"

"It's God."

"Okay."

"God is a madman. He lost his mind, like, a billion years ago. Just before He, you know. Created the universe."

It was Rosa's turn to say, "I like it. Does He, what? I'm guessing he eats the spaceman?"

"He does."

"Peels him like a banana."

"You want to draw it?"

She reached out and laid a hand on his cheek. It was warm and still dewy from the shower, his stubble pleasantly scratchy under her fingertips. She wondered how long it had been since she had last touched his face.

"Sam, come on. Stop for a minute," she said.

"I need to get this down."

She reached out for the pencil and arrested its mechanical progress. For a moment he fought her; there was a tiny creaking of splinters, and the pencil began to bend. Finally, it snapped in two, splitting lengthwise. She handed him her half, the skinny gray tube of graphite glinting like mercury rising in a thermometer.

"Sammy, how did you get him off?"

"I told you."

"My father called the mayor's mother," Rosa said. "Who was able to manipulate the criminal-justice system of New York City. Which she did out of her deep love of René Magritte."

"Apparently."

"Bullshit."

He shrugged, but she knew he was lying. He had been lying to her steadily, and with her approval, for years. It was a single, continuous lie, the deepest kind of lie possible in a marriage: the one that need never be told, because it will never be questioned. Every once in a while, however, small bergs like this one would break off and drift across their course, mementos of the trackless continent of lies, the blank spot on their maps.

"How did you get him off?" Rosa said. She had never before so persisted in trying to get the truth out of him. Sometimes she felt like Ingrid Bergman in *Casablanca,* married to a man with contacts in the underground. The lies were for her protection as well as his.

"I talked to the arresting officer," Sammy said, looking steadily at her. "Detective Lieber."

"You spoke to him."

"He seemed like an all right kind of guy."

"That's lucky."

"We're going to have lunch."

Sammy had been having lunch, on and off, with a dozen men over the past dozen years or so. They rarely displayed any last names in his conversation; they were just Bob or Jim or Pete or Dick. One would appear on the fringes of Rosa's consciousness, hang around for six months or a year, a vague mishmash of stock tips, opinions, and vogue jokes in a gray suit, then vanish as quickly as he had come. Rosa always assumed that these friendships of Sammy's—the only relations, since Joe's enlistment, that merited the name—went no further than a lunch table at Le Marmiton or Laurent. It was one of her fundamental assumptions.

"Well then, maybe Daddy can help you out with this Senate committee, too," Rosa said. "I'll bet Estes Kefauver is a terrific Max Ernst fan."

"Maybe we should just get hold of Max Ernst," Sammy said. "I need all the help I can get."

"Are they calling in *everyone*?" Rosa said.

Sammy shook his head. He was trying not to look worried, but she could tell that he was. "I made some calls," he said. "Gaines and I seem to be the only comics men that anyone knows they're calling."

Bill Gaines was the publisher and chief pontiff of Entertainment

Comics. He was a slovenly, brilliant guy, excitable and voluble the way that Sammy was—when the subject was work—and, like Sammy, he harbored ambitions. His comic books had literary pretensions and strove to find readers who would appreciate their irony, their humor, their bizarre and pious brand of liberal morality. They were also shockingly gruesome. Corpses and dismemberments and vivid stabbings abounded. Awful people did terrible things to their horrible loved ones and friends. Rosa had never liked Gaines or his books very much, though she adored Bernard Krigstein, one of the E.C. regulars, refined and elegant in both print and person and a daring manipulator of panels.

"Some of your stuff is pretty violent, Sam," she said. "Pretty close to the limit."

"It might not be the stabbings and vivisections," Sammy said. And then, licking his lips, "At least not only that."

She waited.

"There's, well, there's, sort of a whole chapter on me in *Seduction of the Innocent.*"

"There is?"

"Part of a chapter. Several pages."

"And you never told me this?"

"You said you weren't going to read the damn thing. I figured you didn't want to know."

"I asked you if Dr. Wertham mentioned you. You said . . ." She tried to remember what exactly he had said. "You said that you looked, and you weren't in the index."

"Well, not by name," Sammy said. "That's what I meant."

"I see," Rosa said. "But it turns out there is a whole, actual *chapter* about you."

"It's not about me *personally.* It doesn't even identify me by name. It just talks about stories I wrote. The Lumberjack. The Rectifier. But not just mine. There's a lot about Batman. And Robin. There's stuff about Wonder Woman. About how she's a little . . . a little on the butch side."

"Uh-huh. I see." Everyone knew. That was what made their particular secret, their lie, so ironic; it went unspoken, unchallenged, and yet it did not manage to deceive. There was gossip in the neighborhood; Rosa had never heard it, but she could feel it sometimes, smell it lingering in the air of a living room that she and Sam had just entered. "Does the U.S. Senate know that you wrote these stories?"

"I seriously doubt it," Sammy said. "It was all nom de plume."

"Well, then."

"I'll be fine." He reached for his pad again, then rolled over and rifled the nightstand drawer for another pencil. But when he was back under the covers, he just sat there, drumming with the eraser end on the pad.

"Think he'll stay for a while?" he said.

"No. Uh-uh. Maybe. I don't know. Do we *want* him to stay?" she said.

"Do you still love him?" He was trying to catch her off guard, lawyer-style. But she was not going to venture so far, not yet, nor poke so deeply into the embers of her love for Joe.

"Do you?" she said, and then, before he could begin to take the question seriously, she went on, "Do you still love me?"

"You know I do," he said at once. Actually, she knew that he did. "You don't have to ask."

"And you don't have to tell me," she said. She kissed him. It was a curt and sisterly kiss. Then she switched off her light and turned her face to the wall. The scratching of his pencil resumed. She closed her eyes, but she could not relax. It took her very little time to realize that somehow she had forgotten the one thing she had wanted to talk to Sammy about: Tommy.

"He knows that you adopted him," she said. "According to Joe." The pencil stopped. Rosa kept her face to the wall. "He knows that somebody else is really his dad. He just doesn't know who."

"Joe never told him, then."

"Would he?"

"No," said Sammy. "I guess he wouldn't."

"We have to tell him the truth, Sam," Rosa said. "The time has come. It's time."

"I'm working now," Sammy said. "I'm not going to talk about this anymore."

She knew from long experience to believe this. The conversation had officially come to an end. And she had not said anything that she wanted to say to him! She put a hand on his warm shoulder and left it there a little while. Again, there was a tiny shock of remembered coolness at the touch of his skin.

"What about you?" she said, just before she finally drifted off to sleep. "Are you going to stay for a while?"

But if there was a reply, she missed it.

AT THIRTY-FIVE, with incipient wrinkles at the corners of her eyes and a voice grown husky with cigarettes, Rosa Clay was, if anything, more beautiful than the girl Joe remembered. She had surrendered her futile and wrongheaded battle against the ample construction of her frame. The general expansion of her rosy flesh had softened the dramatic rake of her nose, the equine length of her jaw, the flare of her cheekbones. Her thighs had a grandeur, and her hips were capacious, and in those first few days, a great goad to his renascent love was the glimpse of her pale, freckled breasts, brimming from the cups of her brassiere with a tantalizing but fictitious threat of spilling over, that was afforded him by one of her housedresses, or by a chance late-night encounter outside the bathroom in the hall. He had thought of Rosa countless times over the years of his flight, but somehow, courting or embracing her in his memory, he had neglected to dab in the freckles with which she was so prodigiously stippled, and now he was startled by their profusion. They emerged and faded against her skin with the inscrutable cadence of stars on the night sky. They invited the touch of fingers as painfully as the nap of velvet or the shimmer of a piece of watered silk.

Sitting at the breakfast table, lying on the couch, he would watch as she went about her household business, carrying a dust mop or a canvas bag of clothespins, her skirt straining to contain the determined sway of her hips and buttocks, and feel as if inside him a violin string were being tightened on its key. Because, as it turned out, he was still in love with Rosa. His love for her had survived the ice age intact, like the beasts from vanished aeons that were always thawing out in the pages of comic books and going on rampages through the streets of Metropolis and Gotham and Empire City. This love, thawing, gave off a rich mastodon odor of the past. He was surprised to encounter these feelings again—not by their having survived so much as by their undeniable vividness and force. A man in love at twenty feels more alive than he ever will again—finding himself once more in possession of this buried treasure, Joe saw more clearly than ever that for the past dozen years or so, he had been, more or less, a dead man. His daily fried egg and pork chop, his collection of false beards and mustaches, the hasty sponge-baths by the sink in the closet, these regular, unquestioned features of his recent existence, now seemed the behaviors of a shadow, the impressions left by a strange novel read under the influence of a high fever.

The return of his feelings for Rosa—of his very youth itself—after so long a disappearance ought to have been a cause for delight, but Joe felt terribly guilty about it. He did not want to be that twinkle-eyed, ascot-wearing, Fiat-driving mainstay of Rosa's stories, the home-wrecker. In the past few days, he had, it was true, lost all his illusions about Sammy and Rosa's marriage (which, as we tend to do with missed opportunities, he had, over the years, come to idealize). The solid suburban bond that he had, from a distance, half-ruefully and half-contentedly conjured to himself at night, proved, at close range, to be even more than ordinarily complicated and problematic. But whatever the state of things between them, Sammy and Rosa were married, and had been so for quite a few years. They were unmistakably a couple. They spoke alike, employing a household slang—"pea-bee and jay," "idiot box"—talking on top of each other, finishing each other's sentences, amiably cutting each other off. Sometimes they both went at Joe at the same time, telling parallel, complementary versions of the same story, and Joe would become lost in the somewhat tedious marital intricacy of their conversation. Sammy made tea for Rosa and brought it to her in her studio. She ironed his shirt with grim precision every night before she retired. And they had evolved a remarkable system of producing comic books as a couple (though they rarely collaborated outright on a story as Clay & Clay). Sammy brought forth items from the inexhaustible stock of cheap, reliable, and efficient ideas that God had supplied him with at birth, and then Rosa talked him through a plot, supplying him with a constant stream of refinements that neither of them seemed to realize were coming from her. And Sammy went over the pages of her own stories with her, panel by panel, criticizing her drawing when it got too elaborate, coaxing her into maintaining the simple strong line, stylized, impatient with detail, that was her forte. Rosa and Sam were not together much—except in bed, a place that remained a source of great mystery and interest to Joe—but when they were, they seemed to be very *involved* with each other.

So it was unthinkable that he should interpose himself and make the claim his reawakened love urged upon him; but he could think of nothing else, and thus he went around the house in a constant state of inflamed embarrassment. In the hospital in Cuba, he had conceived a grateful ardor for one of the nurses, a pretty ex-socialite from Houston known as Alexis from Texas, and had spent an excruciating month in the arid heat of Guantánamo Bay trying to keep himself from getting an erection every time she came around to sponge him down. It was like that with Rosa now. He spent all of his time squelching his thoughts, tamping down his feelings. There was an ache in the hinge of his jaw.

Furthermore, he sensed that she was avoiding him, shunning beforehand the unwelcome advances he could not bring himself to make, which caused him to feel like even more of a heel. After their initial conversation in the kitchen, he and Rosa seemed to find it hard to get a second one started. For a while, he was so preoccupied by his clumsy attempts at small talk that he failed to remark her own reticence whenever they were alone. When he finally did notice it, he attributed her silence to animosity. For days, he stood in the cold shower of her imagined anger, which he felt he entirely deserved. Not only for having left her pregnant and in the lurch, so that he might go off in a failed pursuit of an impossible revenge; but for having never returned, never telephoned or dropped a line, never once thought of her—so he imagined that she imagined—in all those years away. The expanding gas of silence between them only excited his shame and lust the more. In the absence of verbal intercourse, he became hyperaware of other signs of her—the jumble of her makeups and creams and lotions in the bathroom, the Spanish moss of her lingerie dangling from the shower-curtain rod, the irritable tinkle of her spoon against her teacup from the garage, messages from the kitchen written in oregano, bacon, onions cooked in fat.

At last, when he could stand it no longer, he decided he had to say *something,* but the only thing he could think of to say was *Please forgive me.* He would make a formal apology, as long and abject as need be, and throw himself on her mercy. He mulled and planned and rehearsed his words, and when he happened to be passing her in the narrow hallway, Joe just blurted it out.

"Look," he said, "I'm sorry."

"What did you do?"

"I'm sorry for everything, I mean."

"Oh. That," she said. "All right."

"I know you must be angry."

She crossed her arms over her chest and stared at him, brow wide and smooth, lips compressed into a doubtful pout. He could not read the expression in her eyes—it kept changing. Finally, she looked down at her freckled arms, rosy and flushed.

"I have no right to be."

"I hurt your feelings. I abandoned you. I left Sammy to do my job."

"I don't hold that against you," she said. "Not at all. And neither does he, I don't think, not really. We both understand why you left. We understood then."

"Thank you," Joe said. "Maybe you can explain it to me sometimes."

"It was when you didn't come home, Joe. It was when you jumped overboard, or whatever it was you did."

"I'm sorry for that, too."

"That was something that was very hard for me to understand."

He reached for her hand, taken aback by his own daring. She let him hold it for nine seconds, then reclaimed it. Her eyes crossed a little with reproach.

"I didn't know how to come back to you," he said. "I was trying for years, believe me."

He was surprised suddenly to find her mouth on his. He put his hand on her heavy breast. They fell sideways against the paneled wall, dislodging a photograph of Ethel Klayman from its nail. Joe began to dig around inside the zipper fly of her jeans. The metal teeth bit into his wrist. He was sure that she was going to pull down her jeans and he was going to climb on top of her, right there in the hallway before Tommy came home from school. He had been wrong all along; it was not anger that she had interposed between them but the pane of an inexpressible longing like his own. Then the next thing he knew, they were standing up again in the middle of the hall, and the various sirens and air-raid beacons that had been going wild all around them seemed to have fallen silent abruptly. She replaced the various things he had left in disarray, zipped her trousers, smoothed her hair. The color on her lips had smeared all over her cheeks.

"Hum," she said. And then, "Maybe not yet."

"I understand," he said. "Please let me know." He meant it to sound patient and cooperative, but somehow it came out as abject. Rosa started to laugh. She put her arms around him, and he rubbed the smeared lipstick into her cheeks until it was gone.

"How *did* you do it, anyway?" she said. The tips of her teeth were stained with tea. "Get off the boat in the middle of the ocean, I mean."

"I was never on it," Joe said. "I went out on a plane the night before."

"There were orders. I don't know, medical certificates. Sammy showed me the photostats."

He put on a mysterious Cavalieri smile.

"Always true to the code," she said.

"It was very cleverly done."

"I'm sure it was, dear. You were always a clever boy."

He pressed his lips to the parting of her hair. It had an intriguing match-head smell of the Lapsang she preferred.

"What are we going to do?" he said.

She didn't answer at first. She let go and stepped away from him, head tilted to one side, arching a brow; a taunting look that he remembered very well from their previous time together.

"I have an idea," she said. "Why don't you try to figure out where we're going to put all your goddamned comic books?"

14

"NINETY-FIVE, NINETY-SIX, NINETY-SEVEN. NINETY-SEVEN."

"A hundred and two."

"I count ninety-seven."

"You miscounted."

"We're going to need a truck."

"This is what I have been telling you."

"A truck and then a whole fucking warehouse."

"I've always wanted a warehouse," Joe said. "That's always been the dream of mine."

Though Joe preferred to remain vague on the subject of just how many comic books, crammed into pine crates of his own manufacture—complete runs of *Action* and *Detective, Blackhawk* and *Captain America*, of *Crime Does Not Pay* and *Justice Traps the Guilty,* of *Classics Illustrated* and *Picture Stories from the Bible,* of *Whiz* and *Wow* and *Zip* and *Zoot* and *Smash* and *Crash* and *Pep* and *Punch,* of *Amazing* and *Thrilling* and *Terrific* and *Popular*—he actually owned, there was nothing at all vague about the letter he had received from lawyers representing Realty Associates Securities Corporation, the owners of the Empire State Building. Kornblum Vanishing Creams, Inc., had been evicted for violating the terms of its lease, which meant that the ninety-seven or one hundred and two wooden crates, filled with comic books, that Joe had amassed—along with all of his other belongings—must either be transported or disposed of.

"So toss 'em," Sammy said. "What's the big deal?"

Joe sighed. Although all the world—even Sammy Clay, who had spent most of his adult life making and selling them—viewed them as trash, Joe loved his comic books: for their inferior color separation, their poorly trimmed paper stock, their ads for air rifles and dance courses and acne creams, for the basement smell that clung to the older ones, the ones that had been in storage during Joe's travels. Most of all, he loved them for the pictures and stories they contained, the inspirations and lucubrations of five hundred aging boys dreaming as hard as they could for fifteen years, transfiguring their insecurities and delusions, their wishes and their doubts, their public educations and their sexual perversions, into something that only the most purblind of societies would have denied the status of art. Comic books had sustained his sanity during his time on the psychiatric ward at Gitmo. For the whole of the fall and winter following his return to the mainland, which Joe spent shivering in a rented cabin on the beach at Chincoteague, Virginia, with the wind whistling in through the chinks in the clapboard, half-poisoned by the burned-hair smell of an old electric heater, it was only ten thousand Old Gold cigarettes and a pile of *Captain Marvel Adventures* (comprising the incredible twenty-four-month epic struggle between the Captain and a telepathic, world-conquering earthworm, Mr. Mind) that had enabled Joe to fight off, once and for all, the craving for morphine with which he had returned from the Ice.

Having lost his mother, father, brother, and grandfather, the friends and foes of his youth, his beloved teacher Bernard Kornblum, his city, his history—his home—the usual charge leveled against comic books, that they offered *merely an easy escape from reality,* seemed to Joe actually to be a powerful argument on their behalf. He had escaped, in his life, from ropes, chains, boxes, bags, and crates, from handcuffs and shackles, from countries and regimes, from the arms of a woman who loved him, from crashed airplanes and an opiate addiction and from an entire frozen continent intent on causing his death. The escape from reality was, he felt—especially right after the war—a worthy challenge. He would remember for the rest of his life a peaceful half hour spent reading a copy of *Betty and Veronica* that he had found in a service-station rest room: lying down with it under a fir tree, in a sun-slanting forest outside of Medford, Oregon, wholly absorbed into that primary-colored world of bad gags, heavy ink lines, Shakespearean farce, and the deep, almost Oriental mystery of the two big-toothed, wasp-waisted goddess-girls, light and dark, entangled forever in the enmity of their friendship. The pain of his loss—though he would never have spoken of it in these terms—was always with him in those days, a cold smooth ball lodged in his chest, just behind his sternum. For that half hour spent in the dappled shade of the Douglas firs, reading *Betty and Veronica*, the icy ball had melted away without him even noticing. *That* was magic—not the apparent magic of the silk-hatted card-palmer, or the bold, brute trickery of the escape artist, but the genuine magic of art. It was a mark of how fucked-up and broken was the world—the reality—that had swallowed his home and his family that such a feat of escape, by no means easy to pull off, should remain so universally despised.

"I know you think it's all just crap," he said. "But you should not of all people think this."

"Yeah, yeah," Sammy said. "Okay."

"What are you looking at?"

Sammy had edged his way out into Miss Smyslenka's office and was untying one of the stacked portfolios. At nine o'clock that morning, on his way into the Pharaoh offices, he had dropped Joe off here, to begin the laborious process of clearing himself out. It was nearly eight P.M. now, and Joe had been dragging, packing, and repacking, without a break, all day. His shoulders ached, and his fingertips were raw, and he was feeling out of sorts. It had been disorienting to come back here and find everything as he had left it—and then to have to begin to dismantle it. And he was stung by the look in Sammy's eye just now when he walked in and found Joe still at work, finishing the job. Sammy had looked pleasantly surprised—not that the job was finished, Joe thought, so much as to find that Joe was still there. They all thought—all three of them—that he was going to leave them again.

"I'm just taking another look at these pages of yours," Sammy said. "This is beautiful stuff, I have to tell you. I'm really looking forward to reading it all."

"I don't think you will like that. Probably nobody will like that. Too dark."

"It does seem dark."

"Too dark for a comic book, I think."

"Is this the beginning? God, look at that splash." Sammy, his overcoat slung over one arm, sank to the floor beside the broad pile of black cardboard portfolios that they had bought this morning at Pearl Paints, so that Joe could pack up his five years of work. His voice turned dark and cobwebbed. "*The Golem!*" He shook his head, studying the first splash page—there were forty-seven splash pages in all—at the head of the first chapter of the 2,256-page comic book that Joe had produced during his time at Kornblum Vanishing Creams; he had just begun work on the forty-eighth and final chapter when Tommy gave him up to the authorities.

Joe had arrived in New York in the fall of 1949 with a twofold intention: to begin work on a long story about the Golem, which had been coming to him, panel by panel and chapter by chapter, in his dreams, in diners, on long bus rides all across the south and northwest, since he had set out from Chincoteague three years before; and, gradually, carefully, even at first perhaps stealthily, to see Rosa again. He had reestablished a few tentative connections to the city—renting an office in the Empire State Building, resuming his visits to the back room at Louis Tannen's, opening an account at Pearl Paints—and then settled in to implement his double plan. But while he had gotten off to a fine and rapid start on the work that would, he hoped at the time, transform people's views and understanding of the art form that in 1949 he alone saw as a means of self-expression as potent as a Cole Porter tune in the hands of a Lester Young, or a cheap melodrama about an unhappy rich man in the hands of an Orson Welles, it proved much harder for him to return himself, even a little at a time, to the orbit of Rosa Saks Clay. *The Golem* was going so well; it absorbed all of his time and attention. And as he immersed himself ever deeper into its potent motifs of Prague and its Jews, of magic and murder, persecution and liberation, guilt that could not be expiated and innocence that never stood a chance—as he dreamed, night after night at his drawing table, the long and hallucinatory tale of a wayward, unnatural child, Josef Golem, that sacrificed itself to save and redeem the little lamplit world whose safety had been entrusted to it, Joe came to feel that the work—telling this story—was helping to heal him. All of the grief and black wonder that he was never able to express, before or afterward, not to a navy psychiatrist, nor to a fellow drifter in some cheap hotel near Orlando, Florida, nor to his son,

nor to any of those few who remained to love him when he finally returned to the world, all of it went into the queasy angles and stark compositions, the cross-hatchings and vast swaths of shadow, the distended
and fractured and finely minced panels of his monstrous comic book.

At some point, he had begun to tell himself that his plan was not
merely twofold but two-*step*—that when he was finished with *The
Golem,* then he would be ready to see Rosa again. He had left her—
escaped from her—in grief and rage and a spasm of irrational blame. It
would be best, he told himself—wouldn't it?—for him to return to her
purged of all that. But while there might have been at first some merit
in this rationalization, by 1953, when Tommy Clay had stumbled upon
him in the magic shop, Joe's ability to heal himself had long since been
exhausted. He needed Rosa—her love, her body, but above all, her
forgiveness—to complete the work that his pencils had begun. The only
trouble was that, by then, as he had told Rosa, it was too late. He had
waited too long. The sixty miles of Long Island that separated him from
Rosa seemed more impassable than the jagged jaw of one thousand between Kelvinator Station and Jotunheim, than the three blocks of London that lay between Wakefield and his loving wife.

"Is there even a script?" Sammy said, turning over another page. "Is
it, what, is it like a silent movie?"

There were no balloons in any of the panels, no words at all except
for those that appeared as part of the artwork itself—signs on buildings
and roads, labels on bottles, addresses on love letters that formed part
of the plot—and the two words THE GOLEM! which reappeared on the
splash page at the start of each chapter, each time in a different guise,
the eight letters and exclamation point transformed now into a row of
houses, now into a stairway, into nine marionettes, nine spidery blood-
stains, the long shadows of nine haunted and devastating women. Joe
had intended eventually to paste in balloons and fill them with text, but
he had never been able to bring himself to mar the panels in this way.

"There is a script. In German."

"That ought to go over big."

"It will not go over at all. It's not to sell." Something paradoxical had
occurred in the five years he had worked on *The Golem:* the more of
himself, of his heart and his sorrows, that he had poured into the strip—

the more convincingly he demonstrated the power of the comic book as
a vehicle of personal expression—the less willingness he felt to show it
to other people, to expose what had become the secret record of his
mourning, of his guilt and retribution. It made him nervous just to have
Sammy paging through it. "Come on, Sam, hey? Maybe we'd better go."

But Sammy was not listening. He was flipping slowly through the
pages of the first chapter, deciphering the action from the flow of wordless images across the page. Joe was aware of a strange warmth in his
belly, behind his diaphragm, as he watched Sammy read his secret
book.

"I—I guess I could try to tell you—" he began.

"It's fine, I'm getting it." Sammy reached into the pocket of his overcoat, without looking, and took out his wallet. He pulled out a few bills,
ones and a five. "Tell you what," he said. "I think I'm gonna be here for
a while." He looked up. "Could you eat?"

"You're going to read this now?"

"Sure."

"All of it?"

"Why not? I give over fifteen years of my life to climbing a two-mile
pile of garbage, I can spare a few hours for three feet of genius."

Joe rubbed at the side of his nose, feeling the warmth of Sammy's
flattery spread to his legs and fill his throat. "Okay," he said at last. "So
you can read it. But maybe you can wait till we get home?"

"I don't want to wait."

"I'm being evicted."

"Fuck them."

Joe nodded and took the money from Sammy. It had been a long
time, a very long time, since he had allowed his cousin to boss him
around in this way. He found that, as in the past, he rather liked it.

"And, Joe," Sammy said, without looking up from the pile of pages.
Joe waited. "Rosa and I were talking. And she, uh, we think it's okay, if
you want to . . . that is, we think that Tommy ought to know that you're
his father."

"I see. Yes, I suppose you're . . . I will talk to him."

"We could all do it. Maybe we could sit him down. You. His mother.
Me."

"Sammy," Joe said. "I don't know if this is the right thing to say, or what the right way to say it is. But—thank you."

"For what?"

"I know what you did. I know how it cost you something. I don't deserve to have a friend like you."

"Well, I wish I could say that I did it for you, Joe, because I'm such a good friend. But the truth is that, at that moment, I was as scared as Rosa. I married her because I didn't want to, well, to be a fairy. Which, actually, I guess I am. Maybe you never knew."

"Sort of a little bit, maybe I knew."

"It's that simple."

Joe shook his head. "That could be or is why you married her," he said. "But that doesn't explain how come you stayed. You are Tommy's father, Sammy. As much or really, I think, a lot more than I am."

"I did the easy thing," Sammy said. "Try it, you'll see." He returned his attention to the sheet of Bristol board in his hands, part of the long sequence at the end of the first chapter that offered a brief history of golems through the ages. "So," he said, "they make a goat."

"Uh, yes," Joe said. "Rabbi Hanina and Rabbi Oshaya."

"A goat golem."

"Out of earth."

"And then . . ." Sammy's finger traced the course of the episode down and across the page. "After they go to all this trouble. It looks like it's kind of dangerous, making a golem."

"It is."

"After all that, they just . . . they eat it?"

Joe shrugged. "They were hungry," he said.

Sammy said that he knew how they felt, and even though he seemed to mean the remark to be taken only literally, Joe had a sudden vision of Sammy and Rosa, kneeling together beside a flickering crucible, working to fashion something that would sustain them out of the materials that came to hand.

He rode down to the lobby and sat at the counter of the Empire State Pharmacy, on his usual stool, though for once without the usual dark glasses and false whiskers or watch cap pulled down past his eyebrows to the orbits of his eyes. He ordered a plate of fried eggs and a pork chop, as he always did. He sat back and cracked his knuckles. He saw the counterman giving him a look. Joe stood up and, in a small display of theatrics, moved two stools down the line, so that he was sitting right beside the window that looked out on Thirty-third Street, where anyone could see him.

"Make that a cheeseburger," he said.

While he listened to the hissing of the pale pink leaf of meat on the grill, Joe looked out the window and mulled over the things that Sammy had just revealed. He had never given much consideration to the feelings that had, for a few months during the fall and winter of 1941, drawn his cousin and Tracy Bacon together. To the small extent that he had ever given the matter any thought at all, Joe had assumed that Sammy's youthful flirtation with homosexuality had been just that, a freak dalliance born of some combination of exuberance and loneliness that had died abruptly, with Bacon, somewhere over the Solomon Islands. The suddenness with which Sammy had swooped in, following Joe's enlistment, to marry Rosa—as if all that time he had been waiting, racked by a sexual impatience at once barely suppressed and perfectly conventional, to get Joe out of the way—had seemed to Joe to mark decisively the end of Sammy's brief experiment in bohemian rebellion. Sammy and Rosa had a child, moved to the suburbs, buckled down. For years they had lived, vividly, in Joe's imagination, as loving husband and wife, Sammy's arm around her shoulders, her arm encircling his waist, framed in an arching trellis of big, red American roses. It was only now, watching the traffic stalled on Thirty-third Street, smoking his way through a cheeseburger and glass of ginger ale, that he grasped the whole truth. Not only had Sammy never loved Rosa; he was not capable of loving her, except with the half-mocking, companionable affection he always had felt for her, a modest structure, never intended for extended habitation, long since buried under heavy brambles of indebtedness and choked in the ivy of frustration and blame. It was only now that Joe understood the sacrifice Sammy had made, not just for Joe's or for Rosa's or for Tommy's sake, but for his own: not a merely gallant gesture but a deliberate and conscious act of self-immurement. Joe was appalled.

He thought of the boxes of comics that he had accumulated, upstairs, in the two small rooms where, for five years, he had crouched in the false bottom of the life from which Tommy had freed him, and then, in turn, of the thousands upon thousands of little boxes, stacked neatly on sheets of Bristol board or piled in rows across the ragged pages of comic books, that he and Sammy had filled over the past dozen years: boxes brimming with the raw materials, the bits of rubbish from which they had, each in his own way, attempted to fashion their various golems. In literature and folklore, the significance and the fascination of golems—from Rabbi Loew's to Victor von Frankenstein's—lay in their soulless-ness, in their tireless inhuman strength, in their metaphorical association with overweening human ambition, and in the frightening ease with which they passed beyond the control of their horrified and admiring creators. But it seemed to Joe that none of these—Faustian hubris, least of all—were among the true reasons that impelled men, time after time, to hazard the making of golems. The shaping of a golem, to him, was a gesture of hope, offered against hope, in a time of desperation. It was the expression of a yearning that a few magic words and an artful hand might produce something—one poor, dumb, power-ful thing—exempt from the crushing strictures, from the ills, cruelties, and inevitable failures of the greater Creation. It was the voicing of a vain wish, when you got down to it, to escape. To slip, like the Escapist, free of the entangling chain of reality and the straitjacket of physical laws. Harry Houdini had roamed the Palladiums and Hippodromes of the world encumbered by an entire cargo-hold of crates and boxes, stuffed with chains, iron hardware, brightly painted flats and hokum, animated all the while only by this same desire, never fulfilled: truly to escape, if only for one instant; to poke his head through the borders of this world, with its harsh physics, into the mysterious spirit world that lay beyond. The newspaper articles that Joe had read about the upcom-ing Senate investigation into comic books always cited "escapism" among the litany of injurious consequences of their reading, and dwelled on the pernicious effect, on young minds, of satisfying the de-sire to escape. As if there could be any more noble or necessary service in life.

"You need something else?" said the counterman, as Joe wiped his mouth and then threw his napkin to his plate.

"Yes, a fried-egg sandwich," Joe said. "With extra mayonnaise."

An hour after he had left, carrying a brown paper bag that contained the fried-egg sandwich and a package of Pall Malls, because he knew that by now Sammy would be out of cigarettes, Joe returned for the last time to Suite 7203. Sammy had taken off his jacket and his shoes. His necktie lay coiled around him on the floor.

"We have to do it," he said.

"Have to do what?"

"I'll tell you in a minute. I think I'm almost done. Am I almost done?"

Joe bent forward to see how far Sammy had gotten. The Golem appeared to have reached the twisting and jerry-built stairway, all splintered wood and protruding nails—it was almost, deliberately, like something out of Segar or Fontaine Fox—that would lead him to the tumbledown gates of Heaven itself.

"You're almost done."

"It goes faster when there aren't words."

Sammy took the bag from Joe, unrolled it, and peered inside. He took out the foil-wrapped sandwich, and then the pack of cigarettes.

"I worship at your feet," he said, tapping the pack with a finger. He ripped it open and drew one out with his lips.

Joe went over to a stack of boxes and sat down. Sammy lit up the cigarette and flipped—a bit carelessly, to Joe's mind—through the last dozen or so pages. He set his cigarette down atop the still-wrapped sandwich and tied the pages back into the last portfolio. He jabbed the cigarette back into his mouth, unwrapped the sandwich, and bit away a quarter of it, chewing while he smoked.

"So?"

"So," Sammy said. "You have an awful lot of Jewish stuff in here."

"I know it."

"What's the matter with you, did you have a relapse?"

"I eat a pork chop every day." Joe reached over into a nearby box and pulled out the jacketless book with its softened pages and cracked spine.

"*Myth and Legend of Ancient Israel*," Sammy read. "By Angelo S. Rappoport." He flipped through the pages, eyeing Joe with a certain respectful skepticism, as if he thought he had found the secret to Joe's salvation, which he was now obliged to doubt. "You're into all this now?"

Joe shrugged. "It's all lies," he said mildly. "I guess."

"I remember when you first got here. That first day we went into Anapol's office. Do you remember that?"

Joe said that naturally he remembered that day.

"I handed you a *Superman* comic book and told you to come up with a superhero for us and you drew the Golem. And I thought you were an idiot."

"And I was."

"And you were. But that was 1939. In 1954, I don't think the Golem makes you such an idiot anymore. Let me ask you something." He looked around for a napkin, then picked up his necktie and wiped his shining lips. "Have you seen what Bill Gaines is doing over there at E.C.?"

"Yes, of course."

"They are not doing kid stuff over there. They have the top artists. They have Crandall. I know you always liked him."

"Crandall is the top, no doubt."

"And the stuff they are doing, grown-ups are reading it. Adults. It's dark. It's also mean, I think, but look around you, this is a mean age we're living in. Have you seen the Heap?"

"I love the Heap."

"The Heap, I mean, come on, that's a comic book character? He's basically, what, a sentient pile of mud and weeds and, I don't know, sediment. With that tiny little beak. He breaks things. But he's supposed to be a *hero*."

"I see what you're saying."

"This is what I'm saying. It's 1954. You got a pile of dirt walking around, the kids think that's admirable. Imagine what they'll think of the Golem."

"You want to publish this."

"Maybe not quite like it is here."

"Ah."

"It is awfully Jewish."

"True."

"Who knew you knew all that stuff? Kabbalah, is that what it's called? All those angels and . . . and, is that what they are, angels?"

"Mostly."

"This is what I'm thinking. There's something to all this. Not just the Golem character. Your angels—do they have names?"

"There's Metatron. Uriel. Michael. Raphael. Samael. He's the bad one."

"With the tusks?"

Joe nodded.

"I like that one. You know, your angels look a little like superheroes."

"Well, it's a comic book."

"This is what I'm thinking."

"Jewish superheroes?"

"What, they're all Jewish, superheroes. Superman, you don't think he's Jewish? Coming over from the old country, changing his name like that. Clark Kent, only a Jew would pick a name like that for himself."

Joe pointed to the stack of bulging portfolios on the ground between them. "But half the characters in there are rabbis, Sammy."

"All right, so we tone it down."

"You want us to work together again?"

"Well . . . actually . . . I don't know, I'm just talking off the top of my head. This is just so *good.* It makes me want to . . . *make* something again. Something I can be just a little bit proud of."

"You *can* be proud, Sammy. You have done great work. I have always been telling you this all along."

"What do you mean, all along, you've been gone since Pearl Harbor."

"In my mind."

"No wonder I didn't get the message."

Then, startling both of them, there was a flat, tentative knock. Someone was rapping on the frame of the open door to the corridor.

"Anyone here?" said an oboe voice, tentative and oddly familiar to Joe. "Hello?"

"Holy Amazing Midget Radio," Sammy said. "Look who it is."

"I heard I might find you boys up here," said Sheldon Anapol. He came into the room and shook hands with Sammy, then shambled over and stood in front of Joe. He had lost almost all of his hair, though none of his bulk, and his jaw, more mightily jowled than ever, was set in a defiant scowl. But his eyes, it seemed to Joe, were shining, full of tenderness and regret, as if he were seeing not Joe but the twelve years that had passed since their last encounter. "Mr. Kavalier."

"Mr. Anapol."

They shook hands, and then Joe felt himself being enveloped in the big man's fierce and sour embrace.

"You crazy son of a bitch," he said after he let Joe loose.

"Yes," Joe said.

"You look good, how are you?"

"I'm not bad."

"What was all that *narrishkeit* the other day, eh? You made me look very bad. I should be furious with you." He turned to Sammy. "I should be furious with him, don't you think?"

Sammy cleared his throat. "No comment," he said.

"How are you?" Joe asked him. "How is business?"

"A pointed question, as ever, from the mouths of you two. What can I tell you. Business is not good. In fact, it's very, very bad. As if television was not problem enough. Now we have hordes of Baptist lunatics down in Alabama, or some goddamned place, making big piles of comic books and setting them on fire because they are an offense to Jesus or the U.S. flag. Setting them on *fire!* Can you believe it? What did we fight the war for, if when it's over they're going to be burning books in the streets of Alabama? Then this Dr. Fredric Stick-Up-His-Ass Wertham, with that book of his. Now we have the Senate committee coming to town . . . you heard about that?"

"I heard."

"They served me," Sammy said.

"You got subpoenaed?" Anapol stuck out his lip. "I didn't get subpoenaed."

"An oversight," Joe suggested.

"Why would they subpoena you, you're just an editor at that fifth-rate house, pardon me for saying so?"

"I don't know," Sammy admitted.

"Who knows, maybe they've got something on you." He took out his handkerchief from his pocket and mopped his forehead. "Jesus, what lunacy. I never should have let you two talk me out of the novelty business. Nobody ever made a big pile of whoopee cushions and lit them on fire, let me tell you." He went over to the lone chair. "Mind if I sit down?" He sat and let out a long sigh. It seemed to begin rather perfunctorily, for show, but by the end it carried a startling cargo of unhappiness. "Let me tell you something else," he said. "I'm afraid I didn't come up here just because I wanted to say hello to Kavalier. I thought I ought to—I thought you might want to know."

"Know what?" Sammy said.

"You remember we had that lawsuit?" Anapol said.

The next day—the twenty-first of April, 1954—the Court of Appeals of the State of New York would finally hand down a ruling in the matter of *National Periodical Publications, Inc.* v. *Empire Comics, Inc.* The suit had, in that time, made its way in and out of the courts, with settlements proposed and rejected, weaving a skein of reversals and legal maneuverings too complicated and tedious to tease out in these pages. National's case, in the business, was generally felt to be weak. Though both Superman and the Escapist shared skintight costumes, immense strength, and the odd impulse to conceal their true natures in the guise of far weaker and more fallible beings, the same qualities and features were shared by a host of other characters who had appeared in the comic books since 1938; or had been shared, at any rate, until those characters, one by one or in wholesale lots, had met their demise in the great superhero burn-off that followed the Second World War. Though it was true that National had also pursued Fawcett's Captain Marvel and Victor Fox's Wonder Man through the courts, a raft of other strong men who favored performing their feats, including flying, while wearing some form of undergarment—Amazing Man, Master Man, the Blue Beetle, the Black Condor, the Sub-Mariner—had been allowed to go about their business unmolested, without any apparent loss of income to National. Many would argue, in fact, that greater inroads into the hegemony of Superman in the marketplace had been made by his successors and imitators at National itself—Hourman, Wonder Woman, Dr. Fate, Starman, the Green Lantern—many of whom were but distortions or pale reflections of the original. What was more, as Sammy had always argued, the character of Superman itself represented the amalgamation of "a bunch of ideas those guys stole from somebody else," in particular from Philip Wylie, whose Hugo Danner was the bulletproof superhuman hero of his novel *Gladiator;* from Edgar Rice Burroughs, whose orphaned hero, young Lord Greystoke, grew up to become Tarzan, noble protector of a world of inferior beings; and from Lee Falk's newspaper comic strip *The Phantom,* whose eponymous hero had pioneered the fashion for colorful union suits among implacable foes of crime. In so many of his particulars, the Master of Elusion—a human showman, vulnerable, dependent on his team of assistants— bore very little resemblance to the Son of Krypton. Over the years, a number of judges, among them the great Learned Hand, had attempted, tongues not always quite firmly in cheek, to sort out these fine and crucial distinctions. A legal definition of the term "superhero" had even been arrived at.* In the end, in its wisdom, the full panel of the Court of Appeals, overturning the ruling of the state Supreme Court, would side against the prevailing opinion in the comics trade and find in favor of the plaintiffs, sealing the Escapist's doom.

Like the news of the Treaty of Ghent to General Lambert at Biloxi, however, word of the court's ruling, when it came, already would have been overtaken by events.

"Today," Anapol said, "I killed the Escapist."

"What?"

"I killed him. Or let's say he's retired. I called Louis Nizer, I told him, Nizer, you win. As of today, the Escapist is officially retired. I give up. I'm settling. I'm signing his death warrant."

"Why?" Joe said.

"I've been losing money on the Escapist titles for a few years now. There was still some value in the property, you know, from various licensing arrangements, so I had to keep publishing him, just to keep the trademark viable. But his circulation figures have been in a nosedive for quite some time. Superheroes are dead, boys. Forget about it. None of our big hitters—*Scofflaw, Jaws of Horror, Hearts and Flowers, Bobby Sox*—none of them are superhero books."

Joe had gathered as much from Sammy. The age of the costumed su-

---

* "A person of unprecedented physical prowess dedicated to acts of derring-do in the public interest."

perhero had long passed. The Angel, the Arrow, the Comet and the Fin, the Snowman and the Sandman and Hydroman, Captain Courageous, Captain Flag, Captain Freedom, Captain Midnight, Captain Venture and Major Victory, the Flame and the Flash and the Ray, the Monitor, the Guardian, the Shield and the Defender, the Green Lantern, the Red Bee, the Crimson Avenger, the Black Hat and the White Streak, Cat-Man and the Kitten, Bulletman and Bulletgirl, Hawkman and Hawkgirl, the Star-Spangled Kid and Stripesy, Dr. Mid-Nite, Mr. Terrific, Mr. Machine Gun, Mr. Scarlet and Miss Victory, Doll Man, the Atom and Minimidget, all had fallen beneath the whirling thresher blades of changing tastes, an aging readership, the coming of television, a glutted marketplace, and the unbeatable foe that had wiped out Hiroshima and Nagasaki. Of the great heroes of the forties, only the stalwarts at National—Superman, Batman, Wonder Woman, and a few of their cohorts—soldiered on with any regularity or commercial clout, and even they had been forced to suffer the indignity of seeing their wartime sales cut in half or more, of receiving second billing in titles where formerly they headlined, or of having forced upon them by increasingly desperate writers various attention-getting novelties and gimmicks, from fifteen different shades and flavors of Kryptonite to Bat-Hounds, Bat-Monkeys, and a magical-powered little elf-eared nudnick known as the Bat-Mite.

"He's dead," Sammy said wonderingly. "I can't believe it."

"Believe it," Anapol said. "This whole industry is dead after these hearings. You heard it here first, boys." He stood up. "That's why I'm getting out."

"Getting out? You mean you're selling Empire?"

Anapol nodded. "After I called Louis Nizer, I called *my* lawyer and told him to start working on the papers now. I want to get some sucker in there before the roof falls in." He looked around at the stacks of crates. "Look at this place," he said. "You always were a slob, Kavalier."

"True," Joe said.

Anapol started to walk out, then turned back. "You remember that day?" he said. "You two came in with that picture of the Golem and told me you were going to make me a million bucks."

"And we did," Sammy said. "A lot more than a million."

Anapol nodded. "Good night, boys," he said. "Good luck."

When he had gone, Sammy said, "I wish *I* had a million dollars." He said it tenderly, watching something lovely and invisible before him.

"Why?" Joe said.

"I'd buy Empire."

"You would? But I thought you hate comic books. You are embarrassed by them. If you had a million dollars, you could do anything else you wanted."

"Yeah," Sammy said. "You're right. What am I saying? Only you got me all stirred up with this Golem thing of yours. You always did have a way of confusing my priorities like that."

"Did I? Do I?"

"You always used to make it seem okay to *believe* in all this baloney."

"I think it *was* okay," Joe said. "I don't think maybe neither of us should have stopped."

"You were frustrated," Sammy said. "You wanted to get your hands on some real Germans."

Joe didn't say anything for so long that he could feel his silence beginning to speak to Sammy.

"Huh," he said finally.

"You killed Germans?"

"One," Joe said. "It was an accident."

"Did you—did it make you feel—"

"It made me feel like the worst man in the world."

"Hmm," Sammy said. He had gone back over to the final chapter of *The Golem* and stood staring down at a panel in which the clapper in the porter's bell on the doorpost of Heaven's gate was revealed to be a grinning human skull.

"Funny about the Escapist," Joe said, feeling that he wanted to get a hug from Sammy but checked somehow by the thought that it was something he had never done before. "I mean, not funny, but."

"Isn't it, though."

"Do you feel sad?"

"A little." Sammy looked up from the last page of *The Golem* and pursed his lips. He seemed to be shining a light on some dark corner of his feelings, to see if there was anything in it. "Not as much as I would have thought. It's been such a, you know. A long time." He shrugged. "What about you?"

"Like you." He took a step toward Sammy. "It was a long time."

He laid an arm, awkwardly, around Sammy's shoulders, and Sammy hung his head, and they rocked back and forth a little, remembering aloud that morning in 1939 when they had borne the Escapist and his company of fellow adventurers into Sheldon Anapol's office in the Kramler Building, Sammy whistling "Frenesi," Joe filled with the rapture and rage of the imaginary punch he had just landed on the jaw of Adolf Hitler.

"That was a good day," Joe said.

"One of the best," said Sammy.

"How much money *do* you have?"

"Not a million, that's for sure." Sammy stepped out from under Joe's arm. His eyes narrowed, and he looked suddenly shrewd and Anapolian. "Why? How much do *you* have, Joe?"

"It isn't quite a million," Joe said.

"It isn't quite—you mean to say that you—oh. That money."

Every week for two years, starting in 1939, Joe had socked money into the fund that he intended for the support of his family when they reached America. He anticipated that their health might have suffered, and that it might be difficult for them to get work. Most of all, he wanted to buy them a house, a detached house on its own patch of grass somewhere in the Bronx or New Jersey. He wanted them never to have to share a roof with anyone again. By the end of 1941, he was putting in more than a thousand dollars at a time. Since then—apart from the ten thousand dollars he had spent to doom fifteen children to lie forever among the sediments of the Mid-Atlantic Ridge—he had barely touched it; in fact, the account had been swelled, even in his absence, by royalties from the Escapist radio program, which had aired well into 1944, and by the two largish lump payments he had received as his share of the Parnassus serial deal.

"Yes," he said. "I still have it."

"It's just."

"Sitting there," Joe said. "In the East Side Stage Crafts Credit Union. Since . . . well, since the *Ark of Miriam* sank. On December 6, 1941."

"Twelve years and four months."

"Sitting there."

"That's a long time, too," Sammy said.

Joe agreed with this.

"I guess there really isn't any reason to leave it there," he said. The thought of working with Sammy again was very appealing. He had just spent five years drawing a comic book; all day, every day, taking a break every now and then, just long enough to read a comic book or two. He considered himself, at this point, to be the greatest comic book artist in the history of the world. He could dilate a crucial episode in the life of a character over ten pages, slicing his panels ever thinner until they stopped time completely and yet tumbled past with the irreversible momentum of life itself. Or he could spread a single instant across two pages in a single giant panel crammed with dancers, laboratory equipment, horses, trees and shadows, soldiers, drunken revelers at a wedding. When the mood called for it, he could do panels that were more than half shadow; pure black; and yet have everything visible and clear, the action unmistakable, the characters' expressions plain. With his un-English ear, he had made a study of, and understood, as the great comic artists always have, the power of written sound-effect words—of invented words like *snik* and *plish* and *doit*—appropriately lettered, for lending vividness to a jackknife, a rain puddle, a half-crown against the bottom of a blind man's empty tin cup. And yet he had run out of things to draw. His *Golem* was finished, or nearly so, and for the first time in years he found himself—as on every level of his life and emotions—wondering what he was going to do next.

"You'd think I would," he began. "You would think I'd be able to."

More than anything else, he wanted to be able to do something for Sammy. It shocked him to see just how beaten, how unhappy Sam had become. What a feat it would be, to reach into the dark sleeve of his past and pull out something that completely altered Sammy's condition; something that saved him, freed him, returned him to life. With a stroke of the pen, he would be able to hand Sammy, according to the ancient mysteries of the League, a golden key, to pass along the gift of liberation that he had received and that had, until now, gone unpaid.

"I know that I should," Joe continued. His voice thickened as he spoke, and his cheeks burned. He was crying; he had no idea why. "Oh, I should just get rid of it all."

"No, Joe." Now it was Sammy's turn to put his arm around Joe. "I understand you don't want to touch that money. I mean, I think I understand. I get that it . . . well, that it represents something to you that you don't want to ever forget."

"I forget every day," Joe said. He tried to smile. "You know? Days go by, and I don't remember not to forget."

"You just keep your money," Sammy said gently. "I don't need to own Empire Comics. That's the last thing I need."

"I . . . I couldn't. Sammy, I wish that I could, but I couldn't."

"I get it, Joe," Sammy said. "You just hold on to your money."

THE DAY AFTER THE ESCAPIST, Master of Elusion, whom no chains could hold nor walls imprison, was ruled out of existence by the New York State Court of Appeals, a white delivery van of modest dimensions pulled up in front of 127 Lavoisier Drive. On its panels, blue script like the writing on a beer bottle said BACHELOR BUTTON DRAYAGE INC. NEW YORK, arched over a painted nosegay of petite blue flowers. It was getting on toward five o'clock of a dull April afternoon, and though there was still plenty of daylight, the van's lights were turned on, as if for a funeral procession. It had been raining in fits all day, and with the approach of dusk, the heavy sky itself seemed to be settling, like a blanket, over Bloomtown, in gray folds and plaits among the houses. The slender trunks of the young maples, sycamores, and pin oaks on the neighbors' lawns looked white, almost phosphorescent, against the darker gray stuff of the afternoon.

The driver cut his engine, switched off the lights, and climbed down from the cab. He cranked the heavy latch at the back of the van, slid the bar to one side, and threw open the doors with a steely creak of hinges. He was an improbably diminutive man for his trade, thick-set and bowlegged, in a bright blue coverall. As Rosa watched him through the front windows of the house, she saw him stare in at his payload with what appeared to be a puzzled expression. She supposed, given Sammy's description, that the hundred and two boxes of comic books and other junk that Joe had accumulated must make a strong impression even on a veteran mover. But perhaps the guy was only trying to decide how in the hell he was going to get all those boxes into the house by himself.

"What's he doing?" Tommy said. He stood beside her at the living-room window. He had just eaten three bowls of rice pudding, and he had a milky baby smell.

"Probably wondering how we're ever going to fit all of that crap into this shoe box," Rosa said. "I can't believe Joe contrived not to be here for this."

"You said 'crap.' "

"Sorry."

"Can I say 'crap'?"

"No." Rosa was wearing a sauce-spattered apron, and held a wooden spoon bloodied in the same red sauce. "I can't believe it all fits inside that one little truck."

"Ma, when is Joe coming back?"

"I'm sure he'll be back any minute." This was probably the fourth time she had said this since Tommy had come home from school. "I'm making chile con carne and rice pudding. He won't want to miss that."

"He really likes your cooking."

"He always did."

"He said if he never sees another pork chop again, it will be too soon."

"I would never cook a pork chop."

"Bacon is pork, and we eat bacon."

"Bacon is not actually pork. There are words in the Talmud to that effect."

They went out onto the front step.

"Kavalier?" the man called, trying to rhyme the name with its French cognate.

"As in Maurice," Rosa said.

"Got a package."

"That's kind of an understatement, isn't it?"

The man didn't reply. He climbed up inside his truck and disappeared for a while. First a wooden ramp emerged from the back, like a tongue, reaching toward the neighbors' Buick, then lolling on the ground. After that, there was a lot of banging and clamor, as though the man were in there rolling around a keg of beer. Presently he emerged, wrestling a hand truck down the ramp, under the weight of a large oblong wooden box.

"What is that?" Rosa said.

"I never saw that at Joe's," Tommy said. "Wow, it must be part of his equipment! It looks like a—oh my gosh—*it's a packing crate escape!* Oh, my gosh. Do you think he's going to teach me how to do it?"

I don't even know if he's ever coming back. "I don't know what he's going to do, honey," she said.

When Joe and Sammy had returned from the city last night with news of the Escapist's passing, they both seemed pensive, and said little before they each went to bed. Sammy seemed diffident, even apologetic, around Joe, scrambling up some eggs for him, asking him were they too runny, were they too dry, offering to fry some potatoes. Joe was monosyllabic, almost curt, Rosa would have said; he went to lie down on the couch without having exchanged more than a few dozen words with either Rosa or Sam. She saw that something had passed between the two men, but since neither of them said anything about it, she assumed it must have simply concerned the demise of their brainchild; perhaps they had engaged in recriminations over lost opportunities.

The news had certainly come as a shock to Rosa. Though she had not been a regular reader since the days of Kavalier & Clay—Sammy wouldn't have Empire books in the house—she still checked in with *Radio* and *Escapist Adventures* from time to time, killing a half hour at a Grand Central newsstand, or while waiting for a prescription at Spiegelman's. The character had long since slipped into cultural inconsequence, but the titles in which he starred had continued, as far as she knew, to sell. She'd assumed, more or less unconsciously, that the heroic puss of the Escapist would always be there, on lunch boxes, beach towels, on cereal boxes and belt buckles and the faces of alarm clocks, even on the Mutual Television Network,* taunting her with the wealth and the unimaginable contentment that, though she knew better, she could never help feeling would have been Sammy's had he been able to reap the fruits of the one irrefutable moment of inspiration vouchsafed him in his scattershot career. Rosa had stayed up very late trying to work, worrying about them both, and then slept in even later

---

* *The Escapist*, starring a young Peter Graves in the title role, 1951–53.

than usual. By the time she had woken up, both Joe and the Studebaker were gone. All his clothes were in his valise, and there was no note. Sammy seemed to feel these were good signs.

"He would leave a note," he said when she phoned him at the office. "If he were. Going to leave, I mean."

"There wasn't any note the last time," Rosa said.

"I really don't think he would steal our car."

Now here were all his things, and Joe was not. It was as if he had pulled a substitution trick on them, the old switcheroo.

"I guess we'll have to just cram it all into the garage," she said.

The stout little mover wheeled the crate up the walk to the front door, puffing and grimacing and nearly running off into the pansies. When he reached Rosa and Tommy, he tipped the hand truck forward onto its bracket. The crate tottered and seemed to consider pitching over before it settled, with a shiver, on its end.

"Weighs a ton," he said, flexing his fingers as if they were sore. "What's he got in there, bricks?"

"It's probably iron chains," Tommy explained in an authoritative tone. "And, like, padlocks and junk."

The man nodded. "A box of iron chains," he said. "Figures. Pleased to meetcha." He wiped his right hand down the front of his coverall and offered it to Rosa. "Al Button."

"Are you in fact a bachelor?" said Rosa.

"The name of the firm," Al Button said with an air of genuine regret, "is a little out-of-date." He reached into his back pocket and pulled out a sheaf of waybills and carbons, then took a pen from another breast pocket and uncapped it. "I'm going to need your John Hancock on this."

"Don't I need to sort of check everything off as you bring it in?" Rosa said. "That's how it worked when we moved out here from Brooklyn."

"You can go right ahead and check that off, if you want to," he said, with a nod to the crate as he handed the packet to Rosa. "That's all I have for you today."

Rosa checked the bill and found that it did itemize a single article, described pithily as *Wood box*. She paged through the other sheets of paper, but they were just carbon copies of the first.

"Where's the rest of it?"

"That's the only thing that I'm aware of," Button said. "Maybe you know better than me."

"There are supposed to be more than a hundred boxes coming out from the city. From the Empire State Building. Joe—Mr. Kavalier— arranged for the shipment yesterday afternoon."

"This didn't come from the Empire State Building, lady. I picked it up this morning at Penn Station."

"Penn Station? Wait a minute." She started to shuffle through the papers and carbons again. "Who is this from?" While the shipper's name was not quite legible, it did seem to begin with a K. The address, however, was a post-office box in Halifax, Nova Scotia. Rosa wondered if Joe had made it that far during his period of wandering, just after the war, and had left this box of whatever was in it behind.

"Nova Scotia," she said. "Who does Joe know in Nova Scotia?"

"And how did they know he was here?" Tommy said.

It was a very good question. Only the police and a few people at Pharaoh knew that Joe was staying with the Clays.

Rosa signed for the crate, and then Al Button jostled and cajoled it into the living room, where Rosa and Tommy helped him to walk it off of the dolly and onto the low-pile wall-to-wall.

"A box full of chains," Button repeated, his hand rough and dry against Rosa's. "Jesus, Mary, and Joseph."

After he left, closing up his truck and winding his funereal way back to the city, Rosa and Tommy stood there in the living room, studying the wood box. It was a good two feet taller than Rosa, and nearly twice as broad. It was made of solid pine, knotty and unvarnished except by the abrading rasp of its travels, dark yellow and stained like an animal's tooth. You could tell somehow, looking at it, that it had come a long way, suffered ill handling and exposure, had ignoble things spilled on it. It had been used as a table, perhaps, a bed, a barricade. There were black scuffs, and the corners and edges were tufted with splinters. If these were not suggestive enough of wide journeying, there was the incredible profusion of its labels: customs stamps and shipping-line decals, quarantine stickers and claim checks and certificates of weight. In places they were layered a few deep, bits of place-name and color and handwriting all jumbled together. It reminded Rosa of a Cubist collage, a Kurt Schwitters. Clearly, Halifax was not the crate's point of origin. Rosa and Tommy tried to trace its history, peeling away at the layers of seal and sticker, timidly at first, then more carelessly as they were led backward from Halifax to Helsinki, to Murmansk, to Memel, to Leningrad, to Memel once more, to Vilnius, in Lithuania, and finally, scraping away now with the point of a kitchen knife at a particularly recalcitrant carbuncle of adhesive paper near the center of what appeared to be the crate's lid, to

"Prague," said Rosa. "What do you know."

"He's home," Tommy said, and Rosa didn't understand what he meant until she heard the sound of the Studebaker in the drive.

J OE HAD LEFT THE HOUSE very early that morning.

For hours after saying good night to Rosa and Sammy, and long after they went to bed, Joe had lain awake on the couch in the living room, tormented by his thoughts and by the occasional brief giggle from the tank of the toilet down the hall. He had arranged for monthly withdrawals to pay the rent on the offices of Kornblum Vanishing Creams, Inc., and had not permitted himself to consider the total sum of the money he had on deposit in a very long time. The variety of the grandiose and homely schemes it had once been intended to fund was extravagant—he had at one time lavishly overspent in his imagination—and after the war, the money always felt to him like a debt owed, and unrepayable. He had bankrupted himself on plans: a house for his family in Riverdale or Westchester, a flat for his old teacher Bernard Kornblum in a nice building on the Upper West Side. He saw to it, in his fantasies, that his mother obtained the services of a cook, a fur coat, the leisure to write and to see patients as little as she chose. Her study in the big Tudor house had a bay window and heavy timbering, which she painted white because she dreaded gloomy rooms. It was bright and uncluttered, with Navajo rugs and cacti in pots. For his grandfather, there were an entire wardrobe of suits, a dog, a Panamuse record player like Sammy's. His grandfather sat in the conservatory with three elderly friends and sang Weber songs to the accompaniment of their flutes. For Thomas, there were riding lessons, fencing lessons, trips to the Grand Canyon, a bicycle, a set of encylopedias, and—that most-coveted item for sale in the pages of comic books—an air rifle, so that Thomas could shoot at crows or woodchucks or (more likely given his tender feelings) tin cans, when they went out, at weekends, to the country house up in Putnam County that Joe was going to buy.

These designs of his embarrassed him almost as much as they saddened him. But the truth was that, as he lay there smoking, in his underpants, Joe was tormented, even more than by the ruins of his fatuous dreams, by the knowledge that even now, down in the mysterious manufactory of foolishness that was synonymous in some way with his heart, they were tooling up to bring out an entire new line of moonshine. He could not stop coming up with ideas—costume designs and backdrops, character names, narrative lines—for a series of comic books based on Jewish *aggadah* and folklore; it was as if they had been there all along, wanting only a nudge from Sammy to come tumbling out in a thrilling disorder. The notion of spending the $974,000 that was steadily compounding at the East Side Stage Crafts Credit Union to float the recommissioned Kavalier & Clay agitated him so much that his stomach hurt. No, agitation was not the honest word for it. What he felt was *excited*.

Sammy had been right about long-underwear heroes in 1939; Joe had a feeling that he was right in 1954. William Gaines and his E.C. Comics had taken all but one of the standard comic book genres—romance, Western, war stories, crime, the supernatural, et cetera—and invested them with darker emotions, less childish plots, stylish pencils, and moody inks. The only genre they had ignored or avoided (except to ridicule it in the pages of *Mad*) was that of the costumed superhero. What if—he was not sure if this was what Sammy had in mind, but after all, it would be his money—the same kind of transformation were attempted on the superhero? If they tried to do stories about costumed heroes who were more complicated, less childish, as fallible as angels.

At last he ran out of cigarettes and gave up on sleep for the night. He pulled his clothes back on, took a banana from the bowl on the kitchen counter, and stepped outside.

It was not yet five o'clock in the morning, and the Bloomtown streets were deserted, the houses dark, furtive, all but invisible. A steady salt breeze blew in from the sea eight miles away. Later, it would bring fitful rain and the gloom that Mr. Al Button would attempt to relieve by turning on the wan headlights of his van, but for now there were no clouds, and the sky that, in this single-story town of stunted saplings and barren lawns, could seem, by day, as unbearably tall and immense as the sky over some blasted Nebraska prairie, was bestowing itself upon Bloomtown like a blessing, filling in the emptiness with dark blue velveteen and stars. A dog barked two blocks away, and the sound raised gooseflesh on Joe's arm. He had been on and around the Atlantic Ocean plenty of times since the sinking of the *Ark of Miriam;* the train of association linking Thomas, in Joe's mind, to the body of water that had swallowed him had long since worn away. But from time to time, especially if, as now, his brother was already in his thoughts, the smell of the sea could unfurl the memory of Thomas like a flag. His snoring, the half-animal snuffle of his breath coming from the other bed. His aversion to spiders, lobsters, and anything that crept like a disembodied hand. A much-thumbed mental picture of him at the age of seven or eight, in a plaid bathrobe and bedroom slippers, sitting beside the Kavaliers' big Philips, knees to his chest, eyes shut tight, rocking back and forth while, with all his might, he listened to some Italian opera or other.

That bathrobe, its lapels whipstitched in heavy black thread; that radio, its lines Gothic and its dial, like an atlas of the ether, imprinted with the names of world capitals; those leather moccasins with their beaded tepees on the vamps—these were all things that he was never going to see again. The thought was banal, and yet somehow, as happened every now and then, it took him by surprise and profoundly disappointed him. It was absurd, but underlying his experience of the world, at some deep Precambrian stratum, was the expectation that someday—but when?—he would return to the earliest chapters of his life. It was all there—somewhere—waiting for him. He would return to the scenes of his childhood, to the breakfast table of the apartment off the Graben, to the Oriental splendor of the locker room at the Militär-und Civilschwimmschule; not as a tourist to their ruins, but in fact; not by means of some enchantment, but simply as a matter of course. This conviction was not something rational or even seriously believed, but somehow it was there, like some early, fundamental error in his understanding of geography—that, for instance, Quebec lay to the west of

Ontario—which no amount of subsequent correction or experience could ever fully erase. He realized now that this kind of hopeless but ineradicable conviction lay at the heart of his inability to let go of the money that he had banked all those years ago in the East Side Stage Crafts Credit Union. Somewhere in his heart, or wherever it was that such errors are cherished and fed, he believed that someone—his mother, his grandfather, Bernard Kornblum—might still, in spite of everything, turn up. Such things happened all the time; those reported shot in Lodz Ghetto or carried off by typhus at the Zehlendorf DP camp turned up owning grocery stores in São Paulo or knocking on the front door of a brother-in-law in Detroit looking for a handout, older, frailer— altered beyond recognition or disarmingly unchanged—but alive.

He went back into the house, tied his necktie, put on a jacket, and took the car keys from their hook in the kitchen. He was not sure where he was going to go, not at first, but the smell of the sea lingered in his nose, and he had a vague notion of taking the car and driving down to Fire Island for an hour, returning before anybody even knew that he was gone.

The idea of driving *excited* him, too. From the moment he saw it, Sammy and Rosa's car had aroused his interest. The navy had taught Joe to drive, and he had taken to it with his usual aplomb. His happiest moments during the war had been three brief trips he had made behind the wheel of a jeep at Guantánamo Bay. That was a dozen years ago; he hoped he had not forgotten how.

He found his way out onto Route 24 without any problem, but somehow or other he missed the turn to East Islip, and before he quite recognized it, he was on his way into the city. The car smelled of Rosa's lipstick and Sammy's hair cream and a salt-and-wool residue of winter. There was almost no one on the road for a long time, and when he encountered other travelers, he felt a mild sense of pleasant kinship with them as they followed the light of their headlights into the western darkness. On the radio, Rosemary Clooney was singing "Hey There," and then when he gave the dial a spin she was there again, singing "This Ole House." He rolled down the window and sometimes there was a sound of grasses and night bugs and sometimes the lowing of a train. Joe loosened his grip on the wheel and lost himself in the string sections of the hit songs and the rumble of the Champion's straight-8. After a while he realized that a fair amount of time had gone by without his having thought of anything at all, least of all about what exactly he was going to do when he reached New York.

Approaching the Williamsburg Bridge—not really certain of how he had managed to find himself there—he experienced an extraordinary moment of buoyancy, of grace. There was a lot more traffic now, but his shifting was smooth and the sturdy little car was adroit at changing lanes. He launched himself out over the East River. He could feel the bridge humming underneath his wheels and all around him could sense the engineering of it, the forces and tensions and rivets that were all conspiring to keep him aloft. To the south, he glimpsed the Manhattan Bridge, with its Parisian air, refined, elegant, its skirts hiked to reveal tapered steel legs, and, beyond, the Brooklyn Bridge, like a great ropy strand of muscle. In the other direction lay the Queensboro Bridge, like two great iron tsarinas linking hands to dance. And before him, the city that had sheltered him and swallowed him and made him a modest fortune loomed, gray and brown, festooned with swags and boas of some misty gray stuff, a compound of harbor fog and spring dew and its own steamy exhalations. Hope had been his enemy, a frailty that he must at all costs master, for so long now that it was a moment before he was willing to concede that he had let it back into his heart.

At Union Square West, he pulled up in front of the Workingman's Credit Building, home of the East Side Stage Crafts Credit Union. Of course there was nowhere to park. Traffic piled up at the Studebaker's rear as Joe trolled for a space, and each time he slowed, the angry fanfare of horns started up again. A bus came roaring out from behind him, and the faces of its passengers glared down at him from the windows, or mocked him in his ineptitude with their blank indifference. On his third time around the block, Joe slowed once more in front of the building. The curb here was painted bright red. Joe sat, trying to decide what to do. Inside the grimy magnificent pile of the Workingman's Credit Building, in the gloomy transom-lit offices of the Crafts Union bank, the account lay slumbering under years of interest and dust. All he had to do was go in there and say that he wanted to make a withdrawal.

There was a rap on the window on his side of the car. Joe jumped, stepping on the gas as he did so. The car lurched forward a few inches before he scrabbled his foot onto the brake and brought it to a halt with a rude little burp of the tires.

"Whoa!" cried the patrolman, who had come to inquire as to just what Joe meant by holding up the traffic on Fifth Avenue like this, at the busiest hour of the morning. He jumped away from the car, hopping on one leg, clutching at his shining left shoe with both hands.

Joe rolled down the window.

"You just ran over my foot!" the policeman said.

"I'm so sorry," Joe said.

The policeman returned his shoe to the pavement, cautiously, then settled his considerable weight onto it a little at a time. "I think it's all right. You ran over the empty bit at the toe. Lucky for you."

"I borrowed this car from my cousin," Joe said. "I maybe don't know it as well as I should."

"Yeah, well, you can't sit here, bub. You've been here ten minutes. You have to move on."

"That's impossible," Joe said. It could not have been more than one or two at the most. "Ten minutes."

The patrolman tapped his wrist. "I had my watch on you the minute you pulled up."

"I'm sorry, Officer," Joe said. "I just can't to figure out what I'm supposed to do now." He gestured with a thumb toward the Workingman's Credit Building. "My money's in there," he said.

"I don't care if your left buttock is in there," the policeman said. "You'll have to get lost, mister."

Joe started to argue, but as he did he was aware that, from the moment the policeman rapped on the window, he had been feeling immensely relieved. It had been decided for him. He could not park here; he would not be able to get the money today. Maybe it was not such a good idea after all. He put the car in gear.

"Okay," he said. "I will."

In the course of trying to find his way back out to Long Island, he managed to get very effectively lost in Queens. He was nearly to the old World's Fair grounds before he realized his mistake and turned around.

After a while, he found himself driving alongside a vast green stretch of cemeteries, which he recognized as Cypress Hills. Tombstones and monuments dotted the rolling hills like sheep in a Claude Lorrain. He had been here once, years before, soon after his return to the city. It had been Halloween night, and a group of the boys from Tannen's back room had persuaded him to join them in their yearly visit to the grave of Harry Houdini, who was buried here in a Jewish cemetery called Machpelah. They had taken sandwiches and flasks and a thermos of coffee and spent the night gossiping about Mrs. Houdini's surprisingly involved love life after her husband's death and waiting for the spirit of the Mysteriarch to appear, as Houdini had promised that, should such a thing turn out to be feasible, it would. At the break of dawn on All Hallows' Day, they had joked and whistled and pretended to be disappointed at Houdini's failure to show, but in Joe's case at least—and he suspected it had been so for some of the others—the show of disappointment had only served to mask the actual disappointment that he felt. Joe did not in the least believe in an afterlife, but he genuinely wished that he could. An old Christian kook in the public library in Halifax had once attempted to comfort Joe by telling him, with an air of great assurance, that it was Hitler, and not the Allies, who had liberated the Jews. Not since his father's death—not since the day he had first heard a radio report about the wonder ghetto at Terezin—had Joe stood so near to consolation. All he would have needed to do, to find comfort in the Christian's words, was to believe.

He was able to find Machpelah again without too much trouble—it was marked by a large, rather gloomily splendid funerary building of vaguely Levantine design that reminded Joe of Rosa's father's house—and he drove through the gates and parked the car. Houdini's tomb was the largest and most splendid in the cemetery, completely out of keeping with the general modesty, even austerity, of the other headstones and slabs. It was a curious structure, like a spacious balcony detached from the side of a palace, a letter C of marble balustrade with pillars like serifs at either end, enclosing a long low bench. The pillars had inscriptions in English and Hebrew. At the center, above the laconic inscription HOUDINI, a bust of the late magician glowered, looking as if he had just licked a battery. A curious statue of a robed, weeping woman was posed alongside the bench, sprawled against it in a kind of eternal grieving swoon; Joe found it quite gauche and disturbing. There were nosegays and wreaths scattered around in various states of decay, and many of the surfaces were littered with small stones, left by family, Joe supposed, or by Jewish admirers. Houdini's parents and siblings were all buried here: everyone but his late wife, Bess, who had been refused admission because she was an unconverted Catholic. Joe read the prolix tributes to the mother and the rabbi father that Houdini had quite obviously composed himself. He wondered what he would have put on his own parents' tombstones had he been given the opportunity. Names and dates alone seemed extravagance enough.

He started picking up the stones that people had left, and arranged them neatly atop the railing, as it were, of the balcony, in lines and circles and Stars of David. He noticed that someone had slipped a little note into a fissure in the monument, between two stones, then saw other messages salted here and there, wherever there was a seam or a crack. He took them out and unrolled the little strips and read what people had written. They all seemed to be messages left by various devotees of spiritualism and students of the next world who offered posthumous forgiveness to the great debunker for having oppugned the Truth that he had, by now, undoubtedly discovered. After a while, Joe sat down on the bench, a safe distance away from the statue of the woman crying out her eyes. He took a deep breath, and shook his head, and reached out some inward fingers, tentatively, to see if they brushed against some remnant of Harry Houdini or Thomas Kavalier or anyone at all. No; he could be ruined again and again by hope, but he would never be capable of belief.

Presently, he made a pillow of his coat and lay back on the cold marble bench. He could hear the rumbling surf of traffic on the Interborough Parkway, the intermittent sigh of airbrakes from a bus on Jamaica Avenue. The sounds seemed to correspond exactly to the pale gray sky that he was looking up at, intermittently bruised with blue. He closed his eyes for a moment, just to listen to the sky for a little while. At a certain point, he became aware of footsteps in the grass beside him. He sat up and looked out at the brilliant green field—the sun was shining now, somehow—and the hillsides with their flocks of white sheep, and saw, coming toward him, in his cutaway coat, his old teacher Bernard Kornblum. Kornblum's cheeks were raw and his eyes bright and critical. His beard was tied up in a net.

"*Lieber Meister*," Josef said, reaching toward him with both hands. They held on to each other across the gulf that separated them like the tzigane-dancing steeples of the Queensboro Bridge. "What should I do?"

Kornblum puffed out his peeling cheeks and shook his head, rolling his eyes a little as if this was among the more stupid questions he had ever been asked.

"For God's sake," he said. "Go home."

When Joe walked in the front door of 127 Lavoisier Drive, he was nearly knocked off his feet. Rosa dangled by one arm from his neck and, with the other, punched him on the arm, hard. Her jaw was set, and he could see that she was refusing to let herself cry. Tommy bumped up against him a couple of times, like a dog, then stepped awkwardly away, backing into the hi-fi cabinet and upsetting a pewter vase of dried marigolds. After that, they both started talking all at once. Where have you been? Why didn't you call? What's in the box? How would you like some rice pudding?

"I went for a drive," Joe said. "My goodness." He saw that they thought he had left them—had stolen the family car! He felt ashamed to be worthy, in their minds, of such suspicion. "I drove to the city. What box? What—"

Joe recognized it right away, with the ease and unsurprise of someone in a dream. He had been traveling inside of it, in his dreams, since the autumn of 1939. His traveling companion, his other brother, had survived the war.

"What's in there?" Tommy said. "Is it a trick?"

Joe approached the casket. He stretched out his hand toward it and gave it a little push. It tipped an inch and then settled again on its end.

"It's something pretty damned heavy," Rosa said. "Whatever it is."

That was how Joe knew that something was wrong. He remembered very well how light the box with the Golem inside had felt as he and Kornblum carried it out of Nicholasgasse 26, like a coffin full of birds, like a suit of bones. The dreadful thought that there might once again be a body nestled in there with the Golem dashed across his mind. He leaned his face in a little nearer to the box. At some point, he noticed, the hinged observation panel that Kornblum had contrived to misdirect the Gestapo and the border guards had been padlocked shut.

"Why are you smelling it?" Rosa said.

"Is it food?" said Tommy.

Joe did not want to say what it was. He could see that they were half-insane with curiosity, now that they had witnessed his reaction to the box, and that quite naturally they expected him not only to tell them what was in the box but to show it to them, right now. This he was reluctant to do. The box was the same, of that he had no doubt, but as to its mysteriously heavy contents, they could be anything. They could be something very, very bad.

"Tommy told the delivery guy it was your chains," Rosa said.

Joe tried to think of absolutely the most dull substance or item the box could plausibly contain. He considered saying it was a load of old school exams. Then it struck him that there was nothing too interesting about chains.

"It's right," he said. "You must be clairvoyant."

"It's really your chains?"

"Just a bunch of iron."

"Wow! Can we open it now?" Tommy said. "I really want to see that."

Joe and Rosa went into the garage to look for Sammy's toolbox. Tommy started to come along, but Rosa said, "Stay here."

They found the toolbox right away, but she would not let him past her back into the house. "What's in the box?" she said.

"You don't believe it's chains?" He knew that he was not a good liar.

"Why would you *smell* chains?"

"I don't know what's in there," Joe said. "It's not what it used to be."

"What did it used to be?"

"It used to be the Golem of Prague."

It had always been rare to catch Rosa without a reply. She just stepped aside, looking up at him, to let him pass. But he did not go back into the house, not right away.

"Let me ask you this," Joe said. "If you had a million dollars, would you give it to Sammy so that he could buy Empire Comics?"

"Without the Escapist?"

"I guess that's the way it has to be."

She worked on an answer for a minute, during which he could see her spending the money a dozen different ways. Finally, she shook her head.

"I don't know," she said as though it hurt her to admit it. "The Escapist was kind of the crown jewels."

"That is what I was thinking."

"Why were you thinking about that?"

He didn't answer. He carried the toolbox back into the living room and, with help from both Rosa and Tommy, succeeded in lowering the coffin to the ground. He lifted the padlock, hefted it, tapped it twice with his index finger. The picks that Kornblum had given him—until now the only relic from that time which he still possessed—were in his valise. It was a cheap-enough lock, and with a little effort he would no doubt be able to get it off. He let the lock drop back against the hasp and took a crowbar out of the toolbox. As he did so, it occurred to him for the first time to wonder how the Golem had managed to find him. Its reappearance in the living room of a house on Long Island had seemed oddly inevitable at first, as if it had known all along that it had been following him for the past fifteen years, and now it had finally caught up to him. Joe studied some of the labels pasted to the box and saw that it had crossed the ocean only a few weeks before. How had it known where to find him? What had it been waiting for? Who could be keeping tabs on his movements?

He went around to the side opposite the padlock and dug with the teeth of the crowbar into the seam of the lid, just under a nail head. The nail whined, there was a snap like a joint popping, and then the entire lid sprang open as if pushed from inside. At once the air was filled with a heady green smell of mud and river scum, with a stench of summer rich with remembered tenderness and regret.

"Dirt," Tommy said, glancing anxiously at his mother.

"Joe," Rosa said, "that isn't—those aren't *ashes*."

The entire box was filled, to a depth of about seven inches, with a fine powder, pigeon-gray and opalescent, that Joe recognized at once from boyhood excursions as the silty bed of the Moldau. He had scraped it from his shoes a thousand times and brushed it from the seat of his trousers. The speculations of those who feared that the Golem, removed from the shores of the river that mothered it, might degrade had been proved correct.

Rosa came over and knelt beside Joe. She put her arm around his shoulder. "Joe?" she said.

She pulled him closer, he let himself fall against her. He just let himself, and she held him up.

"Joe," she said, after a while. "Are you thinking of buying Empire Comics? Do you have a million dollars?"

Joe nodded. "And a box of dirt," he said.

"Dirt from Czechoslovakia?" Tommy said. "Can I touch it?"

Joe nodded. Tommy dabbed at the dirt with a fingertip, as at a tub of cold water, then plunged in his whole hand to the wrist.

"It's soft," he said. "It feels good." He began to move his hand in the dirt, as if feeling around for something. Clearly he was not yet ready to give up on this box of tricks.

"There's not going to be anything else in there," Joe said. "I'm sorry, Tom."

It was strange, Joe thought, that the box should weigh so much more, now, than it had when the Golem was still intact. He wondered if other dirt, extra dirt, had come to be added to the original load, but this seemed unlikely. Then he remembered how Kornblum, that night, had quoted some paradoxical wisdom about golems, something in Hebrew to the effect that it was the Golem's unnatural soul that had given it weight; unburdened of it, the earthen Golem was light as air.

"Oop," Tommy said. "Hey." His brow furrowed; he had found something. Perhaps the giant's clothes had settled to the bottom of the box.

He took out a small, stained rectangle of paper, with some words printed on one side. It looked familiar to Joe.

"Emil Kavalier," Tommy read. "Endikron—endikrono—"

"My father's," Joe said. He took his father's old calling card from Tommy, remembered its spidery typeface and vanished telephone exchange. It must have been secreted, long before, in the breast pocket of

Alois Hora's enormous suit. He reached in and took a handful of the pearly silt, pondering it, sifting it through his fingers, wondering at what point the soul of the Golem had reentered its body, or if possibly there could be more than one lost soul embodied in all that dust, weighing it down so heavily.

THE SUBCOMMITTEE to Investigate Juvenile Delinquency of the Senate Judiciary Committee was convened in New York City on April 21 and 22, 1954, to look into the role played by the comic book business in the manufacture of delinquent children. The testimony offered by witnesses on the first day is much the better known. Among the experts, publishers, and criminologists called on the twenty-first, three stand out—to the degree that the hearings are remembered at all— in the public memory. The first was Dr. Fredric Wertham, the considerable and well-intentioned psychiatrist and author of *Seduction of the Innocent,* who was, morally and popularly, a motive force behind the entire controversy over the pernicious effects of comic books. The doctor testified at great length, somewhat incoherently, but dignified throughout and alive, ablaze, with outrage. Immediately following Wertham was William Gaines, son of the acknowledged inventor of the comic book, Max Gaines, and publisher of E.C. Comics, whose graphic line of horror comic books he quite eloquently but with fatal disingenuity defended. Finally, that day, the subcommittee heard from a society of newspaper cartoonists, represented by *Pogo*'s Walt Kelly and Sammy's old idol the great Milton Caniff, who, with humor, sarcasm, and witty disdain, completely sold out their brothers-in-ink, handing them up to Senators Hendrickson, Hennings, and Kefauver to be publicly and deservedly crushed, should the senators so deign to do.

The events of the second day of testimony, to which Sam Clay had been summoned, are less well known. It was Sammy's misfortune to follow two extremely reluctant witnesses. The first was a man named Alex Segal, the publisher of a line of cheap "educational" books that he advertised in the back pages of comics, who first denied and then admitted that his company had once—*quite by accident*—sold, to known pornographers, lists of the names and addresses of children who had responded to his company's ads. The second reluctant witness was one of the pornographers in question, an almost comically shifty-looking and heavily perspiring walleyed loser named Samuel Roth, who took the Fifth and then begged off with the excuse that he could not legally testify to anything since he was under indictment for smut-peddling by the State of New York. By the time that Sammy appeared, therefore, the mind of the subcommittee was even more than usually preoccupied with questions of vice and immorality.

The key portion of the transcript of the proceedings reads as follows:

SENATOR HENDRICKSON: Mr. Clay, are you familiar with the comic book characters known as Batman and Robin?

MR. CLAY: Of course, Senator. They are very well known and successful characters.

HENDRICKSON: I wonder, could you attempt to characterize their relationship for us?

CLAY: Characterize? I'm sorry . . . I don't . . .

HENDRICKSON: They live together, isn't that right? In a big mansion. Alone.

CLAY: I believe there is a butler.

HENDRICKSON: But they are not, as I understand it, father and son, is that right? Or brothers, or an uncle and a nephew, or any relationship of that sort.

SENATOR HENNINGS: Perhaps they are just good friends.

CLAY: It has been some time since I read that strip, Senators, but as I recall, Dick Grayson, that is, Robin, is described as being Bruce Wayne's, or Batman's, ward.

HENDRICKSON: His ward. Yes. There are a number of such relationships in the superhero comics, aren't there? Like Dick and Bruce.

CLAY: I don't really know, sir. I—

HENDRICKSON: Let me see, I don't exactly recall which exhibit it was, Mr. Clendennen, do you—I thank you.

Executive Director Clendennen produces Exhibit 15.

HENDRICKSON: Batman and Robin. The Green Arrow and Speedy. The Human Torch and Toro. The Monitor and the Liberty Kid. Captain America and Bucky. Are you familiar with any of these?

CLAY: Uh, yes, sir. The Monitor and Liberty Kid were my creation at one time, sir.

HENDRICKSON: Is that so? You invented them.

CLAY: Yes, sir. But that strip was killed, oh, eight or nine years ago, I believe.

HENDRICKSON: And you have created a number of other such pairings over the years, have you not?

CLAY: Pairings? I don't . . .

HENDRICKSON: The—let me see—the Rectifier and Little Mack the Boy Enforcer. The Lumberjack and Timber Lad. The Argonaut and Jason. The Lone Wolf and Cubby.

CLAY: Well, those characters—the Rectifier, the Lumberjack, the Argonaut—they were already, they had been created by others. I just took over the characters, you see, when I went to work at the respective publishers.

HENDRICKSON: And you immediately provided them, did you not, with wards?

CLAY: Well, yes, but that's standard procedure when you've got a strip that isn't, that maybe has lost a little momentum. You want to perk things up. You want to attract readers. The kids like to read about kids.

HENDRICKSON: Isn't it true that you actually have a reputation in the comic book field for being particularly partial to boy sidekicks?

CLAY: I'm not aware—no one has ever—

HENDRICKSON: Mr. Clay, are you familiar with Dr. Fredric Wertham's theory, which he testified to yesterday, and to which, I must say, I am inclined to give a certain amount of credit, having paged through some of the Batman comic books in question last night, that the relationship between Batman and his ward is actually a thinly veiled allegory of pedophilic inversion?

CLAY: [unintelligible]

HENDRICKSON: I'm sorry, sir, you'll have to—

CLAY: No, Senator, I must have missed that part of the testimony. . . .

HENDRICKSON: And you have not read the doctor's book, I take it.

CLAY: Not yet, sir.

HENDRICKSON: So you have never been aware, personally, therefore, that in outfitting these muscular, strapping young fellows in tight trousers and sending them flitting around the skies together, you were in any way expressing or attempting to disseminate your own . . . psychological proclivities.

CLAY: I'm afraid I don't . . . these are not any proclivities which I'm familiar with, Senator. With all due respect, if I may say, that I resent—

SENATOR KEFAUVER: For Heaven's sake, gentlemen, let us move on.

18

I N ALL HIS LIFE up to this afternoon, Sammy had gotten himself loaded only once, in that big house on a windswept stretch of Jersey shoreline, on the night before Pearl Harbor was attacked, when he fell first among beautiful and then evil men. Then, as now, it was something that he did mostly because it seemed to be expected of him. After the clerk released him from his oath, he turned, feeling as if the contents of his head had been blown like the liquor of an Easter egg through a secret pinhole, to face that puzzled roomful of gawking Americans. But before he had a chance to see whether they—strangers and friends alike—would avert their eyes or stare him down, would drop their jaws in horror or surprise, or would nod, with Presbyterian primness or urbane complacency, because they had suspected him all along of harboring this dark youth-corrupting wish to pad around his stately manor home with a youthful sidekick, in matching smoking jackets; before, in other words, he got a chance to begin to develop a sense of who and what he was going to be from now on—Joe and Rosa bundled him up, in a kidnapperly combination of their overcoats and bunched newspapers, and hustled him out of Courtroom 11. They dragged him past the television cameramen and newspaper photographers, down the stairs, across Foley Square, into a nearby chophouse, up to the bar, where they arranged him with the care of florists in front of a glass of bourbon and ice, all as if according to some long-established set of protocols, known to any civilized person, to be followed in the event of a family member's being publicly identified as a lifelong homosexual, on television, by members of the United States Senate.

"I'll have one of the same," Joe told the bartender.

"Make that three," Rosa said.

The bartender was looking at Sammy, an eyebrow arched. He was an Irishman, about Sammy's age, stout and balding. He looked over his shoulder at the television on its shelf above the bar; although it was showing only an ad for Ballantine beer, the set appeared to be tuned to 11, WPIX, the station that had been carrying the hearings. The bartender looked back at Sammy, a mean Irish twinkle in his eye.

Rosa cupped her hands on either side of her mouth. "Hello!" she said. "Three bourbons on the rocks."

"I heard you," the bartender said, taking three glasses from below the bar.

"And turn that TV off, why don't you?"

"Why not?" the bartender said, with another smile for Sammy. "Show's over."

Rosa snatched a package of cigarettes out of her purse and tore one from the pack. "The bastards," she said, "the bastards. The fucking bastards."

She said it a few more times. Neither Joe nor Sammy seemed to be able to think of anything to add. The bartender brought their drinks, and they drained them quickly and ordered another round.

"Sammy," Joe said. "I'm so sorry."

"Yeah," Sammy said. "Well. That's okay. I'm all right."

"How are you?" Rosa said.

"I don't know, I feel like I'm really all right."

Though he was inclined to attribute the perception to alcohol, Sammy noticed that there appeared to lie no emotion at all, none at least that he could name or identify, behind his shock at his sudden exposure and his disbelief at the way it had happened. Shock and disbelief: a pair of painted flats on a movie set, behind which lay a vast, unknown expanse of sandstone and lizards and sky.

Joe put an arm across Sammy's shoulders. On the other side of Sammy, Rosa leaned against him, and laid her head on Joe's hand, and sighed. They sat that way for a while, propping one another up.

"I can't help noticing that I'm not hearing a lot of astonishment from you two," Sammy said at last.

Rosa and Joe sat up, looked at Sammy, and then at each other behind his back. They blushed.

"Batman and Robin?" Rosa said, astonished.

"That's a dirty lie," Sammy said.

They drank one more round, and then someone, Sammy wasn't sure who, said that they had better be getting back out to Bloomtown, since Joe's boxes were coming today and Tommy was due home from school in less than two hours. There followed a general donning of coats and scarves, some slapstick with dollar bills and the spilled ice from a drink, and then at some point Rosa and Joe seemed to remark that they were headed out the door of the chophouse and that Sammy was not with them.

"You're both too drunk to drive anyway," Sammy told them when they returned for him. "Take the train from Penn Station. I'll bring the car home later."

Now came the first time that they looked at Sammy with something approaching the doubt, the mistrust, the pity that he had been dreading seeing in their faces.

"Give me a break," he said. "I'm not going to fucking drive into the East River. Or anything like that."

They didn't move.

"I swear to you, all right?"

Rosa looked at Joe again, and Sammy wondered if it wasn't just that they worried he might do something to hurt himself; perhaps they were worried that, as soon as they left him, he would head up to Times Square and try to cruise a sailor. And then Sammy realized that, after all, he could.

Rosa came back toward him and unfurled a big lurching hug that nearly sent Sammy tumbling off his bar stool. She spoke into his ear, her breath warm and with a burned-cork smell of bourbon.

"We'll be all right," she said. "All of us."

"I know," Sammy said. "Go on, you guys. I'm just going to sit here. I'm just going to sober up."

Sammy nursed his drink for the next hour, chin in his palms, elbows on the bar. The dark brown, sardonic taste of the bourbon, which at first he had found unpalatable, now seemed no different to him from that of the tongue in his mouth, the thoughts in his head, the heart beating imperturbably in his chest.

He wasn't sure what finally started him thinking about Bacon. Perhaps it was the revived memory of that alcoholic night at Pawtaw in 1941. Or maybe it was just the single pink wrinkle that creased the broad back of the barman's neck. Over the years, Sammy had regretted nearly everything about his affair with Bacon except, until now, its secrecy. The need for stealth and concealment was something that he had always taken for granted as a necessary condition both of that love and of the shadow loves, each paler and more furtive than the last, that it had cast. Back in the summer of 1941, they had stood to lose so much, it seemed, through the shame and ruination of exposure. Sammy could not have known that one day he would come to regard all the things that their loving each other had seemed to put at so much risk—his career in comic books, his relations with his family, his place in the world—as the walls of a prison, an airless, lightless keep from which there was no hope of escape. Sammy had long since ceased to value the security that he had once been so reluctant to imperil. Now he had been unmasked, along with Bruce and Dick, and Steve and Bucky, and Oliver Queen (how obvious!) and Speedy, and that security was gone for good. And now there was nothing left to regret but his own cowardice. He recalled his and Tracy's parting at Penn Station on the morning of Pearl Harbor, in the first-class compartment of the Broadway Limited, their show of ordinary mute male farewell, the handshake, the pat on the shoulder, carefully tailoring and modulating their behavior though there was no one at all watching, so finely attuned to the danger of what they might lose that they could not permit themselves to notice what they had.

"Hey, Weepin' Wanda," said the bartender, in a tone of not quite mock menace. "We don't allow crying in this bar."

"Sorry," Sammy said. He wiped his eyes on the end of his necktie and sniffled.

"Saw you on the TV this afternoon," the bartender said. "Didn't I now?"

"Did you?"

The barman grinned. "You know, I always wondered about Batman and Robin."

"Did you?"

"Yeah. Thanks for clearing that up."

"You," said a voice behind Sammy. He felt a hand on his shoulder and turned to find himself looking into the face of George Debevoise Deasey. The ginger mustache had faded and dulled to the color of a turned slice of apple, and the eyes behind the thick lenses were rheumy and branched with pink veins. But Sammy could see that they were animated by the same old glint of mischief and indignation.

Sammy pushed back from his stool and half-fell, half-lowered himself to the floor. He was not quite as sober as he might have been.

"George! What are you—were you there? Did you see it?"

Deasey seemed not to hear Sammy. His gaze was leveled at the bartender.

"Do you know why they have to fuck each other?" Deasey asked the man. He had developed a slight tremor of his head, it seemed to Sammy, which gave him a more querulous air than ever.

"What's that?" the bartender said.

"I said, Do you know why Batman and Robin have to fuck each other?" He took out his wallet and pulled out a ten-dollar bill, nonchalant, building up to the punch.

The bartender shook his head, half-smiling, waiting for something good. "Now, why is that?" he said.

"Because they can't go fuck themselves." Deasey tossed the bill onto the bar. "The way you can. Now why don't you make yourself useful and bring me a rye and water, and another of what he's having?"

"Say," the bartender said, "I don't have to take that kind of talk."

"Then don't," said Deasey, abruptly losing interest in the discussion. He climbed up onto the stool beside Sammy's and patted the seat that Sammy had vacated. The bartender languished for a few seconds in the cold of the sudden conversational void that Deasey had left him to, then moved over and took two clean glasses from the back bar.

"Sit down, Mr. Clay," Deasey said.

Sammy sat, a little in awe of George Deasey, as ever.

"Yes, I was there, to answer your question," Deasey said. "I happened to be in town for a few weeks. I saw you were on the bill."

George Deasey had left the comics business during the war, never to return. An old school chum had recruited him into some kind of intelligence work, and Deasey had moved to Washington, remaining there after the war was over, doing things with men like Bill Donovan and the Dulles brothers, which, the few times that Sammy had run into him, he neither refused nor agreed to discuss. He was still dressed quaintly, in one of his trademark Woodrow Wilson suits, gray flannel with a parson collar and a clocked bow tie. For a few minutes, as they waited for the barman to bring them their drinks—he took his sweet time—and then sipped at them, Deasey said nothing. Finally, "It's a sinking ship," he said. "You ought to be grateful that they just threw you overboard."

"Only I can't swim," Sammy said.

"Ah, well," Deasey said lightly. He finished his drink and signaled to the bartender for another. "Tell me, has my old friend Mr. Kavalier truly returned? Can the fantastic tale I heard possibly be accurate?"

"Well, he wasn't really going to jump," Sammy said. "If that's what you heard. And he didn't write the letter. It was all—my son—it's a long story. But he's living in my house now," Sammy said. "Actually, I think that he and my wife—"

Deasey held up a hand. "Please," he said, "I've heard enough unsavory details about your private life today, Mr. Clay."

Sammy nodded; he wasn't going to argue with that.

"It really was something, wasn't it?" he said.

"Oh, you were all right, I suppose. But I found the pornographer *extremely* touching." Deasey turned to Sammy and licked his lips, as if wondering whether he ought to drop the bantering tone. "How are you holding up?"

Sammy tried again to decide how he was feeling.

"When I'm sober," he said, "I'm probably going to want to kill myself."

"Status quo for me," Deasey said. The bartender smacked down another glass of rye in front of him.

"I don't know," Sammy said. "I know I ought to feel really bad.

Ashamed, or what have you. I know I ought to be feeling what that ass-hole there"—he jerked a thumb toward the bartender—"was trying to make me feel. Which I guess is what I've more or less been feeling for the last ten years of my life."

"But you don't."

"No, I don't. I feel—I don't know what the word for it would be. *Re-lieved*, I guess."

"I have been in the secrets business for a long time now, Clay," Deasey said. "Take it from me, a secret is a heavy kind of chain. I don't cotton very well to these proclivities of yours. In fact, I find them fairly revolting, particularly when I picture you personally indulging in them."

"Thanks a lot."

"But I wouldn't be surprised if it turned out in the end that Senator C. Estes Kefauver and his pals just handed you your own golden key."

"My God," Sammy said, "I think you might be right."

"Of course I'm right."

Sammy could not even begin to imagine what it would feel like to live through a day that was not fueled or deformed by a lie.

"Mr. Deasey, have you ever been to Los Angeles?"

"Once. I sensed that I could be extremely happy there."

"Why don't you go back?"

"I'm much too old to be happy, Mr. Clay. Unlike you."

"Yeah," Sammy said. "L.A."

"And what would you do out there, I wonder?"

"I don't know. Try to get work in television, maybe."

"Television, yes," Deasey said with a show of distaste. "Yes, you'd be very good at that."

THERE WERE A HUNDRED AND TWO after all; the man from the moving company said so. He and his partner had just finished stacking the last of them in the garage, around and on top of and alongside the crate that contained the pearly residue of the Golem of Prague. Joe came out to the driveway to sign for everything; he looked a little funny to Tommy, windblown or something, red in the face. His shirttails were untucked, and he jumped from foot to foot in his socks. Tommy's mother watched from the front door. She had taken off all of her city clothes and returned to her bathrobe. Joe signed and initialed the forms wherever it was required, and the movers got into their truck and drove back to the city. Then Joe and Tommy went into the garage and stood looking around at the boxes. After a while, Joe sat down on one and lit a cigarette.

"How was school?"

"We watched Dad on TV," Tommy told Joe. "Mr. Landauer brought his TV into the class."

"Uh-huh," Joe said, watching Tommy with a strange expression on his face.

"He was, well, he was sweating a lot," Tommy said.

"Oh, he was not."

"The kids all said he looked sweaty."

"What else did they say?"

"That's what they said. Can I read your comic books?"

"By all means," Joe said. "They're yours."

"You mean I can *have* them?"

"You're the only one that wants them."

Looking at the crates stacked like masonry in the garage gave the boy an idea; he would build himself a Bug's Nest.* When Joe went back into the house, Tommy started dragging and shoving the stacks here and there, and after an hour he had succeeded in transferring space from the edges to the center, hollowing out a shelter for himself at the heart of the pile; a hogan of splintery, knotholed pine, open at the top to let in light from the ceiling fixture, breached by a narrow passage whose mouth he disguised with an easily moved stack of three crates. When it was done, he dropped to his hands and knees, and scrambled on his belly through the Secret Access Tube to the Innermost Cell of the Bug's Nest. There he sat, chewing on a pencil, reading comic books, and paying unconscious tribute, in his igloo of solitude, to the ice tunnels in which his father had once come to grief.

As he sat, biting down on the ridged metal collar of his pencil, stirring a sour-tasting electromagnetic ache in the filling of a molar, the Bug noticed that one of the crates that made up the walls of his Nest was different somehow from the others: time-blackened, whiskered with splinters, more spindly-looking than the other crates in Joe's hoard. He rolled onto his knees and inched toward it. He recognized it. He had seen it a thousand times, in the years before the arrival of Joe's things; lying under a canvas tarp at the back of the garage, with a bunch of other old stuff—a fabulous but sadly defunct Capehart self-changing record player, an inexplicable box full of men's combs. The crate had a loose lid of slats, crudely hinged with loops of thick wire, and a clasp of the same crooked wire, tied with a length of green string. French words and the name of France were stamped, or maybe burned into, its sides; he guessed it had once held bottles of wine.

To any boy, but in particular to one whose chronicle was contained in the sound of a roomful of adults falling silent all at once, the contents

---

* At this time in the history of comic books, it was a mark of only the most successful heroes that they had a secret lair. Superman had his Fortress of Solitude, Batman his Batcave, the Blackhawks their windswept Blackhawk Island, and the Escapist his posh digs under the boards of the Empire Palace. These redoubts would be depicted, from time to time, in panels that showed detailed cutaway diagrams of the secret lair, each 3-D Televisor Screen, Retractable Helipad, Trophy Room, and Rogue's Gallery carefully labeled with arrows. Only one of these cross-section plans was ever published for the Keyhole, a special two-page drawing in the centerfold of *Escapist Adventures* #46.

of the wine crate, ossified by dust and weather into a kind of solid unit of oblivion, would have seemed a treasure. With the precision of an archaeologist, mindful that he would have to put everything back just as he had found it, he prized apart the layers, one by one, inventorying the chance survivals of his prehistory.

1) A copy of the first issue of *Radio Comics,* tucked inside a translucent green cellophane school folder. Its pages yellowed and, held in the hand, bulky and swollen. The very source, the beating heart of the old-blanket odor that the box exuded.

2) Another green cellophane folder, this one stuffed with old newspaper clippings, press notices, and publicity announcements about Tommy's grandfather, the famous vaudeville strong man called the Mighty Molecule. Clipped from newspapers all over the United States, the typography queer, the writing style clotted somehow and difficult to follow, filled with obscure slang and allusions to forgotten songs and celebrities. A few photographs of a tiny man in nothing but a breechclout, whose muscular body had a dense, upholstered look, like Buster Crabbe's.

3) A drawing, folded and crumbling, of the Golem, stouter, somehow more countrified-looking than the one in Joe's epic, wearing big hobnailed boots, striding down a moonlit street. The lines, though recognizably Joe's, sketchier, more tentative, nearer to Tommy's own.

4) An envelope containing the torn stub of a movie ticket and a grainy yellowed photograph, clipped from a newspaper, of the glamorous Mexican actress Dolores Del Rio.

5) A box of unused Kavalier & Clay stationery, left over from just before the war, the letterhead a charming group portrait of all the various characters, superpowered and otherwise—Tommy recognized for certain only the Escapist, the Monitor, and Luna Moth—that the team of Kavalier & Clay had come up with in those days.

6) A manila envelope containing a large black-and-white photograph of a handsome man with hair that shone like a sheet of molded chrome. The mouth a hard thin line, but the eyes holding a reserve of delight, as if he is about to break into a smile. His jaw square, chin cleft. In the lower right corner of the picture an inscription, signed *Tracy Bacon*, written in a large and looping hand: *To the man who dreamed me up, with affection.*

7) A pair of heavy woolen socks with orange toes, in a cardboard sleeve printed with two bright orange bands. Between the bands a conventionalized picture of a merry fire in a country hearth and the word KO-ZEE-TOS in big orange letters.

And then, bent and twisted and adrift at the bottom of the box, a strip of four photographs, from a coin booth, of his mother and Joe—grinning, startled by the flash; all tongues and bug-eyes; with their cheeks and temples pressed together; and then kissing, a heroic and heavy-lidded kiss like two people on a movie poster. In the pictures, they looked absurdly skinny and young and so stereotypically in love that it was obvious even to Tommy, an eleven-year-old boy who had never before in his life looked at any two people and had the conscious thought: *Those two people are in love.* As if by magic, he heard their voices, their laughter, and then the knob turning, and the creaking hinges of the door. Quickly, he began replacing the things he had taken from the box.

He could hear their lips meeting and parting with a sticky sound; the clicking of their teeth or the buttons on their clothes.

"I have to work," his mother said at last. " 'Love Made a Monkey Out of Me.' "

"Ah," he said. "Autobiography."

"Shut up."

"How about if I make dinner," he said. "So you can keep on working?"

"Hey, that would be swell. Unheard of. Maybe you want to be careful, I could get used to that."

"Get used to it."

Those two people are in love.

"Have you talked to Tommy yet?" she said.

"Sort of."

"Sort of?"

"I haven't found the right moment."

"Joe. You have to tell him."

The folder filled with memorabilia of the Mighty Molecule's career slipped from Tommy's hand. Photographs and clippings fluttered everywhere, and as he tried to gather them up, he knocked against the crate, and its lid fell shut with a splintery crack.

"What was that?"

"Tommy? Oh, my God. Tommy, are you in here?"

He sat in the dim hollow of his sanctum, clutching the strip of photographs to his chest.

"No," he said, after a moment, knowing that it was, without question, the most pathetic thing he had ever said in his life.

"Let me," he heard Joe say. There was a scrape of crates and some grunting and then Joe's head poked into the Innermost Cell. He had wriggled his way through the passage on his belly. He propped himself on his elbows with his arms tucked under his chest. Up close, his face was blotchy, and his hair was all crabgrass and dandelions.

"Hey," he said. "Hi."

"Hi."

"What are you doing?"

"Nothing."

"So," Joe said, "I guess maybe you heard a few things out there."

"Yeah."

"Can I come in?" It was his mother.

"I don't think there's room, Rosa."

"Sure there is."

Joe looked at Tommy. "What do you think?"

Tommy shrugged and nodded. So Joe pulled himself all the way in and crammed himself, hunched over, up against the side of the Cell, his hips pressed against Tommy's. Tommy's mother's head appeared, her hair hastily and imperfectly tied up in a scarf, her lips showing right through her lipstick. Tommy and Joe each reached out a hand and pulled her in with them, and she sat up and sighed and said, happily,

"Well," as if they had all settled down together on a blanket in the shade beside a sun-dappled stream.

"I was just about to tell Tom a story," Joe said.

"Uh-huh," Rosa said. "Go on."

"That isn't something I—I'm more used to doing it—with pictures, you know?" He swallowed, and cracked his knuckles, and took a deep breath. He smiled a weak little smile, and unclipped a pen from his shirt pocket. "Maybe I should draw it, ha ha."

"I already saw the pictures," Tommy said.

His mother leaned forward to look with Joe at the two people they once had been.

"Oh, my God," she said. "I remember that. It was that night we took your aunt to the movies. In the lobby of the Loew's Pitkin."

They all moved a little closer together, and then Tommy lay down with his head in his mother's lap. She stroked his hair, and he listened while Joe went on unconvincingly for a while about the things that you did when you were young, and the mistakes that you made, and the dead brother for whom Tommy had been named, that unlucky, unimaginable boy, and how everything had been different then, because there was a war on, at which Tommy pointed out that there had also, until recently, been a war in Korea, and Joe replied that this was true, and it was then that he and Rosa both realized that the boy was no longer listening to anything they were telling him. He was just lying there, in the Bug's Nest, holding his father's hand, while his mother brushed the bangs from his forehead.

"I think we are okay," Joe said finally.

"Okay," said Rosa. "Tommy? Are you okay? Do you understand all this?"

"I guess so," the boy said. "Only."

"Only what?"

"Only what about *Dad*?"

His mother sighed, and told him they were going to have to see about that.

20

SAMMY LET HIMSELF into the house. It was past midnight, he was sober as a headstone, and in his pockets there were tickets for the Broadway Limited and the City of Los Angeles. There was a light on in the living room, and he saw that Joe had fallen asleep in the armchair with one of his dusty old books on Kabbalah or whatever it was—Volume IV of Ginzberg's *Legends of the Jews*—pitched like a tent on his lap. A half-empty bottle of Piels sat on a raffia coaster on the deal table beside him. When Sammy came in, Joe roused a little and shifted in the chair, lifting a hand to shield his eyes from the glare of the bulb. He gave off a stale, drowsy smell of beer and ash.

"Hey."

"Hey," Sammy said. He went to Joe and put a hand on his shoulder. He kneaded the muscles there; they felt knotted and hard. "Everyone all right? Tommy all right?"

"Mmm." Joe nodded, then closed his eyes again. Sammy switched off the light. He went over to the sofa, picked up a peach-and-mustard afghan—one of the few things his mother had ever knit and the only visible remnant of her in his life—carried it to the armchair, and draped it over Joe, careful to cover the orange-tipped toes of Joe's stocking feet.

Next Sammy walked down the hall and entered Tommy's bedroom. In the bend of light from the hall, he could see that Tommy had wandered, in his sleep, to the far edge of the bed, and lay with his face mashed against the wall. He had kicked away all the bedclothes; he had on powder-blue pajamas with white piping at the lapels and cuffs (Sammy, naturally, owned an identical pair). Tommy was a very energetic sleeper, and even after Sammy pulled his head away from the wall, the boy went on snuffling, twitching, his breathing so rapid that it sounded almost like the panting of a dog. Sammy started to pull the covers up over him. Then he stopped and just stood there looking at Tommy, loving him, and feeling the usual spasm of shame that it should be while he was watching the boy sleep that he felt most like a father, or rather, the happiest to be one.

He had been an indifferent father, better than his own, perhaps, but that was saying very little. When Tommy was still an unknown fishboy inside Rosa, Sammy had resolved never to let him feel abandoned, never to walk out on him, and until now, until tonight, he had managed to keep the promise, though there were times—the night he had decided to take that job at Gold Star Comics, for example—when it had been difficult. But the truth was that, for all his noble intentions, if you didn't count the hours when the boy was sleeping, then Sammy had missed out on most of his childhood. Like many boys, Sammy supposed, Tommy had done most of his growing up when the man he called his father was not around, in the spaces between their infrequent hours together. Sammy wondered if the indifference that he had attributed to his own father was, after all, not the peculiar trait of one man but a universal characteristic of fathers. Maybe the "youthful wards" that he routinely assigned to his heroes—a propensity that would, from that day forward, enter into comics lore and haunt him for the rest of his life—represented the expression not of a flaw in his nature but of a deeper and more universal wish.

Dr. Fredric Wertham was an idiot; it was obvious that Batman was not intended, consciously or unconsciously, to play Robin's corrupter: he was meant to stand in for his *father*, and by extension for the absent, indifferent, vanishing fathers of the comic-book-reading boys of America. Sammy wished that he'd had the presence of mind to tell the subcommittee that adding a sidekick to a costumed-hero strip was guaranteed to increase its circulation by 22 percent.

But what did it matter? It was better not to have put up any fight at all; it was over now. He had no choice but to set himself free.

Yet he could not seem to get himself out of Tommy's bedroom. He stood there by the bed for a good five minutes, reviewing the history of sleep in this room, from the days of the baby who lay on his belly in the center of an enameled metal crib, legs tucked under him, his big diapered tuchis poking up into the air. He remembered a stretch of what Rosa had termed "the night jeebies," when Tommy was two or three, how the boy would wake, night after night, screaming as if he were being skinned, and blind from the horror of whatever he had just been looking at in his dreams. They had tried a night-light, a bottle, a song, but as it had turned out, the only thing that could soothe him was to have Sammy get into bed with him. Sammy would stroke the boy's hair until his own wrist ached, listening to the tumult of his breathing, until they both drifted off. That was the high point of his career as a father; it, too, had come in the middle of the night, when the boy was sleeping.

He took off his shoes and got into the bed. He rolled over and lay on his back, and folded his hands together under his head to make a pillow. Maybe he could just lie here for a while, before he went to find his suitcase in the garage. He recognized that there was some danger of his falling asleep—it had been a long day and he was bone-tired—which would spoil his plan of getting out tonight, before there could be any discussion of his leaving. And he was not sufficiently convinced of the rightness of his decision to give Rosa or Joe or anyone else the chance to try to dissuade him. But it felt very good to lie down beside Tommy and listen to him sleep again, after so long.

"Hi, Dad," Tommy said, groggy, sounding confused.

"Oh." Sammy jumped. "Hey, son."

"Did you catch the monkey?"

"What monkey is that, son?" Sammy said.

Tommy waved a hand in a circle, impatient at having to explain it all again. "The monkey with the thing. With the spatula."

"No," Sammy said. "I'm sorry. He's still at large."

Tommy nodded. "I saw you on TV," he said, sounding more awake now.

"Yeah?"

"You were good."

"Thanks."

"You looked a little sweaty, though."

"I was sweating like a pig, Tom."

"Dad?"

"Yeah, Tom?"

"You're kind of squooshing me."

"I'm sorry," Sammy said. He inched a little ways away from Tommy. They lay there; Tommy turned over with a little grunt of annoyance or exasperation.

"Dad, you're too big for this bed."

"Okay," Sammy said, sitting up. "Good night, Tom."

"G'night."

Sammy went down the hall to the bedroom. Rosa liked to sleep in a very dark room, with the blinds lowered and the curtains drawn, and it was not without a certain amount of stumbling and groping that Sammy found his way to the closet. He closed the door behind him and pulled the chain for the light. Quickly he took down a scarred white leather valise and filled it from the hanger rod and the built-in chest of drawers. He packed for warm weather: poplin shirts and tropical-weight suits, a vest, undershirts, boxers, socks and garters, neckties, a bathing suit, a brown belt and a black, stuffing everything into the valise with an indiscriminate and careless haste. When he was through, he yanked the light shut and stepped out into the bedroom, dazzled by the roiling Persian-carpet geometries that filled his eyes. He made his way back out to the hallway, congratulating himself on not having woken Rosa, and crept back down to the kitchen. He would just make himself a sandwich, he thought. His mind was already engaged in the composition of the note he planned to leave.

When he got within a few feet of the kitchen, however, he smelled smoke.

"You did it to me again," he said.

Rosa was sitting in her bathrobe, with her hot lemon water, her ashtray, and the ruins of an entire cake before her. The nocturnal luminescence of Bloomtown, compounded of streetlights, porch lights, the headlights of passing cars, the luster of the state highway, and the diffused glow in the low clouds of the great city sixty miles distant, came in through the dotted-swiss curtains and settled ticking over the teakettle and the clock and dripping kitchen tap.

"You have a suitcase," Rosa said.

Sammy looked down at the valise, as if to confirm her report. "True," he said, sounding a little surprised even to his own ears.

"You're leaving."

He didn't answer.

"I guess that makes sense," she said.

"Doesn't it?" he said. "I mean, think about it."

"If that's what you want to do. Joe was going to try to talk you into staying. He has some plan or other. And, of course, there's Tommy."

"Tommy."

"You are going to break his heart."

"Is that cake?" Sammy said.

"For some reason I made a red velvet cake," Rosa said. "With sea-foam frosting."

"Are you drunk?"

"I had a bottle of beer."

"You like to bake when you're drunk."

"Why is that?" She slid across the kitchen table the tumbled remains of the red velvet cake, with sea-foam frosting. "For some reason," she said, "I also seem to have felt compelled to eat most of it."

Sammy went to the kitchen drawer and got a fork. He wasn't in the least hungry as he sat down, but then he took a bite of the cake and, before he could stop himself, had finished what was left. The sea-foam crunched and melted in his teeth. Rosa got up and poured him a glass of milk, then stood behind him while he drank it, ruffling the hair at the back of his neck.

"You didn't say," Sammy said.

"I didn't say what?"

"What *you* want me to do."

He leaned back into her, his head against her belly. He was tired suddenly. He had planned to leave right away, to make his departure easier, but now he wondered if he shouldn't just wait until the morning.

"You know I want you to stay," she said. "I hope you know that. God damn it, Sammy, I would love nothing more."

"To prove a point, is what you're saying."

"Yes."

"About how nobody can tell us how to live, and it takes all kinds, and mind your own damn business. Like that."

She stopped stroking his hair. He guessed she had heard a certain amount of sarcasm in his tone, though he was not feeling at all sarcastic, and in fact, he admired her for what she was and had always been willing to do for his sake.

"It's just," he said, "I think I have another point I need to prove."

There was a cough, and they turned and saw Joe standing in the doorway, hair standing up all over his head, mouth open, trying to blink away something he did not want to see.

"Is he—you aren't *leaving*?"

"For a while," Sammy said. "At least."

"Where are you going to go?"

"I was thinking Los Angeles."

"Sammy," Joe said, taking a step toward Sammy that had something menacing about it. "Damn it, you *can't*."

Sammy drew back a little and raised his arm as if to ward off his old friend. "Take it easy, Joe. I appreciate the sentiment, but I—"

"It is not a sentiment, idiot. After I left you this morning, I went over there and made an offer for the Empire Comics. To buy it. And Shelly Anapol accepted."

"*What?* An offer? Joe, are you *crazy*?"

"You said you had some *ideas*. You said I got you stirred up again."

"Yeah, you did, but, I mean. Jesus, how could you just go and do that without asking me first?"

"It's my money," Joe said. "You have no say in the matter."

"Huh," Sammy said, and then again, "huh. Well." He stretched and yawned. "Maybe I could write the stories out there, and mail them to you. I don't know. We'll see. I'm too tired for this now, okay?"

"Well, you won't leave tonight, Sam, don't be crazy. It's too late. There isn't a train for you to leave with."

"Stay till the morning at least," Rosa said.

"I guess I could sleep on the couch," said Sammy.

Rosa and Joe looked at each other, startled, alarmed.

"Sammy, Joe and I aren't—this isn't because—we haven't been—"

"I know," Sammy said. "The couch is fine. You don't even need to change the sheets."

Rosa said that while Sammy might be fully prepared to embark on the life of a hobo, there was no way in hell that he would begin his new career in her house. She went to the linen closet and brought fresh sheets and a pillowcase. She moved aside the neat pile of Joe's used linens and spread the new ones, tucking, and smoothing, and pulling back the blanket to expose the reverse of the floral flat sheet in a neat diagonal fold. Sammy stood over her, making a fuss over how appetizing it all looked after the day he'd had. When she let him sit down, he bounced on the cushion, slipped off his shoes, and then lay back with the happy sigh of an aching man sliding into a nice hot bath.

"This is feeling very strange to me," Rosa said. She was gripping the pillowcase filled with Joe's old sheets in one hand, like a sack, and dabbing at the tears in her eyes with the other.

"It's been strange all along," said Sammy.

She nodded. Then she handed the sack of dirty linens to Joe and started down the hall. Joe stood beside the couch for a moment, looking at Sammy with a perplexed expression, as if trying to work his way backward, one at a time, through the steps of the clever feat of substitution that Sammy had just pulled off.

When the household woke the next morning, quite early, the couch had been stripped, the sheets left folded on the coffee table with the pillow balanced on top, and Sammy and his suitcase were long gone. In lieu of a note or other farewell gesture, he had left only, in the center of the kitchen table, the small two-by-three card that he had been given back in 1948, when he had purchased the lot on which the house now stood. It was wrinkled and dog-eared and dyed by the stain of long years spent in Sammy's wallet. When Rosa and Joe picked it up they saw that Sammy had taken a pen and, bearing down, crossed out the name of the never-more-than-theoretical family that was printed above the address, and in its place written, sealed in a neat black rectangle, knotted by the stout cord of an ampersand, the words KAVALIER & CLAY.

AUTHOR'S NOTE

I am indebted to Will Eisner, to Stan Lee, and in particular to the late Gil Kane for sharing their reminiscences of the Golden Age, and also to Dick Ayers, Sheldon Moldoff, Martin "Green Lantern" Nodell, and to Marv Wolfman and Lauren Shuler Donner for providing introductions to some of those brilliant creators. Thanks also to Richard Bensam and Peter Wallace for their expert judgments. Roger Angell, Kenneth Turan, Cy Voris, Rosemary Graham, Louis B. Jones, Lee Skirboll, and the heroic Douglas Stumpf all kindly gave me the benefit of their generosity and intelligence by reading drafts or portions of this book along the way. I'm grateful as well to Eugene Feingold, Ricki Waldman, Kenneth Turan, and Robert Chabon for their memories of New York childhoods; to Russell Petrocelli, group rail-trip coordinator of N.J. Transit; and to the past and present members of the Kirby Mailing List (http://fantasty.com/kirby-l).

I would like to thank the MacDowell Colony for providing the magical gifts of space, time, and quiet, and the Lila Wallace–Reader's Digest Fund for its support.

The research for this novel was undertaken primarily at the Doheny Memorial Library at U.S.C., the U.C.L.A. College Library, the Bancroft Library at U.C. Berkeley, the McHenry Library at U.C. Santa Cruz, and the New-York Historical Society.

I have tried to respect history and geography wherever doing so served my purposes as a novelist, but wherever it did not I have, cheerfully or with regret, ignored them.

I have relied on the prior labor of many writers here, but above all on that of the collective authors of the 1939 W.P.A. *New York City Guide* (John Cheever and Richard Wright among them), and on the work of

E. J. Kahn, Jr., Brendan Gill, E. B. White, A. J. Liebling, Joseph Mitchell, St. Clair McKelway, and all the other great urban portraitists, many of them anonymous, who never failed me when I went searching for their lost city in dusty old bound back issues of *The New Yorker*. Other helpful or indispensable books were: *Letters from Prague: 1939–1941,* compiled by Raya Czerner Schapiro and Helga Czerner Weinberg, *The Nightmare of Reason,* by Ernst Pawel, and *Elder of the Jews,* by Ruth Bondy; *The World Almanac and Book of Facts for 1941,* edited by E. Eastman Irvine, *No Ordinary Time,* by Doris Kearns Goodwin, *The Glory and the Dream,* by William Manchester, *The Lost World of the Fair,* by David Gelernter, and *Delivered from Evil,* by Robert Leckie; *The Secrets of Houdini,* by J. C. Cannell, *Blackstone's Modern Card Tricks,* by Harry Blackstone, *Professional Magic Made Easy,* by Bruce Elliott, *Houdini on Magic,* by Harry Houdini, *Houdini: The Man Who Walked Through Walls,* by William Lindsay Gresham, and *Houdini!!!,* by Kenneth Silverman; *Little America* and *Discovery,* both by Richard E. Byrd, *A History of Antarctic Science,* by G. E. Fogg, *The White Continent,* by Thomas R. Henry, *Quest for a Continent,* by Walter Sullivan, and *Antarctic Night,* by Jack Bursey; *New York Panorama,* by the Federal Writers' Project of the W.P.A., *The Empire State Building,* by John Tauranac, *The Gay Metropolis, 1940–1996,* by Charles Kaiser, and *The Encyclopedia of New York City,* edited by Kenneth T. Jackson; *The Great Comic Book Heroes,* by Jules Feiffer, *All in Color for a Dime,* by Dick Lupoff and Don Thompson, *The Great Comic Book Artists* and *Great History of Comic Books,* both by Ron Goulart, *Superhero Comics of the Golden Age: The Illustrated History,* by Mike Benton, *The Art of the Comic Book,* by Robert C. Harvey, The Steranko History of Comics, Vols. 1 and 2, by Jim Steranko and *The Comic Book Makers,* by Joe Simon with Jim Simon; *On the Kabbalah and Its Symbolism,* by Gershom Scholem, and *Gates to the Old City,* by Raphael Patai; *The Big Broadcast,* by Frank Buxton and Bill Owen, *Don't Touch That Dial,* by J. Fred MacDonald, and *The Book of Practical Radio,* by John Scott-Taggart; as well as the following sites on the World Wide Web: Michael Norwitz's *Lev Gleason's Comic House* (http://www.angelfire.com/mn/blaklion/index.html), Bob King's *Houdini Tribute* (http://www.

houdinitribute.com), and Peter Bacon Hales's *Levittown: Documents of an Ideal American Suburb* (http://www.uic.edu/~pbhales/Levittown/index.html).

I have sought to meet the high standards of the amazing Mary Evans for nearly fifteen years, and only to the extent that it meets them can I be satisfied with this work. Kate Medina blessed this voyage when I had no more than a fictitious map to steer by, and lashed me to the wheel when the seas turned rough. I'm indebted to David Colden, for scaring the pants off of Sheldon Anapol. I am grateful to Scott Rudin, for his patience and faith, to Tanya McKinnon, Benjamin Dreyer, E. Beth Thomas, Meaghan Rady, Frankie Jones, Alexa Cassanos, Paula Shuster, Frances Coady, and Reagan Arthur. And, everlastingly, to Ayelet Waldman, for inspiring, nurturing, and ensuring, in a thousand ways, every single word of this novel, down to the very last period.

Finally, I want to acknowledge the deep debt I owe in this and everything else I've ever written to the work of the late Jack Kirby, the King of Comics.

Read on for an excerpt from Michael Chabon's

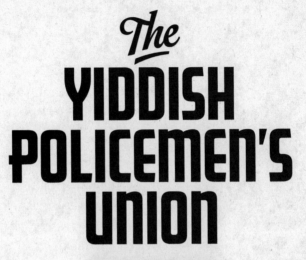

Copyright © 2007 by Michael Chabon.

1

NINE MONTHS LANDSMAN'S been flopping at the Hotel Zamenhof without any of his fellow residents managing to get themselves murdered. Now somebody has put a bullet in the brain of the occupant of 208, a yid who was calling himself Emanuel Lasker.

"He didn't answer the phone, he wouldn't open his door," says Tenenboym the night manager when he comes to roust Landsman. Landsman lives in 505, with a view of the neon sign on the hotel across Max Nordau Street. That one is called the Blackpool, a word that figures in Landsman's nightmares. "I had to let myself into his room."

The night manager is a former U.S. Marine who kicked a heroin habit of his own back in the sixties, after coming home from the shambles of the Cuban war. He takes a motherly interest in the user population of the Zamenhof. He extends credit to them and sees that they are left alone when that is what they need.

"Did you touch anything in the room?" Landsman says.

Tenenboym says, "Only the cash and jewelry."

Landsman puts on his trousers and shoes and hitches up his suspenders. Then he and Tenenboym turn to look at the doorknob, where a necktie hangs, red with a fat maroon stripe, already knotted to save time. Landsman has eight hours to go until his next shift. Eight rat hours, sucking at his bottle, in his glass tank lined with wood shavings. Landsman sighs and goes for the tie. He slides it over his head and pushes up the knot to his collar. He puts on his jacket, feels for the wallet and shield in the breast pocket, pats the sholem he wears in a holster under his arm, a chopped Smith & Wesson Model 39.

"I hate to wake you, Detective," Tenenboym says. "Only I noticed that you don't really sleep."

"I sleep," Landsman says. He picks up the shot glass that he is currently dating, a souvenir of the World's Fair of 1977. "It's just I do it in my underpants and shirt." He lifts the glass and toasts the thirty years gone since the Sitka World's Fair. A pinnacle of Jewish civilization in the north, people say, and who is he to argue? Meyer Landsman was fourteen that summer, and just discovering the glories of Jewish women, for whom 1977 must have been some kind of a pinnacle. "Sitting up in a chair." He drains the glass. "Wearing a sholem."

According to doctors, therapists, and his ex-wife, Landsman drinks to medicate himself, tuning the tubes and crystals of his moods with a crude hammer of hundred-proof plum brandy. But the truth is that Landsman has only two moods: working and dead. Meyer Landsman is the most decorated shammes in the District of Sitka, the man who solved the murder of the beautiful Froma Lefkowitz by her furrier husband, and caught Podolsky the Hospital Killer. His testimony sent Hyman Tsharny to federal prison for life, the first and last time that criminal charges against a Verbover wiseguy have ever been made to stick. He has the memory of a convict, the balls of a fireman, and the eyesight of a housebreaker. When there is crime to fight, Landsman tears around Sitka like a man with his pant leg caught on a rocket. It's like there's a film score playing behind him, heavy on the castanets. The problem comes in the hours when he isn't working, when his thoughts start blowing out the open window of his brain like pages from a blotter. Sometimes it takes a heavy paperweight to pin them down.

"I hate to make more work for you," Tenenboym says.

During his days working Narcotics, Landsman arrested Tenenboym five times. That is all the basis for what passes for friendship between them. It is almost enough.

"It's not work, Tenenboym," Landsman says. "I do it for love."

"It's the same for me," the night manager says. "With being a night manager of a crap-ass hotel."

Landsman puts his hand on Tenenboym's shoulder, and they go down to take stock of the deceased, squeezing into the Zamenhof's lone elevator, or ELEVATORO, as a small brass plate over the door would have it. When the hotel was built fifty years ago, all of its directional signs, labels, notices, and warnings were printed on brass plates in

Esperanto. Most of them are long gone, victims of neglect, vandalism, or the fire code.

The door and door frame of 208 do not exhibit signs of forced entry. Landsman covers the knob with his handkerchief and nudges the door open with the toe of his loafer.

"I got this funny feeling," Tenenboym says as he follows Landsman into the room. "First time I ever saw the guy. You know the expression 'a broken man'?"

Landsman allows that the phrase rings a bell.

"Most of the people it gets applied to don't really deserve it," Tenenboym says. "Most men, in my opinion, they have nothing there to break in the first place. But this Lasker. He was like one of those sticks you snap, it lights up. You know? For a few hours. And you can hear broken glass rattling inside of it. I don't know, forget it. It was just a funny feeling."

"Everybody has a funny feeling these days," Landsman says, making a few notes in his little black pad about the situation of the room, even though such notes are superfluous, because he rarely forgets a detail of physical description. Landsman has been told, by the same loose confederacy of physicians, psychologists, and his former spouse, that alcohol will kill his gift for recollection, but so far, to his regret, this claim has proved false. His vision of the past remains unimpaired. "We had to open a separate phone line just to handle the calls."

"These are strange times to be a Jew," Tenenboym agrees. "No doubt about it."

A small pile of paperback books sits atop the laminate dresser. On the bedside table Lasker kept a chessboard. It looks like he had a game going, a messy-looking middle game with Black's king under attack at the center of the board and White having the advantage of a couple of pieces. It's a cheap set, the board a square of card that folds down the middle, the pieces hollow, with plastic nubs where they were extruded.

One light burns in a three-shade floor lamp by the television. Every other bulb in the room apart from the bathroom tube has been removed or allowed to burn out. On the windowsill sits a package of a popular brand of over-the-counter laxative. The window is cranked open its possible inch, and every few seconds the metal blinds bang in the stiff wind blowing in off the Gulf of Alaska. The wind carries a sour tang of pulped lumber, the smell of boat diesel and the slaughter and canning of salmon. According to "Nokh Amol," a song that Landsman and every other Alaskan Jew of his generation learned in grade school, the smell of the wind from the Gulf fills a Jewish nose with a sense of promise, opportunity, the chance to start again. "Nokh Amol" dates from the Polar Bear days, the early forties, and it's supposed to be an expression of gratitude for another miraculous deliverance: Once Again. Nowadays the Jews of the Sitka District tend to hear the ironic edge that was there all along.

"Seems like I've known a lot of chess-playing yids who used smack," Tenenboym says.

"Same here," Landsman says, looking down at the deceased, realizing he has seen the yid around the Zamenhof. Little bird of a man. Bright eye, snub beak. Bit of a flush in the cheeks and throat that might have been rosacea. Not a hard case, not a scumbag, not quite a lost soul. A yid not too different from Landsman, maybe, apart from his choice of drug. Clean fingernails. Always a tie and hat. Read a book with footnotes once. Now Lasker lies on his belly, on the pull-down bed, face to the wall, wearing only a pair of regulation white underpants. Ginger hair and ginger freckles and three days of golden stubble on his cheek. A trace of a double chin that Landsman puts down to a vanished life as a fat boy. Eyes swollen in their blood-dark orbits. At the back of his head is a small, burnt hole, a bead of blood. No sign of a struggle. Nothing to indicate that Lasker saw it coming or even knew the instant when it came. The pillow, Landsman notices, is missing from the bed. "If I'd known, maybe I would have proposed a game or two."

"I didn't know you play."

"I'm weak," Landsman says. By the closet, on plush carpet the medicated yellow-green of a throat lozenge, he spots a tiny white feather. Landsman jerks open the closet door, and there on the floor is the pillow, shot through the heart to silence the concussion of bursting gases in a shell. "I have no feel for the middle game."

"In my experience, Detective," Tenenboym says, "it's all middle game."

"Don't I know it," Landsman says.

He calls to wake his partner, Berko Shemets.

"Detective Shemets," Landsman says into his mobile phone, a department-issue Shoyfer AT. "This is your partner."

"I begged you not to do this anymore, Meyer," Berko says. Needless to say, he also has eight hours to go until his next shift.

"You have a right to be angry," Landsman says. "Only I thought maybe you might still be awake."

"I *was* awake."

Unlike Landsman, Berko Shemets has not made a mess of his marriage or his personal life. Every night he sleeps in the arms of his excellent wife, whose love for him is merited, requited, and appreciated by her husband, a steadfast man who never gives her any cause for sorrow or alarm.

"A curse on your head, Meyer," Berko says, and then, in American, "God damn it."

"I have an apparent homicide here at my hotel," Landsman says. "A resident. A single shot to the back of the head. Silenced with a pillow. Very tidy."

"A hit."

"That's the only reason I'm bothering you. The unusual nature of the killing."

Sitka, with a population in the long jagged strip of the metro area of three point two million, averages about seventy-five homicides a year. Some of these are gang-related: Russian shtarkers whacking one another freestyle. The rest of Sitka's homicides are so-called crimes of passion, which is a shorthand way of expressing the mathematical product of alcohol and firearms. Cold-blooded executions are as rare as they are tough to clear from the big whiteboard in the squad room, where the tally of open cases is kept.

"You're off duty, Meyer. Call it in. Give it to Tabatchnik and Karpas."

Tabatchnik and Karpas, the other two detectives who make up B Squad in the Homicide Section of the District Police, Sitka Headquarters, are holding down the night shift this month. Landsman has to acknowledge a certain appeal in the idea of letting this pigeon shit on their fedoras.

"Well, I would," Landsman says. "Except for this is my place of residence."

"You knew him?" Berko says, his tone softening.

"No," Landsman says. "I did not know the yid."

He looks away from the pale freckled expanse of the dead man stretched out on the pull-down bed. Sometimes he can't help feeling sorry for them, but it's better not to get into the habit.

"Look," Landsman says, "you go back to bed. We can talk about it tomorrow. I'm sorry I bothered you. Good night. Tell Ester-Malke I'm sorry."

"You sound a little off, Meyer," Berko says. "You okay?"

In recent months Landsman has placed a number of calls to his partner at questionable hours of the night, ranting and rambling in an alcoholic dialect of grief. Landsman bailed out on his marriage two years ago, and last April his younger sister crashed her Piper Super Cub into the side of Mount Dunkelblum, up in the bush. But Landsman is not thinking of Naomi's death now, nor of the shame of his divorce. He has been sandbagged by a vision of sitting in the grimy lounge of the Hotel Zamenhof, on a couch that was once white, playing chess with Emanuel Lasker, or whatever his real name was. Shedding the last of their fading glow on each other and listening to the sweet chiming of broken glass inside. That Landsman loathes the game of chess does not make the picture any less touching.

"The guy played chess, Berko. I never knew. That's all."

"Please," Berko says, "please, Meyer, I beg you, don't start with the crying."

"I'm fine," Landsman says. "Good night."

Landsman calls the dispatcher to make himself the primary detective on the Lasker case. Another piece-of-shit homicide is not going to put any special hurt on his clearance rate as primary. Not that it really matters. On the first of January, sovereignty over the whole Federal District of Sitka, a crooked parenthesis of rocky shoreline running along the western edges of Baranof and Chichagof islands, will revert to the state of Alaska. The District Police, to which Landsman has devoted his hide, head, and soul for twenty years, will be dissolved. It is far from clear that Landsman or Berko Shemets or anybody else will be keeping his job. Nothing is clear about the upcoming Reversion, and that is why these are strange times to be a Jew.